PELICAN BOOKS

AU8

THE LITERATURE OF AUSTRALIA

The Literature of
Australia

∽

EDITED BY

GEOFFREY DUTTON, *ed.*

PENGUIN BOOKS

04129

Bdy

Penguin Books Ltd, Harmondsworth, Middlesex, England
Penguin Books Inc., Baltimore 11, Maryland, U.S.A.
Penguin Books Pty Ltd, Ringwood, Victoria, Australia

—

First Published 1964

—

Copyright © Penguin Books Pty Ltd, 1964

—

Printed in Australia for Penguin Books Pty Ltd
at The Griffin Press, Adelaide
Set in Monotype Times

—

Registered in Australia for transmission
by post as a book

PR
9414
.D8

65-5134

AUSTRALIAN LITERATURE --
ADDRESSES, ESSAYS, LECTURES.

CONTENTS

CONTENTS
PART III

INTRODUCTION

THE primary purpose of *The Literature of Australia* is to fill a gap. For the first time in the history of Australian literature it offers the general reader and the student, in a cheap and compact form, a critical account of the more important writers and their works, with bibliographies that include references to further critical commentaries.

There are already in existence, if not in many cases in print, pioneering bibliographies such as those of Ferguson, Morris Miller, Macartney, and Serle, or histories such as those by Ewers, Hadgraft, and especially Green, and the present book is intended to supplement these rather than replace them. It is the work of twenty-three writers, several of them not only critics but distinguished enough in their own right to be discussed elsewhere in the book. The result has been a multiplicity of insights, and occasional clashes of opinion, but above all a sober admission that Australian literature exists and can be taken seriously in the context of English as a world language. A history of literature written by one man has the advantage of unity of tone and consistency of opinion, but it can be parried as the work of a man with a bee in his bonnet, a happy specialist. A volume written by a couple of dozen experts in various fields cannot be dismissed so easily, especially when they make no wild claims and are in fact sometimes almost unduly severe.

The time is ripe for a volume such as this. Only twenty years ago, a Professor of English, inaugurating the Commonwealth Literary Fund lectures in Australian literature, could say that he was grateful to the C.L.F. for providing the funds, but since they had omitted to provide him with any literature, he would lecture on D. H. Lawrence's *Kangaroo*. Even in the 1940s such a jest was a little excessive (as a glance through the present volume will indicate), but it demonstrates the temper of the times among some who should have known better. A commercial parallel can be found in the story told by a leading Australian publisher of the days in the 1930s when he was beginning as a young traveller for the Melbourne office of an English publishing firm. Before he left the office, his bag was opened by his boss, who withdrew an Australian book from the top of the pile and said, 'Sonny, you'll learn. When you go round the booksellers, show them the Australian books last.' There are now Australian books in the front of every bookseller's display, and in 1962 over a thousand new titles were published in Australia by Australian publishers. In the 1960s the Australian national consciousness demands, and gets, some of the artistic exploration that is a proof of maturity.

All of the critics in this volume are aware of the dangers in chronicling a national literature, and many of them are already on record in print in discussions of the double standard which can lead both to inflation and denigration. The novelist or poet who may mean a lot to Australians, and to Australian history, may well be a pigmy alongside a Fielding or a Wordsworth; to ignore this is chauvinism, but to be cowed by it is to adopt what A. A. Phillips unforgettably called 'the cultural cringe'. It should be remembered, however (and no student of English literature who has suffered, say, *Gorboduc* or *Pamela* is likely to forget it), that tedious works can also be profoundly important in the growth of a national literature. The thorough discussions of nineteenth century Australian literature in this volume whisk no forgotten masterpieces from the dust of obscurity, but they offer plenty of evidence of works that are essential reading not only for an understanding of Australian literature but also of the Australian national character. What also emerges from the general survey of the whole period is the tragedy that so many essential works are out of print, and, owing to high costs and small sales, show no sign of being reprinted. It is one of the minor scandals of the Australian universities that, with a few honourable exceptions, they have made no effort to establish the University Presses that could keep such classics in print.

There are certain omissions from this volume, due partly to lack of space and partly to lack of sufficient research at this stage of Australian history. There is no discussion of Australian language and idiom; despite pioneering work by Sidney J. Baker and Ralph Partridge, we still await some definitive study such as that promised by Professor A. G. Mitchell. The thorniest omission is that of non-narrative prose. It has been argued by Max Harris and others that the best Australian prose of the nineteenth century is to be found not in novels but in journals and reminiscences and historical documents. There are also many fine twentieth century biographies, essays, and histories. Until recent years no one thought of distinguishing 'creative' prose from good prose, and the segregation of narrative prose is full of dangers. But the problem of discussing in the space available all the good Australian prose that has been written was insoluble; many important works are mentioned incidentally in the chapters, especially in Ian Turner's, and references are given in the bibliography. Likewise it has been possible to discuss at length only *The Bulletin* amongst the many newspapers, journals, and quarterlies that have done so much for Australian writing.

Literature in Australia has grown strong from its own roots and its own idiom. Without the need any more to be self-consciously 'Australian' it can take an individual and mature place in the world-wide literature of the English language.

GEOFFREY DUTTON

PART
I

THE SOCIAL SETTING

IAN TURNER

THE celebrated Dr Darwin, as Charles's grandfather Erasmus was known, held high hopes in 1789 for the colony at Sydney Cove:

> ... tumultuous echoes roar,
> And JOY's loud voice was heard from shore to shore –
> Her graceful steps descending press'd the plain,
> And PEACE, and ART, and LABOUR, join'd her train.

Fifty years later, his more celebrated grandson was not so sanguine:

> On the whole, from what I heard, more than from what I saw, I was disappointed in the state of society. The whole community is rancorously divided into parties on almost every subject. Among those who, from their station in life, ought to be the best, many live in such open profligacy that respectable people cannot associate with them. . . . The whole population, poor and rich, are bent on acquiring wealth: amongst the higher orders, wool and sheep-grazing form the constant subject of conversation. There are many serious drawbacks to the comforts of a family, the chief of which, perhaps, is being surrounded by convict servants. . . . I am not aware that the tone of society has assumed any peculiar character; but with such habits, and without intellectual pursuits, it can hardly fail to deteriorate. My opinion is such, that nothing but rather sharp necessity should compel me to emigrate.

> (Charles Darwin: *A Journal of Researches*, 1839)

Erasmus Darwin, from a safe distance, saw no difficulty in applying to the new settlement his confident belief in 'the progressive increase in the wisdom and happiness of [the earth's] inhabitants'; in the harsh, competitive world of the survival of the fittest, there was more room for doubt. But Charles Darwin had misread the signs: already the habits which he deplored were passing, as free settlers took over from the System as the pace-makers of colonial society; while the intellectual pursuits which he valued were beginning to find officials, merchants, and landowners with the leisure to cultivate them.

The 'tone' of colonial society was at first set by the purposes of the British government in establishing the settlement in New

South Wales. The secret instruction of the Lords of the Admiralty to Lieutenant James Cook, in command of H.M. Bark *Endeavour*, had urged him to the discovery of the unknown south-land, an event which they thought might 'tend greatly to the advancement of the Trade & Navigation' of the British Crown: this was one of the last great moments of Mercantilism, but Cook reported to his masters that New Holland (as the land was still known) offered little prospect for their enterprise: 'the Country itself so far as we know doth not produce any one thing that can become an article in trade to invite Europeans to fix a settlement upon it.' So the land was settled, not with traders and their guardsmen, but with convicts and their gaolers: the callousness and the sense of guilt of the gaolers were measured against the sense of grievance and the despair of the gaoled; arrogance, or vindictiveness, or plain cruelty, was met by whining submissiveness, or sullen resentment; and all were subsumed in the bitter violence which clouded over the penal establishments of New South Wales and Van Diemen's Land.

In the sixty-odd years until transportation to the eastern colonies was abandoned, 150,000 men and women came to Australia in chains. They were mainly illiterate peasants, workers, vagabonds, professional criminals, transported for theft or crimes of violence against the person; but among them were a few (English, Scots, Irish, Canadian) transported for political offences, and a few of higher social class, transported for such 'gentleman's crimes' as forgery, embezzlement, or abduction. Most worked with their hands, for government or for the growing class of private landowners; some of the educated were promoted to less arduous positions as overseers or clerks or tutors; a handful, once their punishment had run its course, made their fortunes in trade or on the land. Over the convicts, wielding their power with the rope or the lash or the threat of withheld privilege, were the civil officials and the military; among these were men of education and sensibility, but no leisured class, none for whom literature was more than the writing of a journal or a letter or a despatch. Gaolers and gaoled alike, in these first years, saw their residence as impermanent; they brooded nostalgically over the chances of return (though this was hardly ever possible in practice for the transported); their ties of family and sentiment and culture were with the lands which they still thought of as home.

Aristocracy was not represented in colonial society, which began with the Governor and his entourage, both civil and military – usually middling sort of men, from the families of the gentry, with the grammar school education appropriate to their station and often an interest in the natural sciences derived from long years of observation while at sea or in foreign parts. But there was little time for cultivation of mind or soul: those who had the advantage of education and status were preoccupied, for the first few years, with keeping the colonists fed, maintaining order, and staying alive; later, as the temporary settlement grew into a permanent colony, with making their fortunes. (Indeed, the preoccupation of Australians with material considerations and values has been a continuing theme of inquiring visitors, from the 1820s to the present time.) And this upper class, such as it was, was scarcely less prone to take its respite in unlicensed sex and drink than were the lower orders of colonial society, the soldiers, and convicts. Those who, in the first years, wrote of the antipodes were concerned mainly with the prestige or profit to be won from satisfying that intense interest in the novel and the picturesque, the history of earth and the origins of man, which was a major product of the Enlightenment. And there was much in the new world that was novel and curious – the landscape, flora and fauna, the Aborigines; but those who set out to depict these strange phenomena saw the land through English eyes. They looked at it as visitors, excited by the unfamiliarity of what they saw, sometimes disheartened by the difficulty of what they had to do; but they did not yet look as exiles, overwhelmed by the unfamiliarity and possessed by the intractability of the land – that was to come.

With the convicts, it was quite different. The educated few apart, they came from those strata of the society of the United Kingdom which were quite removed from the cultural patterns of the aristocracy and the middle class. In a sense, they were involuntary outcroppings of the ballad communities which still existed in the towns and villages of England and Ireland, and they brought with them an oral literature which responded quickly and sensitively to their new environment, natural and social, to New South Wales, and the penal system.

The rigours of this System were great, and the demands on both strength and fortitude intense, and these were barely modified by the efforts of the few reformers such as Governor Lachlan Macquarie of New South Wales, and Captain Alexander Maconochie, commandant for a short time of the Norfolk Island convict settlement. But there was little rebelliousness against the system: the only organized revolts were the rising of the Irish prisoners at Castle Hill, near Sydney, in 1804, and the desperate 'battle of the bridge' on Norfolk Island, forty-two years later. Resistance was effectively confined to the continued attempts to escape from the System, by 'bolting', or by piracy of prison ships, or by deliberately seeking sentence of death. There was also the shadowy underground convict elite, 'The Ring', whose members swore (and practised) absolute obedience to their society, and absolute denial of the penal system. The ballads of the convicts expressed their situation: at first, the sentiment was nostalgic, and sometimes mock-repentant, with an ironic acceptance of the moralizing of their judges and gaolers; later (say by the 1820s, although it is impossible to date the ballads precisely), the nostalgia disappeared, and the spirit was hatred or defiance of the authorities, fear or bravado for the brutalities of the System, admiration for those who bucked it (notably the successful escapees), and a bitter humour which set out to subvert the moral values of their betters. This literature was in direct line from that which they had known – the folk ballads, the broadsheets, the lurid stories of the Newgate Calendar; it was perpetuated and adapted by oral circulation in the gaol society,[1] from where it passed into the common stock of the colonial population, about half of which was of convict origin or descent until the goldrushes of the 1850s established a quite new demographic pattern.

Convicts, as assigned servants, or on ticket of leave, or in government gangs, were the unwilling builders of the material foundations of the new society – its farms and towns, its wharves and mines, the roads and bridges and public buildings decreed above all by Macquarie; more and more, they belonged to the new world, but there was no sign of any feeling that the new world belonged to them. The sense of proprietorship was confined rather to the merchant and land-owning class, a few of whom were emancipated convicts, but most of whom (until free immigrants with capital began to trickle, from 1807, and then, a decade later, to flow into the Australian colonies) were former officers and officials who had seen their opportunity and seized it – together with a monopoly of trade and the best of the land

In so far as the British authorities had given any thought to the shape of society in the new colonies almost unknowingly acquired, they had envisaged a self-supporting community of small-holders, the holdings to be distributed as reward for faithful service or good behaviour. But the coincidence of growing demands of the British textile industry, the suitability of eastern Australia for sheep, and the acumen of a few officers of the New South Wales Corps, established a pattern of society far different from the British intention – large holders instead of independent yeomen, pastoral enterprise instead of agricultural, production for an export market instead of for local consumption. This pattern was established in the interregnum which followed the departure of the first Governor, Phillip; it was confirmed by the Rum Rebellion, the failure of Governor Macquarie to make more of his pro-emancipist policy than to introduce a handful of ex-convicts to the pinnacles of colonial wealth, the report to the British government of Commissioner J.T. Bigge, and the victory of the squatters over Governor Gipps.

Early on, the thirst of British manufacturers for wool, and the hunger of Australian wool-growers for land, outran the narrow hinterland of Sydney. Aspiring pastoralists pushed over the mountains, and undertook or financed the exploration of the interior, in search of grass and the waters of an inland sea. Sometimes, but only occasionally, their hopes were realized:

We had at length discovered a country ready for the immediate reception of civilized man; and destined perhaps to become eventually a portion of a great empire. Unencumbered by too much wood, it yet possessed enough for all purposes; its soil was exuberant, and its climate temperate; it was bounded on three sides by the ocean; and it was traversed by mighty rivers, and watered by streams innumerable. Of this Eden I was the first European to explore its mountains and streams – to behold its scenery – to investigate its geological character, and, by my survey, to develop those natural advantages, certain to become, at no distant date, of vast importance to a new people. . . .

(T. L. Mitchell: *Three Expeditions into the Interior of Eastern Australia*, 1838)

The explorers solved the riddle of the inward-flowing rivers, discovered the pastoral possibilities of New South Wales and Queensland, opened up land routes to the unsystematic (and disapproved) settlement from Van Diemen's Land of Portland

Bay and Port Phillip, and to the 'systematic' colony of South Australia. Many would-be settlers were lost in the roving, lightly timbered, and sparsely watered grasslands of the eastern interior, later in the matted jungles of the north and the grassless and waterless stretch of the central desert. Many were killed in frontier skirmishes with an aboriginal population for whom the spread of white settlement meant the loss of their hunting grounds, debasement of their women, and the defilement of their sacred sites. (But more, of course, of the Aborigines were lost: their low level of material culture, and their fragmented social organization, enabled the process of pacification – which, despite a few well-meant but imperceptive attempts at protection, was the dominant theme of white-Aboriginal relations – to proceed almost unchecked; until, over most of Australia, and the whole of the most desirable areas of settlement, only a remnant of detribalized and degraded fringe-dwellers remained.)

During fifty years – with the help at first of convict labour, later of subsidized working-class migration – the woolgrowers made the best of Australia their own, at least to the extent of the occupancy permitted by the pastoral lease.

At the same time, the quality of colonial society was changing. From the end of the Napoleonic wars, a measure of British attention had concentrated on the surprising fact that, almost unheralded, a new outpost of empire had stabilized itself, and promised to add substantially to the prosperity of English manufacture and trade. Beyond the convict origins, gentlemanly adventurers, fortune-seekers and reprobates, canny investors and men of enterprise, ambitious artisans, and increasing numbers of the labouring poor, looked to the Australian colonies as a land of promise. Free settlers flowed into the old penal settlements as well as the new settlements at Melbourne, Adelaide, and Swan River, attracted by the promise of danger and redemption, of work and land and wealth. While the pastoralists fanned out from their beach-heads, the handful of coastal towns grew as commercial and administrative centres for the countryside, and asserted their own needs for clerks and workingmen, merchants, and men of the professions. The demand of the growing pastoral industry (until the depression of the 1840s) for labour and goods and services grew faster than the towns could supply it, while many who came in search of opportunity quailed before the distances together with the lack of amenities of the interior, and the danger of the Aborigines, and clung fearfully to the towns. But from out of these came a class of well-to-do merchants who, with the pastoralists, asserted their right to a voice in colonial government, laid the foundation for the separation of the colonies, established an independent press and judiciary, and a property-based representative government.

These, the established landowners and merchants, contrived to make the land their own, but they were not yet of it. With pride born of pioneering achievement, they asserted its claims:

> Where Sydney's infant turrets proudly rise,
> The newborn glory of the southern skies . . .

but they saw themselves as colonizers, the bearers of an old civilization rather than the creators of a new:

> And, oh, Britannia! shouldst thou cease to ride
> Despotic Empress of old Ocean's tide – . . .
> May this, thy last-born infant then arise,
> To glad thy heart, and greet thy parent eyes;
> AND AUSTRALASIA FLOAT, WITH FLAG UNFURLED,
> A NEW BRITANNIA IN ANOTHER WORLD!

(W. C. Wentworth: 'Australasia', 1823)

Their first accommodation had been hastily improvised of the materials at hand, and had been quite unlike anything they had known; but as they settled into their prosperity in the towns or the closer settled districts, they built themselves approximations of the gracious homes of the English gentry. (Sometimes, indeed, the trappings – the pianos and drapery, the glassware and linen and furnishings – arrived while their owners were still walking on earthen floors.) At first, the education of their children was entrusted to the women of the family, or to convict tutors; but as wealth and improved communications made it possible, their sons at least were sent abroad, while their daughters were educated in the refined studies of French, music, drawing, and the less utilitarian varieties of needlework by governesses who were, preferably, impoverished gentlewomen newly arrived from home. They aspired to create an antipodean replica of the culture from which they had sprung: they relied on the mailships for their music and their reading, and those of them who sought to depict the local landscape in pencil, paint, or poetry were quick to translate it into more accustomed contours. Underlying the seeming stability of the early areas of settlement, there was the loneliness of exile, and, buried still deeper, fear of the Australian unknown – dark uncertainties which they sought to dispel by periodic escape or final return to the homeland, and by recreating familiar social patterns and forcing the strange environment into familiar images and moulds.

But below and beyond this self-created colonial upper class, other patterns were emerging. In Sydney, on the Rocks, there was a lawless, amoral, violent fringe of criminals and ex-convicts, largely illiterate, whose literary currency was the ballads and stories of the convict system, embellished by accounts of men who had escaped from custody and taken to the roads; these carried a defiant challenge that had in it as much of Irish protest against oppression as of the usual criminal's sense of persecution:

> 'I'd rather range the bush around, like dingo or kangaroo,
> Than work one hour for Government,' said Bold Jack Donahoe.

While, on the outback frontier, new generations sought fame or fortune or escape from their past or from themselves, by opening up the land. Settlers, droving their stock and carting their supplies across many miles and months of sparsely peopled country until they reached the limits of settlement and land which could be theirs by right of first occupation; teamsters and timber-cutters, selling their goods and services to the settlers; shepherds and station-hands, working for rations and perhaps £25 a year: among these men, some educated but more illiterate, some free immigrants but more old lags, new values were being created which owed something to the convict society in which many of them had spent their adult lives, but more to the exigencies of the back country environment.

Truth was, [he] had gone short on elementary education. Not that he was lacking in human skill or culture. He could glance at a forest giant and tell which way it would fall to his axe, and how many slabs it would yield to fashion his habitation. He could flay a beast and make from its hide harness and many other things. He could snare a wild horse and convert it into a domestic ally, as there was no outlaw wrapped in hide that could get rid of him while buckle and girth would hold. . . . He could canter over a stretch of country and estimate how many acres it contained, and how many beasts it would graze. He could make a fire in country girth-deep in snow or under pouring rain, and cook a meal at it. There wasn't a beast from the Upper Murray to the Lower Murrumbidgee that he didn't know by the cut of its jib, and no bird could call to its mate, nor outline its wing on the sky at dusk or dawn, without his reading it like the alphabet, and he could not be bushed while the stars shone at night or the sun by day, and when the sun failed the bark on the trees was a compass. . . .

('Brent of Bin Bin': *Up The Country*, 1928)

The first essential was to stay alive. A couple of men, or a handful, living in isolation for months on end, visiting a town at most once a year; travelling immense distances on foot or horse or bullock dray for help or companionship or supplies; working without respite to create a property out of the wilderness of bush; as often as not engaged in a guerilla war which only ended with the virtual extinction of the local tribes: what they valued was the ability and ease which only courage and competence could give, the ready hospitality and the community of their kind. They scorned social pretension, and they were remote, both in spirit and in space, from the culture which was already settling along the coast. The literate few often carried with them well-worn copies of the books they had known, of Shakespeare and the Bible, of Byron and Scott, from which they read for their own entertainment and instruction, and for that of their fellows. But for most what they had of literature was transmitted by word of mouth – again the ballads and stories of the System, but with a smattering of innovation, of ironic jokes at the expense of new-chum immigrants, but just as often at their own:

> Illawarra, Mittagong,
> Parramatta, Wollongong,
> If you wouldn't become an orang-outang,
> Don't go to the wilds of Australia.

They had nothing of formal literary achievement (except for Alexander Harris's fascinating memoirs, *Settlers and Convicts*, first published in 1847). It was many years before the bushmen brought their womenfolk to their new homes, and with them the first refinements of 'civilization'; and it was two or three generations before their descendants, and others who sought to define what was unique to Australian life and culture, canonized the character and achievement of the bushmen in their books.

The Australian colonies had been founded in the brutalities of transportation, and, once established by the forced labour of convicts, had been opened to free settlers. By 1850, nearly half a million men and women (about a third of them under duress) had undertaken the precarious 16,000 mile voyage from the United Kingdom to the Antipodes. Explorers, driven by scientific curiosity, the prospect of fame, the desire for self-justification or the need to possess the land, had circumnavigated the continent and tracked across much of the interior. Administrators and merchants had built monuments to their government or their wealth, often with convict hands. Pastoralists had spread their holdings over several hundred million acres of unknown land. Across a quarter of the continent, the Aboriginal inhabitants had been exterminated. Most men had fought for property, and some for power. The conquest of the land had been a half century of violence: many men had been destroyed, and some had destroyed themselves. But, so far, few had paused to write it down. For the new colonial upper class, the act of possession was necessarily the transplantation of a culture: except for the works of description, designed to satisfy or whet the metropolitan appetite, the journals of the first colonists and the explorers, and the uniformly derivative poems of nostalgia or hope, there was as yet no literary response. The colonies held few attractions for men of literary culture or pretence, and what power of imagery and words the accounts and journals had was incidental to their main purposes of conveying information, awakening interest. It was in the unwritten literature of the lower and further out segments of colonial society that there came the first distinct – and distinctive – imaginative response.

*

Gold had been rumoured since early times, but news of its discovery was at first suppressed. The convict foundations of colonial society would, it was thought, tremble at the first sound of the trumpet. But, by 1851, transportation to New South Wales had been over for a decade; the colonists themselves had struck the final blow to the System, whose effectiveness the British government itself was in any case beginning to doubt, when thousands of them, in Melbourne and Sydney in 1849, demonstrated their refusal to accept a renewal of transportation. The end of the depression of the 1840s had been followed by an increase in free migration, but still the supply of labour, for bush and city, was desperately short. As California had shown, gold was the one sure magnet of population; in 1851, Hargraves's discovery near Bathurst was made public, and the rush began. Soon after, gold was found in much bigger quantities in Victoria, at Clunes and Ballarat and Bendigo.

The effect was immediate. Town and country alike, and the neighbouring colonies, were stripped of their labour, as men of all classes and occupations streamed to the diggings to chance their luck. Then – just as long as it took a ship to get to England and back – came the first of the flood from overseas. A kaleidoscope of race, language, colour swarmed on each new field as news of the discovery became known. Within the two gold decades, the population of the Australian colonies grew fourfold, most of the increase going to Victoria, scene of the richest pickings; in that colony, by 1871, a city of over 200,000 stood on the site John Batman and his ten companions had tentatively selected thirty-six years before as 'the place for a village'.

Life on the diggings was raw. At first, men lived with what they could carry on their backs, or – if they had the money – on horse or dray. Close behind the first diggers came officials and troopers, to arbitrate disputes of the miners, to protect the gold from those who preferred to acquire it with a gun – and to collect the licence fee which became the principal among the many grievances of the diggers against colonial government. On Bendigo and Clunes there was agitation; at Ballarat there was revolt. The suspicion of corruption among the goldfields officials and the licence goad combined with Chartist and continental republican politics and Irish rebellion to lead 'some five hundred armed diggers' to take their oath 'to stand truly by each other, and fight to defend our rights and liberties', as it was read to them by Peter Lalor, brother of the Irish nationalist James Fintan Lalor, and leader of the men under arms who built the Eureka Stockade. The diggers had been prepared to raise their hands and voices in support of the heady programmes of the goldfields radicals, and to demonstrate and petition against the licences and the troopers who enforced them. But when the troopers stormed the Stockade, at dawn on a Sunday morning, only two hundred men were left inside, and these were largely Irish. The fighting did not last for long, nor was it very costly. Less than thirty of both sides were killed in the half-hour which it took the troopers to capture the

Stockade, or died subsequently of wounds. But this was the only armed conflict, between people and government, on Australian soil, and the diggers who died – several of whose names were unknown – passed into the Australian radical pantheon. The goldfields agitation, and the Stockade, secured a redress of the diggers' grievances; the monthly licence was replaced by a yearly Miners' Right, and responsible government (which was already agreed in principle by the British authorities) became an immediate reality and rested on a much broader basis of representation than would otherwise have been the case. And, in later years, old miners 'talked low, and their eyes brightened up, and they didn't look at each other, but away over sunset, and had to get up and walk about, and take a stroll in the cool of the evening when they talked about Eureka . . .' (Lawson: 'An Old Mate of Your Father's,' 1896).

The polyglot communities of the goldfields were too unstable, too heterogeneous, too short-lived to create a literature of their own, but the excitement and wealth of the diggings demanded their own entertainment, and professional entertainers hastened to Australia to skim the cream. In hurriedly erected theatres in Melbourne, Shakespeare or the latest melodrama was played to the accompaniment of a raucous and often ribald commentary from the pit; if the performance met with approval, the curtain call was greeted by a hail of small nuggets, satisfying alike to the self-esteem of the diggers and the cupidity of the performers. While, on the goldfields themselves, grog tents grew into shanties, and shanties into lavish and almost respectable hotels and halls of entertainment. Hotel keepers, seeking the lucrative trade of the successful diggers, competed with one another to hire the best of popular artists: Lola Montez, mistress of King Ludwig of Bavaria, presented her 'Spider Dance' for the diggers, and G.V. Brooke played Hamlet for them. Among the entertainers, one stands out – the 'inimitable' Charles Thatcher, the goldfields minstrel, who sang nightly to audiences of thousands, and everywhere to 'tumultuous applause', his own comments on goldfields society and goldfields life. Thatcher is remarkable because he was almost the only example of a genuinely popular goldfields literature. The rushes brought to Australia the most vivid pens that the country had yet known – those of William Howitt and William Kelly, and of Rafaello Carboni, a Risorgimento Italian, who left a graphic personal reminiscence of the Eureka Stockade. But time was too short, and the call of the new fields too urgent; there was still no leisured class to translate the life of the gold-rushes, the tragedies of failure and success, into imaginative literature; this remained for later generations to re-create, and it was left to a self-opinionated jongleur, whose origin was in the London taverns and music-halls, to leave in a few chap-books a record of how the community of diggers felt about their life. [2]

*

The early rushes were to fields in New South Wales and Victoria; later, and smaller, strikes in the far north of Queensland and South Australia (what is now the Northern Territory was then a part of that colony) drew a few thousands of the more adventurous diggers away from the south-east corner of the continent; but most of the new arrivals remained, and most of the wealth stayed with them. Victoria, the largest gold producer, prospered especially.

Above all, the goldrushes provided the Australian colonies with money for investment, and men to work; and the new colonial prosperity attracted from the United Kingdom still greater supplies of capital and labour. The first excitement over, population and wealth combined to give a sense of permanence to the occupation of the land; the startlingly rapid, yet solid, growth of the colonial capitals provided a new pivot for colonial society.

The pastoralists were well entrenched in their newly-built baronial halls; now that their pioneering was done (except, of course, on the last frontiers in the north and north-west) they retired to the leisured – and isolated – life of rural gentry, emerging only to defend their interests against the land reformers who dominated the colonial parliaments, and for special entertainments, sporting events, and celebrations. Socially, they were the most conservative stratum of colonial society; they aspired to a prestigious education and culture, but not to the searching of science or the storm of creative art.

But, in the cities, men of a kind new to the colonies were coming to the top. Attracted by gold, or the openings for enterprise, or the hope of renewed health, or the wider freedoms of the new world, men of professional and intellectual training and accomplishment began a movement to the antipodes, intending permanent settlement not on the land but in the cities, and determined to pursue their professional and intellectual interests. They were men of considerable energy and vision, and, under their impulsion, libraries, galleries, museums, universities were built; literary and learned societies were founded; periodicals of a serious purpose and even some distinction were published. This was a secular, improving age, and these men of talent were concerned to improve themselves, their fellow citizens, and the society in which they lived – in the first place in material circumstance, but this was only prerequisite to a refinement of the mind, a higher culture. [3] It is true that there was a strong element of practicality in the thinking of the colonial middle class: law and medicine and the natural sciences soon outran in the Universities the traditional Oxbridge disciplines, mathematics and the classics; and, in cultivated discourse, speculations about the material environment and the nature and origins of man outweighed claims of the imagination and the emotions. But the aim was clear. It was, as stated by Robert Lowe (a forerunner of the colonial intellectuals, and later Chancellor of the Exchequer under Gladstone) in his weekly paper, the *Atlas*, in 1845, that 'the ardent minds of the sons of the soil may be prevented from running to waste, may be raised above the unsatisfactory pursuit of sensual enjoyments to revel in the lofty and inexhaustible pleasures of the intellect'. The diffusion of culture was necessary if the Australian colonies were to grow into great and respected nations; while the enfranchisement of the colonial democracy made this a matter of urgency, as the advocates of free, compulsory, and secular education (introduced in most colonies around the 1870s) were not slow to argue:

What I wish to point out is, that democratic institutions such as our own make compulsory education a necessity....In a country... where the highest offices of the State are open not merely in name but in fact to all, it is necessary that there should be no chance of unstructed constituencies returning ignorant representatives....

(C.H. Pearson: *Report on the State of Public Education in Victoria*, 1878)

There was some feeling, on the whole justified, among the educational innovators that the men on the land were neglecting the education of their children because of their preoccupation with 'the growing of crops and the material prospects of their families'; but this could not be said of the new urban working class. These were largely skilled artisans of the building and metal trades, and they shared with the intellectuals a faith in progress and a desire for improvement. When, in 1856, the craftsmen employed on the building of Melbourne University struck work to demonstrate in favour of the Eight Hours' Day, those who led them spoke in terms not only of increased leisure, but of 'social and moral' advance, of fresh opportunities for education and the cultivation of the mind. But, just as the Mechanics' Institutes of the 1830s had failed to attract many mechanics, so now the new attempts to diffuse scientific and literary culture among the working class, through workingmen's colleges, did not succeed. One side of the institutes movement was, however, a great success: the libraries, which sprang up not only in the cities but in small towns throughout the colonies. The colonists had a great hunger for books; but many library committees had crises of conscience when they found that works of philosophy and science and theology gathered dust, while the demand for the popular fiction of the nineteenth century England could not be satisfied.

*

There was then, in the three decades of prosperity which followed the goldrushes, a growing demand for popular literature alongside the growing literacy; but the local audience was still too small to provide financial security, either for authors or for publishers. The colonial novelists, the first of whom appeared in these years, could hope to find serial publication in a local newspaper or magazine, but the returns from these were small, and they had to look to the London houses for publication in book form. [4]

This could not have been as distasteful to these writers as it was to their successors. In the first place, almost all were British-born, and they were concerned as much to interpret colonial life or to touch up a conventional romance with colonial colour for the British audience, as to enrich the colonists' understanding of themselves. Despite occasional lapses of perception, it was not that the environment – at least on the eastern and southern seaboards – was any longer alien: settlement had made it accept-able, and Marcus Clarke, who found the dominant note of the

Australian landscape to be 'Weird Melancholy', nevertheless felt that 'the dweller in the wilderness acknowledges the subtle charm of this fantastic land of monstrosities. He becomes familiar with the beauty of loneliness.' (Preface to *Poems of The Late Adam Lindsay Gordon*, 1880.) Rather it was that these writers still thought in terms of British social conventions: even Rolf Boldrewood, the most Australian of the colonial novelists, could saddle his archetypal wild colonial boy, Dick Marston, with such sentiments as these:

But it's a strange thing that I don't think there's any place in the world where men feel a more real out-and-out respect for a gentleman than in Australia. Everybody's supposed to be free and equal now; of course, they couldn't be in the convict days. But somehow a man that's born and bred a gentleman will always be different from other men to the end of the world. What's the most surprising part of it is that men like father, who have hated the breed and suffered by them, too, can't help having a curious liking and admiration for them. They'll follow them like dogs, fight for them, shed their blood, and die for them; must be some sort of natural feeling. ...

(*Robbery Under Arms*, 1888)

Secondly, they were, or aspired to be, professional writers, and they were very much concerned with the market. It was partly that there was a substantial British sale for works with an exotic spice (this remains true today, as witness the success of many Commonwealth expatriates in London); but it was also that the cultivated colonial audience was quite uncertain of its standards: thus the *Melbourne Review* in 1878:

Almost every colonial author has been harshly treated by the colonial press at first and ... only after great persistence, supplemented by the good opinion of English critics, have any, as a rule obtained press recognition here.

This was the first substantial batch of imaginative writers to concern themselves with the Australian landscape and Australian life – occasionally of the cities (as Catherine Spence), but more characteristically of the System (Marcus Clarke) and the bush (Boldrewood and others), for these were the appropriate settings for romance. Almost without exception, they were men and women of the middle class, reared exclusively (since no other was available to them) in the English literary tradition, aspiring to an audience which shared its preconceptions and to a place in its succession. Some at least enjoyed the patronage of the new urban middle class; but their work remained marginal to the interest of that group in the diffusion of culture. Undoubtedly their poems and stories were well read in their own time; Henry Kendall sold well, Gordon was widely quoted, instalments of Clarke's and Boldrewood's serials were anticipated with some of the eagerness which awaited each new number of *Household Words*. But their impact on urban culture seemed slight: it was among the young men and women of the bush, awakening to literacy in the crude bush schools, and to a dawning sense of belonging to the land, that whatever distinctively Australian note was struck produced (with little regard for its quality) a fervent response.

This was understandable. In the cities, there was broad agreement between the two most articulate social groupings, the mercantile and professional middle class and the skilled artisans, about the sort of society they wanted to build, and this was not far removed from the aspirations of British radicalism. Capital and labour were each to have their place, working together in a spirit of harmony and justice, but Australian society was to be open, with education and the presumed benefits of culture available to all, and adequate rewards for hard work and sound moral principle and talent. In the expansive decades before the crash of 1890, there was in the cities comparatively little disillusion (except in the 'sweated' manufacturing industries) to challenge the reality of this dream. But in the bush it was different, and this for two reasons.

First, there was an unsatisfied demand for land. The end of the easy alluvial pickings on the goldfields had left many thousands of men, accustomed to a rural life, with nowhere to go. True, there was work available, at wages, for the pastoralists; but this did not satisfy the taste for independence. The solution of the urban radicals, who were in any case interested in limiting the economic and political power of the pastoralists, was land reform – breaking up the big estates by the land tax, or by free selection of small agricultural holdings from the pastoral domains. The squatters resisted, but the popular movement overwhelmed them, and when New South Wales's first Free Selection Act was passed in 1861, the bush community sang its praises – 'Now the

Land Bill has passed and the good time has come.' The experiment failed (so decisively that some later commentators have suggested that it could not have been seriously meant to succeed): it was another twenty years before advances in transport and technology, and the growing demand for grain, made it economically possible for agriculture in the eastern states (South Australia had from early times been a large producer of wheat) to hold its own. In the meantime, in parts of New South Wales and Victoria, pockets of rural discontent expressed an unorganized and often criminal protest against the owners of the land.

Secondly, over a large part of the eastern colonies, a capitalist pattern of primary industry was established. On the goldfields, individual alluvial mining was replaced by deep-shaft mining, organized by large-scale entrepreneurs; coal and metal mining went the same way. The gold-induced labour shortage had driven pastoralists to fence their properties, and the day of the shepherd was past. But, as flocks and herds multiplied, there was an urgent demand for new kinds of labour: fencers and well-sinkers; teamsters and drovers; stockmen and shearers. Out of these men grew a new kind of working class, a loose bush fraternity, moving easily from place to place and job to job, that was in its time unique.

These were not distinct groups: the hopeful selector spent much of his time at wage-labour; the bush proletarian was often an aspiring farmer. Between them, they made up a ballad community which inherited something of the pre-gold tradition and had its own brief and vital flowering in the thirty years of the post-gold outback boom. Unlike its European counterparts, this was a nomadic community; its location was the men's hut, or the campfire, or the bush pub, wherever rural workers met. It was eclectic as to sources: it drew its melodies from the popular song of drawing-room or music-hall, or from folksong (commonly Irish), and created its texts by parodying, or by re-writing the more 'literary' productions of the homestead, [5] or by the creation of rough verses of its own. Its language was, however, all its own – colourful and not uncommonly lurid. It had two kinds of 'hero': the bushranger, whom it revered (most of all Ned Kelly and Ben Hall, who may have been, as is often suggested, psychotics; but in this context social psychology is more important than psychopathology); and the 'flash' bushman, whom it cut down to size. Its characteristic attitudes, as evidenced in its yarns as well as its ballads, were admiration for daring and resourcefulness; dislike for the law and the squatter; contempt for the cocky-farmer, the new-chum, and the coloured races; deflation, not unmixed with wry self-recognition, of the blowhard; and a sardonic spitting in the eye of fate, as for example the prayer of 'Holy Dan', a bullock-driver who had seen all but one of his team die in a drought:

> That's nineteen Thou hast taken, Lord, and now you'll
>   plainly see
> You'd better take the bloody lot – one's no damned
>   good to me!

This was a living, unlettered, popularly created literature – the last in Australian history – and it was of considerable importance, because so much of its spirit, and even its language and style, passed into more formal literary expression in the 1890s.

It is not hard to discern these two separate cultures in late nineteenth century colonial Australia. On the one hand, a developing urban culture, especially in Melbourne (metropolitan, preoccupied with intellectual advance, but 'too American') and Sydney (hag-ridden by that 'six-fingered, six-toed giant, . . . the British Philistine'). [6] A British-derived and oriented culture, fostered by the urban middle class, supported by the skilled artisans, directed especially towards reason, progress, and material improvement, at the fringes of which could be seen the beginnings of formal literary creation, not itself city-centred because what was exotic for the British audience (to which one eye was cocked) was in the bush. On the other, the last vigorous fling of a popular rural culture, already tangling with the middle class urban strand, but retaining sufficient of its own identity to make this distinction valid, and containing elements which, for better or worse, set it apart from the mainstream of British literary expression.

Writing some years later – but his comment could well apply – Australia's first notable literary critic, A. G. Stephens, attributed this split to

. . . the dominance of primitive instincts in the country. Those instincts play a larger part in the country than in the cities, since agricultural bush-environment not only fails, as a rule, to stimulate the complex tastes that we associate with civilized life, but gives no opportunity for indulging such tastes when formed.

(*The Red Pagan*, 1904)[7]

An especially acute visitor, Francis Adams (a young English writer and sociologist who had come to Australia in 1884 in search of relief from the ravages of tuberculosis) had, however, already put the positive implication of Stephens's comment at a heavy discount:

And Australia – what a need for Culture is here! I see nothing here of the best, and much of the worst. . . . [The] one commendable wish that the Australians have, is that they really do want the best article in things, and for the best article they are ready to pay. The unfortunate thing is, that there seems nothing in which they are yet qualified to know the best article when they see it! (*Australian Essays*, 1886)

But a great many things changed in Australia between 1886 and 1904, among them the sharp division between the bush and city cultures, the characters of the two principal cities, the capacity of Australians to discriminate – and their readiness to pay.

*

A legend of considerable dimensions has grown up around the 1890s: in these years, people first felt themselves to be Australians, and perceived the six colonies to be one nation; inspired by the ideals of unionism and socialism and nationalism, they saw it as their destiny to 'free from the wrongs of the North and Past / The land that belongs to you,' as Henry Lawson wrote in this first published poem, 'A Song of the Republic' (1887); freed of their old-world blinkers, writers and painters for the first time saw Australia as it really was. Like most legends, this had at least a foundation of historical truth.

At first glance, the optimism of these years seems out of place. By 1889, the boom was showing signs of cracking; banks and pastoral companies, which had financed the pastoral and mining expansion with an open hand, began – as a consequence of the decline of world trade – to call in their loans; then, almost without warning, the recession plunged into the financial crisis of 1891-3, and along with the crisis went a prolonged drought. Caught over-extended, eleven of the major trading banks were forced to close their doors. Company ownership of pastoral holdings grew rapidly – many a 'Kiley's Run' became a 'Chandos

Park Estate'. Manufacturing, which had expanded fast in the boom years, came to an abrupt halt. Tens of thousands of workers, both bush and city, suddenly found themselves without a wage, swelling the numbers of the wan, dispirited 'faces in the street'.

In the years before the crash, mass unions of unskilled workers (miners, maritime workers, bush workers) had been formed; along with the older city unions of artisans, they had taken advantage of the chronic shortage of labour to improve their lot. But, with the first signs of recession, the employers began seriously to resist: their refusal to recognize the right of the unions to speak for their members, the insistence on 'freedom of contract', precipitated a series of large-scale strikes, all of which ended disastrously for the unions. Out of defeat came the resolve of labour to enter politics: the State had ranged itself against the unions; now the unions would organize to win the State.

The ideology of the newly formed labour parties was simple, even naïve. 'Unionism came to the Australian bushman as a religion,' wrote W.G. Spence, a leading officer of both the miners' and the shearers' unions; and at the heart of their religion was the bush ethic of mateship:

It came, bringing salvation from years of tyranny. It had in it that feeling of mateship which he understood already, and which always characterized the action of one 'white man' to another.

(Australia's Awakening, 1909)

Among the leaders of the labour organizations were some who had discovered socialism, and they gave the bush religion their own gloss. 'Socialism . . . is the desire to be mates, is the ideal of living together in harmony and brotherhood and loving kindness,' declared *The Hummer*, an up-country shearers' paper; 'socialism', added William Lane in the Brisbane *Worker*, 'in our time.' The bitter tang of industrial defeat was overpowered by the sweet anticipation of political success:

What are we working for . . .? What is Humanity for? What is Solidarity for? . . . Is it not to free the worker from wage-slavery, to redeem the world from shame and sorrow, to make men manly and women womanly and the little ones full of laughter and life full of love? *(The Worker, Brisbane, 1890)*

33

This was a vision to arouse men's ardour, to set their minds on fire. Australia was a country of workingmen; organized labour could make it their paradise. Distance and isolation – later to be the skeletons at the Australian feast – made a barrier against old-world injustice; in the New World, the People could at last inherit their own.

The first thing about the writers of these years was that their tone of voice was unselfconsciously, unmistakably, and often 'offensively' (as Joseph Furphy said) democratic, lower-class Australian – and this was possibly the first time in any literature that this had been the dominant tone. Not that there were no gradations: Lawson characteristically saw the country from on foot, and his feet were mostly hot and tired and blistered, while his contemporary, and a better balladist, 'Banjo' Paterson, saw it from on horseback; Lawson's future was unlike anything that had gone before, while Paterson's was a return to an idyllic pastoral beginning; Furphy wrote of bullock-drivers, Edward Dyson of miners and city workers, Miles Franklin of remote or feckless station-owners, 'Steele Rudd' of small selectors grubbing a living out of a back-breaking farm. But there was sufficient community of language and sentiment to link all these, and many more, with what was fresh in the nineties air. They were 'battlers' themselves, and their hearts were on that side. Their hope was not in the individualist radicalism of the urban middle class, but in a collectivism which had borrowed some slogans from overseas socialism but owed more to the instinctive solidarity of bush unionism. They rejected old-world models, both literary and social; they spoke the vernacular, and spurned romance. [8] They shared a humour whose central element was an ironic understatement which seemed designed to make more manageable the manifold difficulties of the lives they knew. Their view of human nature was optimistic: there was pathos, even horror and despair, in their work, but not tragedy, for defeat, when it came (as it often did), came from without and not within. And in all this they were close to their people and their time.

In *The Bulletin*, a weekly paper first published in 1880, these writers found a market and an audience, a patron and a guide. The aim of the founders of this extraordinary magazine was to puncture the unhealthy hide of Sydney.

It was a Cant-ridden community. Cant – the offensive, horrible Cant of the badly-reformed sinner – reigned everywhere. There was no health in the public spirit. Socially, politically, all was a mean subservience to a spirit of snobbery and dependency. . . . Sydney, socially, limped in apish imitation after London ideas, habits, and manners. Politically and industrially it was the same. . . . Sydney invited revolt from existing conditions, and *The Bulletin* was the organ of that revolt.

(J.F. Archibald in *The Lone Hand*, 1907)

Among other radical policies, it favoured A Republican Form of Government, Australia for the Australians, and A United Australia and Protection against the World. For itself, it claimed to be

. . . the one phenomenal success in Australian journalism, the one completely non-local and distinctly universal Australasian newspaper. . . . A paper which is at once the most popular city publication and the organ of the intelligent bushman . . . the one most frequently remailed from one reader to another . . . the only well-established Australian journal which, throughout its career, has been consistently Radical.

(*The Bulletin*, 1893)

The description was fair enough; in its time, its influence was huge. *The Bulletin* caught the new popular audience created by universal education; it held them by not talking down to them (as did contemporary British magazines which sought a popular market) but by speaking their language and making articulate their thoughts. [9] Starting with social and political comment, it gradually enrolled as contributors the new imaginative writers who shared its outlook; through its staff-men (notably J.F. Archibald and A.G. Stephens) it moulded their ideas and style.

The point at which the brief dream broke is hard to define: at first sight, the pessimism seems just as unlikely as the earlier optimism. By the mid-nineties, the worst of the crisis and the drought was over; the gold discoveries in Western Australia had helped the economy of all the colonies; labour was represented in most of the colonial parliaments; the unions were re-forming; employment was looking up. But the flush of hope was paling.

First, the labour movement did not measure up to expectation. The succession of strike defeats disheartened many; Will Lane, who had been the movement's heart and tongue, left for Paraguay to found a New Australia, taking with him much of the movement's idealism (and one of the coming writers, Mary Gilmore); while in parliament the bush religion had been transmuted into the pedestrian articles of the labour platform, a ragbag of immediate reforms for which the labour parliamentarians fought a compromising tactical battle from the cross-benches.

Secondly, the federal movement took the fire out of fervent nationalism. The desire to remove the fiscal barrier to intercolonial trade, and the need for a united defence force, had convinced the urban middle class of the importance of federation, but to labour men it seemed that the conservative constitutional safeguards with which federation was embellished (it was derisively called 'fetteration') were designed to inhibit their political advance. The federal movement was middle class in inspiration and direction, but it carried the day. The sentiment of nationhood was strong among workingmen, and especially bush workers; this was the first generation in which the majority of adults were native-born, and the free movement of workers between the colonies had done much to break down former local prejudice. Radical labour opinion supported a united Australia or nothing, but there was sufficient of nationalist appeal in federation to carry a substantial working-class vote:

> And I said to him, 'Jack!' as he gripped my hand fast,
> 'Oh, I hear that our country's a nation at last!'
>
> (Lawson, 'Jack Cornstalk,' 1901)

But the reality was considerably less than the anticipation. The first Commonwealth Parliament, when it assembled in 1901, contained twenty-four labour men, and the first Labor government was formed by J. C. Watson in 1904; yet federation had left a question in the mind of labour: 'An Australian; a citizen of a nation whose realm is a continent and whose destiny is – what?' (*The Worker*, Brisbane, 1901.)

And finally the prospects of the writers themselves no longer seemed so bright. *The Bulletin*, *The Worker* and other radical papers had bought their poems and stories; the recently formed house of Angus & Robertson was publishing their books, and some (especially those of Paterson and Lawson) were selling well; but the returns were not great. Writing in 1899, Lawson estimated that twelve years of authorship had earned him only £700, and meanwhile he had been painter, journalist, timber-cutter, linesman, shearer, unemployed, in three of the Australian colonies and in New Zealand. Lawson is not the best of witnesses – he was never one to drive a hard bargain for his writing, or to husband his money when he earned it – but his comment is not untypical:

My advice to any young Australian writer whose talents have been recognized, would be to go steerage, stow away, swim, and seek London, Yankeeland, or Timbuctoo – rather than stay in Australia till his genius turned to gall, or beer. Or, failing this – and still in the interests of human nature and literature – to study elementary anatomy, especially as applies to the cranium, and then shoot himself. . . .

('Pursuing Literature in Australia,' *The Bulletin*, 1899)

The coincidence of universal education, the spirit of nation, and the organization of labour – especially bush labour – had brought a new voice into literature, one that was earthy, realistic, democratic, optimistic. The rate of infant mortality was still high, but this was a vigorous child. As it grew to a rapid consciousness of its world, its optimism died, but, in rather different forms, its other qualities survived.

*

The welding of the six Australian colonies into a single nation-state swept aside provincial barriers to development and posed political and economic questions on a new and larger scale: the early years of the Commonwealth saw the consolidation of a new pattern of politics, a steady economic diversification and growth, a far-reaching social experimentation, a rapid diffusion of education, and in one sense of culture.

Manufacturing, after the pause of the depression years, was again expanding fast, and concentrating workers and wealth and power in the cities – especially in Melbourne, still enjoying its nineteenth century pre-eminence in light industry, and in the great Sydney-Newcastle-Wollongong complex, where the foundations of a heavy industry were being laid. Primary industry, however, remained the major source of Australian wealth. Gold mining declined steadily, as no new discoveries succeeded the Western Australian strike, but other metal mines were opened up. Wool recovered rapidly from the turn of the century, and to the wool exports, always the main contributor to Australia's export income, were added growing overseas sales of grains and meat, sugar, dried fruits, and dairy products. And meanwhile, to serve these developing industries, transport services spread rapidly around the coast and across the continent; generally, these pivoted on the capital cities, confirming their commercial predominance and inhibiting the growth of rivals.

The great period of railway construction in Australia, linking the primary producing areas to the capitals and these to each other, occurred between 1880 and 1920, culminating in the wartime (1914-18) construction by the Commonwealth of the Trans-Australian Railway which drove for over a thousand miles across the desert (nearly 300 miles without a bend) to link Adelaide and Perth. The spread of railways, from World War I the growing number of motor vehicles, speeded up and fragmented movement across the country, and ended the isolation of the bush communities. Mechanization of farming and the introduction of machine-shearing transformed conditions of rural work and the life of the bush workers. The pioneering days were largely done. Except for the exigencies of drought or flood, diseases of stock or crop, the vagaries of the world market and the imperative demands of mortgagees, rural life was relatively stable; at the same time, rural culture was moving closer to that of the cities.

The spread of the State education network and the closer supervision of curricula brought country children into the mainstream of middle-class, urban ideology. Faster communications carried the newspapers and magazines of the cities to all but the most remote corners of the bush, and brought increasing numbers of bush people on visits to the cities, for business and for pleasure. Travelling entertainers, later films and wireless, ensured that the most up-to-date products of urban mass culture spread more or less rapidly across the land. There were still (as indeed there remain today) many differences of response and taste; but the bush community, aided by universal literacy, was passing from active creation of a hand-tailored culture to passive reception of the ready-to-wear urban commodity.

The pattern of rural production was by now firmly set: it was large-scale and capital-consuming, and this, along with the growth of mining and transport and secondary industry, meant that the population balance was moving decisively against the bush. In the process, the working class was being transformed into (predominantly) an unskilled industrial proletariat; some of this was still nomadic, wandering easily from mine to railway construction site to station or farm, but much of it was now settled in the cities or in the established mining towns, and in larger concentrations than had yet been seen. In political and industrial affairs, this new working class emerged as a more or less united and independent force, but its culture was that provided for it by middle-class educators and, increasingly, by the entrepreneurs of popular entertainment.

The alliance of artisans and the radical middle class, which had carried over into the first Federal Parliament, was shattered by the social polarization which followed in the wake of large-scale enterprise: in Federal and State Parliaments alike, there was a re-grouping into a two-party system of Labor and non-Labor. For the Labor parties, these were years of startling advance. Labor governments – the first of their kind in the world – were formed in the Commonwealth and most of the States before the end of World War I; but these scarcely fulfilled the confident anticipations of the 1890s. Very few of the new Labor politicians shared the feelings of one Queensland bush-worker who declared, as he headed back for his mates in the shearing sheds, that in Parliament 'the friends were too warm, the whisky too strong, and the seats too soft for Tommy Ryan.' Most, on the contrary, were soon reconciled to the electoral and parliamentary tacking and the programme of limited reforms which were seen as the necessary pre-requisites of power; becoming professional politicians, often acquiring private business interests, they lost the respect and confidence of a substantial part of the class and the movement which had created them.

There was some common ground between Labor and non-Labor parties: both accepted a measure of government economic activity and welfare legislation; there was, after some sharp early differences, agreement on the need to protect nascent Australian industry from overseas competition, and the homogeneous Australian population from alien (especially coloured) corruption. Characteristically, however, the non-Labor parties were concerned with economic growth – with the import of capital and labour, the development of industry, the expansion of markets – while the Labor parties were concerned with raising living standards, with social security, and the amelioration of working conditions. For their times, the practical policies which followed from these Labor concerns were by world standards advanced, even unique; they did much to earn Australia an international reputation for radical social experiment. But, within the country, the targets were too close, the pace was too slow, and the compromises were too many for the early excitement and optimism to be sustained.

The years of war and depression confirmed the patterns of urbanization and industrialization, at the same time as they added new elements to Australian thinking.

Nationalism, in its first manifestation, had had about it a decided flavour of republicanism, of 'cutting the painter', but this sentiment had been submerged in the independent nationhood which was symbolized by federation and embodied in the national policies evolved by the first Commonwealth parliaments; with the outbreak of war in 1914, Australian sympathy was overwhelmingly engaged on the side of Great Britain. Later, mounting suspicions about the uneven distribution of the burdens of war and about the purity of the Allied motives led to the rejection by popular vote of a deeper involvement through the formation of a conscript army, to a bitter conflict within the Labor parties which ended in most of the political leaders of Labor transferring their allegiance to a 'win-the-war' party, and to a steady shift of remaining Labor opinion against the war. But the initial response was impulsive and wholehearted.

There was much in it that seemed quixotic; Australian territory was hardly at stake, Australian participation was centred in France and the Middle East, the Australian troops were throughout volunteers. (The amateur status of the Australians set them apart from the soldiers of other nations, and was a matter of great pride, as was their reputation for lawlessness and lack of discipline, and a courage and competency in assault which they believed unparalleled. These were qualities which many commentators have seen as deriving directly from the bush tradition.) There was as well an overtone of affirmation of nationhood in the singleness of the response, together with an undertone of a child staking its claim for parental recognition of its maturity.

There were many who saw as legendary the voluntary commitment of the Australian soldiers, and some, later, who were sad that this sense of purpose and community had flowered most richly in the waste-land of war. In after years, there were many who felt that the nation had been baptized in the blood of the 8,000 Australians – 'they walked and looked like the kings in the old poems', John Masefield said of them – who had lost their lives in the ill-conceived and tragic blunder of Gallipoli. And there were some who, even at the time, doubted that the heroism had been well spent:

> Then call Thou home the bold, young boys again,
>   Who front a ruthless and bewildering fate;
> Call home the young who suffer senseless pain,
>   And leave the war to those who taught them hate.

('Furnley Maurice': 'To God: From the Warring Nations', 1916)

But, however they regarded it, all who lived through it felt that Australian participation in World War I had been a climactic moment in the nation's life.

Equally so the great depression. There had been crisis years before – in the nineties; in the early months of the war, when thousands lost their jobs; in 1919, when inflation and unemployment temporarily ran wild – but there had been nothing like this. The 1920s had been years of rapid growth. The inflow of migrants and capital was substantial. New industries were established, old industries expanded, and all prospered. Several hundred thousand ex-servicemen were re-absorbed into the labour force with surprisingly little dislocation. Encouraged by the confident atmosphere, thousands of men set themselves up as independent artisans or traders. Good seasons and buoyant prices thrust the farmers on to a new crest of optimism. Then came the crash. Doubting the durability of the boom, employers began to demand that their workers accept lower wages and longer hours: in a major series of strikes, during 1928-9, miners, watersiders, and timberworkers were forced to concede defeat. British and American investors began to panic, and overseas loans dried up. The world market for primary products collapsed, and the Australian economy with it. By 1931, almost a third of the work-force was unemployed.

Within a few months of the crisis, thousands were on the road – unskilled labourers, artisans and white collar workers whose jobs had disappeared, farmers who had lost their land, school-leavers and university graduates with nowhere to go:

> Oh, I love King George,
> He's a good friend of mine,
> And that's why I'm hiking
> Down George's main line. . . .

Those still in work clung precariously to their jobs, the men outside the gate always in the corner of their eyes. The workless supported life as best they could – by odd jobs or handouts, on relief work (a Shrine of Remembrance to the dead of World War I was built in Melbourne by the unemployed) or on the dole. In the cities, the unemployed organized to resist evictions, to demand work or at least a larger dole. Throughout the country, a para-military organization, the New Guard, [10] was formed to defend property and propriety against the Australian followers of Lenin and of J.T. Lang, the Labor Premier of New South Wales, whom his supporters declared 'greater than Lenin'. Communism, socialism, anarchism, social credit – outside government, there were plenty of remedies; but inside government no one knew just what to do. The mysteries of deficit financing were not yet understood, and, after the Labor parties had again been split, those who insisted on 'sound finance', that budgets must be balanced, had their way. The nation paid its debts; honour was satisfied, but at the cost of the remnant of optimism which had persisted in Australian consciousness since the days of gold. The slow climb back, as world markets recovered and local confidence was restored, could not expunge the bitter after-taste of the depression.

Indeed, for the writers, unqualified optimism was already well in the past. The plebeian bush voices of the nineties had almost universally rung with hope – so much so that the most original and provocative of contemporary Australian historians, C.M.H. Clark, has declared himself

dumbfounded at their optimism, astounded that belief in material progress and mateship could be their only comforters against earth and sky, man and beast.

(Introduction to *Select Documents in Australian History, 1851-1900,* 1955)

But the dominance of these voices had proved exceptional and short-lived. As in all industrial societies, expanded leisure created a demand for entertainment rather than self-culture, and the satisfaction of this demand soon became a commercial enterprise. The writers of the nineties had sauntered on into the twentieth century; some of them – notably the novelists Joseph Furphy and Miles Franklin and the poet Mary Gilmore – were still to publish their first books. But the spirit which had nurtured them was passing fast. Most of those who continued publishing lost their easy identification with their audience, and with it the faculty for genuinely popular expression which was the hallmark of their writing; anticipating greater rewards, they began to supply the new Australian paperback publishers (notably the N.S.W. Bookstall Co.) with entertaining but empty formula-stories of adventure, humour, or romance.

The strongpoints that they had captured were not, however, altogether lost; at least two of their attributes – an assertion of nation and a faith in social reform – were carried over into the work of the writers who followed them, and to these should perhaps be added a democratic concern to find a popular language and therefore a wide audience. But the new men were writers of a very different kind: while many of them had roots deep in the bush, most were of middle-class origin and of noticeably higher and more systematic education, and almost all sooner or later turned to the cities for their intellectual milieu.

Necessarily, writers of such background were caught between two conflicting impulses – a conflict which is perhaps characteristic of all colonial literatures. On the one hand there were those who felt an urgent need to express the land to which they belonged. Speaking of the writers who were setting out on their course at the beginning of the century, the critic Nettie Palmer said:

Australia was no longer a group of more or less important colonies, hanging loosely together . . . on the ample bosom of Britannia; Australia was henceforth Australia. What that name was to mean it lay in the hands of her writers, above all, to discover.

(*Modern Australian Literature*, 1924)

But there were those who saw this tendency as dangerous and impoverishing, and who demanded that universal standards be applied:

If we ever have an 'Australian' school of literature, it will not be because of the fauna and flora and geography and idioms of Australia which may be introduced. These make nothing in art. . . . It will be because our Australian atmosphere, our national life, occupations, religious and moral ideas, have inevitably and unconsciously created in our eyes and hearts and intellects some difference in our way of regarding things, so that we perceive strength and beauty and pathos in some new light, and adapt our representation thereto.

(T.G. Tucker: *The Cultivation of Literature in Australia*, 1902)

Perhaps few of the creative writers gave direct expression to this conflict, but it is there to see in the body of their work.

To define is to distinguish, and, seeking to define Australia, most writers turned instinctively to the bush, even one so steeped in mythological and literary allusion as Bernard O'Dowd:

> She is the scroll on which we are to write
> Mythologies our own and epics new:
> She is the port of our propitious flight
> From Ur idolatrous and Pharaoh's crew. . . .
> And if we pour on her the red oblation
> All o'er the world shall Asshur's buzzards throng:
> Love-lit, her Chaos shall become creation:
> And dewed with dream, her silence flower in song.
>
> ('The Bush', 1912)

It was not just that the bush and the outback, the distance and emptiness were unique to Australia and that, by re-creating them, writers could at the same time delineate their country and create a new imagery; nor that, by hymning the lives of the pioneers, the explorers, the first settlers, and even the miseries of convict life, they could create a depth of time, a substitute for the 'ancient churches, castles, ruins – the memorials of generations departed', the lack of which many critics believed would inhibit the flowering of an Australian literature; nor even that the industrial cities and mining towns represented the reproduction of Europe in Australia, the denial of the unique. It was also that these writers were beginning to sense that, while in the bush loneliness had a natural origin and was offset by human community, in the new centres of industry the weave of common life and purpose was somehow destroyed and loneliness was absolute. Working-class solidarity was still real, and usually they approved it; but they were no longer part of it, and their isolation was almost complete. And here they met, though from different starting points, with the most personal, the least concerned with immediate realities of time and place, the most desolate of Australian poets, Christopher Brennan, for whom

> . . . a bitter wind came out of the yellow-pale west
> and my heart is shaken and fill'd with its triumphing cry:
> You shall find neither home nor rest: for ever you roam
> with stars as they drift and wilful fates of the sky!
>
> ('The Wanderer,' 1902)

Through four decades, from the foundations of the Common-wealth to the outbreak of World War II, the way of these writers was not an easy one. They needed their own land, yet its intel-lectual atmosphere was too thin for sustenance. The cultivated minority with 'elevated tastes, a lofty conception of writing, a severe standard of criticism, thinking and conversation,' was, Professor Tucker found in 1902, 'disproportionately small'; Australia 'had no culture', it was 'crude, materialistic, Philistine', wrote the dramatist, Louis Esson, explaining his flight abroad in 1905; 'explorers in the interior of the Australian temperament bring back tales of a Great Emotional Desert,' reported A. G. Stephens in 1911. Many Australian writers sought spiritual refreshment at European streams, and a few (for example, Jack Lindsay, Christina Stead) stayed permanently; but most came back to their native creeks and waterholes. One such, the novelist, historian, and critic, Vance Palmer, had declared in his first pub-lished article:

Art is really man's interpretation of the inner life of his surroundings, and until the Australian writer can attune his ear to catch the various undertones of our national life, our art must be false and unenduring.

('An Australian National Art,' *Steele Rudd's Magazine*, 1905)

And then, in London six years later, he had discovered that his ear could attune to no other:

My loyalties were fixed: I had no intention of making a home in London. To me it was a gloomy, friendless place. ... [The] villagers of Hardy's novels were not as near to me ... as the station-folk and camp-blacks of the Maranoa among whom I had been living. ...

('Fragment of Autobiography', *Meanjin*, 1958)

A few (the Jindyworobaks) found the reality of Australia's 'inner life' not in the society they inhabited, but in Alcheringa, in that unity of the Aboriginal material culture and mythology with the natural environment which the coming of the white man had destroyed. But the use of Aboriginal language and imagery remained a cult; for most, the Australian nation meant the Australian common man.

Characteristically, the Australian intellectual of these years was radical in his politics: the heart of this was not so much the guilty paternalistic responsibility *for* working men that was common among European intellectuals, as an often quite humble responsibility *to* them, the creators of the nation's wealth and individuality and ethos. And this involved more than an interest in social reform; in his demand for a 'Poetry Militant', first voiced in 1909, the socialist O'Dowd warned of the danger that, with the problem of physical poverty overcome, there might arise a new division, 'intellectual, artistic, and spiritual starvation among the masses, and among the new castes intellectual, artistic, and spiritual gluttony.' Conscientiously, the writers of this persuasion set out to create a literature which spoke not only of and for the common man, but directly to him; what they had absorbed of the European high culture, they sought to assimilate to the traditions and spirit of the Australian popular culture.

Surprisingly, though, there was still little sign of interest in the life of the cities, or in the cataclysmic events of war and depression. In the early years of the century, those few (Edward Dyson, Louis Stone, C. J. Dennis) who wrote about the city were interested in the exotic larrikin or criminal fringe; later, a couple of novelists only wrote of the war (Leonard Mann, Frank Dalby Davison); a handful were caught up with the drama of the depression (Mann, Palmer, Christina Stead, Kylie Tennant); one or two found some fascination in the rare worlds of the artists and intellectuals (Stead, Dymphna Cusack). But the typical Australian workingman, and the central figure of most creative literature, remained the bush battler; the social conscience of the writers was exercised most on the destruction of man's independence by the spread of capitalist relations. (Examples of work of this kind are Katharine Susannah Prichard's *Black Opal*, Vance Palmer's *Golconda*, Leonard Mann's *Mountain Flat*.)

At both these points, issue was joined. Against the claims of nationalism, the demands of a universal art were counterposed; against the common man's art, an art for the élite, of intellect or sensibility. That is, of course, putting the matter too crudely, for there were many who combined democratic politics with an élitist aesthetic; one such was Victor Daley who, in poems published under his own name, 'tried to make a pleasant garden of dreams', but under a pen-name ('Creeve Roe') wrote fiery verses for the labour press. But, as a description of contrasting tendencies, this can stand.

The counter-theme had many threads. That most clearly defined was the Romance (of satyrs and fauns, buccaneers and bawds, and the lusty giants of pre-Christian mythology) with which the poets and artists of *Vision*, a short-lived magazine of the early 1920s, sought to subvert the laconic realism of most Australian writing – one part of a broader tendency which has been described more precisely by the poet Vincent Buckley as

Vitalism . . . defined, very crudely, as the view which considers the primitive forces of life, amoral and irresistible, more important than the pattern of moral and aesthetic discriminations by which the adult human being lives.

(*Essays in Poetry*, 1957)

The appeal of *Vision* was to the minority who could escape the constraints of social and moral obligation, and find their fulfilment in a riot of the senses.

Just as important was the first clear statement of tragedy in Australian literature, with Henry Handel Richardson's *The Fortunes of Richard Mahony* (1917-29). Before, there had always been conflict, but it had been the conflict of man against nature and man against man. Now, with Mahony, the stage was suddenly filled with a tragic hero of considerable dimension. The social setting was there, in the two worlds (England and Australia) between which Mahony was torn; but the external crisis was only the physical shape of Mahony's inner crisis, and the man was his own destroyer. Richardson's portrait was strong enough to call into question the accepted humanist belief in man as conqueror of his environment and therefore master of his fate.

A third thread was the adoption of a greater literary sophistication, a more esoteric language and frame of reference: a new interest in metaphysics, a personal imagery, a wide range of allusion, the assimilation of Mallarmé and Eliot and Joyce, of Nietzsche and Croce and Freud. 'Art is the expression of the imagination,' wrote Brennan, 'the indivisible energy of the spirit expressing itself in the only way possible, the creation of organic form.' This was not social revelation, but individual and personal. 'My poetry might as well have been written in China as Australia.' The artist spoke for himself, and to the few anywhere who had the wit to hear.

Taken together, this was a formidable challenge. There were many who felt with D. H. Lawrence [11] that Australian democracy was stifling to the creative impulse, tangling everyone in the treacle of a common emotion, flattening the men of talent and sensibility down to the level of the mass, imposing on all its own crude standards of mediocrity and undemanding leisure and material success. No writer could altogether escape the pressure: publishing was impoverished, the rewards of literature were small, the serious writer enjoyed neither status nor prestige, the community of artists was too minute and too scattered to offer emotional security and intellectual support. The difference, however, was in the response. For some, what was necessary was to raise the mass; for others, all that was possible was to consolidate the élite.

*

The outlines were set in the years between the wars; it remains to fill in some more recent detail.

World War II changed Australia in three significant ways. First, the fall of Singapore and the Japanese drive south destroyed the comfortable belief that the Royal Navy was adequate protection for the Australian continent. Isolation, which fifty years before had been a safeguard, was now a threat: the future of Australia could never again be separated from that of Asia. The birth of new and immensely populous nations close at hand, the only slightly more distant rise of Communist China, the fear that renascent Asia would visit the sins of the British father on to the Australian sons, drove the nation into contradictory attitudes of mind: on the one hand, there was the frightened scramble to find another protector, on the other, the half-arrogant, half-guilty bid for the friendship of the new Asia.

Secondly, American co-operation with Australia in the war in the south-west Pacific, and the assumed need for a post-war American alliance, opened Australia to increasing American influence, cultural, political, and economic. American capital has flowed into the country, particularly for the automobile and oil industries, and has been a major factor in post-war Australian growth. Australian domestic politics still approximate to a British model, but in foreign relations Australia has increasingly followed the United States: sentimental declarations that Australians are still the 'Queen's men', and the revivalist atmosphere of Royal tours, have scarcely concealed the reality of British withdrawal from the Pacific, and the Australian turn towards the United States. Culturally, this turn has been almost complete.

Given a choice between American and British film, radio, television, popular music, or literature, Australian consumers overwhelmingly choose the American product; while the plaintive appeals for protection of local cultural enterprise have gone largely unheeded.

Finally, World War II, as did the First, accelerated Australian industrialization, and was succeeded by a period of rapid economic growth. A high inflow of capital and of migrants (almost all European, and predominantly from northern Europe), and buoyant export markets, have provided the basis for an unprecedented affluence which has spread widely through the community. Development has concentrated in the cities and in the south-eastern States; in the north, there is still an 'outback', an exotic frontier element which contributes disproportionately to the Australian self-image. But the consequences of post-war affluence have not been very different in Australia from those in other parts of the capitalist world. Among wage-earners, the balance is shifting noticeably from the unskilled to the semi-skilled and skilled. The growing complexity of industry and government and society multiplies the number of white collar and professional workers. Industrialization demands more specialists, a higher general level of education: schools and universities have grown tremendously, but have contributed to an increasing division of intellectual labour and have done little to check the growing isolation of individuals from the power of effective decision.

Isolation and consequent futility lead men to seek an anodyne: the appetite for mass culture grows; leisure and literacy provide the opportunity for its consumption; automobiles and television offer not only status but escape. Excitement and self-expression find physical outlets, on the roads or in the air, in the surf or on the snow.

Some of the early characteristics remain. Australia is an outdoor nation: people retreat in their leisure from the cities to the beaches or the mountains or the bush; they travel far and make their own way; they live easily with emptiness and distance. There is still a deep underlying concern for social welfare, and it is still the responsibility of government to ensure that this is met. Australian society remains relatively open and egalitarian (although some groups of migrants could become permanently under-privileged, as Aborigines already are); leisure pursuits are great levellers, and given the material opportunity it is not hard for people to pass from one class to another. The egalitarian imperatives are reinforced by the affluent pressures for conformity.

Affluence has not proved such a favourable environment for self-cultivation as nineteenth-century optimism had hoped.

The educational advance, along with technological improvement in the reproduction and circulation of the arts, wider overseas travel by Australians, and the regular inflow of European, American, and Asian artists, have enlarged greatly the audience which lays claim to knowledge and aspires to taste. Artists, producing for the home market, must now expect – as a matter of course rather than as a conscious assertion of superior values – to be judged by international standards. One consequence has been the increasing use and acceptance of an international language; for many, the adjective 'Australian' has acquired the connotation 'second-rate'.

The wider audience has held out for Australian artists (except for those who operate in such fields as theatre, film, and ballet, which require a large capital outlay) new hopes of material security and perhaps success. Publishing, which languished badly before 1939, prospered during the war years when the desperate shortage of shipping space threw Australia back on to its own resources for books. The resumption of large-scale importation in 1946 caused a new slump in local production, and writers – unless they could find a formula which appealed to English publishers – were again hard-pressed. The Commonwealth Literary Fund (an annual government subvention from which are awarded, on the recommendation of an expert committee, fellowships to writers and subsidies to literary magazines and for the publication of works of imaginative literature) kept open some avenues of publication, but the general prospect was far from good. However, Australians 'are, statistically, among the earth's most voracious readers and book consumers. ... In 1961, Australians spent $4 per head on books – in terms of local purchase value the highest book expenditure in the English-speaking world.'[12] Since 1953, more and more of this expenditure has spilt over into Australian books. Whether the audience has increased proportionately or merely absolutely, it is not possible to say; in any case, the disheartening picture of writers searching, often in vain, for a publisher has been transformed in recent years into its opposite.

But affluence has not only enlarged the cultivated Australian audience; it has also produced a pervasive mass culture (over-whelmingly imported) which threatens to create an unbreachable wall between the minority high culture and the mass of the people. The answers that Australian writers have made to this since 1945 have not been essentially different from those of pre-war: either consolidate the minority or elevate the mass. The terms in which these demands have been expressed have, how-ever, varied: as the discussion of Australian literature has grown more articulate, it has also drawn closer to politics. To assert the claims of a national literature has, since 1945, been joined at some points with opposition to the American alliance; the connecting link has been protest against the 'cultural imperialism' of American mass-cult. Conversely, the demand for universal standards, that Australian literature be rescued from its na-tionalist dead-end, has been associated with a new 'radical con-servative' critique of Australian politics and society, and with the claims of an élite culture.

Each side has its problems. One of the demands of social realism is that literature should illuminate the contradictions of contemporary life, and should point to an appropriate resolu-tion. However, affluence is not conducive to radical social action; so that writers of this persuasion have tended to turn to the past, when social conflict was sharper and the lines more clearly drawn. (Perhaps the best examples are Katharine Susannah Prichard's 'goldfields' trilogy, and Frank Hardy's *Power Without Glory*, although it could be argued that the latter is at least as much concerned with the unholy fascination of power as it is with mass politics.) The passion and horror of war, the emotional turmoil of migration, the muted political and indus-trial conflict of recent times, have attracted many of the writers who work within the 'democratic tradition'; in some cases, this has had its limitations:

The trouble with the traditionalists is that they are traditionalists, and have lost the sense of forward movement. They follow the tracks of the pioneers – and they thereby deny the spirit of the pioneers, who followed no man's tracks.

(A. A. Phillips: 'The Literary Heritage Re-assessed,' *Meanjin*, 1962)

This judgement might be applied not only to the more 'political' of post-war writers, but to many of these who are still preoccupied with the Australian environment. Definition remains a major concern of Australian writers – the definition of the nation and the land. There have been vigorous complaints about the unthinking acceptance of a bucolic imagery, and (from James McAuley) about the 'fetishistic attitude to what is indigenous'. The complainants, however, have not themselves escaped the need to define, at least, the spiritual and intellectual desert they sense around them:

> Mentally, they're still in Pliocene,
> A flat terrain, impermeably dense;
> And will be so, until volcanic mind
> Arches its back at brute indifference.
> (James McAuley: 'The True Discovery of Australia,' 1944)

But, complaints notwithstanding, and for all that it sometimes slips over into habit or fashion or exoticism, the fascination with the unique remains. 'Ours is a poetry without echoes,' writes Judith Wright, approvingly. ' . . . may it not be that the only real maturity lies in striking out one's own line, remaining faithful to one's own experience?'

For many, however, wartime and post-war literary pioneering was an Australian rediscovery of Europe. The paintings of the Paris school took Sydney and Melbourne by storm in 1938-9, and almost overnight there was an Australian *avant-garde*. The blues, sociology, cubism, the collective unconscious, atonal music, the classic German film, primitive sculpture, the Id and the Superego, symbolism, surrealism, expressionism – all were avidly absorbed by young artists and intellectuals for whom *avant-garde* meant a revolt against age and provincialism and bourgeois values, a rejection of the market-place and the subordination of art to ideology, a revelation of the senses and the psyche, even a way of life. The Contemporary Art Societies threw brushful after brushful of paint into the faces of the Australian academies, while the irregular but well-produced journal, *Angry Penguins* (1940-6), revelled in the outraged protest it aroused. The excitement of liberation was great, and much of importance was done, but the limitations of intuition as a guide to literary judgement were revealed by the 'Ern Malley' episode, while the difficulty (sometimes incomprehensibility) of its symbolism, language, and imagery limited the participants in the revolt. (See the 'Ern Malley' Poems by A. Norman Jeffares, page 407.)

All the same, it was a valuable clearing operation. Later, many of the *avant-garde* (among others, the poet Max Harris, the artists Arthur Boyd and Sidney Nolan, and the novelist Patrick White, who, although he was not in Australia during the *Angry Penguins* years, had a remarkably similar development) turned the new understanding and techniques they had won towards the problem which has preoccupied the more traditional artists – that of identity. To uniqueness, a new dimension, continuity, has been added, by the identification of the Australian tradition with pre-Christian and Christian traditions, sanctified by age, the transformation of legend into myth. The discoverers of Australia become the ancient Greek voyagers; Judith Wright's bullocky is Moses; Patrick White's Voss and Sidney Nolan's Kelly are Christ. In a sense, this too is a part of the process of definition – the re-definition of the Australian symbol, the discoverer, the pioneer, the bushman, in terms of everyman.

*

Australia is no longer alone: the security and hope of isolation are gone, and with them the dream that, in the future Australia, the millenium will mould the perfect man. Social optimism is qualified by the anticipation of corruption and the fear of annihilation, and by a tragic vision of the individual condition. Those who argue about man's destiny use the language and concepts which divide the world. As in all countries – for an advanced technology has made little difference to this – the number of those engaged in this dialogue is small, but among them are the creative artists. While others dispute affluence and welfare, national safety and international security, conformity and revolt, Australian artists are, on their own account, working their way through one of the hardest of all questions for a once-colonial culture – whether it is possible to say, at the same time, here is an Australian, and here is a man.

NOTES

1. Cf. the story by 'Price Warung' (William Astley), *The Ross Gang 'Yarner'-Ship* (*The Bulletin*, 24 October 1891), which concerns the election of a 'yarner' by a gang of convicts, the qualification for this post being knowledge of 'Frank the Poet's' ballad, *The Convict's Tour of Hell*.

2. See H. Anderson (ed.) *Goldrush Songster* (Melbourne, 1958) for a selection of Charles Thatcher's songs; also the same writer's *The Colonial Minstrel* (Melbourne, 1960) for a brief biography of the entertainer.

3. The discussion in Raymond William's *Culture and Society* (Penguin, 1961) of nineteenth century concepts of culture is relevant for the Australian colonies as well as the United Kingdom; Burke and Mill, Carlyle and Arnold were the starting points for colonial as well as metropolitan discussion.

4. Thus, novels by Catherine Spence, Marcus Clarke and Rolf Boldrewood were all serialized in Australian journals before book publication in London.

5. Compare, for example, the (homestead) text of the song, 'The Wooyeo Ball', in Stewart and Keesing's anthology, *Old Bush Songs*, with the (hut) version 'Euabalong Ball', recorded by A. L. Lloyd on *The Banks of the Condamine* (Wattle Recordings, Sydney).

6. A note for present-day Australian readers: the sequence is right. These views of Melbourne and Sydney, expressed by Francis Adams in his *Australian Essays* (1886), were shared by most visitors at that time.

7. The title of Stephens's book was a pun on his position as editor of the 'Red Page' (i.e. the literary section) of *The Bulletin*, the catalytic weekly founded in 1880. For Stephens, see also Vance Palmer (ed.), *A. G. Stephens: His Life and Work*, which contains, as well as a biographical sketch, a selection of his criticism.

8. But not, at least in Lawson's case, sentiment. In a perceptive comment on one of Lawson's poems, 'Second Class, Wait Here', Joseph Furphy says: 'But in the end he falls into that fatal conventionality, that pseudo-religious sentiment which is so taking, yet so hopelessly relaxing.' See Miles Franklin and Kate Baker, *Joseph Furphy* (1944).

9. On this point, see the article 'The Democratic Tradition' in A. A. Phillips, *The Australian Tradition* (1958).

10. Many critics have seen D. H. Lawrence's *Kangaroo* as an uncanny forecast of the leaders of the New Guard; it seems more likely, however, that Lawrence's study of an incipient Australian fascism was based on his observations of ex-servicemen's organization of the early 1920s.

11. For Lawrence's views on Australia, see his novel *Kangaroo* (1923) and the various references in his letters.

12. Andrew Fabinyi: 'The Australian Book', in *Image of Australia*, a special issue of *The Texas Quarterly*, Summer 1962. Dr Fabinyi, publishing director of a leading Australian house, defends his profession in these terms: ' . . . a genuine, distinctive, indigenous civilisation has emerged and must develop . . . culture and literature are the effective means of national self-expression . . . it is through books that we can conquer worlds for pennies which we could not conquer physically for billions'.

AUSTRALIAN POETRY TO 1920

JUDITH WRIGHT

THE history of Australian poetry from the First Settlement in 1788 until the end of the first world war is largely a study in the adaptation of the European (and specifically English) poetic consciousness and tradition to entirely new, and apparently hostile, conditions. As such, it is an interesting story from many aspects, including the sociological; and if the poetry that was produced during this time is, for the most part, rather of historical significance than great literary value, this was probably to be expected.

It was to be expected, above all, because Australia has seemed from the first so difficult a problem to her settler. It was not only the physical conditions and isolation of the continent which daunted and repelled many of the early settlers, but the psychological climate, as it were, induced by the complete topsy-turvydom of everything to which the European mind was accustomed. There is such a thing, psychologists nowadays announce, as 'culture-shock', induced when migrants enter a new society whose language and customs are wholly unfamiliar; and it is at least temporarily crippling to the sufferer. Much the same effect must have been produced on the convicts, the military, and officials who first landed in New South Wales.

Moreover, as contemporary records show, it took long to wear off. Even near the end of the nineteenth century, writers like Marcus Clarke were making emotional capital of the sheer strangeness and weirdness of the new continent. The unknown is always threatening, and Australia was felt to be both treacherous and bleakly unattractive.

If there were men of a poetic turn among the convicts and soldiers of the first settlement, they had probably no time or inclination to exercise the gift. Mere survival, and a fair share of the rum, perhaps filled the early ambitions of most. However, under the more prosperous and liberal dispensation of Governor Macquarie, at least one convict, Michael Massey Robinson (half-mockingly titled the 'poet laureate' of the settlement) produced a series of birthday odes for various royal personages, which were accorded publication in the *Sydney Gazette*. It is possible, however, that Robinson was also the author of various much less reverential, and much livelier, ballads for circulation at a lower level of society than his 'laureate' odes had in view. 'The Old Viceroy', deploring the end of Macquarie's reign, is an energetic and inflammatory ballad which was attributed to Robinson, as were others.

Another early convict-balladist, Francis Macnamara ('Frank the Poet') though he did not rise to laureateship, produced a number of songs, including a lively account of the seizure of the brig *Cyprus* in Recherche Bay by transported men, and their subsequent escape overseas. The last verse is a fair sample:

> Then sound your golden trumpets, play on your tuneful notes,
> The Cyprus Brig is sailing, how proudly now she floats.
> May fortune help the noble lads, and keep them ever free
> From Gags, and Cats, and Chains, and Traps, and Cruel
> Tyranny.

A few ballads achieved print in various newspapers, but in general this was considerably later than the period of their first circulation: on the whole this earthy and constant undercurrent of song, which of course continued far beyond the days of transportation, was orally transmitted. Most of the ballads appear to have been adaptations of English and Irish originals; but these early songs and recitations had about them an atmosphere of reality which was in general sadly lacking in the productions of more literary-minded men, such as W. C. Wentworth. His chief excursion into verse, during his time at Cambridge in 1823, was a patriotic epic on the subject of 'Australasia', which came second in the competition for the Chancellor's gold medal of that year. Like most of the early attempts at official or serious verse in Australia, it lay under the heavy hand of the current fashion in eighteenth-century versification, which easily betrayed bad craftsmen into pomposity.

Barron Field, during his official residence in New South Wales, produced a volume entitled *First Fruits of Australian Poetry*, in 1819, and reissued it in 1823 with some additions. Though it deserved some, at least, of the disparaise English critics gave it, it has the merit of being the first (and for a long time the only) verse produced in Australia which shows any interest in the 'local productions' of flowers and animals. 'Botany Bay Wildflowers' is appreciatively descriptive of the flora of the sandstone near Sydney, which had sent Banks into professional ecstasies; and it is curious to notice that (except for the wattle, which found its way into poetry comparatively early, perhaps by way of the bush-ballad) there is very little mention of trees, flowers, or birds by name or by recognizable description in Australian verse during the nineteenth and early twentieth centuries. Possibly Field, who knew that he was not destined to stay long in the country, had a sufficiently detached view of such details to enjoy them; whereas for the settlers and convicts alike, Australia seems to have remained for years a hostile arena rather than a countryside allowing of serene appreciation.

Wentworth had been the first native-born Australian to publish any verse; but he was a youth of sufficient wealth and influence to obtain an education and to travel. The first actual book of verse was published by a young man named Tompson, born in Sydney in 1806. He published no more books, but it is possible that his example encouraged a much better young native-born poet, Charles Harpur.

Harpur, son of convict parents, was born in 1813 in the valley of the Hawkesbury River in N.S.W., and lived his early life mainly at Windsor, where his father was schoolmaster. It does not seem that the elder Harpur was himself sufficiently educated to give his sons much more than the three R's, but Charles continued his own education by reading what books he could get hold of in private libraries, probably those of the local clergymen who were acquainted with his father, and by studying as deeply as he could the poetry that they contained.

It seems fairly clear that the young native-born Australians, the 'Currency Lads' of the early nineteenth century, felt a certain solidarity among themselves, and a pride and independence that may have been a reaction against the earlier days of the settlement, when authority and the heavy hand of English officialdom ruled. Whether Tompson's example decided him or not, Charles Harpur seems to have chosen his calling early. His life from his youth onward was to be remarkable for the tenacity and dedication with which he clung to the almost impossible task of laying the foundation for an Australian poetry, under conditions that would have discouraged most writers.

From the age of seventeen (by which time it seems he was already writing, and may have been publishing, verse) the pattern of Harpur's life consisted in repeated, usually unfortunate, attempts to earn a living in Sydney by journalism, acting, and office work, punctuated by withdrawal to the country and a life of hard physical work, frugality, and reading and writing. His ambition and a certain uncompromising pride made him frequently a target for criticism and jealousy, and he was easily wounded into retaliation.

From 1833 onwards, he published work in most newspapers which would accept poetry, particularly those of a radical temper. In early youth (probably before he was twenty) he also wrote a verse play, *The Tragedy of Donohoe*, on the life of the noted bushranger who also figures in the song 'The Wild Colonial Boy'. The play was partly printed in a colonial newspaper, and later achieved book publication under the title of *The Bushrangers*, becoming the first play to be both written and published in Australia by a native-born playwright. This volume also contained about forty poems. His other publications during his lifetime were *Thoughts: A Series of Sonnets* (1845), *The Poet's Home* (1862), and *The Tower of the Dream* (1865). All these publications were very scanty selections, and with a couple of broadsheets, were published either at Harpur's own expense, or by the help of his friends and well-wishers. A project for a subscription volume came to nothing.

A considerable time after his death, his widow managed to arrange for the publication of a collection of his poems, but these were edited by one H. M. Martin, who seems to have had little or no qualification for the task, his chief aim in editing being apparently to remove any passages which might excite controversy, regardless of meaning or unity. It is unfortunate that this volume, printed in 1883, remains the only collection of Harpur's work and has never been reprinted or revised. It is therefore a very misleading guide to Harpur's work and thought.

This fact makes it difficult to document Harpur's real significance as a forerunner of Australian poetry. His manuscripts, however, preserved in Sydney's Mitchell Library, and contemporary newspaper files, make clear the real complexity and breadth of his interests and of his ambitions.

He produced throughout his life not only a considerable number of lyrical and narrative verses (by a few of which, of convenient length for reprinting in anthologies, he is generally known), but a flood of polemical and political verse, lampoons, and topical epigrams, of fierce sincerity and wit not wholly obscured by the ponderous diction of early nineteenth-century verse-journalism. He remained throughout his life (as could not be said of all his early contemporaries) a radical reformist in politics and a believer in Australia's future as a country where equality and liberty might flourish; but his political aims were always subsidiary to his self-dedication to poetry and the search for philosophic and religious truth.

His earliest long poem may have been 'The Kangaroo Hunt', an ambitious attempt to picture the life of his time and the Australian forests as he knew them, which remains unpublished. Harpur says in the manuscript preface to the poem: 'The versification . . . is designedly irregular throughout. . . . I conceived that such an unconfined, many-metred structure of verse as might be varied and paragraphically moulded (after the manner of a musical movement) . . . would be most conducive to effective treatment.' The poem is historically interesting and often well-handled, but relies too much on contemporary poetic tricks like the use of capital-letter abstractions which seem oddly out of place in the poem's setting.

Another long poem, or rather series of poems, on the life and death of Chatterton, 'Genius Lost', is represented in the 1883 volume by a few disconnected lyrics and choruses. The poem as it stands in the manuscript-books is an interesting attempt to use a basically antiphonic plan of monologues and choruses. It seems to have taken its rise from Harpur's own unhappiness and frustration during his early twenties, when as a poor Sydney clerk he came to know something of the difficulties of an unappreciated poet. This poem, too, has never been published in full, and the 1883 volume contains no indication that the subject of the verses was Chatterton. Moreover, this version ends with a poem which was apparently not in the original manuscript, but forms the final section of another poem-series altogether, 'Autumnal Leaves'.

At the age of thirty, after one or two unsuccessful love affairs, Harpur met Mary Doyle, the subject of his sonnet-series 'To Rosa' and later his wife. The sonnets, edited and published in 1948, form almost the only available volume of his verse. They provide a more-or-less connected commentary on his long courtship of 'Rosa' and its fortunes and misfortunes. Since Mary Doyle was the daughter of moneyed settlers, and Harpur was far from being a 'good match', there was opposition to the marriage, and Mary did not finally accept him until seven years after their first meeting.

The 'Rosa' sonnets are competent, pleasantly-turned, and sometimes moving in their expression of his loneliness and frustration:

> I once did think there was no happiness
> In the wide world for me – so harsh its features
> Of social commerce, and its human creatures
> So barren of the will and power to bless ...
>
> *(Sonnet VII)*

Some of them were written during one of his excursions to Sydney, in an attempt to mend his fortunes and make a place for himself in the life of the town:

> Nightly I watch the moon with silvery sheen
> Flaking the city house-tops, till I feel
> Thy memory, Rosa, like a presence steal
> Down in her light: for ever in her mien
> Thy soul's similitude my soul hath seen ...
>
> *(Sonnet XXI)*

But on the whole these sonnets are not characteristic of Harpur at his best. He is happier in longer forms, in which his occasional prolixity and awkwardness are less noticeable.

When *The Bushrangers* was published in 1853, forty poems were included in the volume, some of which attracted a good deal of attention both favourable and unfavourable. The poem 'The Creek of the Four Graves', which has remained his best-known longer work, for the first time indicates the particular quality of his observation of landscape, and his indebtedness to Wordsworth; 'The Bush Fire' is an excellent piece of local description:

> ... huge dry-mouldered gums
> Stood 'mid their living kin as banked throughout
> With eating fire, expelling arrowy jets
> Of blue-tipped, intermitting, gaseous flame.
> Boles, branches – all! – like vivid ghosts of trees.

Another poem in *The Bushrangers* is, 'To an Echo on the Banks of the Hunter', which refers to Harpur's childhood on the banks of another river, the Hawkesbury, and to the change and frustration that his early youthful ambition had met with since those days. The poem has a sombre strength and unity that mark Harpur's thought at its most effective; the echo that he hears on the Hunter's banks and the echo of his own youth in his mind are used to draw the poem to a climax and anticlimax: used, that is, as part of the poem's structure. The last few lines, in spite of a grammatical difficulty which Harpur did not solve until a later version, are a good example of Harpur's middle style.

> ... And so at last
> Have all those glorious hopes become but lonely
> And dying echoes of the hollow past.
> All but one only!
>
> And this around my being only strays
> Like a recurring sound. In lonesome ways
> Like these it moves me still – not as of yore
> Undubiously, though yet its spirit plays
> Upon the same old promise: that when o'er
> My country's homes there shineth riper days,
> Her better sons shall learn at length to prize
> My lonely voice upon the past.

Other poems in this volume include the narrative 'Ned Connor', a fore-runner of later bush-tales in ballad form; an early version of a long poem, 'The Poet's Home', which Harpur later revised, enlarged, and reprinted; and 'The Dream by the Fountain', an important poem in which he expressed his dedication to poetry and in particular to the Australian Muse, the genius of his own country:

> I am the Muse of the Evergreen Forest,
> I am the spouse of thy spirit, lone Bard!
> Ev'n in the days when thy boyhood thou worest
> Thy pastimes drew on thee my dearest regard.
>
> For I felt thee – ev'n then, wildly, wondrously musing
> Of glory and grace by old Hawkesbury's side,
> Scenes that then spread recordless around thee suffusing
> With the purple of love – I beheld thee, and sighed ...
>
> Then would I prompt in the still hour of dreaming
> Some thought of thy beautiful country again,
> Of her yet-to-be-famed streams, through dark woods
>   far-gleaming,
> Of her bold shores that throb to the beat of the main ...

Be then the Bard of thy Country! O rather
Should such be thy choice than a monarchy wide!
Lo, 'tis the land of the grave of thy father!
'Tis the cradle of Liberty! Think, and decide ...

The two main preoccupations of Harpur's verse and life, in fact, both stem from his youth. The first is a love of the mountains and valleys that he knew in the Hawkesbury country, and that appear again and again in his later verses, variously lighted by dawn, noon, sunset, and moonlight, and by the mental light cast on them from his study of Wordsworth's nature-philosophy.

These are the heights described in his 'The Creek of the Four Graves', which

rose crowding with their summits all
Dissolving as it seemed, and partly lost
In the exceeding radiancy aloft.
And thus transfigured for awhile they stood
Like a great company of archaeons, crowned
With burning diadems, and tented o'er
With canopies of purple and of gold.

To the influence of Wordsworth's poetry on his own, we have the witness of a sonnet:

How much, O Wordsworth, in this world how much
Has thy surpassing love made rich for me
Of what was once unprized! ...

His second main theme – the radical libertarianism to which he held all his life, and his dream that Australia might be that liberty's 'cradle' – could have been thought to stem from Shelley, if we had not had Harpur's own assurance that he had not read Shelley before 1842, by which time his own thought had already taken shape and expression. The theme sprang naturally from Harpur's circumstances, as well as from his own fiery idealism. As the son of convict parents, he must have known early the difference between privilege and poverty, and in the Monody written for his father he speaks bitterly of the unhappiness the old man had endured (even though he was one of the more fortunate among the transported men). Harpur, however, developed his theme not through an active political life, but through his gift for writing. It pervades not only the satires and polemical verses he wrote for newspapers, but the whole trend of his thought as a poet.

From a technical point of view, Harpur was influenced chiefly by Wordsworth and Milton (whose prosody is traceable in much of his work, especially the long blank-verse 'The Witch of Hebron' which was the last long poem he completed). The austerities of the blank-verse measure suit Harpur's own mental qualities. He had a strength and severity which made him unable, in his lifetime, to come to terms with the petty materialism and 'cloddishness' of the neighbours his life forced on him, or to defer to the philosophy of 'money's worth' that prevailed around him.

His Wordsworthianism became unfashionable long before the end of his life, when Tennyson and Swinburne were the acclaimed influences. But the early-Romantic view of nature and of poetry, though he adapted it to his own purposes and did not take it over uncritically, gave him two elements most necessary to his position as the first of the Australian poets: an appreciation of the landscape of his country, its mountains and 'yet-to-be-famed streams', and a faith in his own mission as a poet.

The picture he gives of Australia (when all his work, not merely that which appears in the 1883 volume, is taken into account) is a much more faithful and detailed one than his critics have believed. The landscape of this country was difficult both to love and to absorb, as a glance at early painters' attempts to render it will attest. Only after generations of living in it has it finally become part of our vision; and this has come about precisely through the efforts of earlier artists and writers such as Harpur, to grasp and render its qualities. It is scarcely to be expected that any early writer could see it in exactly the light we take for granted today. For one thing, the whole atmosphere of feeling has changed, and since 'we receive but what we give', this alone means that Harpur's landscape was not ours.

For him, the important qualities of Australian scenery were its light (his mountains appear again and again, but always transfigured by different qualities of light) and its solitude. Human figures are always part of his landscapes ('The Creek of the Four Graves', 'A Storm in the Mountains', 'The Kangaroo Hunt', etc.) – but they often seem dwarfed by the sky and the surroundings. His poems on people and events, conversely, ('Ned Connor', 'To an Echo on the Banks of the Hunter', 'Lost in the Bush') often contain sudden glimpses of the surroundings that act as a counterpoint to the story. This vision, of landscape emphasized as it were by human occupation, of humanity against a background of landscape (usually a solitary and strange landscape of trees and hills) is characteristic of Harpur; it is the picture he has handed on to us of the country in which he was born, but which did not yet form a part of the psychological inheritance of his race. It may be contrasted with Kendall's emotionalization, as it were, of the features of his coastal plain in poems in which the rivers or the mountains themselves are the apparent subject, and in which the question of human relationships to the country arises only in so far as the poet himself is always part of the poem. This imparts to it the particular emotional tone of wistfulness, longing, or despair by which the landscape is pervaded. Comparatively, Harpur is a far more objective observer of the life around him than Kendall.

Yet it was, in fact, Kendall's enthusiastic 'discovery' of the elder poet's verses that formed Harpur's chief hope of influencing a younger generation of poets, at a time when, worn out and ill, he had almost come to despair of a hearing. The much younger Kendall corresponded with Harpur for some time, though he only met him once; and in a poem dedicated to him, addressed him as his master and declared him to be 'the Monarch of Song in the land'. Harpur may have had reservations about the rather fulsome style of this young poet, but he replied with a grateful sonnet; Kendall's admiration was perhaps the last pleasure he had.

What took Kendall's imagination in Harpur's poetry was probably less the elder man's method and manner than his dedication to the 'Australian Muse' and his treatment of Australian subjects. Kendall, too, hoped to interpret the new country in verse, and dreamed optimistically of forming one of a band of young poets who should follow Harpur's example. In fact, however, he was virtually the only Australian-born poet of his generation.

He set out on his interpretive task with eagerness. Two at least of his early poems were on themes that Harpur had already treated – 'The Glen of Arrawatta' is a treatment, in Harpur's own favourite blank-verse, of a theme somewhat like that of 'The Creek of the Four Graves', and there are textual correspondences as well. Another early subject was 'The Wail in the Native

Oak'; Harpur's original poem, 'The Voice of the Swamp Oak', was here translated into somewhat gushing Swinburnian measures. If Kendall was taking Harpur as a model, he was also evidently trying to translate him into a more mid-Victorian style.

But Kendall's bent, unlike Harpur's, was rather to the lyric than to narrative or epic verse. His work lacks the backbone, the hard underlying structure, of that of the elder poet, and his style, though he gradually outgrew his early loose and flowery manner, was in general lacking in strength and plainness.

One at least of Harpur's chief preoccupations, that of the future of Australia as a land of political equality and freedom, does not appear in Kendall's verse. The younger poet had none of Harpur's political ardency. Moreover, when Harpur first began to write, Australia was still a largely unknown country, admitting of much more optimistic speculation than it was thirty years later. By that time most of the major explorations were already undertaken; discouraging reports of waterless plains, deserts, failure, and death had put a stop to patriotic hopes for the future of the inland. The discovery of gold had widened the country's horizons and had brought in a flow of migrants and of wealth; but subjects such as these never much interested Kendall. Certainly he wrote – usually to order – a number of patriotic verses, but their sheer badness seems to indicate that his heart was not in them.

An increasing disappointment with the reception of his poetry, and his struggle to make a living, with other personal circumstances, gradually turned his weak but genuine lyric gift more and more inward. The best of his work – such poems as 'Mooni', 'Orara', 'Araluen', and 'Bell-Birds', which celebrate the green solitary valleys and rivers of the coast of N.S.W. – has a corresponding counter-subject in his poems of the inland and of the explorers' journeys, like 'Leichhardt' and 'On the Paroo', which set against the yearned-for rivers and valleys a burning drought-stricken desert in which his explorers almost always perish miserably. For Kendall there seems to be no halfway measure between the coastal Paradise and the hell of the inland, and both are painted in exaggerated colours.

In fact, Kendall's constant identification of his own longings for some Eden of innocence with the coastal rivers, and of his own frustrations with those of the explorers, makes it clear that these landscape-poems are more subjective than objective. So far from being, as has been claimed, the first poet to deal descriptively with the Australian landscape, Kendall internalized it; his landscape-poems are symbolic of his own yearnings and distresses. It is this symbolism, unconscious as it may often have been (though 'Mooni' is clearly an ideal, not a real, river, and visualized as such), that give his poems their pathos and meaning. But to regard him as pre-eminently a poet of the landscape is to miss most of the import of what he wrote.

Technically, Kendall's versification is seldom good, except in those few poems where his personal feeling was so deeply engaged that it carries the poem through successfully on its current. He had a weakness for adjectives, and little capacity to give his verses a firm underlying structure. He is fond of vague and imprecise images, and is seldom exact or forceful. He was much given to self-pity (for which no one need blame him, since his life was lived in most difficult circumstances); but often this self-pity emerges under the guise of compassion for others, and this falsifies much of his writing. In the poem on Leichhardt, for instance, the sentimentalism of the ending, in which he imagines his hero-explorer buried in the rich green landscape of his native Germany, in preference to the desert in which he in fact met his end, is weakening not only to the poem but to the whole initial idea of heroism.

Kendall had much more capacity for lyric writing, and considerably more charm, than Harpur, who is sometimes harsh and pedantic. But he can be even more banal, because more sweetly so, than Harpur; and his lack of capacity to give his work a strong internal structure means that he is out of his depth in poems of any considerable length. In his treatments of Biblical subjects, the shallowness of his feeling reveals his lack of interest; his patriotic verses are examples of pumped-up sentiments and forced rhetoric. These were the verses he wrote to please the public, and their lack of real inner impulse is evident.

His best volume is *Songs from the Mountains*, his third and last. Much of it was written when, after a long and miserable period of breakdown, he regained his serenity and began to live a normal and comparatively untroubled life. The dedicatory poem 'To a Mountain', – which is clearly not addressed to any actual mountain that he knew, but to a symbolic entity – is probably the strongest and best-sustained of his poems. It expresses in a moving and well-managed blank-verse his own sense of having at last risen above his own immediate problems into a serener air:

> ... and from thee, indeed,
> The broad foundations of a finer hope
> Were gathered in; and thou hast lifted up
> The blind horizon for a larger faith.

This was, indeed, the calmest and most successful period of Kendall's life. For various reasons, his poetry was becoming popular, and he achieved, for an Australian poet, a considerable reputation, which has lingered round his name and to some extent prevented a proper assessment of his achievement. The common view, that in his work Australia at last found a voice, does not hold water. As the poet Mary Gilmore pointed out, during his lifetime a great movement towards nationhood was going on, and throughout the country much was happening; the successive waves of settlement were driving out the original inhabitants, both human and animal, and altering the whole face of the country. Kendall saw little of this; his chief preoccupation was, as with poets it is apt to be, with himself and his own problems, and in so far as he wrote of his country she usually stood for some aspect of himself, less of an outer reality than of an inward one. If he was adopted as Australia's poet, it was because Australia began to feel the need of a poet and seized on Kendall to fill the bill, as well as on Gordon. But if he is looked at objectively, it is clear that his best poems are those in which he says least about Australia and most about himself.

In 1870, during his unfortunate sojourn in Melbourne where he tried unsuccessfully to earn a living by writing, Kendall had met the English expatriate, Adam Lindsay Gordon. Gordon had come to Australia seventeen years before, under some unspecified family embargo. He had become a mounted trooper, then a horsebreaker; for a brief time he had entered Parliament in South Australia, but a lack of interest in his Parliamentary career, and a succession of financial troubles, had sent him back to steeplechasing and keeping livery stables. He had always had 'a turn for verse'; as a trooper he had composed verses as he rode along, and no doubt he had heard many of the indigenous ballads that were current in the country. But his ambitions were poetically rather higher than these; he seems to have thought of himself as a kind of second Byron, and the verse he had published, in *Ashtaroth* and *Sea Spray and Smoke Drift*, was influenced largely by Byron and Swinburne.

However, he was now well-known, both as a recklessly daring rider (which in itself endeared him to contemporary Australia) and as the writer of a few ballads which had caught the public fancy, especially 'The Sick Stockrider' and 'How we Beat the Favourite'. Nevertheless, there was no sale for his books, and he was deep in debt on other counts. Kendall greatly admired his verse; and when his last book, *Bush Ballads and Galloping Rhymes*, appeared, it was to become a popular success. But this was too late for Gordon, who, finding himself unable even to pay for the book's publication, had killed himself on the day of its appearance. His suicide was quite possibly a factor in Kendall's own subsequent breakdown.

However, there is no doubt that Gordon's death and the publicity it gave his work had a good deal to do with the sudden posthumous celebrity of his verse. In actual proportion, Gordon wrote little verse that could be called Australian in its subject, and for most of this he himself had little regard (he never cared for 'The Sick Stockrider', for instance, though after his death it became so famous that drovers and boundary-riders all over Australia could recite it). His preference appears to have been for his more pretentious verse.

But he did Australian writing a service at a crucial time, by indicating a new direction of interest. Kendall had been attempting to write much the same kind of verse as might have been written by an English contemporary poet; in spite of a certain success with character-pieces such as 'Jim the Splitter', he had not taken much interest in local event and character, and he knew little of the active life of the country as it then was. It was to this life of the 'back-blockers', the nomad workers, drovers and overlanders, that Gordon's rhymes drew attention.

It may be that the ballads themselves were not very original ('The Sick Stockrider', for instance, has a number of elements that appear in a bush-ballad published five years before *Bush Ballads and Galloping Rhymes*, and no doubt current for years before that) but the fact that Gordon himself was English and already known as a poet of more serious pretensions, and the theatrical Byronism of his character, combined with the genuine swing and excitement of his rhythms, ensured wide popularity for these new subjects and for the first time made the bush-workers interesting in the eyes of the respectable.

Gordon's life and work had another effect: they bridged the gulf between the exile-Australian, who could see little praise-worthy in his country and for whom England was the only criterion of good, and the independent-minded indigene who rejected England and all its works. To the first, Gordon was an important writer because of his English origin, and because his 'serious' work had attracted attention overseas; he had, in fact, a certain snob-value. To the second, Gordon became an idol because of his adoption of Australian balladry and because he was himself a legendary horseman and man of action. The two currents of feeling (which, however contradictory, could exist almost side by side in certain people) once they were united, added force to the impulse towards a new kind of popular poetry. This allowed the acceptance of the more articulate of the 'bush-balladists', and injected a new vigour into Australian poetry, which had hitherto often imitated the subjects and style of late-Victorian English verse.

The effect of this sudden flood of popular verse in the work of the 'Bulletin bards' of the nineties and later was far-reaching. Without this influence, not only Australian writing but much else in Australian attitudes and opinion would scarcely have taken their present shape. Its traces can be seen in the work of numerous present-day writers, and the present-day revolt against 'Austra-lianism' and the 'Australian Legend' is largely directed against the attitudes that stem from the wide acceptance of the values of the 'Bulletin school' that took its rise in the nineties.

Gordon's popularity, then, represented a turning point in the growth of Australian poetry far more decisive than his actual work (which, properly examined, is of very minor value) seems to justify. It is rather as a national figure than as a poet that he is important; but his work gave a remarkable impetus and a new self-confidence to the popular poets, who now saw their oppor-tunity to celebrate the lives of 'the back-blockers' and their hard inarticulate independence.

One of Gordon's earliest and most promising disciples was Barcroft Boake, a young man of naturally melancholy temper-ament, who, after a Sydney upbringing, went to the bush first as a surveyor's assistant, then as a drover and boundary-rider. On a droving trip into Central Queensland, which occupied many months, he discovered for himself the quality of the country and of the lives men were then living there; and he was especially impressed by the fact that Gordon was regarded by many of these men as particularly their poet. Identifying himself deeply with the bush workers and their lives, he saw the effect of absentee ownership and city exploitation. It was the impulse of these experiences of the life of the inland, and his admiration of Gordon, that set him writing, and in the few years of his output he produced some ballads and narratives of considerable vigour and descriptive power, notably 'Corrigan's Gin' and the poem by which he is best known, 'The Land Where the Dead Men Lie'.

This latter poem, with its fierceness and compression, and the economy of the picture it gives of the land 'where the heat-waves dance forever', has a force and unity that outweigh its occasional youthful awkwardness. It anticipates Lawson in its pity and indignation, and outdoes him in poetic achievement.

Like Gordon and Lawson, however, Boake was pessimistic in his outlook on humanity and civilization. His love of the Bush was the obverse of his dislike for the city and its artificialities; the bush life, he felt, was 'the only life'. When the depression of the early nineties left him unemployed in the home of his father, who was also financially distressed, and when he met with disappointment in love, he followed Gordon's example, committing a melodramatic suicide by hanging himself in the loop of his own stockwhip. He was then only twenty-six.

Though Boake was young and comparatively inexperienced, and his work was often naïve and clumsy, it has a brooding force and a vigour of description and narration that might well have made him a much more important figure than Gordon, if he had lived. He was among the earliest of the native-born poets to occupy himself wholly with the interpretation of the life of his own country.

Much of the later *Bulletin*-balladry, even that of Lawson, oversimplified and sentimentalized its subject-matter. The life of the outback was harsh and limited, but the stereotype established by the 'bush bards' was unnecessarily shallow, and it meant that no honest examination in depth of that life was ever undertaken. The originality and strength of a few early ballads were exploited by later writers, and the movement at last petered out. It was revived, however, in a more sophisticated form in the upsurge of writing that began with the early years of World War II, and renewed interest resulted in the collection and printing of much of the original currency of bush-ballads that had antedated Gordon himself.

During the nineties, however, another popular school of verse-writers arose, the 'nationalists' who were mainly represented by James Brunton Stephens and Essex Evans. Both are highly conventional late-Tennysonian romantics, and neither has worn well; but both were much admired in their time. Stephens's 'Convict Once', a long and florid narrative, went into three editions. Both were earnest patriots, writing verses with titles such as 'Ode for Commonwealth Day' (Evans) and 'The Dominion of Australia' (Stephens). If they deserve to be remembered it is partly because the 'nationalist' movement, together with the increasingly sentimental emphasis on the Bush, irritated a few genuine poets into a wholly opposite stance. McCrae, in a violent reaction against the self-satisfied artificialities of both schools, found in Greece and the Middle Ages themes for a reassertion of the basic springs of poetry in the earth and the senses; Brennan, on the other hand, ignoring the Australian scene, turned to Europe and to the whole argument of Western poetic thought.

Brennan, the elder of the two, is also on all counts the weightier poet. Alone in his time and place, he plunged head-foremost into the midst of that movement which was most important in contemporary literature and poetic thought – that is, the Symbolist movement as foreshadowed by Baudelaire and summed up in the work of Brennan's most admired poet, Mallarmé.

It is worth remembering that in the late nineteenth century few writers in England, or even in Europe, thoroughly recognized the significance of the Symbolist movement and its place in the long development of Western poetic thought. That development, when after the end of the early-Romantic movement in England first Tennyson, then Swinburne, Morris, and Rossetti turned more and more away from ideas in the direction of decoration and verbal felicity, had found its growing-point in France. As Brennan recognized, it was Baudelaire's notion of 'correspondences' that gave the impetus to a whole new school of writers and a new poetic view of the relation between man and his world, as between thought and thing, image and experience. 'In our life alone does Nature live,' Coleridge had cried, negating Wordsworth's view of Nature as something apart from man, his 'guide and nurse'; for the Symbolists, nature became a 'forest of symbols', images which intricately re-echoed the truths of human experience.

So Brennan says, in a lecture delivered in 1904:

The law of correspondence has a double action. It charges the outer world with meaning and it awakes meaning within ourselves, helping the mood to disengage itself. When a man lets his soul wed itself to some unified aspect of nature, the vastness of the dawn, or the royal passing of the day, all the pettinesses and vexing trifles drop away: what is left is the purer, intenser mood, the rhythm that is ample enough to sing in tune with that of nature.

(*The Prose of Christopher Brennan*, p. 86)

Poetry, for Brennan, was that which mediated between the 'two lives' of man, the 'outer weariness which made Baudelaire a maniac' and the 'hours of insight'. Its mediation was to be effected by the symbol, the fusion of appearances and underlying truth, 'the meeting-point of many analogies'.

The 'two lives' – the ideal and the real – and their opposition and constant interaction, form the great subject that continually occupies Brennan in almost all his poetry. Speaking later in the same lecture of Blake's symbol of Eldorado or the Golden Age, Brennan says:

Out of this symbol ... grows a myth, for every symbol naturally produces a myth – this time a myth as to the relation between the two worlds. ... The myth is that of the fall of man – in Blake that of his redemption as well – the decay of the Golden Age and its restoration. But this myth is to be read in the same sense as that in which the Gnostics and Neoplatonists reshaped it: the fall is the birth of the soul into matter, which is its bondage.

(Ibid. pp. 88-9)

This, then, was another aspect of Brennan's subject – the soul versus matter, and the necessary reconciliation between the two. Here also the symbol must be the mediator and poetry the reconciling force:

... poetic imagery ... [is] everywhere definite statement of fact. That fact [is], in the case of each particular image or symbol, a harmony

72

between some phase of our spirit and some phase of the universe: the inner fact being corroborated, made more real to us by means of the outer which in turn received its significance from the inner. And the law of correspondences ... means this, – that our spirit is adequate to the whole outer world, and that the whole outer world is a perpetual corroboration of spiritual fact.

(Ibid. p. 160)

It was, then, no less a subject than the 'fall' – the birth of the soul into matter, and its struggle thereafter towards reconciliation – that Brennan chose for his great poem, or poem-series, which was to take up the work that Mallarmé had left uncompleted. That work was to have been 'a myth resuming all the others, without date or place, a figuration of our multiple personality; the myth written on the page of heaven and earth and imitated by man with the gesture of his passions ... a drama, for nature is a drama and as Novalis had said, "The true thinker perceives in the world a continued drama."' (Ibid. p. 145). To the completion of this work Brennan turned his own poetic ambition.

The various sequences of poems which compose *Poems 1913* were written over a number of years, from about 1894 onward. They were not composed in the sequence in which he afterwards arranged them, but taken all together they form a complete and monumental work. Since the ideas that underlie them were, it would seem, already present to Brennan's mind at least as early as 1898, and probably before, it hardly matters that some early poems were subsumed under later sections and vice versa. (Nevertheless, it is true that his early poems are more inclined to floridity and less strongly constructed than the later, so that where poems from different periods are in juxtaposition, the alteration in tone is sometimes jarring.)

The book is made up of a series of sections under four main headings: *Towards the Source*; *The Forest of Night*, which has a number of sub-sections, 'The Twilight of Disquietude', 'The Quest of Silence', 'The Shadow of Lilith', 'Lilith', and 'The Labour of Night', interspersed with three Interludes of two poems each, and introduced by a dedicatory poem to Mallarmé and a 'Liminary'; *The Wanderer*, which marks the end of the logical development of sections; four poems under the general title of *Pauca Mea*, and two Epilogues.

The first section, *Towards the Source*, is concerned with the Edenic myth. It is to a large extent composed of early poems (indeed, it is sub-headed *1894-7*); and since these were written before the death of Mallarmé with his great work left incomplete and destroyed, it is fairly clear that they were in the main not written with the total poem in view. However, it also contains the lyric 'Sweet silence after bells', written in 1913 and far superior in technique and suggestiveness to the rest of the poems in the section, with the possible exception of the lyric titled 'Dies Dominica'. Most of the poems are written in celebration of his love-affair and early marriage, and on the whole the section is not remarkable.

The second section, *The Forest of Night*, is the most difficult and ambitious. It is Brennan's attempt to give an account of man's struggle, since leaving the unconscious joys of 'Eden', with the intractable and ineluctable opposition of his 'first bride', Night. Its central figure, Night personified as Lilith, the demon bride of Hebrew mythology, is Brennan's embodiment of this opposition. Lilith is Night in all her aspects, both negative and positive, abstract and concrete, horrifying and sheltering, hostile and motherly. She is not only the eternal opposition to man's struggle to regain Eden, she is also the only way that leads to Eden; she is not only an implacable enemy but an irresistible lover, continually seeking to win back Adam from Eve's embrace. It is only through increased knowledge, increased consciousness, that she can be defeated and the way to Eden discovered, so Lilith stands for the unconscious opposition which can only be overcome by complete self-knowledge. This self-knowledge implies also complete knowledge of the world, since for Brennan it is man who bestows meaning on the world.

> What do I seek? I seek the word
> that shall become the deed of might
> whereby the sullen gulfs are stirred
> and stars begotten on their night.
> (*The Verse of Christopher Brennan*, No. 42)

So Brennan sets out to trace the various paths by which man has sought to overcome Night and assert dominion; he refers to symbol after symbol and myth after myth that have arisen in the course of the search: the Greek pantheon, Valhalla, Gnosticism, and Neoplatonism, pantheism, the legend of Solomon, alchemy, the religions of Egypt and the Near East – all these and others are woven into the fabric of this long and complex series of poems. Over all of them, however, broods the finally-triumphant figure of Lilith, who has won the victory over all gods and systems yet devised and is still wooing the heart of Adam away from Eve and from his search.

The third section, *The Wanderer*, is written in the first person; the speaker is the Wanderer himself – the unconquered Adam in the person of the poet, finally able to accept that his search may continue for ever without success, but still determined to pursue it. The section is comparatively brief; also its dominant note is simpler and more apparently personal than that of the Lilith sections, less loaded with symbolic figures and images, less dense in thought and language, and therefore more immediately appealing. How far Brennan actually identified himself with the figure of the Wanderer – who stands, not for all men, but for the restless searching mind and the eternally unsatisfied spirit of human consciousness – may be doubtful. The Wanderer is evidently intended to be just as symbolic and generic a figure as Lilith herself. Nevertheless, the poem as a whole is so curiously bound up with Brennan's own life that it might be hard to trace how much the one owes to the other.

Brennan, born in Sydney as the son of Irish immigrants (his father was a Sydney brewer), at one time intended to become a priest. Instead he chose to take a degree course in Arts at Sydney University, and was soon afterwards awarded a travelling scholarship. He went to Berlin University for two years. Here he met his future wife, his landlady's daughter, and also discovered Mallarmé's work, by which he was deeply impressed and influenced. He returned to Sydney in August 1894 (the year in which the first of the poems in *Poems 1913* were written), and after a period of difficulty obtained work as a librarian.

Three years later, his fiancée arrived from Germany and they were married. Meanwhile, a number of the poems which later formed *Towards the Source* had been written, and Brennan's ideas on literature had taken definite shape. He continued writing, and later became connected with the University as a lecturer.

His early poetry testifies to his love of his wife, but they had little in common, and after a few years they began to drift apart. Brennan's violence against the German nation during World

War I was probably exacerbated by, and in turn exacerbated, their relationship.

His reading of Mallarmé, and his interest in the problem of knowledge (the relationship between knower and known, between concept and percept) led him early into attempts to systematize his thought. A paper on 'Fact and Idea', read in 1898, already emphasizes what he was always to assert, that 'concepts have been drawn from experience'; that 'man shapes his reality for himself out of some indifferent *brutum*', (which recalls Coleridge's line already quoted), and that the modern process of analysis 'has been just so much preparation to some greater synthesis – the complete humanization of the Universe, when man shall have attained complete knowledge of himself. ... Man's task is ... to humanize the world; and the challenge proceeds from the Infinite.' (*The Prose of Christopher Brennan*, pp. 5, 9-10.)

This notion of the Infinite as man's constant challenge is embodied later in the ambiguous and shifting nature of the figure of Lilith. Similarly, it may be that his Eve is based on the human reality of his own courtship of his wife. But there are many other symbolic figures and images in the poem; and possibly the most basic of all is the Rose. As Brennan uses it, this symbol is almost, though not quite, synonymous with the other symbol of Eden.

It appears, first, in *Towards the Source* (a sequence which is full of various spring flowers); here it is 'the rose of all fulfill'd delight', and its relationship is to youth, spring, and the flesh. In *The Forest of Night* it appears in another context as the rose-window of the church, now broken and empty:

> A gray and dusty daylight flows
> athwart the shatter'd traceries,
> pale absence of the ruin'd rose.

> (*The Verse of Christopher Brennan*, No. 56)

In this context, the Second Epilogue is relevant, with its tracing of Brennan's early Catholic upbringing; this is perhaps the rose-window of that church

> where I was brought in pious hands,
> a chrisom-child, that I might be
> accepted of that company

> who, thro' their journeying, behold
> beyond the apparent heavens, controll'd
> to likeness of a candid rose,
> ascending where the gold heart glows,
> cirque within cirque, the blessed host ...

The Second Epilogue continues autobiographically to trace Brennan's progress from the Church to the University, where he lost his desire to be a priest and lapsed from his religion, seduced by philosophy:

> and found viaticum and goal
> in that hard atom of the soul,
> that final grain of deathless mind,
> which Satan's watch-fiends shall not find ...

That 'hard atom', he goes on, properly viewed, contained for him

> Eden, clad in nuptial morn—

for he saw the mind as itself a way to conquer the blandishments of Night and rediscover that Eden where knowing and being are one.

The rose-window, the Christian symbol, however, contains in the Lilith sequence only emptiness. Through it is seen nothing but the sky, 'the traitor roses of the wooing dawn', 'the old illusion of the spring'. And through it, lastly, appears the night itself.

> O bleeding rose, alone! O heart of night!
>
> (Ibid. No. 67)

Lilith, then, is triumphant over the Rose. But she is also the way to its renewal:

> Old odours of the rose are sickening: night,
> hasten above the corpse of old delight,
> if in decay the heart cherish some heat,
>
> to breed new spice within the charnel-mould,
> that eyes unseal'd with living dew may greet
> the morning of the deathless rose of gold.
>
> (Ibid. No. 69)

But that morning has not yet come, and the *Forest of Night* ends on a note of uncertainty:

> How long delays the miracle blossoming,
> vermeil and gold, soft fire, flush of the dark ...
>
> (Ibid. No. 84)

The Wanderer sequence contains no reference to the rose. The whole section seems to take place in a bleak and windswept country where no symbols of hope are presented, and the Wanderer knows

no ending of the way, no home, no goal.

Peace can only lie for him in 'the heart of the winds', in a knowledge of his condemnation to perpetual search. The 'deathless rose of gold' has receded beyond his sight.

If Brennan's reputation rested on *Poems 1913* alone, it would still be obvious that in grandeur of conception and breadth of grasp he is our foremost writer. In fact, it is the towering size and the architectural nature of the book that make it so difficult to represent Brennan fairly on any smaller scale, either by criticism or by selection. He is a poet who must be read, and read *in extenso*, to be understood. Though a few of his poems are highly successful as lyrics, they nevertheless lose half their meaning and impact when quoted outside their context. Even within that context, it is not always obvious where their main significance points; for the whole series is intricate in conception and detail and full of reference and cross-reference. It can only be criticized on the same grand scale on which it is conceived.

It was a great misfortune for Brennan that the book was published at a moment that almost ensured its oblivion. World War I broke out and was in full spate before much critical attention could be given to this very demanding work. In Australia it is unlikely that any critic could have been found at the time who was capable of grasping its full meaning; and England and Europe were in no state for critical evaluation of an obscure Australian poet's work. By the end of the war, the mental and emotional climate of Europe had entirely changed, so that any chance the book might by that time have had of critical consideration was greatly lessened. The current of poetry both in France and England had been diverted from its course, and even if it had not been, Brennan's conventional and rather over-blown diction, his formidable scholarship and the high ambition of his subject would by then have seemed very out of date. The *avant-garde* of the twenties was still suffering from the mental shock of war, and eager for a new kind of entertainment, new sensations and rhythms and colours. Justice was never done to the book, from a critical point of view.

Even without the interposition of the war, Brennan's book would probably not have attracted much attention overseas. At the time when he was writing, it would have seemed impossibly pretentious in an Australian poet to expect to be regarded seriously as a contributor to the thought of Western civilization. Also, as a poet, Brennan is not immediately striking or attractive. A. G. Stephens's judgement that his was 'a bush of poetry that smoulders, but does not burn' has often been quoted, and taking Brennan on the small scale that is easiest to apply, it is true enough. Ideally, of course, no critic ought to judge a poet on less than his total output; actually, it happens all the time. A poet who works on the really large scale has very little chance of full comprehension from modern readers.

The actual application of Brennan's poetic thought to the Western poetic situation is direct enough. It is possible to compare the argument of *Poems 1913* to that of Rilke's slightly-later *Duino Elegies*; this fact alone gives a glimpse of Brennan's real stature. But there is no doubt, even though the comparison is valid, that Rilke is the greater poet. His situation in the heart of Europe where the development was going on gives his poetry far greater immediacy, but apart from this, there is seldom a moment or a line in the *Elegies* where Rilke is not acting as one of the great transformers of experience. Brennan had grasped the argument, had even arrived long before at the point round which Rilke's *Elegies* revolve – that of the 'complete humanization of the Universe' as man's task, to which he is challenged by nothing less than the Infinite. But compared to Rilke's struggle and drama, Brennan's exposition seems cold and intellectual.

Rilke, in fact, approached his problem as a poet, who can only reach his answers by humbly undergoing whatever experience is given to him; Brennan approached it as an intellectual and a scholar, so that his attack has too much about it of the mind imposing itself on its material. The formidable array of his instances, the exhaustiveness of his catalogues of symbols, the dragging in, as it were, of everything from the Pyramids to the decline of Western Christian thought, in some sense detracts from the immediate reality of the problem and of the poem. In his eagerness to say everything, Brennan says too much; and 'The Forest of Night', which is one of the most erudite and deeply-considered poems of our time, will always be too densely-packed and too intellectual in concept to be much more than a mine for academic exposition and research. Rilke's struggles and discoveries are far more moving:

> Earth, is it not just this that you want: to arise
> invisibly in us? Is not your dream
> to be one day invisible? Earth! invisible! ...
>
> (trans. J. B. Leishman & Stephen Spender)

And the clotted rhetoric of Brennan's language is itself repellent to modern readers. Where Rilke cries,

> Some day, emerging at last from this terrifying vision,
> may I burst into jubilant praise to assenting Angels! ...

a comparable passage from Brennan would be perhaps:

> How long delays the miracle blossoming,
> vermeil and gold, soft fire, flush of the dark,
> aurora, and ravish of night's mother ark
> still hallow'd 'neath her present cherishing!
>
> The sides of night are anguish'd with this thing,
> unnatural, a fear, a rending: hark,
> dim mutterings; the gulfs are strain'd and stark. ...
>
> (Ibid. No. 84)

There is always about Brennan's poetry a certain heaviness and elaboration, a leaden-footed exploration of all sides of the symbol he is presenting, that make us see it as a symbol only, detached from the reality of human experience that we find so urgently present in Rilke, for instance.

Possibly, Brennan thought too much and was too anxious to make his poetry act as the vehicle for conveying the results of his thought; whereas Rilke at his best seems to see and to utter his insights at one and the same moment. So though the *Elegies* are in fact the result of the most exquisite art, they do not sound so; while Brennan's verses seem meditated by the intellect, translated into 'poetic' language and chiselled, with a view to eternity, into marmoreal form. The impression of artificiality is deepened when we examine his sentential style. There is nothing exclamatory, nothing unpondered, in Brennan's sentences. They stretch at times, almost Jamesian in their architecture, from beginning to end of a single poem, the separate clauses linked by 'because' and 'therefore', the Mallarméan dislocations of syntax which sound far more unnatural in English than in French, too often turning the poem into a kind of language-puzzle for the student to piece together. Rilke was a poet before he was a thinker; Brennan is too often a thinker long before he decides to become a poet.

True, Brennan rejected intellectual analysis, and 'threw overboard the mystics', in favour, so he said, of 'symbolism, that is, poetry'. (*The Prose of Christopher Brennan*, p. 162.) His emphases are usually right; he believes, for instance, in the role of the imagination, not the intellect, in the task of humanizing the universe and uniting soul and matter, man and world, in their final reconciliation. But when he comes to actual practice and instance, he chooses the intellectual and the literary symbol, not the real fact of the real world; he prefers the generalized notion to the thing seen. It was Jug, Fruit-tree, Window, and the rest, that Rilke desired to transform for the Angels; but Brennan's Rose is already a spiritual, not an earthly, flower.

In fact, Mallarméan symbolist theory became for Brennan an intellectual passion that carried his poetry too far into philosophy. 'All theory is bad for the artist,' Synge said, 'because it makes him live in the intelligence'; but for Brennan, the theory was often present before the poem, which came into being to back the theory up. This is why Brennan will probably remain what he has always been, essentially the poet of the academic critics. *Poems 1913*, in spite of its tremendous scope and impressive achievement, remains a book to be respected rather than enjoyed.

Poems 1913 is certainly the book by which Brennan hoped to be remembered; but he had already published a series of fifteen poems, *The Burden of Tyre*, in 1903, which has considerable interest in showing the trend of his thought at the time, and his violent reaction against the jingoism of Australians, and particularly of Englishmen, at the time of the Boer War. Himself an Irish sympathizer, he deeply distrusted English motives and disliked the concept of Empire, and apart from this he regarded the war as unjust and the British attitude as overweeningly arrogant.

The poem, however, takes its stand on higher philosophical grounds than these. It is a bitter arraignment of the material-minded pseudo-patriotism of the day, which Brennan sees as sinning against the dream of Eden which is man's proper search. England ('Tyre') is seen as 'whoring with vision' by misrepresenting purely selfish motives as an assertion of justice, and regarding its needless slaughter as a holy crusade.

But, since Eden is timeless and is untouched by earthly conflicts, Brennan is forced in the end to reject his own hatred. He declares that he will stand apart from 'the old harlotry of right and wrong', even though he must continue to prefer the losing side to that of the winners, with their hypocritical self-justification, and the sheep-like assent of the mob to this betrayal of man's true search. Nevertheless, his disgust with man's repeated betrayal of the Eden-vision leads him to declare that if after the end of this world creation begins afresh and the old story is resumed, he at least will not willingly consent to play his part again.

But in the Epilogue, addressed to 'Eden' itself, his tone changes. Eden may be a realm transcending all wars and conflicts; yet, Brennan declares, all wars spring ultimately from our desire for her. Even he, though he sees the vision more clearly than others, has betrayed her by his dream of revenge against her enemies, since that revenge would itself be a negation of the commands of the vision. Moreover, Eden herself, when the struggle is over,

> changing thy shape to Death and Night
> (for these and thou are subtle kin),
>
> resumest all our waste and new
> conceiving, bring'st to better birth . . .

So the poem ends by denying the emotion that brought it into being, and pleading for forgiveness from the Eden-vision:

> . . . yet if thou befriend
> some note of love, crying in pangs
> of wrath and grief, may echo higher
> than the derided bow that twangs
> against the spectre-walls of Tyre.

It is worth thus summarizing the argument of *The Burden of Tyre*, because the lofty note that we find in it is so completely negated by Brennan's 1914-18 patriotic verses, published later under the heading of *A Chant of Doom*. Both his intellectual and emotional balance seem to have vanished in the gale of hatred against Germany that overcame him during these years; no abuse was strong enough to express his feeling, and even for the time, the violence of his emotion must have seemed intemperate. Nor was it a passing reaction; even in 1918 and after the Armistice, when the rest of the world was sick of slaughter, Brennan is still shouting for more of it:

> For sword and rope are hungry, axe and block
> Demand their grim repast ...

After the insights revealed in *Poems 1913*, this series of verses comes as a considerable shock to the reader. It is not that the sentiments expressed were unusual, but rather that they were the standard sentiments of the worst and most unthinking daily journalism of the time. The series might be better forgotten and left out of account altogether – except that it shows, what otherwise might have gone unnoticed, that Brennan's allegiance to the dream of Eden was an allegiance rather of the intellect than of the whole man – that he too, his personal emotions being involved, could 'whore with vision', as he put it, as 'abominably' as anyone. The pitiful voice of Wilfred Owen, speaking to his slain enemy out of brotherhood and truth, shames this kind of rant and shows more clearly than any critical analysis could, where Brennan fails in the end both as poet and as man. Even, in his own country, the voice of 'Furnley Maurice' pleading for forgiveness for the nations, 'all murdering, none brave enough to cease', should have shamed Brennan's bitter prejudice.

After 1920, Brennan had only a brief recrudescence of poetry, during a late love-affair, and little else remains from these years. There can be no doubt that *Poems 1913* is the volume by which he stands or falls as poet.

The question should be asked: just how much did the fact that Brennan was an Australian, writing in Australia, affect his work and its reception? To begin with, it is clear that Brennan's somewhat abstract poetic thinking, and the form of Symbolism he adopted, were a considerable help to him technically. He was never involved, as other serious poets in Australia have been, in the difficulty of finding imagery in his own environment which would convey the full weight of meaning and association that his poetry needed. An older civilization, a country within which a religion and a culture have grown, whose climates, skies, and landscapes are the natural background for the life and thought of its inhabitants, has not this difficulty, which I have already noted as the greatest obstacle facing European acclimatization in Australia.

But for Brennan, whose poetic premises allowed him to move freely among the symbolic languages of European thought and religion and to ignore his immediate surroundings, the problem scarcely arose. The flowers that so profusely decorate his Eden, in *Towards the Source*, are the symbolic roses and lilies, the familiar field-flowers, of his European inheritance, not the unfamiliar and unsung flowers of his new country – flowers which had as yet no ritual or symbolic significances and no meaningful associations in literature, even in the minds of his Australian countrymen. Moreover, though here and there researchers may triumphantly announce their discovery of some actual detailed correspondence, in the poetry, to Brennan's real environment, the significance of such references is always generalized, rather than personal or particular. So to trace the actual tram-journey he took from the city to the university, past the church where he was baptized, in one of the Epilogues, has only a symbolic significance; the journey provides a convenient means, for Brennan, of contrasting the early simplicity of faith in which he was brought up, with the shoddy and disoriented life of the commercialized modern city, and with the growth of reasoning and detached philosophic inquiry which provided for Brennan's own youth a way that seemed to lead beyond both and provide a possibility of regaining Eden through intellectual enlightenment.

So Brennan's rather rarefied symbolic method allowed him to by-pass certain stubborn obstacles to poetic thought. But its abstraction strengthened him as a poet at the expense of robbing his work, in a certain sense, of the immediacy which can only come of a direct contact with experience on a sensual and emotional level. It adds to the effect of slightly inhuman calculation and distance from fact and daily problems, that keeps Brennan always at more than arms'-length from his audience.

Moreover, his position of, so to speak, suspension between two centuries and two hemispheres meant that he was truly in touch with neither. Over the twenty years which elapsed between his return from Germany, and the publication of *Poems 1913*, the emphasis of the symbolist movement had changed, and the apparent achievement of the nineteenth century was crumbling.

Brennan, isolated as it were with the work of his poetic master, Mallarmé, always before his eyes, remained poetically in the nineteenth century – a fact that is demonstrated not only by his choice of a poetic task, but by his diction and versification, impossibly florid and lacking in intimacy to modern ears. Though he saw that there was a tendency towards breaking up the stricter forms, and away from rhetoric in the direction of immediacy of speech, it did not attract him. He preferred Verlaine's earlier Parnassian manner to his later; and his own poetry abounds in archaisms like 'thou mayst', 'I bid thee', verbs like 'to glad' and adverbs like 'perchance'. His diction alone might have led to his being dismissed outright, as a poet, in the early nineteen-twenties, when his great work at last had a chance of a hearing; that iconoclastic decade was in search of poetry of a very different tone and colour.

In Australia, on the other hand, his very detachment from the tasks that lesser poets saw as important at the time, and his taking part with developments in Western literature that were very imperfectly understood here, even if known, ensured that he has always been more of a legend than of a figure in our literature. His learning seemed more academic than the chaos of information with which O'Dowd packed his radical-political verse; his lyricism with its careful vagueness of suggestion and symbolism seemed less immediately attractive than McCrae's sprightly and uncomplicated songs. If Brennan can ever be said to have had an audience, it was so small as to be scarcely visible.

To return, then, from Brennan to the current of development that continued below his isolated peak.

Early in the first years of the century, McCrae began publishing the lyrics that were collected in 1910 as the first version of *Satyrs and Sunlight*. Seen against the rather dreary and conventional verse of the 'nationalist poets', and the pleasantly hearty Kiplingisms of *The Bulletin* bards, these poems, with their rejection of the balladists' crudities in favour of a more vivid and sensuous concern with life and language, and of nationalisms and political preoccupations in favour of an individualistic gambolling with rhymes and rhythms, offered a new and exciting poetic experience.

Hugh McCrae, a young man who had rejected a settled professional career in favour of a freelance existence on the fringe of journalism and the theatre, had early come in contact with a young artist whose ideas and theories he may not have taken very seriously, but with whom he had much in common. Norman Lindsay was even at the outset of his career a publicist and polemicist with a programme of his own. He and McCrae together conducted a formidable attack on the somewhat fuddy-duddy scene that Australia presented at the beginning of the century.

'When I began to write,' McCrae once observed, 'Poetry wore petticoats.' McCrae's summary treatment of those petticoats may have horrified his Australian audience, but it was Lindsay's theorizing and polemics that probably took the brunt of the hostility of public opinion. Lindsay seems to have cleared a space in which McCrae – never a good protagonist in an argument – was able to sing more or less as he chose. The parochialism of his early audience found a more provocative target in Lindsay's pictures and articles than in McCrae's poetry, even though in a sense McCrae was as much of a rebel as Lindsay.

How much one influenced the other in choice of theme and treatment it is probably not worth while to ask. McCrae was as pictorial a writer as Lindsay was a literary painter. Both were attracted by the imagery of Greek mythology and of medieval legend; and both make of those imageries something purely decorative and physical in their effect, much as did the pre-Raphaelites in England. Their themes, like Brennan's loftier ones, enabled them to work in detachment from the problems of everyday adjustment to life in a new country; and if McCrae's satyrs and fauns and forest-legends look nowadays extremely odd in their transplantation to Australia, it is worth remembering that in essence they represent, not an attempt at a real mytholo-gizing for a real audience, but a way of stating a reaction from certain attitudes and prohibitions that needed opposing.

McCrae's early work is therefore more important than his later, which was in effect not much more than repetition of what he was already doing in the first decade of the century. In 1909, he published a poem, 'The Deathless Gods', which is almost a verbal parallel of Lindsay's manner as a painter:

> O, often I have seen in these new days
> The deathless gods, all naked, without hoods,

> As some old carving, pregnant with the rays
> Of noon ... alive, and singing in the woods ...
>
> Syrinx, to me, unfolded in my hands
> And once again became a laughing girl ...

And his poem 'Ambuscade', published at about the same time, is perhaps the most remarkable of his early poems. Urgently and vividly phrased, the language of the poem re-creates the scene so that we momentarily forget the artificiality of the subject – an attack by centaurs on a herd of mares defended by their stallions – in the actuality of its treatment:

> A roar of hooves, a lightning view of eyes
> Redder than fire, of long straight whistling manes,
> Stiff crests, and tails drawn out against the skies,
> Of angry nostrils, webbed with leaping veins,
> The stallions come!

But the poem gave, as well as a view of what McCrae could do with language, a warning of where his weakness lay. It is the first of a number of poems that seem incomplete, as though the subject had been idly picked up, had struck a few momentary sparks, and had been dropped again and forgotten. It begins without preparation, and on a conjunction:

> Or the black centaurs, statuesquely still ...

And it ends on the half-line quoted above, as though the vision had abruptly vanished and the poet could no longer take the trouble to pursue it.

So, in spite of the gifts he brought to poetry, McCrae remained too desultory, too amateur a writer, to reach any important heights. He demanded little of himself, though he can give much pleasure to the equally undemanding reader, with his love of rhyming for its own sake, his moments of sharp immediacy, and the delightful arabesques he can make with language:

> Look how their shadows run,
>   Swift as she flies from him! –
> Moths in the morning sun
>   Out of a garden dim.
>
> Faint through the fluttering
>   Fall of a flute divine,
> Softly the 'cellos sing:
>   '*Colombine, Colombine.*'

.   .   .

Softly the 'cellos sing
'*Colombine*
Colombine.' . . .

Until the end of his life he continued to shun theory and philosophy, and any kind of earnestness whether about poetry or about life. Brennan's poetic fault was probably intellectualism and a certain ponderousness; McCrae's was a refusal to be preoccupied with anything at all but the passing moment.

Nevertheless, it is possible to see behind his fragmentary, gay, and epigrammatic verses a glimpse of another and frightening world, from which he turns away but which he knows is there. It is in the violence that now and then appears in his verses, the dead hand of Orleans knocking on the door in 'Joan of Arc', the empty echo of 'Never Again':

> She looked on me with sadder eyes than Death,
> And, moving through the large autumnal trees,
> Failed like a phantom on the bitter breath
> Of midnight; and the unillumined seas
> Roared in the darkness out of centuries . . .

This unassimilated vision of horror comes to him seldom, but since nothing in his verse opposes it except sensuous gaiety, when it does come his whole vision seems to crumble before it, like the woman in 'The End of Desire':

> I took her closely, but while yet
> I trembled, vassal to my lust,
> Lo! – Nothing but some sarcenet
> Deep-buried in a pile of dust.

His longest work, *The Ship of Heaven*, is a fantastic play, barely actable but brilliantly light and inventive. His most ambitious poem, 'Joan of Arc', was never finished, and the fragments published are mysteriously disconnected. But his real importance lies in those early years of the century, when he broke through the self-congratulatory parochialisms of Australian literary life at the turn of the century and reasserted the life of the senses and the necessity for poetry to recognize it and do it homage. It was this example as much as anything that allowed the establishment of poetry on a new level, in the nineteen-twenties. The fact that he was a singer, not a thinker, freed the notion of poetry from the portentousness of the Nationalist and radical schools. He simply exemplified, in his joyful rhyming and in his rejection of every kind of statement outside his poetry, how far from poetry many of his early contemporaries in fact were. Perhaps he said nothing memorable, but he sang, when he was at his best, unforgettably.

Australia's only other poet who is above all a singer, John Shaw Neilson, was writing at the same time as McCrae, and was in fact four years older. Neilson, unlike McCrae, was unacquainted with any world outside his own small region; again unlike McCrae, he had practically no formal education and came, not of a cultivated family, but of simple Scottish peasant stock. Nevertheless, the verse he wrote is at least as delicately made as McCrae's, and will probably prove to be more enduring.

For one thing, Neilson was more sincerely devoted to poetry than McCrae ever allowed himself to be. McCrae's detestation of theory and what he called 'philosophy', and the decorative nature of his gift, make his poetry seem always marginal to reality. Neilson, on the other hand, though he was awkward and unassuming, had a high notion of poetry and believed sincerely in its basic function:

> Good brothers of the song,
> Be not too humble; it is you and I
> And a few others lift the world along,

he wrote in an unfinished poem. His poetry was always the most important factor in his life, even though his circumstances prevented him from sparing it much time, and his hard life and poor eyesight meant that much of his work was lost for lack of leisure or of amanuenses to write it down for him.

These factors, too, influenced the kind of poetry he was able to produce. As he himself explained, he had to keep to the simpler rhythms and metres so that he could remember his verses easily, since many of them had to be kept in his head until opportunity came to write them down. Much of his verse is in rhymed couplets, or four-line stanzas with a simple rhyme-scheme; there is often a refrain which serves to remind the hearer of the main theme or to alter or deepen its meaning. These simple, almost archaic forms reinforce one's first impression of naivety; but this is almost at once contradicted or counterbalanced by the subtlety and strangeness of Neilson's perceptions and use of language:

> How should a singer of the cold
> Seeing strange holiness in air
> In his blue famine seek to hold
> Vainly your paradise of hair?

> ('For a Little Girl's Birthday')

In the same way the apparent slightness of his output (he wrote few poems of any great length, and his subjects at first sight often look conventionally easy) is contradicted, on a deeper examination, by the consistency of treatment of his main theme – that of the 'black season' of death and the darkness, opposed by 'the folly of Spring', the unreasoning uprush of creativeness, of spring, dawn, and youth, by which not only the poet, but the world itself, exists.

The best of his poems have themselves something of the subtlety and tender colour, the vague and shifting vibrant light, of a spring morning. They are never muscular either in ideas or expression; their quality is as delicate as something newborn. This special kind of vision and expression is peculiar to Neilson; no other poet in the English language has it in his particular kind. Perhaps it is best exemplified in his poem 'The Orange Tree':

> The young girl stood beside me. I
> Saw not what her young eyes could see:
> – A light, she said, not of the sky
> Lives somewhere in the Orange Tree.

> ... Listen! the young girl said. There calls
> No voice, no music beats on me;
> But it is almost sound: it falls
> This evening on the Orange Tree. ...

Similarly, Neilson's poems often develop, not in a linear or narrative shape, but in a series of curves or loops, as it were, or even in a circular pattern like a web: the first verse states the theme, which is elaborated, altered, re-echoed in later verses, and the last verse may repeat the first either exactly or thematically. A refrain may appear in the first verse (as in 'The Flight of the Weary') and reappear only in the last, or may be repeated and altered throughout the poem. Different voices may take up different themes, in repetition or reply. But Neilson seldom if ever uses the expository method or attempts a linear argument where he does approach these methods, as in 'The Ballad of Remembrance' or 'The Quarrel with the Neighbour', he is seldom successful. His is a passive intuitive method of vision; but when he allows it full play he can produce poetry of an extraordinary, almost surrealistic quality:

> 'Tis no unsalted music
>   The moons bestow,
> 'Tis the untaught eternal,
>   So long, so low.
>
> Time is the old man crying
>   Lives on a string,
> In the eyes of a child fallen
>   We fear the Spring. . . .
>   ('The Scent o' the Lover')

The next verse of this curious poem refers to another of Neilson's poetic peculiarities, his colour-synaesthesia; which he accepted perfectly simply as something natural, and uses in his poetry often with much effect:

> I am assailed by colours
>   By night, by day:
> In a mad boat they would take me
>   Red miles away.

His colour-perceptions, though he did not make any attempt to systematize them, are consistent throughout his poetry. Green is for him the colour of youth and spring, violet the colour of death and of the ground, red stands for strength and violence, white for innocence and childhood, and so on. As he wrote his poetry, unselfconsciously, thinking only of the art and not of the réclame, so he used his perceptions; and he was apparently mildly surprised that others had not the same capacities.

Similarly, other perceptions or ideas are fused, less as simile or metaphor than as identity, in his poems; they abound in phrases like 'the silence honey-wet'; 'the morning was too loud with light'; 'the tremble of the hollow year'; 'I saw the mushrooms hoping'.

Neilson's poetry makes its own special set of demands on the reader, and it has never been popular. It has nothing to do with fashion or with the twentieth century, and it ignores the preoccupations of locality as much as of time. This will, no doubt, prove in time to be its strength; it has been dismissed as weak and feminine by critics interested in the Australian cult of manliness and toughness, which has extended in our own time as far as sadism and unbalance; but it has qualities much more durable than they are aware of. It is both entirely individual, and unafraid of being universal.

Neilson always eschewed politics and polemics, on which ground indeed he would have been miserably misplaced. To look at his work in company with that of his contemporary, Bernard O'Dowd, is to wonder whether the term 'poet' can possibly be applied to both. Two more different writers never existed.

O'Dowd, in fact, began not as a versifier at all, but as a political writer; he then began to turn out a quantity of radical-humanist polemic verse for various journals, and from this developed his first volume *Dawnward?* which was published in 1903. Under the influence of his admiration for Whitman, he seems to have decided to turn himself into a poet, on the wholly theoretical ground that he considered poets to be myth-makers of their societies, and modern society to need a new myth. Rational Socialist humanism and the theory of evolution had outdated Christianity, he argued; therefore new gods were required, and must be invented accordingly by the poets – this, in fact, was the poet's function. When these new abstract Olympians were in turn outdated, the poet must destroy them and invent more.

This reason for becoming a poet, however, did not suffice to make him one. *Dawnward?* while patently earnest and sincere, contains some of the worst verse ever written in Australia (no mean claim). O'Dowd's mind was abstract and unsubtle, and heavily stocked with miscellaneous information gleaned in the course of a University education but unilluminated by any depth of understanding. The poems the book contains are rhetorical addresses from a political platform, in a metre which O'Dowd oddly calls a 'fourteener', but which consisted of a four-line stanza of alternating four-beat and three-beat lines, rhyming abab, and recalling the metre of 'Yankee Doodle'. These lines are crowded with polysyllabic words like 'sybaritic', 'legislative', 'prognathous Neanderthal', and the effect is often rather comic than impressive.

Nevertheless, his later poem 'The Bush' shows that O'Dowd was capable of working much better in a freer and more flexible metre. 'The Bush', though portentously nationalist and didactic, and often ludicrous in its comparisons of contemporary Australia with Periclean Greece, has moments of real relevance to its time, and may have correspondingly fortified the spirits of young men who were attempting to take Australia seriously as a subject for literature.

O'Dowd remains a kind of monument in the history of Australian writing, for he marks the watershed between two centuries. The extraordinary clutter of dead and living mythologies and religions, imperfectly absorbed philosophy and raw political theory which O'Dowd gathered up to clothe man's sudden nakedness in the face of the universe was typical of the confusion and uncertainty of the beginning of the twentieth century. For O'Dowd, Australia, this 'virgin and unhandicapped land of social experiments', was to be the breeding-ground both of the new gods and of the new society. O'Dowd declared himself a disciple of Whitman (who, however, was a hundred times more of a poet than his follower); and in this he exemplified the contemporary influence of American socialist economic theory, as well as of American poetry.

This is a re-emergence into Australian poetry of the old current of Australian radicalism, first voiced by Harpur. Harpur had been an admirer of Emerson, as O'Dowd of Whitman; and Harpur had sung of Australia as the land where in the future

> ... all men shall stand
> Proudly beneath the fair wide roof of heaven
> As God-created equals.

But for Lawson and O'Dowd, writing at the end of the century, the words 'God-created' no longer had the significance they had held for Harpur. In the interval, there had been a tacit substitution; 'God-created' would now have been rendered 'man-created'.

The effect of this shift in emphasis was decisive. It resulted for O'Dowd in a high-flown and over-ambitious attempt to legislate for a society, and to adumbrate a religion, that did not yet exist. For his contemporary, Henry Lawson, it probably contributed to an uncertainty and melancholy of temperament that finally led to personal tragedy.

Lawson, considered as a poet, is not important; his prose is far more telling and apparently far more carefully worked over. In fact, he seems usually to have turned to verse mainly as a weapon of propaganda and a journalistic medium. A few of his better poems, however, such as 'The Sliprails and the Spur', 'The Roaring Days', 'Faces in the Street', and 'Past Carin'', rise above the level of the rest, usually because of their intensity of feeling rather than any technical or poetic gift.

Lawson was, in fact, a man of feeling; a far more human and gentle figure than the colder and more abstract-minded O'Dowd, he came to socialism rather through his affections than his intellect. He felt deeply for his 'lost army' of the poor and exploited (who included himself); but his hope for a future redressing of wrongs and reign of socialist justice seldom seems to amount to conviction. It is doubtful whether he believed sufficiently in the inherent goodness of human nature to trust in a future millennium administered by men; at least his faith was not strong enough to keep his head above the waters of despair.

His contemporary and occasional rival, A.B. ('Banjo') Paterson, was influenced, like Lawson himself, both by the bush-ballads and by Kipling, as well as by Gordon. He was among the leaders of the *Bulletin* bards, and the enormous popularity of his verse reinforced the upsurge of nationalism that occurred about the time of the Boer War, and did much to fix the notion of the Australian as a tough yet sentimental man of action.

Moreover, the movement which Gordon initiated and of which Paterson was the most popular exponent did much to alter the notion of poetry here, away from subtlety, philosophy, and inter-pretiveness and towards simplicity, vigour, and colloquialism. The national legend has long begun to seem unreal, but its legacies (it is worth pointing out) remain, and still act as ferti-lizing influences. Not only elder poets of today, such as Fitz-Gerald and Douglas Stewart and John Manifold, show unmis-takable traces of these influences, but such recent men as Ray Mathew, or Robert Clark, to name only two, would not have written just as they do without the work of the *Bulletin* school behind them.

The 1914-18 war perhaps sobered the 'nationalist' school, but on the whole it left comparatively little mark on Australian poetry. The young Melbourne poet and protégé of Bernard O'Dowd, Frank Wilmot, who wrote under the name of 'Furnley Maurice', published a sincere and interesting, if sometimes naïve, series of war poems under the title 'To God: from the Weary Nations'. The first overtly pacifist utterance in Australian poetry, it pleads for the return of compassion, for 'mercy, not justice' for the misguided nations, 'all murdering, none brave enough to cease'. It is probably the sanest and most sensitive Australian poetry to come out of the first war.

Of the men who fought in the war and returned to write of it, few produced much verse. Vance Palmer's long free-verse poem, *The Camp*, published in book form in 1920, and his well-known 'The Farmer Remembers the Somme', in the same volume; and Leon Gellert's first book of verse, *Songs of a Campaign*, published in 1917, are probably best worth remembering. Both writers are unsentimental, refuse all opportunities for drama, and make their best effects through understatement.

Of the two, Gellert is the more interesting poet, though he produced little more verse of much merit. His 'Before Action', and one or two other poems, are as brief and sharp-edged as the best of Sassoon's war-poems:

> I wondered why I always felt so cold.
> I wondered why the orders seemed so slow,
> So slow to come, so whisperingly told,
>   So whisperingly low.
>
> I wondered if my packing-straps were tight,
> And wondered why I wondered. Sound went wild . . .
> An order came . . . I ran into the night,
>   Wondering why I smiled.

Before 1920, Mary Gilmore, another socialist poet and a friend of Lawson's in his early days, had published only two of her numerous books of verse – *Marri'd* in 1910, and *The Passionate Heart* in 1918. Her lyricism, always warm and humane, and often pointed and forceful as well, her sense of history and her love of country make even her earlier verse pleasant to read. But she gained in strength and economy in her later work; and her influence has been cumulative and personal rather than immediate.

William Baylebridge (Blocksidge), a Queensland-born poet, was overseas between the years 1908 and 1919; but during this time he published, in London and elsewhere, a number of volumes of verse. Of these some are revisions and reprintings of work published earlier, for Baylebridge was seldom satisfied with any version of his work for long.

Probably Baylebridge is our oddest writer. Certainly he considered himself Australia's most important poet and prophet, and took steps to see that Australia should have every opportunity to think so too. His output is large, his style, though cold and grandiose and heavily influenced by Nietzsche, the Elizabethan poets, the Metaphysicals, and various German writers, is pondered and at its best can be impressive. Some of the less tortuous lyrics in his early poems, *Moreton Miles*, have their own epigrammatic force:

> I ask of her like bushmen told
> By travellers of the rain –
> Of overlanding mates of old,
> If stirring yet or slain ... (LIV)

His poem-series for a friend killed in World War I, *A Wreath*, contains sonnets of carefully sculptured strength, sometimes even of grandeur. But in most of his work the proper humility of a poet is sooner or later overcome by the paranoid rhetoric of the political prophet.

If Baylebridge had not had so overwhelming an idea of himself as a thinker, and had practised more flexibility and immediacy of language, he might have become the poet he imagined himself to be. But he appears to have been captivated, possibly during his time in Europe, by his reading of two philosophers, Bergson and the inescapable Nietzsche. From Nietzsche's vision of the *Übermensch*, and from his political and nationalist writings, Baylebridge took very much the same elements as were later to be used in Nazism; from Bergson he took the notion of the *élan vital*, the evolutionary life-force unrolling in time. He combined the two in an exposition of his 'new faith' for humanity, very much as O'Dowd from a different viewpoint might have done. This faith was to be in a transcendence of the individual and the immediate by a greater entity, a kind of collective humanity-at-its-highest, which Baylebridge refers to as The Larger Self, or The Abler Self. This is mankind viewed as a whole, in relation to time and evolution, as a kind of emergent spiritual force:

That abler self is deity, the
Summation Earth's Humanity;
To it alone we homage owe.

(Life's Testament)

But Baylebridge felt that, in some way which he never clearly defined, this Abler Self is itself threatened in our day by 'something sinister' which is 'now emerging': 'forces which seem pledged to destroy much . . . that man in his best manifestations has considered good.' To resist these mysterious forces, man was to strengthen himself by renewing his faith in the Abler Self; and the volume *Life's Testament*, published first in 1914, was intended as a kind of credo to be used towards this end.

Baylebridge never succeeded in making clear in his writing – and probably never to himself – the genesis and function of the various 'forces' his faith postulated. Since all of them appear to have their basis and manifestation in mankind, and mankind is both the instrument for defeating them, and the 'deity' on whose behalf they must be defeated, a vicious circle arises in his argument which vitiates the whole of his thought. He becomes inextricably involved – apparently without ever becoming aware of it – in the solipsist dilemma of modern humanism that Brennan had stated so clearly in *Poems 1913*:

Some throne thou think'st to win
or pride of thy far kin;
this incomplete and dusty hour to achieve:
know that the hour is one,
eternally begun,
eternally deferr'd, thy grasp a Danaid sieve. . . .

(The Verse of Christopher Brennan, No. 68)

This fundamental confusion of thought led Baylebridge into advocating a form of totalitarianism. The arguments in *Life's Testament* and in *The New Life* and *National Notes* are very similar to those used later by Mussolini's apologists and those of Hitler. In this, he was at least early in the field and to that extent could claim originality. The tragedy came later, when he failed during the nineteen-twenties and thirties to recognize the logical weaknesses and inherent dangers in his scheme, even when they were demonstrated before his eyes.

As a poet, he is best represented by a few poems in *Moreton Miles*, *A Wreath*, and a sequence of love-poems, *Love Redeemed*, and in a curious sequence of short epigrammatic verses, *Sextains*, published much later. As a national prophet and political philosopher, his favourite role, he is certainly best forgotten. Even his style, which though involved and affected can be memorable here and there in his non-political verse, takes on a pomposity and inflation in the 'prophetic' books that too clearly betrays his essential lack of humour and humanity.

Looking back from the end of World War I on the growth of an Australian body of poetry, it is interesting to notice how often Australian poets have taken up political attitudes and promulgated creeds and opinions of various kinds, in their attempt to make and interpret a new country. Harpur began it, with his radical egalitarianism based on a view of evolution as a spiritual development, taking its rise in a God whose impulse is towards consciousness and knowledge. For Harpur, justice and equality among men were necessary to fulfil the purposes of a divinized universe; his hope for Australia was that here old tyrannies could be shaken off and mankind attain its 'full stature'. Lawson used his verse as a weapon in the struggle for justice for his oppressed 'Army'. O'Dowd's grandiose projects for a new society, a new religion, and a new literature were intended to exalt Australia to a position of leadership, moral and political. Baylebridge, from much the same premises, arrived at what appeared to be an opposite philosophy. Where O'Dowd believed that the old forms had already crumbled and new must be invented, Baylebridge maintained that the best of the old, 'man in his best manifestations', was to be defended against the forces working for its overthrow, since in it was to be perceived the manifestation of the Abler Self. Both, however, took humanity as their highest value, regarding religion as a product of purely human and secular forces, something as subject to evolution as any other manifestation of life. Both O'Dowd and Baylebridge, moreover, used poetry for political ends, and the poetry disappeared in the process.

The chief hope for poetry as such, at the beginning of the nineteen-twenties, lay in the sweeping vision Brennan had achieved, the lyricism of Neilson, and the rebellious emphasis on pictorial and sensual qualities in poetry that McCrae had used to break through the prosy public-spirited verse of the nationalists. With the impetus given by the discovery of the balladic undercurrent in our literature, and its popularization in the first years of the century, the scene was set for the emergence of poets like R.D. FitzGerald, and Kenneth Slessor, in the decades to follow.

AUSTRALIAN POETRY SINCE 1920

EVAN JONES

It must all have seemed very exciting, literary Sydney in the 1920s: that, at least, is the main impression left by Jack Lindsay's autobiographical volume *The Roaring Twenties*. Lindsay is not alone in seeing his father as the philosopher and arbiter of that decade: 'It is a paradox, indeed, but none the less a fact,' writes Kenneth Slessor, 'that Norman Lindsay has exercised more influence and produced more effect on numbers of this country's poets than any other single individual in Australia's history . . . Norman Lindsay's attitude to poets and poetry . . . has had more to do with a great deal of Australian poetry . . . than is generally realized or admitted'; and Douglas Stewart asserts that 'it is beyond question that the majority of Australian writers – and especially the poets – have accepted him from the beginning not only as an artist but as the fountainhead of Australian culture in our time.'

Ploughing through the turgid and random aphorisms of Lindsay's major manifesto, *Creative Effort*, one might well wonder how this came about. Undoubtedly (as Stewart says), it was partly because of the enthusiasm and encouragement with which he greeted young disciples and quasi-disciples. It was also, undoubtedly, due to the enormous arrogance and assurance that he breathed into them: the artist, he said, transcends petty existence:

> Search for all that common minds reject as useless to the struggle for Existence, and you will find all that serves Life.
> At its highest, where does one find man's effort trend away from the struggle for existence?
> In Creative art.
> Therefore, in Creative art one must find the direction of Life.
> A statement so intrinsically aristocratic must be repudiated by all common minds.
> That is understood.
>
> (*Creative Effort*)

To common minds this might seem extravagantly jejune; but Lindsay's initiates had the assurance that they had uncommon minds. They also had the remarkable assurance that they were virtually alone in possession of them: at no other time have Australians had the confidence, so buoyantly expressed in the pages of the Lindsayite magazine *Vision*, that they were the *Übermenschen* of the cultural world, that the Western cultural heritage had fled a sickened Europe and a vulgar America for these shores.

The evidence is that the poets – quite properly – did not doggedly master the ramifications of Lindsay's aesthetic; but they did absorb its temper. It was for Life with a capital L, but, as the above passage makes clear, Life was sharply marked off from quotidian Existence and, in practice at least, from human experience. The keynote was Gaiety, the worst betrayal was not to be Gay: naturally contemplative men like Slessor and Fitz-Gerald were on these grounds to be hagridden by guilt for years. There was, too, a doctrine of the Image both like and unlike that prevalent in England and discussed by Kermode in his justly well-known book, *Romantic Image*. Unlike, primarily because of Lindsay's emphasis on Gaiety, and his prepossession with the figures of pagan-classic mythology. There is no quicker way to catch the spirit of this than to look at Lindsay's own illustrations for *Vision*: satyrs with dryads, dryads with women, women with fauns; and wilder variations involving centaurs, mermaids, fish and harpies – as well as men and women. At first these drawings amuse with their neat depiction of the gaily lecherous leer or the look of surprised innocence; then they begin to bore, and at last repel. Their emphasis is heavily sexual, for Lindsay laid great stress on the bounties of sexual delight; but the depiction of sexuality is always whimsical, abnormal and finally prurient. No suburban alderman could be shocked by them, for here there is nothing real: and it is just this that in the end makes them deeply shocking.

All this can be seen in the poetry too, especially in the poetry of 'the incomparable Hugh McCrae' (Slessor's phrase). McCrae did not pursue Lindsay's aesthetic very far, for he professed a complete incapacity for, and lack of interest in, intellectual pursuits (and certainly his poetry here bears witness to his verity). On the other hand, he shifted house to be nearer Lindsay, peopled his verse with satyrs and centaurs, and made it almost unremittingly gay. This is the saddest thing. Jack Lindsay quotes a fragment of a love-letter by McCrae which is moving in its simplicity and directness:

I still love you, and can never stop loving you. I see your eyes constantly; and, sometimes, they come between me and the pages of the book I am reading. At other times, I hear your voice, which is different to everyone else's; and, in my dreams, I weigh your black hair in my hand, *constantly adoring you*.

Those words are instinct with feeling, and nothing could more vividly point the poverty and triviality of McCrae's love poetry. Here, as a better-than-average example, is the short lyric 'Reassurance':

> That was a hare (no Satyr as you thought)
> That leaped behind us when we crossed the stile;
> How pale your face is by the March moon caught
> And paler for your smile!
>
> Why needs your timid heart to flutter so?
> My faith! Where does this teasing ribbon run
> Provocative? . . . and what a mulish bow!
> There now . . . 'tis all undone.

It seems to be a sort of self-betrayal; and the evidence is that McCrae was not a happy man, and happy least of all about his poetry. For the main part this is pleasant enough, and sometimes it is rather more. There are poems reminiscent of de la Mare, Belloc and others – not a large claim to make, of course, but it seems too late to make large claims for McCrae. Through all the woods, the deer, the nymphs and the English weather there are glimpses of the man's personality; and there are a number of poems comparatively free from all these trappings, the best of them perhaps being 'Morning'.

None of this explains the intense admiration in which McCrae was held by, amongst others, such markedly more considerable poets as Slessor and FitzGerald. This can only be explained by the fetish of Gaiety which he worked so hard to master, by the remarkable personal charm which still shines clearly from his letters, and by the supposed technical mastery on which H.M. Green lays so much emphasis. That mastery emerges as a scrupulous care for sound effects, a care which runs to waste because it has the merest arbitrary relation to what is being said; and unfortunately, it had a discernible influence on the most promising of McCrae's younger Sydney contemporaries.

This was Kenneth Slessor, who for all that became one of the most notable poets that Australia has produced. From the start, it seems, he shared the current preoccupations: the first poem printed in his collected *Poems* (which are arranged chronologically) is 'Earth-Visitors', a fantasy about the rollicking, wenching, bacchanalian descent of a host of pagan deities on a country town. Dedicated to N.L., it is of course nonsense; and yet it has at once a remarkable vividness and clarity of imagery, and a live, assured movement of language:

> Post-boys would run, lanterns hang frostily, horses fume,
> The strangers wake the Inn. Men, staring outside
> Past watery glass, thick panes, could watch them eat,
> Dyed with gold vapours in the candleflame,
> Clapping their gloves, and stuck with crusted stones,
> Their garments foreign, their talk a strange tongue,
>   But sweet as pineapple – it was Archdukes, they must be.

Except for the 'crusted stones' and the strained exoticism of the last two lines, this is perfectly real: Slessor emerged at the start as a poet with a superb sense for sights and sounds, and with little to do with it but play (fashionable) games. Even this gift was betrayed in the interests of Lindsayian conformity in such hollow roistering pieces as 'Rubens' Innocents', the by-now-notorious 'Thieves' Kitchen' and, worst of all because most ambitious, 'The Man of Sentiment'. Early Slessor can hardly be discarded so long as anybody has the leisure to read it for its moments of vividness; but neither can it be taken very seriously: only one poem, 'The Night-Ride', seems to emerge quite free from the flaws of strained exoticism, strained roistering, and/or strained whimsy.

Slessor was a poet without direction other than that gratuitously offered by Lindsay, McCrae, and *Vision* (which he co-edited). That his poetry came to have a great deal more direction and force was not due to any deliberate break-through: probably no poet can or will offer a cut-and-dried answer to the question 'why do you write poetry', but probably few would disown knowledge of the matter as disarmingly as did Slessor in a radio talk reprinted in *Southerly* in 1948:

I don't propose to discuss the why – that is to say, why poets write poetry, why men and women read it and respond to it. That would be an excursion beyond psychology into the springs of life of which I am not capable. I shall try to talk as lucidly as I can about the tiny area of the How of which I know anything.

This was followed by a rather dismaying discussion, with illustrations, of technical tricks: tricks which Slessor does uncommonly well, but which hardly bear such deliberate pointing at. At no stage did he discuss any of his better poems; but he did say two things of importance:

I think poetry is written mostly for pleasure, by which I mean the pleasure of pain, horror, anguish and awe as well as the pleasure of beauty, music and the act of living.

and

I must write for myself, and speak for myself, and that is why writing poetry is still, I think, a pleasure out of hell.

An insistence on pleasure in these terms is at very best a remote descendant of the Lindsayian emphasis on Gaiety: in combination with pain, horror, anguish, and awe, and the insistence on personal pressure, it is, rather, an atavistic throwback to the great age of Romanticism. And it seems to be no accident that the sense of these things in Slessor's poetry arises at the same time as his often-noted obsession with that obsession of the Romantic poets, the sea: which is not to say, of course, that Slessor consciously turned back to Romantic theories and themes; I think that he probably did not.

Most critics seem, reasonably enough, to date Slessor's emergence as an important poet from 'Captain Dobbin', and to centre attention above all on it, 'Five Visions of Captain Cook', 'Five Bells', and 'Beach Burial'. These are certainly the strongest of Slessor's poems, and those on which his properly high reputation chiefly rests: it is only after saying that as clearly as possible (if briefly) that I can express some dissatisfaction with all but the last of them.

Captain Dobbin is too insistently painted as a wildly quaint and anachronistic figure, and the exoticism of his erstwhile experience is too heavily pointed: these are, one realizes, distancing devices, for Captain Dobbin is clearly a self-projection. That such distancing should be thought necessary betrays a failure of confidence in the vision: partly, at least, it is because Slessor dare not be as ungay as the hero of

> . . . his own Odysseys, his lonely travels,
> His trading days, an autobiography

> Of angles and triangles and lozenges
> Ruled tack by tack across the sheet,
> That with a single scratch expressed the stars,
> Merak and Alamak and Alpherat,
> The wind, the moon, the sun, the clambering sea,
> Sails bleached with light, salt in the eyes,
> Bamboos and Tahiti oranges,
> From some forgotten countless day,
> One foundered day from a forgotten month,
> A year sucked quietly from the blood,
> Dead with the rest, remembered by no more
> Than a scratch on a dry chart. . . .

Even in this passage there is an insistence on the strange names of stars and the exoticism of 'Bamboos and Tahiti oranges'; but for the main part, it is clearly an image of life, and of life as Slessor himself sees it. It may not be gay, but its power and significance are unmistakable: and it seems a pity to have denied them.

'Five Visions of Captain Cook' is not without related failings: it contains, for instance, such disastrously sticky whimsy as

> Two chronometers the captain had,
> One by Arnold that ran like mad,
> One by Kendal in a walnut case,
> Poor devoted creature with a hang-dog face.

> Arnold always hurried with a crazed click-click
> Dancing over Greenwich like a lunatic,
> Kendal panted faithfully his watch-dog beat,
> Climbing out of Yesterday with little sticky feet.

(a striking example, incidentally, of Slessor's virtuosity with sound). Apart from this, the structure of the poem is fragmentary; and despite the striking passages there seems to me to be a final confusion between the historical Cook and Cook the Romantic hero of the poem with whom Slessor is identified – but this is a point which I can scarcely afford to elaborate.

Indubitably, Slessor's greatest poem is 'Five Bells'. It is a meditation on a drowned friend, ostensibly called forth by the ringing of a ship's bell in the harbour below; on his fate and on Slessor's memories of him: and on the unbridgeable gap between these two things. It is superbly and unobtrusively set in time and space as a personal meditation: the poet by his window looks into a night which, to his vision, merges into an endless flux of indistinguishable darkness and sea, a flux in which the drowned Joe is lost, and which is sharply cut off by impenetrable glass from the lighted space in which he himself stands.

The power of the monologue conducted from that standpoint is beyond question; and the reservations I have about the poem can be stated briefly. First, there are a few disconcerting last traces of Slessor's virtuosity, as in the lines

> Deep and dissolving verticals of light
> Ferry the falls of moonshine down . . .

which are a playing with sound that carries no clear and purposeful image (this might be contrasted with the succeeding significant image, 'Night and water/Pour to one rip of darkness, the Harbour floats/In air, the Cross hangs upside down in water'). Second, the talk of time, with its show of philosophical distinctions, promises rather more than it gives. And third, the central sections of reminiscence about Joe seem somewhat random both in direction and detail: a randomness that shows in an occasional slackness of the always fluent blank verse which characterizes the poem. This last reservation, at least, is a serious one, and it detracts from a final estimation of the poem; yet Vincent Buckley's opinion that 'it may not be claiming too much to say that "Five Bells" is one of the two or three best poems written in Australia' does not seem unduly extravagant.

'Beach Burial' is a lesser poem than 'Five Bells', but a more certain one. My only reservation about it concerns the last line: its laconic use of a worthy but sentimental war cliché seems itself more sentimental than the poem deserves. But it is worth quoting in full:

> Softly and humbly to the Gulf of Arabs
> The convoys of dead sailors come;
> At night they sway and wander in the waters far under,
> But morning rolls them in the foam.
>
> Between the sob and clubbing of the gunfire
> Someone, it seems, has time for this,
> To pluck them from the shallows and bury them in burrows
> And tread the sand upon their nakedness;
>
> And each cross, the driven stake of tidewood,
> Bears the last signature of men,
> Written with such perplexity, with such bewildered pity,
> The words choke as they begin –

> '*Unknown seaman*' – the ghostly pencil
> Wavers and fades, the purple drips,
> The breath of the wet season has washed their inscriptions
> As blue as drowned men's lips,
>
> Dead seamen, gone in search of the same landfall,
> Whether as enemies they fought,
> Or fought with us, or neither; the sand joins them together,
> Enlisted on the other front.

Robert D. FitzGerald, a year younger than Slessor, was also a contributor to *Vision* and a member of this loose 'group'. He was much later than Slessor, however, in striking his vein: Slessor's *One Hundred Poems*, to which only three poems have been added to make the collection that now stands, was dated 1919-39; FitzGerald achieved nothing of note until his third book, *Moonlight Acre*, published in 1938, and is still a comparatively active practitioner – his latest book, *Southmost Twelve*, appeared late in 1962.

FitzGerald was affected by the Lindsayian demand for Gaiety, and the enthusiasm for Life: he is at his worst in the well-known sixth poem of the 'Moonlight Acre' sequence:

> Life, toss up your florin;
> 'Heads,' I call.
> Regret be far and foreign
> whichever fall,
> whether for losing or winning
> the stake scarce to be won –
> it's a fine flash of silver, spinning
> in the gay sun.

He never gave over this vitalist and Lindsayian insistence on the delight of the present moment, on clamorous and more or less roistering action. But neither did that alone ever satisfy him: he was, he said, 'of the moon's children', of a reflective cast of mind, and behind and contained in the present instant he saw intimations of other times. So he says in the ninth poem of the 'Moonlight Acre' sequence,

> and Now, holding its breath, reveals
> how each new summer like saved wine
> treasures old summer, and conceals
> springs yet ungathered, and all mine.

At this point, however, his sense of other times was merely *Vision*-ary fantasy: in the fifth poem of the sequence he looks into his lady's eyes and finds them 'black mirrors overcast/by an old past',

> And there's a clashing of arms, a shout
> far from these years; a ship puts out;
> lost to that hour and this,
> doomed lovers kiss.
>
> From night's tower-window leaning down
> there's a soft mouth that meets my own,
> bright as an ancient scar
> from that old war. . . .

In *This Night's Orbit* (1953) he was to comment on all this:

> Duped though we were and now must walk
> beggared these beggars' miles
> with swags of sober sense that balk
> leaping at easy stiles. . . .
>
> When time, the sharper, reached to thieve
> last rags from limbs and back
> we too used sleight-of-hand, a sleeve,
> a fifth ace in the pack.
>
> ('Duped though we were')

FitzGerald's mind seems not to have taken easily to fantasy (compared with Slessor's and even McCrae's, his fantasy is always feeble), and his down-to-earth sense of time and place save him from it not only in his later work, but in the best poems, the tenth and eleventh, of the 'Moonlight Acre' sequence itself. In 'Essay on Memory', a long poem in the same volume, he undertook to inquire more seriously, if rather crudely, into the significant relationship of past and present; and he subsequently displayed a more hard-headed attitude in his continuing concern for the actual past, the past of historical events: a concern culminating triumphantly in his best poem to date, 'The Wind at Your Door', included in *Southmost Twelve* – a poem in which he admits and searches his relationship with a medical ancestor who supervised the flogging of convicts for the New South Wales government.

In all this, we see the very satisfying spectacle of a poet passing patiently and purposefully, over twenty odd years, from poeticizing fantasy to grave and mature reflection. But in other respects the development is not so satisfying. FitzGerald's ideas are not so penetrating that we are likely to read his work for them alone, and their poetic embodiment has disadvantages. He seems almost to have a grudge against the language, a grudge that has been deepened by its recalcitrance over the years till he is prepared to twist and torture it ruthlessly. The most graceful poetry he ever wrote was in the best lyrics of 'Moonlight Acre': this is the opening stanza of the tenth poem:

> Long since I heard the muttered anger of the reef;
> but it was far off even then, so far indeed
> that an imagined murmur, like the ear's belief
> and faith of the night, was mingled with a fuller knell
> throbbing across the silence, and one could not tell
> which sounds were of air stirring, which come at
> the mind's need.

Against this we might set – admittedly an extreme example – a stanza from the title-poem of his latest book:

> But the cold cause-and-effect of mass and force,
> of harnessed action under a shackled sky,
> the powerlessness of will, I still deny,
> who cross the road at choice or hold my course
> and tell the gong of the clock that bangs this beat
> not rope, and better than engine, leads my feet.

This does not quite successfully defy comprehension, but the barbarism of the last three lines seems unjustifiable in any terms. And if FitzGerald rarely tortures the language as cruelly as this, his use of it constantly teeters on the verge of awkwardness and turgidity: this is true even in the case of 'The Wind at Your Door'.

After 'Moonlight Acre' and perhaps its accompanying sequence 'Copernicus', whatever of FitzGerald's poetry survives survives only despite this constant threat. Much, nevertheless, survives quite strongly, and in the most interesting cases it does so mainly because of FitzGerald's command of narrative technique: with the possible exception of Ernest G. Moll's 'Jonah at Nineveh', there are no Australian poems to stand alongside 'Fifth Day', 'The Wind at Your Door' and, above all, the book-length *Between Two Tides* (1952) as narrative achievements. It is these poems and a handful of lyrics that continue to claim our attention.

Rather than any of the contemporaries of Slessor and Fitz-Gerald, it is two younger Lindsayites who stand out, Douglas Stewart and Kenneth Mackenzie. Stewart was already an accomplished poet with books published in New Zealand and England before he arrived in Australia. However, he took to the Lindsay-McCrae atmosphere with zest, though not perhaps with application, and apparently with little thought: though certainly not without a lively intelligence, he seems, both as poet and critic, generally to have regarded thinking as an irrelevance. Extremely fluent, and indeed facile, he has published book after book, most of which take one theme and handle it gracefully, if rather carelessly, for a large part of the volume. He shows a proclivity for fantasy most clearly in *The Dosser in Springtime* (1946); a penchant for graceful but slight nature poems dominates such books as *Sun Orchids* (1952), and *The Birdsville Track* (1955). Before these, he had published in Australia *Elegy for an Airman* and *Sonnets to the Unknown Soldier* (none of which rhymes).

Without doubt, Stewart's most successful volume of poems before the recent *Rutherford* (1962) was *Glencoe* (1947). It contains a series of various ballad forms written with complete assurance in a Scots dialect whose authenticity I cannot question, which as a sequence succeed admirably, and at times movingly, in coherently presenting the story of the Glencoe massacre. But *Rutherford* is his most interesting work. Before this, none of his poems were comic, and none were fully serious either: in *Rutherford*, for the first time Stewart tries, in the somewhat turgid but ambitious title poem, in that very beautiful anthology piece 'The Silkworms', and perhaps in 'The Garden of Ships', to make statements that will stand consideration; and his success is considerable. On the other hand, he has produced also two comic poems, 'Horse' and 'Leopard-skin' which surpass the funniest poems of his friend Ronald McCuaig (who is more notable, in the long run, for the fine nostalgia of 'Au Tombeau de mon Père' than for his comic verse). My preference is for 'Horse', which contains the unforgettable couplet:

> Horse is thinking, of course.
> What are your thoughts, horse?

It might almost be hoped that Stewart will take seriously to writing comic verse.

A less brilliant and prominent figure than Stewart, Kenneth Mackenzie, who was born in the same year, had a much more considerable achievement as a poet until his premature death at the age of forty-one in 1955. Coming to Sydney in 1934, Mackenzie was introduced to, and felt at home in, the Lindsay circle. He had the obligatory interest in sexual love to an almost extreme degree: in a bad joke, he said in the Australian Broadcasting Commission's 'why and how of poetry' series that almost all of his poetry was written in bed. Yet his interest was different in quality from that of his confrères; sexual love in Mackenzie's poetry is represented either as significantly succeeding or significantly failing as a union of two people. The quality of his concern can be suggested by a passage from the title-poem of the second book of poems he published during his lifetime, *The Moonlit Doorway*:

> ... I, the servitor,
> the bolder yet more humble of us two
> who so astonishingly lie together,
> am here no longer; I am in your body,
> and, as the tree grown out of earth is earth,
> so am I you ...

In his poetry, Mackenzie gives sensuality its full value, even at the risk of making it cloying or inflated. At its most exaggerated it retains an air of authenticity: Mackenzie did not invent overwhelming fantasies of Lindsayite sexuality, though, in a poem like 'What the Mirror Said', or even the anthology-piece 'The Moonlit Doorway' itself, the sensuality has become overwhelming and uncontrolled. His love poetry ranges from fulfilment and exultation to bitterness and despair, and from triumph to failure: but it is rarely, if ever, open to the accusations of nastiness or triviality.

This is not to say that it is wholly successful poetry. In his preface to the *Selected Poems* in which Mackenzie is best accessible, Douglas Stewart speaks of his 'fluent and supple use of blank verse': but Mackenzie's blank verse, which dominates his early poems, and especially his love poems, is too fluent and supple by half, and the poems frequently lack tautness and direction. The latest of Mackenzie's poems – those uncollected during his lifetime – contain his greatest successes, and they show us what a loss his death was: poems like the first sonnet of 'Asleep in the Sun', 'Two Trinities', 'An Old Inmate', and 'In the Orchard' show a complete discipline and a very real achievement. 'An Old Inmate' seems to me to be among the most moving poems I have ever read; these are the first two and the last two stanzas:

> Joe Green Joe Green O how are you doing today?
> I'm well, he said, and the bones of his head looked noble.
> That night they wheeled Joe Green on a whisper away
> but his voice rang on in the ward: I'm a terrible trouble
> to all you girls. I make you work for your pay.
> If I 'ad my way I'd see that they paid you double.
>
> Joe Green Joe Green for eighty-two years and more
> you walked the earth of your grand-dad's farm down-river
> where oranges bigger than suns grow back from the shore
> in the dark straight groves. Your love for life was a fever
> that polished your eye and glowed in your cheek the more
> the more you aged and pulsed in your voice for ever . . .
>
> No. I 'ad no dad nor mum of me own –
> not to remember – but still I'd a good upbringing.
> The gran' ma raised thirty-two of us all alone
> child and grandchild . . . Somewhere a bell goes ringing.
> Steps and the shielded lanterns come and are gone.
> The old voice rocks with laughter and tears and singing.
>
> Gi' me the good old days . . . Joe Green Joe Green
> how are you doing tonight? Is it cold work dying?
> Not 'alf so cold as some of the frosts I've seen
> out Sackville way . . . The voice holds fast defying
> sleep and silence, the whisper and trifold screen
> and the futile difficult sounds of his old
> girl's crying.

*

Quite disparate poets came out of Sydney during this time: most obviously, there was A. D. Hope, in many ways the most exciting poet that the country has produced. Hope, who was born in 1907, has said that he began writing poetry at a very early age, but his first book, *The Wandering Islands*, was not published until 1955. Before this, he had some name from fugitive poems published in magazines and anthologies and circulated in manuscript, and a necessarily limited acquaintance with these shows that he went through some phases that he has disowned: he was at one time, apparently, quite a polished Georgian; and at another a quite remarkably slip-shod post-Eliot (and Auden?) modernist. His collected poems however show remarkable formal control and a range of intellectual and especially literary influence and reference unparalleled in the work of any other Australian poet. This, and a certain penchant for satire, have led our glibber critics to speak of him as an intellectual poet harking (deliberately) back to the eighteenth century, to the Age of Reason.

Nothing could be further from the truth. When his younger friend James McAuley wrote a poem, 'The Muse', celebrating poetry as the triumph and culmination of reason working through life, Hope saw fit to match it in a poem which represented the Muse as dark and involuntary instinct always defeated by (reasonable) life: partially powerful though it is, this is by no means one of his best poems: but his work shows that he holds the extreme position it presents. Nor does he believe that these matters can be probed rationally: his answer to such a pursuit is made in the remarkably crude burlesque of 'Return from the Freudian Islands', a poem which he had the grace temporarily but not finally to disown (it was omitted from *The Wandering Islands*, but reprinted in the English edition of *Poems*, 1960). For Hope, the poet's imaginative pursuit is ineffable, and its nature can only be lamely suggested in analogical terms. He is an 'intellectual' poet only in a special and limited sense. If by calling a poet 'intellectual' we mean merely to pay tribute to the power of his intelligence and the range of his knowledge, and to the sheer discipline of his work, then Hope is most certainly an intellectual poet. If, however, by an 'intellectual poet' we mean (as well) one who is concerned to know and even to extend the limits of rational understanding, and to create a vision of rational lucidity and consistency, Hope is not only not an intellectual poet, but is a positively anti-intellectual one.

One of Hope's most important poems is 'The Double Looking-Glass' (published in *Prospect* in 1961), a poem centring on the Apocryphal incident of Susannah and the Elders. It is too complex to deal with adequately here, and it may be that its vision finally precludes an adequate understanding. But the very obscurity of the poem demands some unriddling. This much at least emerges: the secluded garden in which Susannah moves is a garden consecrated to the imagination and shut off from the outside world (though, dismally and significantly, its peace is finally shattered by the philistine elders), a garden in which actuality and the mirror-world of the imagination merge into one; and secondly, the double looking-glass of imagination is the contemplative mind *and* the sexuality of woman as represented by Susannah ('A mirror for man's images of love').

It is a crucial poem because it embodies, and attempts to wed, the two themes that have most concerned Hope: the nature of imagination, and the nature of sexual love. I have already said all that I can afford to about his view of imagination; it remains to describe his account of sexual love, an issue that bulks large enough in his work, though it takes an effort of memory to recall the furore that it quite absurdly raised when *The Wandering Islands* was published. Most critics who have faced the matter at all have side-stepped it more or less gracefully; only James McAuley has attempted rigorously to ask what values underlie Hope's 'preoccupation' with sex. On good grounds, he sees in Hope a Manichean disgust with the physicality of love; but his mistake, I think, is to look for a too simple and programmatic vision: in this matter, as others, Hope is elusive. Nevertheless, his is a real and fairly coherent vision, and a sufficient sympathy with it can elicit a sense of values which seem to me profoundly valid.

McAuley takes as the crucial text 'Imperial Adam', a poem which omits any mention of the Fall, but in which Adam's sexual intercourse with Eve gives birth to the murderer Cain: he concludes, reasonably enough on the face of it, that Hope sees the sexual act itself as the Fall and the source of degradation. The crucial lines, however, are these:

> From all the beasts, whose pleasant task it was
> In Eden to increase and multiply,
>
> Adam had learned the jolly deed of kind:
> He took her in his arms and there and then,
> Like the clean beasts, embracing from behind,
> Began to found in joy the breed of men.

The insistence is not that the deed is dirty (it is clean) or horrible, but that it is merely animal, merely the pleasurable satsifaction of appetite: merely 'the *jolly* deed of kind': and it is this less than human, and less than humanly loving (animals don't love), act that is rewarded by a murderer's birth. Hope does not fail to see beauty and joy and fulfilment in sexual love: where has it been more vividly expressed than in these two lines:

> Now the heart sings with all its thousand voices
> To hear this city of cells, my body, sing.

But, implicitly, he sees a continuum of love, sexual love, and fruition; any break in this chain is more or less disastrous. So the mere lust of Don Juan leads powerfully to his damnation in 'The Damnation of Byron', as the mere sexuality of Adam in 'Imperial Adam' leads to the birth of Cain; so the sterility of love and sexual love in the beautiful 'Chorale' leads to its defeated close:

> Yet within they hear the womb
> Sighing for the wasted seed.
> Love may not delay too long –
> Is the burden of their song.

And so on. Hope very properly sees men and women as sexual beings whose whole life is informed by their sexuality: he does not see sexuality as a thing apart; or where he does, it leads to deprivation. But fine and humanistic as this view is, it feeds back into his denial of the powers of understanding. On the one hand, the distortion of sexuality leads him to say of the besotted Lot, bedded by his ravenous daughters, that only stupor could keep him wise

> In that best wisdom, which is not to know.

And on the other hand, sexual love tends to slide into, not a proper fulfilment of human beings, but an inhuman mystery in which identity is lost: a tendency most marked in that lush poem 'The Lamp and the Jar', in which

> An unknown king, with my transfigured face,
> Bends your immortal body to his delight.

Ultimately, these tendencies are related to a vein of misanthropy in his work which has at its best yielded such a wild comic poem as 'Conquistador', and has at its worst come to full flower in the long 'Conversation with Calliope' (published in an Australian number of the *Texas Quarterly* in 1962), the raffish discursive manner of which does not disguise a distaste for civilized man and all his works any more than it manages to overcome its own vulgarity.

If we are to say (as I would) that Hope has an air of greatness and is the nearest thing to a major poet that this country has yet seen, then we must say it in the face of explicit tendencies which offer abdication, despair and distaste. The grounds on which it might still be said are that in the main he offers, willy-nilly, a complex and valid attitude to human love, and perhaps to the passions in general: if his intellectual framework is perverse, it is still one that allows him to express the most central passions, and he is a poet who, having abdicated reason, writes from the heart. It is at this level that the powerful control and discipline of his poems becomes crucial, bringing order to what might so easily have been a dark chaos:

> This the builder cannot guess,
> Nor the lover's utmost skill:
> In the instant of success
> Suddenly the heart stands still;
>
> Suddenly a shadow falls
> On the builder's finished plan,
> And the cry of love appals
> All the energies of man.

('The Trophy')

The recognition here of the disorder of the passions involved is intense, recognizing a disparity between desire and achievement more complex and more desperate than we commonly care to face: but that recognition brings not defeat and disorder, but a calmly deliberate ordering, a control which masters despair. Nor is Hope's power merely to contain and subdue the disasters of passion: this is the opening of 'An Epistle':

> First, last and always dearest, closest, best,
>   Source of my travail and my rest,
> The letter which I shall not send, I write
>   To cheer my more than arctic night.
> Sole day and all my summer in that year
>   Of darkness, you were here,
> Were here but yesterday, and still I go
>   Rapt in its golden afterglow.
> Caught in the webs of memory and desire,
>   The cooling and the kindling fire,
> Through all this house, from room to room I pace...

Not only are darkness and absence here mastered; they are triumphed over by the remembered and realized human warmth and tenderness with which the passage is instinct, and which emerges so simply and movingly in such a detail as

> The letter which I shall not send, I write
> To cheer my more than arctic night.

Examples could be multiplied at will. To read Hope, as nobody should fail to do, is at worst occasionally to come across disgust, despair, and obscurantism; but at best, and frequently, to find one's own passions enlarged, ordered and clarified, and ennobled in that ordering and clarification.

The names most commonly associated with Hope's are those of the two younger poets who perpetrated the notorious Ern Malley hoax, James McAuley and Harold Stewart. Stewart's first book, *Phoenix Wings*, showed him as a delicate if rather stiff and frigid artificer, at his best in the chinoiserie of some excerpts from 'The Landscape Roll', a work which his second book, *Orpheus*, finds him still pursuing. This second book marks a regression rather than an advance, while subsequent poems like the long 'Ode to the Supernal Swan' and 'The Descent of Manjusri' seem to the uninitiate inhuman in their oriental esotericism and sterile in their formalism.

McAuley has generally, and I think properly, been a more highly regarded poet than Stewart. He, too, has a version of 'the perennial philosophy', but unlike Stewart's his is firmly grounded in Western thought – in Christianity – which might well be thought to offer a better ground for what is still poetry flowering from a Western culture.

McAuley's views are firmly outlined in his book of essays, *The End of Modernity*, and they are profoundly conservative: against what he sees, penetratingly, as the shiftiness and relativism of modern society and its values he sets the idea of a traditional, ordered, and ceremonious way of life. The problem that confronts the reader is to decide how real McAuley's traditional society is, and what are the origins of his vision of it. When, in 'Prometheus/ A Secular Masque', included in his second book of poems, *A Vision of Ceremony* (significant title), his chorus says

> Also I marked how wisely she [Ceremony] prescribes
> Tradition to the uninstinctive tribes

> Of men; to live in a concentric maze
> Of custom while the big flute and the drum
> Proclaim the dance, and well-tuned voices raise
> A shield of sound to ward off what may come ...

one recalls suddenly McAuley's own vivid account of his period in New Guinea and his background of anthropological knowledge: so that if McAuley's vision of the traditional society seems intellectually rather odd, we might realize that it has a more than apparent basis in his own lived experience.

So, too, with the conservatism of his attacks on modern values. The tension that underlies this and its embodiment in his later poetry cannot be recognized without recognizing the startling approaches to modernism in his earlier poetry: that curious sequence 'The Family of Love', for instance, with its brilliant if uncontrolled burlesque of divided views and values in the modern lover, is the most originally and trenchantly 'modern' poem of its decade – in Australia, that is. Again, in 'Dialogue', which begins

> There was a pattering in the rafters, mother,
> My dreams were troubled by the sounds above.
>
> – That is just a young man's fancy, son,
> Lightly turning now to thoughts of love.

and which ends

> And when I woke up in the cold dawn, mother,
> The rats had come and eaten my face away.
>
> – Never mind, my son, you'll get another,
> Your father he had several in his day.

the quality of sick fascination is barely though brilliantly mastered by the wit.

It is, then, primarily himself rather than Vincent Buckley (to whom the poem is dedicated) that McAuley exhorts in 'An Art of Poetry' to

> Scorn then to darken and contract
> The landscape of the heart,
> By individual, arbitrary
> And self-expressive art.

This may have been a necessary step for McAuley: after the sometimes intensely personal poetry of his first book, *Under Aldebaran*, his second presents a poetry from which personal intensity is largely withdrawn, leaving a poetry bare, didactic and frequently over-simple. That the cost was high is registered in one of the few really successful poems of *A Vision of Ceremony*, 'The Tomb of Heracles':

> A dry tree with an empty honeycomb
> Stands as a broken column by the tomb:
> The classic anguish of a rigid fate,
> The loveless will, superb and desolate.
>
> This is the end of stoic pride and state:
> Blind light, dry rock, a tree that does not bear.
>
> Look, cranes still know their way through empty air;
> For them their world is neither soon nor late;
> But ours is eaten hollow with despair.

Since *A Vision of Ceremony*, McAuley has written a book-length poem on de Quiros, the explorer, which can hardly be judged on the few excerpts yet published but which promises to be as formidably passionless as most of the work in *A Vision of Ceremony*; and a handful of lyrics. The best of these – 'Time out of mind' and 'Pieta' – show a new and passionate personal concern, governed by an intense austerity. They augur well: but in the meantime, McAuley's achievement rests substantially on no more than three or four poems from *A Vision of Ceremony*, and a considerably larger number from the earlier book.

If *Under Aldebaran* showed at times an intense concern with what might be called 'morbid psychology', it showed a more frequent concern for the powers of light and reason reaching their culmination in poetry. We can regard this as McAuley's characteristic vein; but if we regard it as boundlessly optimistic in its humanism, we should notice that these forces contend with an almost apocalyptic vision of ruin and disintegration: a key poem, 'Chorale', ends:

> O seraph in the soul, who singing climb
> The orders of creation as a stair,
> And hold a silver lamp above the time
> And places of our deepening despair:
>
> When the delirium swirls within the gyre,
> And comets die, and iron voices wake,
> Be witness to the sun; and mounting higher
> Hold the lamp steady, though creation shake.

McAuley's celebration of rational man is not facile, but is strained tautly against a recognition of the threat of disorder and despair: it is this tension that gives triumph to the calm translucence of his best work. What we find in McAuley's poetry, beyond a mastery of phrase and image, is an achieved wisdom:

> You are yourself; and when we touch
> We understand the joy of being two,
> Not seeking to annihilate
> Distinction, as self-lovers do. The soul
> Is born a solitary; others come
> With foreign gestures to it, which it must
> Learn patiently by heart, or be unjust.
> The god has been a child since men began
> To worship him: he must become a man.

This is from 'The Celebration of Love', a poem that clearly represents McAuley's characteristic virtues at their best. Comparing it with, say, Hope's love poetry, we can see that it recognizes but is unable to embody the full physicality which is an inseparable part of human experience; it offers instead, in the dance of its language and its clear, explicit statement, a serenity and joy which 'are not given, but are truly earned.'

If *Under Aldebaran* was one of the most remarkable first books of poetry published in Australia, it enjoyed nothing like the success of Judith Wright's *The Moving Image*. This first book immediately gave Miss Wright a prominent place in Australian poetry; and indeed, it shows fully developed almost all the qualities embodied in her later four volumes. A poem like 'South of My Days' shows Miss Wright in characteristic vein, and near her best: the opening lines declare its theme:

> South of my days' circle, part of my blood's country,
> rises that tableland, high delicate outline
> of bony slopes wincing under the winter,
> low trees blue-leaved and olive, outcropping granite –
> clean, lean, hungry country . . .

It seems almost to be simple nature poetry, but that phrase 'part of my blood's country' points to the way in which it is more than that: this is not just landscape, it is a way of life, and Miss Wright's achievement lies in suggesting the quality of the life lived in that place, especially in the person of old Dan, the inveterate story-teller:

> Seventy years of stories he clutches round his bones.
> Seventy summers are hived in him like old honey.

That life is slow and reflective; if it has been hard, it has been gentled by the sense of time and memory. This quality is reflected even more in the lingering movement of the long irregular lines than in the explicitness of the reflective statement:

> Oh, they slide and vanish
> as he shuffles the years like a pack of conjurer's cards.
> True or not, it's all the same; and the frost on the roof
> cracks like a whip, and the back-log breaks into ash.

Everything here depends on evocation, not much on the statement – true or not, it's all the same; and this is so of all the poetry in this first volume. The evocation of poems like 'South of My Days', 'Nigger's Leap' and 'Bullocky' is completely satisfying, the philosophizing of the title-poem not: if against old Dan's seventy years of stories, seventy summers, we set

> One ends, another follows; not done with, never done
> The triple fugue of the insatiate body,
> The enfolding heart, the intent and unflinching mind
> building their worlds from night and the light of the sun . . .

we can admire a comparable rhythmic skill and a painstakingness of phrasing, but the epithets seem finally banal, the statement unremarkable.

Woman to Man, Miss Wright's second book, shows a remarkable and entirely persuasive attempt to widen her gift when, in a number of poems, she writes as no one ever has of feminine love and its fruition. The best of these (I would point especially to the delicate first section of 'The Unborn') are perhaps a finer achievement than anything in the first book: but even in *Woman to Man* they have a special and limited place, and apart from them the book offers at best an extension of the achievements of its forerunner, and at worst the febrile gaiety of 'Song in a Wine-Bar', a poem that harks in temper back to the Lindsayites except that it has a bitter underlying cynicism.

After *Woman to Man*, Miss Wright began again to try to renew her poetic vision in a way that has been described by R.F. Brissenden:

Instead of finding eternity in the acts of woman and man, (she) seems to be seeking it in the grain of sand. Flowers, trees, seeds, birds and insects are beginning to displace men and women as the subjects of her poems; and instead of using the cyclic processes of life which these things exemplify to throw light on the problems and questions of human existence, she does just the opposite. Woman and man seem to be no more significant than the cicadas or the cedar trees.

There remains an obvious level of accomplishment, but in her third and fourth books, *The Gateway* and *The Two Fires*, the two really remarkable poems, 'The Traveller and the Angel' and 'The Harp and the King', are both poems of the loss of vision, though their triumph is to face that loss indomitably.

'The Harp and the King' is Miss Wright's most remarkable poem, and very remarkable it is, with a strength and flexibility whose qualities can hardly be exaggerated. In it, the old King Saul implores the Harp to offer consolation for the desolation that his own experience has taught him: but that desolation forces him to reject the Harp's assurances:

> But the old king turned his head sullenly.
> How can that comfort me,
> Who see into the heart as deep as God can see?
> Love's sown in us; perhaps it flowers; it dies.
> I failed my God and I betrayed my love.
> Make me believe in treason; that is all I have.

A relentlessly searching poem, its tragedy (for it is a poem of tragic stature) lies in Saul's triumph in his debate with the Harp. The Harp, indeed, has the final say:

> Wounded we cross the desert's emptiness,
> and must be false to what would make us whole.
> For only change and distance shape for us
> some new tremendous symbol for the soul.

but it is, in its generality, a desperate gesture: Miss Wright's problem has become that of finding an adequate new vision now that she has out-stripped her earlier one. Her latest book, *Birds*, provides only an interlude: composed partly of poems culled from her previous books and partly of new poems, partly of adult poems and partly of poems written explicitly for children, it offers real pleasures but lesser ones: these poems remain modestly but obstinately poems about birds.

The best-thought-of of our woman poets after Miss Wright is Rosemary Dobson, who has published three books of poems.

In her second book, *The Ship of Ice*, she has a sequence of poems called 'The Devil and the Angel'; in the persona of the Angel – clearly the right choice – she says at one point

> This calling-up of souls, in confidence,
> Is sometimes – well, I find it rather trying...

and there is indeed an air of lassitude about her poetry. Generally fine in detail, and sometimes very fine, its characteristic starting-point is from Miss Dobson's appreciation of painting, and in the long run the effect of this is to put her human subjects behind glass: life always seems to be seen at two removes, and this effect perhaps outweighs one's sense of the perfection of the work. David Campbell, similarly, is a poet whose frequent perfection seems to be gained at the expense of sharply limiting the depths he is prepared to plumb, though in other respects he is quite dissimilar from Miss Dobson. His first book, *Speak with the Sun*, showed little sign of his later development: there, the attempt was largely to renew a ballad-like mode. The most notable poem was a war-ballad, 'Men in Green', which certainly lacks Campbell's later polish, yet has a vigour for which we might later look in vain:

> And I think still of men in green
> On the Soputa track
> With fifteen spitting tommy-guns
> To keep a jungle back.

In Campbell's second book he showed, at least in 'Who Points the Swallow?', a fine lyric gift of which there had previously been little suggestion, and in general a more polished and literary approach: there was also a tendency in the title section, 'The Miracle of Mullion Hill', to a rather fatuous indulgence in slip-shod good-humour of an 'out-back' kind. Both tendencies are confirmed to some extent in his third and best book, the recent *Poems*; but the good humour is less slip-shod, and the polish more consistent. A number of these poems succeed in expressing a sheer delight, like 'Bindweed and Yellowtails', which ends

> And these small singers made of light
> That stream like stars between the trees,
> Sum in an inch the long delight
> Of suns and thoughtful centuries.

There are perhaps half a dozen poems as slenderly beautiful as is this one, but they are not poems to look deeply into: a metaphysical-seeming assertion like that of the last line quoted melts easily, in Campbell's work, into the general feeling of the poem. There are a few poems which offer considerably more than this, most notably the third of the 'Songs for the Married Ear', a poem admirably well-modelled on Blake though (reasonably enough) scarcely attempting to offer a depth to match that poet's: Campbell remains, on the whole, a poet who offers us real but minor graces.

John Manifold is a poet who, like Campbell, began by offering a ballad-like poetry, modified, as Campbell's was to become, by more literary models. If he began as clearly a better poet than Campbell, he has ended markedly inferior: nearly all his work of any value is in his initial volume, *Selected Verse*. The second book, *Nightmares and Sunhorses*, shows a general decline which perhaps reflects an accession of political doubt. For Manifold is an intensely left-wing poet, and if the second volume still offers a large proportion of assertively propagandistic verse, it is unable to do so with the hard activist's assurance that marked the earlier work. To Manifold at his best, politics *was* action, and this, rather than more abstruse political ideology, lent him assurance: the importance of action to him came out not only in the political poems but in such a – political pieces as 'Fencing School' and (his best poem) 'The Tomb of Lieut. John Learmouth, A.I.F.', which begins with the assertion that

This is not sorrow, this is work ...

and ends by praising a

courage chemically pure, uncrossed
With sacrifice or duty or career

of which he says

There is no moral, that's the point of it ...

It was this slightly alarming insistence on action for action's sake, and on a world of clear hard surfaces, that gave the best of Manifold's poems, especially some of the ballads and sonnets, a stringent amoral tautness and a rather chill distinction. The irony of Manifold's poetry is that it finally endorses the bitter advice that he offers, surely ironically, to the hirelings of a corrupt old order in 'For the Mercenaries':

Let your achievement be your only myth,
And kill with nothing but a craftsman's pride.

*

Miss Wright, Campbell, and Manifold all live in the country, although Miss Wright's poetry perhaps bears traces of her education at Sydney University and Campbell's of an affiliation with *The Bulletin* as it was under the literary editorship of Douglas Stewart. But with these at least partial exceptions, all the poets so far discussed have their roots in Sydney, and if that city later offered less obvious excitement than it did in the Lindsayian twenties, it remained the centre of whatever poetic excitement the country showed for long after. In 1942, however, C.R. Jury wrote in the opening number of *Angry Penguins*:

If it is possible at this time still to feel the importance of poetry, Adelaide is now in an interesting condition. There are signs here that the imagination is stirring, and that if it has a chance it will give us something of our own. There is genius about the place; and genius as a neighbour is exciting even at this dreadful moment.

That there was genius about the place now seems less than obvious but that there was excitement is indubitable, and Adelaide was host simultaneously to our two most vociferous poetic 'movements', the 'Angry Penguins' and the 'Jindyworobaks'. Natural enemies, the Angry Penguins had on their side an internationalist modernism and an overwhelming preponderance of the excitement; while the Jindyworobaks had a nationalist fervour seeking its inspiration in the land and its original inhabitants, and an underlying staidness. For anyone who would wish our poetry not to be provincial, it is sad to reflect that more poets survived the wreck of the Jindyworobak movement than survived that of the Angry Penguins; but then, the Jindyworobaks were not wrecked so violently, the crew had more time quietly to abandon ship.

Angry Penguins began as the magazine of the Arts Association of Adelaide University, and looked at from these quieter times it looks like essentially an undergraduate magazine: that it was able to create such a furore is a tribute to the energy of its editors, and especially of the indefatigable Max Harris, who quite recently described himself as 'the oldest *enfant terrible* in the business'. As for the quality of the poetry, Harris's own later judgement can stand: 'The Angry Penguin writers built up an astounding monolith of obscure cult-ridden subjectivism, incredible in fervour for such a small country as Australia.' Odd lines here and there show talent, most obviously lines of Harris's own. But it is probably true that the best poems published were those of the fictitious Ern Malley, for although they too were (deliberately) nonsense, they had an occasional edge of wit and satire that distinguished them from the more earnest productions: they were livelier, and Harris could reasonably be congratulated on their publication, though not on the claims he made for them.

Some of the more promising of these writers were killed in the war; the only two continuing as more or less active poets are Harris himself and Geoffrey Dutton. Harris has never recovered his excitement, and seems rather lost without it. Dutton, on the other hand, seemed at best a strained and factitious quasi-surrealist, and was much later to write far more successfully in the lucid and well-mannered travel sections of *Antipodes in Shoes*, the the second of his three books of verse, and as far removed from his first in tendency as possible.

If more erstwhile Jindyworobaks remain in practice, only one of them is more notable. Roland Robinson's previous volumes were recently collected with new poems to form a book called *Deep Well*, and are meant to form some sort of continuous work. His manner, however, does not provide a great range of variation, and in a continuous reading his delicacy and his colourful exoticism sink into a grey monotone in which the separate poems lose their individuality. This monotony is due to the limited range of his subject-matter: the poems are all concerned with the landscape of Northern Australia and its flora and fauna – apart from himself, the only people in Robinson's poems are aborigines who are almost completely absorbed into their background. Robinson's vision of his country is an intuitive pantheism permeated with aboriginal lore, and this is of limited interest; nevertheless a real sense of Robinson's love for, and perceptiveness about, the country emerges, and the poems are generally fine in detail. If they convey little sense of the excitement arising from Adelaide in the nineteen-forties, they are the best work to emerge from that furore (though Robinson was not himself an Adelaide man), and have been equalled by nothing out of that city since.

In discussing the present writer's one book of verse, a Sydney reviewer suggested that the centre of Australian poetic activities is now to be found in Melbourne. If this is true it has not long been true, and Melbourne has never offered the sense of excitement that Sydney and Adelaide did at different times. For many years Furnley Maurice was regarded as the doyen of Melbourne poets for work that can no longer command attention. Less noticed but a much better poet, Leonard Mann has achieved his best work in his latest book, *Elegiac*: uneven, and frequently simply clumsy, it contains three or four poems that are genuinely notable and which show in that small compass a surprising variety of achievement. The best of them is 'The Fan-Dancer's Conversion', where Mann's very crudeness subserves a poetic savagery that is almost Skeltonic in mode.

Beyond this, whatever poetic history Melbourne had had before the nineteen-fifties is mainly of antiquarian interest; and since then only one poet of fairly indubitable stature has appeared there. Vincent Buckley has published two books of poems, *The World's Flesh* and *Masters in Israel*. The first book was in some ways remarkably promising, but its main interest lies in that: it preludes much of Buckley's development. It clearly showed his dangers, too: an apocalyptic rhetorical tone as in the 'Dedication' to the long 'Land of No Fathers' –

> Friend, in this sun-dark land
> We move to assist a birth
> Bloody, spectacular

and a piling up of factitiously momentous images as in 'All Hands are Numbed'. His successes, other than in fragmentary moments, lay in poems more modest and graceful in manner like 'On an Old Portrait', which begins

> Death shadows her. The shallow Georgian face,
> The slight pin-pointed beauty in each eye,
> Make no pretence of livingness, but stress
> Death, like the late guest of her family,
>
> Smiling the Dürer smile. And here death sours
> No great seabird on her throne of water,
> But a thin Aesop's child; but a frame of hours;
> But beauty's lonely and distressful daughter.

The grace of this is unmistakable, and what might seem the portentousness of the opening phrase is quickly redeemed. Some doubts remain. The Dürer and Aesop references seem only half-assimilated; this is no very striking fault, and one easily overcome. But why *should* the subject of the portrait have appeared a 'great seabird on her throne of water'? This line shows a tendency that Buckley has never quite overcome to present striking and sensuous images whose impressiveness barely disguises a lack of genuine imaginative relevance.

The very title of *The World's Flesh* announced the scope of his poetic ambition: Buckley's attempt, which succeeds more notably in the best poems of his second book, is to recreate the feeling of a whole world complete in its sensuous reality, but recognized as a spiritual habitat. The quality of his success can be suggested by the opening lines of the finest poem in *Masters in Israel*, 'Criminal Court':

> So each man's wounded methodical life
> Will turn him back to the daylight year
> Of air and willows, where the creek
> Was a line of dim topaz and of flow
> Fretting the autumn's mud and leaves;
> Four or five kids in an autumn dance
> Dark with rain . . .

These lines immediately create a sense of a whole scene, which is at once realized objectively and instinct with emotion. Such a success is remarkable and is not untypical; but at times the attempt to create the sense of a whole scene is made at the expense of immediacy. These images show one of Buckley's characteristic procedures:

> The lighting of your throat and arms . . .
> The silvering shadows of her rounded side . . .
> And shadows greening on the cabinet . . .

and

> The rounding light gleams on your rounded thigh . . .

The use of light is almost a painter's effect, and we are left not with the clear substance of the images but with the elusive play of light and shade: Buckley in this way creates an aura which suggests a world extending beyond the immediate image, but he does so at the cost of definition of the sensual world ready to hand.

This strain between a general and an immediate apprehension of the sensual world, however, is certainly not so striking as other strains that are perhaps ultimately related to it. The most obvious of these is the tendency to lapse into a hollowly didactic rhetoric. This tendency is linked, as Buckley is aware, with the role he adopts within the poem: a role which he commonly sees as that of bardic enunciation. Sometimes his acceptance of that role shows an engaging irony, as when in 'Reading to My Sick Daughter' he says

> In that blue gaze
> I'm saviour, songman, epic clown . . .

firmly setting the grandeur of those pretensions in a perspective of innocence and naïvety. Again, in 'Late Tutorial' he recognizes precisely the impossibility of communicating with a simple human audience in large prophetic tones; but in the same poem writes without irony that

> . . . all are twined on the great central tree . . .

a gesture ambitious in rhetoric but hollow in effect: if it means that we are all 'twined' with Christ on the cross, it lacks imaginative realization; if it does not mean that, it is merely vague.

Yet it is certainly not true that in Buckley's poetry the grand manner is only redeemed when it is held taut by irony. Where it succeeds directly, as in the magnificent best passages of 'In Time of the Hungarian Martyrdom', it is where Buckley rises adequately above a self-conscious concern for his own role in the poem – for instance, in these lines given to Christ:

> O frail anonymous prophets of My sight,
> Come to these least, the children of My hand;
> In darkness put on your garments; in anguish, light.
> Come to My shore. There is no other land.

In contrast, in an ambitious failure like the 'Impromptu for Francis Webb' he is only too little the anonymous prophet, the man speaking for men:

> Now I am at my trade of prophecy,
> Old friend, I balance every burning word
> With courteous intent, as it should be,
> In case my anger be too much preferred

Before my love: in case our dream of flesh
Decline to the rotting dust of eyes and hair
Without my voice's witness, and the leash
That reasoned anguish holds upon despair.

This is indeed too much a 'trade' of prophecy. The insistence on the personal role is startling, the suggestion that it is not the voice of the poet speaking for men but '*my*' voice that must bear fruitful witness dismaying; and with this goes a collapse into the strained banality of 'burning word', 'courteous intent', 'the rotting dust of eyes and hair'. 'There is nothing here that they will understand,' the poem begins: on the contrary, the poem offers a great deal that we might understand, but Buckley in his prophetic role stands between what he has to say and his audience.

If Buckley as prophet or bard is an identification that he seems almost to force upon the reader, to lay too great an emphasis on it is perhaps to do him an injustice: it is a role that he adopts in the weakest, not the most successful, parts of his work, and this commonly goes hand in hand with a strained rhetoric and the thumping rhythms into which he tends to lapse. When he is saved from it, as he most often is, it is most frequently by the adoption of a more equivocal tone and rhythm, which serve to establish a more subtle and equivocal persona, as in poems like 'Criminal Court'. Throughout *Masters in Israel*, his great virtue is his sustained attempt to see the human world whole and give it its full value, his most marked weakness a loss of hardness and clarity and immediacy in that attempt. Gustav Cross has suggested that 'perhaps the fault lies in the very intensity of Mr Buckley's vision, which demands a larger rhetoric than he allows himself here.' Yet such a rhetoric seems unattainable, and indeed unimaginable: the fault seems rather to be that Buckley too commonly tries to get his whole sense of a physical and spiritual world, complete, into each poem. This is a strain that they scarcely bear: some poems stand out fully realized and complete, but much of the work blurs back, on closing the book, into an intense and admirable but finally unordered vision. It is in this context, especially, that Buckley's subsequent publication of 'Eleven Political Poems' (in *Prospect* in 1962) is significant: the poems there, at their different levels, are written with a clarity and definition most commonly lacking in *Masters in Israel*; and

at least the best of them, 'Election Speech', nevertheless rivals
in intensity anything that Buckley has yet done:

> He goes in quickly for the kill:
> A fact, a promise, and a jibe.
> I think of nothing; nothings fill
> The image that his words inscribe,
> My skull intoning from the hill.

Of Australian poets, Francis Webb is the one with most
affinity to Buckley: or perhaps that should be the other way
round, for Webb is certainly the more extremely individual poet.
Webb had a *succès d'estime* with his early first book, *A Drum for
Ben Boyd*, but was only later to emerge as a remarkable poet:
this first book followed what almost seems an Australian fashion
of narrative poems told in unsatisfactorily-connected fragments,
but it was essentially a simple poem, written in a good straight-
forward manner indebted to Browning and Robert D. Fitz-
Gerald. An altogether different poet emerged in the long title-
poem of Webb's second book, *Leichhardt in Theatre*. This
poem, too, is in some sense a narrative poem, and it is certainly
fragmentary: but the fragmentation is due not to a simple lack
of structure but to a bewildering juxtaposition of impressions
that is (as the title implies) meant to be in some sense dramatic.
Like Douglas Stewart's narrative poem 'Worsley Enchanted', it
offers a swift variation of tones ranging from comic to tragic:
but the comedy is wilder, the tragedy more intense, irony is
frequent, there is brilliant burlesque, and the command of tone
and diction in all this seems effortless. We are left with the
breathless impression of a poet who can do anything.

But then, we are left wondering what he *has* done. It is only
in two stanzas near the end of the poem, sometimes singled out
for their beauty, that we are offered a clue:

> Study the carved wood and the stirrup leather,
> Debris and trifles matched against your skill:
> These are no fragments you may wedge together,
> Animate, summon by name, equip with will:
> Let what is waste lie waste; yield to the pressure
> And silence of their fate. World, words, are closer.

> It is where sun and world blossom into words
> As a tree's lovely frenzies of bloom divide
> Winter from winter, month from month of birds:

In such clean space the man and his shadow ride.
See them upon the hills, life-sized and breathing,
Where they will go, how perish – this is nothing.

The fragmentary relics and remains that offer objective knowledge, Webb seems to be saying, cannot be reconstructed into a
full and complex heroic vision but can only be pushed aside as
waste. It is, then, only where a poet's vision of the world blossoms
into words that the heroic image can be recreated and stand
clearly to be seen: and that, not the narrative details (where they
will go, how perish), is what matters. For that reason, then, Webb
has avoided coherent narrative order as an irrelevance, and has
gone so far as to remove any sense of a distractingly objective
world by removing the whole action to a 'theatre' (the poem is of
course completely unstageable), where the whole complexity of
the heroic vision that Leichhardt suggests to him can be presented
skeletally by shifts of scene and focus. It is a brilliant and daring
attempt, but an extremely disconcerting one: I at least cannot
begin to say what order and significance finally emerge, but can
as yet only testify to the qualities I have suggested.

All of Webb's subsequent long poems – the excerpts from 'A
View of Montreal' in this book; the radio play that gives his
next book *Birthday*, its title, and 'The Canticle' from the same
book; 'Electric', 'Eyre All Alone', and the title-poem 'Socrates'
from his latest book – present difficulties of a comparable order:
serious critical evaluation of them will demand more sustained
and scrupulous consideration than I or any other critic has yet
given them. It may be that Webb has simply made more demands
on his readers than anybody can meet. Such considerations have
led Chris Wallace-Crabbe to say that 'in concentrating on
Webb's longer poems, I am doing him less than justice. Though
these show his range and ambition, they might suggest that he
is a most impressive failure: a brilliant talent, but lacking control.
The best of his shorter poems show that this is not the case.
In his three later books there are a number of poems which succeed resoundingly.' Indeed, Webb can be dishearteningly difficult
in his shorter poems too, and none of them offers the plenitude of
gifts found especially in 'Leichhardt in Theatre', 'The Canticle',
and 'Eyre All Alone'; but there is a number of clear and unmistakable triumphs among the shorter poems that defies listing. In
some ways, Webb is the most exciting poet that we have yet seen.

Webb is not a Melbourne poet, though he has lived here as well as in Sydney and overseas. If Melbourne is a centre of poetic interest, it is perhaps largely due to Buckley's influence not only as a poet but as a teacher and critic. On the other hand, little of the work of younger Melbourne poets shows much trace of Buckley's poetic influence, and least of all that of the most promising of them, Chris Wallace-Crabbe. Wallace-Crabbe's first book, *The Music of Division*, shows a trenchant clear-headedness, self-awareness, and an awareness of man as a social being: qualities that augur well for the future. The weaknesses there that he has to overcome are an urbanity that is worn too assertively to be altogether convincing, and an occasional almost gauche woodenness that belies it. In 1964 he is publishing a second book; at the same time the Tasmanian Gwen Harwood is publishing her first. Her magazine and anthology appearances, however, have already given her a reputation higher, if anything, than Wallace-Crabbe's. They have shown unusual sharpness of phrasing, a display of learning and a rather bewildering range and depth of personae: how significantly these attributes come together is yet to be seen.

Even a nodding acquaintance with the period of this survey will reveal that there are a great many poets, some of them well-known, whom I have failed to discuss. Many of them I am sorry to have omitted, for their poems have given me pleasure; but much further selection among them could only appear idiosyncratic, while any attempt to include all those who have some right to mention could only result in a rather fruitless annotated catalogue. And no poet other than those whom I have included has, I think, risen more than briefly above the general level represented by the annual anthologies of Australian poetry: a level of achievement that is often likeable, frequently worthy, and most commonly unexciting.

AUSTRALIAN FICTION TO 1920

JOHN BARNES

SURVEYING the 'fiction fields' of Australia in 1856, a local editor, Frederick Sinnett,[1] found them fertile but as yet poorly cultivated. 'The few Australian novels which have been written', he noted regretfully, 'are too apt to be books of travel in disguise', neglecting what he called 'the larger purposes of fiction'. It was inevitable that description, 'local colour', would be the *raison d'être* of novels about Australia for almost a century after the beginnings of settlement. Only when the local civilization had an inner identity and strength (when Australia had become more than merely a derivative of England) could it engage the interest of the creative writer – both local and visiting – at a deeper level than that of description. From the start, popular English novelists used versions of colonial life to provide exotic backgrounds for their formula stories. They were interested merely in the glamour of scenes remote and unfamiliar to English readers. There were also a few novelists whose work had an Australian focus; and, generally, it holds true that they were more interested in the details of the setting than in the narrative, and were using the novel form as a vehicle for impressions and information about the colonies. So it is useless to expect to find works of art among the Australian novels of the nineteenth century. In spite of the impression which lingers, that there is a solid body of Australian fiction in this period, it is only with Furphy's *Such is Life* in 1903 and Henry Handel Richardson's *The Getting of Wisdom* in 1910 that it is possible to think of Australian classics. *Geoffry Hamlyn*, *His Natural Life*, and *Robbery Under Arms* diminish in stature as time passes; they are milestones, but they are not the classics of Australian fiction which they were once thought to be. They hold a considerable interest for us still, because they represent stages in the history of the progress towards an Australian prose tradition. An account of prose fiction in Australia from the beginnings to 1920 inevitably becomes an account of fumbling attempts to discover the artistic possibilities of Australian subject-matter. The 'Australian-ness' of the material (understood in different ways) is the constant problem of the novelists, and it is only towards the end of the period that novels which are neither derivative nor self-consciously Australian become a real possibility.

It is usual to introduce such accounts with some mention of *Quintus Servinton* by Henry Savery, [2] which was published in 1830-1 in Hobart. This relatively undistinguished autobiography, barely disguised as fiction, is an apologia, written by a convict with an eye to his rehabilitation. It is fiction of the most rudimentary kind, with little reference to Australia, but due to the accident of its timing – it is the first novel published in Australia – it has not been completely forgotten. One may admire the spirit of the man who wrote it, and find interest in the circumstances surrounding its appearance, but it is relevant only to the history of publishing in Australia. Charles Rowcroft's volume, *Tales of the Colonies*, 1843, is very much relevant to the history of Australian prose fiction, however, for it takes Australian life as its subject. The book made a big impact on English readers because, as Sinnett pointed out, it described what was new and unfamiliar to them. This was to be the pattern of the fiction for the next decade or so, which Cecil Hadgraft has aptly labelled 'the Guide Book period'. [3]

Tales of the Colonies is intended to be, as Rowcroft says, 'a useful history of a settler's life', a demonstration of 'how much may be accomplished by prudence, industry, and perseverance'. Although under no illusions about the hardships of settlement, or the inferiority of colonial civilization – 'It seems to me, that, voluntarily to remove to a new colony is like putting yourself back in the age of the world for some hundreds of years, by relinquishing the point of civilization and progress reached by the old country' – Rowcroft hoped to promote immigration to Australia. He was appalled by the overcrowded and depressed state of England, 'a country where the greatest of crimes is to be poor', and enthusiastic about the colonies where, it seemed to him, a man might recover his natural dignity, and gain a fair share of worldly goods as well. It is a view of Australia sustained and elaborated by Kingsley and Boldrewood, and unthinkingly accepted by most Australians today. To make his point, Rowcroft tells a success story: *Tales of the Colonies* is supposedly an old man's journal of his life in Van Diemen's Land, the story of how he prospered. One can agree with H. M. Green [4] when he remarks that 'there is no attempt at construction and one damn thing happens after another', but not when he adds, 'just as in real life'. The book swings between propaganda for colonization, in the form of descriptions of phases of settling on the land, and entertainment in the form of exciting adventures. Rowcroft crowds one episode on another – Thornley, the settler, is involved in fights with bushrangers and natives, he is lost in the bush, he is threatened by eagles, he is beseiged by natives and almost burnt to death twice – and all of this is one narrative sequence. Just one damn thing after another! Although the romance is intended to entertain the reader and so make the information easier to swallow, Rowcroft doesn't spare his reader the facts: he even includes a letter to a friend, complete with statistics, to show how profitable a farm can be. The nearest he comes to giving his thesis human substance is in the character of Crab, a reluctant settler, clinging to all his English prejudices against the new country ('fit for nothing but convicts and kangaroos to live in') but unable to leave it in spite of himself. Crab is a 'character', drawn according to a stock comic formula, but Rowcroft writes of him with such affectionate admiration that he is more real than the narrator or anything else in the novel.

Rowcroft (c. 1781-1850) advertised himself as a colonial magistrate, but he did not write out of any deep personal experience of the colonies, in which he spent only four years. As a description of bush life, *Tales of the Colonies* is flimsy and full of improbabilities, but it helped to fix the Englishman's illusions about Australia. A few years later, Alexander Harris (1805-1874) was writing to challenge these same illusions. In *Settlers and Convicts*, [5] (1847) he was, like Rowcroft, writing for the prospective migrant, but his account was at once less narrowly propagandist and more realistic. A good example of Harris's concern to set the record right is his description (probably fictional) of 'Bushrangers as they are', which he introduces in this way:

My object in this publication is to convey an idea of facts as they occur in Australian everyday life; in short, to correct the erroneous statements that are abroad, not to add to them. I spent nearly twenty years of a bush life in New South Wales, during the whole of which time I never sustained the slightest bodily injury from a bushranger; nor did I ever suffer from aggression of higher enormity than some slight theft. So that when, since my return to England, I have met with the tales that are so prevalent respecting their sanguinary acts, I have felt them to be virtually exaggerations. The insulated facts might be true enough, but then they are the exceptions, not the usual custom; and this should have been stated in the narration of them, otherwise that impression comes to be attached to everyday life, which really and properly belongs only to its rarest and merest exceptions.

Harris is frequently instructive and informative in the guide-book manner ('And here I should inform the reader how a damper is made'), and includes one chapter, 'The New Settler', which parallels Rowcroft's letter as a source of good advice to the intending immigrant.

Both *Tales of the Colonies* and *Settlers and Convicts* are offered as colonial reminiscences. With good eighteenth century precedent, Rowcroft pretends to be merely the editor of the journal of his old friend; Harris assumes the guise of 'An Emigrant Mechanic', and sub-titles his book, 'Recollections of Sixteen Years Labour in the Australian Backwoods'. Both writers take Defoe as their master. Harris is the more successful at creating an air of verisimilitude, passing off invention as fact, and is still readable today. He writes a plain, manly prose, more supple and viable than that of Rowcroft, who labours heavily over anything but straight description. Rowcroft was plagued by what he considered to be the necessity of adventures: he could tell an amusing anecdote with some authority, but when he attempted anything on a larger scale his sense of realism completely deserted him. *Settlers and Convicts* is free from the improbabilities of *Tales of the Colonies*, largely because Harris ignored the convention of romance which Rowcroft fell back on. His book is a work of recollections, mingling fact and fiction, and he himself is present in the narrative, no mere cipher or object to whom things happen, but a man of strong feelings and prejudices. His tendency to preach – against drink, prostitution, the penal system – which leads to inflated writing, actually strengthens our impression that we are reading a genuine personal reminiscence.

Settlers and Convicts survives, then, as a fascinating, well-substantiated description of colonial life, with the feel of actual experience about it, in spite of Harris's vagueness about himself at what would be crucial points in a genuine journal. However, Harris's second attempt at using Australian experiences is a failure, and the reasons are not far to seek. In *The Emigrant Family or the Story of an Australian Settler*, (1849) his aim was still to describe colonial life and manners, but instead of the supposed autobiographical journal in the style of Defoe, he made use of the 'romance' – he wrote a novel according to popular specification. The effect of this choice can be gauged from the Preface, where he is almost apologetic:

The main design in the composition of these volumes, and that to which every other has been carefully subordinated, was the delineation of the actual life of an Emigrant Family, and the scenery about their homestead in the Australian colonies, in the middle of the nineteenth century. Of course, all must not expect to meet with a Martin Beck for an overseer: but with the single exception of a character necessary to furnish the tale with sufficient of plot to interest the lovers of romance, everything exhibited is a simple copy from actual daily life.

Harris's uneasiness over the distortion which the writing of a popular novel seemed to involve comes out here. The 'lovers of romance' were in the majority in the small audience for Australian books, and they had a restrictive influence throughout the nineteenth century.

Harris's novel was described in the *Westminster Review* as 'well worth perusal, as well for its literary merits as for the accurate pictures of Australian life and manners'. There is no doubt of Harris's power of observation, but as for the novel's worth, Sinnett's general complaint about Australian novels applies: 'The *dramatis personae* are not people with characters and passions, but lay figures, so constructed, and placed in attitudes, as to display the costumes of the place and period'. This comment applies with even greater force to Rowcroft's second work, *The Bushranger of Van Diemen's Land*, (1846) which is a lifeless combination of romantic improbabilities and local colouring. Rowcroft tries to have it both ways: he creates the archetypal New Chum, blatantly named Jeremiah Silliman, who is ridiculed for having taken his knowledge of colonial life from misleading books, and then involves this farcical figure in a tediously drawn-out plot, crammed with sensation. The local colouring is carried to absurd lengths: at one stage, Rowcroft describes a kind of zoological parade, which is surely unequalled, though it can be paralleled in the other novels of the time. Harris is never as crude as Rowcroft, but his novel is a similar mixture –

partially redeemed, it is true, by the clarity and solidity of his descriptions. The plot which he felt obliged to offer his readers was a burden to Harris. Such talent as he had was for description of facts; the novel form, as he and his readers conceived it, was merely a way of arranging his observations and making them more entertaining.

These works may be taken as representative of the early ventures in fiction in Australia. There is such a dearth of creative imagination that it is futile to catalogue and go through the motions of criticizing the work of novelists before Henry Kingsley. What merit they have is in their description of the colonial scene: it is useless to look for anything approaching imaginative interpretation, even in the work of the best of them, like Rowcroft and Harris. William Howitt prefaced his novel, *Tallangetta, the Squatter's Home. A Tale of Australian Life*, (1857) with the announcement: 'In these volumes it has been my object to depict the various phases of Australian life and character more fully than could be done in my "Two Years in Victoria".' [6] This remark puts the fiction of the period in the right perspective. There are exceptions, of course – James Tucker's remarkable convict novel, *Ralph Rashleigh*, written about 1844, and Catherine Helen Spence's *Clara Morison*, 1854 – but these two novels lie off the beaten track. Tucker's novel was not published until almost a century later, and Catherine Spence (1825-1910) lacked the literary skill which could have made her attitude a potent force in the shaping of Australian prose fiction.

Frederick Sinnett thought *Clara Morison* the best Australian novel that had appeared by 1856, because it was 'not a work of mere description, but a work of art'. The properties of colonial life which Rowcroft and others introduced with such zest – bushrangers, natives, convicts, men lost in the bush, local wild life – are missing from this novel about South Australian life during the Victorian gold rushes, which is firmly centred in the domestic circle. There are no scenes of the diggings: Catherine Spence keeps close to what she has experienced at first hand, and reports through her characters what she knows only at second hand. While we can admire her fidelity to her own experience, and her concentration on people rather than places, there is no doubt that the novel suffers from her self-denying approach. The particular love story she tells is less interesting than the background against which it is set. Moreover, Catherine Spence was not wholly free from propagandist intentions, and not wholly engaged by the plot she built around her characters. Her strongest interest was in public affairs (she made her mark in Australian intellectual life as a reformer), and it is a fatal weakness of *Clara Morison* that the gold rushes are observed primarily as a source of social and political problems. And as the novel goes on, the human relationships become subordinate to the discussion of public issues, with the result that the final effect is rather arid.

The appeal of *Clara Morison* is greatest in the opening chapters where, drawing upon her own early experience, Catherine Spence describes Clara's journey to the colony, and her attempts to find suitable work. Here she gives rein to a lively, satirical wit, and, following Jane Austen, crisply fixes on social pretensions and vulgarity. It is only here, however, that she succeeds in dramatizing her characters, and even then, it is the minor figures – types like Miss Withering, whose fastidious and refined manner masks a bullying nature – and not the principals who come to life. Her emotional scope is severely limited; and while her firm, energetic style is never really dull, neither is it vivid or evocative. Her distinction is her fine, discriminating intelligence. She had a remarkable degree of self-awareness, and in her acknowledged self-portrait, the blue-stocking, Margaret, she described herself very justly:

Her mind was not poetical, nor imaginative; if she was silent, she seemed always to be thinking, never dreaming. Her eyes were never timidly cast down, but bravely looked the whole world in the face, with a steady truth in them which demanded nothing less than truth in return.

No critic could improve upon this as a description of the personality which emerges from the novel.

Admitting its restricted sense of life, *Clara Morison* is a solidly interesting book, written with a degree of competence that is quite uncharacteristic of the time. Catherine Spence is more of a realist – and more of an artist – than any of her contemporaries. Why, then, did she have so little success as a novelist? and why has her work been so neglected? She wrote seven novels, of which only four were published in book form, and two were never published at all. One reason is the imaginative impoverishment which strikes the reader at once. Added to that, there is no strong narrative interest. While she adopts a fairly conventional frame for her story, she refuses its dramatic possibilities. This is admirable in so far as she avoids cheap heroics and sentimentality, but it results in a sense of continual anti-climax. Clara's situation in the Beaufort house, the report of her hero's death, and his sudden reappearance – this is the stuff of melodrama, but it is melodrama thwarted. Perhaps a more important reason is that she was writing the kind of discussion novel that could have only a very limited appeal. Her opinions on colonial life were of interest to only a small audience at home and in England. And she did not picture the sort of Australia that the bulk of the English public believed in and wished to read about. She was detached and clear-eyed, identified with the colony to which she had migrated, 'unavoidably Australian', as Sinnett noted; but it was impossible to expect the novel-reading public at that stage to take Australia for granted. She herself stated the dilemma in which she was placed by the public expectation about colonial novels: 'If stories are excessively Australian, they lose the sympathies of the bulk of the public. If they are mildly Australian, the work is thought to lack distinctiveness.' The readers of the day expected colonial novels to be rich in local colour – why else write about the colonies? – and to confirm their pre-conceived notions about life in the colonies.

In this field, Henry Kingsley (1830-76) has never had any serious competitor. As H. M. Green points out, he opened up areas which the earlier writers like Rowcroft and Harris had only glimpsed. He established the romance of station life, which was the major convention of Australian fiction until the 1930s. Australian prose fiction begins with *Geoffry Hamlyn* in 1859.

Kingsley was uninterested in the prospect of a local literature, however. He was, from first to last, an Englishman visiting the colonies, and he admired colonial life as an extension of England. Once the possibility of a choice of loyalties is proposed, he quickly proclaims his love of England and his pride in his birth-right as an Englishman. The much-quoted sentiments of his hero and heroine, who return to England, are galling to Australian pride, but they are in keeping with the atmosphere of nostalgia for England which pervades the novel. When Geoffry Hamlyn indulges in rhetorical prophecy as he gazes on Melbourne ('I see here the cradle of a new and mighty empire'), Major Buckley, the older man, brings him back to earth with a few patronizing words ('The world is very, very young, my dear Hamlyn') and takes him off to dine at the club. Kingsley seems to go out of his way to assert his English-ness and class snobbery – and yet generations of Australians have delighted in the book. Kingsley ('Good old Tory' was A. G. Stephens's phrase for him) appealed to a strong, deep prejudice in both English and colonial readers: the dream of the leisurely, gentlemanly landed society. What has fascinated Australians is the transplanting of the English dream to an Australian setting. Although Kingsley's remarks about colonials are unsympathetic, and he treats his colonial characters with a superior, almost condescending air, the total illusion is flattering to Australians. An atmosphere of old-world heroism softens and dignifies the local scene.

Unlike Harris and his other predecessors, Kingsley was not interested in writing a guide-book. The harsh, unpleasant realities are kept out of sight; and there is little description of the day-to-day labour on the stations. Kingsley deals only with what is suitable for romance. There is consequently little of that documentation that characterizes earlier novels by visitors. It is Kingsley's strength as a romancer that he pays little attention to the new-ness of Australian society, and is (perhaps surprisingly) little involved in the Australian material he uses. Unlike Boldrewood, he is never distracted from the forwarding of the narrative by the desire to document and explain. The Australian details he selects are there to embellish the romance. In retrospect, it seems to us that he has included almost everything possible from station life – a bushfire, a kangaroo hunt, hostile blacks, convicts, bushrangers, a child lost in the bush – but he disposes these with such tact that we are never wearied nor openly incredulous. It is hard to resist the charm of such episodes as Sam's ride on Widderin, and other boyish day-dreams.

Geoffry Hamlyn was quickly accepted as a local classic. 'The best Australian novel that has been, and probably will be written', said Marcus Clarke, in the Preface to *Long Odds*, (1869), and this was still the general opinion at the time Joseph Furphy was writing *Such is Life*, in which he takes delight in being rude about the book and its author. Furphy would not see the book's virtues as romance, because he rejected that mode of fiction entirely: he wanted realism, and therefore could not stomach 'the slender-witted, virgin-souled, overgrown schoolboys who fill Henry Kingsley's exceedingly trashy and misleading novel'. *Geoffry Hamlyn* was such a powerful influence in Australian fiction, fostering the illusions about Australia which *Such is Life* was intended to puncture, that Furphy felt the need to damn it completely.

Kingsley wrote without any very high conception of fiction, as his handling of plot is sufficient to demonstrate. He is a minor contemporary of Dickens and Thackeray, a successful popular entertainer, making use of his Australian experiences. Whereas Rowcroft and Harris aimed at that section of the English public with some interest in emigration to the colonies, Kingsley wrote for the English public at large. With Marcus Clarke (1846-81), the next important name in colonial fiction, there is a change of emphasis and direction. Although he had lived in Australia and actually wrote *Geoffry Hamlyn* here, Kingsley felt no relationship to the country, and always looked at it from the outside. Clarke's one work of importance, *His Natural Life*,[7] (1874) is, however, grounded in Australian history. Clarke is, in no sense, a follower of Kingsley in the novel; and, indeed, it is almost by accident that he wrote a major Australian novel, for he was essentially a journalist, facile, witty, sophisticated, and reckless. The novel for which he is remembered shows little of this side of him, but it reveals an intensity of compassion and an order of moral awareness that found no place in his more ephemeral writings. Beginning with the intention of writing up Tasmanian convict records, he wrote a serial novel, running on interminably, spinning out an improbable plot, but the resulting book (trimmed for publication), hopelessly flawed as it is, is more powerful than any other Australian novel before *The Fortunes of Richard Mahony*.

By the 1870s, the convict system was a feature of the past, no longer a present shame, and as it receded into the distance it became a suitable subject for historical fiction. Clarke was the first to take the system as his main theme, and to focus on its psychological effects. There had, however, been two earlier works of fiction treating convictism, one of which – Caroline Leakey's *The Broad Arrow* (1859) – was well-known to Clarke. He was unaware of *Ralph Rashleigh* by James Tucker (1808-66),[8] which had been written about 1844, but was not published in full in its original form until 1952. The inflated claims which were made for this novel when it was recently brought to light have provoked an inevitable reaction against it. While it doesn't change our impression of the achievements in fiction in Australia during the nineteenth century – at least, not in any major respects – Tucker's performance in *Ralph Rashleigh* is remarkable for the detachment with which he manages to describe the horrors he had been through as a convict, and for what is, by the standards of the period, a relative literary sophistication. Tucker often writes dully in a stiff, formal style, which reminds us of official reports, yet he shows more awareness of the literary possibilities of his material than the popular authors like Rowcroft and Harris who were his contemporaries.

Tucker's aim seems to have been to produce an entertaining *picaresque*, following, for the most part, the outlines of his own convict experience, but supplemented by imagined adventures. Rashleigh – a cover for Tucker himself – is a likeable rogue, of whose goodness of heart we are never in doubt: psychologically, he is a nebulous creation, barely touched by the formidable sequence of adventures he goes through. The *picaresque* manner is strongest in the opening chapters, set in England, which give an engaging account of Rashleigh's roguery. Tucker knew his eighteenth century authors, and a reader constantly has a feeling of Defoe, Smollett and Fielding – particularly the Fielding of *Jonathan Wild* – close at hand. The flavour of literary derivativeness is weaker when Rashleigh is transported to New South Wales, and the narrative becomes a report on the workings of the convict system from the inside. The very disproportions of the narrative are suggestive of authenticity: some episodes are sharp and immediate, with the sort of inconsequential detail which implies a first-hand report, but others are passed over in the flat, reporting style of the period, as if Tucker had retained no clear visual memory of them. In the long run, this is a major weakness of the novel. Tucker lacked the artistry, the discipline, needed to sift his material and give it a coherent shape. He rambles on, filling out his reminiscences with invention – the amount of romantic 'padding' increases as he gets closer to the circumstances of his immediate past – wasting or spoiling his material. He tries to cram everything in – Rashleigh's life of crime, his suffering in the hulks, the journey to Australia, the Emu

Plains settlement, the convict theatre, harvesting, up-country experiences, adventures with bushrangers, the misery of the coal mines at Newcastle, an escape, adventures with blacks, a heroic rescue. The weakest parts of the book are where Tucker appears to have invented most; in particular, the conventional set of heroics whereby Rashleigh wins a pardon. Isolated episodes stand out, and impose themselves by the sheer horror they contain. It is hard to forget, for instance, the description of how the bushrangers tied the convict overseer to an ant-bed; but incidents like this are not marked by any particular literary skill. The power of such a description comes from the raw material itself: the writing is frequently stilted and tedious.

At the same time, Tucker is capable of using words to good effect. The well-rounded narrative of how the convict players tricked the greedy publican reveals an entirely different Tucker. Most of the memorable passages in *Ralph Rashleigh* present violence and cruelty, but the total effect, in so far as we can talk of a single effect, is one of grim humour. Tucker has a sense of style and, more than that, a sense of the incongruity of his well-bred, formal, allusive style, with its obtrusive literary colouring. It is affected writing, allowing only a very small range of effects. Tucker can be lightly satirical in describing theatrical performance ('But the wardrobe! Oh the wardrobe! No powers of language can enable me to do justice to a description of the wardrobe') and even urbane in describing the sordid homestead of the Arlacks ('The earthern floor of this *recherché* retreat was plentifully strewn with fowl's dung, agreeably chequered by petty lagoons of stinking water.') At times, his irony is bitterly intense, as in his account of a sadistic commandant ('. . . this *splendid specimen* of a British officer. . . .'). This style is for Tucker a defence against the raw and violent life which he is presenting, as if he were reassuring himself and his reader of being civilized. The artificiality seems to be deliberate, a way of distancing himself from the story where it mattered to him.

Ralph Rashleigh is a mine of interesting details about convict life, seen through the eyes of a convict. Tucker sees himself as a victim of the system, and stresses the brutality and tyranny under which he has suffered. Caroline Leakey and Marcus Clarke are similarly impressed by the vicious working of the system (who could not have been?), but they see it from the point of view of the humane outside observer.

Caroline Leakey (1827-81), unfortunately, advances her view of convictism through a sentimental romance, which is distressingly feeble. Her heroine, the victim of an unscrupulous well-born lover, is impossibly idealized and enveloped in a haze of piety: proud and stoical, she bears her undeserved fate nobly, scorning the consolation of religion until at last (of course!) she finds the love of God and dies. The religious pattern is obvious and recognizable, and the real interest of the book lies elsewhere than in the characterization of the heroine. Caroline Leakey's work exemplifies what was a recurring feature of Australian fiction, particularly fiction written by women during the nineteenth century: the defeat of intelligence by a sentimental notion of fiction. She is an intelligent and thoughtful interpreter of colonial society, but when she consciously sets about writing fiction – creating characters and developing situations – she falsifies, and shamelessly plays upon the emotions of her readers. The variation within *The Broad Arrow* is extraordinary. The story of Maida Gwynnham's seduction and despair contains such cheap, sensational writing as this:

You hear no more; the sound fades away with the view, which dissolves itself into a moonlight scene. A female in disguise leans on a gentleman's arm. They hurry by; you trace them to a railway-station; they enter a first-class carriage. The whistle is loud, shrill enough to meet your ear; they are whirled off, and the station melts into an upper chamber. But one figure is there – a female; her black hair floats over her shoulders – her eyes glisten; you have seen those eyes before; they glisten, not now with radiant joy; there is a fire in them that you fancy must scathe the object it shall rest upon. A cup is in her quivering hand; you glance involuntarily towards a phial on the table; there is a label on the phial, and on the label there are cross-bones and a skull; beneath the skull is written, in large black letters, 'Poison'.

This poor stuff is unlikely to make anyone's flesh creep now. If this were all that *The Broad Arrow* contained, it could be dismissed without a second glance. But it includes also a sensitivity to colonial attitudes, which results in a different order of writing. Caroline Leakey perceptively renders the colonial love-hate relationship with England. The former magistrate, Mr Evelyn, tells his newly arrived English niece, whose judgements irritate him considerably, 'Never apply the term Colonial to anything but produce.' And this colonial touchiness about English criticism and unfavourable comparisons is well dramatized in his own conversation with his niece. Caroline Leakey reinforces her interpretation by giving Mr Evelyn a colonial-born wife, who is unmistakably a product of the local civilization. Mrs Evelyn has spent all her life surrounded by convicts, whom she treats with a cool disregard of their feelings ('It's a colonial supposition that prisoners have no feelings . . .' is one of Mr Evelyn's observations which his wife's behaviour bears out all too plainly.) Caroline Leakey's particular achievement is to have shown the place of convictism in the lives of a well-off colonial household. The servants are convicts, the young boy is exposed to the pernicious influence of convict nurses, and no matter how much the locals may think of themselves as pure English, the taint of convictism is there. This is an interesting theme, but the story doesn't develop Miss Leakey's view of colonial society or her criticism of the failure of the convict system to achieve its supposed aim of reform. The possibilities are lost sight of in the religiosity and romancing.

In his Preface to *His Natural Life*, Marcus Clarke claims to be a reformer, but this would seem to be merely a gesture. What moved him was the *spectacle* of suffering which the convict records offered. A. G. Stephens was surely right when he suggested that 'much of the force of *His Natural Life* must have lain *perdu* in the records on which Clarke based his story'. Clarke's skill lay in scene-painting rather than in the delineation of characters in their relationships, and the convict records gave him the human facts which he could dramatize. The improbability and involution of the romance which Clarke invented has been commented on often enough. He was not involved, creatively, with this fabrication, which has a makeshift air about it, as if he improvised as he went along, with one eye on the serial readers. The contorted, sensational plot indicates the quality of Clarke's imagination without the stimulus of actual documents. When he writes about episodes of convict life, he is still sensational, but the effect is to deepen our sense of the inhumanity of the system. His technique of setting a scene and building up to a striking climax is obvious enough. There is, for instance, the unforgettable macabre horror of the cannibalism among the escaping convicts:

The insatiable giant, ravenous with famine, and sustained by madness, is not to be shaken off. Vetch tries to run, but his legs bend under him. The axe that has tried to drink so much blood feels heavy as lead. He will fling it away. No – he dares not. Night falls again. He must rest, or go mad. His limbs are powerless. His eye lids are glued together. He sleeps as he stands. This horrible thing must be a dream. He is at Port Arthur or will wake in his pallet in the penny lodging-house he slept at when a boy. Is that the Deputy come to wake him to the torment of living? It is not time – surely not time yet. He sleeps – and the giant grinning with ferocious joy, approaches on clumsy tip-toe and seizes the coveted axe.

It is theatrical and extreme, and it can still make our flesh creep. It is first-rate melodrama.

Yet *His Natural Life* is greater than the melodrama it contains, and much greater than the triviality of its concluding scenes. The unifying theme is injustice, and injustice is shown as inherent in civilization. The novel is not merely a chamber of horrors: along with the melodrama is a moral sense, imperfectly and intermittently expressed, which implies a deeper level of seriousness. This is to be seen in its clearest form in the account of how Rufus Dawes rescued Frere, Sylvia, and her mother, after they had been left stranded on the coast by the mutinous convicts. The episode assumes the dimensions of a fable: it is the story of Crichton, another version of Robinson Crusoe. The order of society is overthrown by human necessity: Dawes, the outcast, the convict who has been hunted and degraded, recovers his natural dignity and by virtue of what he has been forced to learn in his suffering is fitted to rule, while Frere, with all his civilized accomplishments – his military training, his manners – becomes his subject. The situation is shot through with ironies. The little society – the society of four – is based on Natural Law, but it cannot last: all its members long to return to civilized society. Dawes is committed to civilization, but it can only mean prison and humiliation for him. To be true to himself, to his own essential goodness, he must help the others to return, and so lose his freedom and be once more unjustly punished. Frere's brutal treachery epitomizes the corruption of this society which supports the convict system. The irony is further pointed by what happens when the small company are rescued through Dawes's bravery and ingenuity. Frere's lies, accepted by all, are a 'romance', thoroughly conventional in every respect. That is as far as Clarke goes. The implications of the moral fable are only weakly followed up. Clarke indicts society through the futher revelations of brutality and injustice, and through the contrasting responses of the stock clergymen, Meekin and North, but although there are telling passages, the effect of the castaway episode is lost with the renewed emphasis on plot machinery and the pathos of Dawes's sufferings. Never again does Clarke regain the plainness and concentrated feeling of this single and restricted episode, which stands as an indication of what Clarke might have achieved, had he not spent his energies thoughtlessly and recklessly.

*

Catherine Spence had complained about the unreality of the image of Australia which she found in local writing:

> The one-sided pictures that Australian poets and writers present, are false in the impression they make on the outside world and on ourselves ... What we need is, as Matthew Arnold says of life, to see Australia steadily and see it whole.

This is an admirable general statement, and all the important novelists of colonial life in the nineteenth century, excepting Clarke, would have endorsed it as an aim. *His Natural Life* is the only major work of the period not animated by the desire to present an interpretation of Australia and Australian manners. The three outstanding novelists of the last phase of the century – Rolf Boldrewood, Rosa Praed, and Joseph Furphy – all made substantially the same claim: to be presenting a true picture of Australian life. This is the point at issue between the colonial-minded novelists, like Boldrewood and Rosa Praed, and the national-minded novelists, like Furphy and Miles Franklin, who, together with the *Bulletin* short story writers, rejected the assumptions on which novels about Australia had previously been based. The literary clash, most clearly pointed by Furphy in *Such is Life*, is a reflection of a fundamental cleavage within the local society. By the seventies, the number of local-born was outstripping the number of immigrants. The English 'version' of Australian life could satisfy those who accepted England as 'Home', and formed their expectations of literature from English experience; but it could not long continue to satisfy those to whom England was a distant country, especially not those who, as Francis Adams [9] noted in the nineties, referred to England sarcastically as ''ome'.

As Australian life assumed a more distinct and settled character, a local point of view became possible, and the movement towards greater political independence had its counterpart in literature. By the 1890s, thanks to the spirited leadership of *The Bulletin*, nationalism had become a clearly formulated issue in local writing. Between the two *Bulletin* anthologies, *A Golden Shanty*, 1890, and *The Bulletin Story Book*, (1901), the writers associated with this journal articulated a new version of Australian life. In the Introduction to *The Bulletin Story Book*, A. G. Stephens was able to note that creative work 'which is Australian in spirit, as well as in scene or incident' was at last beginning to be written.

The heyday of *The Bulletin* coincides with that of the colonial romance, the most popular exponent of which was Rolf Boldrewood (Thomas Alexander Browne, 1826-1915), whose *Robbery Under Arms*, serialized in 1882, but not published in book form until 1888, is the best 'Australian romance' in the *Geoffry Hamlyn* line. Boldrewood, who had no love for *The Bulletin* – '... a paper of which I do not approve and for which I declined to write' – represents the colonial spirit against which *The Bulletin* struggled in politics and literature. Because he looked back to the period of his youth, his work shows little feeling for the change that was in the air at the end of the century. *Robbery Under Arms* is, in the words of the sub-title, 'A story of life and adventure in the bush and in the goldfields of Australia.' The Australia that interests Boldrewood is the developing colony, not the emergent nation: he sees Australia as a place for pioneering, one of his central themes being the successful immigrant. As one of his characters in *A Sydney-Side Saxon* says of Australia: 'It's the place for a young fellow to go to that has all the world before him.' All of Boldrewood's heroes, except the Marston boys, are immigrants and retain the feelings of immigrants.

But that does not mean that Boldrewood was unsympathetic towards the local scene. He wrote of England as if his home were there, but he knew more about Australia, and he identified himself with the life here. In *A Sydney-Side Saxon*, although England is still 'home' to the successful squatter, he stays in Australia after making his pile:

But I'm not going home – not a yard. Bandra's quite good enough for me, and as long as I have good health, good children, good horses, with enough to keep me from idling, and the best wife in the world, my home's here in Australia.

The confusion over where 'home' is located characterizes the colonial outlook: the nationalist did not admit any alternative place to Australia. Unlike Kingsley, from whom he took his bearings, Boldrewood was not a visitor to Australia: he was brought to the country as a child, and visited England only once. The England sketched in his novels is the England of the story books. The narrator of *The Miner's Right*, for instance, has a suspiciously conventional memory of the land he is supposed to come from:

> Hour after hour, after my frugal midday meal, I lay on the grass under the vast trunk of the fallen forest-monarch, and dreamed of green England's meads and time-worn crumbling keeps, of the half-royal residences of the great nobles – the time-honoured halls of the squires and country gentlemen. I saw again the ancient gables of Allerton Court, the ivy-buttressed village church, the plodding unambitious farm-labourers, the old women in their caps, the clerk withstanding the ever troublesome boys. . . .

And so on. This is a reversal of the earlier situation in fiction in which it was Australia that was described with romantic vagueness.

Boldrewood's solidly factual approach to the local scene impressed his contemporaries. Even A. G. Stephens joined in the chorus of praise, writing in 1901: 'Browne has invented nothing, but as a recorder of Victorian quasi-Australian life of his time, there is none to rival him.' This is a judgement which evades the critical issue, and actually misrepresents Boldrewood's method. He invented a great deal, and his reconstruction of Australian life, while based on factual knowledge, is tailored to meet the requirements of the romance form. Boldrewood certainly valued his reputation as a faithful recorder of the local scene, and in the Preface to *Robbery Under Arms* he made this claim without qualification:

> But though presented in the guise of fiction, this chronicle of the Marston family must not be set down by the reader as wholly fanciful or exaggerated. Much of the narrative is literally true, as can be verified by official records. A lifelong residence in Australia may be accepted as a guarantee for fidelity as to local colour and descriptive detail.

In *The Miner's Right* he shows every bit as much contempt for the exaggerations of popular romance as Furphy did:

One of those invaluable literary caterers for modern civilization, ever ready to construct historiettes concerning lands which he has never seen and societies which he can never have entered, describes in one Australian novel (save the mark) a lovely and distressed damsel, reft from her friends, and chained to the pole of a tent by a ruffian band of diggers. In another improving tale the prepossessing, if not, perhaps, immaculate heroine, is publicly disposed of by lottery and carried off by the winner. How utterly, childishly impossible such occurrences could have been in the wildest days of mining adventure, let any digger say.

Boldrewood's exasperation here is that of a man who knows at first hand – and *that* was his criterion of truth. Unlike Furphy, he could not see that the truth of his fiction was compromised by his reliance upon stock romance conventions. Plot is largely a matter of exercise, a necessary routine for Boldrewood, whose conception of life and literature seems to have been determined almost wholly by his reading of Sir Walter Scott's romances.

The 'realism' of Boldrewood's novels is severely qualified by his lack of imagination. The documentation of aspects of Australian life had been the main concern of the first novelists, and Boldrewood's work thirty years later represents hardly any advance. Indeed, none of his work has the historical value of *Settlers and Convicts*. He supplies information in a tedious and heavy-handed fashion, sometimes, as in *The Miner's Right*, suspending the plot in order to do so. In this novel, he demonstrates convincingly his knowledge of mining conditions and the technicalities of mining rights, and draws upon known historical events; but the total impression of the novel is one of unreality. Boldrewood had none of Henry Handel Richardson's ability to transmute facts into life-like experience. All that he had to say about Australian life is external to whatever imaginative life his writing possesses.

Robbery Under Arms is easily his best novel. It suffers least from the burden of documentation, it has more narrative interest, and it is more firmly anchored in a credible colonial situation. This is the only work in which Boldrewood comes near to transplanting romance in Australia. The bushrangers were the sort of characters (suitably glamourized and given tone by the presence of the mysterious aristocrat) around whom an adventure story could be built. Boldrewood threw himself into the story with a est that is not found in his other work, which strikes us today as mechanical and tedious. He wrote lamely at the best of times; but in novels like *Robbery Under Arms* and *A Sydney-Side Saxon*, where he adopted the *persona* of an uneducated narrator, he avoids the archaic and redundant polysyllables and ponderous literary references which disfigure the pages of novels like *The Miner's Right* and *A Colonial Reformer*, and which he apparently thought constituted 'style'. *Robbery Under Arms* gains from this uncharacteristic plainness, yet it could not be said that he is very successful in pretending to be a colonial youth: even here, at his simplest, he is obviously literary, striving for an effect. Here is Dick Marston, at the beginning of the novel:

But it's all up now; there's no get away this time; and I, Dick Marston, as strong as a bullock, as active as a rock-wallaby, chock-full of life and spirits and health, have been tried for bush-ranging – robbery under arms they call it – and though the blood runs through my veins like the water in the mountain creeks, and every bit of bone and sinew is as sound as the day I was born, I must die on the gallows this day month.

The similes stick out as being pre-meditated: they don't belong to the character, and it is impossible to imagine them in his mouth. And the rhythm is that of a carefully composed speech, with no suggestion of the narrator's mind about it. The rhetoric has its appeal, of course, but it seems worth noting Boldrewood's limited control of the vernacular, in view of the claim made for him as the creator of the first recognizably Australian characters. Dick and Jim and old Ben Marston are the height of Boldrewood's achievement as a novelist; but it is not a very substantial achievement.

The Marstons come to life comparatively, almost in spite of their creator, who cannot forget that he is a member of respectable society even as he details their lawless adventures. It is a different matter with the aristocratic adventurer, Starlight, who never falls below his conception of a hero. Starlight's courtly affectations and sense of honour are described with almost schoolboyish admiration: here Boldrewood was clearly in his element. All Boldrewood's sympathies were with the gentleman, or rather, 'the "gentleman" of fiction, and of Australian fiction pre-eminently', as Furphy had it. There is an interesting discrepancy between the point of view when Starlight is being the masterly and heroic captain of the band, and when he is playin the part of a new chum or a gentleman swell. On the latte occasions, Boldrewood can poke fun at the Englishman wit agreeable manners and educated accent, who is so out-of-plac in the raw society of the colonies. Similarly, he has it both way in *A Colonial Reformer*, the hero of which is the well-bor Englishman, Earnest Neuchamp (pronounced New Chum), wh is first the butt as a new chum, and then the hero as a successfu squatter. And the plots of the novels contain adventures suitabl for gentlemen, the rescues of beautiful maidens being one c their main outback occupations.

In the nineties, *The Bulletin* once referred to Boldrewood a 'one of the industrious publishers' machines', and, leaving asid *Robbery Under Arms* and *A Sydney-Side Saxon*, his work seems t merit that harsh judgement. His feebleness, even within the limit of his chosen mode, is all too clear today. For his contemporaries he was the foremost Australian writer of his generation. Hi reputation was made, however, in London first; and his succes must have been due, above all else, to the picturesque impressio he gave of Australia. Boldrewood had begun as a writer b writing a sketch of a kangaroo drive, which 'I judged correctly would be among "things not generally known" to the Britis public'. And this habit of looking at Australian life from th outside, as it would appear to the British public, remained wit him. Although his earliest (and best) books were written as serial for Australian journals, they pre-suppose an English conventio about Australia. Boldrewood may even be regarded as the mos successful of the guide-book novelists.

Writing in 1896, Desmond Byrne,[10] a local critic, complained just as Catherine Spence had done earlier, of the highly selective and incomplete view of Australian life to be found in fiction: 'Somehow it is assumed that people in the mother country continue to be interested only in the picturesque, the curious and the unusual in Australian life.' The convention had long been set, and Boldrewood strengthened it. An idea of fiction formed by a reading of Scott and his followers could only prolong this situation. Moreover, as Australian cities grew and society became more and more urbanized, the disappearing life of the countryside assumed a degree of glamour, and stories of pioneering and bushranging could be heroic and satisfy the townsman's desire to escape the present reality. Byrne's urging that Australian novelists at this time should take a lead from the modern American realists and write about the middle-class society of the towns fell on deaf ears.

During the eighties and nineties, the Anglo-Australian romance became fashionable. In London there was an active group of ex-patriates, who exploited this taste, and produced anthologies with such titles as *Oak-Bough and Wattle-Blossom*, directed towards two audiences: an English audience with a taste for the 'local colour' of colonial life, and a colonial audience which was, essentially, an extension of the English audience. The con-tributors are fairly described as hack writers, with the exception of Rosa Praed (1851-1935), who was potentially, though not in fact, a major Australian novelist.

As Mrs Campbell Praed, she published 37 novels, as well as other works, and of these 20 are about Australia or touch on Australia. The pattern of her life is almost exactly opposite to Boldrewood's. Born in Queensland, she lived abroad from 1876 until her death in 1935, making only one visit to Australia (in 1894). By all accounts she was an outstanding woman, and yet her fiction is comparatively disappointing. *Policy and Passion*, (1881), her best novel, written when she was just starting out as a novelist, is full of a promise that was never realized.

The reasons for Mrs Praed's failure to develop as an artist are plain in this early novel. In the first place, she was a victim of what A. A. Phillips[11] has called 'the cultural cringe'. Colonial born, she had no doubt where 'home' was; and her work shows a lively recognition of the differences between English and colonial manners. *Policy and Passion*, written after she had left Australia, focuses on the discontent of a colonial-born girl, daughter of the Premier of the colony. Like Caroline Leakey, Rosa Praed knew the pretensions of Australian 'high society', and she catches them vividly in Honoria's disdain of being called 'colonial'. Honoria, in many respects a self-portrait, is bored and restless with life in the colony, and feels the lure of Europe. 'I am always fancying that we Australians are like children playing at being grown-up. It is in Europe that people live – ', she tells her English suitor. This conviction of the insufficiency of colonial life runs deep in the novel. Having to choose between an Australian suitor and an aristocratic Englishman, Honoria at first rejects the Australian,

although he is clearly qualified to be a local version of th
romantic hero, because her 'troublesome fastidiousness' de
mands 'an aristocratic brow, smooth hands, and Europea
address'. Australian life is crude, unrefined, and uncultured; an
Honoria longs for something better. In the end, however, afte
her aristocrat has acted like a bounder, she marries the Australia
and is able to declare, years later, in characteristically Australia
tones: 'I have never regretted having married an Australian; an
wish for no better fate than to cast in my lot with Leichardt'
Land.' Despite this, and despite Mrs Praed's 'placing' o
Honoria's complaining as a form of immaturity, the novel seem
to endorse her criticism by making the hero and heroine a
acceptable, by supposed English standards, as possible. Honori
is a New World version of the romantic heroine; and Mrs Prae
only makes a pretence of confronting national differences throug
the two suitors. They are cast in the same mould: the Englishman
with a 'tall, broadly built figure, bronzed, high-bred face an
soldier-like bearing'; and the Australian, 'lacking somewhat th
graces of society, but rich in an air of native distinction, and i
the chivalry which arises from intuitive good breeding'. A littl
polish is all the Australian needs. One feels like saying that the
novel ought to be called 'Polish and Passion'!

Rosa Praed was proud of being an Australian, and stressed he
nationality in the Preface to *Policy and Passion*:

It has been my wish to depict in these pages certain phases of Australian life, in which the main interests and dominant passions of the
personages concerned are identical with those which might readily
present themselves upon an European stage, but which, directly and
indirectly, are influenced by striking natural surroundings, and by conditions inseparable from the youth of a vigorous and impulsive nation.

The scenery described here is drawn directly from nature; and the
name of Leichardt's Land – a tribute to the memory of a daring and
ill-fated explorer – is but a transparent mask covering features that will
be familiar to many Australian readers.

It is, however, to all English readers that I, an Australian, address
myself, with the hope that I may in some slight degree aid in bridging
over the gulf which divides the Old World from the Young.

While she writes as an Australian, and is often perceptive about
Australian attitudes, she looks to English readers and, in effect,
adopts the values of the English novel-reading public. *Policy and*

ussion contains the expected features of colonial fiction: the
andsome, aristocratic Englishman, gaining 'colonial expe-
ence'; glimpses of station life, including a kangaroo hunt and
ther adventures; and discussions of how colonial life diverges
om the English norm. The unexpected element is the detailed
ccount of the political life of the colony. Chapter I is presented
hrough the eyes of an Englishman, newly arrived in the colonies,
convenient and well-tried way of focusing on the peculiarities
f colonial life. To interest English readers, she had to look at her
abject from the outside, as it appeared to them, and her ultimate
eference is always England and English expectations. Even that
ould not be so bad if she were not so deeply committed to the
alues of the popular romantic novel.

This is the second crippling inhibition under which she wrote.
Her novels suffer from what George Eliot once called 'the vulgar
coercion of conventional plot'. Her capitulation to the debilita-
ing values of fashionable fiction goes hand in hand with the
cultural cringe'. Mrs Praed does not dwell on the picturesque
aspects of the colonies to the extent that some of her contemporaries did, but her conception of 'human nature' is controlled
by the conventions of the novel of romantic love. Her potential
can be seen in the bold conception of Longleat, the former convict, who has risen to become Premier, and who has the same
sort of truth about him as Boldrewood's Ben Marston. But even
as she describes him politicking, Mrs Praed keeps in mind the
values of her audience:

As he stood in the glare of the declining sun, his head thrown back,
his big chest expanded, with his broad capable forehead, his keen eyes
looking out steadily from under shaggy brows, his under lip slightly
protruding and giving to his coarsely moulded face an expression of
suave self-complacency, in spite of the drawbacks of evident low birth
and vulgar assertiveness, there were in his bearing and features indica-
tions of intellectual power and iron resolution, which would have
impressed a higher-class mob than that now waiting eagerly for his words.

In Longleat she had an excellent instance of Australian values,
but she finally sacrificed him on the altar of respectability in a
grating piece of doublethink. She could not ask her readers to
share her admiration for such a man.

Looking back on her beginnings as a writer, Mrs Praed
regretted the road she had taken:

... had I only been simple and natural, had I only tried to describe what I knew, there was a rich virgin field waiting to be tilled under my very feet. I had the Australian bush with its glamour, its tragedy, its pathos and its humour; I had the romance of the pioneer upheavings and the social makings of a new-born colony – had I but known it, the whole stock-in-trade of the novelist. ... Alas! when I think that in those early days of mine, it never struck me that my worthiest ambition might be to become a genuine Australian story teller! Then it was rather the fashion to despise native surroundings and the romance of the bush. We all wanted to be English. ...

But it is never easy to be simple and natural, least of all in an environment where there is no strong literary tradition. The local scene offered little intellectual nourishment to the young writer of her generation. *Policy and Passion* still has some interest today because she put into it so much of her youthful dissatisfaction with her surroundings. But the influences she came under in England smothered her originality. It was at this time that Henry James was complaining of the degradation of the art of the novelist. The popular novelists, he declared, 'turn out an article for which there is a demand, they keep a shop for a speciality, and the business is carried on in accordance with the useful well-tested prescription'. Under the tutelage of her publishers, Mrs Praed quickly learnt to conform to the tastes of the circulating-library reader in England, and her novels belong with those of such successful authoresses as 'Ouida', whom she particularly admired.

Mrs Campbell Praed's fiction is not devoid of a sense of reality (at least in the beginning) but, she compromised her individuality by accepting the conventions of the romantic novel, and her contribution to Australian literature is much smaller than it might have been. The two lady novelists, with whom her name is usually linked, similarly submitted to the tyranny of convention, but, one feels, with less struggle. In her own day Ada Cambridge (Mrs G. F. Cross, 1844-1926) had a reputation which seems quite undeserved now. It was largely, as she herself admitted in her autobiography, *Thirty Years in Australia* (1903), that she began writing in the 1870s before Boldrewood and others had made their mark. She was an accomplished story-teller, with just enough intellectual independence to make her treatment of religious issues seem daring to orthodox minds. The chronicle of her life in Australia – she came as a young wife of a parson, and made only one trip back to England, in her old age – is much more interesting than her novels, evoking the real in a way that her novels don't, because it aims at being no more than a simple record. She was a less vigorous and complex personality than Rosa Praed, but even so she was more than she seemed to be in her fiction. 'The only reason for the existence of a novel is that it does attempt to represent life', wrote Henry James in his memorable essay, *The Art of Fiction* (1884); but these lady novelists worked on completely the opposite premise. Such life as creeps into their novels is kept in the straight-jacket of the romance plot.

'Tasma' (Mrs Jessie Couvreur, 1848-97), the least productive of this group, has worn better than the other two. Her best novel, *Uncle Piper of Piper's Hill*, (1889) is an assured treatment of Anglo-Australian family relationships in the setting of Melbourne society. The characters here are shrewdly observed, and in her handling of sexual relationships she shows a certain maturity, but the effect is muted; and in this field she achieves less than Mrs Praed, whose own unhappy experiences force their way into her novels in spite of her reliance upon the conventional. 'Tasma's' intellectual interests recall Catherine Spence, but she lacks the energy and originality of mind of the earlier writer, and always keeps the discussion within the frame of the story. There is enough created life in her fiction to make her of interest to the literary historian, but yet too little to make her of more than passing interest. There is nothing really distinctive about her work: she seems to have done all that she could do within the confines of the romance.

The work of these three women novelists appealed most strongly to women. It is relevant that the tone of the *Bulletin* writers, who stand in opposition, is predominantly masculine. The role of *The Bulletin* in Australian writing has never been under-estimated; but it is doubtful if it has been weighed accurately. Francis Adams [12] suggested the right stress when he described *The Bulletin* as the only mouthpiece of originality in the country. Some historians give the impression that the founding of *The Bulletin* in 1880 was followed by a sudden burst of creative activity and nationalist feeling – a kind of literary uprising, in fact, in which the colonial Establishment was overthrown, and a new and democratic order set up. But the 'Bulletin revolution' was a more limited one than this view allows. From the first, it proclaimed the need to stimulate the nationalist spirit, but it was not until the nineties, and more markedly after the Red Page was instituted under A.G. Stephens in 1896, that The Bulletin saw itself as the nurse and guardian of a national literature. The most positive and immediate achievement of The Bulletin was to encourage writers to be original, to ignore the current English fashions in fiction, and so escape the stultifying effect of the Anglo-Australian conventions. The readers of The Bulletin were invited to write for other readers of The Bulletin, and not for English readers. 'Every man can write at least one book, every man with brains has at least one good story to tell; every man with or without brains moves in a different circle and knows things unknown to any other man . . . ' ran one Bulletin notice to contributors. That was the spirit in which The Bulletin encouraged local writing. It released stores of creativity that would have remained untapped. Archibald wanted a paper written largely by its readers, and for a period he seemed to achieve this.

While it had no definite theory of literature, The Bulletin did stand for certain values, both human and literary, which it encouraged in its contributors. The contrast between the two story-tellers in Furphy's The Buln-Buln and the Brolga brings out the essential difference between the writer of colonial fiction in the romance convention and the Bulletin-type writer, working within what may be called the convention of bush realism. Fred Pritchard's lies are consciously literary in composition and romantic in substance, and leave us with the feeling that we have heard them before; but Barefooted Bob's are colloquial in style, shaped from his personal experience, and are evocative of the bushman. It is the bushman, 'the one powerful and unique national type yet produced in Australia',[13] as Francis Adams called him, who dominates the fiction of the Bulletin writers. This means a striking shift in point of view compared with the earlier fiction and that of the Anglo-Australian novelists. Rosa Praed, for instance, admired the bushmen, but she saw them at a distance – as 'crude specimens of humanity'. In the Bulletin fiction, the bushman's viewpoint is a kind of norm, a centre; and readers are constantly being invited to share the bushman's way of looking at things. While the Anglo-Australian novelists explain Australia (from outside, or from within the most English section of Australian society) to English readers, the *Bulletin* writers most frequently seem to be explaining the Australian bushman to the Australian townsman. Lawson, for instance, consciously speaks for the bushman in a story like 'The Union Buries Its Dead': 'This is what *we* are really like', he seems to be saying. And that, too, is the attitude of Joseph Furphy, for whom the bushman was unquestionably the *real* Australian.

The bush story quickly became a convention in the pages of *The Bulletin*. Its basis had been the bush yarn, the sort of story told by Barefooted Bob, and Lawson gets the manner of the yarn perfectly. But apart from him – and the special case of Furphy – the celebrated *Bulletin* short story writers of the nineties (taking *The Bulletin Story Book*, 1901, as representative) seem rather artificial today. *The Bulletin* urged writers to be original, and this striving to be original produces frequent melodrama and farce. At least one of the readers of the day complained, in *The Bulletin* itself, of the poverty of imagination which these stories revealed. 'The *Bulletin* short story', he wrote, 'works up to "He is dead" or "He is dead drunk" – this being a generalization of the two favourite climaxes – one some "novel" accident, the other a "sell".'[14] Stephens, it is relevant to note, considered that Archibald's instinct was for melodrama; and certainly, *The Bulletin* stories include a surprising amount of melodrama, partly encouraged, perhaps, by Archibald's advice, 'Boil it down', which led his contributors to over-value terseness, and effects of sudden surprise and revelation.

Generally, it is true that *Bulletin* stories are fragmentary and episodic. 'Australian writers run too much to the easy, detached realistic sketch – ', observed Stephens[15] in 1897, 'not too much if it is considered that they are young and learning, but too much if they are judged without reference to local considerations, as artists merely'. And he had a similar comment when introducing the stories in *The Bulletin Story Book*, of which he remarked that 'many are absolute transcripts of the Fact, copied as faithfully as the resources of language will permit'. An enthusiasm for the facts of the local scene, local colour, is certainly there. In a way, *The Bulletin* short story represents a second literary discovery of Australia.

Stephens referred to the local writers as learning their craft, but it was just this that *The Bulletin* did not encourage them to do. Most of the writers had little staying power, and *The Bulletin* emphasis on brevity led them to be fragmentary, and even slick. They can evoke the local scene with impressive intimacy, but they fail, on the whole, to penetrate very deeply. The stories tend to be anecdotal, and deficient in their handling of human experience at a deeper level. *The Bulletin* stress on originality extended beyond choice of subject to a rejection of English models and influences which could have been fruitful. The anonymous critic in *The Bulletin* made this point with some force:

The Bulletin makes strong demands for originality. Some time ago it said no one was great through imitation, which I deny. . . . If a man is true to himself he will attain all the originality he is capable of. Seeking it, he merely lands in eccentricity and gets farther and farther from the common ground of humanity, where all Art has its power. There is nothing more pitiful than the desire of half-read small-brained creatures of originality. They seek some sensational effect in some accident; they get a small smattering of cheap science and work it in, and call that original. The result is melodrama – without the good there is in stage-melodrama.[16]

This criticism is extreme, but it cannot be disregarded. Except for Lawson and Furphy, *The Bulletin* group included no really original writers, strong in the resources of their own imagination. The colonial romances had followed English modes and reproduced English attitudes, which *The Bulletin* rejected. Furphy recognized, as no one else in that period did, that the English language itself implied a tradition. In his isolation and insecurity he felt the need to relate his work to that English tradition; but it was a conscious effort. Almost all the colonial romancers – at least those worth remembering – had been educated within the English tradition. England was real to them through its literature, if not through personal experience. But they did not keep alive the English tradition in Australia: they merely imitated. The relationship between the colonial and the home literatures is a complex one. By virtue of the language itself, Australian writing was part of English writing; but by writing of the local life in a consciously English way and according to English expectations, the colonial romancers denied themselves the chance of making any contribution to the English tradition. *The Bulletin*'s stress on local independence, originality, was a refreshing change from the imitativeness of the fashionable novelists, but it had the unfortunate effect of encouraging a kind of contempt for what is called 'literary', which has lasted to this day.

'It will be the fault of the writers, not of the land, if Australian literature does not by-and-by become memorable', wrote Stephens in the Introduction to *The Bulletin Story Book*. One essential condition was being fulfilled: writers were beginning to feel themselves to be Australians. But still a surprising amount of the fiction in that collection reads like English fiction transplanted to a local setting, accurately specified in all its details. Dorrington's celebrated story, 'A Bush Tanqueray', is perhaps the clearest example of this. In the same place, Stephens emphasized the possibilities for prose writers in Australia, and his words sound strangely like those of Mrs Campbell Praed, writing at the same time: 'Every man who roams the Australian wilderness is a potential knight of Romance. . . . The marvels of the adventurous are our daily commonplace'. Against this, one might set Furphy's account of how eagerly Stephens and the other townsmen of *The Bulletin* office listened to his stories of life in the Riverina. Lawson and Furphy stand out from their contemporaries by the authenticity of their bush manner. The rest of *The Bulletin* story-tellers tend to be local colourists, of varying competence, whose work is superior to that of their Anglo-Australian contemporaries, because they are closer to local ways of feeling and seeing. At best, they seem capable of only fragmentary insights.

Only one important novel came to light under *The Bulletin* stimulus – Joseph Furphy's *Such is Life*, which was written by 1896, but was not published until 1903, by which time it had been significantly revised. Although little appreciated in his lifetime, Joseph Furphy (1843-1912) has now eclipsed Lawson, once The Australian Writer, and is now recognized as a major Australian novelist. His influence on Australian writers in this century, however, has been more in terms of personal attitude than of artistic achievement: he has been admired as the exponent of characteristically Australian attitudes. The value of *Such is Life*, however, does not lie in its explicit Australianism – Furphy is articulate in defining local as contrasted with English attitudes, and caricatures English types as a way of asserting his anti-colonialism – but in its solid and intimate recreation of life as it was felt by a bushman. It is a novel which gives permanent expression to an indisputably *local experience* of Australia.

In every way it is a remarkable novel. Furphy was, as he said himself, 'Half bushman and half bookworm'. His scholarship – which is humourously paraded (and so defended) through the *persona* of Tom Collins – has something compulsive about it, and is for Furphy a kind of passport to literature. He constantly calls up his reading, particularly Shakespeare and the Bible, and seeks to give his writing intellectual weight by comment, ranging from the philosophical to the merely playful. Unlike his *Bulletin* contemporaries, he was widely read and sophisticated in his literary tastes. *Such is Life* bristles with shrewd criticism of the prevailing fashion in novels; and the very structure and narrative method constitute a protest against the falsification of life to be found in the romance. His aim is to give 'a fair picture of Life', to interpret and not merely record what life in the bush seemed to him to be like. It is a novel of big intentions. 'Such fiction', he wrote of *Such is Life*, 'may be truer than truth itself, since the latter, often anomalous and untypical, is always part-hidden from view.' Pretending to be merely a chronicler, setting down a sample of his experiences, Furphy attempts to illuminate the way in which things happen. He is all artifice. He scorns the temptation to make life fit the romance convention, but he succumbs partially to the temptation to be ingenious in his method of oblique plot development. He overdoes his effects – the concealed plotting is too complicated, the joke of the lost trousers is too long, the digressions and the comic pedantry and word-play become tedious – but by contrast with his predecessors and contemporaries, he is refreshingly aware of the possibilities of the novel form.

Such is Life represents an achievement of considerable magnitude, all the more impressive when the circumstances of Furphy's own life are noted. He wrote in almost complete isolation from the literary life of his day, absorbing *The Bulletin* point of view, without accepting its conception of style. No Australian novel is richer in local colour, but Furphy was never a local colourist. As his title alone suggests, he had a high conception of fiction; and *Such is Life* must be regarded as a comment on the nature of experience. The boldness of Furphy's intention stands out in this period. He had a stricter conception of realism than any of his contemporaries. His realism is circumscribed, however, by his anti-English prejudices and his surprising sentimentality in the treatment of women; and his narrative method to be successful requires greater tact than he possessed. The patterning of the novel, moreover, is extrinsic: as we come to perceive it, we are conscious that life has been arranged. Despite Furphy's philosophical concerns, the realism of *Such is Life* is on the level of portraiture; and as such it has never been surpassed. He writes with unchallenged authority of bushmen and their ways. 'Here the author is unconsciously at home ...' he observed in the note which *The Bulletin* used as an advertisement, from which quotation has already been made. And we can agree with him when he goes on to assert: 'Beyond all other Australian writers Tom Collins is a master of idiom'. But while the dialogue of his bushmen is admirably natural, his personal style (of which the Tom Collins version is a near-parody) is a consciously literary style, polysyllabic, measured in cadence, and veering towards the pompous when not held in check by his sense of humour. He did not have the confidence of a Mark Twain in the local vernacular. *Such is Life* is unmistakably Australian in its created life, and unmistakably English in its literary origins. Furphy threw out the debased notion of fiction found in the colonial romances, and looked to the great prose works of the eighteenth century, as well as to the Bible and Shakespeare, for his literary inspiration. But he did not absorb the English tradition as Henry Handel Richardson was capable of doing; and the result is a self-conscious literariness in *Such is Life*. Although he was free of the debilitating sense of colonial inferiority that affected Rosa Praed, Furphy did not have complete imaginative independence. His aggressive Australianism offered him no security as a writer. *Such is Life* reveals not only the 'wavering unease' of the self-educated man, as Cecil Hadgraft suggests, but also the unease of a writer conscious of belonging to a country without its own literary tradition.

Whatever his limitations, Furphy over-tops his contemporaries, including Henry Lawson (1867-1922), who had a more intuitive grasp of character, and was capable of greater delicacy of feeling. Lawson's literary career was one of early triumph, followed by

slow and inevitable decline. He did not develop as an artist: as he
grew older his art became more mechanical and he lost his early
freshness. Stephens once noted that Lawson's prose work consisted of 'isolated sketches, discontinuous episodes, with an
occasional short series of favourite characters'; and he suggested
that it should have been treated in the same way as Steele Rudd's
On Our Selection:

'Steele Rudd's' *On Our Selection* came to its editor as a gathering of
sketches of Queensland farm life. Families with different names were
shown living in similar ways. By the obvious device of concentrating
interest on one set of names, one set of personages, and by arranging
some chronological continuity, some climactic effect; the book gained
the value of unity. . . .
  Lawson's *While the Billy Boils* – with his wealth of material later
available – asked and still asks for similar treatment. A reader of
Lawson's work is continually setting out for short journeys all round
the compass. [17]

Steele Rudd (Arthur H. Davis, 1868-1935) had originally intended
'to tell faithfully all I knew of the life our family and neighbouring families had lived, and were then living on the land'.
His first sketches were in the form of reminiscences, written by
one of the family looking back to the time when Dad and Mum
were pioneers. In these simple anecdotal pieces Rudd discovered
that he had a talent for farce, and his writing became increasingly
contrived as he developed assurance, until he was a prisoner of
his own facility. The Selection stories were immensely popular
because of their simplicity – almost roughness – of style and their
crude humour. The characters Rudd had created with real
affection and pride became eventually caricatures of reality.
Rudd was wholly a product of *The Bulletin*, and his stories
exemplify its artistic limitations. Although he later moved into
the novel, Rudd's forte was the sketch of the kind that made him
famous. *On Our Selection* does have a degree of unity, as Stephens
suggests, but the arrangement does not hide the slightness of
conception. Lawson's art was of a higher order than Stephens's
comparison implies, and while much of his work is in the form
of the sketch, it has a quality of vision that Rudd's lacks entirely.
  In the Joe Wilson stories Lawson approaches the dimensions
of a novel. The narrator, Joe Wilson, is the soft, sentimental
drifter that Lawson recognized himself to be, and the central

theme of the stories (four stories under the heading of 'Joe Wilson' and a later story, 'Drifting Apart') is the disintegration of his marriage through his weakness and selfishness. Although he shows considerable flexibility and self-awareness, Lawson does not fill out the psychological process by which the man and his wife drift apart. The sequence was never completed, and the centre of the story is missing. Lawson is self-regarding: he establishes the narrator's mood of self-pity and self-reproach superbly, but leaves unexplored the experience he has lived through. These stories, as close as Lawson ever came to the scope of a novel, are perhaps the height of his achievement. They have that inimitable quality which has made Lawson so fascinating to later writers and so pervasive an influence: that quiet, unaffected, intimate, conversational tone of voice. Here, at last, is a natural Australian style.

The 'yarning' style conceals Lawson's limited range of experience and his weakness at developing situations. He had no talent for the novel. Other *Bulletin* contributors produced novels, but they are all inferior in construction. Barbara Baynton (1862-1929), for instance, wrote one novel, *Human Toll*, 1907, a shapeless sequence of vivid scenes, which reads like one of her nightmarish stories, expanded and consequently disproportioned. Plot is the difficulty. In Boldrewood's novels, the plot is the machine to move the characters from one place to another, and a frame of time and consequence within which the real interest – the pictorial description of Australian life – can be contained. Despite their realistic intention, something similar happens in the novels of *The Bulletin* writers, in several instances. Randolph Bedford (1868-1941) mingles impossible romance and sharp reporting of local scenes in *The Snare of Strength* (1905), a crudely organized fabrication of his experiences as an election candidate in Victoria and a copper-mine owner in Queensland. Edward Dyson (1865-1931), a much more considerable literary figure than Bedford and one of the major *Bulletin* short story writers, wrote several novels, one of which, *In the Roaring Fifties*, (1906) demands some notice; and here he has a plot which depends upon improbable coincidences as bad as in any Anglo-Australian romance. He gives much more feeling of participation in the life he describes than does Boldrewood in *The Miner's Right*, but fundamentally the novels are similar in placing the emphasis upon reconstruction of historical episodes and local colour.

Except for *Such is Life*, *The Bulletin* inspired no novel which sustains the ideal of realism. Miles Franklin (1879-1954) raised the central issue of local fiction at the time when she wrote *My Brilliant Career*, (1901), which Stephens welcomed as 'the very first Australian novel to be published'. She addressed an introduction to her fellow-Australians, in which she set out, with youthful exuberance, the literary attitude of *The Bulletin*:

This is not a romance – I have too often faced the music of life to the tune of hardship to waste time in snivelling and gushing over fancies and dreams; neither is it a novel, but simply a yarn – a *real* yarn ...

There is no plot in this story, because there has been none in my life or in any other life which has come under my notice.

It is an immature, question-begging statement of realist intentions which she could not fulfil: by chapter VIII she was slipping into the well-worn romance pattern, with a dashing hero on the horizon. *My Brilliant Career* expresses a gifted young girl, frustrated by the poverty and conventional outlook of her family. It wavers between girlish day-dreams and lively comment on the everyday. The book still has an appeal because of the spontaneity and verve with which she revealed herself.

Miles Franklin was a vigorous and witty personality, but she never resolved the emotional confusion which is present in *My Brilliant Career*. There is a curious immaturity and period flavour about all her work: she seems never to have mastered her own experience as a girl, and remained fixed emotionally in the period of her youth. She had grown up with *The Bulletin*, and it represented Australian literature to her. And throughout her long life she clung tenaciously to the view of Australia which it promoted in the nineties, although it became increasingly anachronistic. Her insularity and prejudice, her sentimental feeling for the bush and the bushmen, and her contempt of art, which disfigure the work of her maturity, all have their origin in her attachment to the aspirations of her youth. If Mrs Campbell Praed is a victim of the colonial outlook, Miles Franklin is a victim of the provincial.

*

Henry Handel Richardson (Ethel Florence Richardson, 1870-1946) was (and perhaps still is) something of a problem for those writers and critics who believed that a vigorous nationalism of the

Bulletin variety was essential to the growth of a local literature. Miles Franklin's animus is embarrassingly apparent in *Laughter, Not for a Cage*, where she damns Henry Handel Richardson's achievement:

This author is rated as the greatest novelist Australia has so far cradled, though her Australian birth had nothing to do with her success, nor had the Australian locale in which most of the trilogy is set. And here at last was a work by an Australian in which the English-thinking Australians could take pride, and it is because of its aid in attracting attention to the Australian novel that it is included in these notes.

Henry Handel Richardson did not belong to the *Bulletin*-oriented 'Australian literary tradition', she took no interest in the creation of a national literature, and she personally exhibited none of the admired Australian characteristics. The bush ideal of 'mateship' is irrelevant to her work, which, by its very existence, calls into question the assumptions on which Miles Franklin and her contemporaries tried to write fiction. She is the first Australian novelist whose work does not invite special attention because of its Australian setting. Hers is the first significant Australian contribution to the tradition of English fiction.

H. M. Green points out the lack of craftsmanship among the novelists at the turn of the century, but the poverty of fiction in Australia at this period stems ultimately from deeper causes. Form is an index of the sensibility of the writer; and the literary environment, which *The Bulletin* did most to create, did not nourish the sensibility of the writer. Henry Handel Richardson's literary awakening came after she had left Australia (to return only once, on a fact-finding visit in 1912) and had tasted the richer intellectual life of Europe. Her first novel, *Maurice Guest*, (1908), comes out of the tradition of European naturalism, as her husband has stressed. It is, indeed, a novel in which we are too conscious of literary debts. A. A. Phillips has argued that Henry Handel Richardson was 'personally intimidated by her sense of colonial inferiority', 'an early victim of ... the cultural cringe of the Australian intellectual',[18] and he has contrasted the dullness of her writing with the freshness, vigour and originality of Furphy and Lawson. It is a tempting hypothesis to account for the prominence of cliché in her work, but it hardly recognizes the intensity of her devotion to a conception of art, which involved at its centre a fruitful struggle for self-understanding.

Phillips makes great play of a remark she quotes in her auto-biography, *Myself When Young*. Finding difficulty with a passage of the trilogy she was working on, she exclaimed in irritation to her husband: 'I don't know I'm sure how I ever came to write *Maurice Guest* – a poor ignorant little colonial like me!' It is hard to believe that she (the Laura Rambotham of *The Getting of Wisdom*) ever seriously felt like this. Her husband made the telling reply: 'But emotionally very experienced.' What is most striking is her freedom from the Australian colonial complex, and her absorption in her own private experience. She was not troubled by the colonial relationship – the fact that she went to Germany rather than to England to study when she left Australia may be relevant here – and never felt it necessary to protest or deny her Australian birth. Her own comment on the above episode was that she now became aware of the deep personal sources of her art in a way that she had not been before:

At the moment I rather blinked the idea, being unprepared for it, then went away to my own room to think it over. And the more I thought the more I saw how true it was – though, till now, the con-nexion had never occurred to me. That is to say, I had written *Maurice* quite unaware of what I was drawing on. Later events had naturally had a certain share in his story. But his most flagrant emotions – his dreams, hopes and fears, his jealousy and despair, his sufferings under rejection and desertion – could all be traced to my own unhappy ex-perience. No wonder the book had come easy to write. I had just to magnify and re-dress the old pangs. – But the light thrown by my husband's words did not stop there. It cleared up other knots and tangles in my life, which at the time of happening had seemed stupidly purposeless. Now I began to sense a meaning in these too, to see them as threads in a general pattern. And gradually the conviction deepened that, to a writer, experience was the only thing that really mattered. Hard and bitter as it might seem, it was to be welcomed rather than shrunk from, reckoned as a gain not a loss. . . .

The experience of the adolescent girl that lay behind *Maurice Guest* is portrayed directly in *The Getting of Wisdom*, (1910), which she began to write as a relief from the strain of *Maurice Guest*. It is, as Vincent Buckley [19] says, her *Portrait of the Artist as a Young Girl*, a sharp, economical, penetrating study of herself as an artist in the making. The heroine of the novel is a steady, mar-vellously full self-portrait, in a spirit of ironic comedy. Henry Handel Richardson's truthfulness is here undiluted by the romanticism that weakens *Maurice Guest*. Laura's experience is rendered sympathetically but never sentimentalized or softened; and it is 'placed' by an adult 'wisdom'. The 'wisdom' which Laura gains is the knowledge of how to live in the world, how to conform, and yet preserve her individuality. She is odd and unconventional, a square peg in a round hole. This discovery is 'uncomfortable', but she has learned how to live with this truth. Laura's later discovery that her 'unfitness' for the world of the conventional is the mark of her being an artist is merely hinted at: the fulfilment is to come.

The Getting of Wisdom appeared just over a decade later than Miles Franklin's *My Brilliant Career*, an earlier piece of self-revelation by a woman who felt herself to be a square peg in a round hole. Any comparison would be unfair to Miles Franklin, who was writing as an adolescent. Henry Handel Richardson, by contrast, had a poised insight into her youthful experience, and a complete mastery of her materials. And it is just this adult awareness, this control of the complexity of experience, by which Henry Handel Richardson's best writing is characterized, that Miles Franklin never reached. Both turned to the Australian past for the material of their major work, but their concerns were markedly different. Miles Franklin chronicles the heroic past: her Brent of Bin Bin series and later *All That Swagger* celebrate the pioneers. Henry Handel Richardson approaches the past in a very different spirit. Her trilogy, *The Fortunes of Richard Mahony*, is a child's memorial to a father whom she scarcely knew and whose death she never mourned: it is a laying of ghosts, and the supreme effort of her imaginative self-discovery. 'In setting out to write a novel,' she once said, 'the one thing I know definitely before hand is the end.' And it is the final volume of the trilogy, where she traces Mahony's final collapse and decay, that is unforgettable. Here she atones for her childhood indifference by a compassionate study of Mahony's struggle with pain and encroaching madness. Her father becomes in the figure of Mahony, what he never was in actuality, a hero in her eyes, and all her powers are engaged in making felt the drama of his suffering.

In Richard Mahony, Henry Handel Richardson laid bare with ruthless objectivity that sense of unfitness, incompatibility, which she turned to good account in her own life as a writer. She was her father's daughter ('. . . the person who knew me best always maintained that, in my imaginary portrait of Richard Mahony, I had drawn no other than my own.'). In her father she had a congenial subject for her talents. The story was *there* – it was a *fact* in her own life – and she set herself the task of interpreting it, as she had interpreted her own childhood. Her extreme reliance upon verifiable details is not merely an expression of her naturalistic view of fiction (she does not, after all, interpret life in naturalistic terms), but rather an outcome of her personal involvement.

The Fortunes of Richard Mahony is at the other pole to the fiction of successful immigrants, a staple theme from Rowcroft to Boldrewood. Henry Handel Richardson has described the intention behind the trilogy as being to tell the life-story of a misfit ('The misfits who were physically and mentally incapable of adapting themselves to this strange hard new world'), using 'the changing face of the country for background'. This account fits the first volume, *Australia Felix*, (1917) pretty well. There is a great deal of historical reconstruction, and the promise of a Life and Times of Richard Mahony. By the nature of the theme, however, Mahony must stand apart from the life of the colony, and there is a consequent division of interest. As the novel progresses, however, Henry Handel Richardson makes less attempt to write history, and concentrates on the bringing out of Mahony's own nature. His problem is not merely that he cannot fit into colonial society. As the second volume, *The Way Home*, 1925, establishes with growing force, Mahony can find no 'home' anywhere. His is not the dilemma of the colonist, but the tragedy of the dreamer, the man who reaches out after he does not know what, and cannot accept what life is. In his own words: 'I can assure you, it's no mere spirit of discontent – as some suppose. It's more a kind of . . . well, it's like reaching out after – say, a dream one has had and half forgotten, and struggles to recapture.'

Mahony's restless movement back and forth between Australia and England in search of what he feels to be lacking in himself enables Henry Handel Richardson to criticize both colonial and English life; and Mahony's sensitivity makes for incisive criticism. Though his failure is ultimately to be located in the incompleteness of his own personality, the evaluation of society is no less valid. It is part of his anguish that he should be so acutely aware of the defects of the society he lives in. This aspect of Henry Handel Richardson's work has never received much notice in Australia, yet she is the most perceptive of all the novelists who have treated the Anglo-Australian theme, and the best able embody her criticism in individual experiences.

It is the third volume, *Ultima Thule*, (1929), however, in which this theme slips into the background, that is Henry Handel Richardson's greatest achievement. The story of the beloved misfit of a father takes on near-tragic proportions – but yet it is not tragedy. The apt comparison is with Arnold Bennett's *The Old Wives' Tale* rather than with the novels of Tolstoy and Dostoyevsky. And there is more of Ibsen in Henry Handel Richardson than has so far been recognized. She sees Richard Mahony's misery with stoical eyes, and finds a kind of triumph in his grim endurance of his terrible fate. She attempts too much when she tries to give him a moment of revelation, a kind of Agony in the Bush, and fails at the highest level to illuminate his suffering. The effect of his end is lacerating, without the sense of release, the paradoxical affirmation of life, that tragedy gives. Yet it remains an outstanding work of Australian fiction.

Henry Handel Richardson has remarkable limitations: her use of language is so uneven, her interests so restricted, her handling of detail sometimes so indiscriminate. With all her weaknesses exposed, however, she is unrivalled in her psychological penetration. Australian novelists, with few exceptions, become reticent and evasive in the face of the great central experiences of life. Even Lawson and Furphy tend to skirt the painful and disturbing elements of the bush life they portray, and leave a great deal unsaid. Neither could have handled an episode such as the death of John Turnham in *The Fortunes of Richard Mahony* with the objectivity and poise that Henry Handel Richardson displays.

The other novelists of interest before the 1920s are Louis Stone (1871-1935) and William Gosse Hay (1875-1945), both of whom, like Henry Handel Richardson, stand apart from the 'bush school', and approach the novel in a spirit of dedication. Neither was a popular novelist in a period when the public taste for fiction was formed by *Robbery Under Arms* and *On Our Selection*; and neither brought the novel in touch with the developing Australian society of the twentieth century. In strikingly different ways they turned away from *The Bulletin* line and attempted to break new ground, but in each case there was a complete failure to establish new directions in the novel. The future lay with the second generation of *Bulletin* writers like Katharine Susannah Prichard and Vance Palmer, who were nourished by the sense of local identity which the first *Bulletin* writers had expressed, but free of their literary parochialism.

When Louis Stone published *Jonah* in 1911, A.G. Stephens welcomed him to 'the front rank of Australian authorship', and hoped that he would advance further. But *Jonah* represented the best that Stone was capable of; and it is, indeed, only the first half of that novel, the story of Jonah, the hunchback, and the Cardigan Street 'push', which really matters – Jonah, the business man of the second half, is less interesting and less credible than the outcast. Stone's achievement is a very narrow one: he created the 'larrikin'. This figure (the equivalent of the modern 'teddy boy') had appeared in earlier fiction, but it is Stone's version which has lasted. Stone was a conscientious observer, who spent years making careful notes before he wrote. An Englishman by birth, he lived most of his life in Sydney, and both *Jonah* and his other novel, *Betty Wayside*, (1915), are filled with local colour – but it is local colour with a difference. His novels are void of any feeling of place or community, or social awareness, and imply no point of view on Australian society. The place names, the detail of streets and shops and suburbs, establish the locale as Sydney, without conveying any sense of its particular characteristics. Stone's world is fundamentally novelettish: in *Jonah*, at least in the first part, he is saved from sinking into sentimentality by his enthusiasm for details of low-class life, particularly details of speech, which he has observed with fascination (and even longing) from his position in the middle-classes (Stone was a schoolmaster in real life).

Essentially, Stone was a romantic, a suburban romantic, enchanted by the life of the poor, represented in this novel by Cardigan Street. He has no moral comment on what he describes; he is caught up in the drama of 'life in the raw', and it is sufficient for him to suggest its colour and crudity. The Saturday night shopping spree is 'painted' in strongly sensuous terms:

It was Saturday night, and Waterloo, by immemorial habit, had flung itself on the shops, bent on plunder. For an hour past a stream of people had flowed from the back streets into Botany Road, where the shops stood in shining rows, awaiting the conflict.

The butcher's caught the eye with a flare of colour as the light played on the pink and white flesh of sheep, gutted and skewered like victims for sacrifice; the saffron and red quarters of beef, hanging like the limbs of a dismembered Colossus; and the carcasses of pigs, the unclean beast of the Jews, pallid as a corpse. The butchers passed in and out, sweating and greasy, hoarsely crying the prices as they cut and hacked the meat. The people crowded about, sniffing the odour of dead flesh, hungry and brutal – carnivora seeking their prey.

Such over-writing, straining after a vivid effect, is characteristic of Stone's response to the commonplace; but this passage doesn't do justice to his affection for the people he describes. Although there are acts of violence (the 'push' manhandling the carpenter), and references to the poverty and degradation of the poor, this aspect of their lives has very little reality in the novel. The characters are types in the Dickensian mould. Stone's favourite is obviously Mrs Yabsley, the wise old woman of Cardigan Street, whom he describes with great gusto:

Cardigan Street was proud of her. Her eyes twinkled in a big, humorous face; her arm was like a leg of mutton; the floors creaked beneath her as she walked. She laughed as a bull roars; her face turned purple; she fought for air; the veins rose like cords on her forehead. She was pointed out to strangers like a public building as she sat on her verandah, gossiping with the neighbours in a voice that shook the windows. There was no tongue like hers within a mile. Her sayings were quoted like the newspaper. Draymen laughed at her jokes.

Yet the women took their secret troubles to her. For this unwieldy jester, with the jolly, red face and rough tongue, could touch the heart with a word when she was in the humour. Then she spoke so wisely and kindly that the tears gathered in stubborn eyes, and the poor fools went home comforted.

Despite all the claims made for Mrs Yabsley as a triumph of realism, she is adequately described as a 'character'. Stone simplifies life in a spirit of kindly innocence, and while it is attractive, it does not satisfy for long.

Stone's two novels are full of vivid sketches, with a cartoon-like clarity and exaggeration. They are period pieces – but not in the usual sense of the term. What we retain are, in a way, the most trivial of impressions – Jonah and Ada eating hot green peas bought from the travelling pieman on Saturday night; Mrs Yabsley staggering home with her shopping; Joseph Gridley, the dandy who diets, having a midnight feast of pigs' trotters; the Colonel going shopping – little vignettes in which the humdrum is seen with a wide-eyed delight.

Stone magnifies and romanticizes the commonplace. In completely opposite vein, William Hay seeks to make life conform to an aristocratic ideal. In this respect, his fiction is something of an anomaly in Australian literature, being a total retreat from the present into an impossible, wholly personal dream of the past. Hay could perhaps be dismissed as negligible on the strength of his first three novels, which run to melodrama – *Stifled Laughter* (1901); *Herridge of Reality Swamp* (1907); and *Captain Quadring*, (1912) – but *The Escape of Sir William Heans*, (1919), is a novel of such pretensions and such individuality that it has been compared with, and even preferred to *His Natural Life*; and Hay has been acclaimed as a major novelist. The novel is so challenging in the conception of fiction it exemplifies, that it is impossible to be neutral about it. All one can do is offer one's own impressions, for what they are worth.

Nominally, *The Escape of the Notorious Sir William Heans* (*and the Mystery of Mr Daunt*) – to give the book its full title – is a historical romance about convictism. In spite of its historical accuracy, the portraiture of identifiable characters and places, and the loving evocation of the atmosphere of the convict times, it never establishes a point of view on the past, nor does it approach historical reconstruction, whatever Hay may have thought he was doing. He referred to the work as 'a summing up in one three-volume novel of all the more polite romance and tragedy of the late 1830s in Hobart'. For some readers, this is in itself an indictment of the novel – Hay meant to give full force to the adjective 'polite'! His hero is scrupulously well-mannered, fastidious to the point of absurdity, and noble beyond belief. Sir William Heans is a transported felon who escapes from Tasmania on his third attempt – that is the story. His crime was to have undertaken the seduction of a beautiful, aristocratic woman who, it is broadly hinted, was not entirely innocent. 'I had to find a crime that I could bear in a man for a hero,' said Hay with revealing honesty. Hay's presentation of Sir William is such that the man's crime seems more like a piece of misfortune that he did not deserve. Hay sees him always as the hero, unsullied by the commonness he is forced to walk among, a sort of Sir Charles Grandison, in every way a perfect gentleman. Taking leave of his hero, Hay invites us to admire him:

Writing to his friend Sir Charles of his future prospects and the things a man may do, he reflects incidentally how 'a fellow may engage himself in being simply a generous, temperate, and noble person, passing his leisure in reading and talking for entertainment, and yet fall short of a difficult ideal.' It will serve our turn to suppose he engaged himself in some effort of this nature.

It will not serve Hay's turn, however, to inquire too closely into this 'difficult ideal'!

There have been suggestions that the novel has a moral theme – 'the fall and regeneration', says R. G. Howarth, [20] who sees Heans as 'a man changed for good' – but such interpretations cannot be sustained by a reading of the novel, which is astonishingly trivial when the hypnotic effect of Hay's curious style has worn off. Miles Franklin [21] remarks: 'Sir William and his friends have a weird unsubstantiality in thought and presentation, as if written about by someone mature in the thirties of last century who had experienced nothing since'. But it is hard to believe that anyone ever wrote as Hay does. The novel suffers the fatal defect of hollowness, an absence of felt experience. Hay is completely immersed in a day-dream. His style, so carefully grotesque and archaic, is a way of keeping experience at a distance. His attitude towards writing can be seen in a passage such as this:

Sir William regrets, and so does the writer, that some freer weapon than his is not in the breach to delineate the last incident of that Wednesday night. It seemed to him such a curious and plausible occurrence that happened under his eyes, and partially through him, that he would have wished to make a souvenir of it with some beautiful, monumental prose.

And he follows this comment with a purple passage:

The motionless witch of night, with its grey moon and streaky clouds, its occasional alarms, the ugly and fateful things which it had brought to life, the house yet wanting a master, the pair of brooding women, the sly wretch above, and the uncanny shock he had put upon them (even if his panics were Heans' strange ally), these were but the brooding beginning to the singular end.

All Hay's energies went into the erection of this 'beautiful, monumental prose', this great white elephant.

Sir William Heans is sometimes discussed as if he were an interesting creation, but he is really no more than an attitude of fastidiousness. Hay is infatuated with the *idea* of a gentleman. Much of the nobility of Hay's own nature (he sounds an attractive personality) undoubtedly went into the making of the character, but it becomes trivial in the process. Moreover, Sir William's nobility is merely posited, never proved in the event. There is a stillness and remoteness about the action of the novel, even when violent events, such as the drawn-out struggle in the stable, are being described: life is slowed down and reduced to the notation of Sir William's impeccable costume, his impeccable manners, his impeccable sentiments. Hay is positively excited by the refinement of his hero:

Sir William was superb at this moment. He had put up his glass, and hiding his trembling lips with his hand, stared the man wanly in his large, bland, conciliating, brisk, yet bothered face.

'I,' he said, with a short laugh, 'will barely be taken for the blackmailer. It is a man named Heans, Sir William Heans, and quite well known to O'Crone. It is a heavy blow that Mr O'Crone is to be taken away, and I shall not see him.'

The reader labours in vain to find human significance in the narrative of Sir William's adventures; it is enough for Hay that they are Sir William's adventures.

At times Hay does seem to be moving towards some pattern of significance, but the novel is full of anti-climax. The mystery of Mr Daunt, for instance, turns into mere mystification. This is not to deny Hay's ability to achieve effects of horror and suspense. There are passages where the writing, by its very insistence on certain words like 'pale', 'grey', 'tragic', almost overwhelms the reader's critical awareness of the unreality of what he is reading. The frequent use of such words produces an almost ritualistic effect. We are invited to value the experiences of Sir William as tragic because Hay so often invokes the word. There are continual strings of adjectives to describe characters and their attitudes, creating the illusion of precision and subtle observation; but all the exquisite placing of words produces only a form of decoration, a 'costume style'.

The root of Hay's failure as a novelist is his retreat from experience. He is cloistered, a Pater in the antipodes, painstakingly creating what is a near parody of the Paterian ideal of ecstacy. The influence of Meredith on his style has been noted by commentators, who have been impressed by his craftsmanship; but the elaborate effects are still-born, and never come to life. In his notebooks William Hay once wrote:

I often think there are a great number of scenes and faces we needn't have looked on in our short life in this world. What a pity our eyes ever open on them! I wish I could prevent my sons from seeing them. (12 August, 1918).

It is a nobly misguided attitude for a writer. Hay was a cultured and dedicated man, with everything a writer needs, except the taste for living. He separated art from life, excluding life. He did not see, as Henry Handel Richardson saw, that the artist takes experience, however unpleasant, as the source of his art.

Although he has had something of a revival recently, Hay has not been a potent factor in the development of Australian fiction, and is unlikely to be. He made an ambitious attempt to revitalize Australian writing at a time of degeneracy, by resurrecting the romantic historical ideal of Scott, and reasserting the importance of style; he failed, because he was too remote from reality.

Such an account as this, touching only the major writers, and in most cases only their most important works, is bound to seem unfair and tendentious. Yet a comprehensive annotated list would obscure rather than clarify the true state of Australian fiction during these first eighty odd years, when writers are struggling with the problem of an inherited tradition in a new land. It is possible to make up impressive lists of authors and titles, but the amount of significant fiction is small. By 1920, only Furphy and Henry Handel Richardson in the novel, and Lawson in the short story, had managed to evoke that sense of reality which is the end of fiction; and of none could it be said that his work is a local development, an extension or an enrichment of English fiction. The prospect of an Australian tradition of English fiction is there in their work, but it is only a prospect.

NOTES

1. Frederick Sinnett, 'The Fiction Fields of Australia', *Journal of Australasia*, vol i, 1856.

2. *Quintus Servinton* was re-published in 1962, with a comprehensive introductory essay by Cecil Hadgraft.

3. Cecil Hadgraft, *Australian Literature, A Critical Account to 1955*. All later references to Hadgraft are to this volume.

4. H. M. Green, *A History of Australian Literature*, vol i. All later references to Green are to this volume.

5. Alexander Harris was in Australia from 1825 until 1840. Doubts about his identity, which were raised by C. M. H. Clark in his Foreword to a new edition of *Settlers and Convicts* in 1953, have been disposed of by the publication of an autobiography, *The Secrets of Alexander Harris*, 1961.

6. William Howitt (1792-1879) spent two years in Australia, out of which came *Land, Labour and Gold; or Two Years in Victoria, with Visits to Sydney and Van Diemen's Land*, 1855. Charles Reade used the work as a source book in the writing of *It is Never Too Late to Mend*.

7. *His Natural Life* was originally published as a serial, *For the Term of His Natural Life*, in the *Australian Journal* from March, 1870, to June, 1872. All references are to the shortened version published in book form in 1874.

8. The dates of Tucker's life have not been established conclusively; and his authorship of *Ralph Rashleigh* is still questioned. For the most recent account of the controversy, see M. H. Ellis, 'Dr Roderick's Latest: Who wrote *Ralph Rashleigh*?', *The Bulletin*, 9 February 1963. *Ralph Rashleigh* was first published in an edited and partly re-written version as *The Adventures of Ralph Rashleigh*, with an Introduction by the Earl of Birkenhead in 1929. In 1952 the original text was printed in full as *Ralph Rashleigh, or The Life of an Exile* by 'Giacomo Di Rosenberg' (James Tucker), with an Introduction and Notes by Dr Colin Roderick.

9. Francis Adams, *The Australians: A Social Sketch* (1893), p. 42.

10. Desmond Byrne, *Australian Writers* (1896), p. 19.

11. A. A. Phillips, *The Australian Tradition* (1958). The *Meanjin* article, with which Phillips introduced the term into Australian criticism, is reprinted here.

12. Francis Adams, *op. cit.*, p. 55.

13. Ibid. p. 165.

14. J. G. H., 'Over the Coals', *The Bulletin*, 29 February 1896.

15. A. G. Stephens, 'Alex. Montgomery's Stories', *The Bulletin*, 13 February 1897.

16. See Note 14.

17. A. G. Stephens, 'Henry Lawson', *The Bookfellow*, 30 January 1922.

18. A. A. Phillips, *op. cit.*, p. 78.

19. Vincent Buckley, *Henry Handel Richardson* (1961), p. 21.

20. R. G. Howarth, Introduction to *The Escape of Sir William Heans* (1955), p. xiii.

21. Miles Franklin, *Laughter, Not for a Cage* (1956), p. 160.

AUSTRALIAN FICTION SINCE 1920

HARRY HESELTINE

BY 1920 Australian literature had developed some characteristics peculiarly its own. There were, for instance, the recurring concern with landscape, often leading to contrasting evaluations of city and bush; the repeated examination of that set of social and ethical values subsumed under the term 'mateship'; the marked bias towards the forms and practices of egalitarian democracy; the sometimes chauvinistic nationalism; the special brand of humour; even, as writers like Brennan and Richardson might have suggested, a darker strain of melancholy and pessimism. The exact nature of the pattern into which these elements had combined is still a matter of some debate. But of the whole body of Australian writing up to 1920, at least one thing is clear: it was based almost entirely on a complex of themes and attitudes rather than any originality of aesthetic invention.

For the most part, the writers of the nineteenth century were content to work within the English and European traditions. To be sure, there was a steadily advancing confidence in the Australian forms of the English language; but of any signs of originality in the larger structures of literature there are practically none. The history of Australian poetry from Harpur to Neilson, for example, is the story of a trial-and-error sampling of the major English verse forms from epic through ballad to lyric. It is only in the short story that some claim can be made for the creation of a formally distinctive literature. The short story writers of the nineties – Lawson, Warung, Dorrington, Baynton, and the rest – did develop a literary mode which seems as necessarily Australian in its structure as in its subject matter.

No such claim can be made for the Australian novel up to the beginning of the period under survey in this chapter. Indeed, its history up to 1920 can be told for most purposes in six titles: *The Recollections of Geoffry Hamlyn*, *For the Term of His Natural Life*, *Robbery Under Arms*, *Such is Life*, *Jonah*, and *Australia Felix*. Of these, *Geoffry Hamlyn*, and *Robbery Under Arms* exist by such rudimentary aesthetic conventions as to be beneath (or beyond) any national boundaries. *For the Term of His Natural*

Life retains its power in spite of a hair-raisingly melodramatic approach to plot, which fortunately did not become a dominant feature of the Australian novel. *Jonah* opened up a new subject, the city slums, but no new techniques. *Australia Felix* deepened the imaginative possibilities of Australian fiction. Only *Such Is Life* made a contribution of which the importance was formal as much as anything else; and its form was so individual and eccentric that it has not become the basis of any significant tradition in the development of Australian fiction.

It was only in the decades following World War I that the Australian novel started to manifest a consistent drive towards national forms as well as towards national themes and attitudes. It would be silly to advance inflated claims for the novelists of the twenties and the thirties. Nevertheless, their works represent a collective achievement of real competence and value. Moreover, for the first time in Australian history they displayed enough community of purpose and method to generate a genuine tradition of fiction, a tradition which has been continuous ever since and which provided the foundation for the quickened growth of the 1950s and 60s. Among the forces which led to the emergence of some distinctive narrative forms after World War I, not the least important was the War itself. For all those involved, trench warfare was a violently traumatic experience. For sensitive Australians, perhaps the agony was even more intense than for the troops of other nations. Australians had no national history of battles, hardly any acquaintance with combat. Their participation in the Boer War had scarcely prepared them for the Western Front. The Eureka Stockade could not provide memories of internecine massacre comparable to those of the American Civil War. There is considerable evidence in fiction of the powerful and special effect of the Great War on the Australian imagination.

The effect of the War on individual Australians is documented by such figures as Harry Sievright in Vance Palmer's *Daybreak* (1932) and Greg Blackwood in Katharine Susannah Prichard's *Intimate Strangers* (1937). Both characters suffer long and disastrous after-effects from their military experience, culminating, in Sievright's case, in suicide. Nor are these permanently marked victims of the War alone in the fiction of the twenties and the thirties. But even stronger evidence of its effects on Australian novelists is their almost uniform refusal to make it the subject of their prose. There is nothing comparable to *All Quiet on the Western Front* or *A Farewell to Arms* in Australian literature. It is as if a whole generation of writers by tacit agreement declined to incorporate the Great War into their imaginative fiction. When they wrote of it, they wrote of it directly, as fact and as history. Almost the only novel of any distinction to be inspired by the War was Leonard Mann's *Flesh in Armour*, which appeared in 1932. *Flesh in Armour*, through a character like Frank Jeffreys, records the horror experienced by the sensitive individual. Jeffreys, a decent young school teacher with mild socialist leanings, at last finds the strain of attack and counterattack so intolerable that he shoots himself. However, Jeffreys' pitiful story is only one of several narrative strands in the book, and in the communal response of the Australian troops to the battle fields of France, Mann enunciates a theme of perhaps even greater importance for Australian fiction than the shuddering reaction of the individual. A characteristic sentiment is revealed at the end of Chapter XVII, during a march-past of Allied soldiers:

The line straightened. What relief! They were moving along together. What pride! What relief! Heads up, while the bands blared Tara – tara – They were the Aussies – the Diggers, the Diggers – tara – tara – the Diggers – the Diggers – tara – tara.

Out of the War, that is, there came not only personal horror at European violence but also a dawning awareness of national identity. World War I served to hasten a development in Australian literature for which it was, in any case, probably ripe: the transformation of a pugnacious nationalism into a mature sense of nationhood. The task of transformation seems to have fallen particularly to the novelists. In the perspective of history, the great achievement of the Australian novelists of Between-the-Wars will be seen to have converted the events and experiences of the previous hundred or so years into an image wherein the rest of the nation could find reflected its own identity. The writers of the nineties had been immediately and practically concerned with the conditions of Australian life; their visions were located, if anywhere, in the future. The novelists of the twenties and thirties were concerned to transmute that earlier practicality into an imaginative vision of the country's past and present.

Such a purpose, if not always articulate, was none the less urgent. Sometimes it was given overt expression, characteristically by Miles Franklin, in a letter to Nettie Palmer of July 1931:

We are struggling with the very beginnings of a national school of literature, unforced, self-respecting, but of the soil as Russians are to their soil (I repeat this again and again and again) and we must nurture those who are indubitably of that soil, despite their blemishes.[1]

Miles Franklin was a representative figure in other ways than in her analysis of the literary movements current in 1931. In her life, too, she expressed one of the most remarkable traits of her own and the next generation of writers – their unflagging commitment to the profession of letters at a time when, in Australia, such a commitment could be a matter of great personal hardship. Russel Ward has recorded of Vance Palmer, for instance, that he for thirty years or more consistently refused to take any job lest it interfere with his real work; and his real work was 'to explore and illuminate the nature of this "elusive quality residing in Australians."'[2] Franklin and Palmer were by no means alone in their dedication to the task of bringing Australian fiction to maturity; it would be difficult to deny that they and their contemporaries made a lasting contribution to that end.

All the chief writers of the twenties and thirties brought to their books a deep love of their country and an unremitting zeal for their craft. In response to these twin pressures they fashioned for the first time what can be described as a formal tradition of the Australian novel. The forms that they shaped were basically three – the saga, the picaresque, and the documentary. None was complex in conception or sophisticated in execution; none became the vehicle for the highest flights of literature. Yet all fulfilled a real need in Australia's literary history, often with a great deal more than adequacy. Generated by the same impulses, the three forms were closely inter-related, often occurring within the bounds of the same work. It might be said that the saga resulted when the novelist conceived his material primarily in terms of time; the picaresque, when his imaginings were situated in the dimension of space. Documentation represented a method of handling the material of both saga and picaresque which from time to time assumed sufficient importance to become the definitive element of a novel.

The saga depended on the simplest chronological sequence – the narration of events in the order in which they occurred, over a span of two, three, or even more generations. The result, in its purest form, was the classic pioneering novel which charted the course of an Australian family from its (usually humble) beginnings through a whole maze of good and evil fortune, and against a background of assorted natural phenomena – the inevitable floods, fires, droughts. The formula is a simple one, but it provided machinery large and adaptable enough to contain the purposes of Australian novelists for some twenty years. The rationale of the saga novel has nowhere been better stated than in Chapter II of Brian Penton's *Landtakers*, 1934:

Growing up in a period when Australians had begun to feel in themselves the germ of a new people and to fumble for words to express themselves, I often wondered what roots that new psyche was coming from. Then it struck me that the answer was somewhere in the life of this old man [Cabell, the hero] and his generation. If I could piece together the picture of that epoch as I had inherited it from him – the savage deeds, the crude life, the hatred between men and men and men and country, the homesickness, the loneliness, the despair of inescapable exile in the bush; the strange forms of madness and cruelty; the brooding, inturned characters; and, joined with this, an almost fanatic idealism which repudiated the past and looked to the future in a new country for a new heaven and earth, a new justice; on the one hand the social outcasts, men broken by degradation and suffering, on the other the adventurers: blackest pessimism balancing the most radiant optimism – if I could only *see* all this, then I would understand.

This passage is preceded by one which indicates how closely the saga form was allied to the need for documentation:

Perhaps I ought to make it clear that very little of this story is imaginative. Until a few years ago there were quite a number of old people in our district who had been with Cabell in the early days. They were all good story-tellers, and it needed very little to set them going.

It is not surprising that the Australian novel of the twenties and thirties was founded on documentation. How, after all, could the Australian novelist attempt anything else until he had grappled with the most fundamental data available to him? Like the English novelists of the eighteenth century, his first technical essay in transforming fact into fiction was simply to transfer it holus-bolus. And for the Australian novelist, fact meant primarily historical and national fact. When he wished to marshall his data in a spatial rather than a temporal order, his solution was what can loosely be called picaresque narrative. It usually lacked the etymological requirement of a rogue-hero, consisting simply of a character or group of characters presented against a wide-ranging set of environments and involved in an episodic series of actions. Both the environments and the actions were likely to be described in some detail – but detail which aimed solely at enumerating objective phenomena rather than isolating the socially or psychologically illuminating instance.

The typical structure of the Australian novel between the wars points to an extensive rather than an intensive imagination. What might be described as the common style of the period reveals a similar kind of commitment. The saga, the picaresque, the documentary more often than not aim at a neutral manner, which deliberately avoids any idiosyncracy of syntax or diction, which is suspicious of a highly coloured tone or a richly wrought texture. It is, in effect, the style of a deliberated realism, which tolerates the tactical metaphor but only rarely the larger strategies of a complex or sustained symbolism. It is remarkable for a singularly unrelenting earnestness (even when it is being funny) and a heavy reliance on action and dialogue as major methods of characterization.

The dominance of such simple forms, along with their concomitant style, is often read as the sign of a backward provincialism in Australian writing of this period. Yet, if Australian novelists wrote as they did, it was not through ignorance of what was going on overseas. Palmer, Franklin, and Penton, for example, all spent some time abroad, and were keenly aware of the great literary experiments and achievements of their day. They were not literary ostriches with their minds jammed wilfully into arid antipodean sands. They spent their careers working out their own versions of forms passed over elsewhere because those forms were best suited to expressing the most urgent common need of their imaginations – the need for national self-definition and understanding. And if there were any need to save Australian novelists from provinciality, there were several commanding voices within their own shores to draw attention to the most arresting of overseas ideas and experiments. Of the Australian novelists of this period who most deliberately cultivated a cosmopolitan attitude, three at least deserve some mention – Norman Lindsay, Chester Cobb, and Christina Stead.

Norman Lindsay will always retain his place as one of the most influential figures in Australian literature during the first half of the twentieth century. His personal sphere of influence has been extraordinarily widespread and enduring. Douglas Stewart recalls his impact on himself and a young New Zealand friend, and he might well be speaking for many Australians:

> We hungered for revolution – anything that would help us to destroy adult authority and remove from us the icy prospect of having to work for our living. There wasn't anything actually political in *Redheap*, but it proclaimed the freedom of sex, it stood for the wildness and mutinousness of youth, and the glorious Mr Bandparts hurled Christianity and most of the established moralities of the world superbly out the window with his cocoa. It was our *Das Kapital* (and a great deal easier to read); it was our Unholy Writ; it was our banned book and our banner of freedom.

(Stewart: 'Norman Lindsay's Novels', *Southerly*, 1959, no. 1, p. 3)

Both within and without the circle of his acquaintances, Lindsay's influence has consistently been of the same kind – a subversion of the bourgeois restraints of middle class Australian society, an unceasing battle against narrowness in life and art. His crusade has always been carried on in cosmopolitan terms, and has especially been sanctioned by appeals to Nietzsche, who is behind much of the doctrine expressed in *Creative Effort: An Essay in Affirmation* (1920). Lindsay, that is to say, has clearly acted as an antidote against potential provincialism in Australia, and to that extent has performed a real service for Australian letters. Yet the importance of his own contributions to fiction is another question. Even now, when the revolutionary shock has worn off, they begin to appear fairly lightweight performances. Tales such as *The Cautious Amorist* (1932) and *A Curate in Bohemia* (1913) derive their lasting interest less from the weight of their protest than from their bubbling good humour and wit. They provide an oasis of laughter in a period of predominantly earnest fiction. The good humour is carried over into *Redheap* (1930) and *Saturdee* (1933); yet even these accounts of boyhood and adolescence in a country town are characterized not so much by any real imaginative shock as by a sense of pleasure in iconoclasm accompanied by real charm and skill in execution. The later city novel, *Dust or Polish?* (1950), moves Lindsay's milieu to Sydney's semi-Bohemia, continues his great theme of the full liberation of the personality, but still does not suggest a mind driven to the forms of fiction in order to obtain complete expression.

Neither Chester Cobb nor Christina Stead can claim the breadth or acuteness of Lindsay's mind, but both more steadily and intensely sought to convert their creative gifts into literature. And both seem, fairly deliberately, to have made use of contemporary experiments in England and Europe. Cobb's *Mr Moffatt* (1925) appeared only three years after *Ulysses* but makes remarkably competent use of the stream of consciousness technique. The balance between Mr Moffatt's interior monologues and the rendering of external data unmistakably recalls the shifts in Joyce's master work between the mind of Leopold Bloom and the rich sensational life of the Dublin streets. Christina Stead's *Seven Poor Men of Sydney* (1934) also displays the kind of technical sophistication to suggest conscious imitation of outside influences. There is a nicely calculated counterpoint in the narratives of the seven men whose lives are presented in the book; the richly textured impressionistic style is, to a degree, reminiscent of Conrad. *Mr Moffatt* and *Seven Poor Men of Sydney* unwittingly reveal their Australianness in a common strand of melancholy and pessimism; in each case, a central figure is defeated by the circumstances of his existence (in *Seven Poor Men* defeat issues in suicide). Consciously, however, both Cobb and Stead repudiated the land of their birth and pursued their later careers overseas. The fact is, in a way, symptomatic of their relation to the mainstream of Australian writing in the twenties and thirties. It was prepared to entertain outside ideas and techniques, but its major orientation was still predominantly domestic.

The task of advancing Australian fiction along its necessary path fell, therefore, chiefly to the writers of saga, picaresque, and documentary. And among these central writers of the tradition, clearly a number must be accorded positions of special importance. As one who gave the saga its characteristic shape and qualities, Miles Franklin occupies a place of honour – as much by virtue of the persistence of her efforts as by the merit of her individual works. She had started writing well before 1920 – *My*

Brilliant Career was published in 1901; *My Career Goes Bung*, though written at much the same time, was not published until much later (1946). She ushered in her post-war career with the whimsical *Old Blastus of Bandicoot* (1931), but it was not until 1936 that *All that Swagger*, the cornerstone of her achievement, appeared. The novel spans something like a hundred years, from the 1830s to the 1930s, and moves from Ireland to the Murrumbidgee and Monaro districts of New South Wales. The plot is centred in the character of Danny Delacy, who brings his young bride to the new colony, where he becomes a successful, if eccentric, squatter and, in the fulness of time, dies surrounded by prosperity and several generations of the dynasty he has founded.

Into its hundred year span, *All that Swagger* packs a great wealth of incident, of the strenuously physical and exciting nature made so readily available by the circumstances of pioneering. The mass of events, however, is given very little shape beyond arrangement in chronological order. Neither does the style do much to bring the book's material under control. In some random historical summaries which are interjected into the Delacy narrative, indeed, it breaks down into fairly clumsy reportage. For most of the book it is adequate to the demands of a simple characterization and the flow of an unsophisticated plot. Only when Franklin turns her attention to the natural beauty of the region that she loved is her language charged with some lyric emotion.

In effect, much of the appeal of *All that Swagger* resides in its unabashed romanticism. In a sense, it is simply another version of the success story: the poor Irish migrant makes good in a new land. But there is a more particular, and more significant kind of romanticism in the book – a kind indicated by the title itself. This is the saga of Australia on horseback, a nostalgic tribute to the gaiety and swagger that accompanied lives spent largely in the saddle. The values of *All that Swagger* might with some justice be described as chivalric. To be sure, it is a chivalry modified by the physical conditions of the Australian land and the social pressures of Australian democracy, but it is still there: the *élan* of the mounted man, the thrill of the cross-country gallop, even the high standards of public morality. More than chivalric, the book is patriarchal. That grand old leader, Fearless

Danny, is most memorable when in the company of his faithful retainers, the aboriginal Doogooluk and the Chinese Wong Foo. Throughout, he carries something of the air of the benevolent despot. It is certainly Delacy who assures the continuing vitality of the book. He is created simple, but created fresh and alive. With his Irish verve and wit, he epitomizes that blend of dash and democracy which Miles Franklin saw as the special mark of the nineteenth century mounted bushman. After Danny's death, the life fades rapidly from the whole book, which not even the romance between Clare Margaret and Darcy can revive. It sinks to rest with an unconvincing attempt to transfer the swagger of the horseman to the aeroplane pilot, the rider of the skies and new man of the twentieth century.

If, as there can be little doubt, Miles Franklin was Brent of Bin Bin, [3] her place at the centre of the saga tradition is made doubly sure. In a series of five novels, [4] Brent of Bin Bin chronicled the histories of some half dozen families who settled in the same general area as is treated in *All that Swagger*. The Brent books also display the same regional love of place as occurs in Franklin's prose. In general structure they are very similar to *All that Swagger*, recounting a profusion of events with little more order than arrangement in chronological sequence. Their enormous proliferation of characters accords them at least one virtue not present in *All that Swagger*, the sense of the warp and weave of the social fabric of an Australian pastoral community. The limits of observation are so widely extended in time and space that the division of the chronicle into five separate books becomes almost a literary necessity as much as a publishing convenience.

The saga formula was not applied only to the country. In another well known novel of the genre, M. Barnard Eldershaw's *A House Is Built* (1929), the scene is set entirely in Sydney from the 1830s to the 1870s. Its theme is the creation of a commercial rather than a pastoral empire, and again there is an attempt, through some rather crude summary, to relate the fortunes of the Hyde family to the wider history of the nation. This summarizing tendency is sometimes extended to the main narrative, notably in the compression of several quite long periods of time into a very short space of print. There is, however, some kind of a pattern imposed on the material. At the close of the book, it is said of the sole surviving male Hyde that 'He was the mouse that the mountain had brought forth.' The remark suggests a potentially powerful piece of historical irony. For the most part, unfortunately, the irony remains unrealized.

Of all the major saga novels, it is Brian Penton's *Landtakers* which most successfully fuses a thematic pattern with its chronicle material. *Landtakers* has all the standard situations and events – the droughts, the floods, the epics of endurance. But they are all put to the service of a central idea which is powerfully imagined and powerfully executed. The story is of Derek Cabell; its subject is the slow moulding of a man's life by his environment. Cabell, the son of a well-to-do English family, comes out to Australia to make his fortune, with the intention of returning home to the elegant life he feels to be properly his. However, the years, the land, all the rigours of pioneering combine to make him a prisoner in the new land, to work a slow and profound change in his character and attitudes. In the end he renounces England and comes to the realization that 'Perhaps I was always meant to stay.' Penton's vision of nineteenth century Australia is a brutal one – brutal people, brutal deeds, brutal country. Whatever the historical accuracy of his vision, it is transformed into a compelling work of art by virtue of the unremitting harshness of his style and the unswerving honesty of his perceptions. Out of the paradoxes and ugliness of pioneering life Penton has wrought a novel of sustained force and considerable stature.

Because of its sheer bulk, the saga novel sometimes seems to dominate Australian fiction in the two decades between the wars. Nevertheless, there were other writers at work whose contribution was in every way as valuable and significant. Indeed, it could with some justice be argued that the most important single novelist of these years was Vance Palmer, whose work cannot easily be assigned to any single category. Like Franklin, Palmer had started writing before World War I,[5] but it was only after 1920 that he started to produce the works of his maturity. *The Passage*, which appeared in 1930 is a characteristic example of his fiction, and among the best. What distinguishes this book and many of Palmer's novels is an awareness of the great natural forces which move the world, the tide of life which submerges the individual into the species. *The Passage* is set close to the sea, its characters make up a little fishing community on the Queensland coast. The Callaway family, and in particular Lew, are as at home in the water as on land; their affinity with that element is a sure sign of their natural morality, their closeness to the simple and best purposes of life. The idea of the sea as the milieu of natural behaviour and the source of psychic replenishment is not restricted to *The Passage*. It recurs, for instance, in *Legend for Sanderson* (1937) and the *Golconda* trilogy. Through its embodiment in images of ebb and flow, it is extended into most of Palmer's important novels.

In spite of Palmer's perception of the rightness of a close identity with the natural order of the world, it would be wrong to think of him as some kind of biological determinist. Fishermen like Lew Callaway or farmers like Bob Rossiter (in *Daybreak*) certainly seemed to him to draw on the positive sources of life, but for them and for all his characters there also exist the stern demands of a purely human morality. Man, in Palmer's view, cannot take refuge from moral responsibility in his animal nature. If Miles Franklin is at the centre of the saga tradition, Vance Palmer, more clearly than any other Australian writer of his generation, spoke for that liberal humanism which is such an enduring element of Australian literature. Ethical behaviour is, for Palmer, an unavoidable part of man's life. It derives its sanction not from any religious or metaphysical code but from the sense of mutual need that any good man must discover in his relations with his fellows. Many of Palmer's characters, therefore, develop their humanist values out of their first and most powerful personal relationships, with other members of their family. The father-son relation, in particular, is a common basis for ethical attitudes in Palmer's novels, notably *Legend for Sanderson* and *The Swayne Family* (1934).

Palmer's conception of moral behaviour was not limited to the family. It extended throughout the Australian society that was the material for his fiction. His novels, that is, are very much concerned with the idea of mateship. Time and again his heroes draw their strength from a sense of community with their fellows, from a belief that life can be good if only men will learn to act in unison. In spite of the presence of violent events, even catastrophes in their action, Palmer's novels bear witness to an optimistic belief in the rightness of a life lived to the full by physically powerful men, men blessed with a fundamental decency and a notion of fair play.

This somewhat rudimentary ethic is projected into novels whose very structure mirrors their conception. Palmer can certainly imagine vivid personal conflicts, even interior tension, but the dominant impression left by his work is less of any array of 'big scenes' than of the slow, strong development of a central idea. The novels collectively display an impressive list of narrative techniques, but they are submerged in a solidly competent and completely unspectacular craftsmanship. The style, equally, is sturdy, direct, and to the point. It rarely aims at anything more than adequacy, is capable of advancing action at a smart pace, of accurately reporting colloquial speech. The higher flights of imagery or extended symbolism are rigorously eschewed as inappropriate to the craftsman's competence and unassumingly honest vision that Palmer seems to have set himself as his aim in fiction.

Palmer's non-doctrinaire humanism was shared by a number of his near contemporaries, among them Frank Dalby Davison and Leonard Mann. They share the same belief in the fundamental goodness of man, and test it not so much against any intellectual system as against actual Australian situations and characters. Davison's first full-length work, *Forever Morning* (1931), he rightly described as a 'Romance'. It depends on a deliberate simplification of plot and character for the sake of idealizing the life of the small farmer. Something of its purpose and quality can be judged from chapter 13, 'A Bangtail Muster', which is injected into the book wholly and solely for the sake of setting down some of the old bush songs – verses which make simple literature out of simple events. A comparable idyllic quality informs the whole work. It is in his other works – *Man-Shy* (1931), *The Wells of Beersheba* (1933), and *Dusty* (1946) – that Davison has made his most individual contribution to the Australian novel. *The Wells of Beersheba*, a slight piece, is a hymn of praise to the horses of the Australian Light Horse regiments of World War I. From its special point of view, it reproduces the fierce national pride which marked Mann's *Flesh in Armour*. *Man-Shy* and *Dusty* are attempts to render from the inside the needs and primitive motivations of a red heifer and a cattle dog. Davison imagines his way into the animal mind with remarkable insight and complete avoidance of sentimentality. The heifer and the dog are seen as part of the same world of biological necessity

which Palmer, from a different point of view, found so fascinating
At the same time, Davison's prose achieves an unassuming
lyricism unique in Australian fiction of the period. The style itself
asserts the beauty and goodness of the natural law.

Mann is less concerned with the natural law than the world of
men, although his characters are usually brought into scenes of
conflict generated by some fundamental need. Already in 1932
he had made a significant addition to the sum of Australian
fiction with *Flesh in Armour*. During the ensuing decade he
published four more novels, two of which, *Mountain Flat* (1939)
and *The Go-Getter* (1942), can serve to indicate his principal
virtues. *Mountain Flat* is located in an isolated rural community,
of which the inhabitants are drawn from the most diverse racial
backgrounds. The isolation, the closeness of one life to the
next, allow Mann to investigate the hates and rivalries which
can be engendered by a family feud. The locale, too, conveniently
permits Mann to demonstrate the primitive urgency of sexual
desire. Mann develops his themes with honesty of purpose and a
marked directness of perception. Characters, incident, landscape,
are all created largely by means of overt description and comment, which to some extent stand between the heavily charged
emotions of the plot and the reader. This overtness of technique
is even more noticeable but more successful in *The Go-Getter*.
The leading concerns of the book are embodied in its protagonist, Chris Gibbons, a man who learns under the stress of
events that the slick, cynical life of the go-getter cannot lead to
personal fulfilment. Such fulfilment is possible only when he falls
back on the established attitudes of the humanist ethos. The
theme of *The Go-Getter* is embodied in its hero; it is projected
onto a background of Melbourne in the Depression years and
viewed through the lens of social realism. There is a fine particularity in the accounts of the city itself, a deliberately unromantic
documentation of all the circumstances of a poverty-stricken
existence.

In *The Go-Getter* the technique of documentation is successfully put to the service of social realism, even protest. The conjunction of such an attitude and such a technique is nowhere
more consistently displayed in modern Australian writing than
in the novels of Katharine Susannah Prichard. At one level, her
novels of the twenties and thirties provide a series of travelogues

lepicting a wide variety of Australian occupations. *Black Opal*
(1921), for instance, pictures the life of the opal gougers in far
western New South Wales. *Working Bullocks* (1926) gives a
realistic and complete account of the timber industry in the
karri forests of Western Australia. *Haxby's Circus* (1930) takes
its readers behind the scenes of a small travelling circus. This
determined documenting of various phases of Australian life and
work is motivated by an attitude which has clear affinities with
the literary patriotism of the saga novelists. In a letter to Henrietta
Drake-Brockman, Prichard wrote that 'My first resolution was to
see and know Australia.' Drake-Brockman, in turn, has written
of her: 'In all her work resides that deep love of the colour, scents,
sounds, of the Australian countryside itself and an appreciation,
thoroughly Australian, of its harsher aspects.'[6]

Nevertheless, none of Prichard's novels remains completely on
the surface. In spite of a sometimes clumsy technique, they all
seek to penetrate to an understanding of their subject dependent
on something other than a mastery of physical detail. Of all
her novels, the one which has most consistently recommended
itself as the vehicle of a coherent imaginative vision is *Coonardoo*
(1929). This book is set on a cattle station in the north-west of
Western Australia and is one of the first works of creative
literature to attempt a serious treatment of the aboriginal. The
treatment is neither sociological, nor patronizing, but (at least by
intention) tragic. The plot traces out the lives of the white station
owner, Hugh Watt, and the native girl, Coonardoo, whom he has
briefly loved and who gives him her lifelong devotion in return.
The latter part of the book is taken up with Coonardoo's collapse
and final lonely death.

It is a matter of some interest that what is probably Prichard's
most complex attempt at characterization and her most intensely
sustained emotional encounter with her material should be
inspired by a member of a race whose dreaming, whose search
for identity, was accomplished long before white men came to
the Australian continent. Certainly, in her dealings with white
Australians, Prichard has been much less sure of her own imaginative insights. She has turned, instead, to systematic knowledge,
to doctrine. *Intimate Strangers* (1937), for instance, bears the
appearance of a calculated attempt to apply Freudian and
Lawrentian ideas to her fiction. It deals with the deeply personal,

especially sexual, relationship between man and wife. The paradoxical and unsatisfactory nature of modern marriage is indicated
by the title of the book and illustrated in the lives of its two main
characters, Greg and Elodie Blackwood.

In determining the resolution of her plots and the reactions of
her characters, socialism is far and away the most important
doctrinal element in Prichard's work. All of her novels of the
twenties and thirties bear a heavy freight of social protest. Mark
Smith, the working class intellectual and organizer, is a leading
figure in *Working Bullocks*. The miners in *Black Opal* band
together in a display of social solidarity in order to defeat the
representative of American capitalism. The cause of the working
classes provides Greg Blackwood with a sustaining faith at the
end of *Intimate Strangers*. Oddly enough, it is the cause which
is so close to her heart which can lead more easily than anything
else to the failure of Prichard's fiction. She is so deeply committed
to the idea of social revolution that she sometimes allows her
wishes to obscure her understanding. When Prichard goes wrong,
it is because she makes her characters behave in the way she
thinks they should rather than in the way they would, granted
the whole context of their past, present, and actual environment.

Prichard's relative failure with her proletarian heroes is a
curious but not isolated phenomenon. For all its socialist
allegiances, the Australian novel has never shown itself at its
best when essaying political themes. Norman Bartlett somewhat
overstates the case when he writes that 'Australian literature, so
far as I have read it, utterly fails to grapple with the life of
politics.'[7] Yet, it is true that, in spite of their repeated examination of the role of the political reformer, Australian writers have
rarely succeeded in presenting him as other than a walking bundle
of dogmas. Indeed, the chief imaginative discovery that Australian
novelists have made about political activity is its corruption and
brutality. Such are the qualities which are displayed, for instance,
by the political elements in Mann's *The Go-Getter*. Similar
perceptions emerge from *Power Without Glory* (1950) by Frank
Hardy, a much more dogmatic left-wing writer than Mann.
The overwhelming mass of documentation in *Power Without
Glory*, in the end, enforces an acceptance not so much of Hardy's
positive beliefs as his awareness of the power of money and the
corruptibility of most men, particularly politicians. The same

kind of point could be asserted of Dal Stivens' *Jimmy Brockett*
(1951), or of some of the work of Judah Waten, F.B. Vickers,
Dorothy Hewett, and the other writers who continue the tradition
of social protest in Australian fiction. It is one of the paradoxes of
Australian writing that it nourishes an enduring optimism about
the spirit of man and the efficacy of social solidarity yet repeatedly
discovers brutality and cynicism as the mainsprings of political
action.

Of all the modern novelists, perhaps it is Kylie Tennant who
carries her political beliefs most lightly. She produced three
novels during the Depression years – *Tiburon* (1935), *Foveaux*
(1939), and *The Battlers* (1941). All of them reveal strong working
class sympathies; none allows political dogma to stultify its native
wit. Generally, Tennant's socialism seems to be less of the intellectual variety than an emotional identification with the characters
of whom she writes. These characters are almost entirely working
class – from a small country town in *Tiburon*, the urban proletariat in *Foveaux*, the rural unemployed in *The Battlers*. When
they are not, they are frequently the target for Tennant's good
humoured satire. Indeed, her sense of comedy is a leaven at work
throughout her fiction. It is to be found not only in the invention
of some outrageously farcical scenes but in a wide gallery
of characters whose conception and execution is essentially
comic in nature. Nobody has come nearer to providing Australian fiction with an array of Dickensian originals than Kylie
Tennant.

Her characters are typically contained in plots which distil
the quintessence of Australian picaresque: a whole series of
incidents strung together with little causal relation, carrying
the novelist and her characters into a wide variety of circumstances and places, and leading for the most part to an optimistic
conclusion. *Tiburon* presents a mosaic of small town life. *Foveaux*
provides an historical panorama of an inner suburb of Sydney.
The Battlers follows a little band of wanderers through their
adventures in outback New South Wales. Kylie Tennant is not
a great novelist. Nevertheless, her books demonstrate more
clearly and consistently than those of any other writer a recurring
mode of Australian fiction, and do so with unaffected vivacity and
good humour. Dorothy Auchterlonie's comment is amply
justified:

Here is living tissue, raw, crude, and shapeless if you like, but breathes and if you put a knife into it, blood will run out.

('The Novels of Kylie Tennant', *Meanjin*, 1953, no. 4, p. 397)

The novels of Eleanor Dark seem to be much less the result of spontaneous delight in people and places than the conscious exploration of the possibilities of fiction. Perhaps for this reason her work exemplifies with remarkable thoroughness nearly all the vital interests which animated the Australian novel in the years which preceded the Second World War. Her first book, *Slow Dawning*, appeared in 1932 and was followed during the ensuing decade by a steady output which culminated in *The Timeless Land* in 1941. The earlier books, like *Prelude to Christopher* (1934) and *Return to Coolami* (1936), are concerned with personal themes and are clearly influenced by experimental English fiction. Both attempt to contain a personal awareness of time and a measuring of its actual passage within a single narrative framework. The main event of *Prelude to Christopher* has not yet taken place when the novel is brought to its close. It tells the story of the idealistic doctor, Nigel Hendon, his marriage to Linda Hamlin, and his catastrophic attempt to establish an Utopian community on a Pacific island. The book is steeped in ideas about heredity, eugenics, dynamic psychology, and its entire action is compressed into a span of four days. Hendon is involved in a motor accident. His past history and present difficulties are revealed by means of flashbacks and by exchanges between those who are most concerned for his recovery – his wife, his mother, and the young nurse who loves him. In the end, the wife, long tortured by incipient insanity, commits suicide, leaving the way open for marriage between Hendon and the nurse, Kay. Out of that marriage will come a son, Christopher, who gives his name to the whole book. His birth will be the culmination of Nigel's life, for which all the rest has been merely a prelude.

There is a considered ingenuity about the construction of *Prelude to Christopher*. There is a similar sophistication of technique in *Return to Coolami*, which reconstructs the lives and problems of a small family group in a series of flashbacks incorporated into a two-day car trip from Sydney to a country property. The novel bears witness, like all of Dark's earlier work, to a thorough schooling in the techniques of modern fiction. Her works exhibit the virtues of a well-trained and well-stored intelligence applying itself to the task of creating literature.

During the thirties, Dark's conception of her task seems to have undergone some change. Certainly, *The Timeless Land*, which appeared in 1941, manifests a distinct shift from the themes of personal conflict and depth psychology which dominated the earlier books. In *The Timeless Land* her imagination applies itself, with no less deliberation, to the beginnings of the Australian nation. The novel is a thorough-going recreation of the first five years of British settlement in New South Wales, and resumes the chief features of those forms which had dominated Australian fiction in the two decades which preceded its publication. It is documented with a truly impressive accumulation of historical detail. There is the heroic vision of a nation begun in the most adverse conditions yet sustained by the unswerving purpose of its first governor, Captain Arthur Phillip. There is the kaleidoscope of all the elements of the minuscule society. And here is the imagined life of the aborigines, who had come to terms with the land generations before the arrival of the First Fleet. In its determination to do honour to black and white, officer and private soldier, freeman and convict, *The Timeless Land* is one of the most comprehensive attempts in Australian fiction to fuse the diverse elements of the past into an image of national identity. [8]

While the novelists were addressing themselves to the task of developing the kind of formal tradition already established in the short story, the short story writers were free to pursue their own more personal interests. The Australian short story of the twenties and thirties is, as a rule, less ambitious than the Australian novel of the period – even on its own terms. However, in terms of fully achieved art, its successes are perhaps more frequent. In many cases novelist and short story writer coincided in a single individual; and it is a point worthy of note that in such cases the short stories were not uncommonly superior to the novels.

Such a view, for instance, could be argued with respect to Vance Palmer. Palmer published three volumes of short stories – *Separate Lives* (1931), *Sea and Spinifex* (1934), and, near the end of his career, *Let the Birds Fly* (1955) – and it might well be claimed that they contain some of his best writing. A number of the stories reproduce the situations and values of his novels. There are tales of outback hardship and endurance, conscientiously and laconically set down; there are tales of the sea, like 'Seahawk'. But among the most interesting and least expected of Palmer's short stories are those which deal with the delicate sensibilities of childhood and early adolescence. Among the most memorable in this class are 'The Foal', 'The Rainbow Bird', and 'Mathieson's Wife'. They are distinguished by a delicacy of perception not often found in Palmer's longer fiction, by an intensity of rendered emotion, and by some subtlety of presentation and organization. In them Palmer ventured a more richly charged metaphorical and symbolic technique than he normally permitted himself in the novel. There is no complete hiatus between his stories and his novels. Yet in his shorter pieces Palmer did consistently rise to his greatest verbal subtlety and most regularly grappled with a recurring theme in the Australian short story – the painful awakening of the adolescent mind to adult experience.

Frank Dalby Davison, too, has shown more than competence in the art of the short story. He has published one volume, *The Woman at the Mill* (1940). Most of the stories deal with the lives of pioneering small farmers. At their best, they achieve the same controlled sentiment and lyric eloquence as *Forever Morning*, but these qualities are now associated with more realistically motivated situations. However, what is probably Davison's most personal contribution to short fiction can be most readily identified in a story as yet uncollected, 'The Good Herdsman'. [9] Its central character is an old man who has taken up a selection late in life, and who has a feeling for his cattle which goes deeper than the hope of commercial gain. In the end he is forced to sacrifice the beasts that he loves and sell them to a neighbour. The story ends with the sentence, 'Isaac Burgess had no word for the act of renunciation, but he knew its pangs.' Davison's achievement here, and one in which he is unsurpassed, is to make articulate the emotions of those who lack the verbal skills to do so for themselves.

Among the other novelists, Marjorie Barnard published *The Persimmon Tree* (1943); Katharine Susannah Prichard, *Kiss on the Lips* (1932). The title story of Barnard's collection is a finely judged portrayal of a feminine sensibility. A number of Prichard's stories lean more to what might be described as the Lawrentian side of her nature than the political. Of this kind are 'The Grey

Horse' and 'The Cow', which go to the natural world to find some adequate correlative for the powerful needs of her human beings. Other stories deal, like *Coonardoo*, with the aboriginals; others display some sense of comic situation.

There were, of course, many writers at work during the twenties and thirties whose chief (or only) effort was directed towards the short story rather than the novel. Of these, there can be little question that the most accomplished was Gavin Casey. In more recent years, Casey has turned increasingly to the novel form,[10] but the fruit of the earlier part of his career was gathered into two volumes of short stories, *It's Harder for Girls* (1942) and *Birds of a Feather* (1943). In these books, Casey added some original and important elements to the Australian short story. He brought a new source of material – heavy industry – under its surveillance. Much of his best and most characteristic writing is set in and around the goldmines of Kalgoorlie. Even more important is Casey's ability to sustain the realistic mode over much longer periods than his predecessors had attempted. Of its kind, there is probably nothing better in Australian writing than the long story, 'Short Shift Saturday'. A seemingly non-committal manner, a judicious selection of detail, a self-obliterating style, a steadfast withholding from melodrama or the slightest suggestion of narrative contrivance: these qualities combine to make Casey's account of a day in the lives of a miner and his family a thoroughly satisfying work of art. Similar traits are exhibited, at shorter length, in pieces like 'Talking Ground' and 'Compensation'.

Casey's treatment of working men on and off the job, of their relations with their wives and children, is often tinged with a rather sombre hue. However, his awareness of the worries and tensions of living is more than offset by a sparkling sense of humour. His laughter may be evoked by realistic situations – often concerned with gold stealing from the mines, and the contest between the individualism of the workers and the representatives of social authority. Working in a more specialized mode, Casey has also produced some of the most memorable examples of the Australian tall story. 'The Hairy Men from Hannigan's Halt' and 'The Irish Oafs from Ugly Gully'[11] set a standard which other writers have equalled but not, I think, surpassed. Dal Stivens, especially through his character Ironbark Bill, has placed his personal brand on the tall story; Alan Marshall, in

'They Were Tough Men on the Speewah', has provided it with a *locus classicus*. But for sheer exuberance and sustained comic invention, neither writer has bettered Casey's performance.

The tall story was a development of a long established literary form – the anonymous folk yarn. However, towards the end of the thirties there loomed up in the Australian literary landscape a number of landmarks which opened the way to new terrain rather than defined the limits of territory already traversed. In retrospect, some half dozen novels contain unmistakable signs that the aims and purposes that the Australian novel had set itself at the end of World War I had been fulfilled and that it was now ready to move forward to new fields of endeavour and achievement.

The outstanding signpost towards new directions and expanding interests was Xavier Herbert's *Capricornia*, which appeared in 1938. The immediately appropriate comparison for this sprawling work might appear to be with any of the earlier saga novels. And indeed it chronicles some forty years in the history of the Northern Territory, at a time when the Territory was more clearly a frontier society than any other region of Australia. The caste of *Capricornia* is as numerically impressive as in any work of Miles Franklin; its seemingly numberless and intertwining plots create a canvas alive with action. The action is usually excited, exciting, and physical in nature – organized around the railway line, the great stations, the untamed wilderness, and the principal settlements of a society which was still governed in large measure by physical strength.

Nevertheless, within the framework of this rumbustious saga are to be detected elements which belong peculiarly to Herbert, some of them new to the Australian novel. Not least among these is Herbert's social indignation, particularly with respect to the treatment of the natives and half-castes. The whites' pretensions to racial superiority are, in Herbert's eyes, pure untruth or hypocrisy, only to be maintained by an unjust repression of the country's aboriginal people. Any attempt to 'civilize' the tribes is viewed with deep suspicion as being, more likely than not, exploitation under another name. Herbert was not the first to express indignation at the white treatment of the native people, although few had done so with his fierce directness. What is a more individual element in *Capricornia* is his gift of comedy. So thoroughly is the outrageous comedy mingled not only with the social protest but with the entire fabric of the book that, without too great an exaggeration, *Capricornia* might be described as the first great comic novel in Australian literature after *Such is Life*. The comedy of *Capricornia* has this, too, in common with Furphy's – it exists in close alliance with a deeply serious (even pessimistic) theme. In episode after episode of *Capricornia* the best (and the worst) efforts of men are thwarted or even reversed by the operations of indifferent, possibly malign, fate. Herbert analyses the material of *Capricornia* from the point of view of a scientific rationalist and finds little in the evidence before him to indicate that men can in any significant way control the pattern of their lives. In spite of its crowded stage, its rich variety of incident, its plethora of raw comedy, the constant force at work in the whole of *Capricornia* is an inescapable and implacable Nature.

In that fact, too, Herbert significantly widened the scope of the saga novel. If Penton in *Landtakers* had imposed on its pattern of action and adventure a consistent interpretation of specifically Australian life and character, Herbert was the first major writer to make such material the medium for a universal theme. In terms of style, he was less content to work with conventions already to hand. With *Capricornia*, the Australian novel began to free itself from the limits of external realism. Its manner is not uniformly successful, but where it fails, it is likely to do so attempting things new to Australian fiction. The title itself gives some indication of the direction in which Herbert's style was moving. The name 'Capricornia' does not disguise the Northern Territory setting, nor is it intended to. But it does suggest a special angle of vision. So, too, do names like Mark Shillingsworth, Captain Settaroge, The Rev. Simon Bleeter, State Prosecutor Thumscrough. In *Capricornia*, social indignation, comedy, and theme come together in a fictional mode which can properly be described as incipient allegory. The allegory, as yet, is not fully sustained, and is stated with forthright vigour rather than subtlety; nevertheless it is a symptom of new forces at work within the established formal conventions of the Australian novel, forces which, in *Capricornia*, are so strong that they threaten to sweep the conventions away. *Capricornia* is one of the few Australian novels of the twentieth century to suggest an imagination of such bursting energy that it is too big for the narrative in which it is more or less contained.

Herbert's was not the only new voice to be heard in the late thirties. In 1939 Patrick White published his first novel, *Happy Valley*. Although little heeded when it first appeared, this story can, in retrospect, be recognized as the authentic beginning of a career which was subsequently to have a massive impact on the development of Australian fiction. Three years later, in 1942, there appeared a novel which immediately established, and has since maintained, a special reputation among Australian novels – Eve Langley's *The Pea Pickers*. This tale of two young girls who wander through Victoria and New South Wales dressed as boys has not, on the whole, worn as well as *Capricornia*. Its deliberately 'poetic' prose seems at times rather too hectic and over-written. Nevertheless, in her own way Eve Langley was making a useful attempt to widen and deepen the bases of Australian prose style and characterization. Her heroine, Stevie, is motivated in part by the same kind of vision of Australia as animated Miles Franklin. However, Langley's prose much more obviously assaults the texture of the natural world as well as its surface; tries to get at the inner quality of her characters' behaviour as well as its outwardly observable manifestations. In pursuing such ends, Eve Langley was in some degree hampered by an overly-romantic heroine and a prose that could topple over into the effusively literary. Yet granted these qualifications, *The Pea Pickers*, like *Capricornia*, was both a sign and a cause of new developments in Australian writing.

The same claim can be made for the first novel of Seaforth Mackenzie, *The Young Desire It* (1937). *The Young Desire It* deals with the adolescence of Charles Fox, and would appear, thus, to invite comparison with Lindsay's *Redheap*. Of the two, Mackenzie's book conveys the stronger impression of a mind totally committed to fiction as the vehicle for its insights and understanding. Even in his subject matter, Mackenzie explores territory foreign to *Redheap*. *The Young Desire It* is set, for instance, in a large boarding school just out of Perth, and so can deal effectively with the effects of formal education on a growing and sensitive mind. Mackenzie's account of the private agony endured by Charles Fox in his progress through school is enriched by the theme of his sexual awakening. There is an uneasy relationship with a latent homosexual on the teaching staff – a daring subject for an Australian novelist in 1937, and handled by Mackenzie with considerable sensitivity and tact. It is balanced by the joy of Charles's love for a girl he meets while on holidays at home in the wheatbelt. By itself, the subject matter of *The Young Desire It* gives the book some importance. The quality of the writing is equally significant. To this and all his novels Mackenzie brought the equipment of a poet. While *The Young Desire It* may have weaknesses of narrative construction, its strength undoubtedly lies in its rendering of experience through image and metaphor. Mackenzie's prose is at once more subtle and more suave than Eve Langley's. Perhaps his greatest contribution to the growth of the Australian novel in the late thirties lies in the fact that he brought the technique of a refined sensibility to the depiction of a refined sensibility – a conjunction of aim and method never before recorded in the history of the Australian novel.

New writers like Herbert, White, Mackenzie, and Langley were not alone in adding fresh hues to the novel of this period. Miles Franklin, for instance, co-operated with Dymphna Cusack in 1939 to produce *Pioneers on Parade*, which, in its satirical view of ancestor worship, recognizes that her own earlier work might have been too well carried out. A weightier contribution by an established figure was Eleanor Dark's *The Little Company*, published in 1945, four years after *The Timeless Land*. Something of the special nature of this book is indicated by the fact that the hero is himself a writer, whose analysis of the world is itself subject to scrutiny. Such artistic self-consciousness is a real mark of growing maturity in Australian writing. Gilbert Massey, the protagonist of *The Little Company*, has started out simply telling stories, but during the late thirties has become increasingly conscious of the political, social, and economic movements in the world around him; so conscious, indeed, that he suffers a kind of writing paralysis and is scarcely capable of putting two sentences meaningfully together. He spends the early war years as a civilian in Sydney, his own ideas constantly being tested against competing doctrines. In effect, what Eleanor Dark contrives to present through the present difficulties and past history of the Massey family is a panorama of the entire intellectual life of Australia during the twentieth century. *The Little Company* must rank among the first significant novels of ideas produced in this country.

Much of *The Little Company* is concerned with the response of civilians to the stresses of World War II. Not surprisingly, the War found its way much more directly into the history of Australian fiction. Indeed, where *Flesh in Armour* stands virtually alone as a full-length treatment of Australian participation in the earlier conflict, there are some half-dozen accounts of the Australian serviceman in the Second World War which seem likely to have some permanent value. Among them are Lawson Glassop's *We Were the Rats* (1944), Eric Lambert's *The Twenty Thousand Thieves* (1951), and *The Veterans* (1954), T.A.G. Hungerford's *The Ridge and the River* (1952). None compares with the greatest war novels produced in England, Europe, or America, but they do distil something of the experience of Australian troops in action. Many of the qualities embodied in these books are predictable enough: the fierce lust for life, the savagery of killing, the intense sense of comradeship among the men (and distrust of the officers), the toughly defensive laughter. To these can be added some further traits which distinguish the responses of a later generation of diggers from those recorded in *Flesh in Armour*. If the literary record is an accurate one, far more of the second generation of troops went into action with an attitude of cynical realism than had their fathers. Hardly any seem to have enlisted with any expectation of martial glamour and glory – their fathers had told them what to expect. For some, the army represented an escape from a Depression still grinding on into the end of the thirties. Many were sceptical about the outcome of their efforts; again, there was the lesson of Versailles. Those men who are represented as fighting for a cause are frequently aligned with the political left.

Noticeably missing from the fiction of World War II is the excited discovery of nationhood which characterized some of the strongest pages of *Flesh in Armour*. There are more likely to be deflating jokes about 'bronzed Anzacs'. There is, of course, a sense of national pride, but it is worn with an air of settled custom, with a shrug as often as with bravado. Most of these novels afford at least a synoptic treatment of world wide strategies, but their characteristic unit is not an army but a platoon or a section. In this respect, *The Ridge and the River* is thoroughly typical. It is also one of the best of World War II novels, while its author, through two subsequent books,[12] has shown a continuing competence in the craft of fiction. *The Ridge and the River* is set in New Guinea and follows a single patrol by a small group of Australian infantrymen. Its various characters are examined in some depth, provided with a three-dimensional past as well as an uncertain and intense present. All the structural devices of the novel are aimed at compressing the attention within a narrow range of time and space; all the resources of its style at rendering the action in all its immediacy, at bringing the soldiers alive in all their colloquial vigour.

Neither *The Ridge and the River* nor any of its companion novels significantly advanced the artistic development of Australian fiction. They convince, more than anything else, because of their compelling personal urgency. The more lasting effects of the War on Australian writing probably came indirectly, through the revolutionary changes in Australian society, economics, and culture wrought during the years 1939-45. Seaforth Mackenzie had Lloyd Fitzherbert, the hero of *The Refuge* (1954), say of those years:

We knew they were impressive years. But what we did not realize, because of their often brilliantly-lighted darkness, was that they were to impress and alter beyond remembrance the whole mind and manner of the civilian community. (p. 178)

It was to take some little time for the consequences of the War and its aftermath to seep down right through Australian culture and then to rise to the surface again as articulate literature. Meantime, during the forties the continuing vitality and traditions of fiction were transmitted more through the short story than the novel. Davison opened the decade with the publication of *The Woman at the Mill* in 1940. This was followed by Casey's *It's Harder for Girls* and *Birds of a Feather* in 1942 and 1943 respectively. 1943 also saw the appearance of Marjorie Barnard's *The Persimmon Tree*; 1944, a new volume by Katharine Susannah Prichard, *Potch and Colour*.

As well as such established writers, there were some new names to be numbered among the leading short story writers of the forties. Don Edwards' *High Hill at Midnight*, for instance, appeared in 1944; Margaret Trist's *What Else Is There?* in 1946. Also making a worthwhile contribution was Peter Cowan, whose work was collected in 1944, in the volume *Drift*. Most of the stories were set in the Depression years in Western Australia, some in the wheatbelt. Yet they are memorable not for their subject matter alone. At his best, Cowan controls his sometimes earthy realism as well as any Australian short story writer. The style is stripped bare; or, as Evan Jones describes it, is 'brisk, transitive, clear'. [13] Cowan's art has continued to ripen, and he has recently published a second volume, *The Unploughed Land* (1958). Brian James (the pen name of John Lawrence Tierney) is another writer who has continued to publish and mature since the appearance of his early book, *Cookabundy Bridge*, in 1946. This has been succeeded by a novel, *The Advancement of Spencer Button* (1950), and a further collection of stories, *The Bunyip o, Barney's Elbow* (1956). Most of James's stories are set in the same locale – the country town and district of Cookabundy; in fact, he has created a small world of his own, which contains a good deal of wryly comic incident, some few pathetic misfits, and not a little subterranean violence. All James's narratives are subject to the restraint of a style which allows him to bring them to a neat resolution with no hint of melodrama or falsity.

Alan Marshall and Dal Stivens, among other short story writers who rose to prominence during the forties, resemble James in dealing mainly with the country. There the similarities end. Stivens is best known for his tall stories, which at their best achieve notable humorous success by dressing up the outback legends in a garb of hyperbole and racy speech. [14] Marshall is happier with different subjects and in another mode. He has a sure grasp on the lives of the very young, as attested to in stories like 'Tell Us About the Turkey, Jo', 'Crossing the Road', and 'How's Andy Going?'. The first and last of these provide the titles for volumes published in 1946 and 1956. Marshall has made another valuable contribution to shorter Australian fiction in his animal stories like 'Blow Carson, I Say' and 'The Gentleman'. In all his work he is an unashamed optimist, sometimes to the point of sentimentality. To all his writing he brings the easy, unforced air of the bushman about to spin a relaxing yarn. These qualities are carried over into the genre wherein Marshall has made his most individual contribution to Australian prose – autobiography. *I Can Jump Puddles* (1955) and *This Is the Grass* (1962) represent his most substantial work. His single attempt at a novel, *How Beautiful Are Thy Feet* (1949), cannot be accounted a complete success. It is set in a Melbourne boot factory during the Depression years; and again it manifests the problem which has plagued practically every Australian writer of social protest fiction – how to reconcile political belief with direct understanding of character.

Towards the end of the forties, the balance of power in Australian fiction shifted back from the short story to the novel. For convenience' sake, the rise of the exciting new developments in the post-war Australian novel might be dated from 1948, the year of publication of Patrick White's *The Aunt's Story*. On his own merits, White, it might be argued, is the first indisputably great novelist that Australia has produced, the first whose work can properly be judged in an international rather than a national forum. His writing is considered in detail elsewhere in this book, so it is not necessary to do so here. However, in the fifties White did not stand alone; he was very much at the centre of a movement which raised the general standard of Australian fiction to hitherto unattained heights. It will, therefore, be of some value to indicate the qualities that he shares with other writers who have contributed to the spectacular advances in prose narrative during the past ten to fifteen years.

What is probably White's most important contribution to the general development of Australian fiction has been neatly indicated by John Rorke, when he suggests that, before White, Australian novelists used their plots as a means of *celebrating* their subject matter, whereas White uses his as a means of *discovering* the meaning of his material. More strenuously, probably, than any previous Australian novelist, White has brought to his writing

the feeling that art is a very serious thing, a grace and a burden.
('Patrick White and the Critics', *Southerly*, 1959, no. 2, p. 66)

By the strength and controlled complexity of his performance, White has communicated that feeling to many of his contemporaries. If he has had widespread influence on the approach of Australian novelists to their art form, his influence on their style has been scarcely less significant. It has been of a kind best described in his own words when he wrote of the purposes which moved him to compose a book like *Voss* (1957): 'Above all, I was determined to prove that the Australian novel is not necessarily the dreary, dun-coloured off-spring of journalistic realism'. [15] There can be little doubt that he succeeded. *Capricornia, The Pea Pickers, The Young Desire It* had made tentative stylistic innovations, had prepared the way for later linguistic experiments. But it was not until White's novels of the fifties that Australian fiction was granted a full-scale demonstration of a literary mode which did not begin and end in objective, or social, realism. And the impact of White's daring handling of language has been strong enough to move other writers to attempt similar goals.

Just as important as the new dimensions that White has added to the language of Australian fiction is his enlarged concept of character. A figure like Voss, for instance, is immediately remarkable for the scale on which he is imagined and depicted. Whether he be adjudged good or evil, there is no denying his heroic – his larger-than-life-size – stature. This fact, too, is in marked contrast to the typical novels of even the near past. The highest aim of their protagonists is to be of equal stature with the men and women who surround them. Voss's overweening ambition, his prideful exaltation of the individual will, expresses itself not only in his assaults on his fellows but also in his effort to achieve mastery over nature. Voss 'accepted his own divinity' (p. 154); the land 'is his by right of vision' (p. 32). His determination to bend even the Australian land to his own desires presents a thoroughly opposed aim to the purposes of, say, a typical Palmer hero, whose chief wish is to live with his environment rather than to master it; to give himself over to the flow of nature, not to make it subservient to his human strength.

Such inordinate ambition is likely to lead a man to a life of both inner and outer violence; and White's protagonists regularly live to the very limit of their resources. In this, too, they are representative of new forces at work within the tradition of Australian fiction. The novel of the twenties and thirties by no means avoided violence, but it is typically an overt violence – excited and exciting physical action, conflict engendered through the heightening of normal passions, and so on. In the post-war novel, the violence is often located in the characters themselves rather than in their relations with the outside world. In formulating instances of extreme behaviour, the post-war novelists are for the first time incorporating metaphysical analysis as a significant element in the Australian novel. In the fifties, to understand man in purely ethical, social, or political terms was no longer enough. When viewing *homo australiensis* under this light, White in particular has found him not entirely pleasing. Indeed, his recent fiction has been marked by an increasingly bitter assessment of Australian life. Although his satirical thrusts may at times lack charity, they are still symptomatic of a further advance in the novel – the more frequent admission of satire into the canon of successfully achieved art.

It might seem, on the face of it, that the deepened concerns and more highly developed technique of the Australian novel since 1948 have been won at the expense of repudiating some of the central elements of the tradition established after World War I. To a degree, this is true, but only to a degree. Certain social attitudes and subject matters have been called into question, but a continuing and continuous tradition has been guaranteed by the retention of the major fictional forms developed in the twenties and thirties. The saga, the picaresque, and the documentary have been bent into some strange new shapes, but their fundamental outlines still seem capable of containing Australian fiction as it seeks after new imaginative insights. What, after all, is *The Tree of Man* but a two-generation saga? What *Voss* but an historical chronicle? What, even, *The Aunt's Story* but bizarre picaresque? And it could be argued with some validity that all the major post-war novels pursue their several ends within the structural conventions crystallized during the preceding quarter century. The tradition which was hammered out in the years following 1918 apparently retains sufficient vigour, suppleness and harmony with the modern mind to continue as the formal basis of the most adventurous Australian writing.

Two of the younger writers who have been most closely identified with Patrick White in the new directions taken by Australian fiction are Randolph Stow and Christopher Koch.[16] Of the two, Stow has so far made the more substantial contribution, having published four novels to Koch's one. All of Stow's books are situated in Western Australia – in the Geraldton district, or further north into the Kimberleys. His treatment of landscape is one of the most striking features of his prose. That his talent in this regard goes beyond graphic description is suggested by the title of his first novel, *A Haunted Land* (1956). Poetic evocation of landscape is consistently linked with the tortured quality of the lives which are played out on its surface. In *A Haunted Land* and *The Bystander* (1957) the setting serves as both atmospheric accompaniment to and partial explanation of the violent actions and emotions which compose their plots. In *To the Islands* (1958) the land assumes even greater importance. The disillusioned missionary, Heriot, journies into the heart of the land; and his physical journey becomes an extended metaphor for the discovery of his own soul. It is a journey which, in the end, takes him 'to the islands', the native phrase for death.

All of Stow's novels take place, as it were, in a haunted land; but it is haunted less by the ghosts of the past than by the unquiet spirits of the present. If landscape helps to provide the books with their prevailing emotional tone, their dominant theme is that of disintegration brought about by self-destructive pressures within the individual. In *A Haunted Land* Andrew Maguire rages against the early death of his wife, and in insanely demanding the love and loyalty of his children succeeds only in destroying the family. Heriot, tortured by his doubts, deliberately walks out of his mission to die. No Australian novelist has had a more vivid awareness than Stow of the obsessive, irrational needs of the human heart; none has been able to render them at a higher pitch of tension and personal tragedy.

Stow's major characters are all driven beings. In themselves, they are driven to self-destruction; as literary creations, they are driven into the same kind of heroic stature as White's protagonists. In this fact lies one of the chief differences between Stow and Koch. The central figure of Koch's novel, *The Boys in the Island* (1958), is of much more domestic proportions. He is not, however, lacking in sensitivity. Indeed, the novel is primarily the inner biography from childhood to late adolescence of Francis Cullen, who is distinguished from his companions mainly by his more active imagination. The novel opens with a small boy's dream; and to the end, no matter what the claims of the outside world, never forsakes its commitment to the inner life.

In its concentration on youthful experience and in its exploitation of the emotional texture of language, *The Boys in the Island* has some features in common with Mackenzie's *The Young Desire It*. But its emphasis is its own: the concern for the private world of the imagination rather than relationships with others, the sense that there is something special and irreplaceable in the experience of childhood and youth. One of Francis's companions, Shane Noonan, suicides on discovering the dullness and frustrations of adult life. In the end of the book, after a drunken party culminating in a car crash, and after returning from Melbourne to his native Tasmania, Francis is left making the same discovery. *The Boys in the Island* has the distinction of being one of the most consistently and sensitively inner-oriented of Australian novels. It may be, too, that it derives some of its conviction from the fusion of two recurring themes of Australian fiction – adolescence and a profound hopelessness in the face of experience.

The Boys in the Island is a deliberately subjective novel. Hal Porter has pushed the Australian novel even further along the same path. He might be described as a stylist of marginal sensitivity and a chronicler of the marginal sensibility. On the first count, he has conducted some of the most daring stylistic experiments of any Australian prose writer. His richly jewelled diction and convoluted syntax are not a function of dramatic mood and necessity; they provide a means of imposing the writer's temperament on his material. The style, in effect, becomes a vehicle for authorial comment, not a technique for rendering plot and character. Porter's main characters are, in themselves, of a somewhat special kind. In both his novels – *A Handful of Pennies* (1958) and *The Tilted Cross* (1961) – his sympathies are most strongly aligned with the socially or psychologically eccentric. *A Handful of Pennies* presents a gallery of portraits drawn from the Occupation Forces in Japan. *The Tilted Cross* is formally an historical novel (it is set in Hobart of the convict period), but it is less concerned to understand its characters in the context of early Australian society than to develop their latent grotesquerie as thoroughly as possible. The grotesques, however, are not merely exhibited as carnival freaks. They create the mode which makes viable the mythic theme of the novel, a theme of pity and love embodied in a startling use of Christian symbolism. In the close relation between its manner, its symbolism, and its narrative, *The Tilted Cross* is a much more tightly organized work than *A Handful of Pennies* and, partly for that reason, a more successful one. Porter on occasion can suffer from the faults of a too *recherché* attitude towards his material, but there can be no doubt that he is one of the most arresting stylists to appear in Australia since the Second World War.

Stow, Koch, and Porter are those most frequently grouped with White as constituting something of a 'movement' (certainly not a 'school') in Australian fiction during the fifties. What gives their writing some sense of common purpose are the exploitation of style as the definitive element of their art, an increasingly sophisticated manipulation of structure, and a conception of character not anchored to its social and environmental determinants. They also have in common the fact that nearly all their best work has been written in Australia, has been set in Australia, and has been based on some solidly established formal conventions. In so far as their work has represented a challenge to some hitherto dominant elements in Australian fiction, it has been a challenge from within. There is another group of writers (neither a movement nor a school) whose work can be fairly said to constitute a challenge from without. Foremost among them is Martin Boyd. Boyd's career in fiction started in 1925, when he published *Love Gods* under the nom de plume of Martin Mills. Since then his works have appeared in a steady stream, but it seems fair to say that it was not until after World War II that he started to make any important impact on Australian audiences. In 1946, for instance, *Lucinda Brayford* brought him some favourable attention. But the pinnacle of his achievement to date is the tetralogy of *The Cardboard Crown* (1952), *A Difficult Young Man* (1955), *Outbreak of Love* (1957) and *When Blackbirds Sing* (1962).

Right from the very beginning of his career, Boyd has been successful in making literary capital out of a theme that for most Australian writers has been the occasion for *ex parte* argument – the relation between Australia and the parent culture of England and Europe. Adopting neither an offensively Australian bias nor what A.A. Phillips has described as 'the cultural cringe', [17] Boyd has made the tension between old and new the very centre of his subject matter. The characteristic formula of his novels is of a well-to-do pioneering family, studied through several generations, and in their peregrinations between England and Australia. The state room of a P & O liner represents, as it were, the cultural fulcrum of Boyd's art. The competing claims of their English and

Australian homes is one of the chief concerns of the Langton family, whose history from approximately 1860 to 1920 provides the main story line of the tetralogy. A wealthy Melbourne family, they have close European connections, and work out two distinct modes of conduct appropriate to England and Australia.

Boyd himself was born in Switzerland, but belongs to an emigrant Australian family. That his pursuit of his Jamesian theme sets out from an Australian base is adequately suggested by the sentence from Proust which opens *The Cardboard Crown*: 'When we have passed a certain age, the soul of the child that we were, and the souls of the dead from whom we spring, come and bestow upon us in handfuls their treasures and their calamities'. Both Guy Langton, the narrator of *The Cardboard Crown*, and Martin Boyd are sufficiently aware of their Australian childhood and ancestry to leave no doubt of the cultural mainspring of their lives. However, the Jamesian quality of Boyd's work is not restricted to the inter-cultural theme. It is equally to be apprehended in his manipulation of his material. The events of the tetralogy are filtered through the mind of the writer, Guy Langton, who becomes the centre of consciousness for the whole series. He has personal recollections of some of its episodes, has to rely on diaries and reminiscences for others, and is perpetually aware of the colouring lent by youth, age, or special circumstances to the evidence which he reports. As he writes himself, in *A Difficult Young Man*, 'It appears to me that as I proceed with this story I am revealing not only the events of that time, but a process in my own mind, which in turn affects what I record' (p. 53). In the course of these four books, Boyd has achieved a subtle mastery over the technique of the multiple point of view, a mastery unrivalled by any other Australian novelist.

The themes of cosmopolitanism, time, and the irrationality of history are potentially weighty subjects for fiction. Yet a further great virtue of Boyd's writing is the deftness with which he handles them. Perhaps because of his assured temperamental conservatism, Boyd has developed a more consistently urbane style than is to be found elsewhere in Australian prose. His whole work is informed with the sense of a sprightly and acute intelligence which, instead of addressing itself immediately to ideas, plays with unerring assurance over the manners and *mores*, the whole fabric of Anglo-Australian society.

Such a disinterested pleasure in social understanding is rare indeed among Australian novelists, and can perhaps be put down to Boyd's long-sustained contacts with other cultures. Other Australian writers who have striven to advance the Australian novel through overseas alignments have produced qualities quite different. Elizabeth Harrower, for instance, sets her second novel, *The Catherine Wheel* (1961), in London, but social analysis is of only minor interest to her. *The Catherine Wheel* is essentially a love story, and it proclaims the Australian origins of its author, if at all, not through any overt discussion of nationality, but through the deployment of certain themes and attitudes. It is the story of an Australian girl in London and her destructively romantic love for an out-of-work English actor. If an affiliation is sought with any earlier Australian novels, the one which most readily suggests itself is Richardson's *Maurice Guest*. In the main, however, Elizabeth Harrower seems sufficiently sure of herself to ignore her Australian background as a conscious item of her creative apparatus. If it finds its way into her work, it does so unbidden. Essentially, *The Catherine Wheel* is an intense and dramatically realized account of a love affair catastrophic in its emotional demands on its heroine.

If there is any Australian writer who consciously rejects his Australian background for the sake of competing unhampered on the international scene, it is Morris West. *The Devil's Advocate* (1959) and *Daughter of Silence* (1961) are both set in southern Italy; both deal with themes chosen deliberately for their universal relevance. *The Devil's Advocate* is the first Australian novel of any stature to make literature out of Christian doctrine. The theme of *Daughter of Silence* is more ethical in nature – the nature and operation of justice. In the comparisons which he seems to invite (Graham Greene most obviously, with respect to *The Devil's Advocate*), West may not always be the winner, yet he clearly wishes his art to be judged before an international rather than a purely Australian tribunal.

It was hardly to be expected that such varied and powerful challenges to some of the chief elements of the Australian tradition of fiction should go unanswered. In fact, the years since the Second World War have produced their quota of books whose aim is the adequate performance of familiar tasks rather than the opening up of new directions. Further, it is possible to identify a group of social realists who are actively opposed to the beliefs and procedures of Patrick White and his tribe.[18] These writers continue to assert the values of objective realism as a fictional method and political radicalism as a socio-economic stance. Paradoxically, some of these disciples of progressivism have produced work which, alongside the aspirations of White, seems only colourless and old-fashioned. The best of them, perhaps jolted into competitive skill, have produced novels which exploit the methods of social realism with greater depth and acumen than ever before.

Frank Hardy's work is characteristic of the post-war social realists. The publication, in 1950, of his first novel, *Power Without Glory*, was attended with some notoriety: its author was brought to court on charges of criminal libel. That fact alone indicates the powerful muckraking motive which underlay Hardy's approach to writing. It is, in essence, an *exposé* of corruption in the domestic politics of Victoria. After the lapse of a decade, the impact of *Power Without Glory* has considerably diminished. Yet it still impresses as an honest, if clumsy, piece of work, unquestionably inspired by sincere indignation and a desire for reform. Hardy's chief literary strategy is thoroughly familiar in Australian writing – documentation, depending on an overwhelming accumulation of detail. Fiction, under the weight of such a technique, can easily collapse into a mass of undiscriminated data, unless it is buttressed by the author's immediate and passionate interest in his material. Hardy has enough of that kind of interest to retain for *Power Without Glory* some lasting merit as a work of art; its importance as a document in social history may in the long run be even greater.

Hardy has continued to write: short stories; another novel, *The Four Legged Lottery* (1958); autobiography, *The Hard Way* (1961). He has learnt to exercise a higher degree of discrimination and to order his narratives into more shapely patterns, but he has never forsaken his reforming zeal, his programmatic approach to literature. In his democratic attitudes he has been joined by a number of other writers, of more or less skill – F.B. Vickers, Ron Tullipan, Donald Stuart, for example. However, one of the most meritorious contributions to this strand of post-war writing comes from David Martin. A Hungarian by birth, he arrived in this country after the War, and soon acclimatized himself to the

literary scene, aligning himself, in general terms, with the up
holders of the democratic theme. His versions of that theme
display a power and depth equal to any produced by native born
Australians of his generation. His most recent novel, *The Young
Wife* (1962), is arguably the best book in this tradition to appear
in Australia since 1945. Its plot is centred in the lives of migrants
in Melbourne, particularly the Greek and Cypriot communities.
Martin's observation ranges through their clubs, their football
matches, their efforts at cultural assimilation. The several strands
of the novel are drawn together in the narrative of Anna, the
young wife who has come out to marry Yannis Joannides. Out
of her life with her husband, her brother- and sister-in-law, her
friendship with the ex-terrorist Criton, there develops a story
whose climax is tragedy and which ends with the hope of new life
in the birth of her child. The balance between creation and
destruction which runs through the whole novel has its symbolic
counterpart in the staging of Euripides's *Alcestis*, an important
episode in the plot. The classical drama, however, is not experienced as an imposed piece of technical apparatus but as an
integral part of the created lives of the characters. In *The Young
Wife*, Martin approaches the level of tragedy, but he starts from
and never wholly forsakes the observable behaviour of all his
characters. More adequately than any other book of the previous
decade, it vindicates the realistic mode as a means of creating a
powerful and profound work of literature.

Judah Waten has never attempted fiction of the magnitude and
penetration of *The Young Wife*, but in all his work he has exhibited a considerable ability to report on social experience in the
sharply defined black and white of the documentary. His most
recent novel, *Time of Conflict* (1961) can stand as the prototype
of a number of left-wing novels of the fifties. It is set in the
Depression years and follows the career of Mick Anderson, who,
being economically underprivileged, suffers the harsh repressions
of a class-minded economy and legal system. In predictable
reaction against a society which exploits and rejects him, Anderson becomes a Communist, discovering the necessary pattern of
his life in working for social and political reform. For something
like two-thirds of *Time of Conflict*, Waten succeeds in making
Anderson's political attitudes an integral part of the fiction.
Where he fails is in the years of his hero's success, when the

youthful aspirations come up against the actualities of political manoeuvring.

In his short stories, Waten has aimed at more modest targets and has achieved more uniform success. The technique is still based on description of external fact, but it seems to be more happily adapted to the almost plotless vignette which is a typical Waten story. His sequence of such scenes from observed life in *Alien Son* (1952) is especially memorable. The book owes its interest, in part, to the subject matter itself. The pieces make up a loosely connected account of the life of a Jewish boy and his migrant parents in pre-war Australia. In general, the social realists have had more success in the short story than in the novel. Their capacity to handle the shorter form is witnessed by the two collections entitled *The Tracks We Travel*, as well as by the work of Martin and Hardy in this mode. But the realistic short story has had no finer exponent since the War than John Morrison. Morrison has written several novels – *The Creeping City* (1949) and *Port of Call* (1950) – as well as short stories. But it is in the latter form that his work is seen at his best. His latest collection, *Twenty-Three* (1962), is thoroughly characteristic. [19] In it are to be found examples of Morrison's best loved themes and subjects. He writes of the waterside workers, their occupations and political beliefs (a subject he had notably treated in the earlier, well-known 'Going Through'). Elsewhere, in a story like 'Black Night in Collingwood', he deals with the domestic lives of working men; 'To Margaret' reveals a more sentimental side of Morrison, his affection for people and love of natural things. All the stories are infused with an unassuming but penetrating understanding of human behaviour; their art consists in bringing the understanding so close to the surface of an apparently simple technique that it is transparently and immediately available to the reader.

If the stories in *Twenty-Three* represent one important element in our current literature at its most attractive, qualities of an entirely different nature are resumed with equal adequacy in Hal Porter's collection, *A Bachelor's Children* (1962). Written over a period of something like twenty years, these stories provide an accurate gauge of the increasing influence of linguistic experiment, sophisticated wit, and a satire which singles out for attack bad taste, ugliness and stupidity. Brilliance is not a word that comes readily to mind with respect to the bulk of Australian short stories, even the good ones. But at their best, Porter's stories are undoubtedly brilliant performances, with a high degree of conscious virtuosity. Between them, *Twenty-Three* and *A Bachelor's Children* represent the two extremes in the range of the current Australian short story. If E. O. Schlunke's two volumes – *The Man in the Silo* (1955) and *The Village Hampden* (1958) – are taken to represent the mean between the two limits, then these three writers can be thought of as providing a cross-section of the best that has been done in this genre since the War.

If the history of Australian fiction in the fifties can be largely interpreted as a set of creative pressures and counter-pressures brought about by the advent of a number of new writers, it would be wrong to think of the period as belonging entirely to the new men. During those years a solid contribution was made by a number of writers who had served their apprenticeship in the craft before 1939. It was not until after the War, for instance, that Katharine Susannah Prichard and Vance Palmer essayed what are perhaps their most ambitious projects in fiction. Unfortunately, with Prichard ambition no longer equalled accomplishment. Her trilogy – *The Roaring Nineties* (1946), *Golden Miles* (1948), *Winged Seeds* (1950) – aims at providing a comprehensive, fictionalized history of the West Australian Goldfields, filtered through a Marxist view of the class struggle. The trilogy fails as literature because of its immense overburden of material. [20] It carries all the documentary weight of *Power Without Glory*, but hardly ever delivers the sense of passionate stir which saves Hardy's prose. Palmer's trilogy is relatively more successful. *Golconda* (1948), *Seedtime* (1957) and *The Big Fellow* (1959) chart the career of Macy Donovan from his beginnings as a union organizer on an outback mining field to his assumption of the highest political power, as Premier of his State. As usual with Palmer, these books seem to have in spite of their length only modest aspirations – to tell what the author sees as the truth of the situation as directly and accurately as possible. Yet they do provide a convincing account of the patterns of political power, not least because public life is continually being intermingled with private relationships. Macy Donovan is essentially a politician, but Palmer does not delineate the political features of the man to the exclusion of all others.

Prichard and Palmer were not the only writers to extend their careers through the war years into the fifties. In 1959 Leonard Mann published his *Andrea Caslin*. Eleanor Dark's good humoured *Lantana Lane* appeared (with the air of a distinct lowering of pressure) in the same year. In works like *Time Enough Later* (1943), *Ride on Stranger* (1943), and *The Honey Flow* (1956), Kylie Tennant continued to mine the lode of Australian picaresque – with virtually no development of technique but with unabated verve and common sense. Dymphna Cusack produced *Say No to Death* (1951) and *Southern Steel* (1953). Before his unhappily early death, Seaforth Mackenzie contributed two further novels to the sum of Australian fiction – *Dead Men Rising* (1951) and *The Refuge* (1954). The former, one of the most interesting of Australian war novels, is based on the uprising of Japanese prisoners in Cowra, N.S.W. *The Refuge* takes its title from the sanctuary afforded by Australia to the Europeans who fled from Hitler's Germany. The public theme is reinforced and mirrored by the relationship between the hero, a journalist, and a refugee girl. In both novels, Mackenzie continued to manifest a style at once evocative, supple, and sinewy. In both he showed a real advance in powers of narrative construction and a willingness to explore the violence within the individual as a source of insight and understanding.

Of all the pre-war novelists who continued to write after 1945, none has added more considerably to his stature than Xavier Herbert. *Seven Emus* (1959), a slight and relatively unsuccessful piece, was followed in 1961 by the massive *Soldiers' Women*. *Soldiers' Women* is set in a wartime city in eastern Australia – clearly modelled on Sydney. Its pleasure seeking women and hordes of American servicemen furnish Herbert with sufficient violent action and enough plots to equal the profusion of *Capricornia*. However, the various narratives are held together in a much more satisfying design than in the earlier novel, and for several reasons. For one thing, Herbert has learned to exercise a much stricter structural control over his material. He is at pains to create a stable framework (indicated by such unifying symbols as the flashing lighthouse) for the wildly fluctuating fortunes of his central characters. Further, the plots of *Soldiers' Women* illuminate and reinforce each other through their mutual dependence on a basic theme much more clearly than in

Capricornia. Soldiers' Women is developed as a complex piece of counterpoint on the motif of love. All its varieties from animal lust to the deepest spiritual affection find their way into the book, and are intensified by the desperate atmosphere of war.

Herbert's advance in architectural control is not the only significant development in this novel. The incipient and sometimes crude symbolism of *Capricornia* has now become a thoroughgoing stylistic mechanism for stating and clarifying his judgements of his theme. The battering rhetoric of *Soldiers' Women* varies from the mock- to the genuinely heroic; the whole apparatus of animal imagery is a consistent means of creating and evaluating character. In this novel Herbert has invented a powerful instrument for embodying his scientific humanism, a stylistic achievement as unique in its way as any of Patrick White's. The twin phenomena of *Soldiers' Women* and *Riders in the Chariot* are likely to make 1961 something of a landmark in the history of Australian fiction.

Thus, as the period under review came to a close, it was distinguished by the appearance of two of the most important novels of the post-war years. However, the current strength of the Australian novel does not depend entirely on isolated performances of major pretensions. Since the Second World War there has developed a broad base of solidly competent popular fiction, created by authors who make no inflated claims for their work but who do achieve a uniformly high level of craft skill. Novelists like D'Arcy Niland, Ruth Park, Jon Cleary, Tom Ronan, and Olaf Ruhen, for instance, do not attempt to write masterpieces. Yet they provide a matrix of fictional expertise in which the masterpieces may be more easily nourished. Perhaps an even more encouraging sign of the health of Australian fiction in the early 1960s is a phenomenon noted by Nancy Keesing [21] – the number of very good, minor novelists who are getting into print. There is, for example, Ethel Anderson's charming set of comic vignettes, *At Parramatta* (1956); or the sensitive regionalism of Colin Thiele's *The Sun on the Stubble* (1961); or the poetic vision of the land in Frank Kellaway's *A Straight Furrow* (1961); or the acute social insight of George Turner's *A Stranger and Afraid* (1961).

A common feature of the work of many of the younger writers is an individual self-assurance which allows them to escape from the conscious national purposes of the novelists of the twenties and thirties. Often they escape into that interest in the texture of society which has long been recognized as one of the central features of English fiction. The point is neatly brought home in the three novels so far produced by Thea Astley – *Girl with a Monkey* (1958), *A Descant of Gossips* (1960), and *The Well Dressed Explorer* (1962). The fascination with the dynamics of social behaviour is not always disinterested; satire, a branch of fiction in which Australian writing has been markedly deficient, is also finding new vitality. In the early 1960s a satirical vision is not only playing an increasingly important role in White's novels or Porter's stories; it is finding expression in such works as Robert Burns's *Mr Brain Knows Best* (1959) and David Forrest's *The Hollow Woodheap* (1962).

It is to be hoped that the increasing incidence of satire is the sign of a society sufficiently self-confident to tolerate and respect criticism of its own institutions and practices. A further hopeful sign of the maturing of Australian literary culture is to be found in the concurrence of this often harshly satirical critique with a vision that can properly be called tragic. For novels like *Voss*, *Soldiers' Women*, *The Tilted Cross*, and *The Young Wife* do propose the standards of tragedy as the appropriate critical criteria by which they should be judged. Whatever the state of Australian culture at the end of the period under review, it is clear that in terms of achieved works of fiction, in complexity of technique and judgement, and in the scope and depth of the fictional environment, it was far more richly endowed than at the beginning. Nevertheless, if the novels and short stories of the twenties and thirties have begun to pale as they recede into the past, high honour should still be accorded them, both collectively and individually. It was the men and women who committed themselves to writing in the years after World War I who, for the first time, created a coherent tradition of Australian fiction; a tradition which has grown steadily and continuously ever since and which, although repudiated in some of its particulars, continues to provide a firm basis for the achievements of the present and the promise of the future.

HARRY HESELTINE

NOTES

1. Miles Franklin's letter is quoted in an article by Marjorie Barnard, 'Miles Franklin', *Meanjin*, 1955, no. 4, p. 470.

2. Russel Ward, 'Vance Palmer: *Homo Australiensis*', *Meanjin*, 1959, no. 2, p. 240. Russel Ward acknowledges T. Inglis Moore as the source of the comment cited here.

3. Marjorie Barnard, a personal friend of Miles Franklin, accepts her identification as Brent of Bin Bin in the *Meanjin* article cited above. So does Beatrice Davis, chief reader for Angus &Robertson, writing in *Southerly*, 1955, no. 2 pp. 83-5.

4. The five related Brent of Bin Bin novels, in order of publication (which does not follow the chronological sequence of the plot) are: *Up the Country* (1928), *Ten Creek Run* (1930), *Back to Bool Bool* (1931), *Cockatoos* (1954) and *Gentlemen at Gyang Gyang* (1956) Brent wrote a sixth novel, *Prelude to Waking* (1950), which bears only a very slight relation to the main chronical series.

5. Palmer's first published fiction was the collection of short stories, *The World Of Men*, which appeared in 1915. His work before 1920 is considered elsewhere in this guide.

6. Prichard's letter is quoted in an article by Henrietta Drake-Brockman, 'Katharine Susannah Prichard: The Colour in Her Work', *Southerly*, 1953, no. 4, p. 215. Drake-Brockman's remark occurs in the same article, on p. 216.

7. Norman Bartlett, 'Winds of Change in the Australian Novel', *Australian Quarterly*, December 1960, p. 82.

8. Eleanor Dark has written two sequels to *The Timeless Land*: *Storm of Time* (1948) and *No Barrier* (1953).

9. Since this chapter was written, Davison has collected 'The Good Herdsman' in *The Road to Yesterday* (1964).

10. Casey has written five novels: *Downhill Is Easier* (1945), *The Wits Are Out* (1947), *City of Men* (1950), *Snowball* (1958), and *Amid the Plenty* (1962).

11. 'The Hairy Men from Hannigan's Halt' is printed in *Coast to Coast, 1953-54*; 'The Irish Oafs from Ugly Gully', in *The Tracks We Travel*, 2nd series.

12. *Riverslake* (1953) and *Sowers of the Wind* (1954).

13. Evan Jones, 'The Anatomy of Frustration: Short Stories of Alan Davies and Peter Cowan', p. 21. Printed with Wallace-Crabbe, 'Order and Turbulence: the Poetry of Francis Webb', as Australian National University *Commonwealth Fund Lectures 1961*.

14. Stivens's most important short stories are collected in the following volumes: *The Tramp and Other Stories* (1936), *The Courtship of Uncle Henry* (1946), *The Gambling Ghost and Other Tales* (1953).

15. Patrick White, 'The Prodigal Son', *Australian Letters* i, no. 3 (April 1958), p. 40.

16. The connection has been most strongly urged by Vincent Buckley, in his article, 'In the shadow of Patrick White', *Meanjin*, 1961, no. 2, pp. 144-54.

17. See the essay, 'The Cultural Cringe' in A. A. Phillips, *The Australian Tradition: Studies in a Colonial Culture* (Melbourne, 1958), pp. 89–95.

18. See, for instance, David Martin, 'Among the Bones', *Meanjin*, 1959, no. 1, pp. 52-8.

19. Morrison's two earlier collections of short stories are *Sailors Belong Ships* (1947) and *Black Cargo* (1955).

20. I am registering, I think, a majority opinion of Prichard's Goldfields trilogy, but not a unanimous one. Jack Lindsay, for instance, in his article, 'The Novels of Katharine Susannah Prichard', *Meanjin*, 1961, no. 4, pp. 366–87, maintains that 'K.S.P. gets into her full creative stride with the trilogy'.

21. Nancy Keesing, 'Australia's "Unlucky" Novelists', *Southerly*, 1962, no. 2, pp. 84-9.

PART
II

THE COLONIAL POETS

BRIAN ELLIOTT

A CHANGE has taken place in the past quarter of a century in what readers have taken to be the nature and function of poetry in Australia. To some extent, it has amounted to a repudiation of the old anthologies for the excessive regard they paid to mediocrity, as though it had amazed and gratified their editors to discover that Australians had at any time shown themselves so fundamentally different from apes and monkeys as to possess any faculty at all for rhyming and rattling. Critically this is hardly a just view, but it may be understood to be more or less inevitable at present; it is merely the perspective of reaction that sets things in that light. If, however, one makes an effort to step beyond prejudice and attempt some kind of an interim, plain assessment of the period from which the anthologies drew most of their bulk if not their strength – yet perhaps some of that too – one is forced in candour to agree that, of a great deal once esteemed, only a little now seems worth preserving for intrinsic reasons, and a little more for historical ones. The question is, upon what principles to select them? The best way, it seems to me, to come to a quick but sound and just evaluation of the Colonial [1] period as a whole, is to single out for notice some half-dozen poets, three of whom – Harpur, Kendall, Gordon – may be considered in their context major writers, the rest interesting and influential minor ones, and leave the preliminary examination at that. It should not, however, rest there permanently; interest in Colonial history must eventually become more consuming, and as the perspective clears the demand will be for a broader range and more precise knowledge. These few principals, however, we may be sure will remain. When inquiry goes beyond them – when the anthologies themselves come under examination, when the newspapers and journals of the day are recovered from dust to trace trends and developments (if not for the discovery of forgotten treasure), then we may suppose the nature of the interest will have broadened and developed; the quarry will be poetry, not merely the poets; history, culture, the frontier itself. This survey is only concerned with the poets; it is accordingly limited to the

227

few individuals among them who stand out, Harpur, Kendall, Gordon, and the attendant figures of J.B. Stephens, G.G. McCrae, and George Essex Evans. These are all Colonial Romantics, and belong entirely to the nineteenth century in sentiment and outlook. Other names might be added but these seem fully typical and sufficient to outline the essential characteristics of the period. It would be appropriate to include some estimate of the importance of Colonial ballad poetry, both of the 'folk-song' and *The Bulletin* types, which provides a lively background to more consciously literary poetry throughout the period. But that is a large subject and demands separate treatment; which will be found elsewhere in this volume. Here I must confine myself to paying a tribute to the vitality of the ballad, which assuredly had a tremendous effect upon the course of poetic development at all levels of sophistication in its day, and whose impact is even now only beginning to be accurately assessed. It has necessarily had to be excluded from discussion here.

*

Charles Harpur (1813-68)

As a poet Harpur was neither great nor glorious, but he did truly describe himself as 'an Australian'. [2] Unlike most other Australian poets, he lived almost all his life in the country. Yet in spite of the poverty of his colonial education and the rarity of his sophisticated contacts, his was a literary mind and imagination, and poetry was his life. He followed several careers – schoolmaster, sheepfarmer, government official – and seems to have been competent at all, but was only happy in the exercise of his imagination and sensibilities; an attitude not easy to sustain under pioneering conditions. It was his personal distinction, but his Colonial cross, that he had to work out his problems for the most part quite alone. He had an articulate brother and was in touch with literary friends in Sydney: but he seems to have been retiring by disposition, and always most at ease in the company of his two passionate inspirations, nature and the English poets. He married, but after long delays: as a young man he promised to be a better poet than provider, as his early sonnets suggest. [3] Poetry absorbed him, and he wrote it constantly. Of what he left, only a comparatively little is really first rate, even by Colonial standards, but there is a quality in his least distinguished verse that is very remarkable in such a man, living at such a time. He seems to have *thought* poetically; at any crisis, he turned to poetry for expression and relief, if it were merely to scribble a few lines which he later threw away. His sensitivity was in excess of his originality, and yet that must not be too severely minimized: it was an original enough way of assimilating Colonial experience, to make poetry of it. The life seems to have dried up his emotions somewhat, and his shy disposition perhaps prevented him from enlarging them by fruitful contact with society. In his later pieces especially he conveys an impression of lively intelligence and a manly morale; but also a touch of hypersensitivity offset by grievance, a too ready acceptance of inevitable defeat. His long work 'Genius Lost', [4] ostensibly concerned with the sorrows of Thomas Chatterton, reflects this mood. But before a Colonial poet is blamed for such a retreat from glory, we should fairly assess the odds against him; they were heavy.

It is an inference easily gathered from his writings, that his childhood was free and happy, his youth less so, and his maturity troubled and frustrated. But how ordinary a Colonial pattern this was! It seems clear that his most serene poems were either written early, or reflect early experience. His well known 'Midsummer Noon' is the poetry of a boyhood rapture. The descriptive poem 'A Storm in the Mountains', begins thus:

> A lonely boy, far venturing from home
> Out on the half-wild herd's faint tracks I roam;
> 'Mid rock-browed mountains, which with stony frown
> Glare into haggard chasms deep adown;
> A rude and craggy world, the prospect lies
> Bounded in circuit by the bending skies . . .

To point out that his childhood was spent in intimate communion with rivers, hills and crags, is not to make a Wordsworthian of him; he did what other Colonial boys did, gazing 'with a keen wondering happiness' ('A Coast View'), on every new prospect. But as literary experience opened up to him, naturally he found Wordsworth congenial. He admired and emulated him; but other literary influences also appear – Coleridge, Keats, and especially Shelley. Even so, Harpur's romanticism is conservative, and still retains something of an earlier cast; there is more of Gray or Collins in it than of – for example, Tennyson, his contemporary. His versification is sober and steady, with an eighteenth-century reticence, though he handles blank verse very freely and at times quite beautifully. We may admire the virtuosity of a Colonial poet who can at the same time discipline his verse, and give it the relaxed tone of simple unaffected speech:

> My dear, dear Charley! can it be that thou
> Art gone from us for ever? Whilst I sit
> Amid these forest shadows that now fall
> In sombre masses mixed with sunny gleams
> Upon thy early grave, and think of all
> The household love that was our mutual lot
> So late, and during all thy little life –
>
> (From a *Monody* on the death of his son)

The best and most spontaneous writings of Harpur are in blank verse, and in a similarly quiet tone; he is not easily represented in short fragments, for that reason.

Harpur was beset by the dilemma which troubled all Colonial poets: which audience to address? What subjects to choose? Ambition spurned the boorish Colonial mob and craved literary laurels, the reward of literary endeavour. But romantic beauty is romantic truth, and how shall the Colonial poet fare if he deserts what he knows and understands, for what is expected by the sophisticated, but beyond the range of his experience? Quantitatively, ambition generally prevailed; yet time has given the victory to quality. In general, only that part of Harpur's poetry which treats of Australian subjects seems to have any prospect of survival. Elaborately planned and carefully executed poems like 'The Tower of the Dream' or 'The Witch of Hebron' have only the interest of Colonial curiosities; but a poem like 'The Creek of the Four Graves', a plain blank verse narrative of a tragic incident in pioneering life – an attack by natives on a party of landseekers – belongs permanently to the Australian repertoire. Though short, it is a kind of miniature Australian epic in effect; but it achieves this power through simple meditative sincerity and plain narrative, not from any ambitious literary pre-arrangement of the effects. The poet speaks of a known and loved landscape:

> Before them, thus extended, wilder grew
> The scene each moment and more beautiful;

> For when the sun was all but sunk below
> Those barrier mountains, in the breeze that o'er
> Their rough enormous backs deep-fleeced with wood
> Came whispering down, the wide up-slanting sea
> Of fanning leaves in the descending rays
> Danced dazzlingly, tingling as if the trees
> Thrilled to the roots for very happiness . . .

– but this poem, too, should be taken as a whole, and not split into fragments. A poem like 'The Dream by the Fountain' is interesting because it exhibits the indecision of the poet's mind. 'Thought-weary and sad', he retreats in classic style to the lonely bush and sleeps by a waterhole (which he calls a fountain); there he is visited by 'the muse of the evergreen forest', replete with lyre, who proceeds to soothe and encourage him, exhorting him to

> Be then the Bard of thy Country! O rather
> Should such be thy choice than a monarchy wide!

Whereupon, mute with love, he gazes upon her 'soul-moulded charms':

> Deeper they glowed, her lips trembled, and, sighing,
> She rushed to my heart and dissolved in my arms!

'So perish all artificial poetry!' was the sentiment of some of his critics. Kendall thought 'The Tower of the Dream' a literary triumph. But G. B. Barton was more discerning. He praised 'The Creek of the Four Graves', but said of the rest:

Suffering in the first instance from a narrow culture, he never seems, unfortunately, to have found the limits of his power, nor the direction in which it lay.

(Barton, *Poets and Prose Writers of New South Wales*, 1866)

It was true. But it was true of others besides Harpur.

*

Henry Kendall (1839-82)

Harpur was twenty-six when Kendall was born, but there was some similarity in their background and a fairly intimate literary friendship developed between them. Both represented a New South Wales point of view. The earlier settlement still retained the thread of its association with the eighteenth century; its cultural roots were pre-Romantic. Melbourne was entirely a nineteenth century and (the pun is unavoidable) Victorian foundation; its outlook was post-Romantic. There is a continuity between Harpur and Kendall which is broken when we come to Gordon.

Kendall's childhood was spent among mountains. The death of his father brought misfortune to his family, but, while it seems to have made a lonely wanderer of him, brought him into contact with a landscape which was to dwell with him all his life. At the age of fifteen he went to sea for two years on a whaling cruise, as cabin boy in a ship owned by his uncle. But except for the poem 'Beyond Kerguelen', which conveys no biographical information – though it remains one of his best impressionistic mood-poems – nothing much came of this experience. Returning to Sydney, he found common-place employment and began to write verse. The fluency of his verses at once brought him to the notice of a small circle of literary personalities in Sydney. Henry Parkes published some of his verses in *The Empire*, and by 1861 there were proposals for the publication of a volume. *Poems and Songs* appeared in 1862. In the meantime he had managed to interest the editor of the London *Athenaeum* (the *Cornhill* turned him down), who published a few pieces and made some encouraging remarks. [5] These, no doubt, Kendall over-rated, since afterwards he never ceased to complain about

> the life austere
> That waits upon the man of letters here.
> (*Selected Poems of Henry Kendall*, 1957, p. 41, also 51, 70)

When the encouragement of such friends as Parkes, J.L. Michael and Henry Halloran failed to create a literary living for him, he went to Melbourne, where he met congenial friends at the Yorick Club, but had no better success. Indeed, Melbourne proved a hopeless, heartless commercial city; in Sydney, with good friends to urge it, a poet might hope for recognition and a government situation. Harpur had been appointed to the Gold Commission; Kendall himself held a minor clerkship before he left. Nor were the days of benevolence over. Returning to Sydney, he found a friendly pair of brothers, timber merchants, who gave him employment, sent him into the country far away from the demon alcohol, and made him and his family as comfortable as possible in the circumstances. But it was still austere.

Kendall's life story is depressing. It is true that any colonial 'man of letters' had a thin time of it, so long as he persisted in dedicating himself to so profitless a career. But it is hard to repress some impatience with Kendall's failings. He had no formed philosophy, no conspicuous intellect, only an abundance of poetical feeling and a heady, intoxicated taste for dactylic rhythms. [6] Yet this waste of his talent, rightly regarded, was pathetic or even tragic; one may ask in vain, what else – in the colonial circumstances – could have come of it? It is best, therefore, not to scrutinize too closely the man, but look only at the poetry – and only at the best of that.

His best is in a few poems, and they are mostly early, or at least not very late. His most ambitious poem was 'The Glen of Arawatta', which forms a kind of companionpiece to Harpur's 'Creek of the Four Graves'. It was several times revised, indicating that he rested his reputation upon it. It has some striking and moving passages. The following will represent its strength and weakness:

> There, in the shelter of a nameless Glen
> Fenced round by cedars and the tangled growths
> Of blackwood stained with brown and shot with grey,
> The jaded white man built his fire, and turned
> His horse adrift among the water-pools
> That trickled underneath the yellow leaves
> And made a pleasant murmur, like the brooks
> Of England through the sweet autumnal noons.

A splendid gift for verse and description is precipitated into bathos by a hopelessly inept simile. It is difficult to discover if it represented a naïve, literary longing in the poet – a hankering, after the lost European nostalgias, seemingly the common possession of all poets except the hapless Australian – or if it was part of a shady design, even more naïve and silly, to curry favour with English readers. Charity favours the former; but Kendall constantly repeated the tactic, as when in 'Bell-Birds' (one of his most evocative pieces), he irritatingly explains that spring comes at the wrong end of the year in Australia:

> The silver-voiced bell birds, the darlings of daytime!
> They sing in September, their song of the Maytime . . .

In 'Mooni', the month is not even named, but referred to as 'English April's sister'. But enough of these flaws and short comings; they do not prove conclusively that Kendall was a bad poet, only that he was a Colonial one, in whom the Colonial uncertainties had a devastating impact.

It would be possible to quote lines from Kendall to show how derivative he was – from E. A. Poe, from Shelley, from Tennyson or (but his style was formed before he discovered him) Swinburne. One could show from his competition poem, 'The Sydney International Exhibition'[7] (1879), that even so late his sense of fitness was so poor that he imagined formal poetry demanded an antithetical couplet style; or from the early 'The Muse of Australia' (inspired by Harpur's 'Dream by the Fountain'?), how easily contented he could be to repeat the most motheaten clichés and literary toys; and how completely devoid he was of a sense of the ridiculous:

> I know she is fair as the angels are fair,
> For have I not caught a faint glimpse of her there;
> A glimpse of her face, and her glittering hair,
> And a hand with the harp of Australia?

All this is fair enough; and yet something may be set against such destructive criticism. The core of Kendall's poetic sensibility is found in his failures. They are real, and so is his sense of them – or rather, so is his evaluation of failure as the predominating experience of Colonial art. Accordingly, what is destructible in him is easily destroyed; what is of more value needs some acuteness of perception, and much sympathy, for its appreciation. But it exists. In attempting to establish his own nostalgias, Kendall's most serious disappointment (or lapse) was in failing to define positively his native emotions. This was why he touched facts so lightly and embraced the excitements of metre so readily. Hypnotized by sheer poeticism, he attempted to bring the landscape he was familiar with, into line with the landscape he had never seen; and so really achieved objectivity in neither.[8] But if he thus fell between the stools, he was acutely aware of his own frustration. In the poem last quoted we find the lines –

> I never can reach you, to hear the sweet voice
> So full with the music of fountains!
> Oh! when will you meet with that soul of your choice,
> Who will lead you down here from the mountains?

– that is (to unravel the rhetoric), when will poetry learn to come down to earth in Australia, and to deal directly and simply with local experience? The traditional forms are too artificial; yet he cannot reject them absolutely. In a later context (two linked 'Prefatory Sonnets' in *Leaves from Australian Forests*, 1869) he confesses ruefully,

> I purposed once to take my pen and write,
> Not songs, like some, tormented and awry
> With passion,

– he means, like Gordon's, or those of the other quasi-European poets who insisted so often upon striking up in melancholy keys –

> but a cunning harmony
> Of words and music caught from glen and height,
> And lucid colours born of woodland light
> And shining places where the sea-streams lie. . . .

But the purpose did not hold. Why? The inspiration of glen and height, woodland, &c., was real and present; but the design misfired. He was not equal to it; not the facts, but the power to present them failed him. He explains his inability, since he cannot account for it otherwise, as a falling off of youth and energy:

> But this was when the heat of youth glowed white;
> And since I've put the faded purpose by.

Hence he has 'no faultless fruits' to offer his reader, but

> certain syllables
> Herein are borrowed from unfooted dells
> And secret hollows dear to noontide dew; . . .

– he feels he has captured something, but not the large, the generous, the great vision; his poetry falls short of the sublime. Perhaps it was a mistake to seek after the sublime – but at any rate, he did, and the failure to find it was his tragedy. Had he always been content with a humbler vision, as in the simple and sensitive lyric 'Araluen', the story might have been different:

> River, myrtle-rimmed, and set
> Deep amongst unfooted dells –
> Daughter of grey hills of wet,
> Born by mossed and yellow wells –

– these are the 'unfooted dells' to which the later poem no doubt refers; and repetition does not kill the phrase. If this is a

fair view and summary of Kendall's poetry, the purest of his art
is found in the lyric 'Orara', the burden of which is the exquisitely
poignant realization that ultimate poetical consummation lies
beyond him, and, it would seem, beyond the range of all Colonial
poetry. The country that lies above the waterfall may be imagined
but never entered:

> I cannot with my feeble feet
>   Climb after my desire . . .
>
> And therefore though I look and long,
>   Perhaps the lot is bright
> Which keeps the river of the song
>   A beauty out of sight.

*

Adam Lindsay Gordon (1833-70)

Gordon was six years older than Kendall, but his career was
shorter, began later, and ended sooner. He must nevertheless be
considered the definitive Australian Colonial poet. He was the
most typical and most vigorous, from both the contemporary
and the historical point of view. When in the later 1860s he began
writing for publication, he achieved some small esteem but not
much success, and fear of the failure of his 1870 book (containing,
ironically, his best, and ultimately most widely acclaimed poems)
undoubtedly hastened on his impatient and unhappy end. After
his death his Colonial reputation soared; his supremacy was
unquestioned, and remained long at its height. He seemed to
epitomize the Colonial mood. His suicide stunned the Colonial
audience; but also, perhaps, added to the force of his poetry. It
made him appear in the light of a martyr, antique, pagan, and
stoic, as well as a credible bushman and man of his time. [9] He had
asked the questions the age was asking, and answered them with a
desperation not unfamiliar to the rest. The frontier, bewildered
but naïvely philosophical, shaken by the mere accidents of
environment out of all civilized complacency, felt bound to
wonder continually, how precious is a man's life? What sufferings, physical or mental, may he endure? What need he not?
What virtue, and what beauty, lies in agony? In loneliness,

frustration, deprivation, boredom? What are the elementals, the fundamentals, without which he can no longer persist? In what landscape of the mind or the eye may he dwell and survive? Gordon's great claim to recognition as a poet never depended upon technical proficiency, hardly upon poetic sensibility – what he had of it was crude and undeveloped, though vigorous and insistent. It was rather the simple fact that he became the mouthpiece of his day and generation. He stands apart from Kendall by reason of his forthright personality; he never hesitated at a word or boggled at a sentiment – however banal. Though his rhymes were 'rudely strung', 'rude staves, roughly worded', his heart was in them and open to every reader. Douglas Sladen wrote, 'In Gordon the man overshadowed the poet, in Kendall the poet the man . . . Kendall wrote like a poet who had been to the races; Gordon like a poet who had raced.' This was *bien trouvé*; but it is well to remark also that Gordon's links with tradition were more immediate. He had been drilled in the orthodoxies of verse (Latin and English) like every other British schoolboy – he had never to invent an excuse for poetry, like a young Colonial. It was natural for him to lisp in numbers of some sort – rough ones contented him. Nothing will come of an attempt to find subtlety in Gordon; his technique is his own, but skilful we need not call it. The frontier asks for plain meanings and candid thoughts, open emotions and clear purposes. It does not niggle about imperfections of detail. It values truth but is not much aware of sublimity. It measures emotion by its strength rather than its complexity. It draws no fine distinctions between eloquence and rhetoric, or between morals and sentiments, and always esteems vitality above finesse. The sensations of life are reduced to their primary proportions. Gordon's talent was so exactly suited to these circumstances, that it may be worth while emphasizing also some exceptional aspects of it. The frontier has its own kind of bravura; but Gordon, though essentially popular, is never vulgar. (Though he writes about horses, he is never horsey.) The frontier is given to certain mildly sinful amusements such as bragging and boasting, drawing the long bow, swearing and swagger – these human frailties are not without their interest, and the later balladists made good capital out of them. But Gordon, without ever claiming superiority, and without the slightest priggishness, never committed them; at least, not in his verse, and probably not at all. As a youth he wore no halo; he was up to tricks and got into a scrape over a race-horse, and he had an interested, if not a roving eye for pretty girls – he would have tumbled a chambermaid and thought nothing of it; but none of this, unless, perhaps, some obscure and remorseful backward glances, got into his poetry. There was a great deal more of the puritan than of the rake in him. He was not a clever man, and neither handsome nor particularly sociable; but he was natural in his manner, gentle, plain, and fundamentally decent. He appealed to the Colonial spirit because it was recognized that he summed up what was good in it, and most vital.

Born in the Azores, he was taken to Madeira, but mainly brought up in England. His father, a retired Indian Army officer, taught Oriental languages at Cheltenham College. The mother was wealthy but eccentric. Lindsay's school career at Cheltenham, and later at Woolwich, was chequered, and he was taken away; finally, after the racing trouble already alluded to (of which the details remain obscure, but it appears a prosecution was only avoided by some careful manoeuvring, and a little judicious expenditure), he was sent out to South Australia. He expected to stay only a year or two, but in fact never returned. [10] His career in Australia was a varied one. He began in the Mounted Police (refusing to use influence which might have gained him a commission); left this for the life of a horse dealer and trainer; then, inheriting a small fortune from his mother, bought property and became a Member of Parliament. After his investments collapsed he drifted back to horses, and attempted to conduct a large livery stable in Ballarat. That also failed, and he went to Melbourne to live on what he could pick up from riding, dealing, and journalism. He was informed of his interest in a small Scottish estate, called Esslemont, a Gordon property which, by the old law on entail, should have come to him. But when he contested it, he discovered that changes in the law had invalidated his claim. He was now hopelessly in debt and at his lowest ebb; the decision arrived at the same time as his *Bush Ballads* came off the press. Troubled at his inability to pay the costs, and at the bleakness of all his future prospects, he rose early, left his wife sleeping, made his way to the tea-tree scrub by the beach at Brighton, and shot himself. It was a Roman gesture, whose violence was in pathetic keeping with the spirit of his poetry.

Three of four publications of Gordon's stand out. The early sequence, *The Feud* (1864) is of some importance because it illustrates the nature of his interest in poetry. Coming across a collection of engravings depicting incidents in a Scottish ballad, of which he remembered the gist but not the actual text, he wrote his own version to fit the pictures. He always remained attached to the legendary and the heroic, and outside his few unpolished Colonial masterpieces, this was the subject matter in which his imagination flourished best.

In 1867 he published two more ambitious books, which exemplify antipodal tendencies in his style. The verse drama *Ashtaroth* was described by Francis Adams as 'Gordon's appalling imitative parody of *Faust*'.[11] We may wonder what agony of creation it cost him, and how it fitted into the kind of life he led; in the end it is only a reminder of the pathetic futility of his concern for poetry of the heroic kind. Even when he managed it with greater success, as he did in the later 'The Rhyme of Joyous Garde' (a poem on the remorse of Lancelot, from Malory), the result was out of the Colonial context and doomed to be forgotten. But in the other book, *Sea Spray and Smoke Drift*, he captured something of greater value.

The character of this volume needs to be made clear. It was here that Gordon established his bona fides with the Colony. Mostly it consists of very slight poems, but their style harmonized with their purpose. Some were mere poetical exercises, written it would be hard to suggest how long ago; there are some pieces which obviously recall *The Feud*; one or two fairly lively heroic pieces (especially the military ballad, 'The Roll of the Kettle-drum, or The Lay of the Last Charger' – sufficiently esteemed to be provided in some later editions with illustrations); and some personal, reflective pieces cast in characteristic mood:

> The cold grey mist from the still side
> Of the lake creeps sluggish and sure,
> Bare and bleak is the hill side,
> Barren and bleak the moor.
>
> 'Wormwood and Nightshade'[12]

But the bulk and best part of the volume consists of two sets of sporting poems – or more accurately, pieces contributed to the columns of a sporting paper, *Bell's Life in Victoria* (in 1865). 'Ye Wearie Wayfarer' and 'Hippodromania' are most uneven performances as poetry, but neither do they make any pretences. They represent very well the sporting journalism of the day, which often appeared in verse form; they purpose to give the reader no more than a sporting man's reflections on a number of topics, some directly connected with racing interests, some quite detached and personal, but all reflective, discursive and informal. This is Gordon's casual poetry, 'sitting loosely in the saddle all the while'. It is here that he appears most relaxed and Colonial. It is here, too, that he drops to his most banal depths:

> Question not, but live and labour/Till yon goal be won. . . .&c.
> (*Ye Wearie Wayfarer*, Fytte VIII, entitled
> 'Finis exoptatus (A metaphysical Song)'.)

But it is also here that we find some of the most intimate impressions of Colonial life and landscape, and glimpses of the poet's brooding personality:

> Rest, and be thankful! On the verge
>   Of the tall cliff rugged and grey,
> At whose granite base the breakers surge,
>   And shiver their frothy spray,
> Outstretched, I gaze on the eddying wreath
>   That gathers and flits away,
> With the surf beneath, and between my teeth
>   The stem of the ancient clay!
> *Hippodromania*, Part One, 'Visions in the Smoke'.

Manner and diction may be uncouth, but the visions are clear, and the sentiments true. Considering its origin and purpose, this sporting poetry retains a mint-new brightness – although most of it is penny-farthing in quality. But it is not offered as the best of Gordon. The third volume, *Bush Ballads and Galloping Rhymes* (1870) contains almost all his poetry that he himself wished to be regarded seriously.

There is not a great deal of it, but a few pieces stand out. In its day 'The Sick Stockrider' seemed to epitomize the mood and atmosphere of Colonial experience. Essentially a bush poem, it is impressionistic, reminiscent, relaxed, familiar; its great significance, however, lay not in what it was, but what it did. This poem alone captured, defined and established for its period the local image and fixed the hitherto hesitant, wavering local nostalgias. Henceforward no Colonial poet could write without remembering it; it represented an emotional point of rest, an end to lost poetical causes and a new creative beginning. The 'Dedication' with which the volume opened added something like a critical reinforcement; it contained some of his reasoning about poetical experience in Australia – the bases of its inspiration, and the purposes it served for the spirit – and amounted to a defence of what might be considered the poetry of a vigorous but restless interim; not to be compared with the great tradition of English poetry, but a sturdy new growth of a new kind.

> Enough. In return for your garland –
> In lieu of the flowers from your far land –
> Take wild growth of dreamland or starland,
> Take weeds for your wreath.

But this was modest.

Gordon made two striking but indispensable discoveries: first, he discovered the Colonial audience itself, the heart of Colonial moral and aesthetic awareness, and words (however rough) through which to reach it; and second, the warmth and vitality of the Australian light, especially the archetypal of the summer sky and the long horizon: 'the sky-line's blue burnished resistance . . .'

Nothing in all Colonial poetry matches in importance Gordon's signal achievement, the fixation of the Australian image. Emotionally, he simply spoke as he felt: the mood of his best work is conversational; its philosophy stoically grim, but spontaneously articulate; its visionary content based upon a broad impressionism; the keynote brightness and sunlight, starlight, a high luminosity in the air.

After the local poems, the rest are of less interest; but he himself probably thought more casually of those than of 'literary' poems like 'The Rhyme of Joyous Garde'. 'The Romance of Britomart', a ballad of martial romance in the seventeenth century (Britomart is a horse), may still be read with some excitement, though the genre itself has lost its gloss.

Though he could be maudlin and he could be trite, there is nothing vicious in Gordon. His freedom from pretence is refreshing. No poet was ever less vain; there have been prettier talents, with less humanity, than his. A tag from 'Hippodromania' will serve to close this note, and is its own comment:

> Alas! neither poet nor prophet
> Am I, though a jingler of rhymes –

'Tis a hobby of mine, and I'm off it
    At times, and I'm on it at times ...

But with song out of tune, sung to pass time
    Flung heedless to friends or to foes,
Where the false notes that ring for the last time
    May blend with some real ones, who knows?

*

James Brunton Stephens (1835-1902)

James Brunton Stephens came to Australia as tutor to a squatter's children, in 1866. Travelled and educated, he settled in Queensland and became successively a schoolmaster and government official; finally he became Under-Secretary in the Chief Secretary's office. As a poet, his main interest lies in the way he illustrates the phenomenon of Colonial adaptation. Beginning with a lofty, but fully metropolitan conception of poetry, he attempted to make a grand-scale use of a Colonial subject matter and produced in *Convict Once* (1871) a poetical 'romance' (or novel in verse) centred upon the strong emotions of a mature woman who, having once been convicted of a passionate crime, attempts, but unsuccessfully, to rebuild her life by ruining the happiness (and stealing the lover) of the innocent girl to whom she is appointed tutor. She fails – her dark passions boil up – the end is noble resignation, and suicide. This spectacular performance upon the high ropes of melodrama fell conspicuously flat, and Stephens at once forsook the altitudes. However, he still felt his talent required a certain range, and his next publication, *The Godolphin Arabian* (1873) was also one of some length, narrative and discursive in style, though much nearer to earth. Instead of the lugubrious hexameters of *Convict Once*, it was cast in *ottava rima*, and it aimed, not at melodrama, but wit and humour; its literary ancestor was *Don Juan*, even if its prevailing humour, perhaps, approached rather nearer to *Punch*. It was light, bright, amusing, and deserved to be better known than it was. But again, it did not strike the popular fancy sufficiently to be much noticed. When he wrote again, he was careful to hit the vein with poems like 'The Black Gin', 'My Chinee Cook', and 'My Other Chinee Cook' – verses so near to the ballad style, in their rattle and comic force, that Stephens really ought to be given more credit for his innovations. These were his main Colonial successes, vying with such other pre-*Bulletin* ballad triumphs as Marcus Clarke's 'Bill Jinks' and Garnet Walch's 'Little Tin Plate', 'Wool Is Up', &c. Stephens thus exhibits a sad descent from metropolitan poetical respectability, and even his descent did not bring him to the *true* ballad humour – a Brett Harte facetiousness is not the true Australian humour – but he does very well exemplify the process of Colonial acclimatization.

*

George Gordon McCrae (1833-1927)

George Gordon McCrae's significance has been eclipsed by that of his son, Hugh. But though they are no longer read, his contributions to Colonial poetry were interesting; at least they have some importance in a history of lost causes. Hugh McCrae's *My Father and My Father's Friends* (see his *Story-book Only*, 1948) gives an impressionistic picture of literary life in his father's time (some of the flourishes are Hugh's, but he captures the spirit of the past). As a poet, G. G. McCrae's claims to notice are mainly based upon two works published in 1867, *Mamba* and *Balladeädro*, both attempts at subjects taken from Aboriginal life and legend. McCrae had grown up in fairly close contact with the natives near his home on Mornington Peninsula, and could speak of them with sympathy and understanding. However, these poems were doomed to be praised and forgotten. Nor were they the first attempts of the kind. G.W. Rusden's *Moyarra*, written about 1851 or earlier, was for its time an enterprising essay in this field (a narrative of tribal love and vengeance, fairly authentic in data); and J. Sheridan Moore's *Spring Life Lyrics* (1864) contained a sketch for a poem on a totemic theme and a short essay urging the claims of such poetical materials. But all of these essays came too early; Stephen's 'Black Gin' and the ballad 'Black Alice' were more to the Colonial taste. Of McCrae's later poems, not much need be said. *The Man in the Iron Mask* attempted once again the long, poetical narrative 'romance'; but not with any success. His *Rosebud from the Garden of the Taj* poems were only keepsakes, and the 1915 collection, *The Fleet and Convoy* only showed that he outlived his period.

*

No account of Colonial Australian poetry can be complete without some allusion to the pervading melancholy of the lyric mood which appears in it throughout the period. This has been much misunderstood, even if, on the whole, justly repudiated. A full treatment would demand a study to itself, but in brief it may be accounted for under three heads. First, it is a historical survival; the thinning-out of the contact with metropolitan culture necessarily produced an intellectual back-lag in the Colonies, as a result of which the poets continued to accept stimuli which, in England, had long been considered *vieux jeu*. The pleasures of melancholy were exploited by Milton ('Il Penseroso'), by the eighteenth century poets (Young, Gray, Collins), and still in some measure by the Romantics; but the Victorians were inclined to question them. In Australia there was still considered to be poetical grist in this mill when the grain was of local growth. Second, the embarrassing discrepancies between metropolitan and Colonial landscape could often best be offset by claiming that the grotesque antipodean anomalies of nature were, not perhaps beautiful in themselves, but endowed with a special passionate interest. Because the position was obscure and inexplicable, the Colonial sensibilities could most easily find expression in terms of 'beauty in ugliness' – something which was felt to have a powerful affinity with 'happiness in sadness'. In the third place, the element of melancholy does truly represent a certain mood of the landscape, especially the vaster, more open aspects of it, where the imagination is aware of a pathetic contrast between the limitless magnitude of nature and the powerlessness of the isolated human spirit. It is true, however, that this emphasis on poetical melancholy with much repetition became trite, and often merely habitual. Kendall protested, even while he himself luxuriated in it. George Essex Evans asked, in 'An Australian Symphony',

> Broods there no spell upon the air
> But desolation and despair?

He suggested that the 'mournful keynote' might have its origin, not in 'the pure depths of Nature's heart', but in 'the heart of him who sings'. Yet for all his anxiety to change the tune he also struck the same note:

> The solitude spread near and far
> Around the campfire's tiny star,
> The horse-bell's melody remote,
> The curlew's melancholy note
> Across the night.

There was, in fact, no cure for this disease, as long as the Colonial mood of mind prevailed. But the rising temper of Nationalism (already alert in Brunton Stephens's 'The Dominion of Australia', 1877) began to turn the substance of the complaint to a more aggressive account as the Colonial spirit faded. Hence the disappearance of the abject note of apology, and the substitution of a new tone of proud defiance:

> I love a sunburnt country . . .

It was the achievement of the Colonial poets to create the vision and define the emotions of the archetypal Australia.

NOTES

1. The term 'Colonial' itself changed its focus. Its strongest denotation at first was 'distant from the metropolis'. Then the metropolitan allusion partly drops away, and a certain pride of location comes into play, as in *The Wild Colonial Boy*; and later, 'Colonial architecture'. Before federal unity 'Colonial' could often be used interchangeably with 'Australian', sometimes even carrying an overtone of easy affection or national sentiment. Nowadays we are emerging from a phase of resentment of the word, and a certain picturesqueness is creeping back among its implications.

2. See J. Normington-Rawling, *Charles Harpur, An Australian* (Sydney, 1962).

3. *Thoughts: a Series of Sonnets* (1845). But see *Rosa: Love Sonnets to Mary Doyle*, (Melbourne, 1948).

4. Unpublished as a whole, but fragments appear in the posthumous *Poems* (1883).

5. The *Athenaeum* article of 24 September 1862, is reprinted as an appendix to Douglas Sladen's *A Century of Australian Song* (1888). In his letter to the editor, Kendall states his age as eighteen (I have not yet reached my twentieth year). He was actually twenty-three in 1862. He was born on 18 April 1839.

6. 'He touched the lyre with something of the lyric musicality which made Shelley the father of the dactylic modern measures.' Sladen, *Century*, Introduction, p. 17.

7. ' . . . magnificent – we should say, perhaps the finest prize poem written in the English language.' Sladen, *Century*, Introduction, p. 17.

8. In a few popular pieces, ballads and rural jingles (for example, 'Jim the Splitter'), Kendall tried to come to grips with some of the plainer aspects of Colonial life and character; but there are not many of these pieces, and they do not seem very typical. Kendall looked at facts with a watery and bibulous eye, and did not like them much.

9. See Sladen, *Century*, p. 497. Margaret Thomas concludes a short, shocked lyric on 'Adam Lindsay Gordon':

> Hush! where the wattles wave, at last
> He rests in his own adopted land,
> Poet, crowned, thro' the centuries vast,
> Altho' he died by his rash right hand.

10. Of his reasons for remaining in Australia, little can be discovered. See my 'The Friend of Charley Walker', *Australian Letters*, vol. iii, no. 3 (1961), p. 32. At the crucial time Gordon lost touch with his parents, somewhat mysteriously. A despatch containing money (maybe the provision for his fare) was misappropriated by a trusted intermediary; but no details survive.

11. Francis Adams, *The Australians, a Social Sketch* (London, 1893), p. 121.

12. The description appears to refer to Mount Gambier.

HENRY KINGSLEY, MARCUS CLARKE, AND ROLF BOLDREWOOD

F. H. MARES

NONE of these writers was born in Australia, and all are different in the degree of their attachment to the country. Kingsley stayed for five years as a young man and then went 'home'. Clarke came as a youth, and though he remained for the rest of his life, was never quite free from the sense of exile. Boldrewood came as a young child and his ties were to the land where he grew up, not where he was born. As a consequence their attitudes and problems as novelists are different. Kingsley is an English novelist, working inside an established and accepted tradition, Clarke is unsure of his situation, while Boldrewood is a colonial writer.

Kingsley is to be considered as an Australian writer only in the sense that in two or three of his novels he wrote about Australia, and at that time a distinction between an 'Australian novel' and 'a novel about Australia' was not – and perhaps could not have been – thought of. In the preface to his own first novel in 1869 Marcus Clarke called *Geoffry Hamlyn* 'the best Australian novel that has been, and probably will be, written'. 'Rolf Boldrewood' in *Old Melbourne Memories* (1884) praised it as 'that immortal work, the best Australian novel, and for long the only one.' The book was admired and influential, the happy return of all the main characters, when they have made their fortunes in Australia, to affluence, ease and a proper social status in England, was no blemish. Not until the nationalist nineties does the 'democratic . . . (and) . . . offensively Australian' Joseph Furphy attack Kingsley on patriotic rather than literary grounds. In *Such is Life* Kingsley's hero appears as 'Hungry Buckley', the ancestor of the grotesque Maud Beaudesart, who clings savagely – since all else is lost – to her gentility and her superior social status.

Henry Kingsley's own attitude to Australia is not clear. The younger brother of Charles Kingsley, he was born in 1830. He left Oxford without a degree and apparently in some sort of disgrace in 1853, and emigrated: in 1858 he returned. He gained no success in Australia. Boldrewood was taking up new land in the Western District of Victoria when he was eighteen; Marcus Clarke was well known in the Bohemian literary circle in Melbourne in his day; but Kingsley's life in Australia is hard to trace. There are glimpses of him as a gold miner, a station hand, a trooper in the 'Sydney' Mounted Police, hints that he was a storekeeper and a sundowner, but little clear evidence, and in that little none of achievement. Even the sheep-station where he is reported to have written most of *Geoffry Hamlyn* has two different owners and two different locations. In one case his stay lasted 'several months' in the other 'nearly a year'. [1]

In *The Boy in Grey*, [2] a strange fable of politics for British youth, Kingsley's hero, Prince Philarete, follows the footsteps of 'the Boy in Grey' all over the world, observing the white man shoulder his burden of colonization and civilization. Finally he comes to Australia.

All the male adult colonists were down on the shore; and every man had brought his grandmother, and every man had brought an egg, and was showing his grandmother how to suck it.

'Come here,' they cried, as Gil and the Prince coasted along; 'come here, you two, and learn to suck eggs. We will teach you to suck all kinds of eggs, not merely those of the emu and the talegalla, but those of the blue-throated warbler. And we will teach you to suck eggs which we have never seen.' (p. 47)

This, I suppose, is the obverse of the native-born's irritation with the immigrant who is quite sure that the way things are done in England is not just the best, but the only possible way. Kingsley gives us the response of the educated Englishman of the period to colonial self-assertiveness. But this is only part of his response; the Prince sails on to a bare and terrible coast that resembles the shores of the Great Australian Bight as Kingsley described them in 'Eyre's March'. Here he lands, and travels on (assisted by the emu-wren, the black cockatoo and other creatures) into the desert. He sleeps by 'the creek Mestibethiwong, the Creek of the Lost Footsteps' where

lay a human figure on its side, withered long since by rain and sun, with the cheek pressed in the sand. So lies Leichhardt, so lay Wills.

(p. 57)

The Prince is equal to his ordeal, and so can travel on into the great forests and mountains where he finds the Boy in Grey, who, it obscurely appears, represents 'common people', and the consummation of the pilgrimage takes place.

Yet there was a light growing in his eye, and before he could tell what that light was, he was out of the dark wood on to a breezy down, where the night wind sighed like old memories in the grass. Before him was a profound valley, dark as the pit, and beyond that a vast alp leaping up into the black sky with sheets of snow. That was the light. . . . Around him, hundreds of miles in every direction, was an ocean of rolling woodlands, untrodden by human foot. The solitude of the plains is terrible, but the solitude of the mountain forest is overwhelming. (p. 62)

The Prince and the Boy in Grey embrace and lie down together.

Kingsley's talent soon declined. *The Boy in Grey*, which first appeared serially in *Good Words For The Young* in 1869 and 70, already shows that 'deterioration . . . of imagination and right judgement, together with a lack of concentration', (Ellis, p. 102) apparent in his later work. In its idealization of boy friendships it can also be taken as evidence of the temperamental difficulty with which Kingsley was burdened. His life indeed was a sad one. The returned prodigal from the colonies had an initial success with *Geoffry Hamlyn* and *Ravenshoe*, then there was a slow decline: marriage to a wife who became a chronic invalid led to debts, a forcing of the powers of the writer and a decline in popularity as a consequence – and so the process went on: recourse to the jug of rum and water by the author who worked all night, the accepting of editorial work for which he had no talent, family estrangements over borrowed money, and an early but anticipated death from cancer of the tongue at the age of forty-six.

The Boy in Grey is an eccentric minor work, but this strengthens the evidence it offers that Kingsley's imagination had been deeply stirred by his Australian experiences. The climax of the allegory of the political ideal is the trial in the desert (it is strange to think of Kingsley – 'so lies Leichhardt' – anticipating the theme of *Voss*), its consummation, high in the Australian Alps. Only two of his novels, *Geoffry Hamlyn* and *The Hillyars and the Burtons*, are set, in large part, in Australia (though there is a brief episode in a third, *Reginald Hetherege*) but the idea of Australia is much more commonly present, and casual references appear often. In *Ravenshoe* – with *Geoffry Hamlyn* his best work – at the crisis of the novel when Charles Ravenshoe has learned that he is not a gentleman but the son of a servant, he thinks often of emigration. He hides himself in London working as a groom while his friends and relations look for him; he is nearly found – and at this point the action is held up while a returned missionary talks about the Australian Aborigines. Perhaps Kingsley thought better of an intention to move the action of his second book to Australia, as he had done in his first – he goes to the Crimean war instead – and these references are the relics of that changed intention. It is safe to conclude, at least, that for Kingsley Australia was a place of refuge and regeneration.

Henry Kingsley's style is fluent, familiar, and agreeable, and he has some narrative skill, both in the direct recounting of action and in ringing the changes from chapter to chapter and from one to another in a large cast of characters, so that interest and suspense are both maintained. His observation is often acute, and he has a good ear for dialogue at times, but his adventurous episodes are told only for their own sake and his major characters are stereotypes with little inwardness of their own. As Hadgraft[3] wittily makes clear, by quoting the ambiguous part of a description of a collie dog, they are admirable animals, prizewinners for size and shape and physical prowess. Metaphysically they are drastically limited by the conventions of Victorian propriety. This is so strong for Kingsley that he is constrained to apologize in a footnote for recounting an authenticated case of convict cannibalism and to dissociate himself – the writer – from the expression of scepticism by one of his creations, Lord Saltire in *Ravenshoe*. The ideal nature of the Victorian gentleman is nowhere defined, but everywhere assumed, so that the reader may well find it tiresome:

On every button of his clean white coat, on every fold of his spotless linen, in every dimple of his close-shaved, red-brown face, was written in large letters the word Gentleman.

(*The Hillyars and the Burtons*, p. 2)

Part of the charm of *Geoffry Hamlyn* is related to this simple moral vision: good triumphs, evil is destroyed or converted to goodness, rewards and punishments are distributed with equity. It is all simple, and there is lots of healthy open-air exercise in the meanwhile: pioneering, riding, hunting kangaroos, fighting blackfellow or bushrangers. At another level it is the protestant myth of *Robinson Crusoe* – a book to which Kingsley wrote an introduction, and edited for Macmillans. The closely connected group of families leaves the old world of Devonshire under difficult circumstances for which they are to blame in some degree. They retire to the simplicities of a pastoral life which is innocent and free, though beset by many dangers, where they must get back to basic things. They succeed, virtue and industry are rewarded, and they return rich and re-established to their old homes. The novel is an ironic contrast to Kingsley's own life in Australia, but it would appear to have some correspondence to reality in the golden age of the squatters, before the discovery of gold: the world nostalgically recalled by Boldrewood in *Old Melbourne Memories*. At a different social level the great tradition of 'mateship' is certainly adumbrated in Kingsley's idealization of male friendship, even if, as in the case of Tom Williams' devotion to the apparently dying Erne Hillyar on the Omeo goldfields, there are also overtones of the feudal vassal's fealty to his lord.

Kingsley is better as an observer than an interpreter. His plots, relying on melodrama and the long arm of coincidence, and his main characters, idealized and stiff, are the stock in trade of his period, but he has a new scene and a new society. He has an eye for scenery in any continent, but seems to be particularly moved by the high forest scenery of Australia, as in the description of the meeting of Hamlyn with Major Buckley's pioneering party, or George Hawker's desperate flight over the watershed between the Snowy and the Gates of the Murray after the defeat of the bushrangers. The emerging society that he records has implications for the future that he does not see or is not interested in, but which are all the same preserved in his reporting.

But at the end of this week, as the three were sitting together, one of those long-legged, slab-sided, lean, sunburnt, cabbage-tree-hatted lads. . . . who were employed about the stable and the paddock, always in some way with the horses; one of those representatives of the rising Australian generation, I say, looked in, and without announcing himself or touching his hat (an Australian never touches his hat if he is a free man, because the prisoners are forced to), came up to Jim across the drawing-room, as quiet and self-possessed as if he were quite used to good society, and, putting a letter in his hand, said merely, 'Miss

Alice', and relapsed into silence, amusing himself by looking round Mrs Buckley's drawing-room, the like of which he had never seen before.

(*Geoffry Hamlyn*, p. 312)

Kingsley treats 'the rising Australian generation' with some condescension, and does not see it as in any way a rival of the benign authority of the Buckleys and the Brentwoods, but he records not only the outward lack of conventional good manners (and the reason for it) but also the inward decency and self-reliance that make any conventional subservience of employee to employer unnecessary. In *The Hillyars and the Burtons*, though he presents the Burton family as the slightly comic, though deserving, poor in the early stages of the book, he does record their rise to wealth and social eminence in the colonial society of 'Cooksland' and he records it with approval as well as condescension.

Kingsley can still be read with pleasure for his easy humour, his exciting narratives, even for his pathos and melodrama: for the connoisseur of Victorian fiction he has a flavour that should not be neglected. In Australian writing his importance is that of a pioneer. The first man to make popular with a wide public the Australian scene and situation; the first to embody the colonist's malaise that has been so important a theme in Australian writing: the search for 'home'.

*

Marcus Clarke is both a better and a worse writer than Henry Kingsley. He is essentially a journalist; his writing for the Melbourne papers is lively, entertaining, often 'smart' in an unscrupulous way, local and topical – and consequently ephemeral. As a novelist he is opportunist: his first novel, *Long Odds*, later called *Heavy Odds*, attempts to take advantage of the popularity of Kingsley's *Geoffry Hamlyn* by showing Sam Buckley in England. His fourth and last completed novel *Chidiock Tichbourne* takes a name from the then topical 'Tichborne case', and as Elliott[4] points out, Clarke had already used the theme of the Tichborne case – impersonation to gain a large inheritance – in John Rex's impersonation of Richard Devine in *His Natural Life*. One of his more outrageous practical jokes as a journalist was to get published in a Warrnambool paper an entirely fictitious account of a rival claimant to Arthur Orton, the butcher from Wagga Wagga, for the Tichborne inheritance. But this witty, bohemian, unscrupulous, bankrupt young man also wrote *For the Term of His Natural Life*, a novel of much greater imaginative power than anything Kingsley achieved.

Clarke's mother died when he was four, his father, an eccentric Irish lawyer living in London, when he was sixteen. The fortune expected proved not to exist, and at seventeen Marcus Clarke came to Australia where some of his senior relatives were already established. He sampled life in a Melbourne bank; he sampled life on a station in the Wimmera for two years, and then, in 1867, he joined the staff of the Melbourne *Argus*. He continued in literary work of various kinds in Melbourne until he died. He married an actress, Marian Dunn, in 1869 and three years later was indulging in a passionate correspondence with her sister, though it came to nothing. The marriage lasted, in spite of Clarke's steadily deteriorating financial circumstances, until he died in 1881. He was plainly a man of great personal charm and some talent, witty, sociable, excellent company and a *bon viveur*, but with a tendency to self-dramatization, to taking romantic attitudes. In early days he swung between eulogizing the bush life, and seeing himself as Ovid among the Goths.

My whole tenor of life changed in a moment. I was forced into a career utterly uncongenial to my tastes. I was somewhat of a swell (God help me!) – I was sent to a land of radicals and mob-law. I was fond of art and literature; I came where both are unknown. I was conversant with the manners of a class; I came where 'money makes the gentleman'. I hated vulgarity; I came where it reigns supreme. . . . I see daily before me a pit into which I dread to fall; the pit of vulgarity, ignorance, slovenliness and radicalism.[5]

In *Human Repetends*, a story appearing in the *Australasian* in September 1872, Clarke seems to be drawing on memories of childhood in his widowed father's household but is almost certainly exaggerating the irregularity of his life then.

I was thrown when still a boy into the society of men twice my age, and was tolerated as a clever impertinent in all those witty and wicked circles in which virtuous women are conspicuous by their absence.[6]

There is a ring of self-pity in this not attractive in so determined a Bohemian as Clarke. It is sentimental.

The original serial version of *His Natural Life* was completed when Clarke was twenty-six; two years later it appeared in volume form in the much revised and shortened version in which it is now known. The revision removes from the beginning of the book a series of adventures in Europe leading up to the transportation of the hero and substitutes the much shorter Prologue recounting the quite different circumstances in which Richard Devine sacrificed himself to protect his mother's good name – an affair it would be an understatement to call melodramatic. Relics of the original version can be observed in the later one, for example the references to alchemy at the end of chapter XII of Book II. The end is also truncated: originally Dawes survived the wreck and after many adventures, including Eureka Stockade, returned to fortune and respectability in England. What go out are the conventional complications and coincidences of the plot, the extensive history of Victoria of the final chapters and the happy ending of a melodramatic Victorian novel. What is left is the story, with a few residual trimmings of romantic plot, of the protracted agony of the convict Rufus Dawes in the clutches of the penal system. Undoubtedly, in writing this Clarke's mind and imagination were deeply stirred, and he produced what is still – with all its glaring and obvious faults – a novel of great power. Although the concluding chapters of the novel in its serial form were plainly inferior, it is said that Clarke only altered his happy ending after strong pressure from friends. Perhaps he did not fully realize what an achievement the convict sections of the novel were. In the preface to his novel Clarke claimed

to illustrate in the manner best calculated, as I think, to attract general attention, the inexpediency of again allowing offenders against the law to be herded together in places remote from the wholesome influence of public opinion, and to be submitted to a discipline which must necessarily depend for its just administration upon the personal character and temper of their gaolers. (p. 5)[7]

Elsewhere he says that the House of Commons reports on transportation 'make one turn sick with disgust, and flush hot with indignation.'[8] All the same, *His Natural Life* is not a novel of social protest, its tone is too dark for that. The reformer, however terrible the evils he attacks, must leave room for hope. Hope, for Rufus Dawes, is reduced to nothing. The final kindness one man can do for another is to murder him.

When Troke came in the morning he saw what had occurred at a glance, and hastened to remove the corpse of the strangled Mooney.

'We drew lots,' said Rufus Dawes, pointing to Bland, who crouched in the corner farthest from his victim, 'and it fell upon him to do it. I'm the witness.'

'They'll hang you for all that,' said Troke.

'I hope so,' said Rufus Dawes.

The scheme of escape hit upon by the convict intellect was simply this. Three men being together, lots were drawn to determine whom should be murdered. The drawer of the longest straw was the 'lucky' man. He was killed. The drawer of the next longest straw was the murderer. He was hanged. The unlucky one was the witness. (p. 386)

Even murder, in this case, is an act of charity, and shows the possibility of good in those who commit it, but no facile change of system could provide for it. Only the dypsomaniac, free-thinking parson, James North, who has been to the bottom of his own shame and suffering, can begin to approach these men, and some are beyond even him. The beast in man is most manifest in Gabbett who persuades others to attempt an escape in his company and proceeds to eat them to sustain his own life in the bush. John Rex, less gross and more genteel, is as utterly and unscrupulously devoted to his own well-being, whatever the cost to others. Not all are bad, but the good are weak and ineffectual, and the penal system strengthens evil. The regulation-bound Major Vickers can do little against officers like the coarse and brutal Burgess or the more ingeniously sadistic Frere. The sequence of events in the plot which brings Dawes further and further into the power of the system and of Maurice Frere is, at a realistic level, almost incredible, but this scarcely worries the reader, for the emotional logic of the book requires this steady destruction, which Dawes's periodic reassertions of his native virtue only make more poignant.

Clarke's style can be sentimental or melodramatic; he often overwrites, but on the whole has a gloomy power that is answerable to his subject. His imagery generally points and reinforces his preoccupation with the essential evil in the heart of man. A crucial point in Dawes's degeneration comes when he is ordered to flog Kirkland who, subjected to homosexual rape in the yard, has cried to be let out: this was the crime for which he was to be punished. The sadism of those participating in the ritual is well suggested in Clarke's comparison of the flogged back to a delicacy.

'Ten!' cried Troke, impassibly counting to the end of the first twenty. The lad's back, swollen into a lump, now presented the appearance of a ripe peach which a wilful child had scored with a pin. Dawes, turning away from his bloody handiwork, drew the cats through his fingers twice. They were beginning to get clogged a little. (p. 264)

Successful, too, in its grand-opera manner, is the description of the storm in which the prisoners who are later to be Gabbett's victims escape from Port Arthur.

The next instant Burgess saw a wild waste of raging sea scooped into abysmal troughs, in which the bulk of a leviathian might wallow. At the bottom of one of these valleys of water lay the mutineers' boat, looking, with its outspread oars, like some six-legged insect, floating in a pool of ink. The great cliff . . . seemed to shoot out from its base towards the struggling insect, a broad, flat straw, that was a strip of dry land. The next instant the rushing water, carrying the six-legged atom with it, creamed up over this strip of beach; . . . amid the thunder-crash which followed upon the lightning . . . the billow rolled onwards . . . and the whole phantasmagoria was swallowed up in the tumultuous darkness of the tempest. (p. 314)

Clarke did not establish the pattern of the convict novel, and the theme has been treated with distinction by writers who have come after him. The measure of what he did in *His Natural Life* (the savagely ironic title of the book weakened by its later extension) is that even today we see the convict period through Clarke's imaginative synthesis of the facts of brutality and pathos into a vision of man's potentiality for evil.

*

Thomas Alexander Browne, who wrote under the name of Rolf Boldrewood, was a happier and less divided man than Henry Kingsley or Marcus Clarke. He is also a good deal less interesting. He was born in England in 1826, but his family had reached Australia before his fifth birthday, and he grew up and went to school in Sydney, staying there even after his family moved to the new settlement of Melbourne in 1839. In 1844 he became a 'squatter' in the Western District of Victoria and prospered there for a number of years. In 1860 came *My Run Home*, though the faintly fictionalized account of his trip to Europe was not written until 1874. In 1861 he was married, and a few years later bought a property in the Riverina which he had to give up after severe drought in 1869. He was a police magistrate in various parts of New South Wales, finally at Albury, until he retired in 1895 and went to live in Melbourne, where he died at the age of eighty-eight in 1915. His writing career began when he was in his forties and he published the last of his twenty-odd volumes, many of which first appeared as serials, in 1905. Many of his articles have never been collected from the journals and newspapers in which they first appeared.

In spite of his place of birth and that trip 'home' Browne had no divided loyalties: his home was in Australia. He sometimes brought his characters from England at the beginning of a novel, but only in a few minor cases did he follow the convention of *Geoffry Hamlyn* and send them 'home' wealthy at the end. His emigrants are settlers. He had a tendency that is something of a besetting sin with colonial writers, that of dressing a good deal of history, travelogue, documentary or serious instruction in a little rather thin fiction. Thus *The Squatter's Dream* as Morris Miller [9] says 'from some aspects might be regarded as a *vade-mecum*' for the pastoralist, *The Sealskin Cloak* is 'an archeological tour' through Egypt and Ceylon. He makes much use of his own reminiscences, frequently introduces historical persons, and often, as in his treatment of the goldfields scene in *The Miner's Right*, spends far more space than is justified in elaborating the background of his story.

Boldrewood was a popular writer, writing with ease what was easily read. In tastes and opinions he was at one with his public. The moral world of his novels is perfectly sincere and entirely conventional. *Robbery Under Arms*, the most famous of them, is a story of bushrangers, told retrospectively and penitently by Dick Marston, one of the gang, most of it while he is in prison waiting to be hanged: of course he isn't, but atones for his life of crime with twelve years in gaol, and at the end of the book comes out to marry the girl who has waited for him, whose love has saved him from despair (her name is Grace) and off they go to Queensland to start a new and better life. The moral simplicities of Kingsley are often ludicrous, but at times there is a tension behind his writing that suggests a darker insight. In *Robbery Under Arms* there are no depths; everything is what it seems; the violent adventures, the Byronic poses of Captain Starlight, the repentance, all have equal value, though as Hadgraft points out, the periodic intrusion of pious reflection becomes a little tedious. The style is appropriate to the narrator; colloquial and relaxed with a good deal of easily used Australian idiom. Place and period are presented accurately, if romantically. On the whole his low-class dialogue carries more conviction than that of Kingsley or Clarke, but there is not much behind it. *Robbery Under Arms* is a tale that could be put into the hands of any schoolboy with some assurance that he would enjoy its lively action and adventure and that it would do no harm to his morals.

NOTES

1. For these various accounts see S. M. Ellis, *Henry Kingsley 1830–1876*, Grant Richards (London, 1931), pp. 48–9; and Rolf Boldrewood, *Old Melbourne Memories*, (London, 1896), p. 172.

2. All references to the works of Henry Kingsley are to the page-number of the appropriate volume in the collected edition – Ward, Lock and Bowden (London, 1894 onwards).

3. Cecil Hadgraft, *Australian Literature*, (London, 1960), p. 44.

4. B. R. Elliott, *Marcus Clarke*, (Oxford, 1958), pp. 157, 201 It is pleasant here to acknowledge also my debt to Dr Elliott for advice and assistance privately given.

5. Ibid. p. 69.

6. Quoted from *The Marcus Clarke Memorial Volume* ed. Hamilton Mackinnon, (Melbourne, 1884), p. 17.

7. Page references are to the edition of *His Natural Life* published by Hallcraft, (Melbourne, 1949).

8. Elliott, *op. cit.*, p. 162.

9. E. Morris Miller, *Australian Literature*, (Melbourne, 1940), pp. 418, 421.

BALLADS AND POPULAR VERSE

EDGAR WATERS

ADDISON noted in 1711 that the broadside street ballads were the darling Songs of the common People. A century later they were still the darling Songs of the common People of England, and by now of English-speaking Ireland as well. For a vast audience in cities and towns – most of the working class, and its fringe of criminals, vagrants, and the destitute – the broadside ballads were the chief form of entertainment available. They were also an important source of information; with their sensational accounts of murders and hangings, battles and scandals, the street ballads were in a very important way forerunners of the popular newspapers.

Most of the convicts and poor free settlers who reached Australia in the earlier periods of British settlement came precisely from those places and those classes in which the broadside ballad most flourished. No ballad press grew up in Australia, to reprint the broadsides of the British Isles, or new ballads of native murders and scandals. But it would be a fairly safe guess, even if there were no more evidence, that the common People of England's new colony would have carried a stock of broadside ballads from their native lands, held in memory, to be sung in their new land and passed on to new generations. There is in fact evidence of two kinds to confirm the guess.

One kind of evidence comes from nineteenth century comment on the singing of bush workers.

The other kind of evidence comes from the folk song collecting of the middle of the twentieth century. The first of Australian folk song collectors was the balladist A. B. Paterson; he published a collection of *Old Bush Songs* in 1905. Paterson's interest lay in preserving native texts. *Old Bush Songs* was undoubtedly widely read, for there were seven editions in thirty years; at the same time, rather oddly, little further work of collecting was done for half a century after its first publication. Since the end of the second world war a number of societies and individual collectors have added greatly to knowledge of oral song traditions in Australia, at least in the eastern mainland states. Their work has shown that

Paterson had by no means recorded all the native texts, and that survivals of traditional song from the British Isles are still quite numerous. Almost all the latter are English or Irish broadside ballads of eighteenth and nineteenth century origin.

It was a matter of course that ballads should be made by the convicts and the population of bush workers and dungaree settlers into which the old lags merged and in which they at last disappeared, though not without trace. Songs have always been a vital part of the culture of the unlettered. Since the songs they carried with them from their homelands were chiefly the street ballads, it was equally a matter of course not only that they and their children should go on singing these street ballads, but also that they should re-make some of them into ballads about their new land; and that they should make their wholly new ballads in the old styles.

The ballads which are fairly certainly convict-made can be numbered off on the fingers of one hand. Perhaps it is surprising that so many have survived for us. All but one of them are in Irish street ballad styles. Before the gold rushes, something like half the population was Irish, if not by birth, then in great degree by cultural background. The Irish street ballad was to remain probably the strongest of all influences on bush song making until near the end of the nineteenth century.

None of the surviving convict-made ballads can have been written earlier than the 1820s. Gentlemanly observers noted that convicts were making ballads before this time, but did not think their words worth the trouble of recording. We need not be in any doubt that they made a powerful appeal to the people who sang them. The most widely sung of them all was the ballad of the convict bushranger Jack Donahoe; it survived in oral tradition into our own day (in North America as well as in Australia). It has been said that the government banned the singing of 'Bold Jack Donahoe'. A formal interdict is undocumented and unlikely, but a Riverina bushman recalled that as late as the 1890s the police took their own steps at least to discourage the singing of ballads of convicts and bushrangers in public places. One of his mates spent the night in the lock-up after singing 'The Wild Colonial Boy' (which, apparently in the 1870s, took the place of 'Bold Jack Donahoe' as the chief of bushranger ballads). Ballads of convicts and bushrangers, this bushman said, were known as *reason songs*; this is the name the Irish gave to some of their songs in the Penal Days. Folk song adds a good deal to our knowledge of parts of history which are not well documented in the printed record.

The bushranger ballads made their appeal to bush workers and dungaree settlers alike; it is likely that many of them were made by the latter class. But most of the songs with native texts are occupational songs of the bush workers: stockmen, drovers, shearers, teamsters, nomadic station hands, and swagmen. The bush workers seem to have been making songs about callings more respectable than bushranging at least as early as the 1840s.

By the 1860s and 1870s, the bush workers seem to have created a considerable body of songs about their callings. Some of the most widely sung of them were made over from street ballads of the British Isles. So, 'The Banks of the Condamine' – also called 'The Banks of Riverine' – has been recorded by song hunters from Victoria to the Northern Territory. It is a dialogue between a shearer (sometimes a horsebreaker) and his girl, who wants to go out on the job with him. It is re-made from an English street ballad, 'The Banks of the Nile', which is itself the offspring of a long line of ballad dialogues between a girl and a lover departing for the war, a line that reaches back to Elizabethan broadsides. It is one of the rather rare bush love songs. They are rare, of course, because a shortage of marriageable women made lifelong bachelorhood the lot of many bush workers. 'The Wild Rover' is a sentimental English street ballad about a penitent prodigal; with only the slightest of verbal changes, its theme and manner seemed so completely to belong to the bush workers that Paterson included it in his *Old Bush Songs*, apparently with no suspicion of its English origin.

Not all the English and Irish songs re-made in Australia were of street ballad origin. The ancient 'Ram of Derby' became 'The Ram of Dalby' and 'The Ram of Albury'. A number of sailor songs were made over. Considerable numbers of sailors deserted British ships in Australian ports (which may explain why one or two of them became known as shanghai ports), and no doubt the best way to avoid arrest and retribution was to strike up-country as soon as possible.

A good many of the home-grown texts are come-all-ye ballads in form. The history of the come-all-ye is obscure; it appears to be of late eighteenth century birth, with the English street ballad and some native Irish form of song for its parents. It rapidly spread from Ireland, and became the favoured ballad form of many ballad-making communities. From 'Bold Jack Donahoe' onwards a great many of the bushranger ballads are come-all-ye's. But the bush workers used it for telling stories of all kinds. One of the more notable of the Australian specimens of the come-all-ye is 'The Cockies of Bungaree'. This tells of a nomadic bush worker fallen amongst hungry farmers, and finding some amusement in the contemplation of his own hardships and the squalors of the cocky's life:

> His homestead was of surface mud and his roof a mouldy thatch,
> The doors and windows hung by a nail, with never a bolt or a catch;
> The chickens walked over the table, such a sight you never did see –
> One laid an egg in the old tin plate of the cocky of Bungaree.

The finding of humour in realistically observed physical hardship is a constant characteristic of popular Australian humour. This fits, and could be used to reinforce, the argument that 'you can't win' is an attitude deeply rooted in the Australian character.

No doubt migrants continued to carry English and Irish street ballads and country folk songs to Australia all through the nineteenth century. But folk song collectors in recent years have found very few traditional songs from the British Isles amongst pastoral workers. It is in farming communities that the ballads from the British Isles are chiefly found today. From about the 1890s onward, the street ballad and the come-all-ye began to lose their importance as models for bush song making; they were replaced by the songs of the popular stage.

In the 1840s Sydney's pubs had their free-and-easies, where a man might drink his beer and join in the singing, with a 'professional gentleman' at the piano to assist. Some pubs had more ambitious saloon theatres, with professional singers and comedians engaged. Here the bush worker, down from the back country, sometimes listened to the 'popular songs of the day'. Pretty certainly, if he were fond of songs, he would learn one or two of the popular songs of the day to carry back up country with him. Perhaps if the gold rushes had not changed, if not everything in Australia, then certainly the whole nature of popular entertainment in Australia, suddenly and dramatically, Australia might have developed a native equivalent of the English music hall and the American black-face minstrel show; with bush songs influencing its repertory as the street ballads did the music hall and Negro folk song the minstrel show. But the crowded goldfields could afford to pay many entertainers, and they came flocking from England and the United States, the music hall entertainers and the burnt-corked 'niggers', along with the Shakespearean actors and the operatic sopranos and the virtuosi of the violin. The possibility, small enough in any case, of an indigenous style of popular stage entertainment developing – being forced to develop – soon disappeared. The goldfields entertainers, chief of them an Englishman, the 'inimitable Thatcher', produced an enormous body of topical song. Some of it is still entertaining, and most of it fascinating for its documentation of life on the diggings. But in style they are all copied from English and American songs of the popular stage. The stimulus given to the production of topical popular songs by the feverish life of the diggings died as the diggings died, and nothing like it has existed since in Australia. Minstrel shows touring the bush occasionally contrived songs about bush life, and a few – a very few of these – passed into the oral tradition of the bush. The pantomimes of a later period produced a few lively topical songs, and in the 1880s and the 1890s the variety stage exploited the larrikin in a few feeble imitations of the coster songs of the London music halls. But for the most part, since the time of the gold rushes until the present, Australia has been content to import its requirements of 'pop' song from the British Isles and – increasingly – from the United States. Australia was one of the countries to be first affected – and most deeply affected – by the growing internationalization of the market in the popular arts.

No doubt the decline of audiences on the gold diggings pushed the entertainers who had flocked to amuse the diggers out into tours of bush towns. As road and rail communications improved, so touring companies of entertainers visited country towns more and more often. So, bush workers who had once had to make their own entertainment, found themselves more and more often able to exercise the privilege of paying for professional entertainment. So also, of course, the popular songs of the day began to appear more and more frequently in the repertory of singers round the campfire or in the shearers' and 'traveller's' huts. In some degree, they pushed the older bush songs and the street ballads of the British Isles out of the bush singer's repertory. But the life of the bush worker was still very different to that of the urban audience for whom the stage songs had been created; so they still felt the need to create songs of their own. But now the tunes of their songs, and the models for their words, were taken largely from the songs of the popular stage.

The folk song scholars have always been reluctant to admit the street ballads within the pale of folk song, even though they may have been long in oral circulation. They have been even more reluctant to admit that songs based upon models from the popular stage, or our modern 'pop' repertory, might qualify as folk song. Arguments about definition can be left aside here.

What is more important here is that, working from their new models, the bush workers were able to make songs which expressed their feelings and their attitudes to life as adequately as those which they had based upon the country songs and street ballads of the British Isles. One example will have to serve; take a verse from 'Click Go the Shears', which derives its tune and some hints for its words from Henry Clay Work's song of the time of the American Civil War, 'Ring the Bell, Watchman':

> The colonial experience man, he is there of course,
> With his shiny leggings on, just off a horse;
> Glancing round the floor like a real connoisseur,
> Brilliantine and scented hair and smelling like a whore.

Very poor verse, no doubt, though like the verse of most songs, it sounds far better when sung than when read; and the fullness of its meanings will not be apparent to anyone not acquainted with the social history of the bush workers. But the bush song maker, after all, was concerned only with an audience of his fellows. To them, it would convey more than adequately a number of things: the shearers' general dislike of Pommies and their particular contempt for the gentlemanly English dilletante; their rejection at the same time of his comprehended claim to social superiority and his uncomprehended claim to superior cultivation; their sense of exasperation at the contrast between his sweet-smelling parasitical cleanliness and their own honest workers' smelliness.

Whatever their models and sources, the traditional songs of the

bush have little literary, or musical, grace about them. A literature can function only within the limits of the culture it serves;
the cultural milieu of the bush workers did not encourage grace
or subtlety or much tenderness. But the bush songs have vigour
and the authentic, sweaty smell of a hard life about them that
will make them attractive to some readers – or better, listeners –
for all that they lack, and for all the crudity of what they have.

*

Historians of Australian literature have sometimes written as
though the bush ballads of Paterson, and others of his kind, were
a wholly native development in literature. There can be little
doubt that, in some senses and in some degree, the literary bush
ballads did have their roots in bush folk balladry. It would have
been odd indeed if men living in the bush in the last quarter of
the nineteenth century had not known the bush folk ballads; odd
if some of them, at least, had not had the folk ballads in mind
when they began themselves to write verse narratives about bush
life which were intended for reading or recitation rather than
singing.

But Adam Lindsay Gordon, who is commonly and reasonably
enough considered the pace-setter for the mob of galloping
rhymesters – more numerous than a Melbourne Cup field – who
came after him, was no simple bush worker; he had the education of an English gentleman, and aspired to compose in classical
languages as well as in the vernacular. Nor were Paterson and
Farrell, who led the main part of the field as it came along more
than a decade after Gordon had published his *Bush Ballads and
Galloping Rhymes* in 1870, simple bush workers who knew no
more of poetry than the songs they heard from drovers and
shearers, or the simple verse they recited from their school
primers at outback schools. Both were men of fairish education
and by profession journalists in a day when journalists perhaps
were better read – at least in the English Poets – than journalists
are today. One of Gordon's four ballads is set in England; of the
three which have bush settings, one, 'From the Wreck', is
Browning's 'How they brought the good news from Ghent to
Aix', transmogrified. When Farrell published his *How he died and
Other Poems* in 1887, the reviewers noticed likenesses not only to
Gordon – and Byron, of course – but also G. R. Sims, Bret Harte,

and John Hay; one English and two American balladists whose verses have a great deal in common with those of the bush balladists. When the Red Page of the *Bulletin* reviewed Robert Service's *Songs of a Cheechako* in 1910, it observed:

In style and humour, Service resembles 'Banjo' Paterson, and both are of the tribe of Kipling. These three are the best-sellers amongst living rhymsters; so that there need be no misapprehension as to the kind of verse the public likes.

While the bush ballad flourished, Australian reviewers showed themselves to be well aware that it was merely the local sub-species of a kind of verse that flourished throughout the English-speaking world.

After Percy's *Reliques* had made its impact on the poets of the Romantic Revival, after the publication of the *Lyrical Ballads*, ballad-writing became a literary fashion; and it remained a literary fashion for more than a century. True, most of the ballads of the nineteenth century poets are now little read (by anyone) and less regarded (by critics). But enough of the iceberg shows in current anthologies for even the casual reader of poetry to assure himself easily that everyone was writing ballads.

Adam Lindsay Gordon, after all, was doing no more than to use the style approved by his poetic betters for new themes when he wrote his bush ballads. And indeed another gentlemanly new chum had been before him, in the person of Alexander Forbes, who published some ballads of bush life in the 1860s; and the native-born Charles Harpur had been before Forbes, with a ballad – or at any rate, ballad-like verse narrative – of bush life called 'Ned Connor', published in 1853. And further – this is a warning against too easily seeing singularities in cultural processes – just about the time that Gordon was writing his Australian version of 'How they brought the good news from Ghent to Aix', Joaquin Miller was writing his American Western version of it, called 'Kit Carson's Ride' (but Miller was living in London at the time and says that he got Browning's blessing for his imitation.)

The mysterious thing about the new kind of popular literary balladry, written by such men as Sims and Harte, is that it appeared with such remarkable suddenness. Harte published his first book of ballads about Californian mining life, *The Heathen Chinee*, in 1871; in the same year John Hay published his *Pike*

County Ballads, and Will Carleton published his first collection of dialect ballads about Michigan farming life. James Whitcombe Riley soon followed where Carleton led. Sims says that he was stimulated to writing his ballads by the first appearance of Hay's *Pike County Ballads*. There had been things like their ballads before, but not a whole school of ballad-writers of this kind.

The emergence of this new school of balladry may have had something to do with developments on the popular stage. Sims says that his ballads 'were never put forward by me as poetry', but were intended for writers who wanted something dramatic; they 'were recited at matinees, and one or two of them were particularly popular at the professional benefits which were common in those days'. In Australia, *The Bulletin* recorded that in 1885 a visiting English actor recited Farrell's 'How he died' at a benefit performance, and 'had the house noisy for "more" when he had finished'. Ballad recitations came to form a normal part of the entertainment offered at the Grand Sacred and Classical Concerts which the Sydney variety theatres presented on Sundays.

It may be, also, that the new kind of popular balladry was a response to the demands of a new popular audience for poetry, which grew up with the spread of literacy. In a time when there is no popular audience for verse, except the verse of the pop songs, it is hard always to keep in mind that less than a century ago, there was a mass audience for poetry; but it was so. This might explain why, in spite of the example of Gordon, in spite of occasional imitations of Harte, the main flood of the bush balladists did not rush down upon the columns of *The Bulletin* until the second half of the 1880s. The success of *The Bulletin* itself probably indicates that it was only in the 1880s – it was established in 1880 – that a sufficiently large audience of literate native-born Australians had been created, by the school reforms of the previous decades, to support a popular journal of its serious-minded kind.

In any case, in the fifteen years following the publication of *Bush Ballads and Galloping Rhymes*, Gordon found no followers in Australia. The few ballads about the bush from the 1870s more often show the influence of Bret Harte than Adam Lindsay Gordon.

The Bulletin provided a stable and practice-track for the main group of bush balladists. The early 1880s sees the writers groping about in search of a style for verse narratives of bush life. The influence of Hood, Gilbert and Scott is as noticeable as that of Gordon or Harte. The first real sign of the flood to come appeared in 1886, with 'A Dream of the Melbourne Cup: a a long way after Gordon'. It was by Paterson, though signed with a pseudonym, 'The Banjo'; the name of a racehorse of Paterson's fancy.

Paterson was not only early on the scene, with only Gordon and Farrell as bush balladists of any note before him; he is also, by unanimous voice, chief of the bush balladists. The verses which he published regularly in *The Bulletin* from 1886 onward were collected in 1895 into a book called *The Man from Snowy River*. Its success was altogether remarkable; no later collection of bush ballads had anything like it. The first edition sold out in a fortnight; ten thousand copies were sold in its first year. An English edition was published in 1896, and an English reviewer claimed that Paterson had a bigger audience than any living poet in the language except Kipling (whose own verse was already strongly influencing Paterson). It was not only the most successful collection of bush ballads ever published; it was also, in terms of sales, one of the most successful books of any kind ever published in Australia.

The balladists who had followed Paterson in the pages of *The Bulletin* soon followed *The Man from Snowy River* with ballad books of their own. In 1896, there came Dyson's *Rhymes from the Mines* and Lawson's *In the Days when the World was Wide* (Lawson had published a mixed collection, *Short Stories in Prose and Verse*, in 1894 without much success); in 1897, Barcroft Boake's *Where the Dead Men Lie and Other Verses*; in 1898, Ogilvie's *Fair Girls and Grey Horses*; in 1899, Brady's *The Ways of Many Waters*. Before 1900, most of the important balladists had published their first volumes of verse, and Paterson, Lawson, Ogilvie, and Brady followed with second volumes in the early years of the twentieth century. A perceptive critic might have predicted when these second volumes appeared that the great days of the balladists were already over, for these broke no new ground, but plodded along in the same rutted tracks. The innumerable amateur poets of the outback have gone on turning out ballads by the bale ever since, many of them not falling far below the general standard of the 1890s. But only Gerard, in his ballads of the *Light Horse in Palestine*, and O'Brien, in his ballads of farming life, have had anything to say that was not said better in the 1890s.

The name *bush ballad* is misleading in both its terms. Many of these ballads are lyrical more than narrative. And some of the titles quoted just above will have suggested to the reader that the balladists rhymed tales of miners and sailors, as well as bushmen. Lawson especially, and one or two others as well, wrote ballads of urban working-class life. Misleading as the term may be, it is too late to change it now. And after all, the name gets to the heart of the thing; the bush was not the only theme of these writers, but it was the central theme of the school, and they were at their best in ballad narratives.

Many of the balladists are still widely read. Thousands of Australians who would be scared stiff of climbing onto a horse's back can recite from memory Paterson's long ballad of that reckless horseman 'The Man from Snowy River'. Paterson's collected verse goes on, and on, selling at a rate that must be highly satisfactory to its publisher. Some critics, though not unwilling to grant the balladists their due few words of praise for simple vigour, are dismayed by their great and long-continued popularity. Others, perhaps not much more impressed by the literary skill of the balladists, see in their continued popularity a pleasing evidence of the continuity of Australian cultural traditions; in this view, the ballads still form a cohesive cultural function. And certainly, as long as 'The Man from Snowy River' and 'Clancy of the Overflow' go on gripping the imaginations of large numbers of Australians, the legend of the bushman will continue to colour the popular image of Australia and Australians.

*

C. J. Dennis, like Paterson and Farrell, spent a good deal of his working life as a journalist. He was a journalist in verse, able to turn out rhymed topical comment that reads as easily as it is quickly forgotten. His first collection of more ambitious verse, *Backblock Ballads and Other Verses*, was published in 1913. There was nothing in most of the backblock ballads to distinguish them from the usual run of bush ballads, though a few showed an unusual interest in the niceties of colloquial speech, and a few a rather unusual interest in themes of farming life (Dennis had clearly been reading such Americans as James Whitcombe Riley, as well as Kipling and his Australian contemporaries). They failed to impress. But some of the other verses, dealing with Melbourne larrikins and written in language which purported to be the speech of Melbourne larrikins, met with a response that encouraged Dennis to write more in the same style.

It has been mentioned earlier that attempts were occasionally made to portray the larrikin on the variety stage. Norman Lindsay and other *Bulletin* artists found the larrikin a most rewarding character for their 'joke blocks'; so rewarding that these often appeared under a generic caption 'In Push Society'. Lawson, Milton Macgregor, even Paterson, had dealt with the Sydney larrikin in verse, and Louis Esson had done the same in Melbourne. Lawson had written a number of short stories about the Sydney larrikins, and Dyson a whole book of stories – *Fact'ry 'ands* – about Melbourne workers who, if not larrikins of the pushes, belonged on the fringe of larrikin society. Dennis was working in an established tradition when he published his first larrikin piece, *Doreen*, in *The Bulletin* in 1909.

Four of the five larrikin pieces in *Backblock Verses* were loosely linked in theme, and printed under the general title, *The Sentimental Bloke*. What Dennis did, when he set to work to write more larrikin pieces after the publication of *Backblock Verses*, was to construct a loosely knit story by adding more episodes to these four; a story which told how the tough Bloke from the push fell in love with a decent working-girl, Doreen, of his reformation, into a decent working-man and marriage.

Now Dennis did not have a wide first hand experience of bush life, but he had even less first hand knowledge of larrikins. In fact, he is said to have met only one specimen of the class when he began writing his larrikin verses. But a great deal of Dennis's verse was inspired more by his reading of other people's writings than by his observation of life. Most of the other writers and artists who had dealt with the larrikin had dealt in realistic, if sympathetic, observation. Realistic observation was not open to Dennis, who at no time seems to have sought first-hand knowledge of the pushes; he preferred to deal in sentiment. Other writers had been at some pains to reproduce larrikin speech with accuracy; Dennis constructed a literary dialect which owes as much to the speech of the London stage-costermonger as it does to the Melbourne larrikin. But when *The Songs of a Sentimental Bloke* appeared in book form in 1915 his fellow-writers did not seem to see the faults which now seem so glaring. Lawson wrote an introduction for the book, in which he spoke of the Bloke as the most perfect portrait of the larrikin achieved, better even than his own 'beloved Benno'.

The success of *The Songs of a Sentimental Bloke* with readers was startling; far more startling than the success of *The Man from Snowy River*. More than sixty thousand copies were sold in Australia and New Zealand in eighteen months. Dennis followed it up with *The Moods of Ginger Mick*, telling in the same style of the adventures of the Bloke's larrikin mate as a soldier. It sold more than forty thousand copies in six months. Both books were printed in pocket editions for sale to the army, and there is plenty of evidence that they were widely read in the army.

It is difficult to see the reasons for this remarkable popularity. Presumably, the conditions of war had something to do with it. One army officer had said before the war that the larrikins would make excellent soldiers; since it gave them a legitimized outlet for their aggressiveness, no doubt they did so. Maybe the war not only made the larrikin who fought and died for his country instead of bashing his fellow-countrymen unexpectedly appear a good fellow at heart after all. Maybe those qualities of the larrikin which had appeared so undesirable in any member of the community before now seemed to be the qualities which the times demanded of all men.

But it would seem that large numbers of respectable Australian men have always liked to feel that they are really larrikins at heart. In both world wars, given some licence as soldiers to behave in rather irresponsible ways, they have been quick to play out the part. *The Songs of a Sentimental Bloke* would no doubt have made its appeal to this feeling at whatever time it had appeared. It was Dennis's good luck that the book was published in war-time.

Dennis's appeal has not lasted as well as Paterson's. But *The Songs of a Sentimental Bloke* still sells well, and recently recordings of recitations from it have been published, and a musical comedy based upon it has met with some success. Dennis's verse seems shallow even when compared with Paterson's; but the feelings to which it appeals are deep-rooted.

Dennis went on writing and publishing verse, and so did some of the bush balladists. But *The Moods of Ginger Mick* was the end of the great boom in Australian popular verse. Set aside the amateur balladists and song-makers of the bush, and Australia produces no popular verse today; not even her own pop songs. There are many odd things about this burst of verse-making. Odd that it should have flourished alongside a busy popular theatre in which Australian-made songs barely found a place; odd that verse should have flourished more than fiction. Odder still that so many of the literary historians should go on speaking as though the bush ballad were somehow uniquely Australian, and miss the fact that it is Dennis's larrikin verses which in fact are unique. For there seems to be nothing quite like them anywhere else. Could it be that the literary historians are, in their own way, as much in the grip of the legend of the bush as the uncritically enthusiastic readers of bush ballads whom they so often deplore?

THE BULLETIN – J. F. ARCHIBALD AND A. G. STEPHENS*

S. E. LEE

TOM INGLIS MOORE has suggested, half seriously, that Archibald and Stephens should be honoured (along with Captain Cook!) in any service of remembrance for the founding fathers of Australian literature.[1] Cook because his discovery of Botany Bay began it all; Archibald because his *Bulletin* 'directed the nationalist energies of the eighties, the nineties and first decade of this century into the first substantial creation of a national literature'; and Stephens because, as Archibald's literary editor, he 'stimulated, assessed and shaped our literature in a way that no individual has ever done since'. J. F. Archibald (1856-1919) was actively associated with *The Bulletin* for the first twenty-two years of its existence (1880-1902), during which time his was the guiding hand; he was the inspired enthusiast who provided the push and drive, the elemental energy and vitality that helped transform a modest under-capitalized Sydney weekly into the most widely-read and popular – certainly the most influential – national magazine in Australian journalistic history. A. G. Stephens (1865-1933) was Archibald's 'Junior sub-editor', and for ten crucial years (1896-1906) editor of the famous 'Red Page', *The Bulletin*'s literary soul, where for the first time creative writing in Australia was subjected to discriminating and challenging criticism and the voices of serious thinkers and writers like Brennan, O'Dowd, Furphy, Daley began to be heard by a growing and informed audience.

When *The Bulletin* was founded by John Haynes and Archibald in 1880 Australian literature was in a state of decline. The poets Harpur and Gordon were dead and Kendall was to die in two years. None of these had found a true Australian voice, imitating too closely the techniques of contemporary English landscape, narrative and lyrical poets. Clarke's novel *His Natural Life* had appeared in book form in 1874 and Kingsley's *The Recollections of Geoffry Hamlyn* in 1859 (Kingsley, like Gordon was an English-

*The author wishes to thank the Trustees of the Library of N.S.W. for permission to quote extracts from MSS in The Mitchell Library and to acknowledge his indebtedness in many ways to the staff of that Library.

man), but Boldrewood's *Robbery Under Arms* was not to appear till 1888. Short stories worthy of the name had not yet been printed: Lawson was but a twelve-year-old school boy. In general, Australian literature could be described as being in a stage of literary dependence on the mother country: the pioneer stage that all colonial literatures seem to pass through, as V. F. Calverton's *The Liberation of American Literature* and J. P. Matthews's more recent comparative study of the development of Australian and Canadian poetry in the nineteenth century, *Tradition in Exile*, seem to demonstrate. Our thesis here is to show how *The Bulletin* first under Archibald's and later Stephens's influence jolted writers out of this ineffectual imitation of home models; and, after a period of rather blatant almost hysterical nationalistic revolt with undue emphasis on the home product, led them some of the way towards the more adult stage of unself-conscious Australianism, where, while there is no mistaking the writer's Australian origins, the whole of English and continental literature is felt to be a common heritage. White's *Voss* and FitzGerald's *The Wind at Your Door* owe something to the faltering even stumbling footsteps of Archibald's and Stephens's protegées. For, before a national literature can come into existence – as Matthews put it, before 'the unself-conscious vision of the poet, who does not have to keep looking at his feet, may have free play' – there must be this earlier period of tentative fumbling. The strong individuality of present-day Australian writing which Judith Wright [2] and others have remarked upon as a sign of our literary maturity is first noted in *The Bulletin* of the nineties.

*

Some confusion surrounds the history of the early *Bulletin* because the principals have left contradictory and incomplete statements. I am inclined to accept Stephens's version 'based upon the personal accounts of its four corner-stones Haynes, Archibald, Traill, and MacLeod'. He modifies somewhat the role of Archibald in the early days in an unpublished note 'Australian Journalism – Some *Bulletin* Reminiscences' written on the occasion of MacLeod's death in 1929 and preserved in 'James Tyrell's Collection of the Papers of A. G. Stephens' in the possession of the Mitchell Library, Sydney:

The one and only 'founder' of *The Bulletin* was John Haynes, an Irish journalist of ability and experience who, in 1880 was sub-editor of *The Evening News*, a daily newspaper in Sydney. Archibald was then a clever youngster of 24, cub-reporting on the *News* at 30s. a week and space rates.

Haynes was a mature man with many friends in Sydney. He saw a chance of starting a weekly paper with Roman Catholic support, in opposition to *The Protestant Standard*, a vigorous weekly organ of the other religious side. The religious feud was bitter in New South Wales in those days. MacLeod was also a member of the Catholic faith. Denunciations of Orangemen and 'The Yellow Pup' were a staple of the early days of *The Bulletin*.

Haynes had virtually no money; but he secured promises of advertising aid and obtained the support of Archbishop Vaughan. The first issues of *The Bulletin* were printed in the office of *The Express*, the Archbishop's own organ. Archibald joined the paper as sub-editor; and the two men worked day and night to gain credit and keep going. Haynes canvassed for advertisements while Archibald minded office; both wrote furiously and enlisted contributors.

Though he relied on Irish and Catholic support, Haynes had no intention of making *The Bulletin* a purely religious organ. He had seen many Californian papers in *The Evening News* office; and his model was *The San Francisco News-Letter*, a very bright news-and-comment weekly of the eighties with the motto 'Boil it Down'. The name was borrowed from *The San Francisco Bulletin*. Haynes was a Free-Trader; and *The Bulletin* started as a Free-Trade paper, opposing the early Protectionists in Victoria.

In another note Stephens adds:

Father Leonard, director of *The Express*, came through the office one day and saw *The Bulletin* proofs. Scandalized, he stopped the printing. The paper was then printed in a lane down by the *Tivoli Theatre* in Castlereagh Street.

Haynes and Archibald were ebullient journalists but impractical businessmen; so in 1881 W. H. Traill, a journalist of some substance, was invited in as proprietor and manager. In 1882 he became editor when the other two were imprisoned for failing to pay the costs in a libel action – occasioned ironically enough by Traill's report of alleged saturnalia at Clontarf picnic grounds. Traill set the business on its feet, gained a start which his rivals could not peg back, by importing the most modern printing and reproducing machinery then available, and by enticing on to his staff two fine illustrators, 'Hop' from America and Phil May from

England. Traill told Stephens (in an interview published in the *Bookfellow* of 25 July 1907):

> For five years and four months I controlled *The Bulletin*. It would have died over and over again but for me . . . I was managing director, editor, printer and everything else.

That Traill was not 'everything else' became apparent when he sold out in 1887 to take up pig farming. The brilliant mercurial Archibald then became editor in name, and with solid managerial control from William MacLeod, who had bought out Traill's interest and then given a large parcel of the shares back to Archibald to encourage him to better efforts, *The Bulletin* established itself as a household word throughout the whole of Australasia. Archibald needed 'the heavy ballast' of men like Traill and MacLeod, otherwise his unrestrained exuberance and brilliance would have destroyed the journal – in libel suits, if nothing else.

So for sixteen years Archibald and MacLeod worked in perfect partnership. But Archibald exhausted himself physically and mentally, and by 1903 there had been a distressing breakdown, MacLeod's handling of which caused a life-long estrangement between the partners. [3] Archibald sold out in 1914, threw himself enthusiastically into the war effort, and was back in journalism again as literary editor of *Smith's Weekly* when he died in 1919. It was fitting that he should die in harness, for as he once declared:

> To a man born with ink in his blood, the mercurial enthusiast whose spine tingles at the rhythm of a set of fiery or pathetic verses from a new-found pen or at the roar of a dispassionate leader – what a music is that of the press and what a fragrance the inky odour of a dingy printing office.

*

All accounts of the great years in the two decades from 1887 agree that *The Bulletin* was Archibald's paper: '*The Bulletin* is my book' he used to say. Stephens who made no fewer than twenty books from its pages has commented, with a generosity of mind that Archibald seemed to inspire in all his associates:

> *The Bulletin* by virtue of contrast indeed became a better book than any of the books that have been made from it. With Daley, Paterson, Dyson, Lawson, Boake, Ogilvie and a stalwart crowd besides – competing together in a variety of moods, styles and subjects – *The Bulletin*

of the nineties reached the highest pitch of characteristic Australian verse.

And Sir Frank Fox wrote in 1907:

J.F. Archibald I have heard described as 'the most brilliant editor of a generation'. As an editor he had pre-eminently the journalistic *flair*. He knew news and he knew men and their minds. 'I have never put a good thing into the waste-paper basket but once', he said, jokingly, one day, 'and that was a bull-pup.' In truth his instinct for a bright thing and his knowledge of the public taste seemed infallible. Under his fostering editorship grew up practically all the literature that Australia has yet produced . . .

Fox was to recall many years later in some notes published by Walter Stone:

There (at *The Bulletin*) began a term of work under ideal conditions. A. was so unselfish, so magnanimous, so industrious in seeking to impress the spirit of (*The Bulletin*) that I was made to feel an associate rather than a pupil and to be one of the 'team' with a full share of responsibility. Also I became aware of the high degree of talent already in the office. A. was most generous in appreciation of my efforts and I could see that he expressed this in quarters outside the office.

(Biblionews, May 1960)

This ability to sense talent and the 'gift of appreciation and the will and capacity to express it', which won loyalty and inspired his colleagues with the same kinds of burning ideals and enthusiasms, were his greatest strengths. Further, his men were allowed remarkable freedom in which to develop special talents or pursue personal enthusiasms. As an example Stephens recalls that the Red Page was 'regularly and entirely set in type without the editor seeing the copy. When the page was ready in proof I submitted it to A. who struck out items twice in ten years.' (One of these items, incidentally, was a bitter and personal attack on A.G.S. by Lawson in 1899 which Stephens was prepared to print – as he did earlier attacks by Daley and Brereton – and had actually set up in proof.) Then there was the same gift of inspiring writers to do of their best 'No freelance, however humble sent anything of worth to the paper and failed to hear about it' says Mrs MacLeod,[4] and the encouragement came in hand-written letters, as Stephens recalls:

'Love letters' Dyson called them, thrilling to the touch ... As Frank
Morton put it, for the encouragement of editors, *The Bulletin* treated
its contributors like men; not like cattle.

(*The Bulletin*, Jubilee Number, 29 January 1930)

Archibald was famous too among his fellow workers 'as a
condenser and improver of style' – a 'literary cobbler' he used to
call himself: soling, heeling, and repairing for others. Here the
emphasis was always on brevity and neatness, with his father's
advice often passed on:

Be terse; give forceful word-pictures; and omit as many words as
you can. Edit your own work severely.

The effect of his prescriptions on *Bulletin* prose writers, including
Lawson, has been severely criticized. But the young Lawson was a
relatively untutored writer – as his friend Brereton tried to tell
him – and like the early Neilson probably needed the kind of help
an Archibald provided. Mrs MacLeod repeats an old *Bulletin*
legend when she states:

[Lawson's] writings always had to be carefully doctored; few knew
how much of his early fame was attributable to Archibald's loving
attention. Lawson gave heart and insight to what he wrote, but it was
Archibald who gave it polish.

The 'frail, nervy, mercurial, intellectually arrogant' little man
'full of likeable little vanities' and resentments against people,
institutions, and 'colonial' modes of thought kept his own name
out of *The Bulletin*. He boasted:

During the twenty-six years of his connection with *The Bulletin* no
word of its editor ever appeared in that paper, nor has anything been
printed about him in any other paper with his consent. ...

('The Genesis of *The Bulletin*', *The Lone Hand*, July 1907)

His reason?

In this world it is only the unknown which is terrible. It is often the
business of a newspaper editor to be terrible.

Nevertheless, his personality comes through unmistakeably, as
the serious-minded Englishman Richard Jebb noted in 1905:

The specialities of the paper are its style – a grotesque and cynical
humour bearing the impress of a single and erratic genius – its uncompromising radicalism and its violently anti-British tone.

(*Studies in Colonial Nationalism*, 1905)

His resentments – against cruelty, oppression, wealth, jingoism, established religion, and conformism – explain many of the extremist *Bulletin* policies. He had a passionate hatred of flogging and capital punishment; and of the judiciary that administered them. The harshness and barbarity, he felt, stemmed back to the 'convict system', which he regarded as eternally to the shame of England. He was so appalled that his contemporaries knew or cared so little about our 'shameful origins' that he pushed through as the first *Bulletin* book a strident exposure of the system entitled *The History of Botany Bay* [5]:

We did not make our history. We only tell it. We merely flay the carcase of the hybrid and moribund monstrosity now on our demonstrating table and dissect the congested organism underneath!

Later on, of course, he was to foster Price Warung's remarkable series of short stories entitled *Convict Days*. Perhaps the Anglophobia underlying the rabid nationalism is thus explained. But there was a sentimental side to the nationalism too, as this account of 'The Genesis of *The Bulletin*' shows:

For *The Bulletin* the name originally designed was *The Lone Hand*. Circumstances conspired to prevent a formal christening, but all its years of battle, the paper, though *called The Bulletin* was *The Lone Hand* in truth and fact, fighting at all odds whenever it could for the weaker side, shouting discords that were heard above the droning chorus of the influential and 'respectable', and ever cheering for the little dog that had its foot in the big dog's mouth. It was always the ideal of *The Bulletin* to heed not the clamour immediately surrounding it, to despise the threats and mutterings of the servile crowds of the cities . . . *The Bulletin* as its blood hissed at the savage crimes so enthusiastically sanctioned by hysterical city 'society' and city mobs, and by the callous and selfish city press, ever bethought itself of the unruffled and compassionate atmosphere of the out-back camps. Careless of what the venal cities thought, it addressed itself to its ideal – The Lone Hand – the very salt of the Australian people, the educated independent mining prospector, who, scorning to accept wages from any man, worked on and on from year to year, hoping to the end for the fortune which might never come. The writer never read the title *Bulletin* on that paper. He could only always see *The Lone Hand*.

(*The Lone Hand*, July 1907)

The reference to the solitary bush worker – the lone hand – is rather significant. In *Tradition in Exile* Matthews argues convincingly that the national movement of the eighties and nineties had its roots in the rebellious minds of the descendants of convicts and smaller free settlers, who roamed this outback as nomadic workers – the shearing, droving, fencing, land-clearing 'contractors', the miners, and bullockies who spurned to be tied down to any 'boss' as wage slaves. Their sense of independence had sprung from earlier frustrations – the harsh authoritarianism of the convict system for example. Regular employment in town or in the outback appeared to endanger their independence; so married men built crude horse caravans in which they carted their families from job to job while the unmarried ones – immortalized in Lawson's *While the Billy Boils* – went on foot, 'humping the bluey' as we say. Matthews comments:

These 'sundowners' formed the nucleus of what was to become the Great Bush Myth in Australia. They, far more than their settled brothers who were to outnumber them, were to exemplify the aggressive egalitarianism of the Australian character. . . .

(*Tradition in Exile*, 1962)

The first number of *The Bulletin* carried the statement that the proprietors 'intend giving provincial matters the greatest attention', a policy always kept clearly in view during Archibald's time. *The Bulletin*'s 'consistent and distinctive AUSTRALIAN NATIONAL POLICY' *favoured*: republican government, political reform, land tax, the complete secularization of state education, prison reform, united Australia, and protection; it *denounced*: religious interference in politics, foreign titles, the Chinese and imperial federation. Little wonder Archibald's red-jacketed journal became 'the most widely read, quoted and remailed journal in Australia' – the inimitable 'Bushman's Bible' – for its policy expressed almost exactly the aspirations and prejudices of Archibald's admired bush democrats.

At first *The Bulletin* seemed unaware of the literary potentialities of the nationalism it was so vigorously espousing. As fiction it served up popular, insipid melodramatic romance (*Adrienne* – 'A Love Story of the Lancashire Cotton Distress'); while the verse, Stephens noted, 'represented principally writers born beyond Australia applying a British style to the life of the cities'. It was not till after 1887 when Archibald was firmly in control with the policy of making his paper one written largely by its readers that the trickle of stories from Lawson, Favenc, Price Warung, Dyson, Barbara Baynton, and the bush verses from Paterson, Boake, Ogilvie, Brady, swelled into the most vigorous flowing of folk literature in our history. As Vance Palmer put it:

The tradition of oral balladry and tale-telling was still alive, and bush people responded whole-heartedly to an imaginative rendering of the incidents of their daily lives. In the shearing-sheds, in small country settlements, at camp-fires along countless tracks, existed a scattered audience and an army of potential contributors, and as *The Bulletin*'s national outlook widened it began to draw them into its civilization, at first unconsciously, and then with deliberate intent.

(*The Legend of the Nineties*, 1954)

One of Archibald's strengths was a knowledge of his own limitations and a readiness to admit them. He knew that he was not properly equipped to sift and judge the flood of manuscripts now coming in, particularly those from the more reflective, intellectual and lyrical poets. Folk writing he judged confidently and well – what he liked *The Bulletin* readers liked. But by 1894 he realized that he needed someone with special gifts in criticism and more catholic tastes in writing whose function it would be to give literary direction to the stream of creative writing flowing into *The Bulletin* office. This man was A. G. Stephens.

*

A. G. Stephens had attracted Archibald's attention in 1893 with two hard-hitting political pamphlets and some sardonic contributions ('Fight in the House of Commons') from Fleet Street where he was trying his journalistic luck. So, in 1894 Stephens responded to 'an invitation too flattering to ignore' and joined Archibald's staff as Junior sub-editor. Stephens was then in his twenty-ninth year, Archibald in his thirty-eighth; each, working then at the top of his power, respected the other: 'A. G. S. has distinction' was the senior man's judgement. Not only that, they shared many convictions, political and moral, and found each other's company stimulating and congenial. Their polemical styles were similar. This peroration[6] on 'Young Australia' was written before the men met . . . by Stephens:

Thought here moves with a broader sweep; there is a carelessness of tradition and conventionality that cramp the limits of action. Pastors and masters tell us that young Australia is irreverent or indifferent to things round which for her forbears, for her contemporaries of European race, clusters an accretion of pious and respectable memories. The charge is true; and 'tis not pity that it's true. The precept is good, 'Prove all things'; and it is that which the young Australian follows, still resolving to hold fast to that which is true. But he will not take his truth on trust. No second-hand shams and spurious philanthropies will he swallow, because stamped with the hall-mark of regal or theological approbation the imagination of the age of reason finds in him its concrete embodiment. The age of superstition will decay as the nation gathers strength, and flings off the trammel that would devitalise its lusty vigour.

But Stephens soon showed that his real interests were literary rather than polemical. Having had some success a few years previously with a literary column in William Lane's *Boomerang* entitled 'The Magazine Rifler' ('rifle' in the sense of 'search and rob'!), Stephens pressed for a similar column in *The Bulletin*. A not very enthusiastic management allowed him to take over the space on the inside front cover of the red-jacketed magazine – then being used, not very profitably apparently, for advertising patent medicines, alcohol, nerve-soothing 'galvanic belts' and so on. The column began quietly in September 1894 with advertisements for books; then notes on advertised books followed; and finally 'Literary Notes', which discussed contemporary and local literature without reference to advertised books, merged naturally into the Red Page – a title used for the first time on 29 August 1896, just about two years later.

The Bulletin now had its literary soul. While Archibald's rougher folksy bush ballads and stories continued to be published in the magazine section ('Verse from the Backblocks') the Red Page itself was reserved exclusively for the literary product. Many a well-known O'Dowd, Daley, Brennan, Gilmore, or McCrae poem was introduced to readers regally printed in graceful italics in the top-left hand corner, with perhaps a brief biographical and critical note on the poet; here Brennan's lectures on the French Symbolists first addressed a general audience; here pioneer assessments were made of the local literary product – often followed up with replies by the writers and their supporters and denigrators; and here the best overseas publications, critical and creative, were brought to the attention of local writers and readers. Thus, John Murray's edition of Byron would be recommended on these grounds (Red Page, 15 February 1906):

Byron is one of the authors – like Shelley, Browning, Shakespeare, Spenser, Chaucer, and their high kindred – who by most of us must be read before twenty if they are to be read right through; and to read in fragments and selections is always to risk error. The world of literature is more than too much with us: there are so many journals of interest, that the mere time to study a lengthy classic comes but rarely between youth and age. And it is in middle life that one wants knowledge of the classics to be sure and stimulating. Therefore, ye golden youth! vow to read and meditate your Byron while there is time: this new edition may confirm the vow.

So for ten inspired years using the pseudonym of 'A.G.S.' or 'The Bookfellow' (in deference to Archibald's demands for anonymity) Stephens wielded unique power as a critic at once to be feared (Furphy's 'three-initialled terror') and respected (O'Dowd's 'rhadomanthine Stephens'); as the literary editor who selected work for initial publication in *The Bulletin*; and as the publisher who determined whether your writing was worth preserving in book form. Even an old hand like Daley, Archibald's discovery, found it difficult to get past Stephens as this pathetic note to Archibald shows:

I do not expect you to read anything today. But please read two or three verses. And if you cannot appraise kindly let Boy have something on a/c. If Stephens is in it is another matter. . . .

He ruled as a kind of lesser Cham of Australian letters; when he resigned in 1906, according to *Bulletin* legend over a salary dispute, neither he nor the Red Page were ever to be the same again; lacking *Bulletin* backing his provocative and incisive voice lost its authoritative ring; lacking his brilliance the Red Page became another literary column. Will Dyson writes (1909?):

I have been working through old *Bulletins* looking for my drawings and if it isn't too belated let me offer you belated congratulations on the Red Page of your date and less belated congratulations on the Red Page of today, which is all an enemy would wish it to be.

*

That Stephens was as striking a personality as Archibald, is shown by accounts of contemporaries like Norman Lindsay, Hugh McCrae, Mary Gilmore, and Mrs MacLeod. A big, hand-some, bearded man with disconcerting clear blue eyes, that stared unblinkingly from below a broad-brimmed bushman's hat 'he scared the daylights out of us younger chaps' one confessed to me. Hanson recalls:

Imagine Neptune from Circular Quay, with his blonde beard obli-terating Dowell O'Reilly who walked underneath – or behind – good-ness knows which.

He used the swagger of a shell-back, and to emphasize the part, wore a reefer-jacket many years old; patched about the arm-holes; and with seams stretched due to frequent chest expansions on account of 'tobacco-heart' ... In his cabin up two-pair of stairs at *The Bulletin* office ... he would inflate himself till his body filled every crevice; not leaving space for anyone else. Like a turkey on parade, this inflation made him appear more formidable than he was. And, all the while he wrote passionately in purple ink; the ink once rated housemaid's stuff; but, now, through his adoption, *encaustum* of kings.

(*Southerly*, 1947, vol. viii no. 1)

The Red Page represents Stephens the critic at his liveliest and soundest. There are obvious limitations and prejudices. An anti-intellectual bias, shared with Archibald ('I have nothing against Oxford men. Some of our best shearers' cooks are Oxford men.') caused him to underestimate, at times even patronize, university men like Brennan, Brereton, and O'Dowd; his *Bulletin* brand of nationalism meant that some 'imperialist' writers like Tennyson and Kipling were condemned while other 'nationalistic' ones like Miles Franklin were praised on non-literary grounds; sometimes, writers like O'Dowd were eulogized when working under his *aegis*, but unduly disparaged when they went their own ways; and there were personal idiosyncrasies: almost crankish notions about the relationships between heredity and literature, insanity and genius, meat-eating and sustained literary achieve-ment. Also he worked, *a priori* as it were, from certain rigid, rather narrow theories on the nature of poetry: the importance of thought, imagination, and structure tended to be overlooked and the more obvious and showy elements of melody and 'power-ful feeling' over-rated. So 'sweet singers' like Daley, vaguely melancholic versifiers like Hebblethwaite ('His work is a scholar's poetry, wistful regretful. It's characteristic content is a grave and lofty beauty of the soul.') were overestimated. On the other hand it must be stated that John Shaw Neilson, whose verse illustrated all the qualities A.G. Stephens himself admired and who is still widely regarded as our finest lyrist, was discovered, nurtured, and published by Stephens.

So it is understandable that some of the assessments on poets such as Neilson, Daley, and Brereton are now being seriously challenged. But most of his judgements on prose writers still stand, for example, he anticipated critics like Moore and Palmer by some sixty years in complaining of the sketchy nature of Lawson's early stories ('the reader is perpetually getting up steam for a five minute's journey which brings him back to his starting point') – a sketchiness in part caused by Archibald's own demands for brevity and economy. And, as Vance Palmer pointed out, the validity of his pioneer judgements is attested by his connection with almost all the Australian writers of the time whose names are remembered. We shall be in a better position to check his judgements when research workers have sifted through *The Bulletin* files again; meanwhile Palmer's statement that 'no important work has emerged from the files of those days to accuse him of neglect' is substantially true.

While the literary judgements – like those of any human critic – are open to question, few who know his work would deny that Stephens is our brightest and most stimulating critic. One has to look ahead to the A.D. Hope of the 1940s to find his like in wit and liveliness – though Stephens appears to be more vigorous, less graceful, than his brilliant successor. Both have the gift of the tense, arresting phrase and both sharpen their meanings with witty and homely metaphor. Hope's famous:

The Jindyworobaks might be described as The Boy Scout School for Poetry. They have the same boyish enthusiasm for playing at being primitive . . .

is matched in a dozen places by Stephens who wrote, of Brunton Stephens:

Always he has one solid Scotch foot on the ground of fact. Sometimes he has two: even when his head is in the clouds he gets rheumatical twinges in his poetical feet from earth damp.

or of Henry Parkes' daughter-biographer:

Her literary attitude is that of a votary at a shrine: she's gushful, and feminine, and overwhelmed by the honour of her parentage.

For the full flavour of his style readers should browse through Vance Palmer's *A. G. Stephens: His Life and Work* which collects Red Page and later *Bookfellow* criticism; or better, the collection which Tom Inglis Moore promises. Perhaps this extract from an article on the sonnet will serve to illustrate the characteristic (and embarrassed) 'play' with metaphor as well as any:

Lyric poets are born, sonnet-writers are made. The lyric poet inherits Nature, the sonnet-writer conquers Art. The essence of the lyric is spontaneity – it bushes freshly from some primal source: the sonnet is clothed with artificiality – it is by comparison an artesian jet, sought and striven for, falling into a trim basin and led away in a masonried channel. An epic, to continue the metaphor is some broad majestic Amazon of rivers; a drama (whose soul is conflict – between Man and Man, Man and Nature, Man and Fate) might be likened to the fury of the rapids before the tragic climax of Niagara. And Poesy is the sea whither all waters converge, and in which the metaphor drowns as it deserves to.

Stephens's criticism was indeed 'a lucky gift to the writers of his day'. Many have left on record their thanks and indebtedness, from McCrae ('my father-in-letters') and Gilmore (your criticism 'sends me out into fields that after all are mine own and yet in which I could never have walked – at least just so – but for it') to laconic Furphy (hearing that Stephens was taking leave 'I feel something like a Yankee whose father died right in the middle of the harvest . . . the loss of your censorship entails many scars on the finished Opus'). This despite his severity ('Australia breeds good horses, but nearly all of them are better ridden with a spur') and his constant reference to the best in contemporary continental and English writing 'as a measuring rod to beat those indulging in antics around the parish pump.'

Many of these antics, of course, he was directly responsible for. In a time when printing standards were low and the publication of Australian books a risky as well as frustrating venture he brought out publications such as *A Southern Garland* – a beautifully produced volume which is a treasured book collector's item today. And his success in pushing through the publication of *Such is Life* despite strong opposition from MacLeod is surely one of the triumphs of Australian publishing.

But the publishing activities, important as they are, were merely a secondary function of the criticism. Perhaps he was too much of a critic to be a first rate publisher. For one thing he consistently over-edited ('improved' – without authorization sometimes) his poets, as anyone who studies the manuscripts must note.

Stephens through his Red Page criticism which educated reading taste, as well as influencing writers was an indispensable ally to Archibald. Archibald with his *Bulletin* bards and story writers had bully-ragged Australian literature from its pioneer stage of cultural subservience into its second still immature stage of aggressive national revolt; Stephens pointed to the third and final stage of cultural independence. As Vance Palmer put it, 'An adult literature was coming into being, and Stephens had to act as its herald and expositor.'

NOTES

1. 'A. G. Stephens as Critic', *Prometheus*, (1959).
2. 'Poetry 1959': *C.A.B.*, vol. 25, no. 4, 21 December 1959.
3. MacLeod had Archibald put under restraint in Callan Park Mental Hospital. Stephens has written in his copy of *MacLeod of the Bulletin*: (now in the Mitchell library) 'MacLeod acted; he had to act but he should have acted with heart and intelligence. Archibald grew temporarily "insane" like Julian Salomons. Salomons was often "in restraint", but not in Callan Park public asylum. Archibald was worth £60,000 – enough to pay for an asylum all his own. Although he recovered, the publicity ruined his reputation. "Perhaps it was right to dissemble your love; but, why did you chuck me in Callan Park?" – Archibald.'
4. This and other references to Mrs MacLeod from *MacLeod of The Bulletin*.
5. Reprinted from *The Bulletin*, 1888. Author Arthur Gayll (pseud. F. J. Donohue).
6. Recalling Edmond's Archibald-inspired lines.
> 'The drivel of our fathers hands a dreary legend down,
> Its gods and heroes building out of dolt and ass and clown;
> The facts that never happened and the things that never would
> Are engraved upon the statues of the men who never could.'

LAWSON AND FURPHY

H.J. OLIVER

THE names of Lawson and Furphy are often linked, and undoubtedly the two writers had in common a close association with
The Bulletin, a social outlook that might be best described in
Furphy's famous words 'temper, democratic; bias, offensively
Australian', and a literary skill in prose excelling that of their
contemporaries. In another sense, however, no writers could be
more dissimilar. Of Lawson, H.M. Green could truthfully say
that 'the marvel is that he managed to do so much with so scanty
an intellectual background',[1] whereas many readers of Furphy
complain (probably wrongly) that his learning is a handicap to
his art; and while Lawson was good only in the short flight ('He
[Archibald] didn't think me capable of sustained work in literature; and he was right'), Furphy needed room to move and,
in spite of the brilliance of some of the single episodes in *Such is
Life* and *Rigby's Romance*, is of little account as a writer of the
short story.

Lawson began his literary career before Furphy. His first published work was a poem, 'Song of the Republic', printed in the
special 8-Hour Day issue of *The Bulletin* in 1887; and his reputation was made by poems such as this and 'Faces in the Street'
and 'The Army of the Rear'. As Dr Colin Roderick has said,
'we judge wrongly if we fail to appreciate the social efficacy of
such writings'[2] and it is not difficult to imagine the impact in
1888, of a poem beginning

> They lie, the men who tell us in a loud decisive tone,
> That want is here a stranger, and that misery's unknown

and lamenting the existence, in a country young and promising,
of the harshest poverty and extreme class-divisions (of the kind
later described in 'Second Class Wait Here').

Incidentally, the reader of the modern edition of Lawson's
Poetical Works will not find the lines just quoted: he will find
instead what George Robertson persuaded Lawson to substitute
in 1916, 'They lie, the men who tell us, for reasons of their own' –
which, Robertson told Bertram Stevens (who didn't agree), 'is a

great improvement. I "lent" Harry a fiver on it, anyway!' Some
sub-editing was certainly necessary: Lawson's spelling was uncertain, and when he wrote 'The Army of the Rear', he thought
'rear' rhymed with 'blare' – 'and when I found out it didn't it
gave me agony of soul for many years'. [3] Nor must it be believed
that Lawson always gave in (when he *was* consulted!). 'No!', he
once replied sharply to Robertson, 'this thing is personal and we
mustn't weaken the poem (and it is one) for anybody. . . . This
is not a bloody Sunday School pome.' Nevertheless, the modern
reader has to face the fact that the Lawson he reads has often
been edited, revised, 'regularized', and bowdlerized. Even the
famous 'Out Back', as now reprinted, is a stanza short; and in a
surviving stanza

> It chanced one day when the north wind blew in his face
>   like a furnace-breath,
> He left the track for a tank he knew – 'twas a shorter
>   cut to death;
> For the bed of the tank was hard and dry, and crossed
>   with many a crack,
> And, oh! it's a terrible thing to die of thirst in the scrub
>   Out Back

the second line originally read – and surely ought to read – 'He
left the track for a tank he knew – 'twas a short-cut to his death'.
The 'revision' (David McKee Wright's) runs the risk of implying
suicide and reduces the tragic irony of what Lawson wrote. A final
example may be taken from the prison poem 'One-Hundred-and-
Three'. Lawson wrote:

> The brute is a brute, and a kind man kind, and the
>   strong heart does not fail –
> A crawler's a crawler everywhere, but a man is a man
>   in gaol;
> For forced 'desertion', or drunkenness, or a law's
>   illegal debt,
> While never a man who was a man was 'reformed' by
>   punishment yet –

but the last two lines are now omitted, presumably because they
were too 'personal'. (Lawson's correspondence with George
Robertson over this one poem, or over 'Black Bonnet', would
provide enough material for a valuable book.)

Even after we have allowed for the fact that some of Lawson's verse has been spoiled, however, we still cannot think of him today as an important poet. We grant that his best verse has genuine feeling, whether the emotion expressed is affection for an individual (as in his finest love poem 'Do You Think that I Do Not Know?' or the lines to his daughter, 'Bertha') or, as it more often is, indignation at the sufferings of the many – the army of the rear, the women of the bush, and the men in 'Starvinghurst' (Darlinghurst) Gaol:

> The clever scoundrels are all outside, and the moneyless
>   mugs in gaol –
> Men do twelve months for a mad wife's lies or Life for
>   a strumpet's tale.

Indeed, he was entitled to claim, as he claimed in 'The Vanguard':

> They say, in all kindness, I'm out of the hunt –
> Too old and too deaf to be sent to the Front.
> A scribbler of stories, a maker of songs,
> To the fireside and armchair my valour belongs.
> Yet in campaigns all hopeless, in bitterest strife
> I have been at the Front all the days of my Life.

We grant also that his bush ballads are good in their kind. As will already be obvious, however, Lawson's rhythms are rarely, if ever, subtle; the metre (particularly the anapaest) is frequently the wrong one for the subject; the pathos (even in 'The Sliprails and the Spur') is too often close to sentiment; and the language is trite:

> There are boys out there by the western creeks, who hurry
>   away from school
> To climb the sides of the breezy peaks or dive in the shaded
>   pool,
> Who'll stick to their guns when the mountains quake to the
>   tread of a mighty war,
> And fight for Right or a Grand Mistake as men never fought
>   before.

Moreover, the once famous 'Star of Australasia', from which those lines are quoted, is one of the best proofs that even when Lawson had a promising rhetorical theme (the prophecy that Australia's rise to nationhood would be speeded up by participation in a World War) he was unable to *develop* it. Poems that

are better in other respects because they are humorous (such as
'When Your Pants Begin to Go') have this same weakness in
development, and 'The Teams', so vivid in its description and
atmosphere, collapses into a final stanza of moral comment.
Having said this, one may allow Lawson his defence, in his lines
'To my Cultured Critics':

> You were quick to pick on a faulty line
>   That I strove to put my soul in:
> Your eyes were keen for a dash of mine
>   In the place of a semi-colon –
> And blind to the rest. And is it for such
>   As you I must brook restriction?
> 'I was taught too little?' I learnt too much
>   To care for a scholar's diction!

In a different mood, Lawson confessed to dissatisfaction with
his own work – and he may not have been referring only to the
verse. Applying to the Governor of New South Wales, Lord
Beauchamp – and not in vain – for financial assistance to go to
London, he wrote:

I am, because of the prices paid literary men here, obliged to publish
rubbish – or, at least, good ideas in a hurried and mutilated form – and,
because of the reputation I have gained in Australia, I am forced to
sign hurried work – else I can't get it published at all. That's the
cruellest part of the business. [4]

His prose, however, hardly needs the apology.

Thinking particularly of the prose, A.G. Stephens has con-
ceded the point that Lawson made against his cultured critics
and has drawn a slightly different conclusion. 'After the Dickens
and Harte and Poe and Kendall and Australian Journal of his
boyhood', Stephens has written, 'he read few books; his mind
was not widened by literature; he used his eyes, he listened as he
could, and remembered all he saw and heard'. [5] Lawson's first
great gift as a writer of prose was indeed that he based his writing
not on literature but on what he saw and remembered.

Stephens was not the last reader to add that Lawson did not
see very far. ('Inevitably his view of life was limited, however
keen.') The complaint is justified but it is not crucial. Lawson's
second gift may be said to be the very sincerity, as well as the
economy and general skill, with which he reproduced one,
harsher, aspect of Australian life. Even though we now under-

stand that the famous controversy between Lawson and Paterson on the nature of the outback was, in a sense, stage-managed, each writer was, in a more important sense, speaking sincerely: Lawson did see the bareness and the hardship where Paterson saw the beauty and the gaiety. Lawson had no reason to dissemble when he wrote from Hungerford on 16 January 1893 to his aunt 'You can have no idea of the horror of the country out here. Men tramp and beg and live like dogs'.

A typical Lawson scene is that of the first few paragraphs of 'The Selector's Daughter':

She rode slowly down the steep sidling from the main road to a track in the bed of the Long Gully, the old grey horse picking his way zigzag fashion. She was about seventeen, slight in figure, and had a pretty freckled face with a pathetically drooping mouth, and big sad brown eyes. She wore a faded print dress, with an old black riding skirt drawn over it, and her head was hidden in one of those ugly, old-fashioned white hoods, which, seen from the rear, always suggest an old woman. She carried several parcels of groceries strapped to the front of the dilapidated side-saddle.

The track skirted a chain of rocky waterholes at the foot of the gully, and the girl glanced nervously at these ghastly, evil-looking pools as she passed them by. The sun had set, as far as Long Gully was concerned. The old horse carefully followed a rough bridle-track, which ran up the gully now on one side of the watercourse and now on the other; the gully grew deeper and darker, and its sullen, scrub-covered sides rose more steeply as he progressed.

The girl glanced round frequently, as though afraid of someone following her. Once she drew rein, and listened to some bush sound. 'Kangaroos,' she murmured; it was only kangaroos. She crossed a dimmed little clearing where a farm had been, and entered a thick scrub of box and stringy-bark saplings. Suddenly with a heavy thud, thud, an 'old man' kangaroo leapt the path in front, startling the girl fearfully, and went up the sidling towards the peak.

'Oh, my God!' she gasped.

Or again, in the oft-quoted words from 'The Union Buries Its Dead':

I have left out the wattle – because it wasn't there. I have also neglected to mention the heart-broken old mate, with his grizzled head bowed and great pearly drops streaming down his rugged cheeks. He was absent – he was probably 'out back'. For similar reasons I have omitted reference to the suspicious moisture in the eyes of a bearded bush ruffian named Bill. Bill failed to turn up, and the only moisture was that which was induced by the heat ...

– and the atmosphere of that story is sustained until the very last word, when the tale-teller, remarking that the name on the coffin was known not to be the 'real one', concludes:

We did hear, later on, what his real name was; but if we ever chance to read it in the 'Missing Friends Column', we shall not be able to give any information to heart-broken mother or sister or wife, nor to anyone who could let him hear something to his advantage – for we have already forgotten the name.

Even 'That There Dog Of Mine' once could have been used to illustrate this merciless realism. As printed in *While the Billy Boils* and *The Prose Works*, it ends with the doctor setting the dog's broken leg 'out in the yard' while its shearer-master, who would not stay in the hospital unless the dog stayed too, is cared for inside. As originally written, the story had an additional paragraph saying that this wasn't true; the hospital wouldn't allow the dog to stay, the injured shearer walked on and died on the track, and those who expressed their indignation at the incident weren't told that when the body was found the dog was still with it – and eating it.

It may be admitted that occasionally Lawson does fall into the 'pathetic fallacy'. More often his eye is keen and his memory is accurate when he pictures the working conditions in the shearing shed of the nineties and in the Grinder Bros. coach-factory, or the living conditions in the slums of Sydney ('Jones's Alley'), in the cheap Sydney boarding house ('Board and Residence'), in the out-back pub ('An Incident at Stiffner's'), in the steerage of the ship going from Sydney to New Zealand, and even in Darling-hurst Gaol (as in one of the uncollected prose sketches called 'Going In').

His third great gift was the sympathy with which he drew the characters of those who, in such conditions, survived. (Those who did not survive are not always drawn with the same skill: senti-mentality sometimes takes over when the story involves a death.) It is sympathy, in both the original and the modern meanings of that word, that makes possible such a story as 'The Drover's Wife', immortalizing the stoic courage of the bush wife who sits up all night watching for the snake that is known to be under, or behind the wall of, the hut. Her husband, having failed to make a living from the impossibly poor land, is away droving – as usual:

She is used to being left alone. She once lived like this for eighteen months. . . . The last two children were born in the bush – one while her husband was bringing a drunken doctor, by force, to attend to her. . . . One of the children died while she was here alone. She rode nineteen miles for assistance, carrying the dead child.

'"Water Them Geraniums"' is a second well-known illustration of this theme.

Among the other men and women whom Lawson sees as making survival possible are those who, however eccentric they may be, forget their own interests when there is an emergency – such as 'Brighten's Sister-in-Law' or the drunkard Doc Wild ('They buried him with bush honours, and chiselled his name on a slab of blue-gum – a wood that lasts' – in the story 'Middleton's Peter'); those who are true to their 'mates' [6]; those who, having paid too great a penalty for a mistake, spend the rest of their lives trying to make up for it ('Telling Mrs Baker' – but 'The Hero of Redclay' is too melodramatic a treatment of a similar theme [7]); and many a bush husband or father, neighbour, mother or wife. He can even find it in his heart to draw sympathetically those who survive by their wits (particularly the 'sharper', Steelman, of the New Zealand stories).

Most of all he admires, and perhaps he draws most successfully, those who get by because of something like his own acceptance of fate and slightly twisted sense of humour – and the greatest of these are Mitchell and the various characters who seem to be portraits of Lawson's father. 'An Old Mate of Your Father's' is, in this sense and others, the central Lawson story; and the phrase that best indicates its tone (is it an illusion to believe that it is Lawson's favourite phrase?) is 'Ah, well!':

And, again they'd talk lower and more mysterious like, and perhaps mother would be passing the wood-heap and catch a word, and ask:
'Who was she, Tom?'
And Tom – father – would say:
'Oh, you didn't know her, Mary; she belonged to a family Bill knew at home.'
And Bill would look solemn till mother had gone, and then they would smile a quiet smile, and stretch and say, 'Ah, well!' and start something else.

Lawson's greatest technical problem, in deciding how to treat
such themes, has been well defined by A. A. Phillips: 'He had to
learn how to be successfully "slight", to find just how little plot
he could afford to use without risking the collapse of the structure'. Vance Palmer has also noted that 'Many writers only
find their own style after a painful effort in sloughing the false
skin of accepted convention, but Lawson fell into a natural
stride from the beginning'. [8] Certainly he did not turn to other
writers as models: he could not, like a Katherine Mansfield, learn
from a Chehov. An occasional story is reminiscent of Bret
Harte or of Dickens, but Lawson worked out his own methods.
Perhaps it was from the typical bush 'yarn' of his day that he
learnt the value of first-person narration in giving verisimilitude
and of laconic periphrasis or understatement in giving true
emphasis ('She wasn't tongue-tied and had no impediment in her
speech'; '[he] will probably end as an habitual criminal, either
at the head of some department like the Lands or Post Office,
or in Berrima Gaol'). Whether from this source or another, he
also learnt the value of dramatization in gaining vividness. There
is, however, no one technique that could be said to be Lawson's.
As he experiments, we find in his stories nearly every degree of
plot or plotlessness; and interestingly, except perhaps in pure
farce, such as 'The Loaded Dog', the stories are best when the
plot is slightest. To be sure, in such a successful story as 'Mitchell
on Matrimony' there is the surprise announcement that Mitchell's
marriage ended when his wife left him 'for – another kind of
fellow', but that information only emphasizes the true theme and,
with a nice touch, Lawson ends the story with Mitchell seeming
to turn his back on the past with the inconsequential: '"Why
don't you finish your tea, Joe? The billy's getting cold"'. 'The
Iron-Bark Chip', which depends entirely on plot, is quickly forgotten, and 'Andy Page's Rival' fails if the ending is intended as
a surprise.

My own favourite is 'Hungerford', which has no apparent
plot at all. From the indefinite 'you' of the opening sentence:
'One of the hungriest cleared roads in New South Wales runs to
within a couple of miles of Hungerford, and stops there; then
you strike through the scrub to the town', Lawson modulates to
the first-personal 'we': 'We found Hungerford and camped there
for a day. The town is right on the Queensland border, and an

interprovincial rabbit-proof fence – with rabbits on both sides of it – runs across the main street'. There are a few anecdotes; a few serious comments: 'I believe that Burke and Wills found Hungerford, and it's a pity they did; but, if I ever stand by the graves of the men who first travelled through this country, when there were neither roads nor stations, nor tanks, nor bores, nor pubs, I'll – I'll take my hat off'; some significant but seemingly casual giving of information about the local water, and costs, and storekeepers; a brief but pointed exchange of opinion with 'an old man who was minding a mixed flock of goats and sheep' – an exchange which reveals how 'tough' the conditions were for the man without a job; and finally the paragraph about the trooper who, because 'one of us was very deaf' thought a conversation was 'a row', but, reassured, 'left us, and later on we saw him sitting with the rest of the population on a bench under the hotel verandah. Next morning we rolled up our swags and left Hungerford to the north-west'. There is indeed 'namoore to seye' – except that the original readers of the story in *The Bulletin* would have had no illusions on the question whether things were any better elsewhere.

The quotations from 'Hungerford' and the other short stories may have made one final point clear. Perhaps because he was uncorrupted by too much reading of bad literature in his youth, perhaps because he aimed so often at the illusion of the spoken word, perhaps even because he learnt to read by getting ahead of his mother with that model of English narrative, *Robinson Crusoe*, Lawson at his best was the master of a magnificent, simple, prose style. A reader who opens Bret Harte at any page will notice the cliché in every paragraph and will understand why Australian critics shudder when they hear Lawson referred to as 'the Australian Bret Harte'.

*

Lawson was so successful in making his stories sound artless and natural that some readers thought Lawson was artless; Furphy was so successful in making his masterpiece *Such is Life* appear formless that many of his readers and critics believed that Furphy had no sense of form and that *Such is Life* was to be appreciated only as a picture of life in the Riverina and northern Victoria in the bullock-driving days. It has been one of the tasks of later criticism to prove – and it was part of the genius of A. G. Stephens that in 1897 he must immediately have seen – that *Such is Life*, even as first written, had in fact a most subtle and original plan, and that good as Furphy was as a 'local-colourist', he was much more than that. As he told Miles Franklin, a great novel needs in addition to 'word-painting', 'a rational appraisement of the value of life, and a definite theory of its purpose'.

Furphy wrote to Stephens (2 May 1897): 'The plan of the book is not like any other that I know of, – at least, I trust not'. The last thing that he wanted was the artificiality of the plot of the average novel, for, as A. K. Thomson has well said, 'He could see that the plot, in the ordinary sense of the term, falsified and distorted the novel; and being a humorist, he constantly measured all things against hard facts'. [9]

Accordingly, he made *his* novel look as little like the orthodox one as possible. He created, to tell the story, the character 'Tom Collins' (that being the traditional bush-name for a teller of tales), and had Collins announce:

I purpose taking certain entries from my diary, and amplifying these to the minutest detail of occurrence or conversation. This will afford to the observant reader a fair picture of Life, as that engaging problem has presented itself to me.

Twenty-two consecutive editions of *Letts's Pocket Diary*, with one week in each opening, lie on the table before me; all filled up, and in a decent state of preservation. I think I shall undertake the annotation of a week's record. A man might, if he were of a fearful heart, stagger in this attempt; but I shut my eyes, and take up one of the little volumes. It proves to be the edition of 1883. Again I shut my eyes while I open the book at random. It is the week beginning with Sunday, the 9th of September.

As soon as Collins has told in detail the events of 9 September, however, he discovers that the events of 10 September are not suitable for expansion:

At the Blowhard Sand-hill, on the night of the 10th, I camped with a party of six sons of Belial, bound for Deniliquin, with 3,000 Boolka wethers off the shears. Now, anyone who has listened for four hours to the conversation of a group of sheep drovers, named, respectively, Splodger, Rabbit, Parson, Bottler, Dingo, and Hairy-toothed Ike, will agree with me as to the impossibility of getting the dialogue of such *dramatis personae* into anything like printable form. The bullock drivers were bad enough, but these fellows are out of the question.

He decides that for Chapter II he will expand the entry under 9 October and for Chapter III 9 November and so on:

The thread of narrative being thus purposely broken, no one of these short and simple analyses can have any connection with another – a point on which I congratulate the judicious reader and the no less judicious writer; for the former is thereby tacitly warned against any expectation of plot or denouement, and so secured against disappointment, whilst the latter is relieved from the (to him) impossible task of investing prosaic people with romance, and a generally hap-hazard economy with poetical justice.

Chapter III, however, has to be extended to cover the events of 10 November, to make sense; and finally for Chapter VII Collins decides that 9 March is quite unsuitable, and takes as his text 28 March instead, assuring us that by 'this arbitrary departure in dates' we shall, coincidentally, meet again one or two characters to whom we have already been introduced.

This, of course, is all camouflage; and the real plan and aim of the novel remain to be defined. The title is the first clue: whether or not Furphy knew that 'Such is Life' were supposed to be the last words of the bushranger Ned Kelly, he certainly knew that they form the usual expression of surprise at the connection or seeming lack of connection between events, or the apparent lack of justice in life.[10] The second clue is in the opening paragraphs of the novel, in which Collins talks about determinism and free will, cause and effect; and the third, I still believe, is in a passage later in the book in which Collins concludes that life consists of a series of major and minor alternatives, that 'each undertaking, great or small, of our lives has one controlling alternative, and no more', and that 'such momentous alternatives are simply the voluntary rough-hewing of our own ends. Whether there's a Divinity that afterwards shapes them, is a question which each inquirer may decide for himself'. Life is like a railway track with a series of junctions; at each one you may turn left or right, but once having chosen, you may not return; life consists, in fact, of 'the unfettered alternative, followed by rigorous destiny'.

The question has quite properly been raised whether, since Collins is a character in the novel and since he is so often wrong about the very story he tells, any passage of *his* philosophizing may be taken as announcing the theme of the novel. I think, however, that it can be so taken. Furphy may well have commented that wisdom comes out of the mouths of babes and fools; and Furphy is all the more likely to be serious when Collins is clowning (as he clowns about his railway-line theory here, with its single lines and double lines, and 'a bright little loco., in holiday trim, dazzling you with her radiant head-lights, and commanding your admiration by her 'tractive power'). Moreover there is the perfect parallel of Rigby in Furphy's second novel, *Rigby's Romance*. Rigby is certainly a character: 'I deliberately intended Rigby', Furphy told his friend Cathels, 'as a man of offensively large information'. He was amused when Kate Baker thought that Rigby was modelled on Cathels and he would have been horrified at any suggestion that Rigby was a self-portrait. He can also say, however: 'I flatter me that Rigby says the last word on the Ethics of State Socialism'. One may argue that Tom Collins similarly goes as far as Furphy thought anybody could go towards expressing a 'philosophy' of life; and every single incident in *Such is Life can* be interpreted in terms of the unfettered alternative followed by rigorous destiny.

Without carrying the argument quite so far, it may at least be maintained that basically *Such is Life* is a series of variations on the theme of *responsibility*; and the variations are arranged, almost in musical fashion, to give the greatest range of mood and effect. Furphy begins with a comic statement of the theme, with the story of the bullock-drivers' near-escape from having their teams impounded. This is followed by a tragic variation, the story of the death of the blind swagman, who would have survived had not Tom Collins, not knowing he was blind, thought to have done him a good turn by letting him rest until dusk. Chapter III then gives a comic variation, with the superb account of how a trivial decision not to light his pipe led Collins to lose his trousers (and to many an accident thereafter). The next variation on the theme may be called 'romantic', since it continues the story of the lover Warrigal Alf (and includes by contrast the account of the bush marriage of Sollicker and 'Helenar', misinterpreted, as usual, by Collins, who does not see that the marriage was most unromantic). Chapter V gives us another comic variation on the theme, in the story of the rounding up of all the 'trespassers' in search of grass for their hungry animals; and by what must be deliberate design, the most tragic of all the variations – the story of the death of Mary O'Halloran, itself 'caused', in a sense, by Collins's generous decision in Chapter II – is set against that comic background. The tragic story of one lost child is followed by the comic story of another one; next there is another tragic version; and the chapter is rounded off with the somewhat bitter comedy of the impounding. Chapter VI can then be in the key of comic romance, so to speak, when Collins's 'romance' with Mrs Beaudesart ('Mrs Bodysark') at the romantically named 'Runnymede' is a kind of parody not only of Furphy's own story of Warrigal Alf but also of Henry Kingsley's novel *Geoffry Hamlyn*, which Furphy hated so much and at which, he told Cathels, he 'wanted to get a cowardly welt ... *à la* Fielding-Richardson': Mrs Bodysark is Furphy's idea of Kingsley's Miss Buckley, as that young lady might have developed in real life (as distinct from a nineteenth century novel). The final chapter gathers all the threads together, if I may change the metaphor, although Collins himself never sees the connections between the tales he has been telling.

Only if it is granted that Furphy's method of construction was that of theme and variations, I believe, will it be understood how, without ruining the construction in any way, he could introduce the story of Mary O'Halloran only at the time of the final revision, and transfer the 'lost child' group of stories from Chapter I to Chapter V, and how, at this same time, he could drop completely the character Peterson. Peterson, another bullock-driver, had been wrongly imprisoned for allegedly assaulting a girl and as a result had 'gone off his head'; and I would suggest that he had been put in the novel in the first place because he illustrated not so much 'the injustice of the law' as this same theme of rigorous destiny and responsibility (or the lack of it) for one's fate. [11]

Perhaps because he felt that this method of construction was in itself not enough, Furphy also bound his novel together by weaving through it one continuous love-story (based, he said, on real-life) – which Collins tells without knowing that he is telling it. (As Furphy put it to Cathels: 'It was not a collection of lies, but one long, involved lie'.) First Collins hears how Cooper, living on the Hawkesbury, had a sister Molly, whose face was disfigured by a horse and who was jilted by her lover three years later; and he learns that the lover married a worthless woman but left her and was last seen bullock-driving in the Bland Country. He also learns that Cooper hates the name Alf, and that Molly was unusually tall and strong for a girl, and loved music.

In Chapter IV, Warrigal Alf, in a state of delirium, imagines he hears the voice of a woman he loved; and he tells Collins that he once lived on the Hawkesbury but left an unfaithful wife and regards all his ills as punishment for 'one deliberately fiendish and heartless action'. Collins, all mixed up between this and the Ouida novel he has been reading, about a 'tawny haired tigress with dark slumbrous eyes', gives a completely misleading account of Alf's life-story to the grazier Stewart of Kooltopa; and Stewart's passing comment that Alf came from the Bland Country six or seven years ago does not mean anything to him.

In Chapter VI, Collins meets the boundary rider 'Nosey Alf' – a curious kind of boundary rider who keeps a hut clean and tends a flower garden, has a beautiful voice but won't sing when women are near, has a 'rippling laugh', and a figure that 'tapers the wrong way' and a face that is disfigured but is 'more beautiful, otherwise, than a man's face is justified in being'. Collins does not place any special significance on Nosey Alf's inquiries about Warrigal Alf but answers them with his usual facetiousness and inappropriate circumlocutions: intending to say that Warrigal Alf has gone to Queensland, he volunteers the information that 'These wool-tracks, that knew him so well, will know him no more again for ever. He's gone to a warmer climate' – and is surprised by Nosey Alf's violent reaction to this and to the further information that Warrigal Alf is now a widower and was once within yards of this very hut. We, however, are interested to learn, in Chapter VII, that Nosey Alf has since been seen 'sixty or eighty mile beyond the Darling', heading north, for Queensland.

By telling his story in this way – and there are other, less important, examples – Furphy is using a technique that is comparable with, but not the same as, others used before and since. Conrad's Marlow, for instance, was a narrator who did not know *all* the facts about the story he told, as in *Lord Jim*, and whose account therefore had to be supplemented by the accounts of others – and by the reader. Furphy's Tom Collins is a further refinement – the narrator who doesn't even know that he *is* telling one story and sees none of the connections between the various incidents he tells, or mis-tells. The reader, as it were, works the story out for himself – and because he has to work it out for himself, believes it (much as Henry James maintained that the reader of

The Turn of the Screw who imagined the evil for himself would be much more convinced that it was evil than he would have been by anything James could name). It also goes without saying that some of the pleasure of rereading *Such is Life* is the pleasure of being one jump, or several jumps, ahead of the narrator Collins; as in a subtly orchestrated symphony or opera, one recognizes with particular pleasure the chords that one knows will later swell into a full melody.

Perhaps it is also only on rereading that one learns to appreciate the Furphy style that so many have found unreadable. The point is that the ponderous polysyllabic style (whether it came naturally to Furphy or not) is here attributed almost entirely to the misguided Collins (a Deputy-Assistant-Sub-Inspector, a Government official of the Ninth Class), to the learned English B.A., Willoughby, and to those who occasionally flatter Collins by trying to imitate him: Thompson, for instance, with his 'I found myself at Moama, with one hundred and ten notes to the good, and the prospect of going straight ahead, like the cube root – or the square of the hypotenuse, is it? I forget the exact term, but no matter.' Thompson's own natural style of speaking, however, is simple and direct; and no reader should fail to observe that it is Thompson who tells the moving story of Mary O'Halloran, and that some of the comedy of the novel comes from the very contrast between Collins's diction, on the one hand, and the simplicity of Thompson or the sanguinary conversation of the bullock-drivers, on the other. Nor should there be any misunderstanding nowadays about Furphy's methods of handling that sanguinary conversation. Furphy's American admirer, Hartley Grattan, could not have been more wrong than when he said that 'Collins was a bit of a Victorian and could not bring himself to write – much less print – two words which occur in the conversation of the "dinkum Aussie" hardly less frequently than commas and periods on the printed page: hell and bloody'.[12] Grattan completely missed the fun of the mock-modest '(adj.)', of the satire on literary convention, and of all the 'elegant variation' that is so much more amusing than mere repetition of 'hell' and 'bloody' would have been. 'An easy and not ungraceful clatter of the adjective used so largely by poets in denunciation of war', and 'I have taken some trouble in weeding the language of Jack's confession, so as not to destroy its consecutiveness' are only two examples of the method. The second is taken from Collins's version of ex-sailor Jack the Shellback's account of the hunger of the man-o'-war hawk – a memorable instance not only of Furphy's incomparable humour but also of his skill with language as such. 'Beyond all other writers', Furphy himself claimed in his 'synopsis-review' drafted at the request of *The Bulletin*, 'Tom Collins is a master of idiom'.

It was in 1897 that Furphy wrote to *The Bulletin* to ask what he should do with the newly-completed *Such is Life*; it was 1903 before the novel was published (and published only because Stephens insisted that *The Bulletin*, which was not normally concerned with novels, could perform a service to Australian literature by risking the almost certain financial loss). Between 1897 and 1903 the book was twice revised. The surviving pages of the original manuscript in the Mitchell Library suggest that when Furphy typed his manuscript he made only a few unimportant changes; the fuller but still incomplete typescript, also in the Mitchell, shows, when compared with the printed text, that the second revision involved tightening-up, occasional verbal improvements, some minor omissions and – as has always been known – two major 'cuts' that reduced the book by one third. Rather than 'emasculate' his novel everywhere, Furphy eliminated two whole sections which, with further additions and omissions, became in time the separate novels, *Rigby's Romance* and *The Buln-Buln and the Brolga*. The former was first published in serial form in the Broken Hill *Barrier Truth*, to which Furphy presented it as a tribute to the democratic spirit of the western miners, and was not issued complete in book form until 1946 (in spite of all the efforts of Kate Baker to keep Furphy's reputation alive); the latter was not published at all until 1948.

No admirer of Furphy would be without these 'anabranches' of *Such is Life*, but the pleasure he has from them may be compared with the pleasure that an admirer of *Henry IV* has from *The Merry Wives of Windsor*. *The Buln-Buln and the Brolga* gives us further interesting glimpses of the boyhood of Tom Collins; and nothing in *Such is Life* is better than some parts of *Rigby's Romance* – such as the self-educated bullock-driver Dixon's version of the story of Moses, which gave him 'a (sheol) of a (adj.) fright', or his account of his misplaced attempts to adapt Rochester's technique in *Jane Eyre* to his own romance with a school-teacher ('I'd come to the (adj.) conclusion that clever, edicated gurls doesn't believe in a (adj.) walk-over. ... On'y, sometimes it don't work properly. *Varium et mutabile semper* (adj.) *foemina*'). Furphy himself, in certain moods, claimed that *Rigby's Romance* was better than *Such is Life* – but this was during the period when he was tired of waiting for the publication of his first book and was working on the second.

Both the later novels are top-heavy. *Rigby's Romance* is in the form of what its editor has called a 'symposium', with Dixon, Thompson and others telling love-stories, while they fish on the banks of the Murray; gradually, however, it all but becomes a monologue by Rigby on the subject of the 'true' Christianity, State Socialism, 'working toward the elevation of the human race as a whole'. Rigby thus quite forgets his appointment with Kate Vanderdecken and thereby deprives the romantically minded Collins of the pleasure of 'the delicate web of heart history' which he had expected to be 'unfolded' for his 'edification'. The 'lines of life' of Rigby and Kate may indeed 'have been insensibly converging' for more than twenty-three years, but Rigby's forgetfulness and other seemingly trivial circumstances mean that once again the unfettered alternative has been followed by rigorous destiny. 'State Socialism', however, is the main theme, and *Rigby's Romance* is perilously close to being what Furphy himself disliked, 'the Novel With a Purpose'. *The Buln-Buln and the Brolga* consists largely of the lies of the buln-buln (or lyre-bird), Fred Falkland-Pritchard, and the attempts by the brolga, Barefooted Bob, to hold his own in such company – together with further instances of Collins's uncanny ability to distort the truth *without* trying. The best single part is Bob's account of his disgust with a performance of *Hamlet* in Melbourne – reminding one inevitably of, and in humour not far behind, Partridge's version of Garrick's *Hamlet* in Fielding's *Tom Jones*.

Collins and Thompson are met again in some of the best of Furphy's short-stories, such as 'High Art' and 'The Bullock Hunter', but most of them – which he apparently intended for a collected volume to be called *Here Be Truths* – are conventional and lack the antiseptic irony of the longer work. Conventional, also, are most of Furphy's poems, collected and published by Kate Baker in 1916; the modern reader will probably approve only of the semi-jocular 'Brahm' (on the theme 'Nothing exists but Brahm') and 'The Schoolhouse on the Plain' – particularly, perhaps, the stanzas describing the scene when divine service is held in the Schoolhouse on Sundays:

> There the boys deal glances fond, and the girls, of course, respond,
>   In spite of the indifference they feign;
> Whilst the mothers of the youth listen to the word of truth,
>   Till they feel about as innocent as Cain;
> And the toddlers play bo-peep, and the rude forefathers sleep,
>   Being bosses of the Schoolhouse on the Plain.

The literary allusion in the second last line is sufficient reminder that Furphy had a combination of qualities that is rare in literary history. We may apply to him the words used by Stewart to describe Warrigal Alf in *Such is Life*: 'Fine combination of a cultivated man and an experienced rough-and-ready bushman'. The parallel that Hartley Grattan thought was closest in American literature was Herman Melville; without necessarily accepting this, one may suggest that the combination of the scholar with the man of action is always particularly valuable if it comes at the stage of development that Australian literature had reached when Furphy wrote *Such is Life*.

NOTES

1. *A History of Australian Literature* (Sydney, 1961), I. p. 354.

2. Royal Australian Historical Society, *Journal and Proceedings*, 45.3. (1959), p. 136.

3. Mary Gilmore has gone on record as saying that she was responsible for Lawson's error here: he accepted without question her wrong pronunciation.

4. Letters to Lord Beauchamp, 19 January 1900. (See also 'Pursuing Literature in Australia', *Bulletin*, 21 January 1899.) All letters cited in this chapter are quoted from the originals in the Mitchell Library, Sydney, or the National Library, Canberra.

5. Quoted from the typescript in the Mitchell Library.

6. I do not overlook Dr H. P. Heseltine's caveat in his article 'Saint Henry, Our Apostle of Mateship' (*Quadrant*, V.i, 1960-1, pp. 5-11). The 'mateship' theme must certainly not be treated as if it were the only one in Lawson.

7. 'The Hero of Redclay' is one of the stories on which Lawson based his unpublished play, *Pinter's Son Jim*, the manuscript of which is in the Mitchell Library. The play was written for Bland Holt, when Lawson was in New Zealand in 1897; Holt paid Lawson an advance on the play but returned the manuscript to him.

8. Phillips, *The Australian Tradition* (Melbourne, 1958), p. 3; Palmer, *National Portraits* (Melbourne, 3rd edition, enlarged, 1954), p. 163.

9. 'The Greatness of Joseph Furphy', *Meanjin Papers*, II. iii (1943), pp. 20-3.

10. See A. G. Mitchell, '*Such is Life*: The Title and the Structure of the Book', *Southerly*, IV.iii (1945), pp. 43-59.

11. I differ here from John Barnes, 'The Structure of Joseph Furphy's *Such is Life*', *Meanjin*, XV.iv (1956), pp. 374-89.

12. 'Tom Collins's *Such is Life*', *Australian Quarterly*, September 1937, p. 75. One hopes that Grattan would have been amused by Furphy's allusion (in an undated letter to Cathels) to 'Titania and B-tt-m'.

CHRISTOPHER BRENNAN

G. A. WILKES

TAKEN as the foremost Australian poet of the twentieth century, Brennan wrote his verse substantially in the nineteenth. In the same decade in which Henry Handel Richardson was widening the scope of the Australian novel by her study of the French, Russian and Scandinavian masters – publishing her translations of Jacobsen and Björnson in 1896, and beginning *Maurice Guest* in 1897 – Brennan was writing the early poems that drew the response from Mallarmé '*Il y a entre vous et moi une parentée de songe*'. [1] He began the serious writing of verse in 1891, issued his first volume in 1897, and by 1902 had his work substantially complete. Although it was not published until 1914 – or effectively restored to print until 1960-2 – Brennan's poetry is still to be understood in relation to the intellectual modes of the later nineteenth century.

As an undergraduate at the University of Sydney, Brennan had been converted to agnosticism in 1890, from reading Herbert Spencer's *First Principles*. His first serious attempt at verse, 'Farewell, the pleasant harbourage of Faith', followed the next year. Brennan now committed himself to a voyage over 'the misty seas of thought' into the 'vast Unknown', in this romantic rhetoric dramatizing the plight of man in the universe of Herbert Spencer, the 'vast Unknown' being Spencer's version of the Absolute (variously defined in the philosophy of the day) as 'the Unknowable' or 'the Unknown Reality'. If this sonnet makes no particular claim for Brennan as a poet in 1891, it does present him already in his role of 'confirmed metaphysician'. [2] All his subsequent effort is to fill the formless aspirations of this time with substance and meaning.

Brennan left Australia in 1892 on a travelling scholarship, and in the two years he spent in Berlin he found in French poetry of the later nineteenth century a reflection of his own metaphysical search. He became convinced that the single impulse behind all the writers of the 'symbolist' and 'decadent' schools was an aspiration to some pitch of experience, some ideal of beauty that ordinary life denied. It was expressed in Gautier and Huysmans in the resolve to explore experience to its limits, disregarding moral law; in the *Axël* of Villiers de l'Isle-Adam it took the form of a disdain of the material world, and an effort to create a personal, hermetic world transcending its tawdriness; in Flaubert's *Salammbô* it was expressed in the rediscovery of the pagan past as 'noble and nude and antique'; and in Baudelaire's *Les Fleurs du Mal* in the presentation of the world as we know it in terms of mockery and violence, for its denial of the ideal beauty. In Mallarmé Brennan found this ideal beauty formulated as Eden, the symbol of the lost paradise itself, and through Mallarmé he came to read all poetry as a history of mankind's dream of the Absolute. The same dream was reflected in myth, in fables of the Golden Age and the Land of Heart's Desire, and attested in everyday life in the feeling most men have of the imperfection of this life, and in their sense of some fuller life transcending it. All Brennan's poetry – and his metaphysics also, from 'Fact and Idea' onward – came to be governed by the sense of a primal harmony lost, and of a further synthesis that man is journeying towards, tormenting him as a vision of perfection he can apprehend but not attain. As he wrote later:

We use poetry to express not the perfect Beauty, but our want of it, our aspiration towards it. Setting it far off in some imagined empyrean, the poet may even by a paradox, treat with fierce irony of life devoid of all shadow of it or desire for it. More often his theme will be the tragedy of such beauty as this world affords, or the fate that dogs the soul intoxicated with perfection. (*Prose*, p. 19.)

Through Brennan's immersion in contemporary French literature in 1892-4, the 'vast Unknown' – the impersonal Absolute of the 1891 sonnet – was endowed with humanity and meaning. These literary influences cannot be separated from Brennan's personal experiences in Berlin, especially his love for Anna Elisabeth Werth. His betrothal to her made 1893 a signal year in his life, recalled in the poem which stands on the threshold of the collected *Poems*, titled simply 'MDCCCXCIII: A Prelude':

> Sweet days of breaking light,
> or yet the shadowy might
> and blaze of starry strife
> possess'd my life;
>
> sweet dawn of Beauty's day,
> first hint and smiling play

of the compulsive force
that since my course

across the years obeys;
not tho' all earlier days
in me were buried, not
were ye forgot.

Brennan's early poems arose from his separation from Elisabeth, as he returned to Sydney in 1894 to wait three years for her to join him. *XVIII Poems: Being the first collection of verse & prose*, was issued in an edition of eight copies in March 1897, then superseded in July by *XXI Poems: Towards the Source*. Brennan was given to quoting the dictum of Novalis, that 'Every beloved object is the centre of a Paradise', and these love lyrics eventually declare themselves as an exploration of love as one of the avenues to the Absolute, one of the ways of realizing Eden.

In his articles on 'Newer French Poetry' in 1899, Brennan described the emergence in French verse in the later nineteenth century of the symbolist *livre composé*, 'the book of verse conceived and executed as a whole, a single concerted poem' (*Prose*, p. 289). *XXI Poems: Towards the Source* (1897) is his own attempt to acclimatize the form. It is not (as *XVIII Poems* had been) a simple collection of verses, but a studiously patterned sequence, with the poems grouped in three movements, with an envoi. In October 1897 Brennan was already contemplating 'a second and enlarged edition, wherein the unity of the book shall be more apparent',[3] and by 1898 a more ambitious design had begun to unfold before him. Its focus was the poem 'Lilith', to which the projected fourth section of *Towards the Source* became an introduction, and the further growth of the cycle through 1898 and 1899 may be followed in Brennan's MSS. The successive plans show him shifting poems from one place to another as the cycle evolves, writing additional pieces to fill in blanks in the structure, and supplying 'interludes' to link one movement to the next. In 1900 Brennan turned aside to write *The Burden of Tyre*, a sub-cycle occasioned by the Boer War, but in 1902 the composition of *The Wanderer* brought the scheme almost to completion. The two smaller units subsequently added, *Pauca Mea* and *Epilogues*, absorb a few later poems and provide a retrospect on the whole action traversed.

In the volume eventually published in 1914, Brennan is therefore sharing Baudelaire's resolve 'to desert the separate *genres*
and to condense all his poetry into one book which shall have its
unity and its secret architecture' (*Prose*, p. 328). *Poems* (1913) is a
single poem in five movements, separately titled, with the text
printed in two kinds of type – ordinary type for the text proper,
and bold face (rendered as italic in Chisholm and Quinn) for the
epigraphs and interludes that make the transitions, providing in
sum a synopsis of the whole development. The pursuit of the
Edenic vision, in its various guises, gives the book its more
essential coherence, approaching Brennan's ideal formulation of
the *livre composé* as

the sublimation of a whole imaginative life and experience into a subtly
ordered series of poems, where each piece has, of course, its individual
value, yet cannot be interpreted save in its relation to the whole.

(*Prose*, p. 329)

The initial movement, *Towards the Source* (1894-7), preserves
seventeen poems from the 1897 sequence (one re-written) and
adds thirteen others. Their immediate appeal is as a series of
love lyrics, belonging mostly to the 'four springtimes lost'
between Brennan's leaving Berlin in 1894 and Elisabeth's arrival
in Australia in 1897. His inscription in her copy of the 1897 text
best captures their feeling:

> The soul, that yearns for sharpest fire
> of sweet attainment, dreams in thee
> a sweet beyond its last desire
> & peace more deep than song or sea.

It is not merely the prospect of fulfilment in love that dominates
the series, but the prospect of a fulfilment beyond it. In the title,
'source' is used in the sense of a well or fountain, perhaps recalling the 'La Source' motif (a nude figure beside a spring) of
Clodion, Ingres, and Courbet, but made more significant by
Brennan's view of the Fountain of Youth as one of the equiva-
lents, in myth, for the lost paradise. He held that Mallarmé
lived 'to turn the steps of a generation towards the source,
towards Eden' (*Prose*, p. 282), and the aspiration of *Towards the
Source* is to realize Eden in human love.

In the first of its three movements, the sense of separation and
disenchantment prevails: the poet is an outcast from happiness,

and his plight is dramatized – by a technique possibly taken from Swinburne – through a *persona* of agelong experience:

> Where star-cold and the dread of space
> in icy silence bind the main
> I feel but vastness on my face,
> I sit, a mere incurious brain,
>
> under some outcast satellite,
> some Thule of the universe,
> upon the utter verge of night
> frozen by some forgotten curse.
>
> The ways are hidden from mine eyes
> that brought me to this ghastly shore:
> no embers in their depths arise
> of suns I may have known of yore.
>
> Somewhere I dream of tremulous flowers
> and meadows fervent with appeal
> far among fever'd human hours
> whose pulses here I never feel:
>
> that on my careless name afar
> a voice is calling ever again
> beneath some other wounded star
> removed for ever from my ken:
>
> vain fictions! silence fills my ear,
> the deep my gaze: I reck of nought,
> as I have sat for ages here,
> concentred in my brooding thought.

It is an exile made more painful by remembered joys ('tremulous flowers and meadows fervent with appeal'), and crossed with yearning for their recovery. In the second movement these conflicting impulses produce the stalemate of *ennui*. Brennan interpreted the *ennui* of Baudelaire and his generation as a recoil from the squalor of ordinary existence, as compared with the fuller life the poet has glimpsed, and he follows Baudelaire and Verhaeren in fixing on the city (in 'The yellow gas is fired from street to street') as the place where the vision is most cruelly thwarted, and 'our paradisal instinct starves'. This mood is thrown off in turn, in the final movement, by a reversion to the woodland scene, and memories of 'the clear enchantments of our single year'. With the prospect of the lovers being reunited, the concluding poems are dominated by the idea of nuptial fulfilment, with its attendant imagery:

> thou common dayspring cease;
> and be there only night, the only night,
> more than all other lone:
> be the sole secret world
> one rose unfurl'd,
> and nought disturb its blossom'd peace intense . . .

In the terminal epilogue to the *Poems*, Brennan speaks of having found Eden 'clad in nuptial morn', as 'my own, my bride' – as though the aspiration of *Towards the Source* had been rewarded. This is less clear in the sequence itself, and a comparison of the 1897 and 1914 versions is instructive. The first, written and published before Brennan's marriage, ends in a mood of anticipatory fervour; in the second there are hints of severance and disquiet in the poems added later, and at the end the quest is resumed. The sequence as a whole betrays a movement from innocence to experience, as the *persona* (in such pieces as 28 and 29) comes to reflect upon the romantic ardours that had earlier possessed him, in growing wistfulness and disenchantment. A passage which Brennan marked in his copy of Arthur Symons' *The Symbolist Movement in Literature* (1899) best sums up the history traced:

All love is an attempt to break through the loneliness of individuality, to fuse oneself with something not oneself. . . . It is a desire of the infinite in humanity, and, as humanity has its limits, it can but return sadly upon itself when that limit is reached.

With the passage from *Towards the Source* to *The Forest of Night*, the character of the cycle changes. The lyrical phase now over, Brennan attempts a dramatic projection of the theme through myth – the myth of Lilith. He used this fable to dramatize the eternal relationship of mankind to Eden. As the first bride whom Adam renounced for a human mate, Lilith represents the transcendent life that man has forfeited (or the initial state from which he has fallen). As Adam is powerless to obliterate all memory of his first bride, Lilith also represents the unsatisfied longings by which men are tormented, the vision of the ideal that dogs the soul intoxicated with perfection. As this vision destroys all other satisfactions, Lilith may appear to fallen man in malevolent guises (siren, lamia, vampire), and his fear of darkness and the void, which are her realm, suggests this underlying threat to the security of his daily round. Although deserted by man, Lilith has finally a desire that answers his, and their reunion would be the recovery of the paradise lost.

The Forest of Night has an intricate structure – it is a miniature *livre composé* in itself – with four sub-cycles and a series of 'interludes' to connect them. In *The Twilight of Disquietude*, the introductory phase, all the despairs thought to have been assuaged in *Towards the Source* well up again, then as the scope widens, *The Quest of Silence* begins the exploration of the legends pre-figuring Lilith. They converge in *The Shadow of Lilith*, where the master-myth is dramatized. The passages in ordinary type are now the speeches of the participants, and the passages in bold face the commentary of an impersonal chorus, and the drama itself proceeds through three 'acts', in MS. designated 'The Watch at Midnight', 'The Voice of Man', and 'Lilith'.

It begins at a stage when part of the action has already elapsed. Adam, deserting Lilith, has fallen from his primal state, and now is joined to his human bride and lapt in the pleasures of the garden. 'The Watch at Midnight' is a series of poems in diverse stanzaic forms, dimly suggesting the location, and tracing the first stirrings of disquiet. 'The Voice of Man' ('O thou that achest, pulse o' the unwed vast') is the watcher's soliloquy as he grapples with the memories that haunt him, and strains to identify the presence that visits him in dream. The new life he has chosen has its delights

> ... I am born into dividual life
> and I have ta'en the woman for my wife,
> a flowery pasture fenced and soft with streams,
> fill'd with slow ease and fresh with eastern beams
> of coolest silver on the sliding wave

but still he must 'sicken with the long unsatisfied waiting'. Torn between the two impulses, Adam finally chooses the life offering the more tangible rewards:

> Kingdom awaits me, homage, swords, liesse,
> battle, broad fame in fable, song: shall I
> confide all hope to scanty shapes that fly
> in dreams, whom even if they be all I know
> not, or fore-runners of the One? I go,
> shaking them from my spirit, to rule and mould
> in mine own shape the gods that shall be old.

– the decision marked in one manuscript, '*il gran rifiuto*'. [4] The final 'act' is the oration ('Terrible, if he will not have me else') in which Lilith declares all the hidden ways of her power, mocking human aspiration in all its forms and promising to reduce it to nothingness. The drama ends in a feud between Lilith and man – though she still sorrows in exile, 'mournful till we find her fair'. *The Labour of Night*, the concluding sequence, is a dismal chronicle of the lot of mankind since, from the princes of magic and heroes of fable to the humble tillers of the soil, all victims of the same hunger, all labourers before the dawn.

The cycle was originally meant to end at this point, for in none of the extant plans is any development beyond *The Forest of Night* (1898-1900) envisaged. But by 1902 an additional chapter had sprung into existence, published in outline in *Hermes* that year, under the title *The Wanderer*. It came from the coalescence in Brennan's thinking of the Pragmatist metaphysic of F.C.S. Schiller with the theory of the subconscious mind, as explained in his presidential address to the Philosophical Society in 1903 (*Prose*, pp. 39-48). *The Wanderer* nevertheless explains itself: it is a semi-narrative sequence, the Wanderer setting out in the dusk of an autumn evening, and as he glimpses the firelit windows along the way, longing passionately to share the security and content of other men, as a refuge from the winds that drive him on his lonely road. In the eighth poem of the series, a counter-movement begins. The warmth and comfort of the fireside, once enviable, come to seem the haven of the 'souls that serve', withholding their hands from life; the Wanderer feels a surge of confidence that he is not as they. The climax is reached in 'O desolate eves along the way, how oft', as *il gran rifiuto* is cancelled. As the chill blast that in the *Koran* presages the end of the world blows out of the west, and as in another dimension the rival powers join in the *Götterdämmerung* and the armies clash at Roncesvaux, the Wanderer's drama is brought to an issue:

> O desolate eves along the way, how oft,
> despite your bitterness, was I warm at heart!
> not with the glow of remember'd hearths, but warm
> with the solitary unquenchable fire that burns
> a flameless heat deep in his heart who has come
> where the formless winds plunge and exult for aye
> among the naked spaces of the world,

far past the circle of the ruddy hearths
and all their memories. Desperate eves,
when the wind-bitten hills turn'd violet
along their rims, and the earth huddled her heat
within her niggard bosom, and the dead stones
lay battle-strewn before the iron wind
that, blowing from the chill west, made all its way
a loneliness to yield its triumph room;
yet in that wind a clamour of trumpets rang,
old trumpets, resolute, stark, undauntable,
singing to battle against the eternal foe,
the wronger of this world, and all his powers
in some last fight, foredoom'd disastrous,
upon the final ridges of the world:
a war-worn note, stern fire in the stricken eve,
and fire thro' all my ancient heart, that sprang
towards that last hope of a glory won in defeat,
whence, knowing not sure if such high grace befall
at the end, yet I draw courage to front the way.

In the finale, 'The land I came thro' last was dumb with night',
the vision is dispelled in the clear light of day, and the road lies
plain ahead. It is the same road. The difference is that the Wanderer is now at peace within. Once having recognized that 'his
house . . . is builded upon the winds, and under them upon the
storm', already 'Man the wanderer is on the way to himself'
(*Prose*, pp. 42-6).

Brennan's work apart from *Poems* (1913) consists of the two
volumes of war verse, *XV Poems: The Burden of Tyre* (1903) and
A Chant of Doom (1918); the half serious *A Mask* (1913), written
in collaboration with Brereton; and a good deal of occasional
and informal verse that has not been fully collected. [5] Besides
making verse translations from German, French, and Italian, he
wrote original verse in French, Latin, and Greek. But it is on the
1914 cycle – with perhaps the handful of lyrics of 1923-5, occasioned by his love for 'Vie' – that Brennan's reputation must rest.

There are some respects in which his work now seems 'dated'.
The quest for Eden as the ideal perfection is nourished by nineteenth century conceptions of the Absolute, as its expression is
shaped by the romantic literary tradition in France and England
at the time. The climate of the nineties may be recognized in
Towards the Source, with its *fin de siècle* sensibility and use of

fashions like the rondel; the presentation of Lilith as enchantress and inscrutable beauty reflects the cult of the Fatal Woman, as analysed by Mario Praz; and although the metrical freedom of *The Wanderer* has made it seem the most contemporary of Brennan's poems, his management of the technique of the *persona* and the 'heroic' style stamp it as a period piece still. These historical circumstances must be recognized, if Brennan's work is not to be approached with false expectations.

What must chiefly be recognized, however, is the mode or genre in which he elected to work, his adoption of the *livre composé* as his chosen form. This too is to be understood historically, as Brennan's response to the problem of the long poem. He began to write at a time when the major forms – verse drama in the manner of Swinburne, verse narrative on the scale of Morris – seemed to have exhausted themselves, and to have become impracticable to a contemporary. To replace them, Brennan looked to the 'symphonic' poem, the 'new ideal of the concerted poem in many movements' (*Prose*, p. 178). Foreshadowed in Rossetti's original plan for *The House of Life*, as in Swinburne's theories of the ode, it had been most nearly achieved in such a structure as Regnier's *Tel qu'en songe*. Here

a great human event . . . viewed broadly enough to be almost abstract, hence a symbol, mythical, is developed through a series of poems, which thus are equivalent to a drama. The images are chosen and assorted so as to render the mythical character of the theme (knights, princesses, satyrs, centaurs), the metres vary from the massive alexandrine in the great impersonal moments to the loosest *vers libres*, controlled only by the emotion, in the shorter lyrical passages.

Such a design preserves the individual genres, but uses them as elements in a larger configuration – 'the unity of the book, its symphonic character, remain' (*Prose*, p. 290).

Poems (1913) is an attempt to realize this form, and a separate study might be made of the modulation of the versecraft to the changing phases of the theme. The romantic aspirations of *Towards the Source* are caught in the constricted form of the quatrain, as its more languid moods take the cast of the 'Patmorian ode' (e.g. poems 19, 27); the style of 'Lilith' is consciously ritualistic, varying from the oracular and declamatory effect of the major speeches to the fragmentary *vers libre* of the lyrical passages; the frustration of the Edenic dream through *The*

Labour of Night is reflected in the sonnet pattern that is scarcely varied throughout, and the emancipation that comes with *The Wanderer* is felt in the freedom of its blank verse. There are occasional lapses and falterings, as the necessity to sustain a structure seems to have led Brennan to retain some inferior pieces (Nos. 46, 84), or to write others as though by an act of will (Nos. 62, 66, 69). The more congested passages in 'Lilith', and some inflated moments in *The Wanderer*, betray the occasional insecurity of the heroic manner. The scheme is however one which allows for calculated discord – the barrenness of the 'Wisdom' series is the effect consciously sought – and these local infelicities are still to be gauged through the concerted effect of the whole. Brennan is to be evaluated not as the author of a number of poems, but as the architect of a single poem.

The effect exerted by this poem is gradual and cumulative, reinforced by the systems of imagery running through from first to last, so that an understanding of any one poem presupposes an understanding of all the others, before and after it. 'An obscure beauty luring to long reverie over its complex significance', Brennan held, 'is the symbolic ideal.'⁶ The cycle has a harmony that deepens with successive readings, as at the same time the inclusiveness of the myth and the dramatic presentation magnify its range. *Poems* (1913) is in one sense a confessional sequence, a chronicle of 'the fate that dogs the soul intoxicated with perfection'. But the paradisal instinct is also presented as common to all men, shaping their creeds and legends down the centuries, a vision extending from the first dawn of creation to the final catastrophe, from which a second Eden may arise. Brennan once described Baudelaire, in his pursuit of 'an ideal which should be the consummation of all desire', as making of himself 'the test-case of humanity' (*Prose*, pp. 331-2). The phrase might be applied to the *persona* of Brennan's cycle, as the allusive technique draws the experience of all men, of past ages and other nations, into the compass of his own, projecting one man's odyssey as the odyssey of Man. This is something no single poem could achieve – only literature, as a whole, might achieve it – but it is still possible for the single poem to be touched by the grandeur of the attempt.

NOTES

1. As cited by R.B. Farrell in *The Union Recorder* (Sydney University) for 22 June 1950. Some of Brennan's letters to Mallarmé are printed in the *Australian Quarterly*, xix, 1947, pp. 27–39.

2. *Prose*, p. 40. All quotations are from the two-volume edition of A.R. Chisholm and J. J. Quinn, *Verse* (Sydney, 1960) and *Prose* (Sydney, 1962). The sonnet is given in the introduction to the *Verse* (p. 16), misprinting 'mighty seas' for 'misty seas'.

3. From a manuscript draft of a 'Prospectus' in the Mitchell Library.

4. *Inferno*, III 60–1. Dante reserves a special place in hell for those who on earth lived without praise or blame, having from cowardice made 'the great refusal'.

5. Almost a thousand lines of verse omitted from the Chisholm and Quinn edition were printed in *Southerly*, xxiii, 1963, pp. 164–202.

6. As reported by G.P. Donovan in *Blue and Blue* (1932), p. 31.

HENRY HANDEL RICHARDSON

LEONIE KRAMER

It has long been accepted that Henry Handel Richardson is one of the most important figures in the history of Australian fiction; yet though her claim to this distinction has never been challenged, neither has her place in the history of the Australian novel been accurately defined. Like so many Australian writers, she has been a victim of critical indecision, not because there is doubt as to the value of her work, but because there is doubt as to the relevance of much of it to Australian literature. In the treatment of her writing can clearly be observed the embarrassing problem of definition. Should all her novels be discussed in the context of Australian literature? Or should only those parts of her work which are Australian in setting be considered in detail?

These questions have naturally arisen (in the mind, among others, of H. M. Green), because of Richardson's four novels only two are set in Australia; and of her small collection of short stories only the long story 'The End of a Childhood', which continues the life of Cuffy beyond the end of *Ultima Thule*, has a distinctively Australian background. Of the rest, her so-called musical novels *Maurice Guest* and *The Young Cosima* belong geographically to Germany. Further, Richardson herself adds to the critical problem, since she left Australia at the age of seventeen, to return only once for two months in 1912. She was, in a word, an expatriate writer; and she was so not only by virtue of her self-imposed exile, but temperamentally. Certainly, after her husband's death she wrote that she would like to leave England and come to Australia; but her autobiographical essay *Myself When Young* (1948) makes it clear that her childhood in Australia was, on the whole, an unhappy one; there is no reason to suppose that she would have dissented very strongly from Richard Mahony's view of Australia.

The tendency, then, for critics to concentrate their attention upon *The Fortunes of Richard Mahony* is not entirely explained by the fact that this is her most ambitious and comprehensive novel; it is also a result of a natural tendency to attach more significance to a novel of distinctively Australian relevance, both as fiction and as a chronicle of the turbulent years of the nineteenth century – a period which saw not only the rapid material progress of the colony, but also the struggle for political independence and democratic government. This critical bias, though understandable, and partially justified, does however obscure the extent to which Richardson is a consistent writer, both in aims and methods; and it makes the problem of assessing her status as a novelist virtually impossible, by creating an artificial division between her works. It is therefore the intention, in this chapter, to consider her work as a whole, in the belief that to do so is to see her Australian novels in perspective.

Henry Handel Richardson (Ethel Florence Lindesay Richardson) was born in Melbourne in 1870. Her early childhood was disturbed by many changes of environment as her mother followed the declining fortunes of her husband, Dr Walter Richardson, the model for Richard Mahony. Possibly her most settled years were those few she spent from 1882 at the Presbyterian Ladies' College in Melbourne. At seventeen she left on a tour of Europe, and was entered as a student at the Leipzig Conservatorium. Here she met her future husband, J. G. Robertson, later to become first professor of German at London University, whom she married in Dublin in 1895. The first eight years of her married life were spent in Europe, chiefly in Germany. In 1903 she returned to England. From 1910 to 1933, apart from brief visits to Europe and to Australia, she lived in London. After her husband's death she moved to Sussex, where she died in 1946.

There seems little reason to doubt that Henry Handel Richardson turned to writing as a career after her disappointment with herself as a musician. She has described in *Myself When Young* her temperamental inadequacies as an executant musician; and she there makes it clear that in the first instance writing was in the nature of an escape from the intolerable demands of musical life. In writing she found solitude and contentment.

She began her serious literary career as a translator, first of *Niels Lyhne*, by the Danish novelist J. P. Jacobsen. This was published under the title *Siren Voices* in 1896. In the same year there appeared her unsigned translation of *Fiskerjenten* by Björnstjerne Björnson, under the title *The Fisher Lass*. From *Niels Lyhne* she derived what might be described as a philosophy of fiction which was to influence her own practice as a novelist most strongly.

This book, she remarked in her introduction, introduced her to a 'romanticism imbued with the scientific spirit, and essentially based on realism.' In her own novels she was later to exploit, in various settings, these two qualities, romanticism and realism; her central characters are romantic in conception, but they inhabit no unreal or ideal landscape. They are defined and placed in an actual setting, precise in all its details, and described with scientific accuracy.

Henry Handel Richardson was a slow and careful writer, and her handful of short stories and four novels occupied over thirty years of her life. She began work on her first novel *Maurice Guest* (1908) some time in 1897, though she interrupted her writing of this from time to time to turn her attention to her short autobiographical novel *The Getting of Wisdom* (1910). In all her writing Richardson seemed to need the support of facts. They were the necessary foundation for the 'scientific realism' at which she aimed; and where facts could not, for whatever reason, be derived directly from her own experience, she sought them in historical documents and records. For *Maurice Guest*, however, she needed no such external aids. When she began the novel, she was still close to her own experience as a student in Leipzig; and it is reasonable to suppose that in describing the background of the story she called more upon memory than upon imagination. Of all her novels *Maurice Guest* is the richest in atmosphere, life, and movement. It breathes the excitement of student life; it captures the city of Leipzig in all its seasonal moods, and it plunges the reader into the centre of its musical world. Students practising, teachers, student recitals, opera, glimpses of musicians – these are presented with all the ardour of affectionate recollection. In *Myself When Young* she describes her years in Leipzig as the happiest she had known, and her enthusiasm for the stimulating life she lived there lends vitality to the pages of the novel.

Yet *Maurice Guest* is a sombre novel. The musical life of Leipzig forms a vivid background for the depiction of a destructive passion. The hero Maurice Guest is the victim of obsessive love which turns to insane jealousy and suspicion and finally leads to his suicide. In her depiction of the relationship between the two central characters, and in the detailed accuracy with which she recounts the deterioration in their relationship, Richardson shows the extent of her interest in scientific realism. Patient accumulation of detail lends her characters the force of real life.

Their central situation, however, is a romantic one. Though Richardson is often painfully honest in her depiction of feeling and mood, her accuracy is directed to the nostalgic theme of the vanity of human wishes. Louise Dufrayer the Australian heroine resists marriage and the formalizing of love for fear that by being made lawful it will lose its spontaneity. Passion without responsibility is her desire. She craves for permanence, but it is the permanence of an ideal not of an actual world. She is the romantic introvert, feeding upon her own moods and desires, turning others into fuel for her own passions, seeing them not as themselves, but merely as instruments of her own fulfilment. The tragedy turns then upon the clash between the demands of the real world, and the apparently self-sufficient world of passionate love. In the intensity of a selfish and consuming personal relationship, values become distorted; until the perfection the lovers so earnestly sought vanishes in scenes of hatred and recrimination.

This is the central dramatic action of the novel, and it is played out against a rich and changing background. The accuracy of Richardson's descriptions is matched by the objectivity of her presentation of character. On her central characters she passes no judgement. She is content to draw attention to their temperamental differences – the one, an essentially ordinary, practical young man caught up in a situation he can neither understand nor sustain; the other, seeking 'more than life' and considering the world well lost for love. Underlying her analysis of character is a preoccupation which appears in some form in all her novels. It is a preoccupation with failure. In this theme of the novel Richardson reveals her interest in the qualities that are summed up in the word genius. Maurice Guest fails in his profession, in his love, and in his attempt to hold onto life. Pursued by the consciousness of his own inadequacy he gives up the struggle to transcend his limitations. His failure is persuasively and poignantly depicted; and if the genius of his successful rival Schilsky is asserted rather than demonstrated, we are at least led to believe that it consists largely in an ability to flout the conventions of ordinary life. Schilsky makes his own rules, and he is driven on by a power which Richardson was more fully to represent in her last novel *The Young Cosima*.

After the turbulent passions of *Maurice Guest*, *The Getting of Wisdom* seems little more than a diversion; and indeed Richardson was working on it concurrently with the former novel, and seems to have thought of it as light relief from the sterner task. She wrote

I persist in thinking of it as a *little* work. . . . Just a merry and saucy bit of irony. How *can* people take it so seriously?
(Nettie Palmer: *Henry Handel Richardson, A Study*, 1950, p. 195)

One answer to this question must surely be that it is taken seriously because it is autobiographical; and critics are eager for any scraps of information about an author as reticent as Henry Handel Richardson. *The Getting of Wisdom* is the story of Richardson's years at Presbyterian Ladies' College in Melbourne in the 1880s. It has some historical interest as a record of education in a girls' school in the nineteenth century, but more as portrait of the 'odd and unaccountable' Laura Ramsbotham, with her triumphs and defeats, her miseries and passions. Laura suffers the humiliations and enjoys the successes that come the way of any school children; she is not, in fact, nearly as unusual as her creator seems to think; and when in *Myself When Young* Richardson looks back on her school days and recollects yet again that she was looked upon as odd, it is difficult to avoid the conclusion that both at the time and later she exaggerated her own nonconformity. This is perhaps one of the most revealing implications of the book.

There is, however, another revelation which throws unexpected light on the morbid insights of *Maurice Guest*. In *Myself When Young* Richardson explains that *Maurice Guest* had come very easily to her, because in writing it she recollected a schoolgirl passion for a young clergyman; so that in describing Maurice Guest's hopeless love she 'had only to magnify and redress the old pangs.' Especially when one recalls that Richardson was at work on the two novels at the same time, it is reasonable to find links between them. In her depiction of Laura Ramsbotham's jealous and absorbing passion for a schoolgirl friend, Richardson is analysing precisely the same kind of temperament as that of Maurice Guest. Laura's passionate attachment, which fills her whole mind and makes it impossible for her to work except in the middle of the night when her friend is safely asleep, is that of an adolescent *Maurice Guest*; and there would be no incongruity in transferring from the *Getting of Wisdom* to *Maurice Guest* the quotation from Nietzsche which heads a chapter describing Laura's torments: 'Gut und Böse und Lust und Leid und Ich und Du.'

As in *Maurice Guest* one can detect a concern with the question of genius and talent, of success and failure, so in *The Getting of Wisdom* Richardson enunciates through Laura an elementary theory of fiction. It can be surmised that in so doing she was exploring the implications of her interest in Jacobsen's combination of realism and romanticism in *Niels Lyhne*; and whether Richardson herself as a schoolgirl had come to the same formula as that which seemed to guide Jacobsen, is less important than the fact that she chooses to stress her heroine's realization that though truth and honesty may be admired in real life, they are not a guarantee of literary distinction. Through Laura's experience of a school literary society Richardson outlines a simple view of the essential quality of fiction – that it should at least give the appearance of truth 'without being dull and prosy'.

Laura meets with success in her combination of a real setting and an invented plot – a story of the kind that her creator was currently writing. So *The Getting of Wisdom* becomes more than a story of school life, more even than an exercise in fictional autobiography. It embodies a view of fiction exemplified, with varying degrees of success, in all Richardson's novels, including this one. What particularly distinguishes *The Getting of Wisdom* from her other works is its tone of light, comic irony. In *Maurice Guest* she had shown her capacity for tragic irony – the novel is full of episodes which gain significance from their prophetic quality, and their anticipation of the final tragedy. But in *The Getting of Wisdom* her irony is that of comedy. Laura becomes aware of the incongruities of life in a series of painful revelations; but with them she acquires wisdom. Richardson, while showing clearly enough Laura's sensitive suffering, does so from the point of view of a detached, amused observer. Were it not for her display of humour in this novel, one might indeed suspect her of not possessing it.

Humour is certainly not a prominent element in the work by which she is best known, *The Fortunes of Richard Mahony* (1930). The three novels which make up this trilogy occupied her for nearly twenty years of her life; she was already involved in the writing of the first volume *Australia Felix* (1917) when she visited Australia in 1912 to refresh her memories of the landscape and to check her facts. *The Fortunes of Richard Mahony* opens at the height of the Ballarat Gold Rush in 1852 and covers over twenty years until the death of its hero. It has been variously described – as a book about money (by J. G. Robertson),[2] as an historical novel, as fictional biography. It is indeed all these and more; and that various descriptions of it are possible does not mean, as has been supposed, that it is confused in its direction. *The Fortunes*, like *Maurice Guest*, is a book about failure. Its central character, Richard Mahony, is in many respects a very exact representation of Richardson's father. He is also an attempt on Richardson's part to see into the life of those to whom success in the new world came hardly, and lasted only briefly.

In form *The Fortunes* follows a pattern commonly met with in Australian fiction, that of the chronicle. It is inevitable that this should be so, since Richardson follows history, and does not seek to impose her own pattern upon the order of events; rather she is content to unfold the story, adopting the attitude of a detached and objective observer, and speaking, as she hopes, 'for the generation of whom the works are written.' (Palmer, p. 194) If in spite of her determined detachment, something of her own attitude may be detected in the trilogy, it is by implication rather than by direct statement, by a subtle alteration in the tone of her prose.

From one aspect, it may be profitable to regard *The Fortunes* as the last and greatest in the line of emigrant novels. Mahony is not simply a misfit by nature. Like Laura Ramsbotham, he is considered by his fellows to be odd and unaccountable. When he is first introduced as a Ballarat storekeeper, he is a strangely incongruous figure. No reasons are advanced for his abandonment of his profession, nor for his apparently voluntary exile; but one is at liberty to suppose that the restlessness which drives him throughout the novel, had already seized him before the book opens.

Regarded from this aspect *The Fortunes* can be interpreted as an unusually thorough analysis of the geographical disorientation which had engaged the attention of earlier novelists, notably Henry Kingsley, and was later to occupy Martin Boyd. This theme is built into the structure of the novel. In *Australia Felix* Mahony voices his dissatisfaction with life in the colony, and the end of this novel marks his departure for England – 'home'. In *The Way Home* (1925) his temporary pleasure in the greenness of England and in its civilized society turns to irritation at its provincial narrowness; and Mahony returns with gladness to the country whose crudities he had so willingly fled. In this book Mahony travels a second time to Europe, only to be forced back to Australia by financial disaster. The last volume *Ultima Thule* (1929), shows the Australian countryside at its worst; its dust and dryness reinforce Mahony's mental distress; and there is little doubt that he is finally broken as much by his environment as by his own morbid sensitivity.

Thus the restlessness of Mahony's temperament is displayed in the shifting locale of the novel, while, as in *Maurice Guest*, irony supplies the tension missing from incidents and unexpected twists of plot. The title of the trilogy and of its separate parts is ironic. Mahony's misfortunes are more evident than his fortunes. *Australia Felix* is for him and for the many victims of gold fever, a land of curses rather than blessings. The Way Home is a way of disillusionment. Home, whether it be the Ireland of his birth, the Scotland of his university days, or the England of his green memories, offers him no welcome and affords him no comfort. Time has destroyed the memories of youth, and the softness of dreams has turned to ugly reality. The final irony is Ultima Thule. At the height of his prosperity Mahony plans a house to be called Ultima Thule, in which he will spend his last years in comfort, able finally to cultivate his long-neglected intellectual pursuits. But the dream of Ultima Thule becomes the reality of madness, and his last resting place is a lonely grave 'indistinguishable from the common ground.'

In its preoccupation with the physical environment, and in its analysis of colonial society and its attitudes, *The Fortunes* shares common ground with other Australian novels earlier and later. But important though these themes are to the trilogy itself, and to its place in Australian fiction, they are so only in so far as they arise from the study of character. 'I never cease to believe', wrote Richardson, 'that character-drawing is its (the novel's) main end and object, the conflict of personalities its drama.' (Palmer, p. 192) It is the character of Mahony from which these themes draw their life; and although *The Fortunes* has been variously interpreted and assessed, and no doubt will continue to be, Mahony stands as one of the memorable characters in Australian fiction.

The impressive reality of his character, however, is the result not of bold imaginative ventures, nor of flashes of insight – though these are present at times – but of the patient accumulation of detail. When she came to write *Myself When Young* Richardson admitted that her father was the model for Mahony, and that she had been helped in her reconstruction of his character by old letters and diaries; and since her historical material for *The Fortunes* was imported with strict accuracy into the novel, it may be supposed that at least some of the biographical material was similarly used. In *Ultima Thule* she describes with painful accuracy the stages of Mahony's mental deterioration, and supplements her own memories of her father's last years with reading in psychology. Yet though Mahony is created and developed by recording minute and literal details of his thought and behaviour, he is no mere collection of attitudes and opinions.

As in *Maurice Guest*, so in *The Fortunes*, Richardson's naturalistic technique, her 'scientific realism', serves a romantic theme. Like Louise Dufrayer, though for very different reasons, Mahony is an incurable romantic. Distant pastures are always greener to his eyes; his pursuit of a dream leads to his flight from reality. 'I see him as a seeker', Richardson wrote. [3] He was never, she thought, equal to the demands of life. Neither was Louise Dufrayer. Mahony believes, as does she, that he belongs in a world not subject to the pressures of ordinary life; but whereas Louise, having secured her ideal world, wants it never to change, Mahony sees 'Panta rei' as the eternal truth, and 'semper idem' as 'the lie we long to see confirmed'.

Herein lies his romantic dilemma – there is no permanence, but the longing for it drives him on. This dilemma is accentuated by the circumstances of his life, and by his geographical bewilderment. But it is, one might say, an inherent attitude. Mahony could say, with Manfred, 'I have not loved the world, nor the world me'. Even in his loneliness there is more than a suspicion of Byronic temperament; of a contempt for the world which is a protest against the world's indifference and disapproval. His failures seem to him not personal defeats, nor products of his own inadequacies, but blows delivered by a crude and insensitive society. Henry Handel Richardson's achievement in *The Fortunes* is without doubt the creation of this tragic figure, unable to resolve the dilemmas of his own making.

With the trilogy Richardson exhausted the material which she derived from her own experience. *Maurice Guest* had sprung immediately from her life in Leipzig, though its emotional roots went further back into her adolescence. *The Getting of Wisdom* was a direct exploitation of her childhood. As she herself wrote 'it contains a very fair account of my doings at school and of those I came in contact with.' (*Myself When Young*, p. 70) In *The Fortunes* she was able to draw on family documents, and also on the memories of her father; and to use herself in childhood in the person of Cuffy. Further, she was able in a sense to use her own temperament, for she did not deny J.G. Robertson's assertion that 'in drawing Richard Mahony I drew no other than myself.' These three novels, so different in character, illustrate Richardson's devotion to the fact. Whatever imaginative content she managed to pour into her novels, she needed, it seems, both the stimulation and the certainty of the known and recorded. To this stimulus she owed both the best and the worst of her writing.

Of her volume of short stories, *The End of a Childhood* (1934) little needs to be said. Richardson is not a distinguished practitioner of the art of the short story, as this volume testifies. In four chapters *The End of A Childhood* she takes up the story of Cuffy a year after Mahony's death, but this is an unsatisfactory fragment, and when one considers the date of its composition, and the fact that Cuffy is a self-portrait, it seems almost like a last attempt to squeeze material out of her own memories, before her final entry into history with *The Young Cosima*. The earliest story in this collection is 'Mary Christina', originally published in 1911 under the title 'Death'. One story has thematic interest, especially in relation to *The Young Cosima*. 'Succedaneum' separately published under the title 'Substance and Shadow', in 1934, is the story of 'that most distracted of mortals, the creative artist whose inspiration has failed him.' It is tempting, though doubtless unwise, to see here Richardson herself, who after the completion of the trilogy entered on a period of barrenness. At the same time she was meditating the story of Cosima Liszt, and the theme of the young composer who finds his inspiration again through love, and having done so rejects his personal and social responsibilities, has an obvious bearing on the theme of her last novel.

It is not easy to see why she embarked on her last novel *The Young Cosima* (1939). It is a failure, but an illuminating one. 'It has been a very heavy job,' she wrote, 'and I'm thankful to be rid of it.' (Palmer, p. 201) And she goes on to say, as though in extenuation of her imaginative failings, 'Built though on a solid basis of fact, and therein lay the toil, for it meant including Richard Wagner's life as well, and the books on R. W. run into hundreds.' A toil it certainly seems to have been, and it makes heavy reading. She acquired a library of books on Wagner and the musical life of the times for reference, and annotated these with her usual conscientiousness. But the result is a book which succeeds neither as fiction nor as musical history. It marks Richardson's complete enslavement to facts, and her incomplete mastery of the art of transmuting them into palatable fiction. The wheel has come full circle. In *The Young Cosima* she plays the part of Laura Ramsbotham, who has not yet learned what it is to be true, yet not dull and prosy.

Yet *The Young Cosima*, both in theme and technique, is a logical end to Henry Handel Richardson's creative activity. It has already been remarked that in *Maurice Guest* she tentatively explores the question of genius. *The Young Cosima* is virtually an essay on this subject. Richardson is interested in the young Cosima von Bülow who left her talented husband, and flouting the conventions of her time, went to the genius Richard Wagner. In Richardson's eyes, she is given a mandate for her action, when von Bülow, speaking of Wagner, says: 'The truth is, it doesn't matter a brass farthing what a man of this vast, stupendous genius says or does. . . . His mere presence is a gift to thank the gods for. . . . Even suppose he were a liar and a thief, his lies should be winked at, his thieving condoned. . . . To such a man ordinary standards can't be applied.'

In the proposing of this view Richardson reaches the height of her romantic doctrine. It is already implicit in the relationships of *Maurice Guest*. Maurice, the talented and conscientious student, yields to Schilsky, the unscrupulous genius. It may be suspected that even in *The Getting of Wisdom*, Henry Handel Richardson makes out a tentative case for the disconcertingly unconventional child rebelling against a conventional setting. But in *The Young Cosima* she justifies the ruthlessness and independence of genius, and at the same time advances a theory of possession. Wagner is depicted as the victim of his creative gift, impelled by a force outside himself, an all-powerful 'blind genius'. He is indeed the Nietzschean Übermensch, absolved from the duties and responsibilities of ordinary life, and from the moral censure of ordinary human beings.

The work of Henry Handel Richardson, then, whether Australian or European in setting, displays a preoccupation with certain themes, and a consistent, though not uniformly successful approach to the writing of fiction. The world of Richardson is inhabited by two kinds of people – those who live and abide by the standards and demands of ordinary life, and those who legislate for themselves. Her failures – Maurice Guest and Richard Mahony – have aspirations beyond their talents. Her successes, Schilsky and Wagner, even Louise Dufrayer, succeed by a ruthless disregard for convention, and by surrendering themselves to what they believe to be a 'call'. It is ironical, though not perhaps surprising, that Richardson should have more success with her failures then with her geniuses. To the doomed aspirations of Maurice Guest and Mahony she gives eloquent expression; Wagner, even though speaking in words sometimes close to his own, seems more often frenzied than inspired.

Richardson was conscientious to a fault in her pursuit of objectivity and factual accuracy. Her imagination worked more freely at elaboration than invention. In *Maurice Guest* she drew not only on places, but on people she had known, with sufficient accuracy to give offence to some (*Myself When Young*, p. 103). *The Fortunes of Richard Mahony*, especially in its first part *Australia Felix*, is documented from a wide variety of historical sources. For *The Young Cosima* she collected a library of some 70 books. Hers is no impressionistic evocation of background and atmosphere, but a carefully constructed scenario, reliable as well as decorative.

This accuracy of detail, both in description of landscape and of character, is one of Richardson's great merits as a novelist. At the same time it imposes a restraint upon her writing, and makes for stylistic clumsiness. *Maurice Guest* and *The Getting of Wisdom* are freer from these faults than her other two novels. Though her

writing, especially in scenes involving Louise Dufrayer, is sometimes extravagant and over-emphatic, the novel moves with ease
and assurance, and it is easy to believe that, as she said, she found
it no trouble to write. In *The Getting of Wisdom* too she displays
the same easy stride, though her style is not free from awkwardness and the inversions which later became a mannerism. In
The Fortunes the style is much more uneven, and at times is a
serious obstacle to the appreciation of character and narrative
comment. In *The Young Cosima* the constructional gaucheries,
clichés and flatness of language are even more noticeable, and
lend to the novel a ponderous and stilted air.

'To have to speak in person is to me the most abhorrent of
tasks. I must have a mask to hide behind.' (Palmer, p. 200) This
comment points to the neutral pose adopted by Richardson in all
her novels. Not only is she the objective recorder; she is also the
impartial observer. She presents conflict without bias; on the
important moral issues raised by her novels she passes no editorial comment. Only by a slight edge in her writing, and some
external evidence, can it be assumed that her sympathies are with
the dreamers of the world, not with the practical men and women
of action, however worthy they might be. But this is ultimately of
less importance than the fact that Richardson shows in all her
novels an awareness of moral problems and their implications
rare in Australian writing of the time. She shows further an
attachment to the individual personality and to personal relationships, which in Australian fiction have often been pushed
into the background by landscape, or the depiction of social and
regional groups. She does not, it is true, reach the highest levels
of achievement. Her imagination is constrained by her literal-
mindedness, and her style does not permit her the penetration
her theme often demands. But her searching analyses of human
vulnerability, and her grasp of the nature of creative activity lend
her novels a special distinction in a literature, which especially
at the time she wrote, was for the most part content to exploit
the environmental oddities of Australia, and neglected the
exploration of those human dilemmas which recognize no
geographical barriers.

NOTES

1. In a letter to Nettie Palmer. See Nettie Palmer, *Henry Handel Richardson, A Study* (1950) p. 196.
2. In his essay 'The Art of Henry Handel Richardson', *Myself When Young* (1948).
3. In the unpublished diary of her 1912 visit to Australia.

ROBERT D. FITZGERALD

A BACKGROUND TO HIS POETRY

DOUGLAS STEWART

ROBERT DAVID FITZGERALD is a surveyor by profession. So was his father, Robert David FitzGerald, before him: he was a surveyor in the New South Wales Public Works Department before he became Deputy Chief Engineer. And so was his grandfather, Robert David FitzGerald, the founder of the Australian family: he was Deputy Surveyor General of New South Wales, and employed his spare time – and, I suspect, much of his professional time also – in making himself the first and foremost expert on Australian orchids:

> In a fork on a blackbutt twig attention
> was high as the wagtail's disc of a nest.
> Tread quietly there; speak low; who'd mention
> cast-off places? Life was a quest;
> and sight was intent on bird or creature
> where bird and found thoughts were new. What power
> had the pull of the past against all nature,
> that orchid, opening in flower?

But sight, in a Deputy Surveyor General, was also presumably fixed from time to time on or through or by a theodolite – I am not quite sure how that noble instrument works. And certainly that is the case with FitzGerald the poet. In fact once when I had remarked how excellent a portrait Philip Lindsay had drawn of him in his autobiography – six feet tall and loping down George Street swinging a theodolite over his shoulder to the peril of all other pedestrians – FitzGerald wrote to me saying that the description was most inaccurate: 'I would never have risked damaging a theodolite.' When, at the beginning of 1963 he was leaving for America to make an appearance at the University of Texas, I wrote a piece for the *Australian Surveyor*, 'a quarterly publication devoted to the interests of the surveying profession in Australia', about the influence of his profession on his poetry; and, though I did it lightly enough, for the occasion, the more I have thought about it, the more significant this line of approach seems to be: as a clue to at least one of the sources of both his subject-matter and his style. Who else but a surveyor could have written, in an epigram on 'Experience':

> In always a fumbled and strange task,
> not scribed to a template, squared or planned,
> and never drafted at the desk,
> this tool shapes clumsily to the hand.

Or who else, unless some actual navigator or maker of nautical instruments, would have written the passage in 'Heemskerck Shoals' which shows so precise an understanding of the importance of inventing the chronometer:

> You might read
> a morning height of the sun, like that at noon
> for latitude, compound and interlock it
> with tabled declination, then oppose
> hour-angle to ascension – very close,
> and very pretty; but time stayed out to mock it!

The *Australian Surveyor* is a fascinating little magazine. I had no idea until I glanced through the December 1962 issue, in which my own contribution was really the only one I could understand, what abstruse and monstrous calculations surveyors are expected not merely to comprehend, but also, presumably, to enjoy. I do once remember meeting FitzGerald in Sydney when he was off to measure up a new skyscraper in which all the window-embrasures were a fraction out of plumb, so that thousands of pounds worth of ready-made windows would have to be scrapped unless the building could somehow be rectified, but I had no conception of the calculations which the poet must have been called upon to perform. To take one of the lighter pieces of reading in the *Australian Surveyor*, 'a simple comparison of Single T_4 with Single T_3 and with simultaneous reciprocal T_3 azimuths' – that is enough. . . .

The fact that FitzGerald probably understands this strange piece of English prose not only enormously sends up my respect for his capacities divorced from his poetry, but also helps to explain to me why, having no mathematical ability whatever, I never could quite grasp his vision of eternity in that most haunting poem 'The Face of the Waters':

> For eternity is not space reaching
> on without end to it; not time without end to it,

> nor infinity working round in a circle;
> but a placeless dot enclosing nothing,
> the pre-time pinpoint of impossible beginning,
> enclosed by nothing, not even by emptiness –
> impossible. . . .

FitzGerald has explained this poem to me a dozen times, carefully, in words of one syllable suitable to my understanding. Sometimes, for an instant, I have it. Then it goes again, darting off into the outer darkness like an azimuth. All I know for certain is that it is indeed a most haunting poem. It makes me feel, as D.H. Lawrence said of the quantum theory, that space is alive, 'like a goose'. It makes me feel that FitzGerald was personally present at the creation of the universe:

> Once again the scurry of feet – those myriads
> crossing the black granite; and again
> laughter cruelly in pursuit; and then
> the twang like a harpstring or the spring of a trap,
> and the swerve on the polished surface: the soft little pads
> sidling and skidding and avoiding; but soon caught up
> in the hand of laughter and put back. . . .

And, if I shall never really understand the mathematical part of the poem, unless FitzGerald merely means that 'a placeless dot enclosing nothing' *is* impossible, so that you don't have to bother about it anyhow, I am at least able to follow his vision of life in all its multitudinous complexity emerging from 'the agony of not-being', which is the core of the poem's meaning:

> once again
> a universe on the edge of being born:
> feet running fearfully out of nothing
> at the core of nothing:
> colour, light, life, fearfully
> becoming eyes and understanding: sound becoming
> ears . . .
>
> . . . the part breaking through the whole;
> light and the clear day and so simple a goal.

How curious, incidentally, are the different ways in which poems find their way to the light! FitzGerald once told me that he dropped upon the theme of another of his finest poems, 'Fifth Day', about the trial of Warren Hastings, when he was up at the Sydney Public Library for no other purpose than to study different systems of shorthand: a most peculiar hobby, which I take to be a reflection of that same mathematical turn of mind that has made it possible for him to be a surveyor. Joseph Gurney, who reported the Hastings trial, was the inventor of a shorthand system – and, I should say, reporting a trial that lasted for seven years, needed to be! As for 'The Face of the Waters', one day I met FitzGerald and he said that he thought his verse was getting too 'tight' and he felt he was going to write something quite free and irregular in form. The next thing was this beautiful poem which, though strictly enough controlled, varies in line-length and music like one of Wordsworth's odes. FitzGerald had sensed the music in his mind before he knew what he was going to write about. Most curious; the whole poem must have been there, somewhere, at the back of his mind.

I don't recall whether FitzGerald's poetry at that time was in fact getting too 'tight'. He has regretted to me sometimes that he 'simply doesn't see' the orchids and the wildflowers which so enchanted his grandfather, and he says in one of his poems:

> Not an observant man,
> I let go by
> much that the mind can
> take in at the eye.

That could be argued. In another poem in the same book – his latest, *Southmost Twelve* – his mind is receiving some extremely exact observations from the eye:

> Thick dust on Paddy's lucerne, burr
> and bracken and long grass,
> blown from the wheels of that great stir
> that men make as they pass,
> paint red the roadside; but beyond
> how clean are leaf and frond! ...

and his Fijian landscapes in *Moonlight Acre* are full of the charm of moonlight, bush, hills, and the sea.

But I think it is true that, after his early love-poems in *To Meet the Sun*, and after *Moonlight Acre*, there has been a hardening, a loss of lyrical quality in his poetry; and this, perhaps, we could attribute in part to the discipline of his profession; to mathematics. His verse is never rigid or mechanical, for there is a great deal more than mathematics in FitzGerald's composition. It is always alive, individual, full of energy. But it is disciplined. He likes to get straight to the point, in hard, clear thought. And he is not greatly concerned with the charm of nature: he is more interested in his ideas about trees or flowers or wagtails or cicadas than in the things themselves. 'And after all,' he says of Tasman, and perhaps also of himself, 'one was a practical man.'

But if these are the limitations which come from a practical and mathematical turn of mind, they are also, simultaneously, virtues. There is nothing wrong with clarity. There is nothing wrong with hardness. There is no weakness in FitzGerald's poetry; there are no holes in it; there is no lushness. It is firm. It is economical. You can throw any stones you like at it, and you won't knock chips off it. It seems to me no accident but entirely fitting that in his latest book he should have turned time and again to rock as his favourite symbol and that he should describe rock as being – of all unexpected adjectives – 'comfortable':

> This comfortable rock
> of all our origins,
> the immemorial clock
> whereunder time begins. . . .

I wonder if we could attribute in part to his profession, to his lifelong training in precision, not only the firmness of each individual line he writes, but the firm construction of each poem as a whole, particularly such longer and later poems as 'Fifth Day' and 'The Wind at Your Door'? I don't know quite what a surveyor does when he surveys a road or a boundary but I imagine it is partly a mathematical problem and partly creative. You see the thing in your mind's eye and you say: This is the way to work it, this is how it must go. It is a matter of sticking to the point. The poet writing a short lyric does not have any great difficulty in arriving at his solution; but in complex narratives such as 'Fifth Day' and 'The Wind at Your Door' the difficulties can be enormous. There are obstacles like mountains in the way; there are tempting bypaths everywhere; it is more like moving an army down the road than the single person of a lyric; and all the time, while you are trying to keep your main theme moving straight ahead to its logical conclusion, there is the problem of speaking clearly in rhyme, in an intricate stanza form, so that it all seems natural and inevitable. Of course all poets who attempt large narrative construction have to face these problems: but whether or not surveying has had anything to do with it, Fitz-

Gerald seems to me to have solved them with quite unusual success. He said to me when he was writing *Between Two Tides*, his epic poem on Tonga, that he was not satisfied to write a long poem in a series of vivid snapshots, which had been the prevailing method in Australian narrative poems: he wanted to go straight through from beginning to end.

But technical matters, like mathematics, are a cold subject. What interests me in the profession of surveying in relation to FitzGerald's poetry is not only that it is a mathematical and constructive profession but also that it is adventurous. It takes the surveyor away from his desk and out into the open air. And, in fact, a great many of FitzGerald's landscape poems have come from his surveying excursions. I don't think we should give his profession the sole credit for taking him to Fiji in his youth, since I suppose he might well have stayed in Sydney; but at any rate surveying and his own naturally adventurous disposition did take him away into those far, high, rainy mountains; and that adventure is one of the most important and fruitful sources of his poetry. It gave him a string of admirable short poems running right through his work from the lovely 'Copernicus' sequence in *Moonlight Acre* to 'Embarkation' and 'Relic at Strength-Fled' in *Southmost Twelve*; it gave him, since it was off Fiji that Tasman was nearly wrecked, the narrative 'Heemskerck Shoals'; and it gave him his most ambitious poem *Between Two Tides* which, though it happens to be set in Tonga, could only have been written by a poet whose interest had been aroused in the native peoples of the Pacific. 'Tongans have probably become Fijians,' he admits in an amused footnote.

This long narrative deserves more consideration than it has yet had in Australia. It was slighted when it was first published in 1952 and I have not yet seen anybody get around to second thoughts about it. It may seem a little out of the way in Australia, where there is not much awareness of the Pacific islands. Had it been published in New Zealand, where Tongans (or Fijians), despite their admixture of Melanesian blood, can readily be accepted as cousins of the Maoris, and are as basic to the tradition of the country as the convicts, explorers, pioneers, and voyagers are to the Australian tradition, it might have had a much warmer reception. How Australia would have welcomed a poem of this length and this quality on, say, Macquarie!

Between Two Tides is drawn from *An Account of the Natives of the Tonga Islands*, a fascinating book which has interested writers as diverse as Byron and R. M. Ballantyne, compiled by John Martin, M.D. from the narration of Will Mariner who, as a boy, was adopted by the Tongans after they had massacred the rest of his ship's company. It is partly a study of Mariner, the English boy compelled to join in native wars and treacheries, partly a study of the native chief Finau who adopted the boy and whose ambition was to subdue the scattered tribes and make himself king of all Tonga. Though New Zealanders would see Finau very much as a Tongan Te Rauparaha, this is the aspect of the story which seems out of the way in Australia; yet FitzGerald himself sees Finau as the equivalent, in little, of Caesar or Alexander; and, driven by the logic of violence from one treacherous murder to the next, portrayed as vividly as he is, he should not really be more remote to us than that Scottish savage, Macbeth:

> . . . That tale was Finau's –
> except as, mystically, it was man's, the spirit
> caught in old struggles of right with wrong for mastery –
> and was the tale of a patriot urged the one way
> by ambition and by ideals; until the two
> split open upon mistrust set in the path
> by unpredictable rancours in his blood;
> then driven by ambition and darker torments
> to the dark act. . . .

I think the poem is weakened to some extent, not by the foreignness of Finau, but by the division of themes in it between Mariner and Finau; or because Mariner, if properly a part of the main theme, is rather sketchily portrayed. FitzGerald's insistence on telling the story from the outside, not using the interior monologue of Browning, has kept him at some distance from Mariner. The youth's problems are stated; but he does not come to life in the way that Finau does. Nevertheless Finau remains. In *Between Two Tides* there are many sustained passages of FitzGerald's best writing, in thought and characterization no less than in verse-craft. And, a substantial and ingeniously constructed narrative poem of nearly three thousand lines, this is the kind of work that gives a poet stature.

Of course you would have to go a long way beyond surveying, and the simple adventure of walking over the mountain tops of Fiji, to get all the weight of thought that is expressed in this poem; and, in fact, there is a lot more than surveying in Fitz-Gerald's background. His father and his grandfather were, as well as surveyors, Irishmen: something which FitzGerald has never forgotten. Once in Dublin I went looking for the 'Strand Street house' which in one of his poems he said his grandfather had sold as a token of his final decision to settle in Australia; and found it, too; or thought I had; only when I wrote to FitzGerald about it he said the right Strand Street was in Tralee. They came from deep down in Kerry. I think it must have been Mary Ann Bell who put me wrong; for FitzGerald's great-grandfather married her, it seems, in Dublin:

> Were I scribe or historian, sure I could take you
> to those days and Dublin and welcome enough,
> using brogue in your ears for the magic to make you
> smell turf and fine horses, hear jigs and discourses,
> see wigs and bright waistcoats, drink porter, take snuff;
> as it is – well, imagine a molten variety
> of all kinds of gentry and heroes pell-mell,
> and know that the toast of that crazy society
> and queen of the city was Mary Ann Bell.

FitzGerald's father and grandfather were, too, men at the top of their profession. His grandfather, besides compiling his great work on Australian orchids, corresponded with Charles Darwin and illustrated for von Mueller, in a series of hundreds of exquisite little watercolours which have never been published, the whole range of Australian wildflowers. They were highly distinguished civil servants and men of culture, living in an atmosphere of colonial aristocracy in the old stone houses of the Sydney suburb of Hunter's Hill. And here, I take it, is the source of two of the principal themes in FitzGerald's poetry: his concern for Australia's national destiny, which inspired some of the most memorable passages in 'Essay on Memory', and his insistence on standards in human conduct. He writes, to use two strangely old-fashioned words, like a patriot and a gentleman. 'Attitude matters: bearing,' he says in 'Fifth Day':

> Attitude matters: bearing. Action in the end
> goes down the stream as motion, merges as such

with the whole of life and time; but islands stand:
dignity and distinctness that attach
to the inmost being of us each.
It matters for man's private respect that still
face differs from face and will from will.

It is important how men looked and were.
Infirm, staggering a little, as Hastings was,
his voice was steady as his eyes. Kneeling at the bar
(ruler but late of millions) had steeled his poise;
he fronted inescapable loss
and thrown, stinking malice and disrepute,
calmly, a plain man in a plain suit.

FitzGerald has said to me sometimes that his own favourite among his poems is 'The Hidden Bole', a poem of some length in which the dancer Pavlova is taken as the symbol of life dancing out of chaos and where the imagery, in places, foreshadows 'The Face of the Waters'. Many critics, with only his earlier work available when they wrote, have chosen 'Essay on Memory' which won the national 150th Anniversary competition and which takes for its theme the influence of all the past, 'the dead time's will', on present-day mankind. My own favourite, if it is not some of the early Fijian landscapes, for which I have a nostalgic affection – and anyhow they are very good poems – is the fluid, visionary, and mysterious 'The Face of the Waters'. But I think that the poem that best illustrates most of his best qualities at their best is 'The Wind at Your Door', which is printed in *Southmost Twelve*. If it does not, like 'The Hidden Bole' and 'The Face of the Waters', probe into the beginning of the universe, nevertheless it continues the theme from 'Essay on Memory' of the past influencing the present. It is flawless in technique and construction. It deals with some great, if grim, adventures. It recall old days in Ireland. It is concerned with Australian nationhood. Its ultimate theme is human conduct; and, dealing with the flogging of an Irish convict, the whole is embodied in a terse, vivid, and most moving narrative:

There, over to one corner, a bony group
of prisoners waits; and each shall be in turn
tied by his own arms in a human loop
about the post, with his back bared to learn
the price of seeking freedom. So they earn

> three hundred rippling stripes apiece, as set
> by the law's mathematics against the debt. ...

> That wind blows to your door down all these years.
> Have you not known it when some breath you drew
> tasted of blood? Your comfort is in arrears
> of just thanks to a savagery tamed in you
> only as subtler fears may serve in lieu
> of thong and noose – old savagery which has built
> your world and laws out of the lives it spilt.

FitzGerald was born in Sydney in 1902. He has published five books of verse, steadily growing in accomplishment. As Dylan Thomas once usefully remarked, 'Poetry is not for gold medals,' and I don't know whether he is to be placed first among contemporary Australian poets, or simply among the first three or four. Somewhere around there. It depends what qualities you happen to be looking for: and if it were solidity of achievement and the feeling of spaciousness and stature, FitzGerald would be hard to pass by. Apart from the pleasure which his poems have given me, my own gratitude to him is largely professional. He sets a standard. When you can write poetry as well as Fitz-Gerald does in 'Fifth Day' and 'The Wind at Your Door', you can really write poetry.

KENNETH SLESSOR AND THE POWERS OF LANGUAGE

CHRIS WALLACE-CRABBE

EVERY poet searches for a poise in which 'language' and 'life' are inseparable, in which the process of perception and what is perceived are in harmony as they so seldom are from day to day. And this, finally, is how the greatest are distinguished: their weaving is such that raw experience and conscious art have become warp and woof of the one seamless robe. We cannot separate their attitudes to life from the shape and texture of their poems.

But such complete achievement is depressingly rare and, for the most part, we must be satisfied with poetry that tends to lean one way or the other: towards life, like *The Prelude*, or towards language, like 'The Scholar-Gipsy'. It is not surprising that this leaning, this uncertainty of poise, is all the more marked in Australia. Amid the still-fluid conditions of 'a half savage country', [1] one would naturally expect statements about experience to come first and the little refinements of art to trail behind. And the truth of this supposition is borne out, not only by obvious primitives like Baylebridge and O'Dowd, but in the best poetry of Brennan and FitzGerald, in the rough-hewn early work of Hope and the later lyrics of Judith Wright. The characteristic Australian poem is one in which there is just enough art to hold the job together: whether it gives voice to prophecy, belief or intimate emotion, it is unlikely to be remarkable for delicacy and precision.

In the midst of such a climate, Kenneth Slessor looks very much an odd man out. Reading his later poetry, in particular, one might easily believe that he had strayed to these shores from some more verbally sophisticated milieu, from the United States, say, or even New Zealand. And in surveying the full body of his work, as represented in *Poems* (1957), [2] one could only be reinforced in such a judgement. For that collection charts the career of a man who acquired his artistic confidence first, and only slowly gained a measure of experience with which his art could be confronted. The verbal dandy appeared first: the poet followed after.

Even Slessor's own admissions, the revelations of an article written in his maturity,[3] will encourage us to think of him as arch-experimenter and craftsman in words rather than as prophet and *poète maudit*. In this article he makes it clear that he is not to be drawn into a discussion of his poetic 'vision' at all. Questions of commitment and vocation are easily shrugged off.

I don't propose to discuss the Why – that is to say, why poets write poetry, why men and women read it and respond to it. That would be an excursion beyond psychology into the springs of life of which I am not capable.

So, after one vaguely religious gesture in the direction of 'the springs of life', the poet discusses the ways in which he is guided by considerations of *form* and *experiment*. His essay is essentially a technical discussion, though he naturally enough insists that technique must be purposeful, expressive. For all that he describes the writing of poetry as 'a pleasure out of hell', it is towards language as a medium and a challenge that he directs his attention here, not to the plain stuff of life.

The poet who can write in one of his earliest pieces,

> Now the tiles drip scarlet-wet,
> Swim like birds' paving-stones, and sunlight strikes
> Their watery mirrors with a moister rivulet,
> Acid and cold.

> ('Winter Dawn')

is already making of his diction a fine and flexible instrument which will be capable of transforming all manner of material into poetry. He is also, we might add, tightening his grasp on one thing he knows to be real, so that he may have some means of evaluating the ephemeral spectres of life. In the later poetry, one often feels that nothing but Slessor's verbal precision could salvage anything from the temporal flux.

Much of his early writing leaves an impression that we might define as painterly rather than poetic. In such poems as 'Pan at Lane Cove', 'Marco Polo' and even the more substantial 'Realities', the paraphrasable content is trivial and banal: Slessor's art here is found largely in his disposition of pictorial elements, of leaning statues, dark hedges, and formal pools touched by moonlight, or those remarkably intensified details which arrest the reader's attention in the first stanza of 'Pan at Lane Cove':

Scaly with poison, bright with flame,
Great fungi steam beside the gate,
Run tentacles through flagstone cracks,
Or claw beyond, where meditate
Wet poplars on a pitchy lawn.
Some seignior of colonial fame
Has planted here a stone-cut faun
Whose flute juts like a frozen flame.

Slessor is not interested in the respective values involved in the worlds of Pan and of Lane Cove; he is interested in the picturesque possibilities which their juxtaposition raises. For comparisons with these poems, one goes not to poetry but to painting: to Norman Lindsay, of course, as the immediate influence, and farther back to Rubens and Watteau. But not to Poussin, it seems important to add. For Poussin, although he evokes the Virgilian glamour of a mythical past, is unwaveringly rational and precise. His paintings are pervaded by that sense of intellectual purpose which we miss altogether in the young Slessor, who wants no more than to evoke the glamour for its own sake. The past which he calls up is a cornucopia of glittering images and evocative stances.

Where the picturesque was his sole concern, Slessor's talents were undeniable. There is something of permanent value in the vividly patterned images of 'Nuremberg' and 'Next Turn', for all the remoteness of both lyrics. But where he sought to be explicit and give voice to an attitude, he merely revealed the crude simplifications of adolescent escapism:

And, tired of life's new-fashioned plan,
I long to be barbarian.
I'm sick of modern men, I wish
You still were living, Kublai-Khan!

('Marco Polo')

A more ambitious, less self-contained poem is 'Earth Visitors', the title-poem of Slessor's 1926 collection. It is dedicated to Norman Lindsay, and the whole substance of the poem plainly acknowledges a young man's debt to the guru of Springwood and to all that the short-lived Lindsayite journal, *Vision*, represented. [4]

The first four stanzas are very good indeed. They comprise an account of a kind of Golden Age – a Golden Age which cannot be identified with the classical reign of Saturn, seeming rather to fall in some period of fairy tale Medievalism (some of the detail, particularly in the second stanza, smacks of Restoration England, however). If the historical origins of Slessor's nostalgic vision are blurred, the actual detail emerges with unusual particularity and coherence. The mysterious, unearthly riders gallop down through the first nine lines with all the immediacy of their physical action dramatized in the energetic verbs, 'gusting', 'rang', 'swept', 'blown', and 'stamping'. And, amid the rich colouring of stanza two, we find an image that is to recur frequently in Slessor's work: the window or barrier of glass which separates two worlds. Outside are the *hoi-polloi*, representatives of the mundane, while the gorgeous visitors perform inside, 'dyed with gold vapours in the candleflame'. Between these two groupings, the 'thick panes' intervene.

The past to which the poem harks back, then – it is significant that *gold* is mentioned no less than four times – was one in which humdrum existence was alleviated by some kind of supernatural intervention. This intervention is typified by Mercury's ravishment of a farm-girl and by a scattering of brilliant memories after the event. And it is seen as bringing to humanity not the Yeatsian possibilities of knowledge and power, but unforeseen beauty.

In the last part of 'Earth Visitors' the nature of Slessor's nostalgia becomes explicit. For the one god who still comes down to earth, the last representative of the riders, is none other than Venus, knocking at the artist's studio window. Beauty, it seems, is the product of an eroticism which is now almost completely lost to mankind. And the lameness of this conclusion finds expression in a sudden enfeebling of the verse. The language has become vague and conventional. Instead of 'Post-boys would run, lanterns hang frostily, horses fume,' we now have the unexpressive gesture, 'When darkness has arched his hands over the bush'; and the description of Venus is a mess of lifeless, sentimental clichés. The poet's imagination has slyly rejected the inadequacy of his overt conclusions.

A much finer poem from this period is 'The Night-Ride'. It is successful *not* because Slessor has bluntly set out to find a viable analogy for his vision of life, but because it starts from a clear definition of local and specific perceptions. His magnificent verbal gifts are no longer wasted on the erection of pleasure domes in Neverneverland, but are devoted to recording the colours, shapes, surfaces of familiar things. One is first of all aware of a particular country station meticulously yet selectively sketched in: yellow lights, silver milk-cans, smoke, luggage, anonymous travellers.

These first eight lines could almost be read as pure impressionism. Almost: but there is about the organization of detail an emotional weighting which is somehow suggestive, even mildly sinister. Yet the poet does not overplay his hand; we do not have to be painfully solemn in our reading of 'All groping clumsily to mysterious ends,/Out of the gaslight, dragged by private Fates,' It is just after these suggestions that the note of the poem does unmistakably deepen with 'shakes', 'plunges', 'cry out', and 'nothing but blackness'. Before, we were aware of Slessor's role as the detached, civilized observer, but here the detachment is lost. The poet's emotions and the movement of the train are inseparable.

We can account for the accelerating intensity of 'The Night-Ride' by regarding it as a sustained metaphorical account of Slessor's view of life as a process. His language focuses so hard on the train journey that the journey becomes the whole direction of a life (there are interesting parallels here with similar journeys in Eliot and Hope, though each of the three draws from his journey a markedly different set of values). And the direction is consistent with that which can be found in a great deal of Slessor's poetry: life is a rapid journey towards oblivion; other people and the bright surfaces of things are perceived through an intervening pane of glass; memorable experience consists of transient flashes amid a general obscurity of 'grey, rushing rivers of bush'.

The progression here, a progression from vivid perception towards a drugging sleep, is finally reversed – reversed, that is, without being negated – in one of Slessor's most brilliant late poems, that rhythmical and syntactical triumph, 'Sleep'. The swaying, evocative lines of this lyric carry the developing logic of three kinds of human situation. A voice speaks with soothing authority,

> Do you give yourself to me utterly,
> Body and no-body, flesh and no-flesh,
> Not as a fugitive, blindly or bitterly,
> But as a child might, with no other wish?

and in the course of the poem the voice seems not only Sleep
addressing the sleeper, but also woman to lover and mother to
foetus. In all three cases, the implied listener is held, enveloped,
in a harmony of pulsing forces. And in each case these forces are
protectively maternal, holding the listener back from the harsh
facts which await him, and which are realized in the new, stark
rhythm of the last stanza:

> Till daylight, the expulsion and awakening,
>   The riving and the driving forth,
> Life with remorseless forceps beckoning –
>   Pangs and betrayal of harsh birth.

Manifestly it is the best of all fates not to be born, not to be
separated, not to wake up. In both these poems the most expressive passages reach towards the oblivion of the womb.

The threats of darkness and oblivion, transient phenomena and
a baffled observer: from these preoccupations most of Slessor's
poetry has been made, the flamboyant and the sardonic alike.
The poems of his 'middle period', those first published in *Cuckooz
Contrey* (1932), show little intellectual advance on the earlier
work; they do however show that he has learned to use language
with new precision and point. And one poem shows a good
deal more than this.

The influence of Pound's *Lustra* and of 'The Love Song of
J. Alfred Prufrock' plays an unmistakable part in this poetry.
The unrealized fleshpots of yesteryear are giving way to wry
monologues which eschew the excesses of Victorian Romanticism
('That's what we're like out here,/ Beds of dried-up passions.')
without completely shedding its self indulgences. In 'Talbingo',
'Toilet of a Dandy', 'Metempsychosis' and particularly 'Elegy
in a Botanic Gardens', the reader is aware of a familiar kind of
alliance between weary disenchantment and a nervously alert wit:

> to the Tristania tree
> Where we had kissed so awkwardly,
> Noted by swans with damp, accusing eyes,
> All gone to-day; only the leaves remain,
> Gaunt paddles ribbed with herringbones
> Of watermelon-pink. Never before
> Had I assented to the hateful name
> *Meryta Macrophylla*, on a tin tag.
> That was no time for botany.

347

The world of Tristan and the narratives of Courtly Love are no more than the faintest of echoes. A fine control of tone enables the poet not only to strike a balance between, but to fuse, his sense of emotional frustration and his unqualified delight in the objects of perception: objects reproduced with such precise brush-work as 'Gaunt paddles ribbed with herringbones/Of watermelon-pink.' Slessor's exemplars have taught him how to detach and delineate the precisely relevant detail.

But Eliot and Pound could not find Slessor's path for him. (It is worth noting that 'The Old Play', his most ambitious Eliotic experiment, falls in a heap, a disastrous mess of *pasticcio* and confectionery.) The finest thing in *Cuckooz Contrey* is also the most thoroughly original poem in that volume – 'Five Visions of Captain Cook'. Here at last, especially in the magnificent fifth section, sharp observation and a fastidious fingering of words are involved in something of the first importance, because here at last Slessor's awareness of life has caught up with his mastery of language.

'Five Visions' is a concentrated drama of enterprise, action, memory, decay, and death. Seeing its development in the starkest light, Charles Higham has called the poem

as harsh a statement of fatalism – hedonism's inevitable aftermath when the pleasures of youth and health have gone – as we are likely to get in poetry. [5]

Yes, one may say, the poem indeed reminds us that life declines into death; and it concludes with the portrayal of a blind old salt droning away at his tales of past adventure. But the weight of the poem primarily reinforces our awareness of the flux and variety of life. Cook has mapped, and snored, and given orders, and made his vital choice, before we come to the balancing conclusion of part V. So when Home drunkenly screeches,

> 'Then Captain Cook,
> I heard him, told them they could go
> If so they chose, but he would get them back,
> Dead or alive, he'd have them,'

his words receive rich confirmation from what has already been presented.

The poem ends with the memory of Cook's death and the image of Home's decline, for this is how life itself ends. And in

the poem at large, as in the old man's consciousness, the fulness
of life is vividly displayed while the 'vague ancestral darknesses'
exist no more than slenderly. Home lives in the past because this
is to live with Cook's (and his own) vital exploits: and if he is
now a fuddled old man, those exploits are still not cancelled out.
The five visions are, as little in the early poetry was, visions of a
world of experience; Cook's *Endeavour* is not 'a painted ship
upon a painted ocean' but a familiar ground of human action.

The verse in part V has become a robust and flexible medium.
Slessor is now capable of setting down a human situation in bold,
concise outline:

> Darkness and empty chairs,
> This was the port that Alexander Home
> Had come to with his useless cutlass-wounds
> And tales of Cook, and half-a-crown a day –
> This was the creek he'd run his timbers to,
> Where grateful countrymen repaid his wounds
> At half-a-crown a day.

Irony here is not a device to permit detachment; it represents a
simple plea for human justice. Every detail, including the soured
repetition of 'half-a-crown a day', is completely functional.

Where the earlier gaudiness makes an appearance, it serves a
new kind of purpose:

> he lived like this
> In one place, and gazed elsewhere. His body moved
> In Scotland, but his eyes were dazzle-full
> Of skies and water farther round the world –
> Air soaked with blue, so thick it dripped like snow
> On spice-tree boughs, and water diamond-green,
> Beaches wind-glittering with crumbs of gilt,
> And birds more scarlet than a duchy's seal
> That had come whistling long ago, and far
> Away.

The brilliancies of Home's vision make a sharp contrast both
with the tawdry inn and with the real Pacific Ocean – as it was
seen in parts II and IV, for example. The blind man's memory is
throwing up wishful fantasies in which air, trees, water, birds, all
are transformed into jewel-like emblems whose only life is a
factitious one. Their very brilliance is a measure of the degree of
escapism involved.

But this is not the whole story, for Home's sustaining memories are composed of facts as well as fantasies, of lived conflicts as well as halcyon days. Within a few lines we are caught up in a recapitulated narrative of violent physical action. The different quality of the old man's memory at this point is made clear by the rhythmical tightness that is achieved: there is in the verse a sense of flexed muscles and abrupt shocks. Half-line jolts against half-line, phrase against phrase, in the rush of events leading to Cook's death in the Sandwich Isles. Action is here presented without a rhetorical pattern or a false logic being superimposed. The figures of marines and savages ('puzzled animals, killing they know not what . . .') are caught up in a brief anonymous struggle, and then, on Cook's death, the memory fades and peace settles down once again, accompanied by the inexorable flow of the sea.

> and a knife of English iron,
> Forged aboard ship, that had been changed for pigs,
> Given back to Cook between the shoulder-blades.
> There he had dropped, and the old floundering sea,
> The old, fumbling, witless lover-enemy,
> Had taken his breath, last office of salt water.

Certainly there is a burden of fatalism apparent here. It does not, however, emerge from the poem anything like so dominantly as Higham suggests. After all, 'Five Visions of Captain Cook' has not been concerned with hedonism but with heroic achievement. Against the old age of Alexander Home we may set the end of part I, 'So Cook made choice, so Cook sailed westabout,/ So men write poems in Australia' and all the positive accomplishment displayed in the first two Visions. However essentially pessimistic he remains, Slessor has discovered in the figure of Cook a vitality which immediately finds its way into the poetry.

Among the poems which Slessor published after 1933, there are four which can be said to mark the climax of his career. In these four poems, 'Sleep', 'South Country', 'Beach Burial', and 'Five Bells', the poet is completely at ease in the shaping of his experience. All the slack of his talent is taken up, his talent no longer dissipating itself in merely virtuoso effects.

It is surely no accident that these poems are among the last that Slessor wrote before falling silent. All four are marked at least by despair and frustration, perhaps by 'a faint ground-bass of disgust with life'. [6] Two are elegies, one depicts life as a betrayal and the fourth, a masterpiece of expressionist landscape, ends with a strange, anthropomorphic vision:

> While even the dwindled hills are small and bare,
> As if, rebellious, buried, pitiful,
> Something below pushed up a knob of skull,
> Feeling its way to air.

('South Country')

'Five Bells' is generally, and rightly, acknowledged to be Slessor's greatest achievement. After a few loose gestures in the first three stanzas, it is hard to find a flaw in the poem's shaping. The form is musical, organic, even to some extent cyclic; like a more famous poem that was perhaps being written at the same time, Eliot's *Four Quartets*, 'Five Bells' demonstrates the possibilities of this kind of form for metaphysical meditation. For the poem is far more than an elegy for a dead friend: it is an intensely dramatic meditation in which Slessor gathers up all his previous suggestions about time and flux and the value of life in a godless universe.

The poem opens with bells, darkness and water, and these recur again and again with further accumulations of meaning as the elegy progresses. The bells record man-made time as well as tolling for Joe's death; darkness punctuates time, surrounds the life of man and awaits him at its end; while water has been the instrument of death (Joe was drowned in Sydney Harbour), of the frustration which is revealed on the Moorebank journey, and of progressive enervation ('sponge-paws of wetness, the slow damp/ That stuck the leaves of living,'): water, above all, suggests the temporal flux upon which all men, including Joe, his stone-cutting father, and the speaker himself, are borne toward 'the pygmy strait' and annihilation. The whole movement of the poem, its meditative undulation, embodies this vision of time, 'the flood that does not flow'.

It is the paradox of a 'flood that does not flow' which stands at the heart of 'Five Bells'. The structure is *both* progressive and cyclic; Joe both is and is not recalled from oblivion; life is both meaningful – as testified by the speaker's vivid memories of Darlinghurst, Moorebank, and Melbourne – and meaningless. On the one hand, Slessor creates meaning in the act of commemorating Joe's death; on the other, the elegy is saturated with premonitions of his own extinction, just as it is saturated with rain, damp, and Harbour water. Towards the end, empathy with Joe has become so complete that the poet's own fate comes to be the real concern of the poetry:

> I felt the wet push its black thumb-balls in,
> The night you died, I felt your eardrums crack,
> And the short agony, the longer dream,
> The Nothing that was neither long nor short;
> But I was bound, and could not go that way,
> But I was blind, and could not feel your hand.
> If I could find an answer, could only find
> Your meaning, or could say why you were here
> Who now are gone, what purpose gave you breath
> Or seized it back, might I not hear your voice?

But only faint, distant sounds are heard, and the poem ends with the cold ring of bells. There is no realm of vigorous action, like Cook's, to set against the loss of contact that finds enunciation here.

'Five Bells' is the final triumph of Slessor's powers of language. He has made his world fully articulate and has thus set the seal upon his small but distinguished *oeuvre*. Having reached this point, he can hardly be expected to write further, unless he is to retreat once again into that conscious dandyism which stood condemned years ago in his glimpse of 'the Corpse in Evening Dress' sneering from the Great Harry's dressing-room mirror.

NOTES

1. Ezra Pound, '*E. P. Ode pour l'Election de son Sepulcre*'.
2. From 1944, Slessor's collected poetry was to be found in *One Hundred Poems*. In 1957, with the addition of three later pieces this became *Poems*, which remains the only available collection.
3. 'Writing Poetry: the Why and the How', *Southerly*, 1948, no. 3, pp. 166–77.
4. *Vision*, a jaunty, polemical journal, ran to four issues in 1923-4. It was edited by Frank Johnson, Jack Lindsay, and Slessor.
5. 'The Poetry of Kenneth Slessor', *Quadrant*, 1959–60, no. 1, p. 71.
6. Vincent Buckley, 'Kenneth Slessor: Realist or Romantic?', in his *Essays in Poetry, Mainly Australian* (Melbourne, 1957), p. 121.

JUDITH WRIGHT

MAX HARRIS

IN the Penguin *Modern Australian Verse* eight of the sixty poets represented are women: in the Oxford *Book of Australian Verse* there are eleven women in the total of seventy poets represented. This seems a not altogether unworthy tally for a country which is notoriously rugged, masculine, and illiberal in its approach to cultural phenomena.

The explanation for Australia's present strength of women poets – Judith Wright, Rosemary Dobson, Nan McDonald, Nancy Cato, Elizabeth Riddell and others – goes back into a colonial past and involves some understanding of the psychology of 'frontier' societies, even where the frontier is as pronouncedly urban as was the Melbourne of the 1850s and thereafter.

No matter how assiduously the nineteenth century squattocracy tried to restate the conventions of wealthy English country life, no matter how energetically mercantile wealth was expended in Melbourne to create great town houses in which salons for choice cultural spirits could be conducted, the terms of Australian life remained obdurately materialistic, isolated, and contemptuous of the luxury of high sensibility. It was possible to mimic the trappings of life 'at Home' in England but among men there was no silken dalliance, no taste for the elegant refinements of Victorian life even among the classes wealthy enough to indulge in such seeming fripperies. It was a masculine and immeasurably practical world in nineteenth century Australia.

It was the women who daydreamed about the educated social life of the homeland eleven thousand miles away. They never lost their sense of colonial exile: they battled in a variety of antipathetic environments to hold on to their Englishness, the delicacy and sensibility of their Victorian femininity. In consequence there is a feminine tradition in Australian poetry which is not only distinct from but runs counter to the male tradition of robust balladry, and outdoor narrative. Ada Cambridge and Catherine Martin became celebrated in circles of refined taste for the gentility of their verse, their capacity to write of love and the emotions in a climate hot and hostile to such lady-like things. As

Geoffrey Dutton has observed, Australia has little to show in the way of love poetry apart from the feminist tradition which culminated in the stuffed-owl excesses of Zora Cross.

With the decline in the twentieth century of the bush ballad and the 'outbackery' tradition of *The Bulletin*, it became clear, in the nineteen-forties, that Australian poets would need to build a more subtle complex of factors into the hearty conventions of the national poetic idiom. A sense of environment and landscape had to be partially retained, but interpreted through the identity of the poet himself, related to a personal vision and to systems of belief and complex habits of thought. In short a tradition that was at its best virile and spirited, at its worst intolerably shallow, had to be replaced by a poetry in depth.

The process had been inaugurated by Brennan, Slessor, and FitzGerald, all poets of remarkable stature, complexity, and skill – but, and this does not detract from the essential worth of their poetry, all reticent in dealing with personal emotion.

Here was a chance for the feminist tradition to develop a new and startling life. It only required women writers with an unselfconscious sense of personal passion and a powerful capacity for emotional identification to spring up to endow the modern Australian image with a new and, oddly enough, more sophisticated dimension.

It was Judith Wright who appeared on the scene in the nineteen-forties. A sense of personal presence in the colonial scene, intellect, a formidable technical proficiency, and an implacably passionate sensibility combined to give Australia the finest work it has ever had from a woman poet. It was little wonder that the historian H.M. Green in 1950 declared, with perhaps excessive certainty, 'Judith Wright is among the leading poets writing in English today'.

All the circumstances of family background, upbringing, and personal history, combined to endow Judith Wright with the kind of qualities that would make for a sophisticated and vibrant poetic talent; her personal life has combined an intimate familiarity with the Australian environment and a sophisticated intelligence.

One of the strangest things about Judith Wright is that she has no juvenilia to show, no period of youthful and immature development. She appeared on the Australian literary scene with her alents fully grown. Some of her most successful and enduringly beautiful poetry appeared before she was thirty years of age, and was published in *The Moving Image* in 1946.

The poetry in *The Moving Image* is comparatively free of the biological-centredness and physical passion that developed in later years. It lacks the complexity, the dark and yet urgent presence of the poet herself in the poems. Yet it has another quality, a quality which Judith Wright shares with Slessor – it is magnificent poetry of projection, of subtle and unobtrusive self-identification. No one could mistake 'South of My Days', 'Bullocky', 'Brother and Sisters', 'The Remittance Man', 'Half Caste Girl' or 'The Idler' for a kind of reportage poetry. The poet is there, not in the poems as a character, but within the characters themselves, and within the framework of the language. It is a measure of the complex nature of Judith Wright that the poet who is capable of losing herself within the subject of the poem can, almost in the same breath, produce a love poem of the most turbulent subjectivity.

The character sketches of the *Moving Image* period are easily the finest things of their kind in modern Australian poetry. For a young poet, the care and technical skill command the utmost respect. For instance, take the totality of 'Brother and Sisters':

> The road turned out to be a cul-de-sac;
> stopped like a lost intention at the gate
> and never crossed the mountains to the coast.
> But they stayed on. Years grew like grass and leaves
> across the half-erased and dubious track
> until one day they knew the plans were lost,
> the blue-print for the bridge was out of date,
> and now their orchards never would be planted.
> The saplings sprouted slyly; day by day
> the bush moved one step nearer, wondering when.
> The polished parlour grew distrait and haunted
> where Millie, Lucy, John each night at ten
> wound the gilt clock that leaked the year away.
>
> The pianola – oh, listen to the mocking-bird –
> wavers on Sundays and has lost a note.
> The wrinkled ewes snatch pansies through the fence
> and stare with shallow eyes into the garden
> where Lucy shrivels waiting for a word,

and Millie's cameos loosen round her throat.
The bush comes near, the ranges grow immense.

Feeding the lambs deserted in early spring
Lucy looked up and saw the stockman's eye
telling her she was cracked and old.
                                    The wall
groans in the night and settles more awry.
O how they lie awake. Their thoughts go fluttering
from room to room like moths: 'Millie, are you awake?'
'Oh, John, I have been dreaming.' 'Lucy, do you cry?'
– meet tentative as moths. Antennae stroke a wing.
'There is nothing to be afraid of. Nothing at all.'

This poem, along with all the human-descriptive poems in
The Moving Image concentrates on a sense of life lost, of desolation, of deprivation. The people who inhabit these poems are
both human and ghostly at the same time. They are all outside
the Heraclitean flux, lost from or separated from time. This
mood rings true in early Judith Wright because a sense of colonial
history is bred well and truly into her bone. Her prose volume of
family biography, *Generations of Men*, illustrated how acute an
instinct she has for the values and human details of the past.
Millie, Lucy, and John are not fancifully dreamed up as images
and symbols, but are recalled from an actual past with such
seeming authority that a sense of the poet's presence in the milieu
is created. The mention of the Sunday pianola brings into the
poem the interpolation 'oh, listen to the mocking-bird', a detail
so fine, a line from a song actually played on the pianola, that the
reader feels, with the poet, intimately involved with the brother
and sisters. Judith Wright has the surest possible instinct for
significant detail.

Also with the surest possible hand Judith Wright has created a
technical framework for a kind of poetry which could quite
easily have slipped over into the abyss of nostalgic sentimentalism.
'Brother and Sisters' is written in a comparatively free run-on
form. It is near to the conversational, but not too near. The skill
lies in the detached quality of the verse: the emotional tone of
the poem is not 'loaded' with technical accentuation. 'Remittance
Man' leads off with the same story-telling tone.

The spendthrift, disinherited and graceless,
Accepted his pittance with an easy air.

> Only surprised he could escape so simply
> From the pheasant shooting and the aunts in the close.

The emotional tensions within the poem are built up with a kind of theatre architecture, a series of building climaxes and development from low-keyed passages.

With the famous anthology piece 'Bullocky' she has chosen, and chosen deliberately, the obvious technical form for the poem. With four heavy stresses to each line and heavy alternate rhymes the poem is almost insultingly onomatopoeic in its suggestion of the plodding bullock team:

> Beside his heavy-shouldered team,
> thirsty with drought and chilled with rain,
> he weathered all the striding years
> till they ran widdershins in his brain:

But there is virtuosity in the change of stress and temper in the last two stanzas,

> Grass is across the waggon-tracks,
> and plough strikes bone beneath the grass,
> and vineyards cover all the slopes
> where the dead teams were used to pass.
>
> O vine, grow close upon that bone
> and hold it with your rooted hand.
> The prophet Moses feeds the grape,
> and fruitful is the Promised Land.

The deliberate archaism of 'where the dead teams were used to pass' leads cunningly into the ironic biblical invocation of the last stanza.

The major poem of this 1946 period is 'South of My Days' and here Judith Wright's ghost-calling sounds louder and nearer. The poet is present overtly in the poem –

> South of my days' circle, part of my blood's country,
> rises that tableland, high delicate outline
> of bony slopes wincing under the winter.

Here the evocation of old Dan and his memories, his mustering yarns, serves a more personal purpose than the mere animating of the dead and dying past. Judith Wright is anticipating her later preoccupations. The landscape she is discovering is an inward one. The imagery inspired by past and environment is about to serve to describe the problems of her personal identity.

In this process something is lost and something gained. Judith Wright begins to be a poet who explores deep and troubled depths within her own identity. Although she writes some magnificently tense and sustained verse in *Woman to Man* and *The Gateway* and *The Two Fires* it is doubtful if she ever wrote with simpler and more enduring cunning than she did in *The Moving Image*.

*

The eyeless labourer in the night,
the selfless, shapeless seed I hold,
builds for its resurrection day –
silent and swift and deep from sight
foresees the unimagined light.

This is no child with a child's face;
this has no name to name it by:
yet you and I have known it well.
This is our hunter and our chase,
the third who lay in our embrace.

This is the strength that your arm knows,
the arc of flesh that is my breast,
the precise crystals of our eyes.
This is the blood's wild tree that grows
the intricate and folded rose.

This is the maker and the made;
this is the question and reply;
the blind head butting at the dark,
the blaze of light along the blade.
Oh hold me, for I am afraid.

This is an historic poem in Australian literature. It created in its day an immediate impact. Love poetry had been part and parcel of the lyrical mode of expression which had achieved its greatest flowering in the works of John Shaw Neilson. But the qualities of *Woman to Man* are passionate, tender, hard, yet feminine. The most frequent critical comment made about Judith Wright was that in her poetry she succeeded in creating a satisfying fusion of passion and intellect. This is certainly true of *Woman to Man*. But this determination to think about the quality of her feelings brought tremendous stresses and strains which eventually told on both her language and technique. Although in *Woman to Man* (1949), *The Gateway* (1953), and *The Two Fires*

(1955) there is a mass of poetic material of breathtaking diversity, too many of the poems are unnecessarily flawed.

It seemed that Judith Wright had acquired the habit of standing too close to her material, her inward concerns took ratiocinative expression in poetry, her voice became shrill, her need for emphasis and effect led her into technical tricksiness. It was obvious she found the inward-looking process a more treacherous business than the outward-looking innocence of 'South of My Days'.

See the kind of thing that has happened in stanzas from various poems from this period:

> All things that glow and move,
> All things that change and pass,
> I gather their delight
> as in a burning glass.
>
> . . .
>
> Strong as the sun is the golden tree
> that gives and says nothing,
> that takes and knows nothing;
> but I am stronger than the sun; I am a child.
>
> . . .
>
> Standing here in the night
> we are turned to a great tree
> every leaf a star,
> its root eternity.

In *Woman to Man* the influence of Blake has been obvious and destructive. Whereas Blake's 'I' is mystical and universal, Judith Wright's is personal and highly conscious of itself. In attempting to face the modern dilemma of the gulf between passion and intellect Judith Wright knew what had to be said, but had lost touch with the appropriate language to say it. Derivative writing, such as the Slessor-ish 'Song in a Wine Bar' shows her plight. A cheapening of technical effects is frequently perceptible.

> But the sad river, the silted river,
> Under its dark banks the river flows on
> The wind still blows and the river still flows.
>
> ('Old House', *The Gateway*, p. 13)

The search for effect is here obvious, the laborious repetitions and the internal rhyme. Likewise the imagery tends to be constipated. Judith Wright was motivated by passion, despair, a complex sense of the destructive interactions of love and life, of life and death, but it seemed these compulsions exhausted her capacity for rightness of image, her previously sure visual sense,

> I dream of hills bandaged in snow
> Their eyelids clenched to keep out fear.
> When the last leaf and bird go
> Let my thoughts stand like trees here.
> ('Eroded Hills', *The Gateway*, p. 12)

'Hills bandaged in snow' is a laborious conceit: the poet has been able to imagine hills with eyelids, but the reader is struggling to establish any sort of equation of his own. However, in *The Gateway* Judith Wright broke out of her highly personal concern with birth, sex, ecstasy, fear, and feminism, transferring these preoccupations to the universe, to the life of trees, flowers, birds, and the bitter changes of the seasons. But she still could not completely recover her youthfully sure sense of language. There is a sincere ring in her cry –

> Then I could fuse my passions into one clear stone
> and be simple to myself as the bird is to the bird.

*

Within two years of *The Gateway* Judith Wright had rediscovered her poetic direction, completely outgrown her biological hysteria and produced in *The Two Fires* (1955) her finest poetry since the early perfections of *The Moving Image*. She is now 'the wise woman from the land past joy and grief'. The verse has a beautiful sense and flow: the mood is compassionate and thoughtful: her themes are the contemplation of anything and everything in the world of her immediate experiencing. If Slessor was her soul-mate in the early years, it is now R.D. FitzGerald whose point of view she shares. The mood is resigned and quietistic, the poetry beautifully constrained.

> So moves in me time's purpose, evil and good.
> Those silent tracts eternity may give;
> But the lame shadow stumbles at my back,
> Still sick for love: the battle of flesh and blood
> Will hardly come to quiet while I live.

In this memorable 1955 collection, which could well be described at this moment of time as her middle period, not only has Judith

Wright discovered a language of philosophical reflection, but she has also discovered within herself the sensibility from which the pure lyric springs. The lyric had never seemed natural to Judith Wright's poetic style although it constantly preoccupied her as the final and most perfect mode of expression. In her previous two volumes she had often adopted a statuesquely Blake-like pose and produced lyric effusions of embarrassing artificiality. 'For the Loved and the Unloved' represents a kind of lyric writing true to Judith Wright's own modes of poetic thought, faintly didactic but finely wrought and delicately assured for all that –

> Love in his alteration
> Invents the heart to suit him:
> Its season, spring or autumn
> Depends on his decision.

'For Precision', 'The Two Fires', 'The Man Beneath the Tree', 'Sanctuary', 'Landscapes' all achieve a memorable finality of statement, a reconciliation of the poet with herself. The feminism has disappeared, for 'flesh has now become time's instrument'. In addition the colonial Australianism of the early years has reappeared, not as hauntingly as in the early work but just as effectively.

Seven years after this resurgence of her powers, her personal world clarified and reconciled, Judith Wright published a new collection, *Birds* (1963). These accomplished little exercises need not largely concern the student of her writing. The poet is merely keeping her hand in. For Judith Wright is so completely a poet that she will continue to develop in one direction or another until she comes to final terms with time.

DOUGLAS STEWART

JAMES MCAULEY

In all parts of his work, in poems, plays, short stories and criticism, Douglas Stewart is recognizably the same mind. There is variety, there may be changes or unresolved problems; but there is no baffling incoherence, and no falsity or pretence. We encounter a mind of considerable integrity, dealing honestly with its world and its audience of readers.

Stewart's critical prose is not the most important part of his work, but it is convenient to look at it first, for it tells us what he looks for in literature, and thus indicates the canons by which he would wish his own work to be judged. The critical writings published under the title *The Flesh and the Spirit* (1948) represent his position very well; subsequent uncollected critical writings do not show any radical change in outlook.

Stewart requires of major poetry that it be an 'art which accepts and presents a heroic image of the life of man' (p. 88). In all poetry, minor or major, he responds to what is vigorous and life-affirming: 'that note of arrogant vitality' and 'joyous gusto' (p. 88) are two of his approving phrases. He is against what he sees as self-pity, railing at life, defeatism, glumness, or limpness. He accuses art and literature in our time of tending to two vices: the rejection of life, and the flight into subjectivism. Both are to him forms of escapism. He wants poetry to be objective, and prefers it to be resolutely this-worldly. He detests confusion and obscurity, believing that poetry requires discipline and control, 'the isolation and clarification of the image' (p. 15). He is interested in three distinct kinds of poetry: narrative, dramatic, and lyrical. He distrusts the overly didactic and the abstract.

Stewart's literary values come from within the romantic stream. At the head of the stream is Sir Walter Scott with his narrative forms, his contact with the ballad tradition, his healthy vigour, and his mixture of romance and realism. But downstream, as we are reminded from time to time, are camped the Australian vitalists, including Norman Lindsay and Hugh McCrae, and the stream is not the same after it has passed them.

It is possible to regard Stewart's main intuitions as radically sound while admitting that there are crudities and limitations in the way they are developed and applied. Thus, since 'the denial of life always pales before affirmation', C.J. Brennan is therefore inferior to Hugh McCrae. Is there, he asks, any poetry branching from Baudelaire that is not fundamentally a surrender to death? (p. 70). Evidently not, but then, 'Baudelaire, after all, was a silly fellow' (p. 215). Norman Lindsay is 'the fountain-head of the Australian culture in our time'; his main attraction to poets is that 'he paints women', and these pictures have a 'religious importance' which has not been sufficiently noticed (pp. 275-7). Pope and Dryden on the other hand are 'masters of artificial metre', and know 'nothing whatsoever about natural rhythm' (p. 153); but then Pope is 'not a true poet' (p. 72). Dr Johnson is characterized by 'rumbling platitudes' (p. 188) and 'professional pietism' (p. 130). Roman poetry was born 'exhausted' (p. 227). It would be easy to use a necklace of such indiscretions to hang Stewart as a critic, but it is more important to acknowledge the soundness of his main critical sentiments, however limited by prejudices.

One of Stewart's critical articles in *The Flesh and the Spirit* should not be overlooked: his comments on verse technique, called 'Tricks of the Trade', which shed light on his own practice. Stewart calls the normal syllabic-accentual kind of English verse by two names which are opprobrious in his critical vocabulary, 'artificial' and 'academic'. The interplay between metrical pattern and actual speech-stress essential to this kind of verse is to him a confusion unaccountably persisted in by most poets. What he finally recommends, however, is not a metre based on pure speech-stress but a balance between 'artificial metre' and 'natural rhythm'. In practice this means *loosened* verse, hovering between reliance on measurement by actual speech-stresses and measurement by the syllabic-accentual code.

There are unacknowledged problems in this sort of hybrid metric. In the first place, measurement by counting actual speech-stresses has a deceptive clarity when offered as a principle of scansion. When we try to apply it we find we are often uncertain which syllables are to be regarded as carrying a sufficient degree of stress to be counted. In fact we have to cheat by working in reverse: we assign a stress or withhold it by reference to the number of stresses we think the line is *meant* to carry. Thus in Stewart's poem 'Lady Feeding the Cats' the following lines have syllables whose metrical value can be assigned only if we know that we are to find neither more nor less than five stresses in the line.

          ?
(1) Uphill past the Moreton Bays and the smoky gums

          ?   ?
(2) Those furtive she-cats and those villainous toms

                 ?
(3) Some recollection of old punctilio.

More serious is the danger of monotony. In the search for naturalness, the variability of the verse is indefinitely increased; and this, paradoxically, tends to make any particular variation less felt, less significant, and therefore less interesting. Furthermore the loosening of the metric threatens to let in rhythmic clichés which are hard to avoid and become tiresome. That Stewart is a sensitive craftsman in verse, and at his best superbly fine, is evident from some of the passages I shall quote; but it is a question whether, in the dramatic verse especially, he has entirely overcome the problems inherent in loosened verse. One may take as a test passage this from *The Golden Lover*:

WHANA: Each night you will come to me, each morning go home
       To the Maori village and your people. Ho, you devil,
       You will have that fat husband in a fit! For that alone
       I love you and will do what you wish. But not for long.
       Eh, you can try it! He will roll on the ground
       And bite himself like a dog chasing its tail
       When you say farewell each evening. You will drive him mad.
       You are wicked, Tawhai, and I love you.
TAWHAI: It will do him good.

Stewart's non-dramatic verse can be roughly classified as narrative poems; poems in a popular quasi-traditional vein with or without fantasy; humorous or satirical poems; meditations and situation-pieces; nature studies, chiefly lyrical; love poems. These categories tend to overlap or mingle.

Among the narratives *Glencoe* (1947) has pride of place. Stewart tells us [1] that it was a 'given work', composed in five days amidst other business: 'it seemed that all I had to do was to take down the ballads as they came'. The complex events leading to the massacre have been rendered with marvellous simplicity and sureness. The style is a natural continuation from the ballad tradition and Scott, and it has great force, swift movement and deep feeling. At the climax of the poem is a stark threnody which shows how at certain moments Stewart's talent reaches back authentically to its high sources.

> Sigh, wind in the pine;
> River, weep as you flow;
> Terrible things were done
> Long, long ago.
>
> In daylight golden and mild
> After the night of Glencoe
> They found the hand of a child
> Lying upon the snow.
>
> Lopped by the sword to the ground
> Or torn by wolf or fox,
> That was the snowdrop they found
> Among the granite rocks.
>
> Oh, life is fierce and wild
> And the heart of the earth is stone,
> And the hand of a murdered child
> Will not bear thinking on.
>
> Sigh, wind in the pine,
> Cover it over with snow;
> But terrible things were done
> Long, long ago.

Glencoe came as a decisive advance from the early volumes of poetry, and marked the beginning of his period of greatest strength, which happily continues, so that his most recent volume, *Rutherford* (1962), is his best. Not that the earlier volumes should be dismissed: they all contain individual successes as well as offering the interest of following a developing talent. In the early volume *The White Cry* (1939), for example, there is a near-perfect lyric called 'Look Now for Country Atlas' which ends:

> Look now for country Atlas:
> Lightly enough he bears
> Who moves among dark trees
> His world of simple cares,
> The wood to warm him by,
> The paddock thick with grass,
> The stack not built; but I,

True load not shouldered yet
And nowhere here to find,
Feel the red-brown light a burden
Lowering on my mind,
And walk with heavy tread
Homeward from farm and Atlas
To glass and book and bed.

In the volume immediately preceding *Glencoe*, the poems published in 1946 entitled *The Dosser in Springtime*, the interest is still rather in the ways in which a developing talent is searching than in actual achievement. Here a main feature was the attempt to 'come to terms with the balladists' – the Australian balladists – as Stewart had said we must do. (*The Flesh and the Spirit*, p. 68). So we find him extending his use of colloquialism, employing vigorous rhythms and refrains, and at times indulging in quasi-legendary fantasy, in order to create a sort of literary populism. The results remain hybrids, uncertain in tone, prolix and wilful. The real success along this line came much later in the play *Fisher's Ghost* (1960) where a traditional vein succeeds, and the fun really is fun:

He was a ticket-of-leave man
Came out by the ship *Atlas*;
His slayer was also a convict,
He had no fellow-feeling alas.

But out of the hole sprang Fisher,
It was a welcome change,
And on that fence by Fisher's Creek
He waited for his revenge.

The vein of humour or comedy, edging towards satire, is evident in a good deal of Stewart's work, and provides sunlight and salt. It is not so easy, however, to find a complete instance in which the humour is satisfying throughout. 'The Bishop' is a deft and enjoyable poem:

I mightn't have liked the bishop alive but I
certainly like him dead,
The good old man in his suit of bronze with the
pigeon on top of his head.

But the interests of life-affirming and of civilized banter are not well served by the vulgar misconception inherent in lines like:

> And a saint alive is a narrow saint, soaring
>   alone like a steeple. . . .

A similar poem, 'Heaven is a Busy Place', begins at this level of facetiousness:

> Heaven is a busy place.
> Those in a state of grace
> Continually twanging the harp.
> And Court at eight-thirty sharp . . .

though it recovers half way through:

> Sir, I would make my petition:
> Love and fulfilled ambition;
> Some friends to be partly protected,
> Some enemies grossly afflicted . . .

In general the humour and comedy are most satisfying when they are an element of dryness or laughter within a more complex whole that disciplines uncertainties of taste.

It is an element for instance in some of the lyrical nature studies. The sonnet 'Familiars', addressed to David Campbell is a delightful instance:

> To each his symbolic creature. But was it quite fair
> That in one morning fishing the mountain water,
> Out of some lair in the rocks or hole in blue air
> To me should have stumbled this dark and humble ant-
>   eater
> So clumsy and prickly and wary, hasty to hide,
> Fumbling the stones and driftwood with his black claw,
> While my companion meets round the mountainside
> 'The biggest reddest fox I ever saw.'
> That dark and secretive creature snuffling for danger,
> Hugging so close to earth and the roots of the rocks,
> Spiny all over for tooth or touch of the stranger
> – I do detect some resemblance . . . and that great fox
> That bites the rabbits, makes farmers' pullets tremble
> – Well, if the cap fits, wish you good hunting, Campbell.

In the poem 'To Lie on the Grass' an essentially comic vision, resembling Swift's alterations of scale, is used with light seriousness. An analogy of proportion (as the ant seems to me, so I in turn may seem to . . .?) is used to hint a comment on human life:

> To lie on the grass and watch,
> Amused and indifferent,

367

> The fever that drives the ant
> To nowhere that matters much;
>
> Oh, to be half asleep
> In the peace of the sunlit pasture
> Is to lie like a lion at leisure
> Where the little kingdoms creep,
>
> And suddenly to be confused
> By a prickle of spine and hair
> And a notion of eyes in the air
> Indifferent and amused.

The comic is also an element within the complex whole of that imaginatively alive poem 'Terra Australis', in which two dreamers who sailed to found perfect communities are imagined as meeting in mid-Pacific, in that region of existence where ghosts re-enact their lives. Characteristically, Captain Quiros and William Lane [3] are dreamers still, who do not quite accept that they are dead and that their dream is unrealizable. Their equality in opposite directions is wittily presented.

To return to the nature-studies. It may be that the best of these are the finest part of Stewart's poetry. Certainly his distinction in this field deserves to be stressed. 'The Silkworms' moves with great delicacy (with a most beautiful handling of the natural speaking voice and phrase in flexible and expressive verse) as it suggests by analogy the pathos of the human condition and the metaphysical abyss surrounding it. An earlier poem, 'A Robin', is a delicate realization of a scarlet robin bathing in a mountain rock-pool. The human meanings are so lightly held that any attempted explication must seem intolerably clumsy. I quote the second half of it:

> The robin darts to bathe
> Breast-deep in the sky's reflection,
> And all that icy trance
> Breaks in most sweet destruction.
>
> Little, oh, little enough
> To fill the heart's great need,
> But when he has splashed his wings
> And dipped his dainty head
>
> And spilled the drops down his back
> And flown as quick as he came,
> There is no need any more
> To wish the mountains to flame,

> For still it seems in the pool
> That breast of crimson glows
> And over the whole cold sky
> Runs wave after wave of rose.

Another bird poem I should like to single out is 'A Flock of Gang-gangs', full of acute observation, dry humour, and real exhilaration. The anthropomorphic vision is used to no more than the needful extent to help us identify ourselves with the birds while still acknowledging the otherness of their life (this is a condition of success in such poems); and the verse is of the sort that only a long-practised hand and ear can find:

> Sleeping or dancing, gossiping or loving
> In that white tree with sun and blue sky over,
> All of one mind, it's certain they are having
> A great day to remember by the river.

Among other very beautiful poems I would mention 'The Snow-gum' describing the tree with its shadow on the snow, a poem in which any symbolic or analogical suggestion remains so implicit that it cannot be pinned down and stated:

> Out of the granite's eternity,
> Out of the winters' long enmity,
> Something is done on the snow;
> And the silver light like ecstasy
> Flows where the green tree perfectly
> Curves to its perfect shadow.

By contrast, where the anthropomorphic vision becomes too insistent one gets embarrassing pawky humouristics ('The Lizards'), and where the analogy is ill-judged one gets verbose twaddle ('The Rivers').

Separate consideration is due to the collection of poems called 'The Birdsville Track', which represent a search for significant images in the stony desert and semi-desert inland country. Like most travel or place poems, they are notations that fall a little short of full poetic existence. But the exploration of images is striking:

> It tore a great gap in her mind
> Harsh as the loose sheet of iron that bangs in the wind

and

> The bright-red dresses of the gins
> Flowering in that hot country
> Like lilies in the dust's soft pond.

It is in regard to meditations such as 'Fence' (which is one of the evidences of an increasing influence of Frost) or of situation – pieces with a strong meditative content, such as 'Easter Island', that current opinions of Stewart's achievement seem most to vary. The examples I have mentioned are from the volume *Rutherford*, whose title poem is probably the strongest evidence to offer for Stewart's ability in this field. *Rutherford* is a meditation in the form of a personality-revealing monologue. The balance between interest in the person of the great New Zealand physicist and concern with the problems faced by the world in consequence of his atomic research is well kept. If it be objected that the thought is not notably profound or original, one may sufficiently answer that the business of poetry is generally with the commonplaces: the poetic task is to make us 'imagine what we know' as Shelley said, and feel what we thus imagine; and this is what Stewart has done. His main device in this imaginative realization is impressive and powerful: the recurring image of the wheel, which has a truly structural function in the poem, binding together the waterwheel and other things made by Rutherford's father, who was a wheelwright, and the galactic wheel of the universe, and the planetary system, and the solar course, and the tiny system of the atom. It is this that lifts the poem above flat discursiveness and gives it imaginative strength and coherence.

In my opinion it is in the best of the non-dramatic poems that Stewart's talent rises to its finest achievement. Nevertheless a great deal of his energy has been devoted to the writing of verse-plays. Though the attempt to make poetic drama successful in the modern theatre seems to me a lost cause, Stewart was not necessarily wrong to follow his impulse in this direction. The limitations in purely theatrical terms of his plays do not deprive them of value as poetic constructions, nor as explorations of character and human values, nor even of dramatic quality in a wider sense. Two of the plays, *The Fire on the Snow* and *The Golden Lover* were written as radio plays; the others were designed for stage performance.

The Fire on the Snow (first performed 1941) can be presented on a stage but its essentially broadcast character appears in the first speech of the Announcer who acts as chorus:

> I am to break into the conversation
> With a word that tastes like snow to say;

> I am to interrupt the contemplation
> Of the familiar headlines of the day ...

an Audenesque idiom of which there are other traces throughout. The title gives one aspect of the theme: man's courage and endurance, his capacity to make and abide by an heroic choice, his ability to turn defeat and death into a victory of the spirit.

> Triumph is nothing; defeat is nothing; life is
> Endurance; and afterwards death. And whatever death is,
> The endurance remains like a fire. ...

Stewart insists on this as the property of man:

> No bird and no beast
> That lives an unthinking life can know such delight.
> It's reserved for the saint, the martyr, perhaps for the
> soldier
> On the peak of death: and women tortured by cancer.

In the lines just quoted one of the problems of sheer vitalism or life-affirming is evident: the inner differentiation of motive and moral content is flattened out. Vitalism lacks a principle of significant discrimination. So too in Wilson's speech later we are told:

> Endurance may have a meaning
> For men in the snow as for saints and martyrs in flames.

The play isolates the quality of heroic fortitude so drastically as to disconnect it from other purposes or values: it becomes virtually autonomous and self-justifying 'on the plane of pure action'. The expedition to the Pole is like the ascent of Everest, a pure exercise in daring, an assertion of will. In Scott's case it is underlined by the fact that Amundsen got there first and rendered the journey futile.

Another aspect of the play's theme is the question of leadership. The Announcer – whose view of events is meant, one supposes, to be authoritative – subsumes all the members of Scott's party under the leader's mind and will:

> This journey is one man's dream
> As it is one man's burden
> And the man is Scott, the leader.
> The others do what they're bidden,
> Bearing their share of the load,
> But cannot tell what it means.

And again Scott is described as the master,

> As every dreamer has been
> Who ruled men's minds or bodies
> Who had no will of their own.

At the end of the play, however, Wilson, in a passage which also carries authority, asserts a view which seems incompatible with this: instead of the image of the leader animating the inert, we are given the image of a community of men, each finding his own personal meaning and motive, and making his choice:

> All of us chose to do it,
> Our own will brought us, our death on the ice
> Was foreseen by each of us: accepted.

But there is no sign that this clash of interpretations is fully meant, or worked out dramatically. That is to say the Scott Announcer view is not tested *against* the Wilson view, or reconciled with it.

A third aspect of the theme is that it proceeds by presenting a man enclosed in a dream, a dream which is fated to fail; and then we are shown the breaking of the dream, and the necessity of accepting the harsh terms of reality:

> They turn their backs on the Pole,
> They turn their backs on a dream,
> They are coming down, now.

A fourth aspect is the contrast between life in the wilderness, where the heroic has its natural context, and life in civilization. This is also a contrast between direct simplicity and hampering complexity. Scott says:

> We're a long way from England now. At last
> I can start to think clearly, free from encumbrances.

These aspects which I have pointed out in *The Fire on the Snow* form a Stewartian complex, and one or all of them recur in the later plays. In the other radio play, *The Golden Lover*, first performed 1943, the emphasis is on the contrast between the impossible dream and the need to accept reality. Tawhai, the young Maori wife feels the call of an ideal untrammelled passion, as offered by her fairy-lover; but in the end she renounces it in favour of life with her own people and her foolish old husband. As Stewart says, in the preface he added to the 1962 edition, 'it is a play about the acceptance of life'.

Ned Kelly was first performed in a broadcast version (1942) but is meant for stage performance. Here all four aspects of the theme of *The Fire on the Snow* re-emerge and undergo considerable development: the value of courage, bravado, daring action, considered in themselves; the relation of the leader to those who are animated by his mind and will; the breaking of the dream against actuality; the contrast between the wild and the tame, the bush and the town, the natural and the artificial. *Ned Kelly* is Stewart's big achievement in poetic drama. The faults as a theatre-piece matter little if one admits that modern poetic drama is inviable anyway. More important as a drawback is an undeniable tendency to excessive wordiness. Lines that are not without graphic quality or other merit may nevertheless contribute to a cumulative sense of oppression as each character plunges into a speech in which phrase after phrase is generated in relentless concatenation:

> The traps out hunting the gang all over the country,
> Climbing the mountains, sweating across the plains,
> Fishing the creeks for bushrangers, turning up stones,
> Poking their noses warily into the caves
> For fear they were bitten . . .

But these limitations do not alter the fact that Stewart has taken one of the few pieces of something like folk-tradition in our history, and used it to examine the issues which he feels are central to Australian life. It is difficult to do justice to Stewart's achievement in a short commentary, precisely because the play does not have the rather over-simple treatment of *The Fire on the Snow*. Here the drama becomes a complex *critical* testing of the values and attitudes involved. Our sympathies are swung to and fro as different aspects are lighted up. The romantic stereotypes are not left unchanged or unchallenged. There is Kelly as the symbol of vitality challenging the mean and tame:

> . . . the smug little men who read about him at breakfast
> While their wives read them – they are the ones who
>   hate him,
> And what they hate is what they fear in themselves
> And what they fear is what deep down they love:
> The man that stands up straight as a man in the sun
> And dares to be himself.

There is Gribble's counter-assessment:

> The words you say, the motives that drive you to murder
> Are mad and terrible abstractions . . .

> You think you're free
> Because you sleep in the bush, but you're bound in
> nightmare. . . .

We are given a 'revolving view' of Kelly: we also see him from within; and at the end of this process we can appreciate the full significance of Byrne's comment:

> Ned's is a bitch legend. Wrong from the start.
> But Australia's in it. . . .

And of Ned's reiterated, 'It all went wrong'. It must be admitted that here and there a false note of strident nationalism is sounded as when Byrne asks the bank clerk:

> Living, when was the last time you felt
> Australia burning your mind like a gun barrel?

But against that are genuine evocations of the Australian environment:

> Miles of emptiness;
> Nothing but gum-trees whichever way you looked,
> Ridge after ridge, the waves of trees that drown us;
> Gum-trees ahead, gum-trees behind your back,
> And out to the east, and burning away to the sunset. . . .

There is an alertly intelligent exploration of character and of moral issues through the development of situation and dialogue. (Even if one feels at times that the movement is repetitively circular, returning to aspects already dealt with, there is nevertheless an overriding evolution as Kelly heads towards his climax of desperation). There is also a control, admirable if not infallible, over tone and level, and a ready use of colloquial idiom in effective verse.

Shipwreck does not have the same density of interest as *Ned Kelly* though the characteristic Stewartian complex appears in its theme. The question of the value of sheer vitality is again posed in a context of criminal violence; the meaning of leadership is put in question by the legitimate leader, Pelsart, on the one hand, and the lawless leader Cornelius on the other; the impossible dream enclosing Cornelius is broken upon actuality; and throughout the contrast of lawlessness and law, and of the wild against the tame, is stressed – in this case reaching its climax in the butler's action which defeats Cornelius (exactly as the mild schoolteacher's action defeats Kelly). The strength of the play lies in the presentation of Cornelius as a character with some complexity and enigmatic quality in his motivations. But in general the play seems to me to have been overmastered by the raw potentials of its 'colourful' theme; as if the superficial and ready-made interest offered by shipwreck, violence, treasure, lust, had inhibited the generation of the kind of interest the play should have, namely, an interest arising from poetic realization and intellectual and moral tension.

Fisher's Ghost, subtitled 'an historical comedy', is the latest play so far. It is an entertainment, enjoying the advantage of freedom from the demands of conventional drama, and worked out in a free mingling of prose and colloquial verse, in which, as we have already noted, the ballad style is pleasantly used.

Finally we must note that the diversity of Stewart's output includes short stories. He has published one collection of these, *A Girl with Red Hair* (1944) and has continued to write others. In the published collection, 'The Whare' and 'The Medium' and 'The Bishops Shoot a Godwit' stand out, and would seem much stronger if freed from the surrounding ones, which do not, as these do, succeed in the short story's task of illuminating motive and character, or exhibiting a contest of values, within the compass of an incident.

Surveying Stewart's work generally, one can see that there are aspects of it that seem to fit some of the critical preferences that have been current in recent years. In his own way he is concerned with life-enhancement, with colloquial idiom, with the concretely particular, with the popular tradition, with nostalgia for an earlier and more 'organic' community. But it is also evident that Stewart starts from a different base, and is travelling on a different errand with a different direction, from what many critics have in mind. His control of diction tends towards clarification, rather than an intrication of colliding possibilities. His interest in larger forms, in the narrative and discursive modes, though not so unusual in Australia, is still unfashionable. His strong feeling for heroic action, panache, and the qualities of leadership would hardly pass as an 'adult' or 'civilized' 'stance' among the Exclusive Brethren of criticism, who care for none of these things; his ironies are not directed to having things both ways, and blocking all roads to decision. He is a Cavalier among Roundheads, a Celt among Saxons. Though a discriminating selection

is needed if he is to appear to his best advantage, the main thing
to be said is that Stewart's work is a large part of what is interesting and likely to be durable in contemporary Australian literature.

NOTES

1. Introduction to *The Golden Lover*, 1962 edition, p. 7.
2. Quiros hoped to found a colony, thinking the island of Espiritu Santo was the
continent of Terra Australis. William Lane led an expedition of Australians to Paraguay
to form a socialist utopia.

THE POETRY OF A. D. HOPE

GUSTAV CROSS

IT is unfortunately a fact that as yet very few of the best modern Australian poets have been prolific enough to demand the kind of critical attention that has been lavished upon the work of their English or American counterparts. A.D. Hope would seem to be a case in point, for set alongside the several volumes of R.D.Fitz-Gerald or Judith Wright – near contemporaries with whose names his is customarily bracketed as the foremost of Australia's practising poets – his output appears comparatively meagre. To date Hope has published only two collections of his work, the second of which reprints all but fourteen of the forty-two poems in the first book, with the addition of barely twenty more, yet the curious thing is that to read either volume is to be immediately aware of a commanding poetic presence. His is a highly distinctive voice – he could never be mistaken for some other poet – and he leaves one in no doubt as to the urgency and importance of what he has to say. His appeal is directly to the intellect, and it is for the quality of the intelligence informing every line that his poetry has first to be admired. With subsequent readings the admiration becomes transferred to its rightful object – the sheer artistry of the poems themselves. Hope's work is remarkable not only – as his best critic puts it – for its strength and solidity, [1] but for the mastery of its design. It is not a design that the poet superimposes upon the intellectual framework of his poetry, but one that is in absolute accord with it. To have contrived to bring about in his best poems such complete fusion of form with content is by no means the least of Hope's accomplishments. Had he done no more than this tribute would yet have to be paid to his very considerable poetic achievement.

For upwards of a dozen years or so before the publication of his first collection, *The Wandering Islands*, in 1955, Hope's poetry was well known to readers of the Australian literary journals, and he was already beginning to be recognized by all but the most backward-looking critics as being among the more interesting and important of contemporary poets. Coming across his poetry for the first time in the magazines of the late forties or early fifties, the post-war generation found Hope significant and exciting largely because he broke new ground. He was clearly one of the 'new men', one of the leaders – along with Harold Stewart and James McAuley – of what J.D. Pringle has since aptly labelled 'the counter-revolution' in Australian poetry. [2] This was far less the conscious and concerted literary movement that this label suggests than the spontaneous reaction of three very dissimilar poets – Hope, Stewart, and McAuley had at that time little in common beyond a desire to discomfit the editor of *Angry Penguins* – yet their work indicated that poetry in post-war Australia was about to develop in an entirely different direction. The so-called revolution took on two distinct forms: on the one hand it sought to discredit the strident Australian nationalism and obscurantism of the Jindyworobak brigade, while on the other it exposed the shallow pretentiousness of the surrealist nonsense which the neo-Apocalyptics of the forties attempted to palm off as poetry on an uncritical and gullible public. Hope was from the first active on both fronts, both as poet and critic, without, however, resorting to the extreme measures of McAuley and Stewart. (In retrospect the Ern Malley hoax appears an irresponsible and puerile prank, a disservice to poetry itself in a country as yet all too reluctant to give it a fair hearing.) Hope's weapon was not parody, but satire, a mode for which there was little precedent in previous Australian poetry, while his dissatisfaction with 'experimental' verse – too often, he has claimed, a cloak for metrical incompetence – found expression in his adherence to strictly regular or traditional forms. For a decade or more before English reviewers began to trumpet the virtues of the 'new smoothness' of the fifties as exhibited in the poetry of Larkin, Davie, Enright, and Wain, Hope was already exploring and exploiting the rich resources ready to hand in the traditional measures of the English poetic past.

Hope's critics have called him many things: an intellectual poet, a philosophical poet, a neo-Augustan, a Romantic, a sex-obsessed poet, a Manichaean, a Puritan, a lyric poet, and a satirist. All are partly true, yet it was his satirical vein, one suspects, that first won him admirers – and notoriety. Irreverence – proverbially a feature of the Australian national character – has all too infrequently found its way into Australian writing, and the irreverence of Hope's satirical verses appealed with the same

immediacy as the lighter verse of the early Auden, with whose
work Hope's has obvious affinities. In such satires as 'The Return
from the Freudian Islands' and 'Conquistador' Hope rivals
Auden's wit and facility with rhyme, and, it must be admitted, in
slighter pieces like 'The Brides' or 'To Julia Walking Away' he
displays not a little of Auden's undergraduate silliness. Yet to
dismiss these poems – as Hope's detractors have tended to do –
as being merely 'Audenesque' is as critically inept as the claim
that has frequently been put forward that Hope is first and foremost a satirist. He himself tucks his satirical pieces away at the
end of his collections, and he has seen fit as yet to publish only
fragments of his mock-epic, 'Dunciad Minimus', a satire highly
esteemed by those among whom it has enjoyed manuscript
circulation, but which scarcely calls for comment here. Despite
his command of invective, Hope's satires too often betray an
uncertainty of direction, and his shafts seem loosed indis-
criminately at a multiplicity of targets, more in the style of an
Elizabethan railer than of the Augustans whose manner he
imitates. Although mention must be made of his satires later on,
it is nevertheless as a lyric poet that Hope must primarily be
considered.

The theme to which Hope most constantly recurs in his poetry
finds its fullest expression in the poem which gives its title to his
first book, 'The Wandering Islands'. It is a theme which he
shares with many major writers of the twentieth century: human
isolation, the inability of one human being ever to establish
complete communication with another. The intolerable loneliness that is an inescapable condition of the human predicament
is nowhere expressed with greater poignancy than in the opening
stanza of this poem:

> You cannot build bridges between the wandering
>   islands;
> The Mind has no neighbours, and the unteachable
>   heart
> Announces its armistice time after time, but spends
> Its love to draw them closer and closer apart.

Occasionally, surprised by 'the sudden ravages of love,' one
human castaway may be swept momentarily within hailing distance of another, yet the poem holds out no hope of any ultimate

deliverance from the solitary confinement to which humanity is condemned:

> An instant of fury, a bursting mountain of spray,
> They rush together, their promontories lock,
> An instant the castaway hails the castaway,
> But the sounds perish in that earthquake shock.
>
> And then, in the crash of ruined cliffs, the smother
> And swirl of foam, the wandering islands part.
> But all that one mind ever knows of another
> Or breaks the long isolation of the heart,
>
> Was in that instant. The shipwrecked sailor senses
> His own despair in a retreating face.
> Around him he hears in the huge monotonous voices
> Of wave and wind: 'The Rescue will not take place.'

Although not all his poems are as profoundly pessimistic as this the possibilities of rescue remain always remote or uncertain. Hope's sense of man's estrangement or alienation in a universe indifferent if not actively hostile to human life emerges most clearly in one of his best – and best-known – poems, 'The Death of the Bird':

> A vanishing speck in those inane dominions,
> Single and frail, uncertain of her place,
> Alone in the bright host of her companions,
> Lost in the blue unfriendliness of space. . . .
>
> Try as she will, the trackless world delivers
> No way, the wilderness of light no sign,
> The immense and complex map of hills and rivers
> Mocks her small wisdom with its vast design.
>
> And darkness rises from the eastern valleys,
> And the winds buffet her with their hungry breath,
> And the great earth, with neither grief nor malice,
> Receives the tiny burden of her death.

Here the feeling of loss and hopelessness that pervades these stanzas is heightened by the imposition of a strict metrical order; only art can charter the trackless wilderness.

In a perceptive appreciation of Hope's first collection of verse S.L. Goldberg commented on the book's three-fold structure, pointing out that the poems with which each section begins are directly concerned with art or the artist, thereby constituting as it were the overtures in which are announced themes to be subsequently developed. [3] Although the arrangement of the poems in Hope's later collection, *Poems* (1960), is quite different – the inferior 'Heldensagen' which opened the third section of *The Wandering Islands* is omitted altogether – it is true to say that next to human isolation the poet is preoccupied with the workings of the creative imagination and the peculiar relationship between the creator and the thing created. While recognizing man's plight to be desperate, in poem after poem Hope affirms his faith in the regenerative powers of art. Through poetry itself the human spirit may be liberated and reinvigorated; daring to plumb the hidden depths of his own despair, the poet brings back from the sacred fount the precious restorative waters that may yet irrigate the arid and 'unteachable' heart. By infusing new life into the ancient myths of the race the poet helps to keep alive that sense of the wonder and mystery of being in a world materially wealthy but spiritually impoverished. The point is made most explicitly in the first poem of the first section of *The Wandering Islands* – it opens Part Two of the second collection – 'Flower Poem'. Hope angrily contrasts the academic 'appreciation' of the poem as cultural exhibit with a true realization of poetry's life-giving powers. Despite the somewhat shrill over-statement of the opening stanzas the poem is central enough to demand quotation in full.

> Not these cut heads posed in a breathless room,
> Their crisp flesh screaming while the cultured eye
> Feeds grublike on the double martyrdom:
> The insane virgins lusting as they die!
> Connoisseurs breathe the rose's agony;
> Between their legs the hairy flowers in bloom
>
> Thrill at the amorous comparison.
> As the professor snips the richest bud
> For his lapel, his scalpel of reason
> Lies on the tray; the class yawns for its food –
> Only transfusion of a poem's blood
> Can save them, bleeding from their civilization –
>
> Not this cut flower but the entire plant
> Achieves its miracle from soil and wind,
> Rooted in dung, dirt, dead men's bones; the scent
> And glory not in themselves an end; the end:
> Fresh seeding in some other dirty mind,
> The ache of its mysterious event

As its frail root fractures the subsoil, licks
At the damp stone in passing, drives its life
Deeper to split the ancient bedded rocks
And penetrates the cave beneath, it curls
In horror from that roof. There in its grief
The subterranean river roars, the troll's knife
Winks on his whetstone and the grinning girls
Sit spinning the bright fibre of their sex.

No poem better illustrates Hope's strengths and limitations; the initial stridency and uncertainties of tone are amply redeemed by the assured control of the conclusion. Despite a few minor imperfections (the last line of the first stanza is unnecessarily crude) 'Flower Poem' is Hope's most moving statement of his conviction that poetry, welling upwards from its mysterious source in 'the foul rag-and-bone shop of the heart', has the power to arrest the spiritual haemorrhage of an age prepared to heed its message. Yet the poet's penetration into these forbidden realms is fraught with difficulties and danger; he is like the diver in 'The Coasts of Cerigo', who, finding the fabled Labra sleeping on the ocean bed, flings away his bag of pearl and snatches her in his arms:

Their bodies cling together as they rise
Spinning and drifting in the ocean swirl.
The seamen haul them in and stand to see
The exquisite, fabled creature as she dies.

But while in air they watch her choke and drown,
Enchanted by her beauty, they forget
The body of their comrade at her side,
From whose crushed lungs the bright blood oozing down
Jewel by ruby jewel from the wet
Deck drops and merges in the turquoise tide.

Conscious of the incalculable risks he runs, and always aware of the improbability of success, the poet endeavours to forge from the impermanence of experience the permanent perfection of art. The creative spirit is nobly celebrated in an excellent poem, 'Pyramis, or The House of Ascent', in which Hope suggests that the poet is driven on by the same demonic urge that impelled the Pharoahs to erect imperishable monuments in the desert:

I think of other pyramids, not in stone,
The great, incredible monuments of art,
And of their builders, men who put aside

Consideration, dared, and stood alone,
Strengthening those powers that fence the failing heart:
Intemperate will and incorruptible pride.

The man alone digging his bones a hole;
The pyramid in the waste – whose images?
Blake's tower of vision defying the black air;
Milton twice blind groping about his soul
For exit, and Swift raving mad in his –
The builders of the pyramid everywhere!

In this vision of the artist's work as the assertion of his individual
pride and will S. L. Goldberg has detected signs of that dangerous
modern heresy of the Artist as Hero, claiming the poets mentioned
in the last stanza – Blake, Milton, Swift – as indicative of the
sterility to which this leads, [4] yet one has only to think of Yeats,
with whom Hope shares this vision, to realize that sterility is not
a necessary outcome; rather in both poets from just such pride
and will has stemmed their finest work. In his moving tribute,
'William Butler Yeats', Hope pays homage to the poet who in
this century has had most to tell us of the supremacy of art:

> To have found at last that noble, candid speech
> In which all things worth saying may be said,
> Which, whether the mind asks, or the heart bids,
>   to each
> Affords its daily bread . . .

Poetry is a highly specialized way of establishing communication between wandering islands, but in many poems Hope
explores the possibilities of communion between man and
woman through the act of love. Sexual imagery figures largely in
his verse, shocking many Australian readers and setting a recent
academic critic the curious task of totting up the number of
anatomical references. [5] Although Hope undoubtedly delights in
shattering the image of smug respectability that is fostered by
Australia's antiquated censorship laws, his celebration of the
joys of sexual union in such poems as 'Chorale' or 'The Gateway' is prompted by much more than a desire to shock. He
habitually equates art with love, creation with procreation, and
it comes naturally to him to write of the one in terms of the other.
In 'The Lamp and the Jar' sexual fulfilment and the satisfactions
of art are one:

> And I, the lamp before the sacred ark,
> The root of fire, the burning flower of light,
> Draw from your loins this inexhaustible joy.
> There the perpetual miracle of grace
> Recurs, as, from its agony, the flame
> Feeds the blind heart of the adoring dark;
> And there the figures of our mystery,
> The shapes of terror and inhuman woe,
> Emerge and prophesy; there with the mark
> Of blood upon his breast and on his brow,
> An unknown king, with my transfigured face,
> Bends your immortal body to his delight.

Hope's attitude to sex, however, is seldom as unambiguous as this. The sexual embrace may be no less unalloyed with danger than the courtship of the Muse (love and death are equated in 'The Coasts of Cerigo'), and the fruits of either union are of a dubious nature. In 'Imperial Adam', Hope's most perfect poem, the innocent joyfulness of Adam's first sexual congress with Eve is paradoxically responsible for bringing evil into the world. In taut stanzas that counterpoint the poem's sensuousness, the myth in which one critic has found evidence of Hope's Manichaeism [6] unfolds against a backdrop as richly crowded as a Baroque painting of Paradise:

> From all the beasts whose pleasant task it was
> In Eden to increase and multiply
>
> Adam had learned the jolly deed of kind:
> He took her in his arms and there and then,
> Like the clean beasts, embracing from behind,
> Began in joy to found the breed of men.
>
> Then from the spurt of seed within her broke
> Her terrible and triumphant female cry,
> Split upward by the sexual lightning stroke.
> It was the beasts now who stood watching by;
>
> The gravid elephant, the calving hind,
> The breeding bitch, the she-ape big with young,
> Were the first gentle midwives of mankind:
> The teeming lioness rasped her with her tongue,
>
> The proud vicuña nuzzled her as she slept
> Lax on the grass; and Adam, watching too,
> Saw how her dumb breasts at their ripening wept,
> The great pod of her belly swelled and grew,

> And saw its water break, and saw, in fear,
> Its quaking muscles in the act of birth,
> Between her legs a pigmy face appear –
> And the first murderer lay upon the earth.

What in a lesser poet might have seemed a shaggy-dog ending is transformed by Hope's precise utterance and unanswerable logic into an inevitable transition from love to death.

Like Yeats, Hope is often drawn towards mythology for his symbols, and the myths to which he turns – in 'Circe', 'Pasiphae', the two poems on 'Lot and his Daughters' – are of 'the sudden ravages of love' in the guise of death. He never for long allows us to forget that the pleasures of art or of the flesh afford only temporary solace. Foster as he may the illusion of communion with his fellows, unregenerate man remains forever a wandering island, embarked already, as in 'The Death of the Bird', upon his lonely, last migration towards easeful death. In 'The Return of Persephone' it is Hermes' demand that she return with him to the kingdom of the living that persuades Persephone that she is in love with Dis, the God of Death:

> Even as she turned with Hermes to depart,
> Looking her last on her grim ravisher
> For the first time she loved him from her heart.

Again, less seriously, death as lover figures in 'Totentanz: The Coquette', in which the skeleton awaits his mistress's return from the ball:

> Past Midnight! Silent in her charming room,
> Nobly proportioned, feminine, richly plain,
> One elegant femur balanced across its twin,
> Sits her lank guest in the deep armchair's gloom,
> The dandy's pose, one hand upon his cane,
> A bald skull and a melancholy grin.

She returns and undresses, to feel suddenly his bones about her nakedness:

> Stiffly she stands, considering awhile
> The challenge of the male, the frank embrace.
> Then, on one shuddering, voluptuous breath,
> Leans back to her gaunt lover with a smile,
> Half turning, with her plenitude of grace,
> In sensuous surrender to her death.

The neatness of Hope's versification lends an air of flippancy to this horror story, but the poem is merely a lighter variation on his most dominant theme. Hope's mastery of verse techniques occasionally tempt one to take less than seriously or to dismiss as pastiche some of his more sustained pieces. For example, his longest poem, 'An Epistle: Edward Sackville to Venetia Digby' or 'The Elegy: Variations on a theme of the Seventeenth Century' remind one so constantly of Donne or Marvell that it is difficult to regard them as original productions. Yet these poems, and the Drydenesque 'An Epistle From Holofernes' are splendid examples of Hope's grace and wit. The last named, particularly, is significant for its attempt to derive from the myth of Judith and Holofernes a hopeful conclusion:

> If in heroic couplets, then, I seem
> To cut the ground from an heroic theme,
> It is not that I mock at love, or you,
> But, living two lives, know both of them are true.
> There's a hard thing, and yet it must be done,
> Which is: to see and live them both as one.
> The daylight vision is stronger to compel,
> But leaves us in the ignorance of hell;
> And they, who live by star-light all the time,
> Helpless and dangerous, blunder into crime;
> And we must learn and live, as yet we may,
> Vision that keeps the night and saves the day.

The unsatisfactoriness of Hope's satire has been remarked upon, yet his criticism of modern society is often trenchant and nearly always amusing. As might be supposed from the importance which he attaches to art, Hope hates those aspects of the new technocracy that degrade or debauch the human spirit. Advertising, television, cultural middlemen and popularizers, materialism, psychiatry and other abuses of our time he drowns with a torrent of invective:

> But chiefly the Suborners; Common Tout
> And Punk, the Advertiser, him I mean
> And his smooth hatchet-man, the Technocrat,
> Them let my malediction single out,
> These modern Dives with their talking screen
> Who lick the sores of Lazarus and grow fat . . .

Yet as satire this seems rather random stuff: one suspects that Hope, like a modern Jaques or John Marston, quite enjoys indulging in the licence that satire traditionally allows. He is capable, too, of some disconcerting contradictions. In 'Standardization' instead of 'darkly brooding on this Modern Age' Hope points out that no manufacturer can compete with Nature in 'the mass production of shapes and things':

> She has standardized his ultimate needs and pains.
> Lost tribes in a lost language mutter in
> his dreams: his science is tethered to their brains,
> his guilt merely repeats Original Sin.

In 'Australia' – a poem for which many of his countrymen refuse to forgive him – he begins with a bitter denunciation of the land's deficiencies:

> They call her a young country, but they lie:
> She is the last of lands, the emptiest,
> A woman beyond her change of life, a breast
> Still tender but within the womb is dry;

> Without songs, architecture, history:
> The emotions and superstitions of younger lands.
> Her rivers of water drown among inland sands,
> The river of her immense stupidity

> Floods her monotonous tribes from Cairns to Perth.
> In them at last the ultimate men arrive
> Whose boast is not: 'we live' but 'we survive',
> A type who will inhabit the dying earth.

> And her five cities, like five teeming sores
> Each drains her, a vast parasite robber-state
> Where second-hand Europeans pullulate
> Timidly on the edge of alien shores.

Then, in a desperate attempt to have it both ways, Hope does a surprising about-face:

> Yet there are some like me turn gladly home
> From the lush jungle of modern thought, to find
> The Arabian desert of the human mind,
> Hoping, if still from deserts the prophets come,

> Such savage and scarlet as no green hills dare
> Springs in that waste, some spirit which escapes
> The learned doubt, the chatter of cultured apes
> Which is called civilization over there.

With the last line Hope throws away the measuring-stick which he apparently used in earlier stanzas, and the poem loses its point.

Modern Australian literature would be poorer without Hope's satires, but they are more to be commended for the courage with which they combat the false values of Australian suburbia than for their intrinsic poetic worth. It is for his craftsmanship and the integrity of his vision in his lyric poetry that Hope can claim to rank among the foremost of modern Australian poets. He writes with intelligence and passion of the themes with which mankind is most preoccupied: creation, love, and death. In a recent essay he wrote as follows:

A man who has continually before him a vision of the world as a whole, or whose mind is continually occupied with the great questions which involve the variety, the complexity or the mystery of the whole world of man, a sense of the past, the future and the present as one process – in short, a man obsessed with the passion for a synoptic view – cannot write the slightest of poems on the most particular of themes without reflecting this ruling passion. [7]

Hope is a poet with such a vision, and even his slightest poems reflect his ruling passion: to have given it exquisite utterance in a dozen or more poems makes it imperative that he now be considered among the best poets writing in English today.

NOTES

1. Vincent Buckley, 'A. D. Hope: The Unknown Poet', in *Essays in Poetry Mainly Australian* (Melbourne, 1957), p. 143.

2. J. D. Pringle, *Australian Accent* (London).

3. S. L. Goldberg, 'The Poet as Hero: A. D. Hope's *The Wandering Islands*', *Meanjin*, 1957, no. 2, pp. 127–39.

4. Ibid. p. 133.

5. Cecil Hadgraft, *Australian Literature: A Critical Account to 1955* (London, 1960), p. 198.

6. James McAuley, 'Literature and the Arts', in *Australian Civilisation*, ed. Peter Coleman (Melbourne, 1962), p. 132.

7. A. D. Hope, 'Notes on Poetry', *Meanjin*, 1962, no. 2, p. 169.

JAMES McAULEY: THE LANDSCAPE
OF THE HEART

DAVID BRADLEY

IN a recent lecture,[1] James McAuley discussed George Eliot's latter-day search for three principles that were the unquestioned possessions of St Teresa of Avila: '*a unified world view, a soaring ardour of heroic self-dedication and an opportunity of producing significant social results.*' He might well have been speaking of his own preoccupations in life and art.

McAuley proclaimed his search for a unified world view by embracing the Catholic faith in 1952, an event of vital importance in his poetry and of some significance in Australian literary history. His search for the second of St Teresa's possessions he has gradually revealed in the process of writing a poetry which everywhere displays a strenuous spiritual discipline; and through his editorship of the quarterly review, *Quadrant*, he entered the world of social action and has tried to stimulate an intelligent and orderly return to the ideals of traditional Western civilization.

He is the more remarkable as the most ardent upholder of the European tradition in Australia because, unlike most Australian intellectuals, he has not studied overseas. His present deep awareness of the spiritual tradition and spiritual malaise of the West was found, not in Europe, but, much closer to home, in the jungles of New Guinea in the years during and immediately after the war:

I could see exemplified in the small field of New Guinea the great drama of the disintegration of traditional cultures, and the groping for the means of creating a new social order in the modern world. It became for me a period of intellectual crisis, because every question about the nature of men and society was opened up.

('My New Guinea', *Quadrant*, 1961, vol. v, no. 3, p. 25)

Poets have an uncanny knack of finding just those situations in their lives which will bear fruit in the development of their art, and McAuley is no exception. Poetry is for him a movement of the whole man. His early poetic thought was nourished by a vision of the cyclical upheaval and stagnation of society and a concern for the revolutionary rôle of the poet, and it was tempered in practice by his professional life as Senior Lecturer in the Australian School of Pacific Administration and his first-hand experiences of the social ferment of New Guinea. His fully-developed aesthetic theory in *The End of Modernity* asserts the visionary and intuitive nature of poetry and speaks of the craft of the poet as 'a "mystery" requiring self-dedication which is ratified by exceptional experiences', yet he nevertheless sees the vital sap of poetry flowing from the traditional values of Western society:

Under strong poetic inspiration ... the mind ... tends to reconstitute the hierarchy of being which scepticism has levelled to the ground and to lay hold on the ancient symbols by which men once understood *who they are*. [2]

His political concern is with the organic life of society, just as in poetry he is concerned with the indivisible unity of the human personality in a world which is seen to have essential metaphysical significance.

As a literary figure his influence in Australia has been very considerable. As a poet his output has been small, and all but a very few of his poems are flawed in major or minor ways, but in his three published volumes of verse – *Under Aldebaran* (1946), *A Vision of Ceremony* (1956), and *Captain Quiros* (1964) there is always present the indisputable power of a transforming vision, and a mastery of lucid and candid statement. We do not sense in McAuley's verse a struggle with the disparate elements of experience, but rather the workings of a highly conceptualizing mind in search of luminous symbols through which its gains may be interpreted and recorded.

The sense of intellectual clarity which results, as also his constant experimenting with fixed verse forms and his subdued and noble music, earn him, in the present state of criticism, the label of 'classicist', but this I believe is a misconception. McAuley is the most inward and subtle of Australian poets, and the prime function of his verse (if we must apply labels) is romantic or symbolist. One finds it continually recalling the cadences of Wordsworth, Tennyson, Yeats, and the English 'Metaphysicals', and the vision of diverse European influences, notably Rilke, Mallarmé, and the French Symbolists. Yet he owes very little of importance to any other poet or school, and the individuality of his imagination speaks vividly through those symbolic *constants* (the Blue Horses, the alternate fires of the star Aldebaran, Mercator – the world's false prophet, the dance, the cosmography of love, the Hydra, the wounded Hero, the loom of Penelope, the labyrinth, the swan, the bird of paradise) which are the milestones along his progress of introspective discovery; a progress we may trace out as a continuous redefinition of the attitude of the whole man.

The earliest of the published lyrics in *Under Aldebaran*, written during McAuley's undergraduate years, are romantic in inspiration, but they are already far from the lush yearning typical of such productions. There is, from the beginning, a strong sense of form, a metaphysical wit and toughness of perception: a poetic imagination nourished by Rilke and an intelligence trained by contact with the empiricism of Professor John Anderson. The vitality of most of the early poems might indeed be described in terms of a conflict between the empiricist intellect and the transcendentalist instinct; a conflict which can be clearly seen in the lyric 'She Like the Moon Arises:

> She like the moon arises
> And tranquil sees beyond dark window-bars
> The exquisite circumspection of the stars
> Treading the heavenly floor.
>
> And insolent hope surprises
> My sole heart that darkness held in pawn
> And spreads the spurious glimmer of a dawn
> Upon the infinite, the nevermore.

McAuley records that he lost his faith at the age of 15 as a result of reading *The Golden Bough*, [3] but it is apparent from this poem that there remained to the poet promptings of that inspiration which seems to apprehend a world of spiritual meanings, and an imagination not to be satisfied with Anderson's explanation of the world as an immense series of very complex facts, of which the mind of the observer is only to be thought of as another complex fact. Even so, the breakthrough of mind into the pure dawn of contemplation is, as yet, rejected as 'spurious', and the fragile image of the stars 'treading the heavenly floor' is finally shattered by the rejection of 'nevermore'.

The same conflict is evident in the most achieved of all these poems, 'Envoi', in which McAuley develops a brilliant *paysage*

intérieur – a technique that is the strength of his mature poetry –
in which he intimately relates his developing aesthetic with the
landscape of Australia: a landscape at first seen as

> A futile heart within a fair periphery

but later as an image of that bareness of spirit which might un-
willingly provide the sinew of a new poetry of the heart:

> Beauty is order and good chance in the artesian heart
> And does not wholly fail, though we impede;
> Though the reluctant and uneasy land resent
> The gush of waters, the lean plough, the fretful seed.

'Beauty is order . . .' is a note that will rest unsounded in his
verse in the years immediately following (1939-42), while he
turns to a period of intense introspective exploration and diligent
apprenticeship in form. This is a poetry of erotic discovery, sometimes rapturous but with an intellectual honesty that defines
sharply between love and lust, even in the height of passion, and
a spirit often shadowed by tones of guilt and spiritual emptiness.
At the same time, the social intelligence moving behind the verse
is experimenting with a notion of poetry as part of an *omnium
gatherum* of revolutionary theories. This appears in 'The Blue
Horses' as a vision of cyclical social upheavals brought about by
the operation of 'that animal imaginative passion which creates
the forms of a culture, but will not rest in them'. [4] The symbol
which links the transforming power of poetic imagination with
the periodic shattering of the bonds of social custom, he found in
Franz Marc's well-known painting, *Tower of Blue Horses*.

McAuley was probably thinking of this period in his own
development when he wrote of the general tendency in modern
literature to seek for a 'principle of personal and social integra-
tion, hence creativity and joy'. Such a principle, he claims, must
be 'transfiguring and salvific' and the search for it will at first
involve 'an erotic divinization, which however, breaks down into
disillusion and severance and the vain hope of somehow attaining
the longed-for divinization in authentic form'. [5]

At that time, however, the poet was content to think of 'animal
imaginative passion' as the spring of poetry. He hails the revolutionary cracking of the bonds of custom in 'The Family of
Love' (otherwise a rather jejune allegory of McAuley's flirtation

with Freud, Marx, and Nietzsche) as a kind of poetic release into the fulness of experience:

> The World's the thing; Mercator its false prophet,
> We scramble on a flat projection of it.

In 'The Blue Horses' he celebrates the power of the imagination to reintegrate a world 'stampeded on the hooves of fate':

> For in the world are spaces infinite
> And each point is a mighty room
> Where flowers with strange faces bloom
> In the amazing light;
> And every little crystal minute
> Has many aeons locked within it
> Within whose crystal depths we see
> Times upon times eternally.

And finally, through the apocalyptic visions of 'The Incarnation of Sirius', he finds the symbol for this notion of cyclical upheaval quenched by periods of established custom in the varying brightness of the star Aldebaran:

> The stars that with rebellion had consorted
> Fled back in silence to their former stations.
> Over the giant face of dreaming nations
> The centuries-thick coverlet was drawn.
> Upon the huddled breast Aldebaran
> Still glittered with its sad alternate fire:
> Blue as of memory, red as of desire.

The 'Incarnation of Sirius' (1944) belongs to a later period than 'The Blue Horses' and bridges a revolution in McAuley's development, a revolution that he notes himself by giving the precise date of December 1943 to the poem 'Revenant', although the effective little poem does not itself reveal whether the experience it records is to be understood in this generalized way. Certainly there were outward revolutions enough. McAuley married in 1942 and was to spend the years of the war as (so he afterwards described it) 'a performing flea in A.A. Conlon's remarkable circus, the Australian Army Directorate of Research', which took him alternately to New Guinea and to Southern Command Headquarters in Melbourne where he worked together with his friend and fellow-poet Harold Stewart. This is the period of the Ern Malley hoax (see following chapter) and a good deal of light-hearted and scabrous verse, of which the only example to find its way into print was the delightful satirical fragment, 'The True Discovery of Australia', where, as a modern Gulliver, he genially reviews Australian littleness:

> North-east across the water, Brobdingnag
> Casts its momentous shadow on the sea
> And fills the sky with thunder; but they smile
> And sit on their verandahs taking tea,
>
> Watching through the pleasant afternoons
> Flood, fire and cyclone in successive motion
> Complete the work the pioneers began
> Of shifting all the soil into the ocean.

The serious poems of the years after 1944 mark a great leap forward in style. They are mostly short lyrics, simple and formal in shape, with a natural ease of rhyme, a quiet epigrammatic quality and an effortless music, which invite reading rather than description. The first poem of the series and perhaps the finest, 'The Muse', proclaims the new-found mastery:

> She is Penelope, patient to resume
> The threads of language, though each night her toil
> Unravels and hangs trailing from the loom.
> Yet still she hopes, content to spoil,
> Until the wanderer whom the gods exiled
> Comes to his kingdom, and her waiting's done:
> The fabric holds, the gods are reconciled.

Also, in 'Missa Papae Marcelli', 'New Guinea Lament', 'Absence', and 'O Clear Day' there is a mastery of simple and sensuous language which is, at the same time, pliable enough to carry the burden of impassioned thought, paradox, wit or precise statement.

The finest achievements of the new poetic language are to be seen in the three longer poems: 'Henry the Navigator', 'The Celebration of Love', and 'Chorale'.

'Henry the Navigator' celebrates the great Portuguese prince who 'saw no distant seas, yet guided ships'. The figure of the hero-explorer, whose world-creating imagination is driven by a resolute intellect, will become of central importance in McAuley's poetry, and will stand as the symbol of the endeavour of the whole man, but for the present these themes are not explicit. There is, instead, an interesting but unintegrated flourish in the poem, appearing as no more than an arabesque in the praise of

Prince Henry's heroic enterprise: an image of the mapmakers who draw 'those Mappa Mundi where the soul finds its similitudes'. The tension of these ideas in the poem is unresolved and marks a sort of instability in both idea and language that we will return to later.

'The Celebration of Love' is a beautiful epithalamion, which carries an ingenious and 'metaphysical' argument about the nature of love to a lyrical conclusion. It begins with a superb meditative passage where the spirit of place finds expression through the pressure of the evolving thought and in which the trance-like inwardness of the best of McAuley's verse is beautifully illustrated:

> All things announce her coming and her praise:
> The evening sun, awake in bright dry air;
> The invisible patterns of the wind, that fade
> To stillness and then faintly reappear,
> Alternate as my hope; the gradual shade
> That moves across the lucerne-flats; the sheer
> Cloud-shapes, leaning on the stony sill
> Of distant ranges folded in blue haze;
> The river, gliding smoothly as my will
> Beneath the solitary heron's gaze;
> The trees upon the hill: the living day's
> External presences attend and bless
> Her coming with an inward happiness.

This is his first sure and untroubled evocation of the landscape of the heart, but the rest of the poem is less certain in its direction and lacks any firm sense of structure. The second stanza, while technically effective, is over-populated with Australian fauna. The central sections, in which the Map of Love is traced through a series of paradoxes stuffed with scholarly allusions, in order to prove the necessary two-ness of lovers, produces a sense of verbal gestures rather than real feeling – an impression that is helped by genuine obscurity of syntax in the *Coda*. Perhaps the point is best illustrated by the fine closing panegyric:

> Worlds rejoice
> To find their lost identities restored
> To morning brightness by a clear voice
> Recovering the creative word.
> Now with uplifted heart, at light's increase,
> I praise in you the stars and waterfalls,

> The slow ascent of trees, swiftness of birds,
> The innocence and order, the wild calls. . . .

No one could, of course, maintain that this passage lacks feeling; but one might draw attention to the lack of precise significance in its rhetoric. If Donne praised his mistress's voice 'recovering the creative word' we would at once sense the immensity of the compliment in a reference to the Logos; or, if he should speak 'with uplifted heart' we would recognize the gesture of prayer or religious exaltation. Now, obviously, McAuley means to say a great deal more than that he is wakened joyfully in the morning by someone calling his name – but how *much* more, no one, probably not even the poet could determine. Geoffrey Dutton was, I think, wrong, in chastising McAuley for using language of traditional religious significance in his religious poetry, but he might have pointed to the difficulty of the poet who is trying to express the natural religious feelings engendered by profound experience, in a language which cannot be divorced from its traditional significance, and which thus forces the poet into saying both more and less than he wants to.

The difficulty of writing a secular epiphany is made explicit in the beautiful philosophical meditation, 'Chorale'. The theme of this poem is concerned with the function of poetic inspiration in a world bound by otiose custom. The creative animal imagination is celebrated in terms of the vital heat of the sun:

> The secular sun, the hot glow of creation,
> The pride of life and lust of liberty
> Rising and setting in each generation
> Still feed the living force of poetry . . .

so that for the imagination fed by intellectual passion

> The universe becomes an algebraic
> Choir of symbols, dance and counterdance,
> Colours and forms in shimmering mosaic:
> Man enters it as an inheritance.

This might be taken as an affirmation of a broad humanism. Yet the poem concludes on a rush of feeling in a totally opposite direction, though it is to some extent prepared for in the elaborate opening passage of submarine imagery in which the vital heat of the sun in a declining age is seen transferred to the contemplative ambience of the moon by a reverse process of alchemy:

> Yet while his golden energy is drowned
> His sister moon performs her transmutation
> Converting it to silver triple-crowned,
> As human lust is changed to contemplation.

The rush of counter-thought which echoes this at the end of the poem is in the form of a passionate prayer:

> O seraph of the soul, who singing climb
> The orders of creation as a stair,
> And hold a silver lamp above the time
> And places of our deepening despair:
>
> When the delirium whirls within the gyre,
> And comets die, and iron voices wake,
> Be witness to the sun; and mounting higher
> Hold the lamp steady, though creation shake.

This sudden incursion of religious reference appears to be a violent back-pedalling, a nostalgic memory of the hierarchial universe present to St Thomas. The rhetorical movement of the passage is compelling but the meaning is simply obscure. There is no means of knowing whether the apparent antithesis between the secular sun of the early section and the sun to which the soul must bear witness in the last stanza is a genuine opposition or not. McAuley himself later wrote of this passage: 'I should have been hard put to justify intellectually the hymn to poetry which, as it were, broke through from the depths of my inner convictions'. [6]

I offer these comments as exegesis rather than criticism (though they are perhaps fundamental criticisms of McAuley's work at this period) and I have discussed the poems out of their proper sequence in time, in order to make the point clearer. Each poem represents a poetic stance, a coherent order of language imposed on the multitudinousness of life, but each is unstable and McAuley's fertile mastery of technique appears now to be threatened by division of feeling about the functions of poetry and by an attraction to the language of hallowed associations as a meaningful symbolism not yet fully recognized as religious. The poet-navigator is continually being drawn aside from the language-chart of the 'real' world to wonder at those strange sea-beasts in the margin, where the soul 'finds its similitudes'.

Later, McAuley for a time experimented with classical myth and wrote fragments of dramas and epics in 'Philoctetes' (1945),

published in *Under Aldebaran*, and 'The Hero and the Hydra',
written in 1947-9 but not published until 1956. They are impressive poems which develop a dignified reflective mode of discourse. But the dramas are not dramas, even though parts of
'Prometheus' appear to be closely modelled on Aeschylus, and
the epic fragments are not epic. Although the classical myths are
useful to some degree in helping to objectify the autobiographical
impulses behind them, the same contradictions exist within this
form as in the previous poems. McAuley is very conscious of
reviving a dead convention. For the living power of myth is in
its relation to some commonly understood ritual, whence it
receives perpetual refreshment. The poems are continually
questioning their right to speak for the heart in its complexity:

> The myths are void, their patterns wear away
> To markings on the street where children play.
>
> ('Prometheus', Chorus III)

The hero Philoctetes is even made to reject his proper rôle in the
Homeric story with the cry:

> The myths are lies:
> Men must either bear their guilt and weakness
> Or be a servile instrument to powers
> That darken knowledge and corrupt the heart. [7]

But the dramatic choruses nevertheless contain moving evocations of the beauty of life attuned to age-old ritual. The epic
fragments, pressed to prefigure a Christian symbolism, are made
to yield complex instances of the function of guilt and rejection
of guilt in the life of heroic endeavour, especially in the image of
the Hydra, that taint of unredeemed desire or original sin, which
drives the Hero to madness and despair. In 'The Tomb of
Heracles', McAuley finally rejects the heroic stance as the antithesis of poetry:

> The loveless will, superb and desolate.
> This is the end of stoic pride and state:
> Blind light, dry rock, a tree that does not bear.

The revolution in his poetry that springs from this impasse goes
beyond the bounds of literary discovery, since it concerns the
profound experience of Christian conversion. But it brings a new
simplicity and joy into his verse, and a sense that, in returning
to the Christian fold, there have been made available to him a

sense of the true dignity of poetry, a significant language and the living power of childhood dreams and imaginings.

The poems in which this process of discovery is recorded were written over nine years, spanning the period of the classical poems, [8] and collected together as 'Black Swans' in *A Vision of Ceremony* (1956). In these poems McAuley celebrates the unity of vision which his new faith makes available. In 'New Guinea', an epitaph for Archbishop de Boismenu, who had a profound influence on his life, he appeals for the miracle of Christ to descend into the spirit of Australian rule in that country in order to replenish the vacancy of our materialist spirit:

> Only by this can life become authentic,
> Configured henceforth in eternal mode:
> Splendour, simplicity, joy – such as were seen
> In one who now rests by his mountain road.

The same chord is sounded in 'An Art of Poetry', in which he sees the force of poetry deriving from the creative Word (which he can now confidently capitalize). For the heart directed by faith, the world is now an infinitely rich script of symbols which require but the barest recording in order to shine with transparent truth. Splendour, simplicity, and joy are the possessions equally of the life directed by faith and of the poetic imagination:

> . . . universal meanings spring
> From what the proud pass by:
> Only the simplest forms can hold
> A vast complexity.

> ('An Art of Poetry')

The poet's confident recovery of an art of language is linked with Christian conversion in the autobiography, 'Celebration of Divine Love':

> Now is the three-hours darkness of the soul
> The time of earthquake; now at last
> The Word speaks, and the epileptic will
> Convulsing vomits forth its demons. Then
> Full-clothed, in his right mind, the man sits still,
> Conversing with aeons in the speech of men.

The truth of this transfiguring vision in McAuley's own verse can be experienced by anyone who will turn to the poems 'Mating Swans', 'Tune for Swans', 'Nativity', and 'To the Holy Spirit', all lyrics of unusual purity and acute natural observation. Nearly all the others in this section seem to me to be flawed either by needless ingenuity, or by the triteness that undoubtedly does sometimes attend the language of traditional religion (for there is also a journalism of piety) or by the elaborate forcing of natural images to yield divine truths. But there is in many of them a tenderness and a humility (one might say a transparent innocence), so that to read them is to love the man without necessarily being convinced of the truths held by the poet.

The theme proposed in 'The Royal Fireworks' – 'The heart is born to celebrate' – might be taken as the motto of McAuley's later work, but the heart's celebration is far from being a spontaneous overflow of powerful feeling. Rather it involves the recognition by intellectual discipline of that divine order in the world, which is, indeed, apparent to the creative animal imagination, but which is only transfigured into art by the action of Grace. As it is put in 'An Art of Poetry':

> Scorn then to darken and contract
> The landscape of the heart
> By individual, arbitrary
> And self-expressive art.
>
> Let your speech be ordered wholly
> By an intellectual love;
> Elucidate the carnal maze
> With clear light from above.

At the same time, McAuley characteristically became an apologist for his recovered faith, and, in a series of poems and essays, turned to review his earlier tenets from a position of such assured Truth that even his admirers among the young Catholic writers were left puzzled and even hostile. In *Reflections on Poetry* (1953) he wrote of the near impossibility of finding a language of generally understood spiritual significance:

The positivism of the modern mind constitutes an anti-poetic . . . it is the great un-Culture of modern times . . . an opinionated scepticism which will not stay to consider fundamental truths, yet is excessively credulous of ready-made current ideas. . . . Where the sub-conscious presence of the traditional views of life has become faint, the mind may suffer an atrophy that humanly speaking becomes incurable.

This essay afterwards formed the basis of a collection published as *The End of Modernity* (1959), in which McAuley argues persuasively the metaphysical bases of art and society, the need for a return to traditional concepts of the nature of man in a coherent spiritual culture, and the rôle of poetry as the expression of man's highest natural capabilities within such a culture.

In verse he made an amusing, if rather disastrously generalized attack on modern un-Culture in 'A Letter to John Dryden' (1953-4) where the intellectual passion is too casually worn and does little to redeem the witty pedantry of imitating 'The Hind and the Panther' in unaugust and necessarily un-Augustan couplets.

The most perfect of all the poems of this period, and perhaps the finest of McAuley's achievements so far, is 'A Leaf of Sage' (1953), a tale from the Decameron, which has a narrative light-ness, a delightfully fresh Chaucerian quality, which almost com-pletely transforms and objectifies the ever-present biographical impulse; but as well as formal satire and medieval tale, *A Vision of Ceremony* includes other experiments with traditional forms of verse, as though McAuley were here reviewing his new mastery of language before turning to the long-cherished project of writing an epic.

It is interesting to observe, as McAuley himself suggests, [9] that Australian poetry belongs more truly to the tradition of the nine-teenth century than does modern English poetry, not least in the sense that the poet assumes the quasi-religious task of drawing Man back to the resources of that stable and universal Self which the age of machines and individualism has deprived him of. And there is still an interest among Australian writers in that great regenerative epic that Arnold and Tennyson and nearly all their contemporaries planned and failed to write.

McAuley's *Captain Quiros* (1964) belongs in this tradition, stimulated partly by classical precedent, partly by a view of the usefulness of poetry – narrative being supposedly its most avail-able form for the general reader – partly by his opinion that the traditional forms of poetry may also be the proper forms for this or any age.

The subject chosen is a natural one for an Australian poet – the discovery of the South Land and the significance of that dis-covery, and hence of modern Australia, in the history of the human spirit. As his hero-navigator he chooses the last of the great Portugese discoverers Pedro Fernandez de Quiros whose ambition it was to build the New Jerusalem in the South Seas, and who therefore serves as an adequate symbol of McAuley's search for those spiritual ends (mentioned at the beginning of this essay as belonging to Teresa of Avila) that had now come to dominate his mind. The poet does not speak through his hero, but chooses a minor rôle, accompanying the voyage in the character of Belmonte, de Quiros's secretary and historiographer (he was also a poet), while the expedition itself becomes a metaphor of the poet's regenerative purpose:

> Our voyage was to be a solemn rite,
> A passing through the waters to rebirth
> In a new world, created in despite
> Of the demonic powers that rule the age.

The narrative is deployed in four main movements: the first, the voyage of Alvaro de Mendana to settle the Solomon Islands, with its disastrous ending in the massacre at Graciosa Bay. On this first voyage Quiros is present as pilot major, and, though we hear little of him, it is to be understood that on this voyage his powers of heart and mind are tempered, that he learns the nature of command and the complexities of power, discovers his personal calling and comes to understand the contradictions of his own civilization in contact with the people of Chief Malope's island.

The second movement is the voyage directed by Quiros to establish Christ's kingdom in the South Seas, and its failure after the gorgeous ceremony of the founding of the New Jerusalem on the island of Espiritu Santo. The third movement is the questioning of Quiros's defeat and a record of his frustrating years spent in the venality of the spiritual and temporal Courts of Europe, attempting to fit out the second expedition, on which he eventually died. The last section is a prophetic death-bed vision of the 'heartland of the South', its history and its wished-for redemption.

The theme of the first two sections is brought to a devotional climax and the third section is prefigured in the prayer of St Ignatius that Quiros utters at the founding of the city:

> For this grace only shall these servants pray:
> That they may give and never count the cost,
> That they may fight when everything seems lost,
> Heedless of wounds, unshaken by dismay.

Yet the third panel of Ignatius's triptych Quiros cannot yet see: to labour and not to ask for any reward. The perfection of his spiritual temper will lie in the realization that the *search* is all-important, that the City of God cannot be squarely built by the hands of fallen humanity.

As a record of a spiritual journey, *Captain Quiros* is deeply impressive and there are scores of passages in it as fine as anything McAuley has ever written, notably the 'Proem', which does achieve something of the sublime serenity to which the whole aspires:

> Four ships on the calm Pacific fold
> Smooth water at the stem, scarce making way.
> Cloud presences on the horizons hold
> With changing tints unchanging shape all day.
> A frigate-bird soars, keeping the fleet in view.
> Far out, the only island in the blue,
> A basking whale sends up a palm of spray.

But the writing of reflective narrative is notoriously difficult, and the task of composing a meditative epic in which the whole powers of the poet's imagination are brought to bear on a Summa of his own psychic development, and projected through an historical narrative which links in a single vision the sixteenth and twentieth centuries, the divine and human and the struggle of cosmic forces of good and evil, is staggering in its immensity. If one's judgement must finally be that the poem as a whole fails, and fails in simple and quite obvious ways, it must be a judgement which acknowledges the magnitude of the attempt.

The most successful passages are, interestingly enough, the landscapes, such as that of the site of the new City, where the poet is drawing on personal reminiscence:

> And still the living waters hurried down
> To where the teeming fish leapt in the bay;
> The native gardens covering our town
> Showed fruits and flowers in splendid disarray.
> Small flocks of green and scarlet parakeets
> Flashed in the air above the future streets,
> And odorous basil flowered along the way.

Or in that of Quiros's first visit to Malope's island:

> The air hangs heavy like a warm wet cloth,
> Torn by the cockatoo's occasional scream;

But where old gardens lapse to undergrowth
Or the thick bush is cloven by a stream,
As large as birds, the perching butterflies
Parting their wings disclose in brilliant dyes
The secret inner surface of a dream.

One senses that it is only in such passages that the poet feels free of architectural problems. In other places the immense calculation that goes into the technique of a long poem – calculation evident in the carefully-muted poetic diction, the seven-line stanza, long enough to express a complete thought yet not too long to weary the reader's attention (it seems to me uncomfortably *short*), the flatter passages of narrative tinged with a suppressed irony – all this tends to depress the poem and the net spread to trap the sublime entangles the narrator.

The major flaws, however, are flaws of construction, McAuley has not solved the problem of how to carry a simple action through any sort of development, or to build a drama whose values are apparent without the need of commentary. The dramatic and narrative aspects of the story are continually sacrificed in order to retain the essential subjectivity of the poem. The device of an accompanying narrator means simply that Quiros gets lost, and a story that begins in the first person lapses into omniscience only at the risk of absurdity (as any novelist must learn). McAuley's Belmonte cannot be imagined to know three-quarters of the things he does know. He never even appears to be intimate with his master, yet he can describe his inmost thoughts, often expanding them in images of great sensitivity.

But the greatest failures are dramatic. We are not allowed to be participants in the action and there is little sense of characterization. When there is direct speech it is scarcely possible in any human tongue and is usually a mere précis of what might appropriately have been said, while in their dying words both Quiros and the aged Father Commissary seem to be contending for the indisputable title of old John of Gaunt.

These things may appear trivial, but they are important in a poem which inevitably fails if it does not *convince*. They also mark the omnipresence of the lyrical or autobiographical element in McAuley's verse. The writer is too close to his narrative to dissociate those parts that must be made clear as action from those that may be dissolved in contemplation.

Thus his broader dramatic control over the reader's sympathies is also uncertain. One such instance is vital to the poem. The natives of Malope's land are given pride of place, and their stable and custom-bound society, moving to ancient seasonal rhythms and rituals, is made to sound paradisally attractive. Chief Malope himself (after he is murdered by the Christians) is even given the accolade of a reception into heaven at the hands of the Virgin. The point of this is, of course, that the coming of the true faith will complete the pattern of the old, deformed by fear and superstition. But on the other hand the contradictions of Christian civilization – 'that babel-tower of avarice and clamour' – are vividly displayed, so that it is only by an act of will that the reader comes to accept the missionary purpose of Quiros and his few Franciscan monks as anything but an unmitigated disaster for the native races. Especially since the Church, as a human organization, is everywhere in the poem viewed with a suspicion approaching despair. The sympathetic reader will, of course, adjust to McAuley's mature and complex study of the divine purpose at work in human affairs, but the poem nevertheless fails in its dramatic articulation.

To attempt a summary or a prediction of McAuley's achievement at this stage is barely possible. His recent poems have returned to the mode of the meditative lyric, but he is still at midway of his working life and his poetic style has already undergone a number of far-reaching revolutions. His current poetic theories point in the direction of a new classical rhetoric, and many of the poems in *A Vision of Ceremony* have indeed the virtues (*salsus*, *claritas*, *urbanitas*) that Quintilian commends to the orator. We might take the 'salt' to be their intellectual strenuousness and supernatural typology, the 'urbanity' to lie in the poet's intense awareness of his society and his acceptance of the hard labour of communication in an age of 'iron voices', and the 'luminosity' to draw its power both from the exceptional experiences of the artist and the spirit of love which is now seen as the spring of a poetry whose function is to celebrate the divine order of the universe.

But in the poems themselves all these qualities are dissolved in the poet's response to life. If he retreats from the arbitrary individualism of the late Romantics, his poetry is nevertheless introspective and transcendental in tendency. If he stops short of the private and mystical modes of vision of Rilke's later work he is not therefore a classicist. If his verse is everywhere sane, controlled by the intellect and rejoicing in professional expertise, it does not seek merely to rest on traditional symbols or established truths, but takes as its motto 'the sober drunkenness' of the Ambrosian hymn:

laeti bibamus sobriam ebrietatum spiritus.

McAuley is still a navigator and the truths of the poetic imagination must still bear the test of arising from the whole man. The problem that now confronts him (as he expresses it in the Preface to his *Selected Poems*) is 'the struggle for an adequate symbolism'. So far, it seems to me, his attempt to expand a strenuously-won private symbolism into a myth that will speak at large to mankind has been only partly successful, but the gains on the way have been in those lyrics or meditative landscapes of the heart in which the unity of symbol and idea produces a serenity or enchantment by which we are offered poetic truth in its most radiant garment of contemplation.

NOTES

1. An inaugural lecture as Professor of English in the University of Tasmania, delivered in April, 1963, and entitled 'A Critical Excursion: Edmund Spenser and George Eliot'.

2. From 'The Perennial Poetry' in *The End of Modernity* (Sydney 1959), p. 139; originally published as 'Reflections on Poetry' in *Meanjin*, 1953, no. 4, pp. 431–41.

3. From *My New Guinea*.

4. In a note to *The Blue Horses* in *Under Aldebaran*, (Melbourne, 1946), McAuley wrote: 'I had in mind Franz Marc's painting, *Tower of Blue Horses*, which seemed to me a symbol of that animal imaginative passion which creates the forms of a culture but will not rest in them, eternally invoking chaos against the simplifications of reality on which custom depends. It has no morality, but creates moralities and destroys them.'

5. From 'The Pyramid in the Waste, an introduction to A. D. Hope's poetry', in *Quadrant*, 1961, no. 4, pp. 61–70.

6. From a broadcast talk, printed in *The A.B.C. Weekly*, 6 October 1956.

7. Lines that A. D. Hope ultimately chose as the sardonic epigraph for *The Wandering Islands*, dedicated to McAuley and published in 1955 after his conversion to Catholicism.

8. With the exception of 'At Dawn', which, as Mrs Dorothy Green has pointed out to me, was reprinted from *Four Poems in a Series*, published in the University of Sydney magazine, *Hermes*, vol. xliv, no. 2, 1938, without substantial alteration.

9. Although McAuley usually makes this comment in pejorative contexts, as in *The End of Modernity*, p. 62: 'For poetry the consequences of the fixation of the Australian cultural matrix at a late nineteenth century level of Progress and Enlightenment have been unfortunate.'

THE ERN MALLEY POEMS

A. NORMAN JEFFARES

IN 1944 Max Harris, the editor of *Angry Penguins*, an *avant-garde* magazine originally published in Adelaide, later in Melbourne, received a letter signed by Ethel Malley, enclosing two poems by her brother Ern, who had died the previous year, and asking whether the poems had any merit. Mr Harris asked to see the rest of Ern Malley's work and also inquired for some details of his life. A circumstantial letter followed: the poet had been a mechanic and an insurance agent and had died of Graves's disease; he had never said anything about writing poetry. The rest of the poems [1] were read by Mr Harris and his partners, John Reed, Sunday Reed, and Sidney Nolan, and they decided to include them in the autumn issue of *Angry Penguins* in 1944, which had a reproduction of a Sidney Nolan painting for its gay cover.

Dr B.R. Elliott, then a lecturer at the University of Adelaide, suggested the poems were a hoax:

> Malley! orphicular wraith, whose diapason
> Astral is cotyledon to no plucked guitar,
> Xoanon in my antique land, Aum's avatar –
>
> How have you anger of the maculate seas,
> Accessory the chain and anchor and all the
> Rose exfoliate leaf by petal warm
> Renounced invulvate with the grave disease?
> Ischiatic, corpulent, dog-toothed with sunken knees
> Scabrous – this check have you cashed,
>   O furciform?
>
> Homunculus, hail! You deft epitome
> Of Tamburlaine and Twankydil's apt dwarf!
> And yet on Taverner's Hill no syndrome
> Xists I warrant of your polymorph.

The actual authors of the poems, James McAuley and Harold Stewart, wrote a statement, published in *Fact*, 5 June 1944, to explain that they had been carrying out 'a serious literary experiment.' They disliked the gradual decay of meaning and craftsmanship in poetry, and they regarded *Angry Penguins* and its editor as representing an Australian example of the literary fashion, current in America and England, which seemed to them to 'render its devotees insensible of absurdity and incapable of ordinary discrimination.' They wanted, they wrote, to discover whether those who wrote and praised current work of the kind they themselves disliked could tell the real product from deliberately concocted nonsense. They created 'Ern Malley' and said they produced his tragic life work in one afternoon with the aid of a chance collection of books such as the *Concise Oxford Dictionary*, a collected Shakespeare, and a *Dictionary of Quotations*:

We opened books at random, choosing a word or a phrase haphazardly. We made lists of these and wove them into nonsensical sentences. We misquoted and made false allusions. We deliberately perpetrated bad verse, and selected awkward rhymes from a Ripman's *Rhyming Dictionary*. The alleged quotation from Lenin in one of the poems, 'the emotions are not skilled workers' is quite phoney.

They finished the poems, wrote a *Preface and Statement*, and elaborated the details of the poet's life. They had decided to write poems with no coherent theme, to take no care of verse technique and to imitate 'the whole literary fashion as we knew it from the works of Dylan Thomas, Henry Treece and others.' They ended their statement by arguing that literary movements such as Dadaism and Surrealism and that of the New Apocalypse school (to which they thought the *Angry Penguin* writers corresponded) were like European political parties; that the Ern Malley poems were not psychological documents and that they were devoid of literary merit as poetry.

The next issue of *Angry Penguins* carried a full critical discussion. The most interesting contribution to this was Sir Herbert Read's comment, which dealt with the problems created by parody, in which the parodist may, especially when the art parodied is experimental and unconventional, end up by deceiving himself. Sir Herbert defended the use of prose quotations, remarking 'In poetry, in art generally, it is not the originality of the unit that matters, but the genuineness of the total conception.' He went on:

If a man of sensibility, in a mood of despair or hatred, or even from a perverted sense of humour, sets out to fake works of imagination, then if he is to be convincing he must use the poetic faculties. If he uses these faculties to good effect, he ends by deceiving himself. So the faker of Ern Malley.

Then the police of South Australia joined in the fray, charging Mr Harris, on 5 September 1944, with having published fourteen 'indecent advertisements', seven of them in Ern Malley's 'The Darkening Ecliptic'. The trial has been described as taking place in 'the period of the last great outburst of Australia's renowned cultural Philistinism', and it is instructive to read some of the ludicrous statements by Detective Vogelsang, the only witness for the prosecution, as well as the judgement of the magistrate, Mr L. E. Clarke, S.M. Witnesses for the defence included Dr B. R. Elliott, Professor J. I. M. Stewart ('Michael Innes'), Dr R. S. Ellery, and Mr John Reed. The South Australian Police Offences Act of the time, however, allowed no defence on the grounds of literary or artistic merit. (Indeed, when the Act was altered in 1953 the successful efforts of some sensible Members to carry an amendment exempting cases where literary or artistic merit was involved, led to much display of feeling in the local press and parliament, and the Premier, Sir Thomas Playford, himself brought forward another amendment with interesting definitions of 'offensive'.) Mr Harris was found guilty and fined £5 with the alternative of twelve weeks' imprisonment.

After the trial not much more was heard in Australia of Ern Malley; but in 1952 Mr Harris, Mr John Reed, and Mr Barrie Reed produced a new jointly edited literary journal under the title of *Ern Malley's Journal*, as a sign of their belief in the merit of the poems. These, however, were not included in the *Penguin Book of Australian Verse* of 1958, despite some interest in them outside Australia; but in 1960 Mr John Thompson produced a documentary radio programme about the hoax, entitled 'The Ern Malley Story', for the Australian Broadcasting Commission, and in this he interviewed many of the persons involved. Some of their comments are included, along with Ern Malley's poems, a detached account of the affair by Mr Harris, and a summary of the trial in *Ern Malley's Poems* (1961).

What of the poems themselves? They begin with 'Durer: Innsbruck, 1495', a simply contrived poem, with effective lines, dealing with an Australian attitude to Europe, a novice's to a long history of art, and, presumably, to poetry, also. The writer is 'The black swan of trespass on alien waters'.

The 'Sonnets for the Novachord' indicate the 'serious frolic' of the authors. For the magistrate trying the case brought against Mr Harris, 'Sweet William' produced a task of interpretation 'rather like trying to unravel a crossword puzzle from a newspaper with the aid of only half the clues, and without the satisfaction of seeing the solution in the next issue.' The implications of 'Boult to Marina' have been carefully explained by Mr Clarke, without any implication that there is humour in the poem with its swaggering echoes of a mixed Fletcher-Flecker strain of poetry. 'Sybilline' has further echoes, of Eliot among others, and both this poem and 'Night Piece' have an oracular yet conversational tone. Here is 'Night Piece':

> The swung torch scatters seeds
> In the umbelliferous dark
> And a frog makes guttural comment
> On the naked and trespassing
> Nymph of the lake.
>
> The symbols were evident,
> Though on park-gates
> The iron birds looked disapproval
> With rusty invidious beaks.
>
> Among the water-lilies
> A splash – white foam in the dark!
> And you lay sobbing then
> Upon my trembling intuitive arm.

This poem disturbed Detective Vogelsang because the events of the poem appeared to take place in a park at night:

They were going there for some disapproved motive. Because of the disapproval and the nature of the time they went there, and the disapproval of the iron birds make me say it is immoral. I have found that people who go into parks at night go there for immoral purposes. My experience as a police officer might, under certain circumstances, tinge my appreciation of poetry.

'Documentary Film' has an air of undergraduate cleverness about it, a casual wit that emerges more clearly in 'Palinode':

> Remember, in any event,
> I was a haphazard amorist
> Caught on the unlikely angles
> Of an awkward arrangement. Weren't you?

'Baroque Exterior' and 'Perspective Lovesong' are cryptically obscure poems, echoes of Tennyson in the latter mingling with 'Blue Angels' and 'Moorish Idols'. 'Culture as Exhibit' is, perhaps, the most famous of all the poems, because of its lines taken from an anti-malaria pamphlet and its apostrophization of the Anopheles mosquito. This was a joke widely appreciated by many who never read the poems. 'Egyptian Register' looks forward to some of Harold Stewart's subsequent poetry, while 'Young Prince of Tyre' uses Australian material:

> He the dark hero
> Moistens his finger in iguana's blood to beseech us
> (Siegfried-like) to renew the language. Nero
> And the botched tribe of imperial poets burn
> Like the rafters. The new men are cool as spreading fern.

'Colloquy with John Keats', which contains the 'phoney' saying attributed to Lenin, has itself something sensible to say though some of its vocabulary smacks of mere cleverness. 'Petit Testament' returns to Eliot and to, presumably, some echoes of Dadaism, with its final 'Beyond is anything.'

The poems cannot be quite so easily written off as their authors would wish. They were better fabricators than they expected themselves to be, just as their fabrications were received with more kindness and respect than they expected. Professor McAuley's argument, put forward in the radio interview, is that there are two kinds of process that lead to artistic production, one pseudo-inspiration – an exciting surrender to irrational forces – and the other genuine inspiration, based upon conscious use of the shaping intellect. The hoax, however, seems to have been undertaken in a spirit of conscious criticism just as much as in a process of creation of the train-of-imagery kind. As Dr Elliott remarked of the poems, the rational content is incoherent, but the drift is intelligible. They contain some memorable lines as well as some lively imagery, which has a collage-like effect, sometimes gaining its results by yoking heterogenous ideas and images together, not perhaps as reminiscent of Dylan Thomas's sensuous emotive skill as the authors imagined, but all done, as Professor McAuley confessed, 'in a rather high-spirited fashion'.

The Chattertonian critical issues were obscured at the time of the hoax by the action of the zealous police. What has emerged from the dust? Professor J. I. M. Stewart regrets the effect the joke had upon the public reception of poetry; Dr Elliott sees it as a major event in Australian literary history, a prophylactic event which made young Australian poets more careful and less precious; Mr Harris regrets none of the enthusiasm with which he welcomed Ern Malley and helped him to fame; and one of the perpetrators claims it was a literary experiment, and the other asserts that 'in this arena of public ideas, movements and so, there has to be a good deal of bashing around, and so long as attack and criticism is not personally biased, hasn't got a malicious character, I think it's just got to be fairly tough.'

It was fairly tough on Mr Harris, tougher than it should have been. Derivative, incomprehensible and often indecent poetry tends to thud remorselessly into the letter-box of any editor of a literary journal which publishes poetry. It is often indecent because it says the kind of things that may be commonplace as conversational remarks in future years, but may well now offend the iron birds who guide the literary taste of the guardians of public morals. It is derivative because those who write it are often young and have not yet achieved a style of their own. It is often incomprehensible because technique is not taught and stupidly despised. An editor who feels he has a duty to allow young poets' work to be tested by publication might well act as Mr Harris did, and act on these generous grounds as well as on the grounds that these poems had a strength and an assurance unusual in an unknown, unpublished and uncriticised poet. It is very easy to be wise after the event: the pity of it all is that Mr Harris (who is a good poet himself) should not have sent Professor McAuley some similar pseudonymous offering and had it published in the journal that Professor McAuley now edits, couched in the kind of conscious poetry he fancies, but concealing subterranean oracular matter. This would probably confirm many readers in a belief that editors *like* or *dislike* a work of art and then justify intellectually the processes by which they accept or reject it. Taste dominates and we might apply to this whole controversy Ern Malley's own phrase, 'The emotions are not skilled workers.'

NOTES

1. The Ern Malley poems, with introductions, critical commentaries and an account of the court case, have been published as: *Ern Malley's Poems*, with an introduction by Max Harris, (Melbourne, 1961).

THE NOVELS OF PATRICK WHITE

VINCENT BUCKLEY

MOST of the interest in Patrick White has been centred on his attitude to Australia and to the creation or re-creation of grandiose myths. The interest is misplaced; for it is neither as a patriotic sociologist nor as a myth-maker in the narrow sense that White is important. His greatness is that of a novelist remarkable among his contemporaries for combining brilliant and wide-ranging comic insights with a world-view of magnanimous proportions and with a serious interest in the resources of language.

It is worth noticing, too, that in his first two novels there is nothing which one could define as a myth-making activity; yet the preoccupations exhibited there, the themes which emerge, the attitudes to humanity which strike us, are similar to those in his later and more substantial works. The later concern with 'myth' does not create those preoccupations, themes, perspectives, but fructifies them – and, at times, distorts them. It is to them that we have recourse if we genuinely want to explore his achievement.

What astonishes us about White's novels is not only his development through his preoccupations but his persistence in them. The last work, *Riders in the Chariot*, reaches its climax in a crucifixion. Myth-making? Possibly. But on the second page of his first book, *Happy Valley*, there is mention of the crucifixion of a roadman by a drover. The image occurs several times in White's work, presumably to express his sense of what is entailed in most personal relationships; and it suggests not only a certain rococo violence in his sensibility but also a certain misanthropy in his conscious attitudes.

Happy Valley (1939) does not express that sensibility or define those attitudes with any power. In it, White has set himself an easier task than he will ever again attempt: to trace certain relationships in a tiny isolated township in the Australian snow-country. The result is that, although all the characters scarify one another, their author is left more scarified than any of them. There is no lasting satisfaction, no way out of the desperate emotional numbness of the snow-country; ambition is a folly, self-indulgence a self-delusion, sexual desire an itch, love an invitation to parasitism or failure. For all the clear outline of its episodes, the apparent confidence of its prose, *Happy Valley* is a weary book: all the wearier in that what force it has is borrowed from other writers. One senses that White is using borrowed modes, even borrowed accents, to release a personal defeatism which they cannot control or define. It is the weariness of an unduly prolonged adolescence.

One catches glimpses of a drily diagnostic power which is later to prove decisive in establishing his greatness. Later preoccupations are mostly here, in an immature form: the preoccupation with emotional incapacity, overripe but unhopeful desire, crucifixion, numbness. The habit is also present of investing his emotions very heavily in the analysis of social pretensions, particularly those of 'Society' women. This habit recurs in each book, each time with a startling savagery; and with it recurs the figure of the male seducer, masculine, hairy, middle-aged, narcissistic and hollow, seen as a woman might see him, but with fascinated dislike.

The chief failure of the book comes, however, from the inertness of the prose, which, though it is from time to time revived with 'Lawrentian' symbolism and perceptions that have the sharpness of broken glass, works against rather than with the diagnosing intelligence. White can neither decisively attach his prose to the created rhythm of his characters' lives nor cleanly detach it from them; the result is that, while he mimes their thinking, he does so simplistically and unevenly; and his own passages of explicit commentary come to seem all the more supercilious and knowing. The book lacks magnanimity; and it proves unable to bear the weight of its author's preoccupations.

The Living and the Dead (1941) is an altogether more ambitious book, more ambitious both in its social range and in the depth at which it attempts psychological diagnosis. It deals with the England of the first third of this century; and its theme (for it is, in a wavering way, a *roman à thèse*) is the way in which emotional death is communicated from one generation to another. The dead, represented chiefly by Catherine Standish and her son Elyot, possess the earth and reduce it; yet the living, represented chiefly by Elyot's sister Eden, may inherit (and renew?) it. They can do so, however, only by moving outside the constrictions of 'Society' and taking breath from the working-class.

So, at any rate, White insists. But the insistence strikes us as nominal. In this book the diagnostic intelligence is savagely at work, probing the corruption of the effete and the 'cultured' more accurately than, for example, Lawrence does in *Women in Love*; yet the diagnosis strikes us as quite deadening in its artistic effect. As one critic has remarked [1]

The characters as a whole are so pallid that there seems to be no striking difference between the living who know themselves and have learned to live with the knowledge, and the dead who know nothing.

The reason is clear; the prose, so remorselessly and glitteringly intent on diagnosis, fails in fact to create the discriminations insisted on. The whole book has a cold, posed, inorganic, mandarin distinction, as though it were a sophisticatedly featureless translation from another language. The glitter of invention is everywhere, frustrating White's attempt to solve the problem of providing a distinctive identity, a speaking-voice, for each of his characters; and he seems unable to come to terms with the maturity of his readers or of his characters.

Still, where corruption and self-delusion are his subject, he shows a brilliant epigrammatic insight, presented with feline care; and, while this shows an almost infallible awareness of pettiness and contradiction, it is used to *fix* the characters like mice, not to use them as the foci of his own creative abundance:

That was before she began, it happened at first slowly, her fingers slipping as surely as a fruit off its twig, her dress the downward flare that brushed his face, he saw, the rushing was the white dress, the head that tumbled with the sickness of a fruit, her voice stretched out in air. For half an hour or more, and at once, in two seconds, he knew that Connie was falling out of the mulberry tree. He shouted at her. Through his anxiety he felt annoyed. Because this was just the sort of thing that Connie Tiarks would do. Connie was a girl. She was sent to exasperate him. (p. 101)

The slow-motion arrest of feeling and sensation ('her voice stretched out in air') is the quality which gives the prose its distinction; but it is also the quality which robs it of economy, and in the end introduces into the enervation of the character's sensibility the enervation of the author's. White has failed to solve the problem of creating a distance for himself and an identity for his characters; and his sensibility is submerged under those of his characters.

Yet we may see in *The Living and the Dead* the beginnings of that process of creative struggle which is to issue in *The Tree of Man* and *Voss*. It is significant that his third novel, *The Aunt's Story* (1948), is in one sense simpler than either of the earlier books, and in another sense more ambitious. It is said that White himself has a special fondness for it; and one can see why. The figure of Theodora Goodman is presented in the foreground, and the great understanding and compassion with which she is treated are reflected in the limpid, controlled precision of the prose. Almost all White's characters are cases of psychic isolation; but Theodora is a case of extreme alienation. In this fact lies the author's creative problem, a problem which seems almost insoluble; for the second half of the novel takes her to the utmost limits of alienation, to madness; and since she *is* the foreground of the novel, White has no set of devices by which her madness can be placed in the perspectives of sanity. In the end, his creative method succumbs to her alienated consciousness, just as in *The Living and the Dead* it had succumbed to the corruptness of the Standishes; compassion is recurrently thwarted by grotesquerie.

The venture as a whole is gallant, and surprisingly successful. The experimental, ambitious character of the work comes from its attempt to render the very texture of an experience as radically alienated as Theodora's; and in this, I think, it is a failure. But its simplicity comes from the unwavering and compassionate focus which, in the first half, it keeps on her; White has wisely and fruitfully drawn back from the synoptic vision of society attempted in *The Living and the Dead* and concerned himself with one consciousness, one destiny. He defines that consciousness, and he defines the world by means of it. The prose presents the radical ambiguity of Theodora's position, but at no point patronizes her; it is less fluid than that of the earlier books, but more precise; it records with great authority the tension in her consciousness between the desire for freedom and the fact of imprisonment:

Viewed this way, the situation was more tolerable. There were times when the morning sang with bulbuls encaged in palms, their throats throbbing from behind green slats, and yes, it was very tolerable. She became lighter now, too. Her arrested black flowed through the afternoon. Even a mahogany tombstone dissolved. She was at most, but also at least, an aunt. She swam down the passage, out of her mother's room, away from the influence of the coffin, and in the suave silence she saw across the bay the pepper trees tossed into green balls by a wind starting, that raked the sea until all the little white boats jumped and fretted and pulled at their moorings to be away. [p. 5].

Nor is White's sensibility confined, here, to such a consciously 'rich' texture of experience: the *humanity* of Theodora's experience also emerges, and at moments we are very close to the human heart-beat:

She had told the story of Meroë, an old house, in which nothing remarkable had taken place, but where music had been played, and roses had fallen from their stems, and the human body had disguised its actual mission of love and hate. But to tell the story of Meroë was to listen also to her own blood, and rather than hear it quicken and fail again, Theodora smoothed with her toe the light on the carpet, and said,
'But, my darling, there is very little to tell.' (p. 13)

To stress that *The Aunt's Story* is the work of a great writer is not to say that it is a great book. In fact, despite the authority with which the author's prose warms and humanizes his concerns as well as defining them, one is perhaps more conscious of the failure than of the achievement. Besides the submergence of its second and third parts in the flow of an alienated experience, White shows again and again that tendency which has so often been taken for mere mannerism but which is actually an inordinate (and perhaps defensive) insistence on *textures*. He is, I think, a victim of a mysticism of objects – or, better still, a mysticism of sensations. Far too many things, objects, are presented as revelations; and it is through an unremitting concern with sensations that they are so presented:

This house was still comfortable with sleep. But the bronze cock flaunted his metal throat and crowed. Somewhere a voice tore itself from a sheet. A thin, dark, perhaps an Indian woman, or a Mexican, lifted her head and looked, rising out of deep darkness, Theodora saw. Theodora looked away thinking that she recognized her own soul in the woman's deep face.
    The bronze cock was screaming. Voices came from kitchens, prominent voices, because they were still feeling their way, and cold, because every morning is the first. (p. 312)

This is unmistakably fine, but only a rigid control keeps it from inanity. It is ironic that where in his mature novels White fails it is because the prose which is so insistently used to discriminate, define, and value *things* surrenders to the endless flow of their textures and so ends by blurring the distinctions between them.

This fault recurs in the three later novels written after his return to Australia; but in them it is at worst incidental and, whatever its cause, has the status only of a mannerism. Each of these is an important work, and the three together constitute White's claim to greatness. *The Tree of Man* (1955) has the virtues of *The Aunt's Story*, lacks its central weakness, and has a much larger range of human implication. It remains for me White's finest work; and one can fairly say that *The Aunt's Story* was the bridge by which he crossed from the disastrous pretensions of *The Living and the Dead* to its magnificent concern with the central problems of humanity. 'What had seemed a brilliant, intellectual, highly desirable existence, became distressingly parasitic and pointless' [*The Living and the Dead*, perhaps], and yielded to 'the stimulus of time remembered'. [2] Yet what is stimulated to existence in *The Tree of Man* is no merely individual time remembered but the rendering and definition of other, representative lives which, being native to his native country, grow out of and transcend his own individual past. It is with *that* he peoples the 'Great Australian Emptiness' while defining the emptiness itself:

> Because the void I had to fill was so immense, I wanted to try to suggest in this book every possible aspect of life, through the lives of an ordinary man and woman. But at the same time I wanted to discover the extraordinary behind the ordinary, the mystery and the poetry which alone could make bearable the lives of such people, and incidentally my own life since my return. [3]

The novel is, for the most part, a much more impersonal work than those final phrases might suggest. The labour which has gone into it is a labour of objectification; a world is created, and in its creation the author's personal tensions become not so much released as transcended. It is interesting, too, that the diagnostic intelligence which has always been evident in his work is now at the service of an 'exploratory-creative use of words upon experience'. [4]

> Never far from the dog the man would be at work. With axe, or scythe, or hammer. Or he would be on his knees, pressing into the earth the young plants he had raised under wet bags. All along the

morning stood the ears of young cabbages. Those that the rabbits did not nibble off. In the clear morning of those early years the cabbages stood out for the woman more distinctly than other things, when they were not melting, in a tenderness of light.

The young cabbages, that were soon a prospect of veined leaves, melted in the mornings of thawing frost. Their blue and purple flesh ran together with the silver of water, the jewels of light, in the smell of warming earth. But always tensing. Already in the hard, later light the young cabbages were resistant balls of muscle, until in time they were the big, placid cabbages, all heart and limp panniers, and in the middle of the day there was the glandular stench of cabbages. (pp. 26–7)

This is no mere surface impressionism; it is vibrant with significance not only for the story of White's characters but also for his view of the reality of which they are part. The images provide a frighteningly precise analogy for what we later see as Amy Parker's emotional development, and one feels that, here, Amy almost senses it. They establish the Janus-faced view of reality which is central to White's whole venture, by establishing at once the striking temporal identity and the ultimate fluidity of *things*. And they use sensations not to submerge but to serve people and things. When we remember *The Living and the Dead*, the surety of the approach is astonishing.

In a similar way, the episodes of flood, bushfire, and drought do not serve the purpose only of adding surface realism or physical violence; they are in the book as organic parts of, indices to, the spiritual life of Stan Parker and his wife. It is through them that we gain access to the emotional states which the characters themselves cannot articulate. And inarticulateness is a large part of the novel's concern; the tree of man grows from and in a dumbness which, though exasperating, is somehow necessary. We realize this from the moment we see Stan selecting his bride almost by chance, very much as he selects his few sticks of furniture, and the lumpy man and his skinny woman go in an awkward less-than-intimacy to win their living from uncleared bush.

In the whole of this first section, the seemingly unimportant or random events are made important by White's splendid selectiveness. The casual exactitude with which the floods are described is the most notable example. There is no inflation into significance, and no glamourizing; but there is a net of significances established, so that we take without question the passage which White offers as the fitting conclusion to the section:

It is not known how or why the district in which the Parkers lived got its name, but it was about the time of the floods that the official voice began to refer to it as Durilgai. And this meant 'fruitful' . . .

(p. 98)

We take it as natural even though the swollen passion of the floods has served only to emphasize the barrenness of Amy and the suspension of the Parkers' marital life. For we have been given a most moving realization, both in sharpness of observed detail and in total rhythmic movement, of the actual life the Parkers led; and it is this life that the episode of the floods reveals at depth. The exactitude is the servant of a vision which cannot be established by that means alone; and such symbolic episodes as those of the flood, the fire, and the drought serve not only to organize and concentrate the observed detail but also to reveal in the lives of the characters a dimension which otherwise would be lacking. They act as symbols of the emotional condition which those lives have reached at a given crucial moment; but, in establishing *that*, they also act as symbols of man's life in what White seems to regard as its essential progress or devolution: the flood, bringing man to the first stage of self-awareness in relation to other people; the fire, exciting his romantic fantasies and purging him of the emotional dross they represent; the drought, accompanying his decline of animal energy to the point where he must attain wisdom or lapse insensately into death. They are symbols of the deepest powers of life breaking into consciousness; and their creative use is, in a sense, as organic as the life they symbolize. They emerge out of the characters' lives, and are not imposed on them.

To say all this is to indicate the novel's main strength, but not its only one. White may not be confined to the means of 'realism', but the precision and economy of his *social* observation, so much finer and more relaxed than anything in *The Living and the Dead*, strengthen, as they are strengthened by, a symbolic habit which otherwise might have been stifling in its suggestiveness. I think particularly of the surety with which the children, Ray and Thelma, are set in those circles of ambition and corruption which are their individual worlds. Here, too, the comparison with the Lawrence of *Women in Love* is not to White's disadvantage:

Then, suddenly, Thelma Parker left the shipping office, where she was getting on, and took a position with a solicitor at a lower salary. She could not have explained with any conviction why she had done this, only that it had to be. Soothed by the smell of discretion and timelessness perhaps. Many of the women clients wore fur coats and pearls, and were ushered out by the partners with signs of discreet intimacy and social connexion, and a touch of dry hands.

In the circumstances, her life at Bourkes' became more and more distasteful. Ammoniac smells from the stables clashed with the lavender water with which she refreshed her long hands, and the hooded horses sidled monotonously out, led by the hairy older men, or with boys up, hunched into shapes of arrogant responsibility. None of this concerned Thelma Parker or was concerned about her, but it was there. . . . (p. 267)

In fact, there is throughout the book a constant yet varied play of the creative intelligence; some readers, finding it rather daunting, would call it unremitting. And, certainly, the novel's undoubted greatness is a flawed one: the over-insistence on certain conceits, the Biblical pretensions which the prose often adopts, the moments of overt superciliousness in the implied comments of the author, these have been often remarked on. Yet, by themselves, they are no more than mannerisms, strains of the surface. Two other failings are more serious, and, indeed, threaten White's whole conception. One is the treatment of the hero, Stan Parker, whose presumed growth in wisdom is not dramatically presented in the narrative; so that his final vision (or revelation?) of God in a gob of spittle is not a culmination of his living but an imposition on the reader. That weakness was no doubt predictable; but it becomes serious when we associate it with another, White's failure at certain crucial moments to deal maturely with the maturity of his characters. He implicitly claims to treat mankind as a whole, to give an account of the human condition as such. But the nearer his characters come to the years of ripening, the more closely life comes to demand of them the responses due to a full maturity, the less certain his prose becomes in delineating those responses. The result is that, while he does not condescend to his characters as he did in the first two novels, he fails at times to preserve the tone of compassionate respect which is due to his profound conception of them.

These, perhaps, are faults of temperament; and, as actual flaws, they seem to me no more damaging than James's or Lawrence's; but, as tendencies, they are perhaps more disturbing, because they threaten the way White may call on his own emotional resources in directly presenting the emotional condition of his characters. They are perhaps responsible for the prose mannerism and the tendency to inflation.

Voss (1957) tackles head-on the question of emotional resources, almost as though White had recognized his own danger and was determined to confront it. His megalomaniac explorer is a figure which might have attained the stature of an Ahab, yet somehow does not. His journeying is superbly presented, yet the man himself is too close to the grotesque to be terrible, as Ahab is terrible. It is heartening that White should have chosen such a subject after the more subdued personalities of *The Tree of Man*; his conception of his hero is as splendidly Nietzschean as Voss's conception of his own destiny. But it founders in the symbolism which is Voss's medium. If Stan Parker's inner being remained too nearly closed off by his own inarticulateness, Voss's inner being is too nearly stifled by the weight of the analogies he is forced to carry. One is the victim of social, the other of symbolist, conventions. For, while the remarkable and varied play of observed detail serves at times to express Voss's inner states, it is also pressed into the service of an allegorizing tendency which, in the end, dehumanizes him. It is a case of two approaches to 'symbolism' coming into contradiction.

If there is a myth-making propensity at work here, there is also the diagnosing intelligence. Voss is not merely a figure of mythic proportions, he is also a case history of Nietzschean man. The novel is an analysis of his compulsive drive to explore the continent, to embrace it, to possess it, to be as a God; yet the prose which analyses his case also creates the stature of his attempt; the writing is at once diagnostic and heroic.

. . . The foreigner himself remained indifferent. Seated on his horse and intent on inner matters, he would stare imperiously over the heads of men, possessing the whole country with his eyes. In those eyes the hills and valleys lay still, but expectant, or responded in ripples of leaf and grass, dutifully, to their bridegroom the sun, till all vision overflowed with the liquid gold of complete union. (p. 165)

White's attitude to Voss runs, as those of the other characters do, from careful and suspicious awe to an almost mocking intimacy. He is as aware as we are that his hero is a grotesque; yet he insists on the epic nature of his spiritual attempt. This fluctuation in his attitudes to his hero is not a disabling weakness; but, in its alternate opening and closing of Voss's inner being, like a systole-diastole, it serves to set his humanity at too uncertain a distance from our own. whom presumably he represents.

We do, however, glimpse in *Voss* the view to which White's savage analysis of 'Society' has been tending: that life can be won only outside 'Society' – and, perhaps, only outside society. One of the things which persuade us of the epic stature of Voss's exploration is the picture White gives of colonial Sydney. Voss explores and, in exploring, affirms the dimensions of human experience whose very existence Sydney denies:

> In the course of ritual, after the ladies had abandoned the gentlemen to the port and everyone had been bored for a little, Mrs Bonner pounced on Mr Topp and smiled and asked: Would he? It was obvious that he had been invited only for this moment. As it was invariably the case, he was neither surprised nor offended, but addressed himself to the pianoforte with such relief that the susceptibilities of his hosts would have been hurt if they had but considered. Mrs Bonner, however, was creating groups of statuary. This was her strength, to coax out of flesh the marble that is hidden in it . . . (p. 90)

Though savage, this is also, in its way, relaxed. However unsure White is in his attitude to Voss he has complete control of the Society which plays foil to his 'hero'. In one sense, Sydney society is compellingly real; in another sense, its unreality guarantees Voss's reality. Certainly, it demonstrates his stature.

Yet, in the end, it is the stature of a mission, a destiny, rather than of a man. And it is significant that Voss's destiny is to invert his own original mission. The determination to possess ends in a being-possessed; the compulsion to lead ends in what Laura Trevelyan calls 'humility'. Predictably, but unpleasantly, Voss becomes a Christ-figure, and re-enacts the Passion; confusingly, too, since, although there is a redemption, it is of Voss rather than by him. It is Laura who cries out the 'It is over'. And one is forced to consider whether it was her willing agony which won for Voss the relative dignity of his simultaneous dying:

> Whereupon, she was moving her head against the pillow in grateful ecstasy.
> Such evidence would have delighted the Palethorpes and mystified the Bonners, but the former were not present, and the latter were drooping and swaying in their own sleep on their mahogany chairs.

So the party rode down the terrible basalt stairs of the Bonners' deserted house, and onward. Sometimes the horses' hooves would strike sparks from the outcrops of jagged rock. (p. 382)

In these final episodes, the stress both on the psychic identification of Laura with Voss and on the Christian 'meaning' of their joint suffering is so strong that one is forced to pass both a negative and an approving judgement: on the one hand, there is something tainted about a creative habit which insists on an allegorical reading and then blurs the meaning it points to; and, on the other hand, there is something uniquely fine about a creative habit which can bring such diverse kinds of life into such a mutually enlivening relationship. The analogy is surely with music, and one feels that White would welcome our drawing it. Yet there are dangers in presenting a heroic theme in a *symboliste* mode; and in *Voss* there is a mandarin quality which is refreshingly missing from *The Tree of Man*.

Riders in the Chariot (1961) returns to deal more directly with the common world; but the return to ways of living which had fructified White's genius in *The Tree of Man* seems to involve also a regression to the modes of perception which unbalanced *The Living and the Dead*. The regression has several symptoms: what in *Voss* had been an extension of metaphor in the direction of allegory now becomes open allegory; White no longer *creates* his themes through image and analogy, he states, repeats, and forces them on us in a crudely allegorical form. The intention is clear: it is to insist that from a corrupt society only a spiritual élite can escape, a tiny élite, whose members recognize one another by some sixth sense, and who are inevitably the victims of society's scorn and hatred. A cabbalistic notion of the struggle between good (esoteric awareness) and evil (society) permeates the whole action of the novel; and one is forced to the conclusion that White's distrust of social institutions has now become something more extreme. This process is seen both in his treatment of society and in the terms in which he presents at least two of his four 'riders in the chariot', Alf Dubbo and Miss Hare.

The depiction of Miss Hare is crucial for establishing the ethos of the novel; she is one of the elect, and yet she is presented in terms so permeated by the sensuousness of corruption that she appears quite as evil as her persecutor, Mrs Jolley. In making her an *illuminé* White is, despite himself, co-operating with the forces of disintegration which the book is devoted to attacking. Paradox could hardly go further. Miss Hare is not alienated, as Theodora Goodman was; she is softened and decaying throughout; and we cannot think of her except in terms of her kneeling in leaves and mould, or 'heaping endearments' on her imprisoned goat.

I feel that this creative flaw is fatal to White's notion of the 'riders'; and it is not surprising that it has its counterparts in other large symptoms of strain: in the ludicrously complete parallel between Himmelfarb's crucifixion and that of Christ, and in the savagely wilful caricaturing of the speech and behaviour of people like Mrs Jolley and Mr Rosetree. There is excess everywhere, excess of ingenuity and of emotion. If this is a *roman à thèse*, the thesis gets less backing from ideas than from uncontrolled emotions, of which the chief seems to be a scorn that strives to be olympian but is merely excessive.

Still the novel has, in parts, a considerable strength; and, paradoxically, that strength is exhibited in the treatment of ordinary lives, in the establishment of the worlds of Himmelfarb and Mrs Godbold (how disconcertingly pointed most of these names are, by the way). Mrs Godbold's reflective moral strength, her amazing fortitude, are communicated to the prose which presents her:

... But it was she, of course, who had to carry her brother. It was not very far, her blurry mouth explained. From that field. To the outskirts of the town. She was strong, but her thoughts were tearing as she carried the body of her brother. It had been different when their mother died, in bed, at night, surrounded by relatives. Children were forgotten. Until, almost at once, the big girl had taken them on. She was lugging her brother around. So that he was hers to carry now. As her feet dragged along the first of the paving-stones, women clapped fingers to their mouths, and ran inside, trampling geranium and pinks, or burst from their cottages to gape at the girl who was carrying a dead boy, the sun setting in the grey streets, filling them for a moment with blood. (p. 267)

This has the tensile but almost simple strength of direct notation. Himmelfarb, a much more complex spiritual case, is presented in a prose supple enough to present both his self-consciousness and the Germany of which he is sharply aware:

But the strange morning was already unfolding, in which any individual might have become exposed to contingency. The evader walked with care, under the naked, cawing elms. It seemed as though he had abandoned the self he had grown to accept in his familiar room. It seemed, also, fitting that it should again be winter when he took the long, undeviating road along which friends had brought him – how long ago, months or years? – to experience silence and waiting. The winter air cleared his head wonderfully with the result that he found himself observing, and becoming engrossed by the least grain of roadside sand. . . . (p. 189)

It is interesting that White's success in this novel should come in the presentation of sanely unassuming personalities and in a mode of relatively simple realism; the rest of the book is undermined not only by over-elaborateness but also by misanthropy.

White's achievement is seen not merely in any one masterwork but in his whole development, fluctuant as that is; so that any account of him must deal with all six novels, and attempt to show the way in which each grows out of and away from its predecessor. As each does so, we see White at once correcting an over-emphasis and exploring new themes, new modes by which to define his preoccupations. The fervour with which he approaches each new task suggests an unusual magnanimity in his view of the novel as a form, and an unusual openness to the demands of experiment. Unlike some great novelists, he does not with each new work ring the changes on a basic situation or situations which it is his concern to delineate. The situations he deals with are, in fact, strikingly varied; it is his preoccupations that remain standard; and we see the novels growing out of one another in a way which first surprises us with its seeming arbitrariness, and then satisfies us with its profound appropriateness. This process continues until his last work. With *Riders in the Chariot*, wide-ranging and substantial though it is in some ways, his creative development becomes unbalanced as the themes and situations are inflated and distorted by his emotions. In his finest work, *The Tree of Man*, those emotions are defined by the situations they energize. In especial, they are defined by the prose; and it is at the local level, in the enormously daring and responsive prose, as much as in his large structural conceptions, that White proves himself a great writer, of the order, possibly, of Conrad.

NOTES

1. R. F. Brissenden, *Patrick White*, A.N.U., 1958, p. 10.
2. Patrick White, 'The Prodigal Son', *Australian Letters*, vol. i, no. 3, April 1958, p. 38.
3. Ibid. p. 39.
4. F. R. Leavis, *The Common Pursuit*, p. 109.

THE NOVEL AND SOCIETY

S. MURRAY-SMITH

THE lack of a leisured class with cultivated tastes, the rawness of colonial society, an impulsive reaction from the over-drawn niceties of an English high culture and, indeed, the very urgency of environmental adaptation and proximity of natural threat: these factors have imparted to the whole corpus of Australian writing a 'social' twist. Even those who have rebelled against a surfeit of 'realism' have, by their very apostasy, emphasized the dominant trend. 'Australian economic history,' says the economist S. J. Butlin in a well-known passage, 'is the major part of all Australian history; from the beginning economic factors have dominated development in a way that should gladden the heart of any Marxist.' It is not difficult, *pari passu*, to draw the same lesson from history of the Australian novel.

There is perhaps a danger here of getting involved in a tautology. If we define Australian writing as writing recognizably about Australia, it will be clear that almost any book we choose will have its strong social underpinnings: *Geoffry Hamlyn* on the manner and morals of squatting expansion, *Richard Mahony* on alienation in a materialistic, expatriate community, and so on. There is not even yet a sense of metropolitan well-being about Australians; we are self-conscious about our country and its geographical and historical setting, and every book is held up, like an egg against a candle, to test the colour of its yolk – to see what it tells us about ourselves. We are, and have been for eighty years, *worried* about identity. No writer has been able to escape.

Despite this inescapable cast imparting some communal significance to nearly all our literature, what we are concerned with here is essentially the literature of 'protest'. Strong polemical and didactic motives have influenced many of our novelists from Marcus Clarke on, yet there is danger perhaps in too crude an emphasis on this. Firstly, our novelists of protest have been very much part of the 'stream'; what basis have we, because perhaps of only slight heightening of emphasis, to categorize them apart? Louis Stone's *Jonah*, for instance, some of the work of Katharine Susannah Prichard, much of the work of Kylie Tennant, perhaps all of the work of Vance Palmer, can hardly be apostrophized as overtly radical. Secondly, we run into trouble with definitions. Is a novel of protest one in which the writer sets off with a definite moral vision to which he subordinates the other aspects of his work? If his protest emerges implicitly, even independently of the author's consciousness, is it still protest? And what is protest? Are Patrick White's extra-political celebrations of spiritual poverty in a denatured world radical and sociological in the way we associate with 'protest'? Must a 'solution' be implied before a work becomes one of protest; and, if so, when does it stop being 'implied'? Has indeed the nature of real protest in our literature been changing for some time? The comparative sterility of much ostensibly left-wing writing, and the failure of too many socially-oriented writers to respond sensitively enough to post-war political, social, and economic movements, raises this question today in an urgent form. It is possible, and probably necessary, to oppose at one and the same time escape into private mazes and a reshuffling of some well-worn radical cards. For those of us who see it as a great thing about Australian writing that so much of it has been concerned with the more-or-less earthy problems of the common man, the chief consolation in this day of so much right-wing and left-wing conformity may well lie, for instance, in the exploratory talents of the Communist Dorothy Hewett (as shown in *Bobbin Up*, 1959), of David Forrest (his quirkish and original satire *The Hollow Woodheap*, 1962), of David Martin, with his feeling for human intimacy in specific social settings (*The Young Wife*, 1962), or George Turner, looking at a country town and the people in it without, perhaps, realizing that he is writing both sociology and politics (*A Stranger and Afraid*, 1961; *The Cupboard Under the Stairs*, 1962). The tradition is not dead, but it is certainly undergoing a metamorphosis.

The first of our novelists to write deliberately in the modern idiom to arouse indignation in the reader was Joseph Furphy, or rather his *doppel-gänger* 'Tom Collins' who wrote *Such is Life* (1903). (I am omitting discussion of Marcus Clarke's *For the Term of His Natural Life* (1874); despite its real literary merits this book, which has something of the nature of a reformer's tract, remains an erratic with little bearing on our subsequent literary history.) *Such is Life* is a work with such a complexity of plot and such a wealth of asides that it will prove a profitable mine for generations yet of Australian critics. Textual exegesis alone will be a decade's work for some single-minded (and perhaps fortunate) scholar. The narrative twists and divides like Furphy's own familiar Murray River; it would be a bold man who would claim that Furphy's main theme was the class struggle or socialism or ignorant oppression, for inextricably mixed up with his sometimes bitter thoughts on these matters is not only an obsessive concern with bog-philosophy (notably questions relating to determinism and free-will) but also a Brahm-like aloofness, supported by the subtlest wit yet met with in Australian writing, which detracts from a general air of 'message'. Yet Furphy *is* angry, and his mild fatalism does not detract from his air of urgency. His radical argument is both general and particular. General in his hatred of oppression and of complacency under oppression; particular in his application of his beliefs to the situation Australians find themselves in. Furphy covered much ground in his arguments, from historical precedent in Wat Tyler ('Each inch of recovered ground cost a hundred lives'[1]) to contemporary sociology, notably the ignobility of what he termed the 'deserving poor' ('Compulsory-contented poverty is utterly, irredeemably despicable ... they richly deserve every degree of poverty, every ounce of indignity, and every inch of condescension they stagger under'). But specifically he spoke to his countrymen, using – as a parable if you like – the struggle of the Riverina bullock-drivers to get a bit of grass and water for their cattle from mean-spirited squatters as a profound lesson for all: 'I tell you that from the present social system of pastoral Australia to actual lordship and peonage is an easy transition ...'

Such is Life is deservedly dealt with at greater length elsewhere in this collection, together with the work of Henry Lawson. Lawson wrote no novels, and would hence seem by definition excluded from a discussion of the novel of protest. Yet it would be ridiculous to omit here the name of the man in whose prose social commitment and art are more successfully linked than anywhere else in our writing. Lawson, whose main work was published in the nineties, has a reputation founded almost exclusively on his short stories. In theme and in characters, as well as in setting, a great many of these stories are linked so as to form a body of connected work; while they lack the overall thematic articulation of most novels they cannot be set aside in any discussion of the literature of protest. Despite his poverty, his radical political convictions and the stormy times in which he lived, Lawson in his stories (generally dealing with the bush worker or the slum-dwellers of Sydney) seldom appears to set off with the idea of a fixed message he had to 'get across'. When we are moved to pity and indignation by the protests that are there in his work, we are thus all the more strongly moved. Arnold Kettle has written that: '*Uncle Tom's Cabin* may enlarge the realm of our knowledge, *Wuthering Heights* enlarges that of our imagination.' One important significance of Lawson in the Australian literary scene is that he is the *only* writer of protest who has been able to take the full step across from Harriet Beecher Stowe to Emily Brontë. This does not make him less committed, but rather more effectively committed, despite ambiguities in his attitude to the working class which I have discussed elsewhere,[2] and despite his sentimentality which Furphy apostrophized when he wrote that 'in battle there is something to do besides pick up the wounded'.

The last fifteen years of the nineteenth century had seen a decisive growth in the political consciousness of the urban and rural proletariat in Australia, caused by the growth of popular education and an organized labour movement, reflecting the failure of democratic land policies and the labour-capital clashes arising from the development of industry, and expressed in the proliferation of radical groups and organizations. Many writers, including Lawson and Furphy, developed from this process and – additionally moved by the utopian visions associated with Australian Federation – powerfully contributed to it. Two relatively minor but important figures in the tradition were Steele Rudd and Edward Dyson, both, like Lawson, and because of the lack of cultural sophistication and literary expertise, writing in a form mid-way between the short story and the novel. Rudd's *On Our Selection* (1899) and Dyson's *Fact'ry 'Ands* (1906) both deal in ostensibly humorous manner with their subject-matter, the former concerning struggling selectors on dusty and impossible farms, the latter with workers in a Melbourne factory. Yet underlying the humour, especially in the former, is a bitter pathos; *On Our Selection* – and perhaps especially to a later generation – implicitly raises the question, time and time again, as to whether Australians had fought for generations to subdue the land in order to be forced to lead the life of coolies. Dyson's book is most notable for its disrespectful attitude to employing authority and factory discipline, and for its sympathetic insight into a new urban type, the larrikin, who expresses the frustrations of Australians, conscious of wider horizons, who are forced into the narrow confines of city lanes and grimy sweat-shops. The theme was carried further but perhaps weakened by the orthodox framework of the romantic novel in Louis Stone's *Jonah* (1911).

With the exception of Price Warung's stories of the convict system, seeking to remind his readers of the cruelties and oppression in which Australian society was first shaped, the writers of this early generation make their chief contribution to the tradition of 'social' writing in the immanence of their demonstration that it was a proper, and perhaps *the* proper object of literature to concern itself with ordinary people in ordinary situations. Here their strength was their insularity; on the whole they came from, or from near, the working class, and the only intellectual in their midst was the editor and critic A. G. Stephens, who did so much to shape their talents. Their strength was their close and intimate involvement in the situations they wrote about; their inspiration was personal experience, their technique leaning towards the documentary. They were essentially the products of a simpler epoch, when the running sores of society were more open to view. They were transferring experience, not transmuting it.

Though the cant phrase has it that the Great War made Australia a nation, in many ways the effect was the reverse. The brave concepts of Eutopia and Hy-Brasil which had sustained so many of our builders in the nineteenth century, from explorers and statesmen to shearers and writers, vanished over-night. Australia shrank. Turkish bullets and German shrapnel killed brave men and braver visions. After the war public life became meaner, the individual less sure of himself, the issues more complex and confusing. Labor was often in power now, but it didn't seem to make any difference. 'Anyone who looks at the history of Australia in this century,' Norman MacKenzie has written, 'is struck at once by the contrast between the mood of optimism when the Commonwealth was founded and the sardonic pessimism of most of the inter-war years – a contrast between the interest in social experiment before the first world war and the complacent conservatism that preceded the second.'

The working-class writer who saw his pen as a pike, and who was the last and finest representative of the nineteenth-century 'self-improver', had in fact reached the end of his tether. Or rather, perhaps, literature ceased to seem relevant to him and he finished his days as a hack on some trade union newspaper. The novel, classically speaking, is a product of the bourgeois epoch *par excellence*. As we have seen, the rebel working-class litterateur felt uneasy in grappling with its implications, with its emphasis on the individual, and with its discipline. Further, literary techniques from overseas had, until now, not been strictly applicable to the Australian situation. Ralph Fox, in listing *Wuthering Heights*, *Jude the Obscure*, and *The Way of all Flesh* as the three greatest books of the Victorian age, claimed that they were 'manifestos of English genius that a full human life in a capitalist society was impossible of attainment'. Even if we want to look at this statement more closely, we can still agree that it is as a critique of a selfish and ingrowing society that we see much of the best in nineteenth century English literature. In Australia, until World War I, we had the vision of a society which, however flawed, was challenging and expansive. The broader, more intellectual criticisms were not relevant.

It was the difficult task set themselves by some Australian writers after the war to re-interpret colonial experience. Hardly again were we to see a working-class writer of protest; the intellectuals moved in, as they had to, in order to grapple at a higher level of art with problems that had become inchoate at a lower. Of course many intellectuals withdrew from the challenge; their imaginations suffused with what pickings of overseas intellectual discourse filtered through to Australia, they sought to create their own cloud-cuckoo-lands in the bohemian attics of Sydney or Melbourne. Such an 'escape', if it was an escape, did not necessarily indicate a lack of radical convictions; with the young Jack Lindsay, for instance, surely it was a romantic revolt against a crude insistence on the banal and material in much of Australian culture in general and literature in particular.

Some, however, set out on the new and intensely difficult path. Katharine Susannah Prichard, whose first published book, *The Pioneers*, appeared in 1915, was herself the pioneer, and her courage, influence and example stiffened the whole growth and development of the social novel in Australia for half a century.

Above all we owe to her that, in bringing a distinguished literary talent to bear on socially-relevant aspects of Australian life, she also brought a cultivated mind well-read in world literature and a determination, despite her political convictions, not to humiliate literature to dogma nor to become the arch-promoter of a 'school'. Her starting points were a deep compassion for man and a profound love of her country, merging, in the fire of her political beliefs, to an anger expressed throughout her work:

And yet there are things in Australia I have hated. To see relief workers, and their wives, living in the western forests under shacks of bagging and boughs, through which the rain streamed – women with babies in their arms. To find abandoned farms and hear stories of a tragic struggle for existence in the wheat-growing areas. To watch men and women and their children sweltering through heat and dust storms in unsanitary hovels on the goldfields. To know that hundreds of Australians, young and old, have lived on the brink of despair because they could not find work or wages to feed and clothe themselves, in this rich and lovely country of ours.

In *Working Bullocks* (1926) Katharine Prichard tells the story of life among timber-getters in the karri forests of Western Australia. The images of the bush, the subtleties of the relationship between man and man, man and job, are skilfully and patiently developed; and, though Katharine Prichard has disavowed being strongly influenced by Lawson, the effect of tradition is there, reborn and matured, whereby a middle-class woman can write, convincingly and without patronage, of the tough lives of tough men in an isolated working-class community. There is politics, of course, but Katharine Prichard made a point ignored by many later writers when she demonstrated in this novel that, if politics is life, then it emerges as life mainly by the interplay of character and personality, of people impinging on people, and not through the juxtaposition, however adroit, of incident and action alone.

The capacity shown here for the sympathetic treatment of even those characters she does not approve is carried further in *Coonardoo* (1929), a tale of cultural clash and tragic love under the shadow of the colour bar in the north-west. 'The author herself', Aileen Palmer tells us, 'draws no moral, makes no accusation, but leaves us with the image of Coonardoo, very thin and wasted with disease, returning ... to die on the earth that was her tribal home.'

Among Katharine Prichard's other books, those that most call for some discussion here are her goldfields trilogy, *The Roaring Nineties* (1946), *Golden Miles* (1948), and *Winged Seeds* (1950). These books she would consider her crowning work, in bringing most effectively into focus both art and truth. Most commentators will disagree, will feel that the authoress herself, because of her lack of personal involvement, turns the wheel full circle and depends too heavily on that documentary quality that our earlier realists depended on because they were too closely involved. These books do lack the artistic unity of her earlier books discussed here, but they remain among the most outstanding of the achievements, not only of the Communist school of social realism, but probably of the novel of protest in Australia. There is a temptation to suggest that they also mark the end of the line, the playing out of that particular lode. It is not just that literary fashion would seem to make it unlikely that we will get social reporting of this kind at this length again: re-interpretation of our experience is now necessary, not abandoning all the older tradition, any more than Katharine Prichard did, but re-assessing and heightening and bringing new ideas both of form and content into consideration.

Like Katharine Prichard, her contemporary Vance Palmer neither shirked the problems of Australian reality nor lacked political convictions with a radical bias. Yet his work has not, on the whole, the social 'bite' of Prichard's. No Marxist, he lacked conviction of the essential unity of art and politics; or perhaps, to be more fair, he just refused to think of the world as a very simple place. But there is an ambiguity, a lack of decisiveness in much of his work that removes it from the sphere of commitment. Where Palmer comes closest, as in his trilogy involving the Queensland labour movement,[3] he does however perform notable service. His dry, ironic sympathetic study of a labour careerist and his dying ideals hits harder than some brasher and more forceful attempts at the same portrait by others.

Prichard and Palmer had arid soil to work in in the twenties, but it might have been thought that the shock of the Depression and the anger generated by it would have spurred a variety of radical writing in the thirties. Strangely enough, this is not so. The thirties was a time of publication of romances, historical and otherwise. It was not, in fact, till full employment and prosperity returned under the beneficent hand of war that Leonard Mann's *The Go-Getter* (1942) appeared (J.K. Ewers has called it 'a sort of Australian *Love on the Dole*'), and not till seven years later that Alan Marshall's satirically-titled *How Beautiful are thy Feet* (1949), describing work in a boot factory at this time, was published. Now, thirty years later, the Depression seems set fair to become a most-favoured-topic among proto-realists, starving for subjects amid the riches of the 'affluent' society.

There is one exception: Kylie Tennant, who is still a youthful influence on the Australian literary scene, published *Tiburon* in 1935. A novel of the unemployed in a New South Wales country town, it was followed by *The Battlers* (1941), employing the same locale, also raising both implicitly and explicitly a number of immediate social questions, and including the climactic device of a strike. This device, previously used by Katharine Prichard in *Working Bullocks*, was to become almost the *sine qua non* of the post-war novel of social criticism as Australian writers envisaged it, a mute expression of the unsophisticated belief that conflicts had to be externalized before they became real. Kylie Tennant varied her target with *Foveaux* (1939), raising the questions of slum reform and municipal politics in an urban Sydney setting, and with *Ride on Stranger* (1943). This latter broke new ground in being in part a satirical comment on the *modus operandi* of certain left-wing groups; Miss Tennant gleefully quoted on the jacket the Communist Sydney *Tribune*'s view that this was: 'A cynical and slanderous novel . . . A more morbid, contemptuous view of Australian life has never been written . . . it is a scandal that valuable paper should ever have been wasted on this irresponsible nonsense.'

Despite the lack of writing on the effects of the Depression, the most important novel published in Australia in the thirties, Xavier Herbert's *Capricornia* (1938), was an outstanding work of social protest, just as was the most important Australian novel of the forties, Frank Hardy's *Power Without Glory* (although published in 1950, it belongs to that decade). *Capricornia* is so *big* a work that it cuts across many boundaries and presents a real challenge to critical analysis. It is, in a way, in its rambling, untidy, episodic structure, a lineal descendant of the rough-hewn works of protest of an earlier period. It is part of a long line of novels, following *Coonardoo*, on Aboriginal and half-caste themes; this has now become the safest and easiest topic for literary indignation, but there is nothing safe, limited or tired about *Capricornia*. It is a story of the cruelty, prejudice, and ignorance of the white man in northern Australia, but it is more than this: a rich and vital mine of character and incident, cultural and personality clashes, it transcends its own theme of protest to speak for its time, as few books in our literature do, and to approach the borders of the classical concept in European literature of 'critical realism'.

Capricornia, unfortunately, marked an end rather than a beginning. It was individualistic, passionate; unselfconscious writing from without the borders of literature itself. Like the frontier of which it spoke, this was a 'one man with his own hands' book, and like the frontier it was an anachronism. For the Second World War created a new base for socially-conscious writing in Australia. The common struggle of all classes to defeat fascism not only promoted a ground-swell of interest in politics, intellectual ideas, and discussion in the armed forces and in the community at large, but re-moralized the whole radical movement and raised again, for the first time in thirty years, Bernard O'Dowd's vision of 'the great Australia yet to be'. Lone wolves were out, and there was to be a coherence – and a flatness – in post-war socially-critical writing that we had not seen before.

The traditional philistinism of the Australian Labor Party, of social-democracy, in this country made it inevitable that the central role here should be played by writers belonging to or influenced by the Communist Party. The genre of protest as promoted by realist writers' groups became probably the strongest single literary influence of its day; and although the general mood of social criticism was undoubtedly also responsible, many writers without strongly-defined personal political views were drawn into its gravitational field. Although in its more extreme form the movement was largely played out by the middle fifties, its contribution to Australian writing was substantial and valuable, and performed the important function of re-emphasizing the political and social responsibilities of the writer. Unfortunately this re-emphasis coincided with (and was in part responsible for) an increasing rarification of literary criticism in Australia, and a dichotomy developed with this withdrawal into the academies which not only has precluded an adequate critical assessment of post-war radical writing, but has also (because of this) harmed the progress of Australian literature itself. A. G. Stephens would never have withdrawn from the dust and heat.

Undoubtedly an important landmark in the history of the Australian novel of protest was Hardy's *Power Without Glory*, another rambling, uneven and amateurishly-constructed novel whose virtues outweighed – or were even assisted by – its vices. Setting out to tell the story of the rise to wealth and political power of an unscrupulous Melbourne ward-boss, the writer does in part fulfil his jejune boast of attempting to follow the example of Balzac: we do in fact get there a sense of social truth, of movement and a kind of dark dialectic. Ironically, though the Marxist view is that Balzac wrote better than he, a believer and a monarchist, knew, Hardy's unfolding denunciation of the corruption of John West is accompanied – as Mr Jack Lindsay and others have commented – by a fascination, almost an unwilling admiration, of the man. At least Hardy brought back into the 'realist' novel the classical concept of the 'hero', even if he is a negative one, and has reminded us – as Mr David Martin has pointed out [4] – that most of our 'protest' novelists have evaded the difficulties of the 'positive' hero by effectively deleting one altogether.

At one time it looked as though Eric Lambert would challenge Hardy for the laurels of the leading writer of the left, but his superior literary skills were eroded by the political effects of this rivalry and by an inability to refresh his subject matter from the source. After the publication of *Watermen* (1956), a light-weight but well-felt story of a fisherman's co-operative, he removed himself from the Australian scene. His main legacy is his two war novels, *The Twenty Thousand Thieves*(1951) and *The Veterans* (1954), both expressing better than has been done elsewhere the sufferings and the sardonic radicalism of the Australian soldier.

The two other major writers of the committed 'left' in the post-war period are Judah Waten and John Morrison. Waten has more intellectual stamina and staying-power than his contemporaries, and though his view of political exigencies has meant a detraction from the artistic impact of his recent novels, *Shares in Murder* (1957) and *Time of Conflict* (1961), they, together with *Alien Son* (short stories, 1952) and *The Unbending* (1954), present an impressive body of socially critical material. In the two latter we also find the most sensitive treatment yet available of the Jewish theme in Australian writing.

Morrison's novels, *The Creeping City* (1949) and *Port of Call* (1950), are not properly representative of the extremely important role of this writer, whose talents are best expressed in his several collections of short stories. Morrison, the only radical writer of our day who is actually a manual worker, expresses better than any of his contemporaries the understanding that it is the long view, the quiet view of life and of people that, finally, wins the day. Pervading all his work is a militant humanism and sympathy for the under-dog, but in reading Morrison one is never conscious of being unduly influenced. He comes closer than any left-wing contemporary to the vital understanding that each man also fights himself.

Other novelists closely associated with the left-wing literary movement, and usually also with the Australasian Book Society (in effect a publishing house for the various groups of 'realist writers') which started operations in 1952, are Ralph de Boissiere (*Crown Jewel*, 1952), Gavin Casey (*Snowball*, 1958), David Forrest (*The Last Blue Sea*, 1959), F.B. Vickers (*The Mirage*, 1955), Dymphna Cusack (*Say No to Death*, 1951; *Southern Steel*, 1953) and Donald Stuart (*Yandy*, 1959). There are also a number of contemporary novelists who have made notable contributions to the literature of protest, but have stood further away from the committed 'left': Tom Ronan, with his remarkable study of the ethics of landed proprietorship, *Moleskin Midas* (1956); Dal Stivens, with his story of 'the last of the "great brutes" of the era of capital accumulation', *Jimmy Brockett* (1951) and Criena Rohan, with her moving plea for young people out-of-joint with society, *The Delinquents* (1962).

In a way it would be unfair to cavil at a radical literary tradition which has given us so much, and which imparts a structural strength to our writing in this country lacking in other parts of the English-speaking world. On the whole our writers face reality; and the sterile aspects of the militant tradition tend gradually to be modified as they lose relevance and impact. Yet several points of a critical nature remain to be made.

First, on the nature of 'protest' in literature itself. Protest neither makes literature, as I have heard some claim, nor does it deny it, as I have heard others. On the other hand protest is a vitally important component in much great literature of the modern era. Many of the greatest novels of Russia, England, and

France, not to speak of the U.S.A., emerge from a dissenting conscience within an assertive and dominant middle-class society; a conscience stirred by real conflicts and struggles and reflecting these in literature. We have never really had an assertive and dominant middle-class society in Australia, in the broader cultural sense, although we have certainly had strong class-conflicts and certainly have a capitalist economy, and a fairly crude one at that. Middle-class writing in Australia has been weak, and proletarian writing has suffered by its weakness. We have not been able to profit by the synoptic social vision of a Galsworthy, Thomas Mann, Balzac, or Tolstoy.

Perhaps this is part of the reason for the chief weakness in our literature of commitment, that failure to give at least an illusion of 'embracing it all'. True, we get hints of this in the work of Henry Handel Richardson, Lawson, Furphy, and perhaps in Herbert, Prichard, Hardy. But for the would-be radical writers of today there are no great *bourgeois* fore-runners of significance to our own, culturally-differentiated society. On the whole we are still nibbling at the corners of the carpet – and not even at all the corners. Think of the vast areas of smugness and babbittry, of cruelty disguised because we have not thought about it, that await even their Sinclair Lewis: the law, the education system, the medical profession, the stock-brokers, the academics, the politicians, the intellectuals themselves! We have hardly started.

It does not matter much that our writers of protest have different aims; that a Hardy or Waten write consciously within an ideological system and want their books to prove that capitalism must be demolished and social-democracy routed, while F.B. Vickers, protesting as an individual, is mainly concerned to say that we should give the half-caste a fair go, and David Forrest, writing more in the tradition of general social criticism, is making fun of stuffed shirts in banks. This is all useful, as long as the fact that the novel of protest is an established genre does not lead to an unimaginative re-stringing of beads on the thread; even, in some cases, to the concept that there *is* no other valid literary motivation.

There are signs that we may look forward in the next few years to a revival at higher level of socially critical writing. Various techniques, sociological and otherwise, are beginning to emerge to help us grapple with the anonymity and complexity of contemporary life; we share fairly healthy political facilities; and education, though tragically backward, is producing intellectual reinforcements. A diversification, both of the subject-matter and the nature of radical writing; a willingness to experiment and to improve the formal techniques themselves: these need not dull the edge of the razor, but rather give it extra cutting power.

NOTES

1. From *Rigby's Romance* (1921), originally portion of *Such is Life*.
2. *Henry Lawson* (Melbourne, 1962).
3. *Golconda* (1948), *Seedtime* (1957), *The Big Fellow* (1959).
4. In his important essay 'Three Realists in Search of Reality', *Meanjin*, 1959 no. 3.

AUSTRALIAN DRAMA

EUNICE HANGER

THE taint of amateurism has clung to Australian drama longer
than to poetry and to fiction. It is only since 1955 that our playwrights have taken the liberty of a professional stance. This is not
surprising: Lawler, our most successful playwright to date, was
not known as a writer until *The Summer of the Seventeenth Doll*
suddenly emerged. Amateur writers, ignoring Lawler's long apprenticeship in the theatre, have tended to think they may also,
with one play, make a fortune. But there will always be amateurs.
What is much more important in recent developments is that a
number of professional writers, including Ray Mathew, Patrick
White, Hal Porter, and Laurence Collinson, all better known for
verse or fiction or both, are also playwrights. It is true, moreover,
that even among our minor playwrights a professional outlook
is being taken for granted. Though they know that the chance of
a great success is small, and that they may seldom achieve any
but Little Theatre production, they practise the craft of writing
plays with the same attention to detail as a good craftsman of any
kind practises. They have ceased to feel the old diffidence about
the fact that they write plays, and in Australia, if you are healthy
and gregarious, it is not simple to practise any art: you have to
mean it.

In the nineteenth century, a bad time for drama everywhere,
much was written in dramatic form, but largely without the stage
in view. To give a picture of what was happening in Australia, one
has to classify roughly, but the picture is not significant, because
all the writing was purely imitative of what was being done elsewhere.

Some of the plays were bookish, long-winded affairs, often in
verse, dramatic only in form. Such was Harpur's blank verse
tragedy, *The Bushrangers*, published serially in 1835 and then
with his poems in 1853. Harpur was no theatrical craftsman, and
the play is a wordy vehicle for a Byronic hero, who hates men
from a sense of injustice; there are creaking comedy scenes in
imitation cockney, and there is the Wordsworth touch in the
softening of the hard heart of man by contact with nature. Harpur

is recorded because this play illustrates a kind, the sort of play written by men who remembered their Shakespeare and thought they could still write five-act plays with many small scenes and with large casts mainly of men, in an age when women were acting, the proscenium-arch stage was established, the theatre-auditorium was enormous, and thus spectacle and ham-acting were the desiderata. Harpur and his kind were literate, literary playwrights.

Much more theatrically workable are the melodramas and farces, such as filled the first book of plays published in Australia, *Plays and Fugitive Pieces in Prose and Verse* (1842) by David Burn, a Scot who had settled as a farmer in Tasmania. Burn did not include in the book his melodrama, also called *The Bushrangers*, his own first play and probably the first play that dealt with contemporary Australia. It is set in Van Diemen's Land in 1825, and its characters include convicts who escape and become bushrangers, the Lieutenant-Governor and his soldiery, some aborigines and some comic new settlers. Unreal though it is by our standards, this play and a farce went on in Edinburgh in 1829. The published volume contains the farce, some historical and tragic plays mainly in verse, and some poems and stories. Most of Burn's plays had brief productions in Hobart or Sydney. Burn is better at burlesque, for the purpose of topical satire, as in the slight but amusing *Sydney Delivered*, which he published under the pseudonym of 'Tasso Australasiatticus' in 1845, than at the heroic style he attempted for *Regulus* and *Loreda*. But the variety of styles he attempted makes Burn a good representative nineteenth-century playwright, and certainly he shows a desire for professionalism in his efforts to combine the traditional and the topical, and to have his plays produced as well as read.

There is not much point in listing more of the same kind of thing, which continued to be done through the century. Some was published, some exists in manuscript, chiefly in the Mitchell Library, and in small doses it is entertaining to read. The heavy poetic stuff breaks invariably into bathos; its blank verse is very blank, it has long exposition speeches, reported narrative, and inversions to preserve metre –

Would that we separated never had!

Attempts to work in local colour provide awkward stuff, especially when decorated with Miltonic tricks –

> Used her contentless tongue with hot fierce words,
> Like hot Australian blasts, unbearable.

The straight melodrama is hilarious, with its tags –

> Go, you hound, and do not darken my door again!

and –

> Thank God, I saved a good woman from your clutches
> tonight!

But we meet now and then a genuine and not contemptible effort to distinguish the new character-types developing in the country, as with Joe, in Cooper's *Colonial Experience* (1869), and Ted, in Sutherland's *Poetical Licence* (1884), both rough diamonds, whose blunt slangy speech offends their parents. The comedy of the melodramas and farces is usually derivative: an aborigine may talk like an American negro, as in *The Duchess of Coolgardie* (1896), by Leigh and Clare, where the black boy speaks of a plant –

> Dat am de Flower ob sleep;

and cockneys make pseudo-Dickensian puns. But refreshing touches are found in the guying of the affected, fastidious new-chum, and in the local oaths of a bullocky called Parramatta Bob, whose guarantee of good faith is

> So 'elp me Parramatta!

and his expression of astonishment,

> Well chuck me into Woolloomooloo Bay!

There are totally unreal settings like 'On the top of Mt Kosciusko', but there is also the genuine local setting such as 'At the Blazing Stump shanty' (a sort of bush pub), and 'The room is divided by flour bags' – an early multiple set! – in *Westman's Jackeroo* (c. 1900) by Cuneo.

Among these writers of melodrama should be remembered Alfred Dampier, an actor-manager who was co-author of a number of plays, such as *To the West* (1896). The style of the melodrama and the farce, or the mixture of the two, continued to hold the stage even into this century, and changed little from the work of Burn and of Tucker's farcical romance of a newchum, *Jemmy Green in Australia* (in the forties). Local colour, in the shape of drought, flood, fire, convicts, bushrangers, and land-speculators, was introduced purely for its sensational appeal. Imitation of English and American melodrama was barefaced.

THE EARLY TWENTIETH CENTURY

In the early years of this century, there was emulation of the
theatre of ideas, of realism, and of the well-made play that went
with it. Australian writers, producers, and critics dreamed of
theatres that would produce Ibsen and Shaw, and of writing their
kind of play; of a poets' theatre like that of Yeats and Synge; of
satiric comedy and comedy of manners, like Gilbert's and Wilde's.
All dreamed of a drama rooted in Australia, including plays of
city and country, low life and high, simple life and sophisticated,
contemporary and historical. Like the 'Bulletin period' in poetry,
but twenty years later, it was a time when writers desired to be
'dinkum', perhaps a little less crudely than the balladists.

Many writers published work in dramatic form which was a
product of social consciousness and the desire to make some significant contribution to the literature of man's quest for a
meaningful existence. Such plays were often fantasy, or in pageant
form, with heavily allegorical and symbolic figures. Their names
indicate their preoccupation with moralizing – *Australia's Part*
(1910), *Homo Sapiens* (1929). But these would be more interesting
to the social historian than to the student of drama. Period interest
apart, they are just dull.

Much more important is the reaction from melodrama, which
produced plays that were without pretentiousness. William
Moore, organizer of the first playwrights' theatre in Australia, is
remembered for his influence on Louis Esson and Vance Palmer
rather than for his own writing, though his tiny one-act, *The Tea-
Room Girl* (1910) is a pretty piece of atmospherics – a Melbourne
café period piece. Between 1909 and 1912 he staged annual 'Australian drama nights', when one-acts by a number of writers
were done. Most of these writers drifted to other media, but
Louis Esson revived the idea of a playwrights' theatre when he
returned from some years abroad, full of eagerness to imitate
what he had seen of the Abbey Theatre. With Vance Palmer and
others he founded the Pioneer Players, a tiny production unit
that lasted in Melbourne from 1922 to 1926. It perished for lack
of money, actors, and the kind of organization that could have
induced audiences to support the venture. For the record, I mention two later attempts to run an authors' theatre: one by Carrie
Tennant in Sydney in 1929, the Community Playhouse; and

Geoffrey Thomas's Playwrights' workshop, in 1953, also in Sydney.

Esson's one-act plays achieve the effect he seems to want: the action, though generally slight or without strong conflict, combines with the 'business', for which he gives detailed directions, and the speech, generally of homely characters, to evoke an atmosphere unique in the sense that it is fresh, individual, non-derivative, Australian, different from the atmosphere of the same situation in another part of the world. *The Drovers* (1909) is set in a camp where an injured drover has to be left to die, attended only by an aboriginal boy who makes a primitive, traditional wail over him, like the keeners in *Riders to the Sea*, lifting one lonely death into the realm of universal mourning. The drovers' talk of the job with its ups and downs, of the fact that there is no help for it – they must abandon their mate – and the touches of quiet comedy that break through in spite of the tragedy: all these are individual and at the same time eternal and general.

In *Dead Timber* (1911) he has another timeless theme, a father's rejection of the daughter who has brought shame on his house by taking a lover. The father is a farmer, narrowed and hardened by his long struggle with the land. In *The Woman-Tamer* (1910) Esson writes a comedy set down-town in the city; a woman chooses a lawless scamp instead of a respectable citizen for her lover.

His longer plays are varied in subject. *The Southern Cross* (1923) tells the Eureka story, and like most of our historical plays has too many characters and scene-changes to be practicable; *Mother and Son* (1923) is a bush drama involving acceptance of the simple life in conflict with the pull of the sophisticated; *The Bride of Gospel Place* (1926) is the most successful in use of realistic speech and method: Lily the girl from the streets and Bush the pug-gangster she loves are driven inevitably and movingly to a tragedy of the slums; *The Time is Not yet Ripe* (1912) is as different as possible, a political comedy of manners, witty and amusing, if unreal.

Esson's ear for speech was not flawless, and he could in his dialogue suddenly become stilted and bookish, as can most playwrights who work without a theatre. Apart from this major weakness, one always feels that Esson was on the right track, and that with favourable conditions he could have been a considerable playwright. He calls up atmosphere easily, he has a strong sense of the kind of situation that creates dramatic tension, and he refuses to cheat, to contrive conflicts or sensational actions that do not arise with seeming inevitability.

Vance Palmer went on writing plays, infrequently, to the end of his career. They include the historical *Hail Tomorrow* (1947), on the shearers' strike, the country comedies, *Happy Family* and *Christine*, and some one-acts, of which *The Black Horse* and *Ancestors* are the best. He tends to lapse into bookish dialogue, so that his plays are readable rather than actable.

A.H. Adams was a determined professional, and published three plays in one volume, as well as one-acts in periodicals. He ranges from farcical political comedy in *Mrs Pretty and the Premier* which was running in London in 1916, to Ibsen-like probing into social and psychological matters, in *The Wasters* (1910). He makes no experiments outside the realistic well-made play, and breaks down on construction, so that the plays lack unity; his social probing sounds a shade derivative; but he was actually a serious professional playwright, and has left us some sort of dramatic picture of what one could call middle- or merchant-class Sydney in 1910.

An abortive movement that might have had interesting results is represented by *Venus and the Wowser* by Bernard Ingleby, published in 1910 in a volume illustrated by McCrae. It is fantasy: Venus visits a town dominated by a Methodist clergyman, and the situation is worked out in a Rabelaisian spirit.

But with the First World War, and the films, came popular patriotism of the narrowest kind, and in 1916 it was possible for a line to be written in a play, to be spoken by a dying German to the Hero – English of course – who has unmasked him –

> If I were not a German, I should like to have been an
> Englishman.

Esson and Palmer could not gather enough strength to make head against the combined effects of the film industry and local apathy. The Pioneers' abortive theatre marks the end of a stage not of development but of failure to develop. From the thirties on, things are a little better.

Bridging the gap are the one-acts, of which some collections were published from 1931 on, and of which the best single writer is Sydney Tomholt, who put out a volume of his own, *Bleak Dawn, and other plays* (1936). He takes his subjects from anywhere in the world, caring only that the situations provide the intensity needed for dramatic tension; and *Anoli the Blind* is a hair-raising piece of atmospherics arising from a version of the eternal triangle. Tomholt has something broader, more cosmopolitan about him than most of his contemporaries in the field.

SINCE 1930

The two factors that have contributed most to the development of our drama are the Little Theatre movement and play competitions; the Elizabethan Theatre Trust [1] has contributed chiefly by way of these two.

The Little Theatre movement began as early as 1908, when groups of people in Adelaide, Melbourne, and Sydney organized amateur production of the kind of plays they wanted to see, which the professional theatre was not showing. These groups, which concentrated on production of Ibsen, Shaw, Yeats, classics and contemporary European, also did some locally-written plays. They were generally called Repertory theatres, but were not professional like English Repertory, while at the same time they had a higher standard of acting and production than English amateur. Such theatres have worked on a subscribing membership basis, and most of the work has been voluntary, spare-time work, often very devoted and strenuous. With many fluctuations and failures, the movement has grown in strength, especially since 1930, till today every town of a few thousand people has one amateur theatre and all the capitals have a number, some in the city proper, some in the suburbs, where they are fed by a local population. Modification of the amateur status has occurred, for instance in the Union Theatre in Melbourne, where students of the University use the theatre, which has a salaried permanent staff, for some months, and for the rest of the year a professional company perform there, touring when the students take over.

The Little Theatres keep audiences interested in the live theatre and aware of current developments in it. Thus, when an Australian play is done, there are audiences to see it. They make some attempt, sporadic in most cases, continuous in a few, to find new Australian scripts and produce them. For a while, in the thirties and forties, they conducted competitions that un-earthed some latent talent; lately, since the Elizabethan Theatre Trust took over the competitions, with bigger prizes offered, the Little Theatres have concentrated on competitions for one-acts. They are still the best hope a local writer has of gaining experience and of having his play staged. They train actors and theatrical personnel, including audiences. From 1908 to 1955 they provided almost the only opportunity for Australian audiences to see new plays, English, American, and European, and thus they alone made possible the appreciative reception accorded *The Summer of the Seventeenth Doll* (1955) and *The Ham Funeral* (1961).

The influence of play competitions is hardly separable from that of the Little Theatres. Out of them, the Playwrights' Advisory Board emerged, a voluntary group headed by Leslie Rees of the Australian Broadcasting Commission drama department, or-ganized to read and criticize play-scripts and sometimes send them to Little Theatres, recommending their production. The Board also organized and judged entries in competitions which it ran, and for which it persuaded big businesses to give prizes. Along with their work goes that of the Australian branch of the British Drama League, whose director, Miss E. Tyldesley (who probably knows more about the theatre in Australia today, its organization and its people, than any other one person), started festivals, began a lending library that includes Australian scripts, and persuaded publishers to put out collections of one-acts and separate long plays. When the Trust began looking for a new Australian play, they tried out a competition-winner, found by the Playwrights' Advisory Board and discovered *The Doll*. Other plays have since been discovered through competitions run by the Trust itself, by the Journalists' Club, and by J.C. Williamson Ltd, and most of these have been judged by Playwrights' Advisory Board personnel. [2]

The competitions of the thirties and forties brought likely writers out of the ruck and gave them some chance to see their plays staged, and sometimes published. Moreover, the criticisms, published or made available to individual competitors, lifted the standard of writing. Mere technical skill does not of course make a good play, but some measure of craft is essential – techniques of exposition, story-telling by dialogue, creating atmosphere, building for climax, conveying and resolving conflict. This had been lacking, and did develop, in the work of writers who began in the thirties and forties and continued to write for the competitions.

Competitions had a less happy effect on the choice of material because conditions of entry generally asked for a theme of national significance or something of the kind, and so historical plays proliferated. There were many on such colourful characters as Bligh, and episodes involving rebellion against tyranny, like the Eureka story; there were plays on more peaceful patriotism like Caroline Chisholm's work with migrant women or Deakin's for Federation. Almost all these plays have enormous casts, a large number of scenes, and change of costume, and are so broken into separate scenes that they lack unity and seem 'bitty'; often they try to use the speech of the period represented, which becomes merely quaint. Many of them have therefore never been put on the stage at all, but most have been adapted for radio production.

The quest for 'typical' Australian material did no worse damage than the ballad craze and the Jindyworobak craze did for poetry. It produced a spate of one-acts dealing with the hardships of pioneering, convict days, loneliness of bush life, and attitudes to World War I and to Anzac Day. Our drama is still being influenced by a reaction against these themes. There were long plays on similar subjects, especially the family play showing three generations settling on the land. Perhaps it was necessary that playwrights should wrestle with this sort of material before they could take their environment for granted and let their characters speak of Toorak or Surrey Hills, the Reef or the Centre, as unselfconsciously as Rattigan would name a London suburb. At all events, it suddenly passed. The contemporary playwright feels no need to set about deliberately evoking the feel of a local setting; he knows it will come through the speech and behaviour he presents, and can let it take care of itself. The best of our contemporary playwrights have become very competent at this. J. P. McKinney does it supremely in *The Well* (1959), where slow-thinking characters punctuate the intolerable leisureliness of their half-communication, with pauses and interrogative repetitions –

Down the well?
Down the well?

The well!
Through the fence and down the well!
You see 'er go down?
No.
How'd yer know?
Seen 'er.
You just said yer never.
Seen 'er down the well.
Funny, to me.

OUR PLAYWRIGHTS NOW

We have never had a school of playwrights. The good plays have been isolated plays by isolated writers. The playwrights are not and never have been a pack, and I suspect that a pack is desirable. Of the writers who have emerged in the last twenty years and are writing with vigour, some live mainly in one city or another – Seymour, Beynon, Hepworth, Collinson, Oriel Gray, Ireland, White, Throssell; some abroad at least part of the time – Catherine Duncan, Dymphna Cusack, Henrietta Drake-Brockman, Lawler, Mathew, Porter; some in the bush or in the small towns – Dann, McKinney. Some are attached to a theatrical organization, some though polite about the Little Theatre do not trust it or have not found it useful. There is endless argument about the desirability of the playwright's soaking himself in a practical knowledge of theatre and of acting and production techniques. Ireland and McKinney are two playwrights who, though they see very few plays, write their own with great detail regarding settings and business; and this detail, while it may have to be modified for a particular theatre, works in principle and can often be followed almost slavishly; it is always relevant to the total interpretation of the play, and imaginatively suggestive to producer and actor.

There are a number of veterans in the field who deserve each a paragraph, if one had space, though they have not yet achieved plays one feels will be in the permanent repertory. George Dann has handled many subjects – the loneliness of life on a small island on the Queensland coast, in *In Beauty it is Finished* (1931), white townspeople's treatment of aborigines, in *Fountains Beyond* (1944), small town comedy, in *Ring out Wild Bells* (1959) and in *Resurrection at Matthewtown* (1958), history in *Caroline Chisholm*

(1943), tragedy in a radio play, *The Orange Grove* (1957). Honesty of purpose and a direct, clear style are always evident, and the most recent play shows great advances in command of the authentic speech Lawler popularized. Oriel Gray has won competitions, but never had the first-class production to make the most of her work – problem plays, like the early *Had we but World Enough* and *Burst of Summer* (1959), both of which study relationships of aborigines and whites; *Lawson*, built round the short stories and the life of Henry Lawson, the most often performed; *The King who Wouldn't*, a witty political satire; *The Torrents* (1955), a period play.

Less orthodox and more experimental, Ric Throssell exemplifies the all-round theatre-man – actor, producer, writer – and most of his plays have been performed at least in his own stamping-ground of Canberra Repertory. *Devil wear Black* (1945) is an amusing satire on dress-selling; *The Day before Tomorrow* (1958) a terrifying anti-bomb play; *Doctor Homer* (1962) a departure from the realistic and well-made style, an extravaganza that has room for song, dance, mime, verse, audience within the audience, and any other technique you can mention, adding up to a crazy morality play, thoroughly theatrical, a sort of satire on advertisement propaganda, clichés, and unacknowledged brain-washing generally. In his earlier plays there has been a weakness, a tendency to use stock rather than freshly-conceived characters; here the stock characters are appropriate since it is a morality play; and the whole thing is full of vitality, rich in comedy.

Henrietta Drake-Brockman and Dymphna Cusack are among a number of professional writers who have published volumes of plays, but do not devote their most serious efforts to this form, finding that novels or short stories give more certain return. Their work is rather slick than penetrating or in any way adventurous.

Others have used verse, suggesting that they took the playwright's job very seriously indeed. Among earlier writing, Hugh McCrae's *The Ship of Heaven* (published 1951) was satire; Jack Lindsay's myths and legends, as in *Helen Comes of Age* and *Hereward* (1929) were erotic nonsense; more recently J.J. Bray and C.R. Jury have been witty, learned, and a shade unpractical in their demands on number of cast, variety of scene, and length of speech, in verse-plays based on history and myths; though

Jury's satires on university and public life, in the posthumously published *The Administrator* and *The Sun in Servitude* (1961), are fully theatrical. Catherine Duncan's *Sons of the Morning* (1946) uses verse in several colloquial yet dignified idioms in her picture of Australian soldiers and Cretans at the time of the evacuation from Crete in the last major war. But of course the best verse plays have been written by Douglas Stewart.

He is also our best radio playwright, and his first success was with a radio play, *Fire on the Snow* (1943), a study in atmosphere and mood rather than conflict, but gripping because of its heroic theme and the poetry of its treatment. *The Golden Lover* (1944) uses poetry, happily, for a comedy based on a favourite theme of Stewart, the conflict of the law-abiding and the adventurous spirit, a theme he handles with tragic conclusion in his two stage plays, *Ned Kelly* (1943) and *Shipwreck* (1947). Stewart's credo, that the artist provides the myths by which the people live, led him to seek out the hero-figure, good and bad, in conflict with society. He gives a poet's liveliness of expression to his characters, and any one speech is good to say and to listen to – colloquial, colourful, with images that catch and cling –

We're four dead trees in a sunset.

He manages the pace of the verse to correspond with mood and with interplay of character. He rises to the occasion when a character has his moment of revelation, as with Sebastian, redeemed by his killing of his soul's enemy –

I am a thing of shame. But so sweet a peace –.

But the two stage plays are flawed because the talk eddies instead of moving into action. When these plays are cut for radio they play better.

Others who have done well in radio and sometimes also in television are Rex Rienits, Musette Morell, Max Afford, Gwen Meredith, Betty Roland – author also of one good stage play of the thirties, *The Touch of Silk* (1942) – and Alexander Turner, whose *Royal Mail* (1944) is a stage play which wonderfully conveys the atmosphere of the West Australian goldfields. It becomes impossible to draw the line between plays and features, and one has then to include some of the work of John Thompson and Ivan Smith, such as the sensitive presentation of Bill Harney, and of the Ern Malley story, and *Death of a Wombat*. Sumner Locke-

Elliot is another radio-writer (now writing for television in U.S.A.) who had one notable stage success, *Rusty Bugles* (1948), which had the luck to be banned for bad language, and filled the theatres thereafter. It was the best realistic play to date.

But the realistic play came of age in Australia with the success of Ray Lawler's *The Summer of the Seventeenth Doll* in 1956. It brought us closer to having a school of playwrights than we ever came before, because writers were encouraged to work in its kind, the well-made, realistic play. *The Doll* presented attractively, in an engaging story full of humour, unexpected turns and twists, violence, pathos, and wry wisdom, the speech of casual-speaking Australians, in such a way that this speech seemed authentic, picturesque, and vital. Lawler taught the contemporary playwright how to write this speech, and that lesson has never to be re-learned. Any playwright of any ability can now use it, and the influence of what Lawler taught is to be seen in the convincing quality of the uneducated speech in all the realistic plays we have had since. The playwrights may not consciously be imitating Lawler. Characters in *The Shifting Heart* (1957) and *The One Day of the Year* (1960) have their own individuality and this includes speech habits. But certain points were learned; how to leave out words, as in

Got no use for anyone can't pull their weight;

how to include and not stress 'language', and the women's mechanical reproaches for it; how to reproduce with interest the repetitions with which we lard our speech when we are not speaking deliberately.

Plays in this tradition have varied in setting, subject, and kind – comedy, satire, tragedy, or blend of any of these. Generally they are hard to classify. They leave a question-mark, a problem not completely solved, an ending neither conventionally happy nor tragic. The characters are picking up the pieces, giving it another go, not taking themselves over-seriously. The settings range from city slums, as in *The Doll*, *The Shifting Heart* (1957) by Beynon, *The One Day of the Year* (1960), by Seymour, to the bush, as in Coburn's *Fire on the Wind* (1958): from well-to-do city dwellings, as in *The Multi-Coloured Umbrella* (1958), to a small-town café, as in Oriel Gray's *Burst of Summer* (1959). Others are set in the homes of orchardists, or in seaside dwellings, where land agents are buying up the small holdings to sell for quick profits. Others are set in ghost towns, or country pubs, or hospitals, or suburban backyards.

Cultivated people sometimes complain that the realistic plays present only the speech of the uncultivated Australian, and while it is not quite true it is near the truth and it is very natural that this should be so. It is easier for the playwright to avoid sounding derivative – as if he is imitating some English or American writer – if he portrays characters whose speech he must find by listening, because it is not his own; that is, if he portrays uncultivated characters, like those he meets and hears in the environment of his play, known and familiar to him, but not to be found in the plays of English and American playwrights. In this way he gains the freshness, the vitality he needs. All too soon it will become easy for the speech idiom founded (or found) by Lawler and re-produced with modifications by all the realistic playwrights to become itself hackneyed and derivative. This will happen when writers take it from books and plays, not from live speech which is always changing, just as there developed a stock stage Irish, Scottish, cockney, and American speech, in poor English plays.

THE OTHER PLAYWRIGHTS

This brings us to writers whose work does not fall into the category of the well-made play – White, Mathew, Collinson, Ireland, McNamara, McKinney, Hepworth. All are reaching for language and a technique of presentation that demand more than realism. They present their figures, scenes, and situations with the touch of exaggeration and of poetry that makes them sometimes grotesques and sometimes symbols. They experiment in form and language, are sophisticated in outlook, and are in line rather with recent European drama down from Pirandello than with the American realistic or brittle-sophisticated. Since some of their work is earlier than the date of the staging of Brecht, Beckett, Ionesco, and Pinter in this country, we must see them as influenced by the Zeitgeist rather than by the work of these.

Patrick White's play, *The Ham Funeral*, written fourteen years before its first production in 1961, is impressive in technique and in the sense of controlled power that informs it. It makes original use of a multiple set, which is here not merely a device to provide five playing areas – basement, stairs, two bed-rooms, landing, and street – but a means of using these areas, with the people in them, to create the world of the play. Triggered off by the first contact the young poet makes with the reality that is the landlord, the action moves the poet and the audience from one attack to another on his fastidious revulsion from human experience; and it is the places, with the people who are inevitably in them, that launch the attack.

Thus White is here in a sense a 'morality' playwright for whom his characters are types of humanity anywhere, like Beckett's. But his second play, *The Season at Sarsaparilla*, is localized in a suburban backyard setting, and local atmosphere is created. There is still originality in treatment, particularly in the counterpointing of situations and relationships in the various family groups whose home life we see from the back doors. White has a gift for comedy, ranging from the macabre to the plain or symbolically bawdy, that enables him to fuse passion and suffering, the idealistic and the earthy, with high-spirited theatricality, as with the relatives and Alma Lusty in *The Ham Funeral*. All the writers in this sec-tion possess this gift in some degree, which is why we may anti-cipate that from them will come the flood of good plays we are needing.

But most of them have so far been little produced. It is too soon to speak of their work in detail. Their strength is their vitality, their strong sense of the theatre, their knowledge that the business of the theatre is entertainment, their willingness to pro-vide pictures larger than life. There are the fights that flare up and subside in Ireland's *Image in the Clay*, the physical contrasts of the healthy and the crippled in his *The Virgin of Treadmill Street*; McNamara's *A Man is a Mountain* mixes impassioned bitterness with gay fantasy and with bawdy comedy; Collinson invites us, in a serious drama, *The Zelda Trio*, and a school farce, *The Syllabus of Love*, to a willing suspension of disbelief so that we may look with astonishment at the mad world of our own per-sonalities; McKinney laughs at and with the simplicities of his bush folk in *The Well*; Hepworth combines song and dance with one catastrophic action to produce the intense compassion of his plays about misfits, *The Beast in View* and *The Last of the Rainbow*.

It is another matter with Ray Mathew, who, though he is still better known as poet and short story-writer, has been writing plays steadily since 1950, beginning with one-acts and then writing at least four full-length plays, apart from radio adaptations and so forth. Each is a distinct kind of play, with different experiments in technique and with different raw material. *A Spring Song* handles the loneliness of bush life and the conflicting claims of personal and family feeling, in six scenes of sun and cloud from a quiet homestead. *We Find the Bunyip* is almost totally a study in atmospherics and character contrasts, with little plot in the ordinary sense; the setting is a bush pub on a hot Saturday night, but this time the tug-of-war is between acceptance and denial of life. *Sing for St Ned* is a play on the Kelly myth; it uses the Brechtian trick of breaking illusion by letting characters talk to each other and to the audience about the characters they are acting and the nature of the Kelly myth; the audience are invited to join in and sing with the characters, who line up for 'The Wild Colonial Boy', restoring gaiety after a moving scene in which a human Kelly is allowed to emerge from the overall cynicism: the play has been done by amateurs, and even so goes well. *The Life of the Party*, which should have been produced first in Sydney, by actors who knew the locale, had a disastrous first production in London in 1961. Set in two flats in King's Cross, it involves a bohemian group of young and middle-aged people, and its conflict is that of domesticity versus the freedom of the male. But this over-simplifies: the frustration and futility of modern living, the essential loneliness of the human condition – a factor in all Mathew's work – the failure of love, and the despair that can lead to suicide, all find expression through the interactions of characters who are intelligent, articulate, and both stagey and charming. For all that it involves deaths, the play is a comedy in the handling, with action that could be tragic coming out as a part of life that must be endured and forgiven: what breaks into pieces must be mended with tears but also with wry laughter. Mathew's command of characterful speech makes the play grip. Properly presented, this sophisticated play, and *We Find the Bunyip* could already have established Mathew as a leading playwright in Australia.

Many people think that the time is past for distinct categories such as English, American, Canadian, and so forth applied to literature. But the country of origin has much to do with the quality of drama. Certainly ours has developed first with writers

who worked from particular places, finding their characters in a
suburb of Melbourne or a part of the bush that they knew, not in
'any suburb in any city' or in something vaguely described as
'the bush'. From precise local definition came authentic speech
and behaviour, learned from observation of life, and not from
imitation of other plays. *The Ham Funeral* may be urged as an
example of a successful play set in a locality not defined, but it is
in an unusual category, that of the modern morality, where
characters are types and symbols more significant than purely
local characters would be. Not many writers have the intellectual
and creative capacity to work well in this medium: generally
attempts to do it produce not the vital landlady and relatives, but
a whole set of characters paler than the pale girl upstairs in
White's play, the least satisfactory character. White himself
moved to the precisely-defined setting in his second play.

Again, recent criticism sees in our latest-produced plays an
abandoning of the tough Australian as protagonist, in favour of a
more subtle and sensitive type: Lawler moves from his cane-
cutters of *The Doll* to writer and actors, in *Piccadilly Bushman*
(1959). Seymour's *The One Day of the Year* sets the educated,
sensitive son against the uneducated, rather stupid father. But
this is not as new as it looks. Back in the thirties there was literary,
non-theatrical drama written by such idealists as Dulcie Deamer,
that was full of frustrated sensitive plants. Much more impor-
tantly, there have been plays since the early fifties – plays which
mainly did not find production – in which there was no question
of the tough Australian appearing as anything but a foil for more
subtle characters. Tony, the school-teacher in Mathew's *Bunyip*,
stands aside to make his wry though affectionate comment on the
commonplace types in the pub. *The Ham Funeral* was written
earlier still. We have simply been slow to discover and put on
these plays.

*

I wrote earlier of two helpful factors in the development of our
drama.

Two hampering factors have been the spread of a small population over a large area, and the 'establishment'. The spread of
population we cannot help, and anyway there is greater concen-

tration now. By 'establishment' in this connection I mean the professional theatrical world, the managers who decide what plays and films we shall see, the controllers of radio and television as mediums of drama, the controllers of publicity and criticism.

Let me add quickly that the Trust found and produced the work of Lawler and Seymour; that J.C. Williamson Ltd did *Rusty Bugles* and *The Multi-Coloured Umbrella*; that some actors do *not* treat acting in a new Australian play as theatrical slumming; that Leslie Rees and the Australian Broadcasting Commission have produced a large number of Australian plays, and that they found Douglas Stewart as a radio-playwright; that some newspaper critics treat Australian plays detachedly, as they treat others. But it is still true that actors do not jump at the chance to create, by playing a new role in a play by a countryman; that the professional theatre headed by J.C. Williamson Ltd has effectively repressed local playwrights from A.H. Adams on; and that the endeavours of the Trust to date have been chancy and unconvincing – at N.I.D.A.,[3] for instance, a list of plays produced by students over two years contains no Australian work at all, which means that actors are being trained only in work that requires anything but Australian speech and behaviour.

Moreover audiences, which constitute a big factor in the establishment, are conditioned by press, radio, and TV to an attitude that works gainst the development of an original local drama. They are easily 'shocked' by settings, behaviour, or language to which they can apply the vague epithets of 'sordid', 'crude', 'disgusting'. They tolerate such material from foreigners, but are uncomfortable if it comes near home. They want to believe 'we are not like that'. The poet and the fiction-writer have long been able to ignore such criticism, and the playwright must ignore it if he is to write what he wants.

Obviously, his business is to make his audiences think about something else. He must make his play so good, so entertaining with its characters and situations and talk, that the audience forget who wrote it. This may not sound idealistic; but the best example is White's relatives scenes in *The Ham Funeral*: to be entertaining, the playwright does not need to lower his flag; he needs only to be very good at fighting under it.

*

Where possible, dates of first production are given with the first mention of a play. Dates of publication are given in the appendix, when publication has taken place. Date of publication is often a long time after writing and first production. Date of writing is necessarily vague, because most playwrights rewrite, wholly or in part, before or after production. Few playwrights can tell one exactly when they first, or finally, wrote a play.

Many of my references are to plays that exist in MS. only. When these are earlier than 1930, they are mostly available in the Mitchell Library. Recent references are to scripts held now in the Fryer Memorial Library at the University of Queensland, by courtesy of the authors. The plays referred to have generally been produced or at least had a rehearsed reading.

I am indebted to Morris Miller's bibliography of drama, to Leslie Rees's book, *Towards an Australian Drama*, and to the courtesy of Mr Campbell Howard, of the New South Wales Adult Education Department, who made his collection of scripts available to me.

NOTES

1. *The Australian Elizabethan Theatre Trust* (*The Trust*, for short) founded in 1955, is supported by government funds and membership subscription. It runs seasons of opera, ballet, and drama in the capitals, and sometimes tours these. Its headquarters are in Sydney, where it owns a theatre, and it supports or half-supports professional or semi-professional theatres in Melbourne and Armidale, as well as Sydney.

2. *J. C. Williamson Ltd* (*J.C.W.* or *The Firm*, for short) is the major and almost the only commercial organization with a chain of theatres in the capitals and a permanent flow of entertainments through these. Thanks to its monopoly, it has effectively dictated the theatrical fare of the Australian people for about sixty years.

3. *N.I.D.A.* stands for *National Institute of Dramatic Art*, and it is one of the major responsibilities of the Trust. It is run at and in conjunction with the University of New South Wales. It provides a two-year course, leading to a diploma, in acting, theatre-techniques, and the history and literature of drama.

PART
III

APPENDIX

COMPILED BY L.T. HERGENHAN

FOR FURTHER READING AND REFERENCE

LIST OF ABBREVIATIONS

A.B.C.	Australian Broadcasting Commission		source are reprints of C.L.F. lectures).
A.I.F.	Australian Imperial Forces	d.	died
		ed.	edited, edition
A.N.U.	Australian National University	*J.R.A.H.S.*	*Royal Australian Historical Society: Journal and Proceedings*
b.	born		
C. OF E.	Church of England		
C.L.F.	Commonwealth Literary Fund	m.	married
Cmwlth.	Commonwealth	R.A.A.F.	Royal Australian Air Force
C.U.C.	Canberra University College, now A.N.U. (Publications from this	sel.	selected, selection
		vol.	volume
		yrs.	years

INTRODUCTION

THE following bibliography is a selective one designed as an introductory guide, and as a ready source of reference for general readers and students. The aim has been to represent as many important authors as possible, but some emerging writers with few book-publications to date could not be included. The Appendix follows the general pattern established by existing *Pelican Guides*; but it departs from them in that it gives a fuller coverage both to authors' works and commentaries on them. This policy was followed because the fullest literary bibliography by E. Morris Miller (1940) is out of print, and because Miller's work and its continuation to 1950 by Frederick T. Macartney necessarily give little representation to some notable contemporary authors, or to the growing body of commentaries published since. Wherever possible, an author's complete works, and most of the recent commentaries on him, have been included. But the bibliography of such a voluminous and much-discussed author as Henry Lawson must perforce be more selective than that of an important contemporary writer such as Patrick White. So far as commentaries are concerned, reviews and short pieces are generally not represented, and the emphasis has been placed on the work produced during the last thirty years or so, because it is more readily obtainable, and of greater interest to the general reader and student, than earlier criticism. Biographical notes have been kept as brief as possible. Collections of essays, and books of a general nature, such as Green's *History*, are usually listed only under *General Studies*, and are not repeated in the lists of commentaries in *Authors and Their Works* except in special cases. In the section on *The Social and Intellectual Setting* preference has been given to more recent and easily available works. Usually the date of first edition only is given for books.

Acknowledgements are due to the bibliography of E. Morris Miller; to its continuation extended to 1950 and edited by Frederick T. Macartney; to the notes in the *Penguin Book of Modern Australian Verse* (ed. John Thompson, Kenneth Slessor, and R. G. Howarth, London, 1961), to the Mitchell Library's *Index to Periodicals* (1944-), to the suggestions of contributors to this present book, and to Michael Roe, Walter Stone, and Pamela Coates.

L. T. HERGENHAN

FOR FURTHER READING AND REFERENCE

The Social and Intellectual Setting

GENERAL HISTORIES

Abbott, C.L.A. *Australia's Frontier Province* (Sydney, 1950)

Australian Encyclopaedia (10 vols., Sydney, 1958)

Barnard, A. (ed.) *The Simple Fleece: Studies in the Australian Wool Industry* (Melbourne, 1962)

Barnard, Marjorie *A History of Australia* (Sydney, 1962)

Berndt, R.M. and C.H. *The First Australians* (Sydney, 1952)

Borrie, W.D. *Italians and Germans in Australia* (Melbourne, 1954)

Butlin, N.G. *Australian Domestic Product, Investment, and Foreign Borrowing 1861-1938/9*, (Cambridge, 1962)

Cambridge History of the British Empire Vol. VII, Pt. I, *Australia* (Cambridge, 1933)

Cilento, R.W. and Lack, Clem *Triumph in the Tropics: an Historical Sketch of Queensland* (Brisbane, 1959)

Clark, C.M.H. *The History of Australia* Vol. I. (Melbourne, 1962)

Clark, C.M.H. (ed.) *Select Documents in Australian History, 1788-1900* (2 vols., Sydney, 1950-5)

Crawford, R.M. *Australia* (London, 1952)

Crisp, L.F. *The Parliamentary Government of the Commonwealth of Australia* (Melbourne, 1949)

Crowley, F.K. *Australia's Western Third: A History of Western Australia from the First Settlement to Modern Times* (London, 1960)

Davies, A.F. *Australian Democracy* (London, 1958)

Davis, S.R. (ed.) *The Australian Political Party System* (Sydney, 1954)

Davis, S.R. (ed.) *The Government of the Australian States* (London, 1960)

Elkin, A.P. *The Australian Aborigines* (Sydney, 1938)

Favenc, E. *The History of Australian Exploration from 1788 to 1888* (Sydney, 1888)

Fitzpatrick, B.C. *British Imperialism and Australia 1783-1833* (London, 1939)

Fitzpatrick, B.C. *The British Empire in Australia: An Economic History 1834-1839* (Melbourne, 1941)

Fitzpatrick, K. (ed.) *Australian Explorers* (Oxford, 1958)

Grattan, C. Hartley (ed.) *Introducing Australia* (New York, 1942)

Greenwood, G. (ed.) *Australia: A Social and Political History* (Sydney, 1955)

Hancock, W.K. *Australia* (London, 1930)

Legge, J.D. *Australian Colonial Policy* (Sydney, 1956)

Madigan, C.T. *Central Australia* (London, 1936)

Mair, L.P. *Australia in New Guinea* (London, 1948)

Miller, J.D.B. *Australian Government and Politics* (London, 1954)

Murtagh, J.G. *Australia: The Catholic Chapter* (New York, 1946)

O'Brien, E.M. *The Foundation of Australia* (London, 1937)

Pike, D.H. *Australia: The Quiet Continent* (Cambridge, 1962)

Pike, D.H. *Paradise of Dissent: South Australia, 1829-1857* (London, 1957)

Roberts, S.H. *History of Australian Land Settlement (1788-1920)* (Melbourne, 1924)

Serle, P. *Dictionary of Australian Biography* (2 vols., Sydney, 1949)

Shann, E.O.G. *An Economic History of Australia* (Cambridge, 1930)

Shaw, A.G.L. *The Story of Australia* (London, 1955)

Spann, R.N. (ed.) *Public Administration in Australia* (Sydney, 1959)

Taylor, T.G. *Australia: A Study of Warm Environments and Their Effect on British Settlement* (London, 1940)

Wadham, S.M., Wilson, R.K. and Wood, J. *Land Utilization in Australia* (Melbourne, 1957)

West, J. *The History of Tasmania* (2 vols., Launceston, 1852)

Wood, G.L. (ed.) *Australia: Its Resources and Development* (New York, 1947)

THE SOCIAL BACKGROUND AND CONTEMPORARY SCENE

Adams, F.W.L. *The Australians: A Social Sketch* (London, 1893)

Allen, H.C. *Bush and Backwoods: A Comparison of the Frontier in Australia and the United States* (Michigan, 1959)

Aughterson, W. V. *Taking Stock: Aspects of Mid-Century Life in Australia* (Melbourne, 1953)

Bean, C.E.W. *On the Wool Track* (London, 1910; revised 1913)

Birch, A. and MacMillan, D. S. *The Sydney Scene 1788-1960* (Melbourne, 1962)

Blainey, G. *The Peaks of Lyell* (Melbourne, 1954)

Blainey, G. *Mines in the Spinifex: The Story of Mount Isa Mines* (Sydney, 1960)

Caiger, G. (ed.) *The Australian Way of Life* (Melbourne, 1953)

Childe, V.G. *How Labour Governs* (London, 1923)

Clune, F. *Wild Colonial Boys* (Sydney, 1948)

Clune, F. *Scandals of Sydney Town* (Sydney, 1957)

'Culotta, Nino' (John O'Grady) *They're a Weird Mob* [novel] (Sydney, 1957)

Fitzpatrick, B.C. *The Australian Commonwealth: A Picture of the Community, 1901-1955* (Melbourne, 1956)

Fitzpatrick, B.C. *A Short History of the Australian Labour Movement* (Melbourne, 1940)

Froude, J.A. *Oceana, or England and Her Colonies* (London, 1886)

Gollan, R.A. *Radical and Working Class Politics: A Study of Eastern Australia, 1850-1910* (Melbourne, 1960)

Grant, J.A. and Serle, G. *The Melbourne Scene, 1803-1956* (Melbourne, 1957)

Greenwood, G. and Laverty, J. *Brisbane 1859-1959: A History of Local Government* (Brisbane, 1959)

Hardy, F.J. *Power Without Glory* [novel] (Melbourne, 1950)

Hogan, J.F. *The Irish in Australia* (London, 1887)

Kiddle, M. *Caroline Chisholm* (Melbourne, 1950)

Kiddle, M. *Men of Yesterday: A Social History of the Western District of Victoria, 1834-1890* (Melbourne, 1961)

Lawrence, D.H. *Kangaroo* [novel] (London, 1923)

McIntyre, A.J. and J.J. *Country Towns of Victoria: A Social Survey* (Melbourne, 1944)

Mackenzie, J. *Australian Paradox* (Melbourne, 1961)

Mackenzie, N. *Women in Australia* (Melbourne, 1962)

Martineau, J. *Letters from Australia* (London, 1869)

Meggitt, M.J. *Desert People* (Sydney, 1962)

Moorehead, A.M. *Gallipoli* (London, 1956)

Pearl, Cyril *Wild Men of Sydney* (London, 1958)

Pringle, J.D. *Australian Accent* (London, 1958)

Scott, E. *Australia During the War*, vol. XI of *The Official History of Australia in the War of 1914-1918*, (ed.), C.E.W. Bean (12 vols., Sydney, 1921-42, and later editions)

Spence, W.G. *Australia's Awakening: Thirty Years in the Life of an Australian Agitator* (Sydney, 1909)

Tew, M. *Work and Welfare in Australia* (Melbourne, 1951)

Trollope, A. *Australia and New Zealand* (London, 1873)

Twain, M. *More Tramps Abroad* (London, 1897)

Twopenny, R.E.N. *Town Life in Australia* (London, 1883)

Ward, R.B. *The Australian Legend* (London, 1958)

THE CULTURAL BACKGROUND AND CONTEMPORARY SCENE

Anderson, Hugh *The Colonial Minstrel* (Melbourne, 1960)

Austin, A.G. *Australian Education 1788-1900* (Melbourne, 1961)

Badham, H.E. *A Study of Australian Art* (Sydney, 1949)

Blainey, G. *The University of Melbourne: A Centenary Portrait* (Melbourne, 1956)

Boyd, Robin *Australia's Home, Its Origins, Builders, and Occupiers* (Melbourne, 1952)

Boyd, Robin *The Australian Ugliness* (Melbourne, 1960; Penguin 1963)

Clark, Kenneth, MacInnes, Colin, and Robertson, Bryan *Sidney Nolan* (London, 1961)

Coleman, Peter *Obscenity, Blasphemy, Sedition – Censorship in Australia* (Brisbane, 1962)

Coleman, Peter (ed.) *Australian Civilization: A Symposium* (Melbourne, 1962)

Ellis, M.H. *Francis Greenway: His Life and Times* (Sydney, 1949)

Fogarty, R.N. *Catholic Education in Australia 1806-1950* (Melbourne, 1959)

Herman, M.E. *The Early Australian Architects and Their Work* (Sydney, 1954)

Holden, W.S. *Australia Goes to Press* (Melbourne, 1961)

Kardoss, J. *A Brief History of the Australian Theatre* (Sydney, 1955)

La Nauze, J.A. *Political Economy in Australia* (Melbourne, 1949)

Leonard French, The Campion Paintings, introduction by Vincent Buckley (Melbourne, 1962)

Mackerras, C. *The Hebrew Melodist* (Sydney, 1963)

McLeod, A. (ed.) *The Patterns of Australian Culture* (London, 1963)

Mayer, H. (ed.) *Catholics and the Free Society: An Australian Symposium* (Melbourne, 1961)

Moore, William *Story of Australian Art* (2 vols. Sydney, 1934)

Nadel, G. H. *Australia's Colonial Culture* (Melbourne, 1957)

Orchard, W. A. *Music in Australia* (Melbourne, 1952)

Paintings of Tom Roberts, with introduction and commentaries by Robert Campbell (Adelaide, 1962)

Palmer, V. *The Legend of the Nineties* (Melbourne, 1954)

Price, A. G. (ed.) *The Humanities in Australia* (Sydney, 1959)

Rienits, Rex and Thea *Early Artists of Australia* (Sydney, 1963)

Sharland, Michael *Stones of a Century* (Hobart, 1952)

Smith, Bernard W. *Australian Painting 1788-1960* (London, 1962)

Smith, Bernard W. *European Vision and the South Pacific 1768-1850* (Oxford, 1960)

Smith, Bernard W. *Place, Taste and Tradition: A Study of Australian Art Since 1788* (Sydney, 1945)

Smith, R. S. *John Lee Archer: Tasmanian Architect and Engineer* (Hobart, 1962)

Spate, Virginia *John Olsen* (Melbourne, 1963)

Stephensen, P. R. *Foundations of Culture in Australia* (Gordon, New South Wales, 1936)

Turnbull, Clive *Art Here* (Melbourne, 1947)

The Arts in Australia (Pamphlet Series), (Melbourne, 1962-)

BIOGRAPHIES, AUTOBIOGRAPHIES, LETTERS, MEMOIRS REMINISCENCES

Adams, D. (ed.) *The Letters of Rachel Henning* (Sydney, 1952 and 1963)

Barnard, A. *Visions and Profits, Studies in the Business Career of Thomas Sutcliffe Mort* (Melbourne, 1961)

Barnard, Marjorie *Macquarie's World* (Sydney, 1941)

Barry, J. V. W. *Alexander Maconochie of Norfolk Island* (Melbourne, 1958)

Barton, R. D. *Reminiscences of an Australian Pioneer* (Sydney, 1917)

Bassett, F. M. *The Hentys* (Melbourne, 1954)

Bates, D. *The Passing of the Aborigines* (London, 1938)

Bennett, M. M. *Christisen of Lammermoor* (London, 1927)

'Boldrewood, Rolf' (T.A. Browne) *Old Melbourne Memories* (Melbourne, 1884)

Bonwick, J. *An Octogenarian's Reminiscences* (London, 1902)

Bull, J.W. *Early Experiences of Life in South Australia and an Extended Colonial History* (Adelaide and London, 1884)

Carboni, R. *The Eureka Stockade* (Melbourne, 1855; 1947)

Chisholm, A.R. *Men Were My Milestones* (Melbourne, 1958)

Crisp, L.F. *Ben Chifley: A Biography* (Melbourne, 1961)

Croll, R.H. *I Recall: Collections and Recollections* (Melbourne, 1939)

Duffy, C.G. *My Life in Two Hemispheres* (2 vols., London, 1898)

Durack, M. *Kings in Grass Castles* (London, 1959)

Eggleston, F.W. *Reflections of an Australian Liberal* (Melbourne, 1953)

Ellis, M.H *John Macarthur* (Sydney, 1955)

Ellis, M.H *Lachlan Macquarie: His Life, Adventures, and Times* (Sydney, 1947)

Evatt, H.V. *Australian Labour Leader: The Story of W.A. Holman and the Labour Movement* (Sydney, 1940)

Fitzpatrick, K. E. *Sir John Franklin in Tasmania, 1837-43* (Melbourne, 1949)

Garran, R.R. *Prosper the Commonwealth* (Sydney, 1958)

Gilchrist, A. (ed.) *John Dunmore Lang, 1799-1878* (2 vols., Melbourne, 1951)

Hancock, W.K. *Country and Calling* (London, 1954)

Harney, W.E. *Life Among the Aborigines* (London, 1957)

Harris, Alexander *Settlers and Convicts* (Melbourne, 1953; first published London, 1847)

Hasluck, A. *Portrait with Background: A Life of Georgiana Molloy* (Melbourne, 1955)

Howitt, William *Land, Labour, and Gold in Victoria* (London, 1855)

James, G.F. (ed.) *A Homestead History* (Melbourne, 1942)

Lang, J.T. *I Remember* (Sydney, 1956)

Lang, J.T. *The Great Bust: The Depression of the Thirties* (Sydney, 1962)

Lindsay, Jack *Life Hardly Tells* (London, 1958)

Lindsay, Jack *The Roaring Twenties* (London, 1960)

Lindsay, Jack *Fanfrolico and After* (London, 1962)

Macalister, C. *Old Pioneering Days in the Sunny South* (Goulburn, 1907)

McCrae, Hugh *My Father and My Father's Friends* (Sydney, 1935; reprinted *Story-book Only*, 1948)

Maclaren, J. *My Crowded Solitude* (London, 1926)

Moll, E.G. *Below These Hills: the Story of a Riverina Farm* (Melbourne, 1957)

Murdoch, Walter *Alfred Deakin: A Sketch* (London, 1923)

Normington-Rawling, J. *Charles Harpur, An Australian* (Sydney, 1962)

Page, E. *Truant Surgeon* (Sydney, 1963)

Palmer, N. *Henry Bournes Higgins: A Memoir* (London, 1931)

Palmer, N. *Fourteen Years: Extracts from a Private Journal 1925-1939* (Melbourne, 1948)

Palmer, V. *National Portraits* (Sydney, 1940; enlarged Melbourne, 1954)

Parkes, H. *Fifty Years in the Making of Australian History* (2 vols., London, 1892)

Parkes, H. *An Emigrant's Home Letters* (Sydney, 1896)

Petrie, C.C. *Tom Petrie's Reminiscences of Early Queensland* (Brisbane, 1904)

Skemp, J.R. *Memories of Myrtle Bank* (Melbourne, 1952)

Sladen, Douglas *Twenty Years of My Life* (London, 1915)

Whyte, W.F. *William Morris Hughes: His Life and Times* (Sydney, 1957)

Wright, Judith *The Generations of Men* (Melbourne, 1959)

Young, G.F. *Under the Coolibah Tree* (London, 1953)

The Literature

BIBLIOGRAPHIES

Anderson, Hugh *A Guide to Ten Australian Poets* (Melbourne, 1953)

'Annual Bibliography', in *Publications of the Modern Language Association of America* (PMLA, Wisconsin, 1958-), [contains an Australian section of critical studies]

Australian Bibliography and Bibliographical Services (Canberra, 1960)

Australian Public Affairs Information Service (*A.P.A.I.S.*), 1945 – ('prepared as a guide to current literature on Australian cultural, economic, political, and social affairs'); published by Commonwealth National Library, Canberra

Australian National Bibliography, 1961-; previously *Annual Catalogue of Australian Publications* (1936-60); Commonwealth National Library, Canberra

Borchardt, D.H. *Australian Bibliography: A Guide to Printed Sources of Information* (Melbourne, 1963)

Ferguson, J.A. *Bibliography of Australia 1784-*, 4 vols., 1784-1850, and vol. V, 1851-1900, A-G (Sydney, 1941-)

Hornibrook, J. H. *Bibliography of Queensland Verse* (Brisbane, 1953)

Index to Periodicals, 1944-, published by Public Library of New South Wales

Miller, E. Morris *Australian Literature from Its Beginnings to 1935, a Descriptive and Bibliographical Survey, With Subsidiary entries to 1938* (2 vols., Melbourne, 1940)

Miller, E. Morris and Macartney, Frederick T. *Australian Literature: A Bibliography to 1938 by E. Morris Miller, Extended to 1950 and Edited With an Historical Outline and Descriptive Commentaries by Frederick T. Macartney* (Sydney, 1956)

Serle, Percival *Bibliography of Australasian Poetry and Verse* (Melbourne, 1925)

Stone, Walter, is editor of a series of *Studies in Australian Bibliography*, published Cremorne, New South Wales, 1954-; details of certain of these bibliographies may be found under entries for individual authors.

Tregenza, J.A. 'A Checklist of non-Commercial Literary Magazines published in Australia 1923-54', *Biblionews* (June 1959)

GENERAL STUDIES

Australian Drama and Theatre, Current Affairs Bulletin, 28 July 1958

Baker, Sidney J. *The Australian Language* (Sydney, 1945)

Baker, Sidney J. *Australia Speaks* (Sydney, 1953)

Baker, Sidney J. *The Drum: Australian Character and Slang* (Sydney, 1959)

Barton, G.B. *Literature in New South Wales* (Sydney, 1866)

Barton, G.B. (ed.) *The Poets and Prose Writers of New South Wales* (Sydney, 1866)

Brereton, J. Le Gay *Knocking Round* (Sydney, 1930)

Brown, Cyril *Writing for Australia* (Melbourne, 1956)

Buckley, Vincent *Essays in Poetry, Mainly Australian* (Melbourne, 1957)

Byrne, Desmond *Australian Writers* (London, 1896)

Coombes, A.J. *Some Australian Poets* (Sydney, 1938)

Cross, Zora *An Introduction to the Study of Australian Literature* (Sydney, 1922)

'Eldershaw, M. Barnard' *Essays in Australian Fiction* (Melbourne, 1938)

Elliott, Brian *Singing to the Cattle, and Other Australian Essays* (Melbourne, 1947)

Ewers, J.K. *Creative Writing in Australia: A Selective Survey* (Melbourne, 1945; revised 1962)

Grattan, C. Hartley *Australian Literature* (Seattle, 1929)

Green, H.M. *Outline of Australian Literature* (Sydney, 1930)

Green, H.M. *Fourteen Minutes* (Sydney, 1944)

Green, H.M. *A History of Australian Literature* (2 vols., Sydney, 1961)

Green, H.M. *Australian Literature 1900-1950* (Melbourne, 1951, 1963)

Greenop, Frank S. *History of Magazine Publishing in Australia* (Sydney, 1947)

Hadgraft, C.H. *Queensland and Its Writers* (Brisbane, 1959)

Hadgraft, C.H. *Australian Literature: A Critical Account to 1955* (London, 1960)

Heddle, Enid Moodie *Australian Literature Now, A Reader's Survey* (Melbourne, 1949)

Hetherington, John *Forty-two Faces* (Melbourne, 1962)

Hope, A.D. *Australian Literature 1950-1962* (Melbourne, 1963)

Howarth, R.G. *Notes on Modern Poetic Technique, English and Australian* (Sydney, 1949)

Howarth, R.G. *Literary Particles* (Sydney, 1946)

Hunt, Hugh *The Making of Australian Theatre* (Melbourne, 1960)

Ingamells, Rex *Handbook of Australian Literature* (Melbourne, 1949)

Johnston, Grahame (ed.) *Australian Literary Criticism* (Melbourne, 1962)

Jose, A.W. *The Romantic Nineties* (Sydney, 1933)

Kellow, H.A. *Queensland Poets* (London, 1930)

Macartney, F.T. *Australian Literary Essays* (Sydney, 1957)

McGuire, P., and others, *The Australian Theatre* (Melbourne, 1948)

McLeod, A.L. (ed.) *The Commonwealth Pen: An Introduction to the Literature of the British Commonwealth* (Ithaca, New York, 1961)

Matthews, J.P. *Tradition in Exile* (Melbourne, 1962)

Miller, E. Morris *Pressmen and Governors: Australian Editors and Writers in Early Tasmania* (Sydney, 1952)

Mitchell, A.G. *The Pronunciation of English in Australia* (Sydney, 1946)

Moore, T. Inglis *Six Australian Poets* (Melbourne, 1942)

Murphy, Arthur *Contemporary Australian Poets* (Adelaide, 1950)

O'Leary, P.I. *Bard in Bondage: Essays* (ed.) J. O'Dwyer (Melbourne, 1954)

Palmer, Nettie *Modern Australian Literature (1900-1923)* (Adelaide, 1924)

Palmer, Vance *The Legend of the Nineties* (Melbourne, 1954)

Phillips, A.A. *The Australian Tradition: Studies in a Colonial Culture* (Melbourne, 1958)

Rankin, D.H. *The Development and Philosophy of Australian Aestheticism* (Melbourne, 1949)

Rees, Leslie *Towards an Australian Drama* (Sydney, 1953)

Roderick, Colin *The Australian Novel (An Historical Anthology)* (Sydney, 1945)

Roderick, Colin *An Introduction to Australian Fiction* (Sydney, 1950)

Serle, Percival *Dictionary of Australian Biography* (2 vols., Sydney, 1949)

Stephensen, P.R. *Foundations of Culture in Australia* (Gordon, New South Wales, 1936)

Stewart, Douglas *The Flesh and the Spirit: An Outlook on Literature* (Sydney, 1948)

Turner, H.G. and Sutherland, A. *The Development of Australian Literature* (London and Melbourne, 1898)

COLLECTIONS AND ANTHOLOGIES

Anderson, Hugh *Australian Song Index, 1828-1956* (Melbourne, 1957)

Anderson, Hugh (ed.) *Colonial Ballads* (Melbourne, 1955; revised 1961)

Australian Poetry (Sydney, 1941-; an annual anthology)

Barton, G.B. (ed.) *The Poets and Prose Writers of New South Wales* (Sydney, 1866)

Beatty, Bill (ed.) *A Treasury of Australian Folk Tales and Traditions* (Sydney, 1960)

Brissenden, Alan and Higham, Charles *They Came to Australia* (Melbourne, 1961)

The Bulletin Reciter (Sydney, 1901)

The Bulletin Story Book (Sydney, 1901)

Christesen, C.B. (ed.) *Australian Heritage* (Melbourne, 1949)

Coast to Coast (Sydney, 1941-; an annual anthology of short stories)

Cowling, G.H. and Maurice, Furnley (eds.) *Australian Essays* (Melbourne, 1935)

Drake-Brockman, H. (ed.) *West Coast Stories* (Sydney, 1959)

Green, H.M (ed.) *Modern Australian Poetry* (Melbourne, 1946)

Hadgraft, Cecil and Wilson, Richard (eds.) *A Century of Australian Short Stories* (Melbourne, 1963)

Heseltine, H.P. (ed.) *Australian Idiom* (Melbourne, 1963)

Hungerford, T.A.G. (ed.) *Australian Signpost* (Melbourne, 1956)

Ingleton, Geoffrey (ed.) *True Patriots All ... A Collection of Broadsides* (Sydney, 1952)

Jindyworobak Anthology (ed.) Rex Ingamells and others (Adelaide, 1938-53)

Moore, T. Inglis (ed.) *Australia Writes* (Melbourne, 1953)

Moore, T. Inglis (ed.) *A Book of Australia* (London, 1961)

Mudie, Ian (ed.) *Poets at War* (Melbourne, 1944)

Murdoch, Walter (ed.) *The Oxford Book of Australasian Verse* (Oxford, 1918, and later editions)

Murdoch, Walter and Drake-Brockman, H. (eds.) *Australian Short Stories* (London, 1951, and later editions)

Osborne, Charles (ed.) *Australian Stories of Today* (London, 1961)

Mackaness, George (ed.) *An Anthology of Australian Verse* (revised Sydney, 1952)

Paterson, A.B. (ed.) *Old Bush Songs* (Sydney, 1905, and various editions)

The Penguin Book of Australian Verse, (ed.) John Thompson, Kenneth Slessor, and R.G. Howarth (London, 1958, reprinted 1961 as *The Penguin Book of Modern Australian Verse*)

Poetry in Australia 1923, preface by Norman Lindsay (Sydney, 1923)

Roderick, Colin (ed.) *Australian Round-Up: Stories from 1790 to 1950* (Sydney, 1953)

Sladen, Douglas (ed.) *Australian Poets 1788-1888* (London, 1888)

Sladen, Douglas (ed.) *A Century of Australian Song* (London, 1888)

Southern Festival: A Collection of South Australian Writing (Adelaide, 1960)

Stewart, Douglas and Keesing, Nancy (eds.) *Australian Bush Ballads* (Sydney, 1955)

Stewart, Douglas and Keesing, Nancy (eds.) *Old Bush Songs and Rhymes of Colonial Times: Enlarged and Revised from the Collection by A.B. Paterson* (Sydney, 1957)

Verse in Australia (Adelaide, 1958-61; an annual anthology)

Wannan, Bill (ed.) *A Treasury of Australian Frontier Tales* Melbourne, 1961)

Waten, J.L. and O'Connor, V.G. (eds.) *Twenty Great Australian Stories* (Melbourne, 1946)

Wigmore, Lionel (ed.) *Span: An Adventure in Asian and Australian Writing* (Melbourne, 1958)

Wright, Judith (ed.) *A Book of Australian Verse* (London, 1956)

Wright, Judith (ed.) *New Land New Language* (Melbourne, 1957)

AUTHORS

ARCHIBALD, JOHN FELTHAM (1856-1919): Editor; b. Kildare, near Geelong; educated Catholic school, Warrnambool; worked casually as journalist and clerk in Melbourne, Queensland and Sydney. In January 1880 with John Haynes started *The Bulletin*; August 1881 W.H. Traill became registered proprietor and manager; 1882 both Haynes and Archibald gaoled for libel;

Traill had become editor, Archibald was his deputy; Archibald edited journal 1886-1902; after years of ill-health he sold out in 1914; 1919 became literary editor of *Smith's Weekly*. Survey of *The Bulletin's* activities and staff is contained in Jubilee Number of 29 January 1930. *The Bulletin* was most influential in promoting a national literature, and issued a number of publications (see G. Mackaness and W.W. Stone, *The Books of The Bulletin, 1880-1952*, Sydney, 1955). Archibald wrote a series of articles (unfinished) on 'The Genesis of *The Bulletin*', *Lone Hand*, July-September 1907.

Commentaries on Archibald and *The Bulletin*:

> *A Word About The Bulletin* [reprint of an article 'The Australian Attitude', from *The Times*, London, 31 August 1903], published by *The Bulletin*, no date
>
> John Haynes, 'My Early *Bulletin* Memoirs', *Newsletter*, April-December 1905
>
> Richard Jebb, *Studies in Colonial Nationalism* (London, 1905)
>
> S.E. Lee, 'On the Genesis of *The Bulletin*', *Drylight* (1961)
>
> Ken Levis, 'The Role of *The Bulletin* in Indigenous Short Story Writing During the Eighties and Nineties', *Southerly* (1950, no. 4)
>
> Vance Palmer, *The Legend of the Nineties* (Melbourne, 1954)
>
> G.A. Wilkes, 'The Eighteen Nineties', in Grahame Johnston (ed.), *Australian Literary Criticism* (Melbourne, 1962)

BARNARD, MARJORIE, see under 'Eldershaw, M. Barnard'.

BAYLEBRIDGE, WILLIAM (1883-1942): Poet; b. William Blocksidge in Brisbane; educated Brisbane Grammar School, and afterwards by private tutor; travelled in Europe and Middle East, returning to Brisbane 1919; afterwards lived in Sydney. Under terms of his will a definitive edition of all his work is now in progress. P.R. Stephensen is the editor. Poetry: *Moreton Miles*, 1910; *Life's Testament*, 1914; *Seven Tales*, 1916; *A Wreath*, 1916; all privately printed. *Selected Poems* (Brisbane, 1919); *Love Redeemed* (Sydney, 1934); *Sextains* (Sydney, 1939); *This Vital Flesh* (Sydney, 1939) also ed. P.R. Stephensen (Sydney, 1961). Fiction: *An Anzac Muster*, privately printed, 1921, also ed. P.R. Stephensen (Sydney, 1962).

Commentaries:

> Brian Elliott, in *Singing to the Cattle* (Melbourne, 1947)
>
> F.T. Macartney, 'The Originality and Philosophy of William Baylebridge', *Australian Literary Essays* (Sydney, 1957)

F. Mackinnon, 'Poetry and Philosophy of William Baylebridge', *All About Books* (November, 1937)

T. Inglis Moore, 'William Baylebridge', *Six Australian Poets* (Melbourne, 1942)

'William Baylebridge number', *Southerly* (1955, no. 3) (Includes articles by Hugh Anderson, Martin Haley, R.G. Howarth, and Judith Wright)

'BOLDREWOOD, ROLF' (nom de plume of Thomas Alexander Browne) (1826-1915): Novelist; b. London; 1831 family came to Australia and settled in Sydney; 1839 family moved to Port Philip district, Victoria; Browne returned to school in Sydney for two years; 1844-6 took up land in Port Fairy district; 1860 visited England and 1861 m. Maria Riley; 1869 gave up farming because of losses; 1871 became a magistrate at Gulgong, and later at Dubbo, Albury and Armidale. In 1860's contributed to *Cornhill*, and later to various Melbourne and Sydney journals; retired 1895, then lived in Melbourne. His many novels include: *Ups and Downs* (London and Sydney, 1878); later entitled *The Squatter's Dream*, 1890; *Robbery Under Arms* appeared serially in *Sydney Mail*, 1882-3, and as a book, 1888; *The Miner's Right*, 1890; *A Colonial Reformer*, 1890; *A Sydney-Side Saxon*, 1891; all published London. Autobiography: *Old Melbourne Memories* (Melbourne, 1884); *In Bad Company and other Stories* (London, 1901).

Commentaries:

'T.A. Browne', *Lone Hand* (February 1911)

Keast Burke, *Thomas Alexander Browne; An Annotated Bibliography, Checklist and Chronology* (Cremorne, 1956)

J.T. Ryan, 'An Australian Novelist: Rolf Boldrewood', *Review of Reviews* (Australasian ed., May 1894)

A.G. Stephens, 'Rolf Boldrewood', in Vance Palmer (ed.) *A.G. Stephens* (Melbourne, 1941)

BOYD, MARTIN (b. 1893): Novelist; b. Lucerne; parents (watercolourists) brought him to Melbourne when six months; educated Trinity Grammar; studied architecture; World War I went to England and enlisted; lieutenant in Buffs regiment, served with Royal Flying Corps; returned to Australia; after 1921 lived in England; 18 months with *British Australasian*; Australia 1948-51. Novels under pseudonym 'Martin Mills': *Love Gods*, 1925; *Brangane*, 1926; *The Montforts*, 1928. Novels as Martin Boyd;

Scandal of Spring, 1934; *The Lemon Farm*, 1935; *The Painted Princess*, 1936; *The Picnic*, 1937; *Night of the Party*, 1938; *Nuns in Jeopardy*, 1940; *Lucinda Brayford*, 1946; *Such Pleasure*, 1949 (U.S.A. ed. entitled *Bridget Malwyn*); *The Cardboard Crown*, 1952; *A Difficult Young Man*, 1955; *Outbreak of Love*, 1957; *When Blackbirds Sing*, 1962. Travel: *Much Else in Italy*, 1958. Autobiography: *A Single Flame*, 1939. All the foregoing published London.

Commentaries:

> Barnard Eldershaw, *Essays in Australian Fiction* (Melbourne, 1938)
> Brian Elliott, 'Martin Boyd: An Appreciation', *Meanjin* (1957, no. 1)
> Kathleen Fitzpatrick, *Martin Boyd and the Complex Fate of the Australian Novelist* (C.U.C., 1953)
> Kathleen Fitzpatrick, *Martin Boyd* (Melbourne, 1963)
> Leonie Kramer, 'Martin Boyd', *Australian Quarterly* (1963, no. 2)
> Brenda Niall, 'The Double Alienation of Martin Boyd', *Twentieth Century* (1963, no. 3)
> C. Wallace-Crabbe, 'Martin Boyd and *The Cardboard Crown*', *Melbourne Critical Review*, 1960
> G.A. Wilkes, 'The Achievement of Martin Boyd', *Southerly* (1958, no. 2; reprinted Grahame Johnston (ed.) *Australian Literary Criticism*, Melbourne, 1962)

BRENNAN, CHRISTOPHER JOHN (1870-1932): Poet and critic; b. Sydney of Irish parents; attended Catholic schools, scholarship to St. Ignatius' College, 1885; 1892 M.A. Sydney University with Honours in Philosophy, then 2 years Berlin on travelling scholarship; 1895 cataloguer at Sydney Public Library; m. 1897; 1909 appointment to University Modern Languages staff; 1920 appointed Associate Professor of German and Comparative literature; 1925 dismissed from University because of intemperance and action by wife to obtain legal separation; afterwards lived by casual teaching and small Literary Fund pension. Poetry includes: *XVIII Poems* (Sydney, 1897) (only 8 copies), and *XXI Poems (1893-7): Towards the Source* (Sydney, 1897); *Poems* (Sydney, 1913); *A Chant of Doom and Other Verses* (Sydney, 1918). Posthumous: *Twenty Three Poems* (Sydney, 1938); *The Burden of Tyre* (Sydney, 1953). Collections: *The Verse of Christopher Brennan*, (ed.) A.R. Chisholm and J.J. Quinn (Sydney, 1960). *The Prose of Christopher Brennan*, (ed.) Chisholm and Quinn (Sydney, 1962).

Commentaries:

A.R. Chisholm, *Christopher Brennan: The Man and His Poetry* (Sydney, 1946); 'Brennan and Mallarmé', *Southerly* (1961, no. 4, and 1962, no. 1); *Men Were My Milestones* (Melbourne, 1958)

M.A. Clark, 'C.J. Brennan: An Appreciation', *Art In Australia* (February 1933)

H.M. Green, *Christopher Brennan: Two Popular Lectures* (Sydney, 1939)

Randolph W. Hughes, *C. J. Brennan: An Essay in Values* (Sydney, 1934)

Alec King, 'Thoughts on the Poetry of Brennan', *Westerly* (1961, no. 3)

James McAuley, *Christopher Brennan* (Melbourne, 1963)

G.B. Philip, *Sixty Years' Recollections and Impressions of a Book-seller: Christopher Brennan* (Sydney, 1939)

Sybille Smith, 'Brennan as Critic', *Quadrant* (1963, no. 1)

A.G. Stephens, *Chris Brennan* (Sydney, 1933)

Walter Stone and Hugh Anderson, *Christopher Brennan: a Comprehensive Bibliography with Annotations* (Cremorne, 1959)

G.A. Wilkes, *New Perspectives in Brennan's Poetry* (Sydney, 1953); and articles in *The Union Book of 1952; Australian Quarterly*, (June, 1959); *Meanjin* (1960, no. 1 and no. 4); AUMLA (1960, no. 14); *Southerly* (1961, no. 2, 1963, no. 3)

Three Chris Brennan Numbers of *Southerly*: 1949, no. 4, including articles by A.R. Chisholm, Margaret Clarke, R.G. Howarth; 1957, no. 3, including articles by James McAuley and R.I. Scott; 1963, no. 3, including articles by G.A. Wilkes, N. Macainsh, W. Kirsop.

'BRENT OF BIN BIN', see under Franklin, Miles

BROWNE, THOMAS ALEXANDER, see under 'Boldrewood, Rolf'.

BUCKLEY, VINCENT (b. 1925): Poet, critic; b. Victoria; educated Melbourne by Jesuit Fathers, and Melbourne and Cambridge Universities; World War II served with R.A.A.F. until invalided out; worked for some time as public servant, now Reader in English, University of Melbourne. Criticism: *Essays in Poetry, Mainly Australian* (Melbourne, 1957); *Poetry and Morality* (London, 1959); *Henry Handel Richardson* (Melbourne, 1961). Poetry: *The World's Flesh* (Melbourne, 1954); *Masters in Israel* (Sydney, 1961).

Commentary:

Penelope Curtis 'Vincent Buckley as Poet', *Quadrant* (1962, no. 4)

Bulletin, see under Archibald, J.F.

CAMBRIDGE, ADA (1844-1926): Novelist; b. Norfolk, England; published hymns; 1870 m. G.F. Goss, Anglican clergyman and accompanied him to Australia where he was minister at a number of Victorian towns; 1893 he became vicar of Williamstown. Ada Cambridge published some novels in *Australasian* that were not reprinted. Novels include: *A Marked Man*, 1890; *The Three Miss Kings*, 1891; *Not All in Vain*, 1892; *Fidelis*, 1895; *A Humble Enterprise*, 1896; all published London. Poetry: *The Hand in the Dark* (London, 1913). Autobiography: *Thirty Years in Australia* (London, 1903).

CAMPBELL, DAVID (b. 1915): Poet, b. Ellerslie station, near Adelong, New South Wales; of pioneering family; educated The King's School, Sydney, and Cambridge University; distinguished athlete; World War II pilot in R.A.A.F., and awarded D.F.C. and bar; now farms property near Canberra; has contributed poems and short stories to magazines. Poetry: *Speak with the Sun* (London, 1949); *The Miracle of Mullion Hill* (Sydney, 1956); *Poems* (Sydney, 1962). Stories: *Evening Under Lamplight* (Sydney, 1959).

CLARKE, MARCUS (1846-81): Novelist, short story writer; b. London, son of barrister; educated Cholmondeley Grammar School, Highgate, with G.M. Hopkins; 1863 father died and Clarke went to Victoria where uncle was a County Court Judge; employment in Melbourne Bank proved unsuitable, as did station work; contributed to *Australian Monthly Magazine*; 1867 on staff of *Argus* and *Australasian*, and undertook freelance journalism; 1868 became owner and editor of *Colonial Monthly*; m. actress 1869; *His Natural Life* serialized in *Australian Journal* (1870-72) which Clarke edited for a time; serial later revised and abridged for book-publication; 1870 on staff at Melbourne Public Library; Australian correspondent of London *Daily Telegraph*; insolvency 1874, and again when he died aged 35. Novels: *Long Odds* (Melbourne, 1869), (English ed. *Heavy Odds*, London, 1896); *His Natural Life* (Melbourne, 1874; London, 1875) re-titled *For the Term of His Natural Life* in 1885 ed. and afterwards; only unabridged ed. in book form (Sydney, 1929); *'Twixt Shadow and Shine* (Melbourne, 1875); *Chidiock Tichbourne; or the Catholic Conspiracy* (London, 1893). Stories include: *Old Tales of a Young Country* (Melbourne, 1871); *Holiday Peak and Other*

Tales (Melbourne, 1873); *Four Stories High* (Melbourne, 1877); *The Mystery of Major Molineux and Human Repetends* (Melbourne, 1881); *Sensational Tales* (Sydney and Adelaide, 1886); *Australian Tales* (Melbourne, 1896); *Stories of Australia in the Early Days* (London, 1897). Essays: *The Peripatetic Philosopher*, by 'Q' (Melbourne, 1867); *The Future of the Australian Race* (Melbourne, 1877). Collections: *Marcus Clarke Memorial Volume*, (ed.) H. Mackinnon (Selections and biographical notes) (Melbourne, 1884); *The Austral Edition of the Selected Works of Marcus Clarke*, (ed.) H. Mackinnon (Melbourne, 1890); *A Marcus Clarke Reader*, (ed.) Bill Wannan (Melbourne, 1963).
Commentaries:

A. W. Brazier, *Marcus Clarke* (Melbourne, 1902)

Brian Elliott, *Marcus Clarke* (Oxford, 1958) (with bibliography)

R. G. Howarth, 'Marcus Clarke's "For the Term of His Natural Life"', *Southerly* (1954, no. 4)

Ida Leeson, '*The Term of His Natural Life*', *All About Books* (15 September 1930)

Hugh McCrae, in *My Father and My Father's Friends* (Sydney, 1935)

Vance Palmer, 'Marcus Clarke and His Critics', *Meanjin* (1946)

L. Rees, 'His Natural Life, the Long and Short of It', *Australian Quarterly* (June, 1942)

L. L. Robson, 'The Historical Basis of *For the Term of His Natural Life*', *Australian Literary Studies* (1963, no. 2)

Samuel R. Simmons, *A Problem and a Solution: Marcus Clarke And the Writing of Long Odds* (Melbourne, 1946)

COUVREUR, JESSIE CATHERINE, see under 'Tasma'

COWAN, PETER (b. 1914); Short story writer; b. Perth; B.A. and Diploma of Education, University of Western Australia; 1943-5 R.A.A.F. Senior lecturer at Scots College, Perth, and tutor at the University. Stories: *Drift* (Melbourne, 1944); *The Unploughed Land* (Sydney, 1958).
Commentaries:

John Barnes, 'The Short Stories of Peter Cowan', *Meanjin* (1960, no. 2)

Evan Jones, *Short Stories of Peter Cowan and Alan Davies* (C.U.C., 1962)

DARK, ELEANOR (b. 1901): Novelist; b. Sydney; daughter of Dowell O'Reilly; educated Redlands, Neutral Bay, Sydney; 1922 m. Dr Eric Payten Dark; lives at Katoomba; winner of Australian Literary Society Medal's for best novels of 1934 and 1936. Novels:

Slow Dawning (London, 1932); *Prelude to Christopher* (Sydney, 1934); *Return to Coolami* (London, 1936); *Sun Across the Sky* (London, 1937); *Waterway* (London, 1938); *The Timeless Land* (London, 1941); *The Little Company* (Sydney, 1945); *Storm of Time* (London, 1948); *No Barrier* (Sydney, 1953); *Lantana Lane* (London, 1959).

Commentaries:

> Hugh Anderson, 'Eleanor Dark: A Handlist of Her Books and Critical References', *Biblionews* (August 1954)
>
> Barnard Eldershaw, in *Essays in Australian Fiction* (Melbourne, 1938)
>
> Eric Lowe, 'The Novels of Eleanor Dark', *Meanjin* (1951, no. 4)
>
> John McKellar, 'The Black and the White', *Southerly* (1948, no. 2)
>
> G.A. Wilkes, 'Progress of Eleanor Dark', *Southerly* (1951, no. 3)

DAVISON, FRANK DALBY (b. 1893): Novelist; b. Melbourne; after education at State schools worked father's property, King-lake; then Gippsland station, and Ringwood orchards; 1908-14 in U.S. where he became printer's compositor; served in cavalry and infantry in World War I; soldier-settler in Queensland; then joined father's real estate business in Sydney; now farming in Victoria; father started *Australian* (became *Australia*) in which *Forever Morning*, 1931, and *Man-Shy*, 1931, first appeared; *Dusty*, 1946, won *Argus* competition. Other novels: *The Wells of Beersheba*, 1933; *Children of the Dark People*, 1936. Stories: *The Woman at the Mill*, 1940. All works published Sydney.

DENNIS, CLARENCE MICHAEL JAMES (C.J.) (1876-1938): Poet; b. Auburn, South Australia; educated State School Gladstone and Christian Brothers' College, Adelaide; various occupations, including journalist, barman, carpenter, clerk, editor of satirical *Gadfly; The Songs of a Sentimental Bloke* (Sydney, 1915), sold more than 66,000 copies; its successor, *The Moods of Ginger Mick* (Sydney, 1916), written expressly for A.I.F., also popular at home and abroad; *The Sentimental Bloke* later dramatized and twice filmed; Dennis was on staff of Melbourne *Herald*, 1922-38. Other books of verse exploited characters from *The Sentimental Bloke*. *Selected Verse of C.J. Dennis*, (ed.) A.H. Chisholm (Sydney, 1950).

Commentaries:

> A.H. Chisholm, *The Making of a Sentimental Bloke* (Melbourne, 1946)

Margaret Herron, *Down the Years: (the Life Story of C.J. Dennis Told by His Wife)* (Melbourne, 1953)

F.T. Macartney, 'Larrikin Literature', *Australian Literary Essays* (Sydney, 1957)

Ian McLaren, *C.J. Dennis: His Life and Work* (Melbourne, 1961)

DOBSON, ROSEMARY (b. 1920): Poet; b. Sydney; grand-daughter of Austin Dobson; educated Frensham School, Mittagong, New South Wales, and Sydney University; studied, then taught, art; 1947 worked for London publishing firm; now lives in Sydney, m. Alec Bolton 1951. Poetry: *In a Convex Mirror* (Sydney, 1944); *The Ship of Ice* (Sydney, 1948); *Child with a Cockatoo* (Sydney, 1955).

DUTTON, GEOFFREY PIERS (b. 1922): Poet, critic; b. Kapunda, South Australia; educated Geelong Grammar School; World War II Fl. Lieut. R.A.A.F.; after war studied at Oxford, then lived in London and South France; 1955 became lecturer in English, Adelaide University, resigned 1962; co-editor and founder of *Australian Letters* and *Australian Book Review;* has promoted Australian Literature by his writings, radio and television talks, and publishing activities; independent editor Australian Penguin books. Poetry: *Night Flight and Sunrise* (Melbourne, 1944); *Antipodes in Shoes* (Sydney, 1958); *Flowers and Fury* (Melbourne, 1962). Fiction: *The Mortal and the Marble* (London, 1950). Criticism: *Walt Whitman* (Edinburgh, 1961); *Patrick White* (Melbourne, 1961). Travel books: *A Long Way South* (London, 1953); *Africa in Black and White* (London, 1956); *States of the Union* (London, 1958).

ELDERSHAW, FLORA, *see below.*

'ELDERSHAW, M. BARNARD' (Flora Eldershaw and Marjorie Barnard): Novelists, historical writers. FLORA ELDERSHAW (1897-1956): b. Darlinghurst, Sydney; B.A. Sydney University, then teacher at Presbyterian Ladies' College, Croydon, New South Wales. M. BARNARD: b. 1897, Ashfield, Sydney, educated Sydney Girls' High School; B.A. Sydney University; libararian at Sydney Technical College and elsewhere. Novels in collaboration: *A House is Built* (London, 1929); *Green Memory* (London, 1931); *The Glasshouse* (London, 1936); *Plaque with Laurel* (London, 1937); *Tomorrow and Tomorrow* (Melbourne, 1947); Criticism in collaboration: *Essays in Australian Fiction* (Melbourne, 1938). By M. Barnard alone: *The Persimmon Tree and Other Stories* (Sydney, 1943). M. Barnard has also written historical works with F. Eldershaw and alone.

ESSON, LOUIS (1879-1943): Dramatist; b. Edinburgh; came to Australia as a boy; assistant at Melbourne Public Library, then journalist; travelled abroad; interested in Abbey Theatre and met Yeats, Synge, and other Irish playwrights; 1922 joined with Wm. Moore, Vance Palmer and Stewart Mackey in forming the Pioneer Players, Melbourne, but group lacked support and disbanded four years later; continued to promote indigenous drama. Drama: *Three Short Plays* (Melbourne, 1912?); *The Time is Not Yet Ripe* (Melbourne, 1912); *Dead Timber and Other Plays* (London, 1920); *The Southern Cross and Other Plays* (Melbourne, 1946 with introduction by Hilda Esson and notes by other writers).

Commentaries:

Keith Macartney, 'Louis Esson and Australian Drama', *Meanjin* (1947, no. 2)

V. Palmer, *Louis Esson and the Australian Theatre* (Melbourne, 1948)

Leslie Rees, in *Towards an Australian Drama* (Sydney, 1953)

FITZGERALD, ROBERT DAVID (b. 1902): Poet, b. Sydney; educated Sydney Grammar School; studied science at Sydney University; as licensed surveyor spent five years in Fiji; at present a senior surveyor in Commonwealth Department of the Interior. 1951 O.B.E. for services to literature. Poetry includes: *To Meet the Sun* (Sydney, 1929); *Moonlight Acre* (Melbourne, 1938); *Between Two Tides* (Sydney, 1952); *This Night's Orbit* (Melbourne, 1953); *Southmost Twelve* (Sydney, 1962). Prose: *Elements of Poetry* (Brisbane, 1963).

Commentaries:

Hugh Anderson, 'Robert FitzGerald, Humanist', *Southerly* (1958, no. 1)

Vincent Buckley, 'The Development of R.D. FitzGerald', *Essays in Poetry* (Melbourne, 1957)

A.R. Chisholm, 'Mr FitzGerald's Essay on Memory', *Australian Quarterly* (September 1938)

T. Inglis Moore, in *Six Australian Poets* (Melbourne, 1942)

H.J. Oliver, 'The Achievement of R.D. FitzGerald', *Meanjin* (1954, no. 1; reprinted Grahame Johnston, (ed.) *Australian Literary Criticism*, Melbourne, 1962)

H.G. Seccombe, 'A Contemporary Australian Poet', *Australian Quarterly* (March 1941)

F.M. Todd, 'The Poetry of R.D. FitzGerald', *Twentieth Century* (Spring 1954)

FRANKLIN, MILES (1879-1954): Novelist; Stella Maria Miles Franklin, b. Talbingo Station, near Tumut, New South Wales; grew up in Goulburn district: freelance writer in Sydney, then went to U.S.A. in 1905 for nine years, while there was associated with women's labour movement, and co-edited *Life and Labour*; World War I honorary helper in England and hospital in Macedonia; remained abroad except for brief visits until 1933, then resided in Australia. Novels: *My Brilliant Career* (Edinburgh, 1901); *Some Everyday Folk and Dawn* (Edinburgh, 1909); *Old Blastus of Bandicoot* (London, 1931); *Bring the Monkey* (Sydney, 1933); *All that Swagger* (Sydney, 1936); *My Career Goes Bung* (Melbourne, 1946). With Dymphna Cusack: *Pioneers on Parade* (Sydney, 1939). Biography: With Kate Baker, *Joseph Furphy* (Sydney, 1944); Criticism: *Laughter, Not for a Cage* (Sydney, 1956). Autobiography: *Childhood at Brindabella* (Sydney, 1963). The Novels of 'Brent of Bin Bin' have been confidently attributed to Miles Franklin. These novels are: *Up the Country* (Edinburgh, 1928); *Ten Creeks Run* (Edinburgh, 1930); *Back to Bool Bool* (Edinburgh, 1931); *Prelude to Waking* (Sydney, 1950); *Cockatoos* (Sydney, 1954); *Gentlemen at Gyang Gyang* (Sydney, 1956).

Commentaries:

A.W. Ashworth, 'Miles Franklin', *Southerly* (1948, no. 2)

A.W. Ashworth, 'Brent of Bin Bin', *Southerly* (1951, no. 4)

Marjorie Barnard, 'Miles Franklin', *Meanjin* (1955, no. 4)

Miles Franklin: A Tribute by Some of Her Friends, (Melbourne, 1955)

Walter Stone: 'Miles Franklin: Biography and Bibliography', *Miles Franklin's Manuscripts and Typescripts* Catalogue no. 47, Berkelouw (Sydney, 1962)

Ray Mathew, *Miles Franklin* (Melbourne, 1963)

FURPHY, JOSEPH ('Tom Collins') (1843-1912): Novelist; b. Victoria, of emigrant parents (Northern Ireland); educated at home and at schools at Kangaroo Ground and Kyneton; worked on father's farm; also undertook saw-milling, operating farm and mine machinery, gold-prospecting; m. 1866; worked selection unsuccessfully; drove bullock teams in Riverina and Hay districts; 1884 worked at brother's foundry, Shepparton; 1905 joined two sons with similar business at Fremantle. Novels: *Such is Life* (Sydney, 1903); with preface by Vance Palmer (Melbourne, 1917); ed. Vance Palmer (abridged) (London, 1937); *Rigby's Romance*, 1905-6 as serial in *Barrier Truth*; abridged with preface by A. G. Stephens (Melbourne, 1921); enlarged edition, (ed.) R.G. Howarth (Sydney, 1946); *The Buln-Buln and the Brolga*, (ed.) R.G. Howarth (Sydney, 1948). Also, *The Poems of Joseph Furphy*, (ed.) Kate Baker (Melbourne, 1916).

Commentaries:

A.L. Archer, *Tom Collins, Joseph Furphy as I Knew Him*, (Melbourne, 1941)

Kate Baker and Miles Franklin, *Joseph Furphy* (Sydney, 1944) (reviewed by A.D. Hope, *Meanjin Papers* (1945, no. 3))

John Barnes, 'The Structure of Joseph Furphy's *Such Is Life*', *Meanjin* (1956, no. 4)

John Barnes, *Joseph Furphy* (Melbourne, 1963)

John K. Ewers, *Tell the People* (Sydney, 1944)

John K. Ewers, *Creative Writing in Australia* (revised, 1962)

C. Hartley Grattan, 'Tom Collins's *Such Is Life*', *Australian Quarterly* (September 1937)

R.G. Howarth, 'Such Was Life in the Riverina', *Literary Particles* (Sydney, 1946)

R.G. Howarth, 'Joseph Furphy. The "Tom Collins" Trilogy', *Southerly* (1951, no. 2)

B. Kiernan, 'The Form of *Such Is Life*', *Quadrant* (1962, no. 3)

Brian Kiernan, 'Society and Nature in *Such is Life*', *Australian Literary Studies* (1963, no. 2)

A.G. Mitchell, '*Such Is Life*: The Title and Structure of the Book', *Southerly* (1945, no. 3)

H.J. Oliver, 'Joseph Furphy and "Tom Collins"', *Southerly* (1944, no. 3)

E.E. Pescott, *Life Story of Joseph Furphy* (Melbourne, 1938)

A.A. Phillips, 'The Craftsmanship of Furphy', *The Australian Tradition* (Melbourne, 1958)

Walter Stone, *Joseph Furphy: An Annotated Bibliography* (Cremorne, 1955)

Bruce Sutherland, 'Joseph Furphy, Australian', *University of Toronto Quarterly* (January 1951)

A.K. Thomson, 'The Greatness of Joseph Furphy', *Meanjin* (1943, no. 3)

Chris Wallace-Crabbe, 'Joseph Furphy, Realist', *Quadrant* (1961, no. 2; reprinted Grahame Johnston, (ed.) *Australian Literary Criticism*, Melbourne, 1962)

'Furphy Number', *Meanjin Papers* (1943, no. 3)

'Joseph Furphy Number', *Southerly* (1945, no. 3)

GILMORE, DAME MARY (1865-1962): Poet; b. near Goulburn, New South Wales, maiden name Mary Jean Cameron; after period as school teacher joined group led by Wm Lane to set up socialist community in Paraguay; there in 1897 she married Wm Alexander Gilmore; returned to Sydney, 1902; for 23 years conducted woman's page in the *Worker*; 1936 created Dame in recognition of contribution to literature. Poetry includes: *Marri'd and Other Verses* (Melbourne, 1910); *The Passionate Heart* (Sydney, 1918); *The Wild Swan* (Melbourne, 1930); *The Rue Tree* (Melbourne, 1931); *Under the Wilgas* (Melbourne, 1932); *Battlefields* (Sydney, 1939); *The Disinherited* (Melbourne, 1941); *Pro Patria Australia* (Sydney, 1945); *Selected Verse* (Sydney, 1948); *Fourteen Men* (Sydney, 1954); *Australian Poets: Mary Gilmore*, sel. and introduced by R. D. FitzGerald (Sydney, 1963). Prose: *Old Days, Old Ways* (Sydney, 1934; reprinted 1964); *More Recollections* (Sydney, 1935).

Commentaries:

R.D. FitzGerald, 'Mary Gilmore: Poet and Great Australian' *Meanjin* (1960, no. 4)

I.M. Foster, 'The Poetry of Mary Gilmore', *Desiderata* (November 1930)

Hugh McCrae, 'Mary Gilmore, Our Great National Poet', *Australian Quarterly* (September 1933)

T. Inglis Moore, 'Mary Gilmore', *Southerly* (1949, no. 3)

Overland (1955, no. 4), tributes by A.G. Mitchell, Judith Wright, K.S. Prichard, Eleanor Dark, Ernestine Hill, and Dorothy Cottrell

GORDON, ADAM LINDSAY (1833-70): Poet; b. Azores, son of retired Indian Officer; at seven went to live in England; educated Cheltenham College and private school in Gloucestershire; interested in sport; withdrawn Woolwich Military Academy for waywardness, sent to Adelaide 1853; two years in Mounted Police, then horse-trainer; m. 1862; 1865-6 member of South Australian Parliament; unsuccessful sheep and property ventures; steeplechase rider; 1867 livery stable at Ballarat; moved to Melbourne, 1868; had contributed to Melbourne periodicals; melancholy increased by failure to obtain Barony; publications financial failures; committed suicide on day of publication of *Bush Ballads and Galloping Rhymes* (Melbourne, 1870). Poetry includes: *The Feud* (Mt Gambier, 1864); *Ashtaroth: A Dramatic Lyric*, and *Sea Spray and Smoke Drift* (both Melbourne, 1867); in 1876 Marcus Clarke added a preface to the latter; *Bush Ballads and Galloping Rhymes* (Melbourne, 1870). Collections: *Poems* (ed.) F.M. Robb (London, 1912); *Poems*, with preface by A.G. Stephens (Sydney, 1918); *The Adam Lindsay Gordon Memorial Volume*, (ed.) E.A. Vidler (Sydney, Melbourne, 1926); *Adam Lindsay Gordon*, (ed.) *Douglas Sladen* (London, 1934). Commentaries:

F. Adams, 'Australian Criticism and the Reaction Against Gordon', *Centennial Magazine* (1889-90)

Edith Humphries, *The Life of Adam Lindsay Gordon* (London, 1933)

Edith Humphries and D. Sladen, *Adam Lindsay Gordon and His Friends in England and Australia* (London, 1912)

Ellen Kaye, 'Life of Gordon', *Australasian* (serialized from August 1933)

Leonie Kramer, 'The Literary Reputation of Adam Lindsay Gordon', *Australian Literary Studies* (1963, no. 1)

G.G. McCrae, 'Adam Lindsay Gordon', *Southerly* (1944, no. 1)

J. Howlett Ross, *The Laureate of the Centaurs* (London, 1888)

Douglas Sladen, *Adam Lindsay Gordon, the Life and Best Poems of the Poet of Australia* (London, 1934) (Westminster Abbey Memorial Volume)

Oscar Wilde, in *Reviews* (London, 1908)

HARPUR, CHARLES (1813-68): Poet; b. Windsor, New South Wales, where father was schoolmaster and parish clerk; 1837-9 Charles was clerk in Sydney Post Office; made friends with W.A. Duncan, editor of *Australasian Chronicle* and *Weekly Register*, who published some of his poems and his first book; also friendly with Henry Parkes, and contributed to his *Empire*; in 1840's schoolmaster and farmer in Singleton district; 1850 m. Mary Doyle; 1859 appointed Gold Commissioner at Araluen, then at Nerrigundah, where he also farmed; appointment abolished 1866; misfortunes in last years, including floods and accidental shooting of son. Poetry includes: *Thoughts: A Series of Sonnets* (Sydney, 1845); *The Bushrangers: A Play, and Other Poems* (Sydney, 1853); *A Poet's Home* (Sydney, 1862); *The Tower of the Dream* (Sydney,

1865); *Poems* (Melbourne, 1883); *Selected Poems* (Melbourne, 1944); *Rosa: Love Sonnets to Mary Doyle* (ed.) C.W. Salier (Melbourne, 1948).

Commentaries:

G.B. Barton, 'Charles Harpur', *The Poets and Prose Writers of New South Wales* (Sydney, 1866)

P.B. Cox, 'Charles Harpur and the Early Australian Poets', *J.R.A.H.S.*, 1939.

J. Normington-Rawling, *Charles Harpur, An Australian* (Sydney, 1962)

C.W. Salier, 'Charles Harpur: A Pre-Centenary Note', *Australian Quarterly*, December, 1943; 'Harpur's Sonnet-Series of 1845', *Australian Quarterly*, September, 1945; 'Life and Writings of Charles Harpur', *J.R.A.H.S.*, (1946); 'Harpur and His Editor', *Southerly* (1951, no. 1)

Judith Wright, 'The Upside Down Hut', *Australian Letters* (1961, no. 4)

Judith Wright, *Charles Harpur* (Melbourne, 1963)

HARRIS, MAX (b. 1921): Poet, critic; b. Adelaide; educated St Peters College and University of Adelaide; co-founder of publishing firm of Reed and Harris; editor *Angry Penguins*, 1941-6, and involved in 'Ern Malley' affair; co-editor and founder of *Australian Letters* (1957-) and *Australian Book Review* (1961-). Poetry: *The Gift of Blood* (Adelaide, 1940); *Dramas from the Sky* (Adelaide, 1942); *The Coorong and Other Poems* (Adelaide, 1955). Novel: *The Vegetative Eye* (Melbourne, 1943).

HAY, WILLIAM GOSSE (1875-1945): Novelist; b. Adelaide; son of Alexander Hay, member of Legislative Council, and of Agnes Grant Hay, author of *After-Glow Memories*; educated Melbourne Grammar School; 1894 Trinity College, Cambridge; 1897 graduated in Arts; gave up studies for bar to devote himself to literature; 1901 returned to Australia and m. Mary Williams; lived at 'Beaumont', Adelaide; and 'Nangawooka', Victor Harbor; visited Tasmania. Novels: *Stifled Laughter*, 1901; *Herridge of Reality Swamp*, 1907; *Captain Quadring*, 1912; *The Escape of the Notorious Sir William Heans*, 1918; reprinted Melbourne, 1955, with critical essays by R.G. Howarth and E. Morris Miller; *Strabane of the Mulberry Hills*, 1929; *The Mystery of Alfred Doubt*, 1937; all first published London. Essays: *An Australian Rip Van Winkle* (London, 1921).

Commentaries:

J.H.M. Abbott, 'William Hay: Extracts from a Memoir', *Southerly* (1952, no. 1)

Brian Elliott, 'The World of William Hay', *Singing to the Cattle* (Melbourne, 1947)

F.T. Macartney, 'Words and William Hay', *Australian Literary Essays* (Sydney, 1957)

'The Original Ending to *Herridge of Reality Swamp*', *Southerly* (1950, no. 2)

'William Hay Number', *Southerly* (1946, no. 3) (Includes articles by R.G. Howarth, F. Earle Hooper, and Uther Barker)

HERBERT, XAVIER (b. 1901): Novelist; b. Port Headland, Western Australia, educated Christian Brothers' School, Fremantle; began science courses at Perth and Melbourne Universities, but abandoned them for freelance writing; employed in Government medical branch at Darwin, and as a Protector of Aborigines; sergeant in A.I.F. in World War II in Pacific area; has contributed many stories to periodicals; writes film scenarios; *Capricornia* (Sydney, 1938), won Sydney novel competition. Other Novels: *Seven Emus* (Sydney, 1959); *Soldiers' Women* (Sydney, 1961). Stories: *Larger than Life* (Sydney, 1963). Autobiography: *Disturbing Element* (Melbourne, 1963).

Commentaries:

Vincent Buckley, '*Capricornia*', *Meanjin* (1960, no. 1; reprinted Grahame Johnston, (ed.) *Australian Literary Criticism*, Melbourne, 1962)

Helen Prideaux, 'Xavier Herbert's *Capricornia*', *Prospect* (1960, no. 2)

HOPE, ALEC DERWENT (b. 1907): Poet, critic; b. Cooma, New South Wales, son of Rev. P. Hope, a Presbyterian clergyman; spent part of childhood at Campbelltown, Tasmania; educated Bathurst and Fort St High Schools, and Universities of Sydney and Oxford; then became teacher New South Wales Education Department; vocational psychologist; lecturer in English and Education, Sydney Teachers' College; m. 1938; Senior Lecturer in English, Melbourne University. Since 1951 Professor of English, Canberra University College (now School of General Studies, A.N.U.). Has contributed many poems and critical articles to Australian periodicals. Poetry: *The Wandering Islands* (Sydney, 1955); *Poems* (London, 1960; New York, 1961).

Commentaries:

> Vincent Buckley, 'A.D. Hope: the Unknown Poet', *Essays in Poetry* (Melbourne, 1957)
>
> S.L. Goldberg, 'The Poet as Hero: A.D. Hope's *The Wandering Islands*', *Meanjin* (1957, no. 2)
>
> James McAuley, 'The Pyramid in the Waste', *Quadrant* (1961, no. 4; reprinted Grahame Johnston, (ed.) *Australian Literary Criticism*, Melbourne, 1962)
>
> D.J. O'Hearn, 'A Note on A.D. Hope', *Prospect* (1959, no. 4)
>
> W.A. Suchting, 'The Poetry of A.D. Hope: A Frame of Reference', *Meanjin* (1962, no. 2)

INGAMELLS, REX (Reginald Charles) (1913-55): Poet; b. Orroroo, South Australia; educated Prince Alfred College, Adelaide, B.A. Adelaide University; many years schoolteaching in Adelaide, 1946 connected with Melbourne publishing house; travelled widely throughout Australia; best known as founder of Jindyworobak movement which took its inspiration from the distinctive qualities of the Australian environment, with special emphasis on aboriginal culture and tradition; killed in a car accident, 1955. Poetry includes: *Selected Poems* (Melbourne, 1944); *Yera* (Adelaide, 1945); *Come Walkabout* (Melbourne, 1948); *The Great South Land* (Melbourne, 1951). Criticism: *Conditional Culture* (with Ian Tilbrook) (Adelaide, 1938); *Handbook of Australian Literature* (Melbourne, 1949). Novel: *Of Us Now Living* (Melbourne, 1952).

Commentary:

> M. Haley, 'King of the Jindies: Rex Ingamells', *Twentieth Century* (1956, no. 3)

KENDALL, HENRY (1839-82): Poet; b. southern New South Wales coast; son of a farmer; family moved to Clarence River, then to Wollongong 1852; 1855 went to sea for two years, then became Sydney shop-assistant; 1859 verses began to appear in Parkes' *Empire*; 1862 verses in London *Athenaeum*; 1863-9 Sydney civil servant; m. 1868 and 1869 took up journalism in Melbourne; period of poverty and intemperance; death of first child; 1870 return to Sydney, increased lapses; 1875 clerical employment at Camden Haven; 1881 Inspector of State Forests; d. of consumption. Poetry includes: *Poems and Songs* (Sydney and London, 1862); *Leaves from an Australian Forest* (Melbourne, 1869); *Songs from the Mountains* (Sydney and London, 1880);

Orara (Melbourne, 1881). Collections: *Poems*, (ed.) A. Sutherland (Melbourne, 1890); *Poems*, (ed.) Bertram Stephens (Sydney, 1920); *Selected Poems*, chosen by his son, with Preface and Memoir (Sydney, 1923); *Selected Poems*, (ed.) T. Inglis Moore (Sydney, 1957).

Commentaries:

Donovan Clarke, 'Henry Kendall – A study in Imagery', *Australian Quarterly* (December 1957, and March 1958)

Brian Elliott, 'The Friend of Charlie Walker', *Australian Letters* (1961, no. 3)

E. Hamilton, 'Henry Clarence Kendall', *Sydney Quarterly Magazine* (1889)

Mrs Hamilton-Grey, *Facts and Fancies About Our Son of the Woods* (Sydney, 1920); *Poet Kendall: His Romantic History* (Sydney, 1926); *Kendall: Our God-Made Chief* (Sydney, 1929)

Frederick C. Kendall, *Henry Kendall: His Later Years, Notes by His Son, Frederick C. Kendall. A Refutation of Mrs Hamilton-Grey's Book, Kendall: Our God-Made Chief* (Sydney, 1938)

Hugh McCrae, *My Father and My Father's Friends* (Sydney, 1935)

A.P. Martin, introductory essay in *Australian Poets 1788-1888*, (ed.) Douglas Sladen (London, 1888)

T. Inglis Moore, 'Henry Kendall: A Bibliography', *Biblionews* (February 1957)

A.G. Stephens, *Henry Kendall* (Sydney, 1928)

T. Thornton Reed, *Henry Kendall* (Adelaide, 1960)

KINGSLEY, HENRY (1830-76): Novelist; b. Northamptonshire; lived as a boy in Devon and Chelsea; brother of novelist, Charles Kingsley; went to Oxford, but without graduating migrated to Australia in 1853; little known of his life here, but joined the mounted police at Sydney, worked on goldfields, and on stations and farms in the Monaro, New South Wales, and in Gippsland and Western Victoria; 1858 returned to England; 1869 editor of Edinburgh *Daily Review*. Novels of Australian interest: *The Recollections of Geoffry Hamlyn*, 1859; *The Hillyars and the Burtons*, 1865; *The Boy in Grey*, 1871; *Reginald Hetherege*, 1874. Stories: *Tales of Old Travel Re-narrated*, 1869; *Hetty and Other Stories*, 1871; *Hornby Mills and Other Stories*, 1872. All published London.

Commentaries:

S.M. Ellis, *Henry Kingsley, 1830-1876: Towards a Vindication* (London, 1931)

J.C. Horner, '*Geoffry Hamlyn* and Its Australian Setting', *Australian Literary Studies* (1963, no. 1)

Leonie J. Kramer, *Some Novels of Henry Kingsley* (C.U.C., 1954)

Michael Sadleir, 'Henry Kingsley', *Edinburgh Review* (October 1924)

Clement Shorter, preface to *Geoffry Hamlyn* (London, 1894)

Bruce Sutherland, 'Henry Kingsley and Australia', *Australian Quarterly* (June 1945)

LAWLER, RAY (b. 1922): Dramatist; second son in family of eight; father worked as council labourer in Melbourne; badly burned in infancy, and until eight was in and out of hospital; went later to school and had to leave at thirteen; worked with engineering firm; first seven plays written between ages of nineteen and twenty-four and all set in England; stage manager Brisbane 1948; 1949 actor and producer in National Theatre, Melbourne; directed professional repertory company at Melbourne University; prize-winning play, *Summer of the Seventeenth Doll*, first produced Melbourne, 1955, London, 1957; (published London and New York, 1957). Other published play, *The Piccadilly Bushman* (London, 1961).

Commentaries:

R.F. Brissenden, 'Some Recent Australian Plays', *Texas Quarterly* (Summer 1962)

P.H. Davison, 'Three Australian Plays: National Myths under Criticism' *Southerly* (1963, no. 2)

LAWSON, HENRY (1867-1922): Poet and short story writer; b. at Grenfell goldfields, son of Norwegian seaman, Larsen; family settled on poor selection in Mudgee district; Lawson received rudimentary education Mudgee schools; hampered by deafness; helped on farm; 1883 parents separated; Lawson joined mother and other children at Sydney; apprenticed to firm of coachpainters; clerk at Newcastle for short time; from 1887 contributed verse and stories to *Bulletin*; 1889 worked in Western Australia; returned to Sydney and wrote for *Republican* and *Worker*; 1892 carried swag from Bourke to Hungerford; 1893 worked in New Zealand in sawmill and as telegraph linesman; mother, Louisa, devoted to Women's Rights, and started magazine, *Dawn*, 1888; her press issued Lawson's first book *Short Stories in Prose and Verse* (Sydney, 1894); m. Bertha Bredt, 1896; 1897 second visit to New Zealand, left Sydney for London, 1900, returned 1902; separated from wife 1903; in difficulties through poverty and drinking; periods in gaol (for non-payment of maintenance) and hospital; 1916 friends secured him position at Yanco irrigation settlement; d. Sydney. Lawson's short stories include: *While the Billy Boils* (Sydney, 1896); *On the Track* (Sydney, 1900); *Over the Sliprails* (Sydney and London, 1900); *Joe Wilson and His Mates* (Edinburgh, 1901); *Children of the Bush* (London, 1902); *Mateship* (Melbourne, 1911). *Prose Works* (2 vols., Melbourne, 1935); Sydney, 1937, 1940, 1948, etc. Lawson's poetry includes: *In the Days When the World Was Wide* (Sydney and London, 1896); *Verses, Popular and Humorous* (Sydney and London, 1900); *When I Was King and Other Verses* (Sydney, 1905); *Poetical Works* (3 vols., Sydney, 1925), with preface by D. McK. Wright, other eds. 1933, 1938, 1947, 1950, 1951, etc. Collections of Lawson's prose and poetry are by no means complete.

Commentaries:

Hilton Barton, 'Lawson's Editors', *Overland* (1957, no. 10)

J. Le Gay Brereton, *Address on Henry Lawson* (Sydney, 1927)

J. Le Gay Brereton, *Knocking Round* (Sydney, 1930)

F. J. Broomfield, *Henry Lawson and His Critics* (Sydney, 1930)

T. S. Browning, *Henry Lawson Memories* (Sydney, 1931)

Edward Garnett, 'Henry Lawson and the Democracy', *Friday Nights* (London, 1922)

H. P. Heseltine, 'Saint Henry, Our Apostle of Mateship', *Quadrant* (1960-1, no. 1)

Bertha Lawson, *My Henry Lawson* (Sydney, 1943)

Bertha Lawson and J. Le Gay Brereton (eds.), *Henry Lawson By His Mates* (Sydney, 1931)

George Mackaness, *An Annotated Bibliography of Henry Lawson* (Sydney, 1951)

T. Inglis Moore, 'The Rise and Fall of Henry Lawson', *Meanjin* (1957, no. 4)

S. Murray-Smith, *Henry Lawson* (Melbourne, 1962)

T. D. Mutch, 'Early Life of Henry Lawson', *J.R.A.H.S.* (1932)

Vance Palmer, 'The Writer, Henry Lawson', *National Portraits* (Sydney, 1940)

A. A. Phillips, 'The Craftsmanship of Lawson', *The Australian Tradition* (Melbourne, 1958)

Marjorie Pizer (ed.) *The Men who Made Australia* (Melbourne, 1957)

Denton Prout, *Henry Lawson: The Grey Dreamer* (Adelaide, 1963)

Colin Roderick (ed.), *Henry Lawson: Twenty Stories and Seven Poems With Observations by His Friends and Critics* (Sydney, 1947)

Colin Roderick (ed.), *Henry Lawson's Formative Years 1883-1893* (Sydney, 1960) reprinted from *J.R.A.H.S.*, 1959, vol. 45, part 3

Colin Roderick (ed.), *The Later Life of Henry Lawson (1910-18)*, (Sydney, 1961), reprinted from *J.R.A.H.S.*, 1960, vol. 46, part 3

A. G. Stephens, 'Henry Lawson', *Art in Australia* (November 1922)

Walter Stone, *Henry Lawson: A Chronological Checklist of His Contributions to The Bulletin (1887-1924)* (Cremorne, 1954)

F. M. Todd, 'Henry Lawson', *Twentieth Century* (March 1950; reprinted Grahame Johnston, (ed.) *Australian Literary Criticism*, Melbourne, 1962)

LINDSAY, NORMAN (b. 1879); Artist, novelist; b. Creswick, Victoria, and educated at Grammar School there; began career in Melbourne, contributing drawings to journals; became illustrator for *Bulletin*; prolific artistic output: oils, water-colors, etchings, book-illustrations; wrote on literature in such magazines as *Vision* (partly founded by his son, Jack), *Lone Hand*, and *Bulletin*. His attitudes are specifically expressed in *Creative Effort*, (Sydney, 1920); *Hyperborea* (London, 1928); and *Madam Life's Lovers* (London, 1929). Novels include: *A Curate in Bohemia* (Sydney, 1913); *Redheap* (London, 1930); *The Cautious Amorist* (New York, 1932); *Saturdee* (Sydney, 1933); *Age of Consent* (London, 1938); *The Cousin from Fiji* (Sydney, 1945); *Halfway to Anywhere* (Sydney, 1947). Also, *The Magic Pudding* (Sydney, 1918).

Commentaries:

C. H. Hadgraft, 'Four Ages – Youth and Norman Lindsay', *Southerly* (1951, no. 2)

J. Hall, 'Norman Lindsay,' *Lone Hand* (February 1910)

Hetherington, John *Norman Lindsay* (Melbourne, 1961)

Kenneth Slessor, 'Australian Poetry and Norman Lindsay', *Southerly* (1955, no. 2)

P. R. Stephensen, in *The Foundations of Culture in Australia* (Gordon, New South Wales, 1936)

Douglas Stewart, in *The Flesh and the Spirit* (Sydney, 1948)

'Norman Lindsay Number', *Art in Australia* (December 1930)

'Norman Lindsay Number', *Southerly* (1959, no. 1) (Includes articles by Kenneth Slessor and Douglas Stewart)

MCAULEY, JAMES (b. 1917): Poet and critic; b. Lakemba, Sydney; educated Fort St High School; M.A. Sydney University;

1938-42 schoolteacher; m. 1942; 1944 with Harold Stewart responsible for 'Ern Malley' poems; during war worked in Australian Army Directorate of Research and Civil Affairs. In 1946 civil appointment as Senior Lecturer in Government, Australian School of Pacific Studies; editor *Quadrant* since inception 1955; 1961 Reader in Poetry, University of Tasmania, then later in same year, Professor of English; has contributed many poems and critical articles to Australian periodicals; convert to Catholicism 1952. Poetry: *Under Aldebaran* (Melbourne, 1946); *A Vision of Ceremony* (Sydney, 1956); *Australian Poets: James McAuley*, sel. and introduced by the author (Sydney, 1963). Criticism: *The End of Modernity* (Sydney, 1959); *C. J. Brennan* (Melbourne, 1963); *Edmund Spenser and George Eliot: a Critical Excursion* (Hobart, 1963). Also with Harold Stewart, introduction by Max Harris, *Ern Malley's Poems* (Melbourne, 1961).
Commentaries:

> V. Buckley, 'Classicism and Grace: James McAuley', *Essays in Poetry* (Melbourne, 1957)
> V. Buckley, 'James McAuley: The Man and the Poet', *Westerly* (1960, no. 3)
> Geoffrey Dutton, 'The Classic Pose', *Australian Letters* (1959, no. 3)
> Charles Higham, 'James McAuley's Discipline', *Prospect* (1961, no. 2)
> Leonie Kramer, *James McAuley* (C.U.C., 1957)
> Harold Stewart, 'The Myth of Prometheus', *Workshop* (vol. 2., no. 2, 1948, a supplement to *Meanjin*)

MCCRAE, HUGH (1876-1958): Poet; b. Melbourne; father, George Gordon McCrae poet and man of letters; educated Hawthorn Grammar; articled to Melbourne architect, but turned to freelance writing and illustration in Sydney; 1914 visited New York; played small parts on Broadway, mainly with Granville Barker company; at Melbourne played lead in silent film on life of A.L. Gordon, and took supporting roles in Shakespearian productions under Ian MacLaren; 1930 went to live at Camden, New South Wales, and later at Sydney. Poetry: *Satyrs and Sunlight; Silvarum Libri* (Sydney, 1909); *Colombine* (Sydney, 1920); *Idyllia* (Sydney, 1922); *Satyrs and Sunlight* (collected poetry), (London, 1928); all foregoing illustrated by Norman Lindsay; *The Mimshi Maiden* (Sydney, 1938); *Poems* (Sydney, 1939); *Voice of the Forest* (Sydney, 1945); *Forests of Pan* (Brisbane, 1944) (sel. by R.G. Howarth of poems from *Satyrs and Sunlight* not previously reprinted); *The Best Poems of Hugh McCrae* (ed. Howarth), (Sydney, 1961). *The Ship of Heaven*, 1951 (play: 'musical fantasy', music by Alfred Hill). Prose: *My Father and My Father's Friends* (Sydney, 1935), reprinted in *Story-book Only* (Sydney, 1948). Commentaries:

A.R. Chisholm, 'Poetry in Australia', *Australian National Review* (July 1937)

R.G. Howarth, 'The Prose of Hugh McCrae', *Southerly* (1954, no. 3)

Jack Lindsay, *The Roaring Twenties* (London, 1960)

T. Inglis Moore, 'Hugh McCrae', *Six Australian Poets* (1942)

Douglas Stewart, 'An Introduction to McCrae', *Southerly* (1962, no. 1)

'Hugh McCrae Number', *Southerly* (1956, no. 3) (Includes articles by O.N. Burgess, R.G. Howarth, Norman and Lionel Lindsay, Kenneth Slessor, and Douglas Stewart)

MCCUAIG, RONALD (b. 1908): Poet: b. Newcastle, New South Wales; educated there and Sydney; wrote for radio; 1939 travelled abroad; 1942 worked for *Smith's Weekly* and *S.M.H.*, then *Bulletin*. Poetry: *Quod Ronald McCuaig* (Sydney, 1946); *The Ballad of Bloodthirsty Bessie* (Sydney, 1961). Essays and Stories: *Tales Out of Bed* (Sydney, 1944).

MACKENZIE, KENNETH ('Seaforth Mackenzie') (1913-54): Poet, novelist; b. Perth, Western Australia, spent boyhood at Pinjarra; educated Guildford Grammar School, then Muresk Agricultural College; studied Arts and Law at University of Western Australia; became journalist, and later agricultural worker. Novels: *The Young Desire It* (London, 1937; Sydney, 1963); *Chosen People* (London, 1938); *Dead Men Rising* (London, 1951); *The Refuge* (London, 1954). Poetry: *Our Earth* (Sydney, 1937); *The Moonlit Doorway* (Sydney, 1944); *Selected Poems* (Sydney, 1961).

Commentaries:

M. Barnard, 'Novels of Seaforth Mackenzie', *Meanjin* (1954, no. 4)

Douglas Stewart, in *The Flesh and the Spirit* (Sydney, 1948)

MANIFOLD, JOHN STREETER (b. 1915): Poet; b. Melbourne; educated Geelong Grammar School and Cambridge University;

teacher and translator until 1939; served with British Army; after war journalist in London, and edited several sixteenth-century musical works; returned to Australia, 1949; now lives in Queensland; authority on Australian folk songs–(ed.) *The Penguin Australian Song Book* (Melbourne, 1964); collects and sings bush ballads. Poetry: *The Death of Ned Kelly, and Other Ballads* (London, 1941); *Trident* (London, 1944); *Selected Verse* (New York, 1946; London, 1948); *Nightmares and Sunhorses* (Melbourne, 1961).

MANN, LEONARD (b. 1895): Novelist, poet; b. Melbourne, educated at State Schools, then Wesley College; LL.B. Melbourne University; served with A.I.F.; after practising for a time at the bar in Victoria, became secretary to various industrial organizations; during World War II managerial position in Department Aircraft Production, then Senior Public Relations Officer of Department Labour and National Service. Novels: *Flesh in Armour* (Melbourne, 1932); *Human Drift* (Sydney, 1935); *A Murder in Sydney* (London, 1937); *Mountain Flat* (London, 1939); *The Go-Getter* (Sydney, 1942); *Andrea Caslin* (London, 1959); *Venus Half-Caste* (London, 1963). Poetry: *The Plumed Voice* (Sydney, 1938); *Poems from the Mask* (Melbourne, 1941); *The Delectable Mountains* (Sydney, 1944); *Elegiac and Other Poems* (Melbourne, 1957).
Commentary:

M. Barnard Eldershaw, 'Leonard Mann', *Essays in Australian Fiction* (Melbourne, 1938)

MATHEW, RAY (b. 1929): Poet; b. Sydney; educated Sydney High School; teacher for three years at small country schools western New South Wales; 1952 abandoned teaching, and has written radio scripts, plays and poetry; part-time tutor Sydney University. Play, *Life of the Party*, was a finalist in London *Observer* competition, and was performed in London. Poetry: *With Cypress Pine* (Sydney, 1951); *Song and Dance* (Sydney, 1956); *South of the Equator* (Sydney, 1961). Stories: *A Bohemian Affair* (Sydney, 1961). Drama: *A Spring Song* (Brisbane, 1961).

'MAURICE, FURNLEY' (Frank Wilmot) (1881-1942): Poet; b. Melbourne; father secretary to first socialist group in Victoria; after education at State schools, worked in E.W. Cole's bookselling business and became manager; published *Microbe* (1901-2);

1932-42 manager of Melbourne University Press; own printing press and used it to publish mainly poetry, including some of his own; contributions to periodicals included critical and other writings in prose. Poetry includes: *Some Verses*, 1903; *Unconditioned Songs*, 1913; *To God: from the Weary Nations*, 1917; *Eyes of Vigilance*, 1920; *Ways and Means*, 1920; *Arrows of Longing*, 1921 (introduction by Bernard O'Dowd); *The Gully*, 1925; *Melbourne Odes*, 1934; *Poems*, 1944 (sel. by Percival Serle). Essays: *Romance*, 1922. All published Melbourne.

Commentaries:

> Hugh Anderson, *Frank Wilmot, Furnley Maurice: A Bibliography and a Criticism* (Melbourne, 1955)
> F.T. Macartney, *Furnley Maurice, Frank Wilmot* (Sydney, 1955)
> T. Inglis Moore, 'Frank Wilmot as Furnley Maurice', *Southerly* (1951, no. 3)
> Vance Palmer, 'Frank Wilmot', *Australian Quarterly* (June 1942)
> Douglas Stewart, 'A Maker of Melbourne', *The Flesh and the Spirit* (Sydney, 1948)

'MILLS, MARTIN' *see* Boyd, Martin.

MOORE, THOMAS INGLIS (b. 1901): Poet, critic; b. Camden, New South Wales; educated Sydney Grammar School and Sydney University; scholarship to Oxford; schoolteaching and lecturing in U.S.; three years Professor of English in Philippines; 1931 joined *Sydney Morning Herald* staff; World War II gunner, and Army Education Service; Senior Lecturer in Pacific Studies, Canberra University College; now Associate Professor, English Department, A.N.U. Poetry: *Adagio in Blue* (Sydney, 1938); *Emu Parade* (Sydney, 1941); *Bayonet and Grass* (Sydney, 1957). Novel: *The Half Way Sun* (Sydney, 1935). Radio verse play: *We're Going Through* (Sydney, 1945). Criticism: *Six Australian Poets* (Melbourne, 1942).

MUDIE, IAN (b. 1911): Poet; b. Hawthorn, South Australia; educated Scotch College, Adelaide, where he has spent nearly all his life, with exception of short periods in Sydney and England; has held numerous jobs, including journalist and farm-hand; 1944 ed. verse anthology, *Poets at War*; associated with Jindyworobak movement. Poetry: *Corroboree to the Sun* (Melbourne, 1940); *This is Australia* (Adelaide, 1941); *The Australian Dream* (Adelaide, 1943); *Their Seven Stars Unseen* (Adelaide, 1943); *Poems: 1934-44* (Melbourne, 1945); *The Blue Crane* (Sydney,

1959); *The North-bound Rider* (Adelaide, 1963). Prose: *River-boats* (Adelaide, 1961).

NEILSON, JOHN SHAW (1872-1942): Poet; b. Penola, South Australia, educated briefly there, and Minimay, Victoria, where father settled on farm, 1881; farm abandoned after about eight years, family moved to Nhill; after Neilson did manual and station work of various kinds; later in life suffered from defective eyesight, sometimes dictated verse; 1922 small literary pension; 1928 attendant at Country Roads Board, Melbourne. 1941, spent some time with James Devaney in Queensland, 1942 returned to Melbourne. Poetry includes: *Heart of Spring* (Sydney, 1919); *Ballad and Lyrical Poems* (Sydney, 1923); *New Poems* (Sydney, 1927); *Collected Poems* (ed.) R.H. Croll (Melbourne, 1934); *Beauty Imposes* (Sydney, 1938); *Unpublished Poems*, (ed.) James Devaney (Sydney, 1947); *Australian Poets: Shaw Neilson*, sel. and introduced by Judith Wright (Sydney, 1963).

Commentaries:

> Hugh Anderson, *Shaw Neilson: An Annotated Bibliography And Checklist 1893-1956* (Cremorne, 1956)
>
> J. Devaney, *Shaw Neilson* (Sydney, 1944)
>
> T. Inglis Moore, in *Six Australian Poets* (Melbourne, 1942)
>
> S. White, 'John Shaw Neilson', *Australian National Review* (May 1938)
>
> Judith Wright, 'The Unshielded Eye: the Paradox of Shaw Neilson', *Quadrant* (Spring, 1959; reprinted Grahame Johnston, (ed.) *Australian Literary Criticism*, Melbourne, 1962)
>
> 'Neilson Number', *Southerly* (1956, No. 1) (Includes articles by Hugh Anderson, A.H. Chisholm, James Devaney, L.I. and R.G. Howarth, and H.J. Oliver)
>
> *John Shaw Neilson: A Memorial* Tributes in prose and verse, with biographical note by R.H. Croll (Melbourne, 1942)

O'DOWD, BERNARD (1866-1953): Poet; b. Beaufort, Victoria, son of police constable who later became farmer; educated State Schools, scholarship Grenville College, Ballarat; B.A. and LL.B. Melbourne University; 1887-1913 Assistant Librarian Supreme Court, Melbourne, then First Assistant Parliamentary Draughtsman; 1931 until retirement in 1935 State Parliamentary Draughtsman. Poetry includes: *Dawnward?* (Sydney, 1903); *The Silent Land and Other Verses* (Melbourne, 1906); *Dominions of the Boundary* (Melbourne, 1907); *The Seven Deadly Sins* (Melbourne, 1909); *The Bush* (Melbourne, 1912); *Alma Venus and Other Verses*

(Melbourne, 1921). *The Poems: Collected Edition*, (ed.) Walter Murdoch (Melbourne, 1941). *Australian Poets: Bernard O'Dowd*, sel. and introduced by A.A. Phillips (Sydney, 1963). Criticism: *Poetry Militant* (Melbourne, 1909). Essays: *Fantasies* (Melbourne, 1942).

Commentaries:

Hugh Anderson, *Bernard O'Dowd (1866-1953): An Annotated Bibliography* (Sydney, 1963)

Brian Elliott, 'The Poetry of Mr Bernard O'Dowd', *Australian Quarterly* (December, 1940)

Brian Elliott, 'Young Democracy: The Early Verse of Bernard O'Dowd', *Singing to the Cattle* (Melbourne, 1947)

Victor Kennedy and Nettie Palmer, *Bernard O'Dowd* (Melbourne, 1954)

F.T. Macartney, in *Australian Literary Essays* (Sydney, 1957)

E. Morris Miller, 'Bernard O'Dowd's Early Writing', *Meanjin* (1949, no. 4)

T. Inglis Moore, in *Six Australian Poets* (Melbourne, 1942)

'O'Dowd to Whitman', *Overland* (1962, no. 23)

F.M. Todd, 'The Poetry of Bernard O'Dowd', *Meanjin* (1955, (no. 1)

'Bernard O'Dowd Number', *Southerly* (1953, no. 2) (Includes articles by Hugh Anderson, Kate Baker, A.H. Chisholm, S.E. Lee)

'Tributes to the Memory of Bernard O'Dowd', *Meanjin* (1953, no. 4)

PALMER, VANCE (1885-1959): Novelist, short story writer, poet, dramatist; b. Bundaberg, Queensland; educated Ipswich Grammar School; clerical and journalistic work in Brisbane, then freelance writing in London; tutor and bookkeeper on Queensland stations; further five years in London; travelled in North and South America; 1914 m. Janet Gertrude Higgins (author, Nettie Palmer); World War I served with A.I.F.; spent some time in Spain, then lived in Melbourne. Novels include: *The Outpost*, by 'Rann Daly' (London, 1924 revised ed. *Hurricane* Sydney, 1935); *The Man Hamilton* (London, 1928); *Men are Human* (London, 1930); *The Passage* (London, 1930); *Daybreak* (London, 1932); *The Swayne Family* (Sydney, 1934); *Legend for Sanderson* (Sydney, 1937); *Cyclone* (Sydney, 1947); *Golconda* (Sydney, 1948); *Seedtime* (Sydney, 1957). Stories: *The World of Men* (London, 1915); *Separate Lives* (London, 1931); *Sea and*

Spinifex (Sydney, 1934); *Let the Birds Fly* (Sydney, 1955). Drama: *The Black Horse* (Melbourne, 1924); *Hail Tomorrow* (Sydney, 1947). Poetry: *The Forerunners* (London, 1915); *The Camp* (Melbourne, 1920.) Also, *The Legend of the Nineties* (Melbourne, 1954); *National Portraits* (Sydney, 1940; enlarged Melbourne, 1954).

Commentaries;

> Frank Dalby Davison, 'Vance Palmer's Writings', *Meanjin* (1948, no. 1)
>
> C.H. Hadgraft, 'The Fiction of Vance Palmer', *Southerly* (1949, no. 1)
>
> A.D. Hope, 'Vance Palmer Reconsidered', *Southerly* (1955, no. 4) (a reply to the following article)
>
> J. McKellar, 'Vance Palmer as a Novelist', *Southerly* (1954, no. 1)
>
> 'Vance and Nettie Palmer Number', *Meanjin* (1959, no. 2) (Includes a Bibliographical Checklist by C.M. Hotimsky and Walter Stone, and articles by John Barnes, Brian Fitzpatrick, A.D. Hope, T. Inglis Moore, Keith Macartney, and Arthur Phillips)

PATERSON, ANDREW BARTON (1864-1941): Poet; b. 'Narrambla', near Orange, New South Wales; brought up Illalong station near Yass; educated Sydney Grammar School; practised as solicitor for some years, and wrote verse about life at Illalong; verse became popular in *Bulletin* under pseudonym 'The Banjo'; first book gained unprecedentedly large public; abandoned law for journalism; war correspondent in South Africa 1899; later went to China and London; returned Australia 1902; 1903 m. Alice Walker. Editor *Sydney Evening News*, 1904, *Sydney Town and Country Journal*, 1907-8; pastoralist for six years; served in 1914-18 war as ambulance driver and in A.I.F.; C.B.E. 1939; d. Sydney. Poetry: *The Man from Snowy River*, 1895; *Rio Grande's Last Race*, 1902; *Saltbush Bill, J.P.*, 1917; *The Collected Verse of A.B. Paterson*, 1921 (numerous reprints, including 1951, with introduction by F.T. Macartney); *The Animals Noah Forgot*, 1933. Fiction: *An Outback Marriage*, 1906; *Three Elephant Power and Other Stories*, 1917; *The Shearer's Colt*, 1936. Ed., *Old Bush Songs*, 1905. All published Sydney.

Commentaries:

> Brian Elliott, 'Australian Paterson', *Singing to the Cattle* (Melbourne, 1947)
>
> John Manifold, 'The Banjo', *Overland* (Spring 1954, and Summer 1954-5)

R.C. Sheridan, 'Banjo Paterson: A Biographical Note [with Checklist of His Books]', *Biblionews* (May, 1951)

PORTER, HAL (b. 1917): Poet, short story writer, novelist; b. Melbourne; lived as boy at Bairnsdale (Victoria); educated there; taught English and modern languages at schools in Victoria, South Australia, Tasmania, and New South Wales; 1949-50 in Japan, teaching children of Occupation forces, and senior Japanese pupils; librarian in Victoria 1954-61; has published numerous poems and stories in Australian periodicals, and won C.L.F. awards. Stories: *A Bachelor's Children* (Sydney, 1962). Novels: *A Handful of Pennies* (Sydney, 1958); *The Tilted Cross* (London, 1961). Poetry: *The Hexagon* (Sydney, 1956). Autobiography: *The Watcher on the Cast-Iron Balcony* (London, 1963). Drama: *The Tower* (in *Three Australian Plays*, Penguin, 1963).

Commentary:

Peter Ward, 'The Craft of Hal Porter', *Australian Letters* (1962, no. 2)

PRAED, MRS CAMPBELL (1851-1935): Novelist; b. Rosa Murray-Prior on father's station in Queensland; some schooling Brisbane; lived on stations until 1868, then Brisbane; 1872 m. Arthur Campbell Mackworth Praed; 1876 they went to live in England, and but for one visit to Australia she lived there until death; long friendship with Justin McCarthy, with whom she collaborated (see *Our Book of Memories*, 1912, ed. by her). Her many novels include: *An Australian Heroine*, 1880; *Policy and Passion*, 1881; *The Head Station*, 1885; *The Romance of a Station*, 1889; *Outlaw and Lawmaker*, 1893; *Fugitive Anne*, 1902; and with McCarthy: *The Right Honourable*, 1886; all published London; *Mrs. Tregaskiss* (New York, 1895).

Biography: Colin Roderick, *In Mortal Bondage: The Strange Life of Rosa Praed* (Sydney, 1948).

PRICHARD, KATHARINE SUSANNAH (b. 1883): Novelist, and short story writer; b. Fiji of Australian parents, came to Australia in her infancy and spent portion of early childhood in Launceston; educated South Melbourne College under poet J.B. O'Hara; journalist in Melbourne, then freelance writer in London; first book, *Clovelly Verses* (London, 1913); *The Pioneers* (London, 1915), won Australian section of Dominion Novel

Competition; 1919 m. Captain Hugo Throssel, V.C., son of second Premier of Western Australia; has since resided at Greenmount, Western Australia; travelled extensively; author of political writings. Other novels include: *Black Opal* (London, 1921); *Working Bullocks* (London, 1926); *The Wild Oats of Han* (Sydney, 1928); *Coonardoo* (London, 1929); *Haxby's Circus* (London, 1930); *Intimate Strangers* (London, 1937); trilogy: *The Roaring Nineties* (London, 1946); *Golden Miles* (Sydney, 1948; *Winged Seeds* (London and Sydney, 1950). Stories include: *Kiss on the Lips and Other Stories* (London, 1932); *Potch and Colour* (London, 1944); *N'goola, and Other Stories* (Melbourne, 1959). Some of these works have been translated into a number of languages. Drama: *Brumby Innes* (Perth, 1940). Poetry: *The Earth Lover* (Sydney, 1932). Autobiography: *Child of the Hurricane* (Sydney, 1963).

Commentaries:

Hugh Anderson, 'K.S. Prichard: A Checklist', *Biblionews* (March 1959, with addendum in July 1959)

H. Drake-Brockman, 'K.S. Prichard: the Colour in her Work', *Southerly* (1953, no. 4)

Muir Holburn, 'Katharine Susannah Prichard', *Meanjin* (1951, no. 3)

Jack Lindsay, 'The Novels of K.S. Prichard', *Meanjin* (1961, no. 4)

Ellen Malos, 'Some Major Themes in the Novels of Katharine Susannah Prichard', *Australian Literary Studies* (1963, no. 1)

Ellen Malos, 'Jack Lindsay's Essay on Katharine Susannah Prichard's Novels', and Jack Lindsay in reply (*Meanjin*, 1963, no. 1)

Aileen Palmer, 'The Changing Face of Australia: Notes on the Creative Writing of K.S. Prichard', *Overland* (1958, nos. 12 and 13)

Richard Sadleir, 'The Novels of K.S. Prichard: A Critical Evaluation', *Westerly* (1961, no. 3)

G.A. Wilkes, 'The Novels of K.S. Prichard', *Southerly* (1953, no. 4)

'Katharine Susannah Prichard Issue', *Overland* (1958, no. 12)

'RICHARDSON, HENRY HANDEL' (Mrs Ethel F. Robertson), (1870-1946): Novelist; b. Melbourne, daughter of Irish doctor who, unsuccessful on the goldfields, prospered in his profession in Victoria; later his health failed, and he became mentally ill; after his death his widow became postmistress; following some private education, H.H. Richardson was sent to the Presbyterian

Ladies' College at East Melbourne; in unfinished autobiography, *Myself When Young*, 1948, she speaks of *The Getting of Wisdom*, 1910, as containing 'a very fair account of my doings at school'; after period as governess, went abroad at seventeen to study as pianist in Leipzig; here met Scottish student (later Professor) of German literature, J. G. Robertson, and m. him 1895; rest of life spent in Germany and England; returned to Australia for one short visit. Other Novels: *Maurice Guest* (London and New York, 1908); trilogy – *Australia Felix: The Fortunes of Richard Mahony* (London, 1917); *The Way Home* (London, 1925); *Ultima Thule* (London and New York, 1929); (revised omnibus edition of trilogy 1930); *The Young Cosima* (London and New York, 1934). Also, *The End of a Childhood and Other Stories* (London, 1939). *Letters of H. H. Richardson to Nettie Palmer*, (ed. K. J. Rossing, Uppsala, 1953).

Commentaries:

Vincent Buckley, *Henry Handel Richardson* (Melbourne, 1961)

Jennifer Dallimore, 'The Malaise of Richard Mahony', *Quadrant* (1961, no. 4; reprinted Grahame Johnston, (ed.) *Australian Literary Criticism*, Melbourne, 1962)

Leonie J. Gibson [Kramer], *Henry Handel Richardson and Some of Her Sources* (Melbourne, 1954)

Maria S. Haynes, 'Henry Handel Richardson [A Bibliography]', *Bulletin of Bibliography* (January-April 1955)

C. H. Hadgraft, 'The Novels of H. H. Richardson', *Southerly* (1948, no. 1)

C. H. Hadgraft, 'Diagnosis of Mahony', *Australian Quarterly* (June 1955)

A. D. Hope, 'H. H. Richardson's *Maurice Guest*', *Meanjin* (1955, no. 2)

R. G. Howarth, 'H. H. Richardson's *Richard Mahony* and *The End of a Childhood*', *Australian Quarterly* (March 1955)

Leonie Kramer, *A Companion to Australia Felix* (Melbourne, 1962)

F. H. Mares, '*The Fortunes of Richard Mahony*: A Reconsideration', *Meanjin* (1962, no. 1)

E. Morris Miller, '*The Fortunes of Richard Mahony*: A Bibliographical Note', *Meanjin* (1948, no. 3)

T. Inglis Moore, *The Misfortunes of Henry Handel Richardson* (C.U.C., 1957)

Nettie Palmer, *Henry Handel Richardson: A Study* (Sydney, 1950)

Edna Purdie and Olga M. Roncoroni, *Henry Handel Richardson: Some Personal Impressions* (Sydney, 1957)

H.H. Richardson, 'Some Notes on My Books', *Virginia Quarterly Review* (Summer 1940)

J.G. Robertson, 'The Art of H. H. Richardson', in H.H. Richardson's *Myself When Young* (London, 1948)

'Henry Handel Richardson Number', *Southerly* (1963, no. 1) ed. G.A. Wilkes; comprises previously uncollected articles and stories.

ROBINSON, ROLAND (b. 1912): Poet; b. County Clare, Ireland; brought to Australia at age of nine; various jobs on stations in western New South Wales; has sampled other occupations, including ballet-dancer, script-writer, railway fettler, greenkeeper; studied painting; usually lives Sydney; during War worked in Northern Territory; m. 1952; 1954 C.L.F. grant to revisit Northern Territory; deeply interested in the aborigines. Poetry: *Beyond the Grass-Tree Spears* (Melbourne, 1944); *Language of the Sand* (Sydney, 1949); *Tumult of the Swans* (Sydney, 1953); *Deep Well* (Sydney, 1962). Books of Native Folklore: *Legend and Dreaming* (Sydney, 1952); *The Feathered Serpent* (Sydney, 1956). Stories: *Black-feller, White-feller* (Sydney, 1958).

'STEELE RUDD' (Arthur Hoey Davis) (1868-1935): Novelist, short story writer, b. near Toowoomba, Queensland; lived on selection with family at Emu Creek; left local school before he was twelve; odd jobs in bush as stockman; 1886-1903 worked Government offices in Brisbane; 1895 contributed to *Bulletin* sketches reprinted as *On Our Selection*, extremely popular; other books continued history of fictional Rudd family; 1904 began publication of monthly, *Steele Rudd's Magazine*; d. Brisbane. Numerous works of fiction include: *On Our Selection*, 1899; *Our New Selection*, 1903; *Sandy's Selection*, 1904; all published Sydney; *Back at Our Selection* (Brisbane, 1906).

Commentaries:

Brian Elliott, 'A Word for Steele Rudd', *Singing to the Cattle* (Melbourne, 1947)

A.D. Hope, 'Steele Rudd and Henry Lawson', *Meanjin* (1956, no. 1)

Vance Palmer, 'Steele Rudd', *Overland* (1959, no. 15)

A.G. Stephens, see *A.G. Stephens: His Life and Work*, ed. Vance Palmer (Melbourne, 1941)

SLESSOR, KENNETH (b. 1901): Poet, b. Orange, New South Wales; educated Mowbray House School, Chatswood, and

C. of E. Grammar School, Sydney; 1920 *Sun* (Sydney) reporter; joint-editor of *Vision*, 1923-4; 1925 worked for Melbourne *Punch* and *Herald*; 1927 joined staff *Smith's Weekly* (Sydney), later became editor; 1940-4 Official War Correspondent A.I.F. Middle East and New Guinea; 1944 rejoined *Sun*, becoming chief leader-writer and literary editor; 1957 transferred to *Daily Telegraph* and *Sunday Telegraph*; 1956-61 editor *Southerly*. Poetry includes: *Earth-Visitors* (London, 1926); *Cuckooz Contrey* (Sydney, 1932); *Five Bells* (Sydney, 1939); *One Hundred Poems 1919-1939* (Sydney, 1944); *Poems* (Sydney, 1957 and 1963). Article: 'Writing Poetry, the Why and How', *Southerly* (1948, no. 3).

Commentaries:

> Vincent Buckley, 'Kenneth Slessor: Realist or Romantic', *Essays in Poetry* (Melbourne, 1957)
>
> Max Harris, *Kenneth Slessor* (Melbourne, 1963)
>
> Charles Higham, 'The Poetry of Kenneth Slessor', *Quadrant* (1959-60, no. 1; reprinted Grahame Johnston, (ed.) *Australian Literary Criticism*, Melbourne, 1962)
>
> R.G. Howarth, 'Sound in Slessor's Poetry', *Southerly* (1955, no. 4)
>
> F.T. Macartney, 'The Poetry of Kenneth Slessor', *Meanjin* (1957, no. 3)
>
> Douglas Stewart, 'Harbour and Ocean', *The Flesh and the Spirit* (Sydney, 1948)

SPENCE, CATHERINE HELEN (1825-1910): Novelist; b. Scotland; came to Adelaide with family in 1839; at seventeen became governess, and at twenty opened a school; 1850 took up journalism; Adelaide correspondent of Melbourne *Argus*; 1859 influenced by J.S. Mill and for the rest of her life active on behalf of Woman's Suffrage, proportional representation, and other social causes. Novels: *Clara Morrison*, 1854; *Tender and True*, 1856; *Mr Hogarth's Will*, 1865; *The Author's Daughter*, 1868; all published London.

Commentary:

> J.F. Young, *Catherine Helen Spence: a Study and an Appreciation* (Melbourne, 1937)

STEAD, CHRISTINA (b. 1902): Novelist; b. Rockdale, New South Wales; schoolteacher, then demonstrator in Psychology, Sydney University; 1928 went to London, then lived in Paris, travelling Europe extensively; visited U.S.A. 1935, then Spain; returned to

U.S.A. 1937; now living in England; m. W.J. Blech ('William Blake'), novelist. Novels: *The Salzburg Tales* (London, 1934); *Seven Poor Men of Sydney* (London, 1934); *The Beauties and the Furies* (London and New York, 1936); *House of All Nations* (New York, 1938); *The Man Who Loved Children* (New York, 1940); *For Love Alone* (New York, 1944); *Letty Fox, Her Luck* (New York, 1946); *A Little Tea, A Little Chat* (New York, 1948). Commentaries:

Christina Stead number, *Southerly* (1962, no. 4)
Colin Roderick, 'Christina Stead', *Southerly* (1946, no. 2)
R.G. Howarth, 'Christina Stead', *Biblionews* (January 1958)

STEPHENS, ALFRED GEORGE (1865-1933): Critic, editor; b. Toowoomba, Queensland, educated grammar school there; at fifteen apprenticed to printing trade Toowoomba, and later Sydney; 1889 returned Queensland and became editor *Gympie Miner*; then sub-editor Brisbane *Boomerang*, a radical weekly; 1891 editor and part-owner Cairns *Argus*; 1893 travelled U.S.A., U.K., France (see *A Queenslander's Travel Notes*, 1894); left journalistic work in London to become sub-editor Sydney *Bulletin* 1894-1906: 1896 instituted famous 'Red Page'; 1907 revived *Bookfellow* which lasted with some gaps and changes until 1925; influential critic and promoter of contemporary literature; edited over thirty publications. Criticism includes: *The Red Pagan* (Sydney, 1904) (criticism from the *Bulletin*); *Victor Daley* (Sydney, 1905); *Chris. Brennan* (Sydney, 1933). Other criticism collected in Vance Palmer (ed.), *A.G. Stephens: His Life and Work* (Melbourne, 1941). Also published poetry, and a novel, *Bill's Idees* (Sydney, 1913).
Commentaries:

'A.G. Stephens', articles by Norman Lindsay and Hugh McCrae, *Southerly* (1947, no. 4)
T. Inglis Moore, 'The Red Page Rhadamanthus: A.G. Stephens', *Texas Quarterly* (Summer 1962)
Vance Palmer (ed.), *A.G. Stephens: His Life and Work* (with foreword Melbourne, 1941)
P.R. Stephensen, *The Life and Works of A.G. Stephens* (lecture published by the author, 1940)
Douglas Stewart, 'A.G. Stephens', *The Flesh and the Spirit* (1948)

STEWART, DOUGLAS (b. 1913): Poet, dramatist, critic; b. Eltham, New Zealand; educated New Plymouth Boys' High

School and Victoria University College; after working for several New Zealand papers, came Sydney 1938, joined *Bulletin* staff, edited its 'Red Page' from 1941 until recently. Poetry: *Green Lions* (Auckland, 1936;) *The White Cry* (London, 1939). All the following published Sydney: *Elegy for an Airman*, 1940; *Sonnets to the Unknown Soldier*, 1941; *The Dosser in Springtime*, 1946; *Glencoe*, 1947; *Sun Orchids and Poems*, 1952; *The Birdsville Track*, 1955; *Rutherford*, 1962. Verse Plays: *Ned Kelly*, 1943; *The Fire on the Snow and The Golden Lover: Two Plays for Radio*, 1944; *Shipwreck*, 1947; *Four Plays* (all the foregoing), 1958; *Fisher's Ghost* (prose and verse) 1960. Criticism: *The Flesh and the Spirit*, 1948. Stories: *A Girl with Red Hair and Other Stories*, 1944.

Commentaries:

David Bradley, 'Second Thoughts about Douglas Stewart', *Westerly* (1960, no. 3)

J.F. Burrows, 'An Approach to the Plays of Douglas Stewart', *Southerly* (1963, no. 2)

H.J. Oliver, 'Douglas Stewart and the Art of the Radio Play', *Texas Quarterly* (Summer 1962)

A.A. Phillips, 'The Australian Romanticism and Stewart's *Ned Kelly*', *The Australian Tradition* (Melbourne, 1958)

Leslie Rees, 'Douglas Stewart and Modern Australian Verse Drama', *Towards An Australian Drama* (Sydney, 1953)

Alan Tory, 'The Shade of Ned Kelly', *Harbour in Heaven* (Sydney, 1949)

STEWART, HAROLD FREDERICK (b. 1916): Poet; b. Drummoyne, Sydney; educated Fort St High School, Sydney University and Conservatorium of Music. With James McAuley, wrote 'Ern Malley' poems. Poetry: *Phoenix Wings: Poems 1940-6*, (Sydney, 1948); *Orpheus and Other Poems* (Sydney, 1956); *A Net of Fireflies* (Japanese paintings with verse translations and an essay) (Vermont, 1960).

Commentary:

Ronald Dunlop, 'Some Aspects of the Poetry of Harold Stewart', *Southerly* (1963, no. 4)

STIVENS, DALLAS G. (b. 1911): Novelist, short story writer; b. Blayney, New South Wales; educated Barker College, Hornsby; on staff *Daily Telegraph* 1939-42; Army Education Service 1943-4; m. 1945; several years with Commonwealth Department of Information. Stories: *The Tramp and other Stories* (London, 1936); *The Courtship of Uncle Henry* (Melbourne, 1946); *The Gambling Ghost and Other Tales* (Sydney, 1953); *Ironbark Bill* (Sydney, 1955); *The Scholarly Mouse, and Other Tales* (Sydney, 1957). Novels: *Jimmy Brockett* (London, 1951); *The Wide Arch* (Sydney, 1958).

STONE, LOUIS (1871-1935): Novelist; b. Leicester, England; came to Australia 1884; lived in Brisbane, then Sydney, where he became State school teacher, eventually at Sydney Boys' High; to study life portrayed in *Jonah* (London, 1911), lived for a time in Waterloo, Sydney. Other novel: *Betty Wayside* (London, 1915). Also wrote plays, but none printed in book-form.
Commentary:

H. J. Oliver, 'Louis Stone', *Meanjin* (1954, no. 3)

STOW, RANDOLPH (b. 1935): Poet, novelist; b. Geraldton, Western Australia, educated Geraldton, Guildford Grammar School, University of Western Australia; 1962 Lecturer in English, University of Leeds. Novels: *A Haunted Land* (London, 1956); *The Bystander* (London, 1957); *To the Islands* (London, 1958 won Miles Franklin Award); *Tourmaline* (London, 1963). Poetry: *Act One* (London, 1957); *Outrider: Poems, 1956-62* (London, 1963).
Commentaries:

Vincent Buckley, 'In the Shadow of Patrick White' [Stow and Christopher Koch], *Meanjin* (1961, no. 2)

G. K. W. Johnston, 'The Art of Randolph Stow', *Meanjin* (1961, no. 2)

David Martin, 'Among the Bones', *Meanjin* (1959, no. 1) (on Patrick White and Randolph Stow)

P. H. Newby, 'The Novels of Randolph Stow', *Australian Letters* (November, 1957)

'TASMA' (Jessie Catherine Couvreur) (1848-97): Novelist; b. London, daughter of Alfred Huybers; came to Hobart when about four; 1867 m. Charles F. Fraser, accompanied him to Melbourne, divorced him several years later; in Melbourne she wrote for *Australasian* and *Australian Journal*; 1873 wrote and lectured in Europe, received from French Government decoration of Officier d'Academie; 1883 visited Australia; 1885 m. Auguste Couvreur. Works: *Uncle Piper of Piper's Hill*, 1889; *In Her Earliest Youth*, 1890; *A Sydney Sovereign and Other Tales*, 1890;

A Knight of the White Feather, 1892; *Not Counting the Cost*, 1895; *A Fiery Ordeal*, 1897; all foregoing published London; *The Penance of Portia James* (London and Melbourne, 1891).

TENNANT, KYLIE (b. 1912): Novelist; b. Manly, New South Wales; educated Brighton College there, and Sydney University; publicity officer of A.B.C. for a time; 1933 m. Lewis C. Rodd; has sought direct experience of many of the places and circumstances described in her novels. Novels: *Tiburon* (Sydney, 1935); *Foveaux* (London, 1939); *The Battlers* (London, 1941); *Ride on Stranger* (Sydney, 1943); *Time Enough Later* (New York, 1943); *Lost Haven* (New York, Melbourne, 1946); *The Joyful Condemned* (London and New York, 1953); *The Honey Flow* (London 1956); *Speak You So Gently* (London, 1959). Play: *Tether a Dragon* (Sydney, 1952).

Commentaries:

D. Auchterlonie, 'The Novels of Kylie Tennant', *Meanjin* (1953, no. 4)

T. Inglis Moore, 'The Tragi-comedies of Kylie Tennant', *Southerly* (1957, no. 1)

WATEN, JUDAH (b. 1911): Novelist, short story writer; b. Odessa, Russia; came with parents to Western Australia, 1914; published story in annual *Coast to Coast*, 1947, and since then has published many stories in periodicals; C.L.F. grant to write novel, *The Unbending* (Melbourne, 1954). He often writes on cultural and political questions and lectures on Australian literature. Other novels: *Shares in Murder* (Melbourne, 1957); *Time of Conflict* (Sydney, 1961). Stories: *Alien Son* (Sydney, 1952).

Commentary:

David Martin, 'Three Realists in Search of Reality' [on Frank Hardy, John Morrison, and Waten], *Meanjin* (1959, no. 3)

WEBB, FRANCIS (b. 1925): Poet, b. Adelaide; educated Christian Brothers' Schools, Sydney; World War II served in Canada with R.A.A.F., afterwards Sydney University for a year, then returned to Canada to work in publisher's office; has since visited Australia and England. Poetry: *A Drum for Ben Boyd* (Sydney, 1948); *Leichhardt in Theatre* (Sydney, 1952); *Birthday* (Adelaide, 1953); *Socrates* (London, 1961).

Commentaries:

Vincent Buckley, 'The Poetry of Francis Webb', *Meanjin* (1953, no. 1)

Sylvia Lawson, 'The World of Francis Webb', *Australian Letters* (1961, no. 1)

WHITE, PATRICK (b. 1912): Novelist, short story writer, playwright; b. London of Australian parents; brought up in Sydney; educated Tudor House, Moss Vale, and Cheltenham College, England; after period as jackeroo at Monaro and Walgett, graduated in Modern Languages, King's College, Cambridge, 1935; remained abroad about fourteen years; travelled in Europe and America; for five years with Intelligence section of R.A.F., Greece and Middle East; after demobilization settled on farm, Castle Hill, near Sydney; 1962-3 contributed stories to Australian periodicals; recently four plays performed in Australia not yet published. Autobiographical article by White, 'The Prodigal Son', *Australian Letters* (1958, no. 3). Novels: *Happy Valley* (London, 1939); *The Living and the Dead* (London, 1941, 1962); *The Aunt's Story* (London, 1948); *The Tree of Man* (New York, 1955; London, 1956); *Voss* (London and New York, 1957); *Riders in the Chariot* (London, 1961). Poetry: *The Ploughman and Other Poems* (Sydney, 1935).

Commentaries:

M. Aurousseau, 'The Identity of Voss', *Meanjin* (1958, no. 1)

Marjorie Barnard, 'The Four Novels of Patrick White', *Meanjin* (1956, no. 2)

R.F. Brissenden, 'Patrick White', *Meanjin* (1959, no. 4)

Vincent Buckley, 'Patrick White and His Epic', *Twentieth Century* (1958, no. 3; reprinted Grahame Johnston, (ed.) *Australian Literary Criticism*, Melbourne, 1962)

O.N. Burgess, 'Patrick White, His Critics, and 'Laura Trevelyan', *Australian Quarterly* (1961, no. 4)

Geoffrey Dutton, *Patrick White* (Melbourne, 1961)

H.P. Heseltine, 'Patrick White's Style', *Quadrant* (1963, no. 3)

Rodney Mather, '*Voss*', *Melbourne Critical Review* (1963)

Colin Roderick, '*Riders in the Chariot*: an Exposition', *Southerly* (1962, no. 2)

John Rorke, 'Patrick White and the Critics', *Southerly* (1959, no. 2)

Peter Wood, 'Moral Complexity in Patrick White's Novels', *Meanjin* (1962, no. 1)

WILMOT, FRANK, see under 'Maurice, Furnley'.

WRIGHT, JUDITH (Mrs J.P. McKinney) (b. 1915): Poet; b. station near Armidale, New South Wales, of pioneering family; educated Correspondence School, New England Girls' School,

Sydney University; after year in England and Europe, stenographic and secretarial jobs, Sydney, 1938-42; statistical research officer, Queensland University, 1944-8; now lives Mt Tamborine, Queensland; has also contributed short stories to periodicals. Poetry: *The Moving Image* (Melbourne, 1946); *Woman to Man* (Sydney, 1949); *The Gateway* (Sydney, 1953); *The Two Fires* (Sydney, 1955); *Birds* (Sydney, 1963); *Australian Poets: Judith Wright*, sel. and introduced by the author (Sydney, 1963); *Five Senses: Selected Poems by Judith Wright* (Sydney, 1963); Family Biography: *The Generations of Men* (Melbourne, 1959). Commentaries:

R.F. Brissenden, 'The Poetry of Judith Wright', *Meanjin* (1953, no. 3; reprinted Grahame Johnston, (ed.) *Australian Literary Criticism*, Melbourne, 1962)

Vincent Buckley, 'The Poetry of Judith Wright', *Essays in Poetry* (Melbourne, 1957)

Charles Higham, 'Judith Wright's Vision', *Quadrant* (1961, no. 3)

F.H. Mares, 'The Poetry of Judith Wright', *Australian Letters* (July 1960)

T. Inglis Moore, 'The Quest of Judith Wright', *Meanjin* (1958, no. 3)

Robert Ian Scott, 'Judith Wright's World View', *Southerly* (1956, no. 4)

Douglas Stewart, 'Judith Wright's Poetry', *The Flesh and the Spirit* (Sydney, 1948)

Richard Wilson, 'The Short Stories of Judith Wright', *Australian Literary Studies* (1963, no. 1)

LIST OF CONTRIBUTORS

IAN TURNER	Senior Lecturer in History, Monash University
JUDITH WRIGHT	See Appendix
EVAN JONES	Lecturer in English, University of Melbourne
JOHN BARNES	Lecturer in English, University of Western Australia
HARRY HESELTINE	Lecturer in English, University of New South Wales
BRIAN ELLIOTT	Reader in English, University of Adelaide
F. H. MARES	Senior Lecturer in English, University of Adelaide
EDGAR WATERS	Leading Australian Folklorist
S. E. LEE	Lecturer in English, Sydney Teachers' College
HAROLD OLIVER	Professor of English, University of New South Wales
G. A. WILKES	Professor of Australian Literature, University of Sydney
LEONIE KRAMER	Associate Professor of English, University of New South Wales
DOUGLAS STEWART	See Appendix
C. WALLACE-CRABBE	Lecturer in English, University of Melbourne
MAX HARRIS	See Appendix
JAMES MCAULEY	See Appendix
GUSTAV CROSS	Professor of English, Newcastle University College, N.S.W.
DAVID BRADLEY	Lecturer in English, Monash University
A. NORMAN JEFFARES	Professor of English, University of Leeds
VINCENT BUCKLEY	See Appendix
S. MURRAY-SMITH	Editor of *Overland*, critic and reviewer
EUNICE HANGER	Senior Lecturer in English, University of Queensland
L. T. HERGENHAN	Lecturer in English, University of Tasmania

INDEX OF NAMES